THE
Clouded
World

THE
Clouded
World

DARKENING
FOR A FALL
AND
EMPIRE OF CHAOS

JAY AMORY

Gollancz

LONDON

Darkening for a Fall copyright © Jay Amory 2008
Empire of Chaos copyright © Jay Amory 2008

The right of Jay Amory to be identified as the author
of this work has been asserted by him in accordance
with the Copyright, Designs and Patents Act 1988.

This edition first published in Great Britain in 2008 by
Gollancz
An imprint of the Orion Publishing Group
Orion House, 5 Upper St Martin's Lane, London WC2H 9EA

An Hachette Livre UK Company

A CIP catalogue record for this book is available
from the British Library

ISBN 978 0 575 08372 1

1 3 5 7 9 10 8 6 4 2

Typeset at The Spartan Press Ltd,
Lymington, Hants

Printed and bound at CPI Mackays,
Chatham ME5 8TD

The Orion Publishing Group's policy is to use papers that
are natural, renewable and recyclable products and made
from wood grown in sustainable forests. The logging and
manufacturing processes are expected to conform to the
environmental regulations of the country of origin.

www.orionbooks.co.uk

DARKENING FOR A FALL

CHAPTER 1

Jetball Cup Final

The attempt on Lady Aanfieldsdaughter's life took place during the jetball cup final.

The match was between the Pearl Town Peregrines and up-and-coming underdogs the Cumula Collective Harpies, and the first half was a close-fought contest. The Peregrines had greater strength in the middle and low fields, as well as the advantage of being the match hosts, with the majority of the crowd on their side. The Harpies, however, were the sharper team and hungrier for victory. The Peregrines had overhauled the current Pan-Airborn Trophy holders, the Northernheights Goshawks, in the league table, but the general view was that that success had made them stale and overconfident. The Harpies had never played in a final before, and the bookies were offering long odds on them winning – but not that long.

Also in their favour, the Harpies had the single best jetball player currently being fielded anywhere, Neriah Tenth-House.

On that fact, Az and Michael could agree. On every other aspect of the match, however, the brothers differed wildly.

'An all-female team will never beat an all-male team,' Michael stated early on in the game. 'I'm sorry, I'm not being sexist, it's just the truth. Neriah aside, they just don't have the speed and stamina.'

'But look at that!' Az exclaimed, pointing. 'Those two Harpy upper forwards are flying rings around the Peregrine defence.'

'But the Peregrine centre back's just intercepted. Stole the ball right out of their hands.'

'He was lucky.'

'Lucky my tailfeathers! He's bigger and meaner, that's – whoa! Did you see that? Az, did you? That was a definite foul. Wing-butt. Referee! Are you blind or something? She wing-butted him! Send her off! Ref!'

'Michael,' said Aurora. 'Down.'

In his agitation, Michael had flapped up out of his seat. Aurora caught him by the ankle and yanked him back into place.

'But she—'

'Mike,' Aurora said, firmly. 'Behave yourself. You are sitting in the dignitaries' box. It's a privilege to be here, and people are watching. You can't carry on like this is just a weekday evening friendly at the local hoopdrome. Some decorum, please.'

'Yes, dear. Sorry, dear.'

Behind the cover of one wing, Michael rolled his eyes at Az.

'Hen-pecked,' Az commented with a smirk.

'Shut it, little bro,' Michael retorted.

'Oh, and for your information, Michael,' Aurora said, 'if an all-female team can't beat an all-male one, how come the Harpies are in the final at all? They've had to overcome several male teams to get here.'

'I, er, what I meant was an all-female team's never won the final.'

'Well, not yet they haven't.' Aurora nodded towards the swirling action of the game. 'But the score's only sixty-fifty to the Peregrines, and the way things are going . . .'

As if to prove Aurora's point, at that moment Neriah Tenth-House soared out of midfield to smack home a spectacular upward drive. The ball whammed into the Peregrines' 20-point frame. The crowd roared. Twelve thousand voices cheered and twelve thousand pairs of hands and wings clapped together deafeningly. Even the home-team supporters joined in, recognising skilled play when they saw it. Neriah celebrated the goal, and acknowledged the applause, by loop-the-looping all the way back to her starting position.

Lady Aanfielsdaughter, who was sitting in the row in front with the mayor of Pearl Town on her left, turned round.

'Enjoying it so far?' she asked Az.

'Very much so, milady,' Az said. 'I couldn't be happier. Comfy seats, great view. If only the Stratoville Shrikes were playing here today . . .'

'Alas, it's beyond even my capabilities to arrange for your favourite team to reach the final. But everything else is fine?'

'Straight up,' Az replied in his impression of a Groundling accent, which he thought was pretty good but which he never dared use in the presence of Cassie or any of the Grubdollar family. 'Matter of fact, I be happy as a coal miner on bath day.'

Lady Aanfielsdaughter laughed, and Mr Mordadson, seated on her right, chuckled softly too. But within seconds the Silver Sanctum emissary was back to scanning the crowd. His eyes, behind his crimson-lensed spectacles, darted to and fro with hawkish intensity. His gaze came to rest on a face here, now a face there, checking, scrutinising, moving on.

Nearby, a man got up from his seat and headed towards the aisle. Mr Mordadson tracked his progress, relaxing only when the man disappeared down a chute that led to the public toilets.

Mr Mordadson was always vigilant, but Az had the sense that today he was being more so than usual. He had been on edge since the Silver Sanctum party arrived at the Pearl Town 'drome. He stuck close to Lady Aanfielsdaughter at all times, never straying further than a wingspan from her side. He was currently behaving less like an emissary and more like a personal bodyguard.

Did Mr Mordadson know something that no one else did, and wasn't telling?

Az thought it very likely.

But that didn't prevent Az from becoming wrapped up in the game, and when the half-time siren blew, he felt exhausted. It was strenuous work, all this hurrahing and yelling. He looked forward to a quarter-hour of rest.

A display of competitive kite-flying had been laid on to keep the spectators entertained during the interval. Representatives from every sky-city entered the playing area, each bearing a kite marked with the insignia of his or her hometown. The kites were launched into the air, and combat commenced.

For a tail, each kite was fitted with a length of twine which was weighted at the end and coated with a mixture of glue, sand and ground glass. The rules of the contest were straightforward. You flew your kite at those of your opponents and tried to cut their control strings with the tail. The ground-glass mixture made the tails razor sharp. Whoever's was the last kite still tethered and aloft was the winner.

The kites flashed and slashed, wheeling around one another like a flock of bizarre, multicoloured birds of prey. Control strings snapped with a twang, and stricken kites spiralled downwards, to be caught by their owners and carried off. It was a frenetic free-for-all. One by one, the kites' numbers were whittled down. Stratoville went. Then Emerald Rise. Northernheights. Pearl Town (a groan of shame from the home crowd). Cloud 9. Azuropolis. Acme Empyrean. Then, to the dismay of Az and Michael, High Haven.

The remaining kites battled on. The people guiding them used every trick they knew: nosedives, cunning feints, sudden reversals of direction. They were remarkably skilled. The kites seemed like extensions of themselves.

One kite came hurtling out from the playing area and swooped towards the dignitaries' box, leaping away again at the last moment with a crack of canvas. Everyone in the box ducked. The tip of the kite's tail had missed Aurora's head by mere centimetres.

'Who's the featherbrained guano-head who did that?' Michael snarled. 'Whoever it is, they'd better not try it again.'

Scowling, he laid a wing protectively around his wife's five-months-pregnant belly.

Az looked at Mr Mordadson. He was eyeing the kite flyer very carefully indeed. Az saw the tendons in the back of his neck flexing. His wingtips were twitching.

The kite zoomed perilously close to the dignitaries' box again. This time the tail lashed at Lady Aanfielsdaughter. There was an audible gasp from the spectators immediately around the box. The mayor of Pearl Town squealed, while Lady Aanfielsdaughter shrank down in her seat. The tail whipped through the air just where her head had been a split second earlier.

'Az!' shouted Mr Mordadson, launching himself up out of his seat. He didn't even look around. 'Get her ladyship out of here. Now!'

The next few moments passed slowly for Az. Horrendously slowly. Like in a dream. A nightmare.

CHAPTER 2

Killer Kite

Az sprang into the seat Mr Mordadson had just vacated. The kite was turning in the air overhead, spinning on its own axis, getting ready to come in for a third time. He noted that it bore the Prismburg insignia. The same rainbow pattern adorned the tailfins of his beloved *Cerulean*. He made these observations even as he seized Lady Aanfielsdaughter by the arm and began hustling her out of the dignitaries' box. He was feeling somehow both calm and panicky at once. He realised the danger the kite posed, and was afraid, but a higher, cooler part of his brain had taken charge and was governing his actions. It was telling him to move swiftly but sure-footedly. To get Lady Aanfielsdaughter to the nearest exit, keeping her head down the whole way, and his own too. To ignore anything else, everything else. To focus only on ensuring Lady Aanfielsdaughter's safety. That was all that mattered.

The kite dived down. Even above the cries of alarm that were rising from all around him, Az could hear the rippling of its canvas, getting louder – all too rapidly louder. A diamond-shaped shadow passed over him. He knew the tail was trailing immediately behind. He and Lady Aanfielsdaughter were still three metres from the exit, a little gate set into the waist-high wooden partition that enclosed the box.

There was only one thing to do. He grabbed her by the shoulders and shoved her face-down onto the floor. Then he threw himself on top of her.

He glimpsed the kite's tail *swissshing* towards them. Instinctively, he put up his right arm to ward it off.

The pain was instant and excruciating. It was unbelievable that anything could hurt so much. From elbow to wrist Az's arm became one huge burning flare of agony. He screamed soundlessly, while blood – his own blood – sprayed his face and his shirtfront. He clutched the arm with his free hand, trying to hold the pain in, like you could with, say, a stubbed toe. It didn't work. The pain would not be contained. His hand came away dripping with warm, red liquid. He rolled onto his back, his mouth still yawning open, trying in vain to get that scream out. He knew the danger hadn't gone away and that he must still guard Lady Aanfields-daughter in whatever way he could. But he couldn't seem to move. Everything had shrivelled down to the pain in his arm, the incandescent throb, the crippling, nauseating, torment that the kite tail had inflicted.

He stared up into the blinding light of the sun. He could hear Michael bellowing: 'He's injured! He's bleeding! Someone do something!' His brother's voice seemed to be coming from a long way away.

Then, slightly nearer, Aurora was speaking to him: 'Az? Lie still. I'm going to have to put pressure on the wound. It's going to be unpleasant but you must keep still.'

'Lady Aan—' Az started to say, but then the agony overtook him, worse than ever. Aurora had begun wrapping a strip of cloth tight around his injured limb.

Meanwhile there was a continuous background thrum, the sound of worried voices, people standing, leaving their seats, taking to the air.

Everything swelled to a crescendo – pain, sounds, the brilliance of the sky.

Az felt like he was teetering on the brink of a great blackness, a dark, cool, limitless void. It beckoned to him, inviting him in. Gratefully, he plunged.

CHAPTER 3

The Fletcher Tank

Cassie frowned at the clouds.

'What'm up, girl?' her father asked. 'You'm got a queer look on your face. Like you just heard a noise and you be'n't sure what it be and where it'm come from.'

'Dunno. It'm nothing, most probably. Just . . .' She shook her head. 'Funny feeling, that'm all. As if there be trouble.'

'There be trouble all right,' said Fletcher, flipping up the visor of his welder's mask. 'And you'm in it, Cass, unless you bring me that spare oxygen canister like I asked.'

Cassie blinked and nodded. She fetched the canister from the concrete loading dock and lugged it over to her brother. Fletcher attached it to one of the tubes from his oxy-acetylene blowtorch and fired up a cone of flame at the nozzle. Swinging the visor back down, he bent to work. Sparks shot from the join he was welding, bouncing off his fireproof gloves and the front of his mask. A lightning-storm smell filled the air.

In the centre of the Grubdollars' courtyard, where *Cackling Bertha* used to reside, a new invention was taking shape. It was a steel cylinder approximately five metres long and three metres tall, with a wheel-lock door at one end. The cylinder was insulated and airtight. Inside there was a narrow bench running along the middle. A rubberised length of pipe protruded from the other end, leading to a motor-powered compressor pump, which was regulated by a timer mechanism.

This was Fletcher's brainchild, a device he had dreamed up during the Grubdollar family's foray into the Relentless Desert five months ago with Colin Amblescrut and Michael and Aurora Gabrielson. It was a pressurisation/depressurisation chamber capable of swiftly acclimatising a person to the difference in atmospheric density between the ground and the sky-cities. He had already dubbed it, rather grandly, the Fletcher

Tank. He had spent weeks developing the idea and building a scale-model prototype, which he had tested out on fieldmice, successfully. The next step was this full-size prototype, which he intended to test out on himself once it was completed. If it worked – and he had no reason to believe it wouldn't – he could foresee a time when there were dozens of Fletcher Tanks installed at the base and summit of every sky-city column. Ground-sickness and altitude sickness would be things of the past. Travel between the Groundling and Airborn realms would be easier and more convenient than it had ever been. All it would require was an hour or so in a Fletcher Tank, and you were ready for whichever of the two environments you had journeyed to.

The social benefits for both races would be enormous. And so, too, would the financial benefits for one Fletcher Grubdollar and his kin.

Which was good because, with *Bertha* gone, the Grubdollars were deprived of their usual means of earning a livelihood. They were desperately short of money. They were, in fact, down to their last few notes, and Den Grubdollar had begun scouting around for a job with one of the local Grimvale industries, in case the Fletcher Tank project didn't pan out for any reason. He had gone to an interview for an above-ground position at one of the coalmines and another as a driver for Roving Sightseer Enterprises, and was waiting to hear back from both those companies. It was humiliating for a lifelong self-employed man to have to look for salaried work. Den had been his own boss for so many years, the idea of being answerable to somebody else did not sit well with him. But needs must.

'It be'n't right, Da,' Cassie said, as they watched the leap and stutter of the sparks from Fletcher's welding.

'This that "funny feeling" of yours?' said Den. 'That'm what you be talking about?'

'No. That were something else.' *Something to do with Az*, she nearly added, but didn't. Her father would think she was going loopy if she told him she had a strong sense that Az was injured and in difficulties. Most likely he would laugh and make some joke about women's intuition and all the daft notions that girls got into their heads. She herself knew she might be imagining things. She resolved not to think about it for now. If Az *was* in trouble, she would know about it soon enough. She was due to meet him in Heliotropia the day after tomorrow.

'No,' she went on, 'what be'n't right is *Bertha* not being here.'

Den sighed. 'I know. Like Robert said this morning, just before him set off for school. He said, "I open the curtains, Da, and it'm always a shock when I see her's not there. Every time, I think someone must've nicked she. Then I remember. Someone did, basically, and now us doesn't have a vehicle to get about in."'

'Unless you count that crappy old half-tarp,' Cassie said, nodding to the little van that was parked snugly in one corner of the yard. It used to belong to Deacon Hardscree and, after the demise of its madman owner, the family had driven it home from the Relentless Desert intending to sell it. Instead, finding themselves in need of transportation after *Bertha* was taken, they had kept it. 'But it'm more than that, Da. I feel the same about *Bertha* as I did when Martin died, almost. Seems ridiculous. She'm just a hunk of old metal. Parts and machinery and that. She be'n't a person.' Cassie told herself she wasn't going to cry. She just about managed not to. 'But still I . . . I miss she, Da. Nearly as much as Mart.'

'Me too. And it be'n't ridiculous. I've never known a time when *Bertha* weren't in my life. Her's part of the family, no question.' Den put an arm around his daughter's shoulders and hugged her roughly. 'But her be gone now. Them Craterhome buggers took she, and us just has to accept that.'

'Why, Da?' Cassie shot back, challengingly.

'You know why,' Den replied.

'No, I don't. I know Robert electrocuted all those folk in Craterhome and I know *Bertha* got confiscated and that were a condition for the police not pressing charges against we. But I also know it be'n't fair. Nobody *died*, did them? Robert didn't kill anyone. And besides, what him did were an accident. I don't see why us should have to suffer like this just because of a mistake.'

'Sometimes life be'n't fair,' said her father. 'Us simply has to put up with it.'

'No, us doesn't. That'm coward's talk.'

'Now, now. I be'n't a coward, girl, and don't you dare be calling I one.' Den looked stern. 'I be just practical. There'm some things you can fight against and others you can't. This'm one of the ones you can't, and you'll only cause yourself misery if you think you can try.'

Cassie huffed but said nothing. Her father was right, of course, but that didn't mean she had to like what he said. It grieved her to think of *Bertha*, out there somewhere, probably in Craterhome, toiling away for someone else, some stranger. It made her heart ache. *Bertha* belonged nowhere but here. No one should be using her but a Grubdollar.

Fletcher finished welding the join. He switched off the blowtorch and inspected his handiwork. The glow of hot metal faded from yellow to orange to dim red, revealing a neat seam between two of the panels on the side of the tank.

'Straight up,' he said, with an approving nod.

Just then, a loud rapping came from the portcullis gate.

Cassie went to open it.

A man was standing in the street outside, holding a large, official-looking brown envelope. His suit was sombre and businesslike, and so was his expression.

Cassie knew – she just knew – this was yet more bad news for the Grubdollars.

CHAPTER 4

Cease-And-Desist

'Miss Grubdollar?' the man said.

'That be I.'

'Miss Cassandra Grubdollar?'

Cassie winced. She hated her full first name.

'Cassie,' she said.

'I'm Wilberforce Plumshoot,' the man said.

'I be sorry to hear that.'

The man twitched his head, then attempted a smile. 'Ahem. Yes. Well. I work for a law firm by the name of Dullgrumble, Pointcut and Blusterby.'

'I be even sorrier, then.'

'We're based in Craterhome and represent a number of immensely influential clients. In fact' – Plumshoot craned his neck self-importantly – 'I'd go so far as to say we are the foremost law firm in the whole of the Westward Territories. I'd be surprised if you haven't heard of us.'

'I wouldn't be,' said Cassie. 'Us doesn't have much dealing with law firms if us can possibly avoid it.'

Her father appeared beside her. 'Cass? Who'm this wormy little chap? What does him want?'

'Mr Dennis Grubdollar I presume,' said Plumshoot. 'I'm—'

'Him's some lawyer, Da. From Tumrumble, Pointless and Gustybum. Did I get that right?'

Plumshoot ignored her. He seemed determined not to become ruffled by her jibes. 'I'm here on behalf of Slamshaft Engineering Incorporated. You've certainly heard of *them*.'

'I has,' said Den. 'Them makes . . . well, pretty much everything that can be made. Us has bought a few of their murk-comber spares and accessories in our time. "Built To The Highest Standards", that'm their

13

motto. Be'n't always true, mind. The number of replacement gasket heads from Slamshaft us has got through. Them splits right down the middle, them does.'

'Be that as it may,' said Plumshoot, 'Slamshaft Engineering have instructed my firm, and my firm have instructed me, to deliver this.'

He held out the brown envelope.

'What'm that?'

'Open it, Mr Grubdollar, and see.'

Den slid a grimy-nailed index finger beneath the envelope flap and extracted the letter inside. 'Smart headed notepaper.' He squinted at the text of the letter, then passed it to Cassie. 'That typing's too tiny, and I can't be bothered to get my reading specs. You tell I what it says, lass.'

' "Dear Grubdollar family," ' Cassie read out. 'Nice start. Polite. "Forthwith heretofore upon receipt of this missive . . ." Is them actually words? ". . . of this missive, you are to refrain from all work upon your pressurisation/depressurisation unit and take immediate steps to dismantle the aforementioned apparatus." '

'Wha-a-at?' said Den.

Cassie read on, her voice growing loud with disbelief and indignation. ' "You are to cease and desist from any operations which might be considered a furtherance of the construction of said apparatus. Any attempts to continue to infringe the copyright of Slamshaft Engineering Incorporated will be met with punitive legal action, up to and including criminal prosecution. Furthermore, you are to undertake to surrender any and all documentation pertaining to . . ." I can't go on.' She waved the letter in Plumshoot's face. 'What be this all about?'

'I should have thought it was perfectly clear, Miss Grubdollar,' said the lawyer. 'The letter is saying—'

'I know what it'm saying. What do it *mean*?'

'That tank you're putting together there.' Plumshoot pointed through the gateway, past Cassie's shoulder, into the courtyard. 'Slamshaft have taken out a patent on the design. It's *their* intellectual property, and they're busy mass-producing it even as we speak. You carry on with yours, and you'll wind up in prison. I can't put it any more plainly than that.'

Or any more smugly, Cassie thought.

'But this'm daft!' Den exclaimed. 'The tank be Fletcher's idea. It'm his baby. Him came up with it, and him's been busy with nothing else this past few months. Slamshaft can't just come along and say it'm theirs and them's making it and him's ripped them off. Can they?'

'Did your son lodge an application with the Central Patent Office?'

'Search I.' Den turned to Cassie. 'Did him?'

14

Cassie shrugged. 'Don't think so. Him never mentioned it. Don't think him realised him had to.'

'Then, in answer to your question, Mr Grubdollar, yes. Slamshaft *can* do this, and are.'

Den groaned. 'I don't believe it.'

'Me either,' said Cassie. She tore the letter to shreds and sprinkled the pieces around Plumshoot's gleaming calfskin shoes. 'That be what I think of your stupid bit of paper.'

The lawyer looked unimpressed. 'The cease-and-desist order still stands, Miss Grubdollar, however you treat the original document by which it was conveyed to you. We will, of course, send you a replacement copy, and charge you accordingly.'

'Why, you scummy little—!' Cassie reached out to throttle Plumshoot, but her father restrained her.

'Clip it down, Cass,' he said. 'It be'n't this snooty runt's fault. Him's just doing his job.'

'Let I at he, Da! Please! Just for a second. Let I give that lousy featherplucker what-for.'

Plumshoot was backing nervously away as Cassie struggled in her father's arms.

'First off, girl, don't swear. Not even in Airborn. And second off, no, I won't let you at he. Save it for later. Us'll sort this out some other way and get angry with the people us should get angry with. What I think us needs to do right now . . .'

Den turned to look at his son. Fletcher was just out of earshot but he had observed what was going on at the gate and seen enough to know he should be worried.

'. . . is us needs to find some way of telling your brother that him's got to start taking his precious prototype apart. And somehow,' Den added grimly, 'I has a sneaking suspicion him's not going to be any too happy about that.'

CHAPTER 5

At The Hole And Shovel

When Colin Amblescrut entered the Hole and Shovel at half past six that evening, he was a little surprised to find Fletcher propping up the bar in the main saloon. He was delighted, too. Fletcher wasn't a frequent pubgoer, so it was a treat for Colin to have his friend there to drink with. Plus, he reckoned he could count on Fletcher to get his share of rounds in. In fact, if luck was on his side, Colin thought he might be able to persuade Fletcher to get *all* the rounds in.

Briefly Colin revelled in the familiar aromas of spilled booze, pipe smoke, pies cooking in the kitchen, and the sawdust that covered the floor. He waved to a couple of fellow-regulars. The pub – his home from home. Then he crossed to the bar. Pulling up the stool next to Fletcher, he nodded a greeting.

Fletcher nodded back, and it was in that moment that Colin realised that his pal was very, very drunk. The whites of Fletcher's eyes were pink and the nod he gave was more a loll of the head than a conscious physical action.

The pub had only opened at six. It had taken some going for Fletcher to get *this* drunk in the space of just half an hour.

'All right?' Colin asked, cheerily but also with curiosity.

'Nope.' Then, as if he hadn't already said it, Fletcher said it again: 'Nope.'

'Oh. Well, what'm you having?'

Fletcher studied his pint tankard, which was nearly empty. Beer-froth webbed the inside of the glass.

'Beer,' he said simply.

Colin gestured to the landlord with a flick of his fingers. 'Two pints of Earthtrembler's Old Peculiar, Gus,' he said. When the drinks arrived, he jerked his head in Fletcher's direction. 'His tab.'

Fletcher didn't hear this, or if he did, he didn't care enough to object.

'So,' Colin said, after he had downed most of his pint at a single gulp, 'want to talk about it, Fletch?'

'Nope.'

'OK.'

After a minute's gloomy silence, Fletcher said, 'Them's shafted me, them has.'

'Shafted you? Who?'

'Slam-bloody-shaft Engineering, that'm who. Shaft by name, shaft by nature.'

'Eh? How come?'

Briefly, and slurring his words somewhat, Fletcher explained about the cease-and-desist order.

'Ooh, that'm nasty,' Colin said, with feeling. He patted Fletcher's arm. 'Right buggers, those big businesses is. The Fletcher Tank were your idea. Us all knows that. And then them comes along and claims it for their own, and there'm nothing you can do about it. How can you? You'm just the little man. The fly under the swatter. The rabbit under the front tyres. The sapling in the avalanche. The—'

'Yes, yes, I get the picture, Colin.'

'Just saying their sort's bullies. Rides roughshod over everyone. Be'n't the way it ought to be, but what can us do? I be sorry, Fletch. You had such hopes for the tank and all. Ah well. Back to the drawing board.'

If Fletcher was comforted by these sentiments, he didn't show it.

'Although, I had a horrible feeling something like this might happen,' Colin went on. He signalled to Gus the landlord, and two more pints of Earthtrembler's appeared. 'Ever since that bloke were round here a while back . . . What were his name? No, it'm gone. But the way him were talking, I had this feeling you had competition. Maybe I should've said something about it to you at the time, only I didn't want to discourage you.'

'Bloke?' said Fletcher, lifting his head. His eyes narrowed. 'What bloke?'

'Just some geezer from Craterhome way. Him were up in Grimvale on a – what were the phrase? – a "fact-finding mission". Said him had heard this area were a hive of innovation. His exact words. A hive of innovation and activity. Said there were rumours that had got as far as Craterhome, about us having some very clever inventor types in our midst. Of course, I couldn't help boasting about my old chum Fletcher Grubdollar and what him were up to at home.'

Fletcher appeared to sober up in an instant. His gaze became steadier and more focused and his speech no longer so thick and stumbling.

'Repeat, Colin, precisely what you said to he.'

'I didn't say anything. Not really. I mean, you swore I to secrecy over the Fletcher Tank, so I weren't about to blab about it to just any old random bod, now were I? All I said to he was you'd had this brainwave, which you'd worked out when us had some Airborn passengers in *Bertha*'s loading bay.' He shrugged. 'What can I say? Pride got the better of I. But I definitely did not tell he any more'n that. Not even after him bought that third pint.'

'Colin.' Fletcher was pronouncing his words very crisply and clearly now. 'Be you quite sure you didn't tell he any more? I want you to think back. Be honest. After the third pint, were there maybe a fourth? A fifth, even?'

'No. Well, yeah. But I stopped at the fifth, definitely. Or were it the sixth?'

'And all this time, while the man were buying you beer, did he keep asking questions?'

'No, him and I were just chatting.'

'Did the subject of the Fletcher Tank come up again?'

Colin racked his brains. 'Now that I recall . . . yup. Once or twice. But only once or twice, no more'n that.'

'You didn't explain the principle of the tank to he? Because I know you know it.'

'Umm . . .' It was dawning on Colin that he perhaps didn't remember the *whole* of his conversation with the stranger from Craterhome. As the evening had worn on, things had become a bit blurry. The man had seemed like nice enough, for a Craterhomer. Friendly and forthright, and his hand had kept dipping into his pocket. Colin hadn't had to shell out once for a drink. Which had made for a memorable evening. Or, rather, an *un*memorable one.

Had he spilled the beans about Fletcher's pressurisation technique? The theory on which the tank's operation was based?

Colin was beginning to fear that he had.

'But it were just some bloke in a pub,' he said lamely.

'Colin, you blithering great idiot!' Fletcher growled. 'Him were an industrial spy! Had to be! Don't you see? Someone in Craterhome must've got wind of what I were up to. Someone at Slamshaft, most likely. And the company then sent a man up to ask around and pump people for information. "Find some local with a taste for the booze," him were probably told, "some brainless hillbilly whose lips'll loosen at the first offer of a pint, and see what you can get out of he." And lo and behold . . . !'

'Now, Fletch,' Colin said, wagging a meaty finger at him, 'I be going to overlook you calling I those names, on account of you's had a skinful and be'n't in your proper head. I realise you might think you's a reason to be

18

cross with I, but really, when you look at it, it weren't my fault. It were yours.'

'Oh yeah? And by what insane process of logic do you arrive at that conclusion?'

'Well, you shouldn't have entrusted I with your secret. I mean, I be'n't exactly known for my reliability. Maybe you should have thought of that before you dragged I in on this whole thing.'

'Dragged you . . . ?' Fletcher was agog. 'You walked in while I were experimenting with the miniature prototype. You barged into my room without knocking and had your nose halfway inside the model before I could stop you. "Ooh, a mouse," you said. "I love mice." '

'And I do.'

'So what were I supposed to do? Make up some absurd cover story for why I had a mouse in a homemade pressurisation chamber or tell you the truth?'

'Probably, the cover story would have been the better idea.'

'Dammit!' Fletcher leapt to his feet. 'This is what I get for hanging around with an Amblescrut.' He jabbed a finger in Colin's chest. 'You and your whole, dumb, too-close-knit-for-comfort clan. You be wasters and scroungers and idlers and no-hopers and – and wasters.'

'You already said wasters.'

'I know. So what? I be sick of it. I be sick of *you*, Colin. You's knackered my life good and proper. You's gone and ruined the one chance my family had left. You . . . you . . .'

Words failed Fletcher, and in their absence all he could think of to do was take a swing at Colin.

His fist collided with the indomitable Amblescrut skull, and of course came off worse. Several of his knuckles split open but he was too angry (and had too much alcohol in his system) to feel the pain. He threw a second punch. This one Colin made the effort to deflect. He'd permitted Fletcher that first hit. In a way he deserved it, and usually his opponents hurt themselves so badly with the initial punch that they never managed a follow-up. But a second blow from Fletcher was a blow too far.

Colin then sideswiped him with the flat of his hand, and instantly Fletcher was face down on the floor. He staggered upright, spitting out sawdust. He reeled at Colin, fists clenched. With a sigh Colin got to his feet and plucked Fletcher up by one arm. Suspended off the ground, Fletcher flailed with his feet and free hand but none of the shots connected.

'Fletch, mate,' Colin said, 'let's get you out of here, eh? Before you does yourself a mischief.'

He carried the still flailing Fletcher to the door and tossed him into the street. Fletcher landed in a heap in the gutter. He tried to get up but the fight had gone out of him. He sat in the roadway, dazed, legs akimbo, while Colin brushed his palms together and went back inside.

Some minutes later, Fletcher finally made it to his feet. He trudged off home, muttering curses about Colin and all the Amblescruts.

Colin, for his part, spent the rest of the evening drinking as heavily as his budget allowed, and when his cash ran out he yanked a distant relative out of one of the snugs and shook him down for a bit more money. He felt bitter at the way Fletcher had treated him, and remorseful that the two of them had fallen out.

Deep down, too, he knew who was to blame. And that made it all the more imperative that he lose himself in the pure, dreamy oblivion of inebriation. And so he did.

CHAPTER 6

Breaking Metal . . . And The Law

CLONNNG!
CLONNNG!
CLONNNG!

It sounded like the tolling of an immense bell. Cassie snapped awake, shot out of bed and hared downstairs in her pyjamas. Her father and Robert weren't far behind.

A few hours ago Cassie had helped a very unsteady Fletcher into bed. Now he was out in the courtyard. He had set up an arc lamp, and by its fierce white light he was assaulting his unfinished Fletcher Tank with a sledgehammer. His face was etched with lines of fury, his teeth bared like fangs.

CLONNNG!

Cassie ran to stop him, but was halted in her tracks by a scowl from Fletcher. He looked so maddened that it seemed possible he might turn and use the sledgehammer on *her*.

'Leave he be, Cass,' Den said softly. 'If someone has to turn that thing into scrap, may as well be Fletch who does it.'

CLONNNG!
CLONNNG!
CRACK!

The Fletcher Tank began to fall apart under the onslaught. Panels flew off, as though the device was some large steel reptile shedding its scales. The door was battered askew and then knocked off its hinges. The bench was reduced to firewood. Fletcher, sweating profusely, kept at it with a relentless energy. The sledgehammer swung and struck, swung and struck.

CRUNCH!
CLONNNG!

THWACK!

Soon neighbours were pounding on the portcullis gate and protesting about the racket at the tops of their voices. Did the Grubdollars realise what time it was? Decent folk were asleep in bed. Did they want the cops brought?

'Go ahead and bring they!' Den roared over the wall. 'See if us cares!'

'All right, us will,' came the reply, but the tone was uncertain. If the Grubdollars weren't worried about the police coming, then what good was the threat?

'Heh,' said Den. 'Called their bluff.'

Finally, after nearly an hour, the Fletcher Tank was a pile of twisted metal. Fletcher, its creator-turned-destroyer, stood over the wreckage, panting hard. The sledgehammer hung slackly in his hands. Cassie went over and took it off him, lifting a burden from him and making it her own. Fletcher acknowledged this feebly, then slumped to the ground and started weeping. Cassie set down the sledgehammer and crouched beside her brother. She held him while he sobbed, clasping his head to her chest. Tears were rolling down her cheeks too.

She looked up at her father and Robert.

'This'm it,' she said. 'Enough be enough. Look at Fletch. Look at we all. Us is a mess. Us can't do without *Bertha*, straight up. It were crazy to think us could.'

'But what would you suggest—?'

'Get she back, Da,' Cassie interrupted. 'Plain as that.'

'Yeah?' said Robert. 'How? Us doesn't even know where she be.'

'And there'm the small matter of us being forbidden by law to run she, let alone look for she,' said Den.

'So what? If the law be in our way, then the law'm wrong.'

'If everybody thought like that, girl, the world'd be chaos, and what would be the point of anything? Society has rules, and us mayn't always like they but us has to live by they.'

'Stuff that!' Cassie shouted. 'Since when has the rules helped we? Since when has sticking to they ever got we anywhere? You went to the Chancel, Da, when it were a Chancel, to rescue I and Fletch and Martin. Remember? That were against the law, surely. You drummed up all those Amblescruts and got into a rumble with the Humanists. I doubt the police would've been any too happy if them'd known about it. Them'd've put a stop to it if them had had the chance. And yet it were still the *right* thing to do. Same when us took on Deacon Hardscree. Him were going to kill you. Him tried to kill nearly all of we, in point of fact. And us did what us had to, to defend ourselves, and him wound up dead, and in the eyes of the law that'm murder, no doubt about it, or manslaughter at least, but us did it all the same. So what be the difference now? When the law don't work, us takes the law into our own hands. It'm the only way.'

Den was quiet for a moment. Stroking his chin with a thumb, he pondered.

'Her's got a point, Da,' said Robert.

'Her has,' Fletcher agreed, sniffing.

'Well?' said Cassie. 'That be three votes in favour, I reckon. What do you say, Da?'

Den studied his offspring, his gaze shifting from one face to the next. It seemed, every time he looked at them, that the three got one more step closer to being adults. Almost as it, when he took his eyes off them for a moment, they accelerated a year in age, becoming less children, more the grown-up people they were destined to be. It made him inordinately proud, and sometimes quietly sad.

'Nobody ever said this family were a democracy,' he said slowly. 'But . . .'

He grinned, revealing all three of his front teeth.

'Let's do it.'

'Yes!' exclaimed Cassie, and she leapt on Den and smothered his stubbly cheeks with kisses.

'I be going to regret this, be'n't I?' Den said, hugging her.

'Probably,' Cassie replied. 'Probably us all is. But wouldn't you rather regret doing something than regret *not* doing something?'

There was, Den thought, simply no arguing with that. There was, indeed, no arguing with Cassie at all. Not these days. Not any more.

CHAPTER 7

The Wingless Patient

A discreet flutter of wings woke Az.

He looked up to see a beautiful woman, standing over him at his bedside. She was checking the dressings on his right arm, which was in a sling suspended from a steel frame. She had neatly styled blonde hair and wore an immaculate white uniform, and the name-badge on her chest (her not inconsiderably large chest) read STAFF NURSE ARIELLA HAATANSDAUGHTER. Her wings were encased in gauze sheaths, just as her hands were encased in thin cotton gloves, for hygiene's sake.

Az, flat on his back, gazed at her for a while. She hadn't noticed he was no longer asleep. Although he felt muzzy and his head ached, it was extremely pleasant to be looking at Staff Nurse Haatansdaughter because she was so very pretty and had an air of such reassuring competence about her. He could have watched her ministering to him all day.

Then his memory served up an image: himself in a similar situation a year and a half ago, coming to his senses on the couch in the Grubdollars' lounge, with Cassie next to him. Cassie wasn't the elegant, well-coiffed, well-endowed creature that Nurse Haatansdaughter was, but she *was* his girlfriend, and Az experienced a sudden, furtive pang of guilt. Not that there was anything wrong with admiring another woman. What was it Michael said? 'Just because you're on a diet doesn't mean you can't study the menu.' But Az and Cassie got together so infrequently that the items on the menu were more than usually appetising, especially one as well served up as Nurse Haatansdaughter.

Finally Az let out a groan, announcing that he was conscious.

The groan was partly genuine. His wounded forearm was emitting dull, sludgy pulses of pain, like someone was reaching in and giving the veins and nerve endings a slow tug at regular intervals. The sensation came and went, but when it was bad it was only just bearable.

'Oh, hello there,' said Nurse Haatansdaughter. The greeting was cooler and brisker than Az would have liked, as was the smile that followed. 'About time you rejoined us.'

'I've got a cracking headache.'

'That'll be the after-effects of the chloroform.'

'Where am I?'

'Hospital, where do you think?'

Her sarcasm cut through the fogginess of his thoughts. He responded in kind. 'Ooh, I'd never have worked *that* out by myself. I meant, which hospital?'

'Pearl Town Mercy.'

'OK. And how am I doing?'

Curtly, Nurse Haatansdaughter filled him in on his medical status:

'You didn't lose the arm, although there was some question over that when they brought you in. It was opened up clean to the bone and a couple of tendons were almost severed. You were lucky. Dr Barpharangesson, our top surgeon, operated on you and saved the limb. The prognosis is good. You ought to make a full recovery.'

'You don't sound too happy about that.'

'It's not my job to be happy or unhappy about how a patient is doing,' said Nurse Haatansdaughter. 'But I admit, I won't be sad to see you leave. It's been bedlam here ever since you arrived. We've been besieged by reporters demanding information about you. They're crowding the entrance lobby downstairs and hassling the staff. That's why you're in a private room, not a ward, and why we're keeping the blinds closed. Everyone wants an interview with you.'

'Well, I'm sorry to be such an inconvenience,' Az said.

'And,' she added, 'as if that wasn't enough, we've got the Silver Sanctum breathing down our necks, asking for updates on your progress every hour, just about. All of which is making it very difficult to get any proper work done around here. I know you're a special case, man of the moment and all that, but even so. It seems to me a great deal of fuss to be making over a kid who doesn't even have . . .' She trailed off.

'Go on, say it. "Doesn't even have wings." '

Nurse Haatansdaughter's face reddened and she became suddenly fascinated by the chart on the wall above the bedstead, as if it contained more than just graphs that plotted Az's blood pressure, heart rate and temperature readings.

Even now, Az thought to himself, *even after all I've done for the Airborn, and the Groundlings, there are still people who think that I'm an insult to our race – who think that I shouldn't even have been born. I could save the world a dozen times over, and there'll always be someone who looks at me and sees nothing but a wingless freak of nature.*

25

He didn't fancy Nurse Haatansdaughter in the slightest any more, but neither did he hate her. If he felt anything for her, it was dull contempt, a weary nothingness.

'Look,' he said, 'whatever you think of me, it doesn't matter. I just need to know, is everyone else OK? What happened after I blacked out at the hoopdrome? Do you know?'

'I'm not sure, but your brother is down in the waiting area. Would you like me to send somebody to fetch him?'

'If it wouldn't be too much bother, Nurse Haatansdaughter.'

CHAPTER 8

One Hundred Per Cent Hero Stuff

Michael looked pale and dishevelled, but also overjoyed to see Az. He said he had been keeping vigil downstairs through the night, surviving on cups of very bad coffee from the hospital cafeteria and doing his best to avoid the reporters. They seemed to be everywhere, popping up from behind chairs and around corners, brandishing their notebooks and sketchpads, asking him if he could spare a moment or two for the *Northernheights News* or the *Stratoville Chronicle*.

'You're the big story of the day, Az,' he said. 'Everybody wants a piece of you. I mean, it's one thing, the stuff you've already done, beating the Humanists and then tackling Naoutha and her gang. Most people have heard of you because of that, even if you're not exactly a household name. But saving Lady Aanfieldsdaughter's life in front of a capacity crowd at the cup final . . . That's a whole new level of celebrity!'

'So I did save her.' Az was relieved and glad.

'Oh yeah. You took the hit from the kite tail that was intended for her. And you bought old Mordy enough time to take down the bloke from Prismburg who was flying the kite. It was one hundred per cent hero stuff, little bro. You should be proud of yourself. You couldn't have played it better – apart from the whole nearly-getting-your-arm-chopped-off bit.'

'Mum and Dad?'

'They're in an airbus even as we speak. Should be here by this evening.'

'And no one else got hurt? Aurora, the baby . . .'

'Nope, no one. Unless you count the Prismburger. Pluck me, you should have seen the way Mr Mordadson laid into him. It was like a harrier hawk on a sparrow.' Michael winced at the recollection. 'I think I heard bones crack, even all the way up in the dignitaries' box.'

'Was it deliberate? He was attacking on purpose?'

'Who, Mordadson? I should say so!' laughed Michael.

'No, birdbrain, the Prismburger.'

'Oh. Don't know about that. Probably – unless he just lost control of the kite.'

'Which isn't very likely. Not three times in a row like that.'

'Yeah, well, either way, Mr Mordadson hauled him off unconscious. I've no idea where he is now. But wherever it is, I bet Mordy's making his life pretty damn uncomfortable.'

Michael grinned.

'More importantly, Az,' he said, 'have you *seen* that nurse of yours? What a bird of paradise!'

'Mike, you're a married man – about to become a father.'

'Still, she's got a lovely pair on her, hasn't she? Of wings, I mean.' He chortled leeringly. 'And what have I told you about diets and menus?'

Az debated whether to reveal the nurse's gaffe about his winglessness, but he decided not to ruin Michael's fantasy. 'She's not my type. I like them earthier,' he said, and left it at that. Anyway, he was more interested in the motivation behind the Prismburger's assassination bid, if that was what it had been. He pressed his brother for further information, although there wasn't much to be had. Michael simply didn't know any of the whys and wherefores of the incident.

What reason could somebody have for trying to kill Lady Aanfiels-daughter, Az wondered. It was inconceivable. It was insane. What would murdering a wise and benevolent leader like her achieve? What could anyone hope to gain from it?

CHAPTER 9

A Mynah Distraction

Lady Aanfielsdaughter herself was keen for answers to the questions which Az was pondering, and Mr Mordadson was doing his utmost to supply them. He, like Michael, had passed a sleepless night, but unlike Michael he had had more to keep him occupied than finding coffee and dodging journalists. He had spent the time interrogating the Prismburg kite flyer in a holding cell at the Pearl Town Alar Patrol headquarters. Now he was back at the Silver Sanctum, with little to show for his efforts but bruised knuckles.

'Tight-lipped so-and-so,' he snarled, before adding, with grudging admiration, 'You have to give him some credit for that. If I'd been him, with what I put him through, I'd have been singing like a canary in no time.'

'Please, Mr Mordadson, spare me the gory details,' said Lady Aanfielsdaughter, with a shudder. 'The less I know about what you sometimes have to do, the easier I can sleep at night.'

'And the relieving of milady's conscience is my only goal in life,' said Mr Mordadson. 'Never mind the state of my own conscience.'

Lady Aanfielsdaughter looked at him askance. It was an uncharacteristic comment and seemed to carry a note of bitter self-pity. But Mr Mordadson's face remained the same as ever, solid, determined, implacable. His eyes were no different behind their shields of crimson glass, calm yet alert. She put the remark down to tiredness. People were not themselves when they hadn't slept. They said things they didn't mean, in ways they didn't intend.

'Your service to me,' she said, 'is never taken for granted. So, did you discover anything?'

'Eventually, milady, yes.'

29

Lady Aanfielsdaughter, who was seated at her office desk, leaned forward, folding her wings expectantly.

'He's a Feather First!er,' said Mr Mordadson.

'Ah. I see. And?'

'And that's it. That's all I could get. I wouldn't even have found that out if I hadn't looked for the tattoo.'

'Tattoo?'

'It was on his upper arm. A lot of Feather First!ers have the tattoo these days, especially the extremist ones. Two wings, side by side, with the filaments arranged so that they look like a pair of F's. Apart from that, though, I know nothing about him. Couldn't even persuade him to cough up his name. The one he gave to the organisers of the kite competition was false. He's not even the real Prismburg kite-flying representative. That's some poor fellow who pulled out at the last minute, claiming illness. I reckon the First!ers "leaned" on him and insisted he put forward their own man as his substitute. I'll learn more in time, don't you worry.'

'I'm sure you will.'

'Yes, he's a tough nut to crack all right. There's something . . . not quite right about him. I can't put my finger on it. The way he stares at me, like he's looking straight through me. The way he doesn't utter a sound.'

'Perhaps he's simply intimidated.'

'Perhaps. Whatever it is, just as soon as I'm done here I'm heading back to Pearl Town for another one-on-one session with him. But I thought it best to report to you in person. I was concerned, too, milady, about your wellbeing, and wanted to see how you are.'

'I'm fine, as you can tell,' said Lady Aanfielsdaughter. She waved in the direction of her office windows. Out on the balcony, two Alar Patrollers stood at attention, their lances at the ready. 'I have protection, which I'm none to happy about but realise the necessity for. I understand you've arranged for a whole contingent of Patrollers to come to the Sanctum, to look after us all. I'm none too happy about that either, but for the time being I suppose I can live with it. No, if there's anyone you should be concerned about, it's Az. I'm just a bit shaken up by what's happened, that's all. He's the one who actually got hurt.'

'Pearl Town Mercy was going to be my next port of call, after the Alar Patrol HQ.'

'Good. I'd go myself, but . . .'

'No, with all due respect, milady, you must stay here for now. There's no sense in you showing yourself in public and exposing yourself to further risk.'

'I'd have thought that's precisely what I should be doing. Proving to everyone that I won't be cowed into hiding from these . . . these terrorists.'

'Later, milady. Not just yet.'

'So what do they want?' Lady Aanfielsdaughter rose and began pacing the floor. 'Till now, the Feather First! movement has been an annoyance and an embarrassment, but hardly a threat. Staging protest rallies, haranguing passers-by with their rhetoric – fine. Airborn democracy permits people to hold differing points of view and express them. Harassing Groundling visitors is another matter, but I thought the Patrollers had cracked down on that and had it under control. Tour parties have Patrol escorts and we're not seeing nearly as many of those unpleasant confrontations as before, Groundlings being called names and pelted with soil.'

'It could be,' said Mr Mordadson, 'that the crackdown itself is the root of the problem. What upsets the Feather First!ers is the notion that Groundlings are our equals and worthy of respect. Giving them any kind of special treatment – Patroller escorts, for example – merely confirms in the First!ers' minds that the authorities are on the Groundlings' side.'

'Well, we are, when it comes to them being victimised.'

'But the First!ers don't see it that way. They see it as bias, Groundlings being given precedence over Airborn.'

'And this so enrages them that they put together a plot to, very publicly, kill me?' Lady Aanfielsdaughter stopped pacing up and down. It made her feel like a prisoner – which she was, to some extent. The Silver Sanctum was a large and luxurious place to be confined in, but it confined her nonetheless. The presence of the Patrollers on guard outside did nothing to ease the impression that she was now, somehow, under arrest. 'It's a desperate step to take.'

'These are desperate people,' said Mr Mordadson. 'Flight Lieutenant Wallimson – remember him?'

'He accompanied you on your journey to Redspire. He was one of them, wasn't he? A First!er.'

Mr Mordadson nodded. 'Thanks to him, our mission nearly failed and I almost died. If he's typical of the movement's more radical wing, then this kind of violent militancy is only going to worsen. You called them terrorists, milady. That, I fear, is what they are becoming.'

'Then what would you suggest I do?'

'Not up to me. You must discuss that with your colleagues here. That's how the Sanctum operates. You make the laws. People like me only implement them. And it's—'

He broke off. Something outside had caught his attention.

'What's up?' said Lady Aanfielsdaughter.

31

Mr Mordadson peered long and hard at the windows. 'Nothing,' he said finally. 'Just a bird, hopping around out there.'

Lady Aanfielsdaughter followed the line of his gaze and, through the filmy curtains which draped the large windows, saw a small bird near the feet of one of the Patrollers. It was pecking around inquisitively, moving to and fro in little skips and jumps. Its plumage was black all over, apart from two long flaps of yellow skin which overhung its eyes, like strange, floppy eyebrows.

'It's just a mynah,' she said. 'I leave seeds out there for the wild birds. It's having a snack.'

'But most mynahs are pet birds.'

'So? Plenty of Sanctum residents own one. Maybe it escaped. I'm sure it'll find its way back home soon. I don't see what's so bothersome about it. Leave it be. Let it enjoy its freedom.'

Because at least it has freedom, she thought. *Which is more than I can say for myself.*

CHAPTER 10

A Mynah Dispute

The appearance of the mynah on the balcony perturbed and aggravated Mr Mordadson for reasons he could not share with Lady Aanfielsdaughter.

He could, however, share them with Farris, Lord Urironson, and shortly he was doing just that, in Lord Urironson's private quarters, to which he flew straight after taking leave of Lady Aanfielsdaughter.

He went storming into the apartment's living room, where Lord Urironson happened to be taking tea at the time. The abrupt, startling intrusion caused him to drop his half-finished cup on the floor, with regrettable consequences for both the cup itself, which broke, and the rug, over which it spattered its contents. Lord Urironson's shoes and trouser legs were tea-splashed too, which he found irksome as he was a man who took great pride in his clothing and personal appearance.

'What the . . . ?' he spluttered.

'You were spying on me!' Mr Mordadson growled. 'That ruddy bird of yours was outside Lady Aanfielsdaughter's office, listening in.'

'I assure you, I have no idea what—'

'Where is it, then?' Mr Mordadson jabbed a finger at the hanging cage which was the mynah's usual home. The cage stood empty, the little door wide open.

'I let Echo out to have a fly around,' said Lord Urironson, recovering some of his customary suaveness. 'He likes to go off and stretch his wings from time to time. Where he is right now, I couldn't tell you. And if you happen to have spotted a mynah hear Lady Aanfielsdaughter's office, all I can tell you is it wasn't Echo, and even if it was, it's merely a coincidence.'

'Coincidence!' Mr Mordadson snorted.

'Besides, how could a *bird* be spying on you? Really, that's an absurd idea. A dumb, ignorant avian? Preposterous.'

'For starters,' said Mr Mordadson, 'it isn't dumb. Mynahs mimic. I've heard your one do it often enough. It rattles off everything anyone's just said. And extremely annoying it is too.'

'And you're suggesting I placed him up there to eavesdrop on her ladyship and report back to me?'

'I'm not suggesting it, I'm saying it. Except your mynah wasn't eavesdropping on just Lady Aanfielsdaughter. It was eavesdropping on the both of us. On *me*, for pluck's sake.'

Lord Urironson blinked, slowly, calmly, infuriatingly. 'The implication being that I don't trust you. That I feel the need to check up on you.'

'Absolutely right.'

'Mr Mordadson.' Lord Urironson got to his feet, bent over with a grunt, and delicately gathered up the shards of broken teacup. He tutted over the state of the rug. Those stains would not come out easily. 'If, as you say, I don't trust you, could it perhaps be because the alliance between us is relatively freshly-formed and we haven't yet fully got the measure of each other? Could it be because, although you've pledged to support me in whatever political manoeuvres I make, we haven't so far had the opportunity to test the validity of that pledge? Could it be that, up till now, you've relayed plenty of inside information to me from Lady Aanfielsdaughter's office but nothing that I've been usefully able to exploit against her?'

'You doubt that I'm loyal to you.'

'Naturally I do.' Lord Urironson gave a cold, canny laugh. 'You don't get to the top of the Sanctum tree without scrutinising and querying the motives of everyone around you, friends as well as foes. To me, a hand-shake is a comparison of strength and a smile is just a way of baring your teeth. I invariably look for the rationale behind every deed, and then the rationale behind the rationale. So when Lady Aanfielsdaughter's faithful sidekick comes and visits me one day and proposes a clandestine joining of forces, of course I have to ask myself why. What does he get out of it? What is his true agenda?'

'I told you,' Mr Mordadson said. 'You know what I'm after. I'm fed up. I'm fed up with being Lady Aanfielsdaughter's strong right arm. I'm heartily sick of having to commit all sorts of foul acts in her name, dirtying my hands so that she can keep hers clean. I decided I'd rather align myself with a leader who isn't afraid to take bold decisions and claim ownership of them, a leader who isn't scared of making hard choices and being answerable for them. I know which way the wind is blowing. I know where the world is heading. You do too. It's heading towards the abyss. Chaos is looming. And in times of chaos we don't

34

need politicians who are reasonable and even-handed. We need firm, forthright governance. Bravery, not sensitivity. Boldness, not caution. And that's where you come in.'

Lord Urironson tried not to look flattered, but he was. 'Nevertheless, your conversion struck me as somewhat abrupt.'

'Listen, I'd just had the guano kicked out of me by a bunch of pterine-heads, all in the service of her ladyship. You saw the state of me after I got back from Redspire.'

'You looked as if you'd had your face slammed against a wall several times, and you were walking like an arthritic old man.'

'Exactly. And on top of that, I had to go through pterine withdrawal. The pirates shot me full of the damn stuff. Overdosed me. I was sick as a parrot for days. And it was while I was shivering and sweating and throwing my guts up that I came to a conclusion. Why, I thought, should I have to put up with this? Not just the withdrawal symptoms. This life of mine. This existence I lead. All the suffering I go through, all on behalf of someone who doesn't strike me as winning material any more. Better I should throw in my lot with a man of the future, rather than a woman of the past.'

'Yet still you work for her, nominally at least. And still you leapt to her rescue yesterday when she came under attack. Can you wonder if I remain sceptical?'

Mr Mordadson let out a testy sigh. 'I'm more use to you, milord, as a double agent. For now, I can do more harm if I'm still under Lady Aanfielsdaughter's wing, so to speak. There's no point in betraying her until I have no alternative. And for that reason, saving her life was utterly in accordance with my current status. It would have been foolish, in fact, to do anything else. It would have blown my cover.'

'Hmmm.' Lord Urironson eyed the other man speculatively from beneath hooded, beetling brows. These made him look not unlike a mynah himself, in keeping with that old adage about pets resembling their owners and vice versa. 'It seems we cannot help distrusting one another.'

'It does seem that way. Perhaps it might help if you yourself were a little more honest with me. For instance, you could tell me where it is you go when you vanish for a couple of days at a stretch, as you have done lately. I don't think anyone else has noticed these "disappearances" of yours, but I have, and I've got to say it's been making me a little tiny bit curious.'

'My secrets should remain mine, for now.'

'But trust works both ways.'

'In time, Mordadson, all will be revealed.'

'All right. If that's how you want it. Never, though, *ever*, spy on me again. Is that clear? From now on, if I see a mynah bird anywhere near me, unless it's yours and it's in that cage, I will cheerfully wring its neck. Understood?'

'In so far as I deny all knowledge of what you're referring to,' said Lord Urironson, 'yes.'

'Good.'

Mr Mordadson exited the apartment in a flurry of featherdown.

CHAPTER 11

(Insert Your Own 'Mynah' Pun Here)

Echo, Lord Urironson's mynah, was no carrier dove or homing pigeon, and certainly no trained falcon. He did not come when called or head swiftly and unerringly back to the place from which he had originally been released. In that respect, he was unreliable. In every other way, though, he served his purpose well.

Lord Urironson had to wait till dusk before being reunited with his pet, but when Echo did finally remember he had a home, he flew back there with a head full of dialogue, and only a little coaxing was required to get him to blurt out what he had overheard. Lord Urironson let the bird perch on his wrist and fed him live grubs. Echo snatched the tiny squirming delicacies from his fingers and gulped them down whole. Between beakfuls, Lord Urironson caressed Echo's throat and spoke to him in soothing, cooing tones, in a manner that seemed genuinely affectionate.

Soon enough the mynah was repeating phrases and snippets from Mr Mordadson's earlier conversation with Lady Aanfielsdaughter.

'The relieving of milady's conscience,' he squawked. 'My foremost priority. *Awrk!*'

And: 'I have protection. *Arook!* Which I'm none too happy about. None too happy about.'

And: 'Violent militancy only going to worsen. *Thweep!*'

And: 'You make the laws. People like me. *Awk!* People like me only implement them.'

Echo was able to replicate not just the words but the voices of the individual speakers, so Lord Urironson could tell which of the statements came from Mr Mordadson and which from Lady Aanfielsdaughter.

Everything the mynah conveyed to him was to his satisfaction. First, Lady Aanfielsdaughter was rattled. That was good. The attempted assassination had put yet another dent in her confidence, a big one, and that was something he could surely use to his advantage. Second, Mr Mordadson was beginning to express his resentment about his position as her emissary, albeit in guarded tones. His patience was wearing thin. He didn't want to be her 'strong right arm' much longer.

'Good Echo,' Lord Urironson said, letting the mynah sidestep off his wrist into the cage. He shut the door. 'Clever Echo. You've done well.'

He was pleased. Mr Mordadson appeared to be on the level, sincere in his desire to ally himself with someone other than Lady Aanfielsdaughter. She herself was weakening. This confirmed what Lord Urironson knew already through his own careful probings among fellow Sanctum residents. Various elders were muttering that Lady Aanfielsdaughter had handled the recent Redspire affair clumsily, and many juniors were saying the same. *Their* opinions counted for less than the elders' but they made up in numbers what they lacked in influence. She should have dealt with the pirates sooner and harder. She should have shown more backbone, and then maybe things wouldn't have gone so badly out of control. Again and again, Lord Urironson was hearing remarks like these. And again and again, he was expressing them himself, softly, subtly, but with vigour.

A mood of restlessness was growing within the Sanctum. Lord Urironson could feel it. A similar mood was growing outside as well, throughout the Airborn realm. The Feather First! attack on Lady Aanfielsdaughter proved it.

If a crisis came now, the Airborn would look to the Sanctum for firmness and resolve. They would look to someone like Lord Urironson to guide them through the emergency.

Luckily, from Lord Urironson's viewpoint, a crisis *was* looming. And not just in the Airborn realm alone. Down on the ground as well.

He wasn't just sure of this.

He knew it for a fact.

CHAPTER 12

Cell Suicide

Mr Mordadson arrived back at Pearl Town Alar Patrol HQ, to be greeted by bad news.

'He's dead,' said Group Captain Kfialson.

Down in the holding cells lay a grisly sight. Sometime during the small hours of the night, the Feather First!er had removed his trousers and looped one leg of them around the bars of the cell window, which was set high up in the wall. With the other trouser leg knotted around his neck, he had flown up to the ceiling, plummeted, and hanged himself.

He lay spreadeagled against the base of the wall, still suspended from his makeshift noose. His face was black, his tongue protruded between his lips, and his eyes bulged like dull marbles, staring in slightly different directions. There was the smell of faeces in the air. The man had voided his bowels at the moment of strangulation.

'For pluck's sake!' hissed Mr Mordadson. 'Wasn't somebody keeping watch over him?'

'Checks at half-hourly intervals, as per procedure,' said Kfialson, indicating the spy-hole in the cell door. 'Unfortunately, it takes a lot less than half an hour to hang yourself.'

'There should have been a Patroller in there with him.'

'He didn't strike us as a suicide risk.'

Mr Mordadson thumped the door in anger. 'Well, that's just great. Not only do we not have a suspect to interrogate any more, we now have a martyr. Once word about this gets out, the First!ers are going to have a field day. We've just handed them the perfect propaganda victory.'

'Erm, it was *his* doing. Our only mistake was allowing him the opportunity to do it.'

'Amounts to the same thing,' snapped Mr Mordadson, and he slammed the door shut on the corpse with a thunderous, terminal clang.

CHAPTER 13

Awash With Blood And Feathers

On his second day in hospital, Az received a stream of visitors.

First were his parents. His mother was nothing but fretfulness and concern. She decided the room wasn't clean enough and the water in the jug by his bedside was stale. She made it plain to every member of staff at Pearl Town Mercy, not least Nurse Haatansdaughter, that they should be looking after her son better.

Az's father was somewhat calmer, though worried too.

'I realise you're an important chap these days, Azrael,' he said while Az's mother was out of the room, hectoring the senior matron. 'You carry a big weight on those young shoulders. But please, for my sake and your mum's, try to be a little more careful if you can. When all's said and done, you're still our boy.' He nodded at Az's arm. 'It frightens us silly, some of the stuff you get involved in.'

'I *was* being careful,' Az joked. 'Didn't help much.'

His father gave a wan smile.

Next in line was Aurora, who brought a bunch of flowers from Lady Aanfielsdaughter and her ladyship's best wishes.

'If she could have given these to you in person, she would have,' Aurora said, arranging the flowers in a place where Az could see them. They were lilies and white lilacs, the lushest, freshest blooms from the Sanctum nurseries, and their perfume was delicious. 'But with the situation as it is . . .'

'It's all right, Aurora. I understand.'

'I'm taking Mike back home, if that's OK with you. Poor man, he's exhausted.'

'That's fine. He deserves a rest.'

Then came Mr Mordadson, looking as angry and as glum as Az had ever seen him. They spent an hour together, discussing the assassination

40

attempt, the assassin's suicide, and the possible consequences of the two events.

'Why would he kill himself?' Az asked.

'He was facing life imprisonment. The courts were certain to convict him, and a crime as serious as his would mean life without possibility of parole. Stuck in jail till he died, in a cell scarcely large enough to spread his wings in. Never to fly in the open air again. Watching his feathers fall out with disuse, one by one. The horror of it was all too much for him. I don't know, I'm just guessing. Who can say what goes through the minds of these extremists? But it's obvious he wasn't the clearest-thinking of people to start with.'

'Yeah. You'd have to be pretty deranged to think killing Lady Aanfields-daughter was a good idea. Tell me, though – you knew, didn't you? That the attack was coming. I saw the way you were watching the crowd at the final.'

'I didn't *know* it,' said Mr Mordadson, 'but I feared that it, or something like it, might happen. Airborn opinion is turning against the likes of Lady Aanfielsdaughter. The First!ers are just the leading edge of a general shift in sentiment. People up here aren't seeing any benefit from the opening up of relations with the Groundlings. All they're seeing is antagonism, disruption and danger. Once we had it pretty cushy. Now we're finding life harder, less settled than ever. We're having to pay for things we used to get for free. All of which is creating resentment, divisions. On the one hand you have Lady Aanfielsdaughter, counselling patience and restraint, promising things will get better. On the other you have the First!ers, who are arguing we were better off before we showed ourselves to the Groundlings and who've now got a dead movement-member to add to their list of grievances, a martyr to the cause. People are starting to take sides. Even within the Sanctum.'

'In the Sanctum?' Az found this hard to believe.

'Oh yes. There are factions, even there. What you've also got to bear in mind is that the Airborn are, in fact, quite a fragmented race. We all look alike and speak the same language, but each sky-city's still a self-contained state with its own customs and internal governance. How different, for example, is somewhere like High Haven from somewhere like Redspire?'

'Very different.' *An ordered, kindly city*, Az thought, *versus a hive of irresponsibility and anarchy*.

'And what about the Cumula Collective compared with, say, Helio-tropia?'

The women of the Collective were an austere, self-denying lot who lived according to very strict rules: a simple diet, modest clothes, a regime of vigorous exercise, everyone doing her fair share of work to keep the

41

city going, and little contact with other sky-cities except when it came to jetball. Heliotropia was all about gambling and leisure and pleasure, a grown-ups' playground.

Mr Mordadson went on, 'The Pact of Hegemony stitched us together, providing a few basic rules we could all agree on and try to keep to. But it wouldn't take much, I feel, for all the good work the Pact has done to start unravelling. It's not as if we even have a shared religion to give us unity. A few myths and legends about our founding fathers, such as Metatron, hardly constitute a belief system, and although there are those who put their faith in a "higher power", there aren't nearly enough for them to be considered anything more than a fringe group. We don't, as a race, have a single overarching, binding philosophy. Do you get what I'm driving at, Az? Do you see what these flaws in our society mean? Do you see where all this uncertainty and destabilisation could be leading?'

'War?'

'The worst kind of war. Civil war,' Mr Mordadson intoned gravely. 'At the very least, civil war. A return to the bad old days, when it was sky-city pitted against sky-city. When the air was awash with blood and feathers.'

'But – but can't we stop it somehow? You and me? Surely we can. Do our usual hero bit and save the day.'

Mr Mordadson looked bleak. 'I don't see how, this time. It's too big. The momentum is building fast – too fast. It may already be too late. All we can do is choose a side, and hope we've chosen right. Whose side would you be on, Az, if it came to it?'

Az thought about it. 'Whichever one you're on, I guess.'

Mr Mordadson hesitated, then smiled crookedly.

'Good answer,' he said.

CHAPTER 14

The Agony Of Commitment

Az's final visitor of the day was a total surprise.

'Cassie!?'

She came in toting an oxygen cylinder and breathing mask. She removed the mask in order to bombard Az with kisses, and after that resorted to it whenever she began to feel light-headed.

'Got a letter, I did,' she told him. 'Personal from Lady A. All the way from the Sanctum to Heliotropia, then down to the former Grimvale Chancel and delivered to my door by an employee there. It said you be laid up in hospital and gave some story about you doing something daft and brave and getting hurt saving her life. And with the letter were a piece of Airborn craftwork, kind of a miniature picture of the sun, done using gold leaf on parchment. Sort of thing that be fetching plenty of notes from a gift-broker – enough money to pay for a train ticket to Granite Plains, which'm at the base of this city, and back.' She grinned, then the grin turned into a yawn. 'It'm a long trip, but here I be.'

'You don't know how much it means to me,' said Az.

'Well, us had a date, didn't us? Couldn't break that, even if it'm not in the usual place. Mind you, I nearly didn't make the final bit of it, thanks to those reporters downstairs.'

'Are they still there?'

'Yup. One of them figured out who I were. Yelled, "There's his Groundling girlfriend!", and suddenly them's all over I like wasps on jam. I be about to tell they precisely what them can do with their questions, and then who should arrive out of nowhere but Mr Mordadson. Him grabs I and flies I through they and up here.'

'Nice of him.'

'I know. I barely got a chance to say thanks before him shot off again.'

'You know Mr Mordadson. No rest for the wicked.'

'So, how long be your arm going to be tied up to that metal contraption?'

'Doctor says it has to stay in the sling for three more days, then I can get up and about. The dressings'll come off in a fortnight. I should be fully healed within a couple of months or so.'

'Be'n't it enough that you'm got no wings? You trying to get rid of all your other limbs as well?'

Az gave a grim chuckle. 'Believe me, it wasn't my idea. If I'd thought for a moment about what I was doing . . . well, I wouldn't have done it. But hey, what's the use of being "pivotal to the future of the Airborn race" if you're not prepared to lose a limb or two in the process?'

Cassie rolled her eyes. 'The prophecy,' she said with distaste. '*That* load of old slag. I thought you'd decided the Count of Gyre and all his accountant cronies was a bunch of nutters. You doesn't still think their super-duper abacus thingy actually, genuinely foretold your future?'

'Please, didn't you hear the inverted commas in my voice?'

'I never can tell with you, Az. Sometimes you says stuff and you doesn't sound like you'm joking but you be, and other times it'm the other way round. After you pulled off that trick with *Cerulean*, finding *Behemoth* even though you didn't know how, you was all "ooh, I must have magic powers or something" for a while. You was halfway believing it meant the prophecy might be true, whereas all it were were dumb blind luck.'

'I know that,' Az said. He felt a little embarrassed. There had been moments, in the wake of the Redspire business, when he was convinced that some supernatural force had touched him as he stood in *Cerulean*'s control gondola, infusing him with the ability to locate the pirates' airship through the cloud cover. He had behaved accordingly, strutting around puffed up with self-importance. It had taken Cassie to bring him back down to earth. Cassie, who had little time for bigheads. Cassie, who repeatedly punctured his bubble by reminding him that he'd had no choice about making the descent through the clouds when he did. It had been either that or have his ship commandeered forcibly by the Alar Patrol.

Gradually Az had come to realise that one extraordinarily lucky break did not make you a harbinger of destiny. He was not gifted in some strange, mystical way. The Ultimate Reckoner's so-called prophecy was just a piece of fancy flim-flam and signified nothing.

He hadn't, however, thrown away the slip of printout paper with the double-ended arrow symbol on it. He kept it safe in a sturdy envelope at the back of his sock drawer at home. Just on the off-chance that there might be something to the prophecy after all.

'That be'n't to say you'm not a major player.' Cassie could see that Az's ego needed boosting. He cherished the hope that a wingless kid like himself could still make a difference in the world. 'Not everyone goes around saving the lives of high mucky-mucks like Lady Aanfieldsdaughter. There'm no doubting you be a pretty cool guy.'

'Yeah, I am, aren't I?' said Az, brightening. 'So, how's life been for you lately? Everybody well at the Grubdollar homestead? How's the Fletcher Tank coming along?'

'Ah. Not so good.'

She told him about Slamshaft and the cease-and-desist order, and also about Colin's careless talk and how it had cost Fletcher his dream.

'Stupid Colin,' said Az. 'And as for those Slamshaft people, who do they think they are?'

'Them thinks them's people who's bigger than we. And them's right. But the good news is, it'm concentrated our minds somewhat. Now us knows what us needs and wants, which be *Bertha* back. Fletch and Da be already over at Craterhome. Them's gone down there by train to nose around and try to find where her's got to.'

'But the legal repercussions if you pinch her back . . .'

Cassie shrugged. 'Her be ours and there'm an end of it.'

'Cassie, I don't want you getting in trouble.'

'Says the boy in the hospital bed with his arm all torn open.'

'No, but seriously. You know what I mean. Look, I've been thinking.'

'Steady there. Mustn't hurt your poor old brain.'

'Ha ha. Listen to me. I know, since *Bertha*'s gone, your family's been struggling to make ends meet. Well, I've got a proposal for you.'

'A proposal?' Cassie pretended to act coy. 'Why, Mr Gabrielson! What'm a girl to say? Shouldn't you at least go down on one knee?'

'Not that sort of proposal,' Az said, blushing red-hot. 'Please, just listen, Cassie. I think there's something we can do about your financial difficulties.'

Her face hardened. 'No handouts, Az.'

'This isn't a handout. What I've been thinking is, how about you all come and live up here?'

Cassie blinked. 'What?'

'You heard.'

'Live up here? In case you hasn't noticed, Az, it be'n't easy breathing at these altitudes.' To illustrate her point, she huffed on the oxygen cylinder.

'But you could acclimatise. It might take a while, but I'm sure it would happen eventually.'

'Groundlings have tried. I heard about one lot, they took up residence in, where was it, Zenith? Azimuth City? Azuropolis? One of those sky-cities with a Z in the name. It were kind of an experiment. Them lasted all of three days there. Spent most of the time throwing up and passing out.'

'I know. But maybe if they'd stuck it out a bit longer . . .'

'And then there's the getting around. Sky-cities be built for the winged, not the wingless.'

'I manage,' said Az. 'Sometimes I need a little help, but even so.'

'And what would us do to earn a living, even if it were possible us could survive up here?'

'You could be, I don't know, official Groundling ambassadors perhaps.'

'Ambassadors? Have you *met* my family, Az?'

'All right, something else then. I could have a word with Lady Aanfielsdaughter. I'm sure she could find you some kind of salaried position.'

'Nope, it'm a handout,' Cassie said, 'pure and simple. And Grubdollars don't do handouts.'

'What was that sun picture Lady Aanfielsdaughter sent you, then, if it wasn't a handout?'

'You'd rather I hadn't come?'

'No. No. But just think about it, Cassie. You could live in High Haven. We could see each other every day. It would be fantastic. None of these long journeys so that we can get together for an hour of less then go our separate ways again.'

He could see she was tempted. It occurred to him that, if Mr Mordadson's predictions of civil war proved well-founded, this was surely the worst time to be inviting the Grubdollars to live in the Airborn realm. Then again, if the guano really was about to start flying, Az wanted Cassie close to him. Otherwise, amid all the chaos, how would they have a chance to see each other at all?

Cassie sighed. 'It'm a lovely dream, Az. I mean it. I'd want it as much as you. But I just can't see how it would work. Maybe the other way round, though – you coming to live down on the ground. That would be possible, wouldn't it?'

Now it was Az's turn to be tempted. But, stiffly, he shook his head. 'I have commitments up here.'

'You does. Just as I has them down there.' She laughed, a hollow sound. 'Us is a right old pair, be'n't us? There'm nothing us'd like more than to be together permanently, and there'm nothing less likely to happen. And yet the more there be to keep us apart, the more us wants each other. What'm up with that, d'you reckon?'

'We're just perverse, I suppose. All the same, Cassie, could you at least—'

At that moment Nurse Haatansdaughter entered. She bustled past Cassie, not even giving her a second glance, took Az's blood pressure, entered the figure on his chart, and bustled out again, without saying anything to anyone.

'She'm friendly,' Cassie noted.

46

'I know. I won the nurse lottery with her.'

'Pity, though. She's a right beauty, straight up.'

'I only have eyes for the girl with her face half covered by a breathing mask.'

'Flatterer.'

'How much longer do you have?'

'About quarter of an hour.'

'Think you could manage some more of that kissing, without getting too short of breath?'

'Why don't you *make* me short of breath, Azrael Gabrielson?' said Cassie, moving over to his bed.

CHAPTER 15

How To Be Outraged

A five-strong delegation of Feather First!ers arrived at the Alar Patrol HQ in Pearl Town, demanding to be allowed to see their imprisoned comrade. They had brought a lawyer with them and argued that the man was entitled to legal representation. It was the constitutional right of every Airborn who had been arrested, however severe his or her crime, to have access to a lawyer. It was enshrined in the Pact of Hegemony.

'What do I tell them?' Group Captain Kfialson asked Mr Mordadson.

'Stall for a while,' was Mr Mordadson's advice. 'They've finally come forward and admitted their lot was behind the kite attack. Let's see what, if anything, they have up their sleeves.'

Kfialson informed the First!ers that the suspect had refused to co-operate; he had not even given his name. Until he chose to be more helpful, there was nothing to be gained by introducing a lawyer into the equation. It would complicate, not simplify, matters.

The First!ers were outraged. They were outraged in such a loud, blustering way that it was quite clear they had hoped and intended all along to be outraged. They shouted phrases such as 'This is intolerable!' and 'It's a travesty of justice!' in the manner of people who had carefully rehearsed how to speak and act outraged. They shook their fists and their wings in a none-more-outraged fashion, and stormed out of the building. As they left, their voices and indignation mounted. Each of them seemed to be trying to out-outrage the others.

'Phew,' said Kfialson.

'No,' said Mr Mordadson. 'Not phew. They'll be back.'

And they did come back, just a couple of hours later, in greater numbers. At least twenty First!ers set up camp on the plaza in front of the Patrol HQ, and this time they had placards. Nice, neat, well-made placards that had obviously taken more than a couple of hours to put together.

The First!ers flew in a circle, brandishing the placards and chanting the slogans daubed on them:

ALAR PATROL UNFAIR

FREE THE FEATHER FIRST! ONE

WHO PATROLS THE PATROLLERS?

'This is a performance,' said Mr Mordadson disgustedly, watching from the vantage point of a high window. 'This is cabaret.'

'I wouldn't pay to go and see it,' Kfialson remarked.

'They want to exploit this situation for maximum publicity.'

'And they're doing a decent job of it. Look.'

Reporters were alighting on the plaza. Their notebooks were out and they were scribbling in them furiously. This would be tomorrow's headlines, all across the Airborn realm.

A few of the First!ers even interrupted their circling and chanting to go over and talk directly to the men and women of the Press. By their body language you could tell they were putting their viewpoint across with vigour and firmness, and the reporters were lapping it up. It was the sort of thing that made for great copy: controversy, protest, an anti-government stance. Whether newspaper readers agreed with the First!ers or not, they would certainly want to read all about it.

'I bet they tipped the reporters off,' said Kfialson. 'Told them they'd be here creating a fuss, come and see.'

'I'd say you're right. Well, there's only one thing we can do.'

'What's that?'

'Try and beat them at their own game. Gather some men, Group Captain.'

'Why?'

'Just do as I say.'

'At least give me some idea what you're up to.'

Mr Mordadson looked shrewd, and also resigned. 'A dozen Patrollers should be enough. Kit them out in full combat gear, including shields. I'm going to start a riot.'

CHAPTER 16

Flying Off The Handle

In full view of the reporters, the Patrollers filed out of their headquarters and moved in on the protesting First!ers. Lances and shields glittered in the late-afternoon sun. Helmet visors and wing hoops shone. The Patrollers divided into two streams and flowed either side of the First!ers, forming an outer circle around them.

The protest continued, the First!ers undaunted. If anything, the Patrollers' show of strength added fuel to the fire. Their chants got even louder and the placards were waved higher in the air. Defiant, the First!ers felt that the Patrollers were proving their point for them. They were being oppressed. The law was treating them harshly, unequally. Any other political movement would be allowed to air its opinions free from such blatant intimidation tactics.

Then Mr Mordadson emerged from the building, launching himself up in an arc, coming down in the midst of the First!ers.

'Right,' he called out. 'Which of you's the ringleader? Come on, there's got to be one of you prepared to speak for the rest. Who is it? Any takers?'

The chanting subsided, the circling slowed and stopped, and eventually a short, sturdy-looking man emerged from the ranks of First!ers and presented himself to Mr Mordadson. He had a florid complexion, the kind that suggested high blood pressure and a quick temper.

Excellent, thought Mr Mordadson.

'Who are you?' the Sanctum emissary demanded.

'You can call me El El,' said the florid-faced man.

'Just El El? No surname?'

'It'll do for now. And who are you?'

'Someone you'd be wise to heed. Well, El El, I have some news for you and your colleagues. Your friend indoors? The one who took it into his head to try and kill Lady Aanfieldsdaughter? He's dead.'

El El blinked. 'I don't believe you. You're lying.'

'Why would I lie? I can take you to view the body, if you like. He committed suicide last night. I think he realised how much trouble he was in, and took the only way out available.'

'Noaphiel,' gasped one of the First!ers.

'Was that his name? Noaphiel?' said Mr Mordadson, keeping his gaze fixed on El El. 'Well, Noaphiel's Noaphiel no more. And you might think that makes him a hero, but me? I call him a rank coward. A right old yellow-bellied sapsucker. Couldn't face his punishment. Couldn't accept the consequences of his actions. So, now that you know you're here complaining about the rights of a dead person' – a contemptuous leer stole over Mr Mordadson's face – 'what are you going to do about it?'

He waited a heartbeat. The colour in El El's cheeks was deepening rapidly, going from red to purple to puce.

'Are you going to take it lying down?' Mr Mordadson said. 'I would, if I were you. Forget Noaphiel, flap off home, give it all up as a lost cause. Because that's what you all are, losers chasing a lost cause.'

'You . . . you . . .' El El spluttered.

Unable to find the right words, he swung his placard at Mr Mordadson instead.

Mr Mordadson could have parried in any number of ways – forearm block, wing block, a flick of the wrist. He could equally have dodged. But he didn't. The placard caught him on the side of the head, a swiping blow. The surface on which the slogan was written was a square of plywood, the edges of which were sharp. The impact hurt and drew blood. Mr Mordadson went reeling to the floor with a loud cry.

The irate El El struck him a second time as he lay in a heap. Mr Mordadson cried out again, loud enough for all the journalists to hear.

Inspired by El El's example, the other First!ers went on the offensive too. They launched themselves at the assembled Patrollers. For several minutes there was pandemonium on the plaza. Placards flew, blows were thrown, First!ers and Patrollers jostled and wrestled. Meanwhile the reporters cowered and jotted.

'Minimum force!' Kfialson ordered. 'Subdue only!'

The outcome, of course, was never in doubt. Combat-trained and fully armed, the Patrollers were unlikely to be beaten by the First!ers, despite being at a numerical disadvantage. It was a case of them containing the chaos in as controlled a manner as possible. First they relieved the First!ers of their placards, then they used their lances to pin them down in pairs, so that they could neither fight back nor fly off. Handcuffs and wing restraints appeared, and soon the twenty-odd political agitators were trussed up like turkeys and squatting in rows, looking ruffled and remorseful.

'Well done,' said Mr Mordadson, aside, to Kfialson. 'You put on a good show. A disciplined response to an apparently unwarranted outbreak of violence. Should play well in the papers tomorrow.'

'What now? What do you want us to do with them?'

'Arrest them, process them, let them go.'

'Let them go?' said the group captain, surprised.

'With a formal caution. Let them limp back to their nests and commiserate with their First!er pals. We've made them look like the aggressors here, and I think they know it. They've lost the moral high ground. They won't pull a stunt like that again in a hurry.'

Kfialson pointed to Mr Mordadson's head. 'That's a pretty nasty cut you've got there. You should get it seen to.'

Mr Mordadson put a hand to the wound, then examined the blood on his fingertips. Finally he said, 'I'll be fine. I've had worse.'

Kfialson detected more than just bravado in the statement. There was fatalism there too. One more injury. So what?

He didn't know Mr Mordadson well, but the impression he had formed was of a dark and very complicated man. He respected him . . . but he wouldn't ever have wanted him as a friend.

CHAPTER 17

And Now For A Round-up Of What
The Papers Are Saying

Next day's newspapers all carried coverage of the riot, alongside articles about the suicide of the Feather First!er in custody. The Alar Patrol had issued an official statement on the suicide of Noaphiel Thothson. His identity had been confirmed by the First!er protestors, and a coroner had supplied a verdict of death by strangulation resulting from an act of deliberate self-harm. The Pearl Town Patrol was exonerated from blame. Little could have been done to prevent the death from occurring.

In the *Northernheights News*, the *Zenith Times*, the *High Haven Mail*, the *Emerald Riser*, in the great majority of Airborn papers, the riot was painted as the product of tempers fraying and insufficient self-control being shown by the First!ers. On the whole, the Airborn press was unsympathetic to the movement. Today phrases such as 'misguided philosophy', 'habitual troublemakers' and 'an outlet for prejudice dressed up as dissent' were bandied about.

There were exceptions, however. The *Cumula Collective Siren* claimed that, even though the First!ers had thrown the first punch, the Alar Patrol must bear some of the responsibility for the riot. Turning out in full armour could, in some sense, be seen as an act of provocation.

Meanwhile the *Prismburg Express*, published in a sky-city where Feather First! activity was frequent and widespread, cast doubt on the coroner's verdict, hinting that foul play might have been involved. The *Express*'s editor was known to harbour First!er tendencies and his opinion pieces often gave veiled support for assaults on Groundling tourists, without actually going so far as to condone the practice.

As for the *Redspire Feedback*, it not surprisingly deplored the Patrol's tactics, calling them 'heavy-handed and excessive'. It also invited its readership to view the First!ers as 'heirs to the spirit of Naoutha Nisrocsdaughter and her gang'. Already Naoutha's pirates were becoming folk heroes in Redspire. Drinking songs celebrated their deeds and honoured them as freedom fighters rather than simply plunderers and thieves. Naoutha herself was regarded as a doomed, damaged beauty who had gone out in a blaze of glory, while the surviving pirates, who were currently languishing in jail, received no end of fan mail from their co-citizens and could look forward to being treated like royalty when they were finally released and sent home. Many Redspirians had adorned themselves with tattoos of Naoutha's symbol, the skull and crossed feathers, to show solidarity. Many believed, too, that Naoutha was not dead. Rumours persisted that she was alive and well and biding her time, waiting till the moment was right for her to make a triumphant return.

Aside from these carping voices in the press, over-all Mr Mordadson's plan paid off. The riot – short-lived though it was – put the First!ers in a bad light. Coming hard on the heels of the attack on Lady Aanfielsdaughter, it confirmed in the public's mind that the movement was a threat to Airborn values.

To the casual observer, it might appear that Mr Mordadson had won a victory.

He himself, though, knew he had won a temporary respite at best. Feather First! would hit out again soon enough. It was a question not of *if* but *when*, not of *why* but *where* and *how*.

CHAPTER 18

Comedown

The train from Granite Plains deposited Cassie at Grimvale station and hauled off north-eastwards in a great swirling huff of steam. She traipsed home on foot, feeling travel-sore and a little thick-headed, as she customarily did after a trip to see Az. Returning to the ground after a brief stay above the clouds was a dispiriting experience. She exchanged brightness for gloom, blue sky for grey, sunshine for, more often than not, rainfall. The world seemed slower down here, the air like treacle. There were few vistas, everything felt enclosed and tight. This was where she belonged, and she was glad to be back. But what did that say about her? Did it imply she was content to lead a limited life, to be happy with less?

Az's suggestion that the Grubdollars should move to High Haven had opened up tantalising possibilities, and Cassie felt guilty because now she couldn't help looking at her hometown with jaundiced eyes. She spotted some hard, lumpy loaves of bread on display in a baker's window – they resembled cooked mud and would probably taste not much better. She saw the rust which pockmarked a tin sign advertising a rattle-lung remedy (it didn't actually promise a cure for the disease but boasted that 'PhlegmPep's patented active ingredient alleviates the worst symptoms and brings blessed relief'). She passed a shabby stray dog curled around itself in an alleyway, nibbling at its own fleas. She heard raucous laughter and off-key piano music spilling out from a pub doorway. She noticed, as if for the first time, the fur of moss and algae that grew on almost every building; the odours of swampy decay from the river and its off-branching canals and drains; the general atmosphere of sootiness, sourness and neglect; Grimvale's lack of polish, compared with the glittering brilliance of the sky-cities.

This feeling of dissatisfaction would pass, she was sure. Her mood would lift. All she needed was a bath to wash off the sweat and grime of the train journey, followed by a good, long sleep, and she would be herself once more.

'Cass! Them found she!'

These were the first words Robert said to her as she emerged at the top of the spiral staircase. He came rushing into the hallway, grabbed her by the waist and swung her round and round in a dance. He was chortling with glee.

'She?' said Cassie. '*Bertha*?'

'Of course *Bertha*, you dingdong.'

'Where? Where be she?'

'Craterhome somewhere.'

Cassie was getting dizzy, being spun like that. She seized her brother's shoulders, planting him to the spot.

'Keep still for a second. Tell I in plain language. Da and Fletch – them's got hold of she?'

'Nope, not yet, not as far as I know. But them sent a telegram. It arrived this morning. Here.' Robert fished a crumpled slip of yellow paper out of his pocket.

Cassie unfurled and read it.

The message was necessarily brief. You paid for telegrams by the word. The more succinct you could be, the better.

```
LOCATED B. IN CRATERHOME + STOP + COME WITH CASSIE
+ STOP + STAYING AT THE BOXES + STOP + DA + STOP
```

'Pack a bag,' Cassie said, tossing the telegram onto a side-table.

'Already did,' said Robert. 'I's been waiting to go since the moment the telegram arrived.'

'Be the half-tarp fuelled up?'

'Full tank, spare cans of diesel in the back.'

Cassie looked down at her rumpled clothing. She could smell her own dried sweat.

Oh well, so much for bath and sleep.

'Then what'm us hanging around here flapping our lips for?' she said. 'Let's hit the road.'

CHAPTER 19

The Journey South

They drove overnight, taking it in turns at the wheel, two-hour stints, one napping while the other steered the half-tarp through the dark. Except that, around midnight, when it was Robert's turn next to take over from her, Cassie let him sleep on. She forged on through the small hours, crossing the Fishkill River and joining the main southbound highway not long after. The going was easier here, the road broader and straighter, less taxing on the eyes and concentration. The half-tarp over-took lumbering juggernauts laden with logs and coal, passenger coaches beetling along with their window blinds drawn, and a few slow-rolling post office traction engines, pulling long lines of wagons filled with parcel freight and letters. These other vehicles were few and far between, though, and for the most part the van had the road to itself. There were long stretches when Cassie could just cruise, watching the signposts count down the kilometres to Craterhome and thinking how good it would be to have *Bertha* back.

Near dawn, they stopped and had breakfast at a roadside way-station. Robert was cross that Cassie hadn't woken him as she was supposed to. She pointed out that, technically speaking, he was too young to be driving on the open road. It was better for that reason if she did the bulk of the journey. Since joining the highway she had spotted a couple of police cars lurking in lay-bys. (They were large machines with charge-cooler V8 engines and a hunched, front-heavy profile that always made her think of an animal crouching, ready to pounce). The last thing they wanted, she told her brother, was for them to get pulled over by a traffic cop and be fined for having an underage driver and have the van impounded. Robert saw the wisdom in this, and reluctantly agreed that she should be in charge of the half-tarp for the rest of the way.

While Robert was finishing off his bacon and eggs, Cassie went to the ladies' room to freshen up. As she opened the door to step out, she happened to catch the tail-end of a conversation between two truckers who had just exited the gents'.

'. . . says them's offering a hundred notes per day if you sign up,' one of the truckers was saying.

'A hundred!' exclaimed the other. 'That'm decent wedge, straight up. But I doesn't have any, as it were, experience. I mean, I's been in a few scraps in my time, but not, you know, serious fighting.'

'Don't matter. You get training. It'm part of the deal.'

'Hmmm. Certainly seems worth thinking about. I doesn't personally have anything against they up there, mind. But if the money'm good as you say it be . . .'

'Think about it,' said the first trucker, patting the other on the shoulder. 'What does you normally clear in a day? Thirty notes at best? Think what you could do with more than triple that. You could buy some nice presents for that sweetheart of yours. *And* have some cash left over for the missus!'

The truckers strode off, chuckling throatily.

Cassie tried to make sense of what she had overheard. Serious fighting? Training? They up there? It didn't sound good. She debated whether to run after the truckers and get them to explain what they'd been talking about, but she knew it wouldn't be any use. There had been a confiding tone to the conversation, a sense of secrets being passed on. She doubted they would be willing to share the information with a 17-year-old girl. They would simply laugh at her and clam up.

Her priority, anyway, was *Bertha*, and soon she and Robert were back on the road. Daylight seeped dully into the sky. The landscape flattened out, becoming fields. Here, shrouded in morning mist, wheat and corn grew, hardy strains that flourished as best they could on the limited sunshine they received, which in places was bolstered by arrays of high-wattage lamps that glared through the night. Also prevalent were crops of root vegetables, which didn't need so much light for photosynthesis, along with the occasional hop orchard and wine vineyard, and now and then a pasture browsed by cattle.

This was the region known as the Massif, and also as the garden of the Westward Territories. It supplied the food needs of the vast majority of the population and was farmed intensively. There wasn't a single available hectare of the Massif, it was said, that wasn't given over to agriculture, and certainly for the next few hours all Cassie saw on either side of the road was that, agriculture. The only buildings she and Robert passed were farmhouses, barns and grain silos. No towns, just hamlets and smallholdings, hunkered close to the soil, crude stone-walled dwellings, part of the earth almost.

Afternoon, almost 700 kilometres on the clock since leaving Grimvale, and the outskirts of Craterhome appeared. At another way-station, Cassie made enquiries about The Boxes. A waitress informed her it was a hotel in the Fourth Borough and gave rough directions.

'Hotel, though,' the waitress added, 'be'n't really the right word for it.'

'What'm the right word then?' Cassie asked.

The waitress paused. 'Not sure if there actually *be* one. Not one you'd use in polite company, at any rate.'

CHAPTER 20

The Boxes

Picture a cube as big as a city block, made entirely of red brick. Picture hundreds of tiny windows, porthole-sized, on each face of this cube. Picture, inside, room upon room, each of identical dimensions, two metres by two metres by two metres. Picture these rooms crammed one on top of another, 100 per storey, in a grid pattern, with corridors running in between, none more than a metre in width. Each floor a twisting, turning, dimly-lit warren. One bathroom servicing every twenty rooms. The cheapest temporary accommodation in Craterhome. Purpose-built to house migrant workers with little cash to spare and no desire to put down roots.

Welcome to The Boxes.

It took Cassie and Robert quarter of an hour to persuade the concierge – a sullen, lank-haired old codger – to reveal which room their father and brother were staying in. It took them another three-quarters of an hour actually to locate Room 6/21. Arrows and numbers painted on the corridor walls sent them in various different directions, promising to get them closer to their destination but failing to do so every time, usually leaving them even further away. In the end they resorted to wandering the floor calling out, 'Den Grubdollar! Fletcher Grubdollar!', much to the annoyance of several residents, who leaned out from doorways and told them to clip it down.

'*You* clip it down,' Cassie retorted, and went on yelling her father's and brother's names until at last a far-off voice boomed, 'Cass? Be that you?'

'It'm me and Robert, Da. Keep shouting.'

Den hollered, 'I's here. Here I be. Over here. This way,' while Cassie and Robert homed in on the sound. Finally they turned a corner and there he was, standing halfway along a corridor, filling it with his broad shoulders.

Much hugging later, Den ushered his children into the very, very humble abode he and Fletcher were occupying. It was furnished with a double bunk bed of reasonable proportions along with a table and chair so small they might have been made for a dwarf. Illumination came from a flyblown, unshaded lightbulb that dangled from the ceiling on a length of threadbare flex.

'No window?'

'That'm an extra half-note per night, Robert,' Den replied. 'Us is on a budget, don't forget. But then who needs windows when there be our very own pet rat thrown in, free of charge?'

'What?'

He indicated a hole that had been chewed out of the wainscot. 'Yup, him's called Colin and him lives in there. Comes out at night and scampers over you while you be sleeping. Friendly beggar, him is. Always want to know what'm going on. In fact, I wouldn't be surprised if . . . Yup. There. Look.'

A sharp nose, whiskers, and a pair of beady red eyes poked out from the hole. No sooner had the rat scanned the room than it snatched its head back out of sight.

'Eurgh!' said Robert.

'Oh, don't be like that, boy. Him's just being inquisitive. Wants to see who the newcomers be. You keep shouting like that, him'll get the impression you doesn't like he.'

'But, Da, it'm a *rat*!'

'Quieten down, or everyone'll want one.'

Cassie was grinning. ' "Colin"? Fletch didn't name he, by any chance?'

Her father stroked his chin in a parody of pondering. 'Ooh now, that never occurred to I. What a queer coincidence. Who'd've thought that two rats might have the same name as each other? Chance in a million, I'd say.'

'Speaking of Fletch,' said Robert, 'where be he?'

'On stakeout.'

'Stakeout?'

'Sure. Down where us found *Bertha*. Him and me has been noting the schedule, the comings and goings, so as us can figure out when and how best to go in and grab she.'

'Where be that?' Cassie asked. 'The comings and goings where?'

'Heh, now here'm some irony,' replied Den. 'Talk about adding insult to injury. After all that's happened this past week, who should turn out to be *Bertha*'s new owners? Go on, take a wild guess.'

Cassie frowned. 'It can't be. Surely not . . .'

'Slamshaft,' said her father with a nod. 'Slamshaft Engineering Incorporated. Her's been put to work over at their main plant in the Second Borough. Them buggers has got her going back and forth, hauling loads like some . . . some motorised pack-mule. And a very sorry sight it be too, a fine old lady like that being reduced to running errands at a factory. Her's been enslaved, her has. Not to put too fine a point on it. Enslaved.' His voice rose. His eyes fired. 'And for that reason, it'm no longer our right to liberate her. Oh no.' He slapped a fist into an open palm. 'Getting her back be nothing less than our *duty*.'

Then, softly, he added, 'Shame it'm going to be next to impossible, though.'

CHAPTER 21

Slamshaft

Den and Fletcher were scarcely two days into their search for *Bertha* when they found her – although it might be as accurate to say that she found them.

They had spent their first day in Craterhome at Hundred Ways in the Third Borough, that nexus of thoroughfares, a perpetual crowded hubbub. Here, they asked around, literally stopping strangers in the street and posing the question: *you spied a murk-comber anywhere round these parts lately?* Not such a long shot. Murk-combers were rare in Craterhome. They plied the Prismburg Shadow Zone, which was some twenty kilometres away, but seldom came into the city itself. Narrow, cobbled streets and bulky, caterpillar-tracked vehicles were not an ideal combination.

A couple of people reported seeing a murk-comber not so long ago, but it soon became clear that, although they *were* talking about *Bertha*, they were referring to her visit a while back, the occasion when Robert inadvertently electrocuted all those citizens, which ultimately cost his family their prize possession. More recently than that, nobody could recall a murk-comber having passed by.

Since the Third Borough was Craterhome's commercial centre, it seemed logical that a practical, hard-working machine like *Bertha* would be there, if she was anywhere. But after a fruitless and frustrating day, Den and Fletcher decided to look further afield. The Second Borough, though nowhere near as industrialised as the Third, contained a number of heavy-manufacturing plants. Some of the largest companies in the Westward Territories sited their main factories there. So that was where father and son headed on day two of the search. They roamed the district all morning, halting outside the larger business premises and peering in

63

through the gates. Fletcher was starting to feel pangs of despair, but his father refused to give in.

'Come on, lad,' he said at one point. 'Let's keep at it. Who knows, *Bertha* could be just around the next corner.'

And as luck would have it, she was.

They were walking towards the largest factory either of them had ever seen or could imagine seeing. It consisted of a dozen zigzag-roofed buildings that loomed like cliffs, each capped by a chimney that towered so high it seemed to scrape the base of the cloud cover. The chimneys blurted sparks and black smoke, and the din of the work being carried out inside the buildings was a perpetual rumble which you felt as much as heard. The very air around the factory shimmered with the low vibrations of industry.

The gate was suitably enormous, like some iron-bar border between nations. Mounted on it was a corporate logo carved in steel, a huge S with a lightning bolt shot through it. Both Grubdollars identified it straight away.

Slamshaft.

Before Fletcher could make a comment – and he had plenty to say on the subject of Slamshaft – a faint yet oh-so-familiar sound caught his attention. It was just audible above the factory's earthquake thrum, a slow, determined chugging with the merest hint of laughter in it. Sad laughter, brave and lonely and forlorn.

His gaze met his father's. Den had heard and recognised the sound too.

'It can't be,' Den breathed.

But it was. Through the gates they saw her trundle into view, lugging a long, tip-up trailer that had been coupled on behind her. Her engine was straining, not just from the burden she was hauling but also from not having had a recent, proper tuning. Her exhausts were coughing fumes. There was a crack in the glass dome of one of her observation nacelles. She seemed to be dragging herself across the factory yard, her tracks slipping and juddering. The trailer alone, unladen, must have weighed three tonnes, and whatever was inside seemed to be adding at least another ten to the tally.

Still, it was *Cackling Bertha*. She had been given a slapdash paintjob and a Slamshaft logo had been added to her side. Still, there she was. And it seemed to the two Grubdollars that her cackle grew louder and stronger as she passed before their eyes, as if she sensed they were there and was calling out to them. Perhaps they imagined this, perhaps not. Either way, they didn't know whether to whoop with joy, or cry.

Then *Bertha* went round the corner of one of the factory buildings and vanished from sight. Den and Fletcher would have remained there, waiting for however long they needed to till she reappeared, had a security guard not spotted them. He came out of his guardhouse, sauntered up to the gate and challenged them.

'State your business,' he demanded, folding grey-uniformed arms over a grey-uniformed chest. 'What does you two want here?'

'I'll tell you what us wants—' Fletcher began hotly, but his father hushed him.

'Nothing,' Den told the guard. 'Us was just leaving, wasn't us, Fletch?'

He steered his son away from the gate, and when they were out of the guard's earshot, said, 'This be'n't the time or the place to cause a ruckus. Foolish to draw attention to ourselves. Us needs to be patient and work out a strategy.'

Fletcher protested, then relented. He saw the logic in what Den was saying.

Since then, he and his father had been taking it in turns to reconnoitre. They'd watched the factory, Fletcher by day, Den by night, in order to familiarise themselves with the pattern of the Slamshaft work schedule and thus establish when would be the right moment to go in and rescue their murk-comber.

Only, thought Fletcher, *there don't appear to* be *a right moment.*

He was sitting in the shelter of a doorway diagonally opposite the factory. The doorway belonged to an undertaker's shop which had gone out of business 'due to bereavement', according to the scrawled note that was fastened to the inside of the window. Presumably the bereavement had something to do with the shop's proprietor, otherwise it would have been an odd reason for an undertaker to close down.

The doorway afforded a good view of the gate but also gave some cover. The security guard manning the gate didn't have a direct line of sight to it.

Having surveyed operations at Slamshaft for three days in a row, Fletcher was coming to the conclusion that the place never worked at anything less than full tilt. His father's night-time observations corroborated this. Trucks delivered raw material and took away finished product round the clock. The workforce arrived and left in overlapping shifts, a twenty-four-hour ebb and flow of labour. The factory did not rest, did not sleep. Everyone knew Slamshaft was prolific – but this? Fletcher hadn't appreciated just how much stuff the company turned out. No wonder its spare parts were notoriously unreliable. It made so many of them, so quickly, that mistakes were bound to happen, flaws inevitable.

Most of the things that left on the backs of the trucks weren't, however, spare parts. They were large objects, items of machinery, perhaps vehicles of some sort, although it was impossible to tell for sure because they were shrouded in voluminous, tethered-down tarpaulins. Slamshaft wasn't known for its assembly-line output. Mostly it made the bits that other people then put together. Yet those shapes on the trucks were evidently whole, completed pieces of mechanical apparatus. Maybe Slamshaft was diversifying its product range. Maybe some of the truck-borne items were even its version of the Fletcher Tank.

The thought made Fletcher seethe, and the anger he felt made him all the more determined that *Bertha* was coming home with him, whether Slamshaft liked it or not.

The problem was, *Bertha* never left the factory premises, which meant that to get to her the Grubdollars would first have to get past the company's security. And security at Slamshaft was extraordinarily tight. Every truck was checked at point of entry, given a thorough going-over to make sure there was nothing and nobody on board that shouldn't be. The same on the way out. As for the workers, each carried an identification pass with a photogravure picture on it. The gate guards were scrupulous about inspecting these. Fletcher had examined the wall all the way around, and it was too high and sheer to climb, and there was broken glass and barbed wire along the top of it for good measure.

It seemed all but hopeless. The factory was in full-time use and there was no easy way in.

Fletcher heaved a sigh.

'That'm a sorry sound,' said a voice nearby.

Fletcher's head snapped round.

He blinked.

'You?'

Looking back at him, with a grin of cocky self-assurance on his face, was a boy of about nine years of age.

Fletcher recognised the boy from his previous visit to Craterhome, and now his hand flew to the pocket where he kept his wallet.

It was still there.

'Oh, don't worry about that,' said the kid pickpocket airily. 'I owe you one from last time. You be safe with I. So, long time no see. How'm it going?'

CHAPTER 22

Toby Nimblenick

Toby Nimblenick – for that was the pipsqueak pickpocket's name – had spotted Fletcher in the undertaker's doorway earlier that afternoon. It was payday at Slamshaft, and Toby had been busy shadowing the workers as they came off-shift from the factory. He'd been focused on relieving as many of them as he could of their wage packets, meaning he hadn't had the chance before now to approach Fletcher and renew acquaintance.

'But I were watching they leaving,' Fletcher said, with mild astonishment. 'Closely. I never saw you.'

'Well, you wasn't supposed to, was you?' replied Toby. 'Wouldn't be much good at my job if people *saw* I. I's a way of being able to just sort of hang around without actually being obvious. In point of fact, I were standing right here for the best part of ten minutes before I spoke to you. Did you notice I?'

Fletcher had to admit he hadn't.

'There you be, then. Point made. So, what brings you to the Big Smoke again? Still looking for your da?'

'Nope, him's off the missing persons list.'

'Glad to hear it.'

'It'm someone else us has lost this time. Only, actually us has just found she.'

'Not that pretty sister of yours?' said Toby. 'Surely her didn't disappear.'

Fletcher laughed. 'Afraid not. Her, us is stuck with. No, it be'n't a person at all. Our murk-comber, *Bertha*.'

'That murk-comber?' Toby said, nodding towards the factory. 'That one I's seen they using in there? Her be yours?'

'Her be.'

'How come Slamshaft has she?'

Briefly, Fletcher outlined the situation. 'And after the cops confiscated

67

she, them must've auctioned she off. Them does that with stolen goods and lost property and the like, if no one comes to claim it. Topping up their retirement fund. Seems kind of criminal, selling off what weren't yours in the first place, but that'm the police for you.'

'Too true,' said Toby. 'One set of rules for we, another for they. It'm like, because them spends their whole time enforcing the law, them gets bored and loses respect for it and reckons them doesn't have to abide by it themselves. Take what happens when them collars you. Off down to the station, and you always gets roughed up a bit unless you bribes they, and sometimes even then. I's seen blokes who hasn't stumped up the necessary, bleeding from head to toe after, ahem, "tripping over and falling down some stairs". No use complaining about it, though. Cops just laughs in your face and beats you up some more if you does.'

He and Fletcher shared a moment's silence, musing on the injustices of the justice system.

'You's figured out how you be going to infiltrate Slamshaft and nick back your *Bertha*?' Toby enquired.

'No,' Fletcher replied, despondently. 'Not a clue.'

'You'd need a worker's pass, maybe.'

'At least.'

'One with a likeness of you on it.'

'That would help.'

'And a set of Slamshaft overalls.'

'If I could get hold of they.'

'Plus some sort of distraction to draw the security guard away from the gate at the crucial moment.'

'So that us wouldn't have to ram it. Yes.'

''Cause that'm a tough-looking gate, straight up. Too much for even a murk-comber to plough through. You'd need to use the control lever in the guardhouse and open it.'

Fletcher nodded. The bobbing of his head slowed and his eyes widened, as he realised what Toby Nimblenick was proposing.

'You can help? You can get hold of this stuff for we?' he said.

'Sure. Why not? And I could do the distracting as well.'

'But . . .' Fletcher peered at the boy sidelong. 'What'm in it for you? Us hasn't got any money. Us can't pay you a note.'

Toby shrugged his bony shoulders. 'I be'n't expecting payment. Remember, like I said, I owe you one. You and your sis could've shopped I to a constable last time. You didn't. Then I ran off from that bloke's store, Barnswallow, with a whole load of cigarette lighters, and that were thanks to you, in effect. Fetched I a tidy sum, them did. So I reckon, I help you now, it'll even things up. Besides,' he went on, with a wicked grin, 'it'll be one in the eye for the cops who flogged your murk-comber to Slamshaft. Kind of natural justice, if you like. What d'you say? Sound good to you?'

'Sounds very good to I,' said Fletcher.

'Let's shake on it then.'

Toby spat in his palm and held the hand out.

Fletcher hesitated, then copied the gesture, and with a mingling of saliva the deal was sealed.

CHAPTER 23

No Hair, Fewer Scruples

At around this same time, just a couple of kilometres away, another kind of alliance was being cemented.

Guests were arriving at a mansion in the exceedingly posh Fifth Borough. Executive-model limousines with wire wheel spokes and wide wooden running-boards glided one after another through an imposing entranceway. The cars rolled along a gravelled drive and slid to a halt in front of a sweep of stone steps that led up to an immense oaken door.

From each limo stepped a man – and in one instance a woman – who was smartly dressed, neatly groomed, and in every way wealthy-looking, with shoes that gleamed with polish, fingernails that were buffed to perfection, and a face which radiated the sort of confidence that only huge worldly success can bring. Each guest swaggered unhurriedly up the steps, perhaps with a glance at a wristwatch or fob-watch to make sure this was after the scheduled time of arrival but not too long after, and certainly not before. None wished to appear as if he or she was not a thoroughly busy person with countless other things to be doing. Equally, none would have missed this meeting for the world. It represented a significant step in a process that was going to change the course of history (and greatly increase each of their personal fortunes into the bargain). Punctual but not too punctual was the way to play it.

The guests were escorted through the mansion by domestic staff. They strolled across marble floors, past oil paintings in gilded frames and alabaster statues on pedestals, from lavishly furnished room to lavishly furnished room, and were unimpressed by all the opulence on display. That suit of armour from pre-Cataclysmic times, complete with brass-trimmed shield and broadsword, hardly merited a second glance, even though there were perhaps three dozen of its kind in existence and half that number in as good condition as this one. The same went for the huge wall-tapestry, a quite superb piece of Pale Uplander craftsmanship, woven from angora goat wool and depicting a hunting scene in such exquisite detail that you could see the sweat on the huntsmen's brows and the fear in the eyes of the stag they were pursuing. The visitors' own homes could boast artefacts that were no less magnificent and expensive. This was how people like them lived, that was all.

On a terrace at the rear of the house they were served drinks. It was a warm, humid evening. Tapers flared in the dusk, giving off a citrus scent that warded mosquitoes away. The mansion's garden had a small lake with a fountain, encircled by drooping willows. The willows were surrounded by other, taller trees whose branches were draped with moss and whose trunks were bulbous with fungus. These trees provided an all-round screen. No prying eyes could spy into the garden, not even with a telescope from one of the houses embedded in the borough's lofty crater sides. Here, there was perfect privacy. What was said, and whoever said it, could remain a secret.

The servants withdrew, and out came the host of the evening, the mansion's owner. He was a tall man with an athletic build. He moved with grace and poise, like a dancer, although in fact he owed his elegance to his rigorous training as a swordsman. He had been a professional fencer, much medalled, before turning to a career in manufacturing, and he still practised regularly with foil and sabre to maintain a high level of fitness. Though in his early forties, he had a physique that would have been the envy of most twenty-year-olds. His face, likewise, was almost wholly unwrinkled. The only thing that gave his true age away was the absence of hair from his head, but then baldness, with him, was less a sign of advancing years than a statement of character. He waxed off the few wisps and tufts that still grew on his scalp, preferring to do without any hair than struggle on with partial coverage here and there. He was an all or nothing kind of man. Ruthless. Either something was useful to him or it wasn't, and if it wasn't then he discarded it without a second thought and without regret.

Dominic Slamshaft was his name, and in the space of just fifteen years he had built up a manufacturing empire that was second to none. Starting out with one, relatively modest tyre-making company, he had expanded and acquired speedily, buying out other firms and folding them into his own until in the end he was able to consolidate all his assets into the monolithic entity known as Slamshaft Engineering Incorporated. He had an acute, inborn business sense which helped him do this, but he also had an absolute lack of scruples. He didn't care if he had to lay off workers when he merged one company into another. He didn't care that he was known in various boardrooms as a bully, a bamboozler and a betrayer, someone not to be trusted and always to be feared. It didn't bother him one bit that Slamshaft products were notoriously unreliable – so much so, indeed, that they were implicated in a number of fatal accidents. There had been court cases. Lawyers had tried to show that a faulty Slamshaft part had led to the derailment of this train or the explosion of that industrial lathe. But nothing had come of these prosecutions, nothing had been proved, and the products still sold. People still bought Slamshaft, in huge quantities, because its prices undercut everyone else's. And that was all that mattered: turnover, profit, income, the bottom line.

Dominic Slamshaft, this mighty, manly magnate, greeted his guests – firm handshakes all round, double handshakes sometimes, or perhaps just the single but accompanied by a grip on the biceps. His sole female guest he kissed on both cheeks.

That was it as far as the social niceties went.

'Gentlemen and lady,' said Slamshaft to his fellow Groundling grandees, 'you know why you're here. The time has come. Tonight, we live in a world at peace with itself. Tomorrow, we start out down the road to war.'

CHAPTER 24

A Friend In High Places

Slamshaft looked from one guest to another, scanning the faces of this unofficial syndicate he had put together, and what he saw there pleased him. Not a trace of apprehension in any of them, not a shred of doubt. They were with him all the way, 100%.

'You, Paul Copperplate,' he said to an elderly man who owned half the newspapers in the Westward Territories, including the prestigious *Crater-home Messenger*. 'Your editors have been hard at work, seeding the soil. I've read, with delight, their numerous editorials and opinion pieces inveighing against our soon-to-be enemy. I've read, too, some wonderful pieces of journalism on the same subject that appear to be unbiased and are anything but. The minds of your readers have at the very least had a shadow of unease cast across them, and your rising sales figures would seem to suggest that either your papers are in tune with the popular mood or vice versa. Bravo.'

Paul Copperplate bowed his white-haired, stoat-like head.

'And you, my old chum and long-time sparring partner Brigadier Jasper Longnoble-Drumblood,' Slamshaft said, turning to a stiff-backed fellow with a crisp moustache and severe crewcut. 'You have been giving us the benefit of your military experience and expertise. You've overseen our training camps and helped knock a ragtag bunch of volunteers into an ordered and disciplined fighting force. I've watched your troops on prac-tice manoeuvres out on the fringes of the Relentless Desert. Impressive. You're to be congratulated on what you've made of them.'

'My pleasure, Dom,' said Longnoble-Drumblood, clicking his heels together. He was an aristocrat of impeccable birth, and the only person present who had inherited his fortune rather than worked for it. 'The job's brought a spring back into this old soldier's stride.'

'The rest of you,' Slamshaft said, 'have provided extraordinarily

73

generous financial backing. It would be unfair to single out any one of you for particular praise, but I must say, Mrs Zelda Graingold, I'm more than grateful to your Perpetual Mutual Bank for the sizeable, no-strings commitment it has made to this project.'

'We anticipate an above-average return on our investment,' said diamond-dripping Mrs Graingold. 'It would have been foolish not to take part.'

'And you, Harry Brickmansworth,' Slamshaft said, addressing a jowly, pot-bellied man with a nose like an overripe strawberry. 'You, too, will reap rewards afterwards for your outlay. When this is all over, Brickmansworth's Construction will have more work than it knows what to do with.'

'I'll drink to that,' said Brickmansworth, draining his tumbler of whisky and refilling it from a silver hipflask.

'All in all,' said Slamshaft, 'I could not be happier with how things are going. I told you a moment ago that tomorrow we start out down the road to war. That's no idle boast. Truly, we've reached a crucial juncture. There could not be a better moment to launch our offensive than now. Our targets are in disarray, beginning to look vulnerable. As a matter of fact—'

'Come on, Dom,' Longnoble-Drumblood butted in. 'Enough of the backslapping. We're dying to meet this "mystery partner" of yours, the one you've been rabbiting on about for weeks.'

'Patience, Jasper. I was just getting to that. As I was saying, disarray. I know this for a fact. I have it on the very best of authority. Because, as I've hinted time and again, I have an inside man. A friend in high places, you might call him. And here he is.'

Slamshaft clapped his hands, and moments later a beating sound could be heard, getting louder. The guests' heads turned, looking this way and that. Eventually all gazes angled upwards, necks craned . . . and there, above, descending at a serene and gentle pace, was a winged figure.

Down from the darkening sky the Airborn came, alighting in the midst of the guests and furling his wings behind him.

'This,' said Slamshaft, 'is the man who has been covertly assisting us above the clouds for several weeks now, and the man who, if all goes according to plan, will soon be crowned absolute ruler of the Airborn realm. Please, all of you, allow me to introduce . . . Farris, Lord Urironson.'

'Good evening,' said Lord Urironson, surveying Slamshaft's guests with a sleek, self-satisfied air. 'It's going to be a pleasure turning the world upside down with you.'

CHAPTER 25

'Heroes'

Not long afterwards, the meeting moved indoors. Dinner was taken in Slamshaft's dining room amid a dazzling, candelabra-lit array of silverware and crystalware. Waiters whispered in and out of the room, delivering course after course and recharging wine glasses. Much of the table talk centred around Lord Urironson, which was just how he liked it. The members of the Groundling syndicate peppered him with questions about Airborn life, and he answered graciously and at length. They enquired about the Sanctum, and he offered them an insider's view of the workings of the place, not neglecting to describe how he himself was respected, revered even, by his fellow residents. Meanwhile he fed scraps from his plate to Echo, whose cage sat on a sideboard in the corner. The mynah perched on Lord Urironson's shoulder, looking wise and curious and every so often whistling or mimicking a phrase of the dinnertime chatter. This enchanted Mrs Graingold, who was sitting on his lordship's right. She declared that she must have one of those birds for herself. Such a darling little creature, and so much more *responsive* than a cat or dog, not to mention so much more intelligent than a mere parrot.

'The wonders you Airborn take for granted!' she said. 'You are so blessed.'

'I'd gladly show you more of them, my dear lady,' said Lord Urironson, exuding charm like an orchid oozing nectar. 'When all this is over and we have a bit more time, it would be my pleasure to escort you around the realm.'

'But I'm a married woman,' said Mrs Graingold, although it didn't sound much like a protest, more like an expression of regret.

'Unhappily married, as I understand it.' The droopy eyebrows waggled.

'Oh, your lordship!' She gave him a teasing shove.

'So it's a date then?'

She didn't say yes, but she didn't say no either.

'At the very least let me find you a mynah of your own, as a gift.'

To that, she did say yes. Mrs Graingold was not the sort who knowingly turned down the offer of a gift.

Once the last dessert plate had been removed, the serving staff were dismissed. Then cigars were lit, the port and brandy decanters began circulating, and weightier topics of conversation were broached.

Slamshaft announced that production of acclimatisation units was in full swing. Lord Urironson could himself vouch that the process of adjusting to the air pressure on the ground was now an easy matter.

'Absolutely,' Lord Urironson said. 'An hour's all it takes, sitting inside that tank. Not altogether comfortable. My ears began to hurt pretty badly at one point. But then it's done, and no ground-sickness. Not a trace. Echo will back me up on that, won't you, Echo?'

'Not a trace, *thweet!*' said the bird.

'Works the other way as well,' said Longnoble-Drumblood. 'We've been testing it in the field. We've had men up to three thousand metres with no ill effects.'

'In aeroplanesh?' said Brickmansworth, who was by this stage completely sozzled. 'In the shky?'

'The units are installed in our aircraft,' Slamshaft confirmed.

'And such aircraft they are!' exclaimed Longnoble-Drumblood. 'Objects of beauty. To watch them take off and soar . . .'

'We've enhanced Airborn design,' Slamshaft said. 'No offence to his lordship, but there's a certain delicacy about most Airborn vehicles.'

'No offence taken,' said Lord Urironson. 'They do the job they're meant to. I realise that, for your purposes, a little added Groundling grit was needed.'

'Couldn't have put it better myself, milord.'

'But hold on a shecond,' said Brickmansworth. 'I didn't know we had planesh already.'

'Of course we do, Harry,' said Slamshaft. 'Oh wait, that's right. You missed our last little get-together a couple of months ago, where I announced that we'd successfully test-flown our prototype.'

'Ill health.'

'Yes, ill health, right,' said Slamshaft, with thinly veiled sarcasm. With Harry Brickmansworth, *ill health* invariably meant chronic hangover. 'Well, as you know, I was able to retrieve specimens from the Relentless Desert. There was that pitched battle between Airborn sky-pirates and some Westward Oil Enterprises roughnecks a while ago, remember? It cost me a small fortune but I was able to get hold of a few of the planes involved and transport them to my research and development workshops. All of them were personal-use craft, small and short-range. They provided the template. My designers then adapted, improved and, above all, enlarged. We've reverse-engineered a fleet of aircraft bigger and robuster than any the Airborn have, and we're mass-producing more of them even as I speak. I'm looking forward to showing them to you in action very shortly. I'm also looking forward to giving you a demonstration of some of our other inventions. I think you'll find them intriguingly volatile. The next generation of ordnance.'

'What's the timetable, then?' the newspaper baron Paul Copperplate wanted to know. 'How soon is this all going to kick off? I ask because, if an attack is to take place imminently, it would be sensible for me to start planting a few stories here and there in the press. You know, along the lines of "Trouble Above The Clouds", "Why We Should Get Involved", that type of thing.'

'Milord?' said Slamshaft. 'This is your department.'

'I'm loath to make predictions,' said Lord Urironson.

'Loath,' echoed Echo.

'But everything seems to be coming to a head, and if events continue as they are – and I intend to see that they do – within a day or so, three days at most, discord and disunity will be rampant among the Airborn. That's the time when somebody could legitimately take matters into their own hands, when somebody could say with some justification that the safety of Groundlings was at stake – that somebody being you.'

'Us,' said Slamshaft, nodding. 'We who have had the foresight to take precautions. We who feared a day like this might come, the Airborn in chaos, a potential threat to us, and took on the responsibility of planning for it. We exemplary citizens.'

'Ush! Yesh!' agreed Brickmansworth triumphantly. He raised his brandy balloon, managing to slop half the contents over his hand. 'A toasht to ush! We ekshempler – ekshlempull – Whatever you jusht shaid we are.'

'How about "heroes"?' Longnoble-Drumblood offered.

'A lot eashier to pronounsh,' agreed Bricksmansworth. 'A toasht to ush heroesh!'

'Yes, why not?' Slamshaft said. He raised his glass too, and the others at the table followed suit. 'A toast to us . . . heroes. And to war. And to the spoils of war.'

'The spoils of war,' everyone repeated.

'The shpoilsh of war!' bellowed Brickmansworth. 'Hurrah!'

'*Awk!* Hurrah!' said Echo.

CHAPTER 26

Chloroform

'Shh.'

An under-the-breath hiss.

A stealthy footfall.

A soft glug of liquid.

A sharp, chemical scent.

A whisper: 'Ready?'

Az snapped his eyes open.

There were people in his room. In the semi-darkness he saw a silhouette he recognised – Nurse Haatansdaughter. He glimpsed a small glass phial in her left hand, a wadded-up piece of cloth in her right. There were men behind her, two of them. Dressed like hospital porters.

He sprang out of bed.

Or rather, tried to. The sling snagged him. All he managed to do was slither part-way out from under the covers before his tethered arm brought him up short. He was left sprawling, half on the bed, half off.

'Dammit, he's awake!' said one of the men.

'Never mind. Grab him,' said Nurse Haatansdaughter.

The men moved in on Az. One went for his shoulders, one for his legs.

Az kicked out, barefoot. The blow connected with a head, but hurt Az more than it hurt the recipient. He felt like he'd broken a toe.

The other man grappled with him, pushing him down onto the mattress and pinning down his free arm. Az writhed, still kicking. He was at an awkward angle, unable to gain any proper purchase on the bed, and therefore any leverage. The sling was holding him back in more ways than one. His opponent had the advantage.

He tried a head-butt, but missed the bridge of the man's nose, which was where the impact would have done the most damage. Instead, there was a clash of foreheads, painful for both of them.

The man cursed. 'He's a maniac. I can barely keep a grip on him. Do it! Ariella, do it now! Quick!'

'All right, all right.'

Nurse Haatansdaughter squeezed past the man, the piece of cloth poised in her hand.

Az knew what the cloth smelled of: chloroform. It brought back a faint memory from his arrival at the hospital – being anaesthetised for the operation on his arm.

He snapped at her hand with his teeth. Pinned down as he was, it was all he could do.

'Argh, you little creep!' Nurse Haatansdaughter said. 'Bite me, would you? I don't think so.'

She slapped him in the face, hard. Sparks shot across Az's vision. He gasped. He gaped.

Then the cloth was over his mouth and nose, clamped firmly. Nurse Haatansdaughter pressed down with all her might.

Don't breathe, Az told himself.

Chloroform fumes trickled up into his nostrils, cold and acrid. He thrashed his head from side to side, trying to dislodge the cloth.

Don't breathe.

Now he could taste the chemical at the back of his throat. It made him want to gag. He fought the reflex.

Don't breathe.

Nurse Haatansdaughter's face loomed over him, filling his vision. Her glamorous features were contorted, a mask of ugly determination.

'Freak,' she intoned. 'Monster. Cripple. This is what you get. This is what you deserve.'

Don't—

But things were dimming. Swimming. The chloroform was starting to take numbing effect. Az could no longer feel his tongue. His brain seemed to be filling up with ice water. He inhaled without even realising it, and the process quickened. A blankness spread through him. The hands that were holding him down seemed to melt away. He was floating. He was adrift.

There was nothing.

Gone.

CHAPTER 27

Prisoner In Prismburg

Then, just like that, he was back awake. Only a few seconds had passed.

Except . . .

Az blinked, clearing his vision.

He wasn't in the hospital room any more. He was on the floor of a tiny backroom. In a private house or apartment, was his guess. This had once been a child's room, judging by the powder-blue wallpaper and the toucan-motif curtains that covered the window. The bare carpet he was lying on had indentations where items of furniture had recently stood.

He'd been taken somewhere else. Where? How long had he been unconscious?

It was broad daylight. Behind the curtains, sunlight bloomed. By the brightness Az reckoned it must be midday at least. He hadn't been out for a few seconds. More like twelve hours.

He became aware of a constriction around his face. He had been gagged with a rag of some kind, a strip of coarse cotton.

He moved.

Or attempted to.

His ankles were bound together with cord, so tightly that it was cutting off the circulation to his feet. His wrists were tied too, but somewhat more loosely. Whereas his ankles were pressed hard against each other, his wrists were secured separately, with a short piece of cord linking them. This, he assumed, was to avoid putting undue strain on his bad arm.

How thoughtful.

For good measure, the two sets of bonds were joined to each other by a third length of cord which ran behind his back. This was threaded through an eye-bolt that had been screwed into the floor.

No doubt about it, whoever had kidnapped him wished him to stay put. He could barely move. He couldn't even crawl to the window to lift up the curtain hem and peer out.

Az didn't need to look out, however, in order to be able to make a reasonable assumption about where he was. All over the walls of the room there were scattered patches of reflected sunlight that bounced in from outside, around the curtain edges. Each little lozenge of light was iridescent, a splash of sunbow colours. In only one sky-city did you get multiple refraction patterns like that, the sky-city where every single building was encased in glass panels and convex mirrors.

Prismburg.

Which gave Az a clue as to who his abductors might be.

Feather First!ers. Who else?

He, after all, had messed up the First!ers' plan to kill Lady Aanfiels-daughter, and Prismburg was a stronghold for their movement. Kidnapping him, then, was the First!ers' revenge. A tit-for-tat gesture. Had to be.

He drew a deep breath through his nostrils and expelled it slowly.

His main goal was to remain calm. He had been held prisoner once before. On that occasion he had felt nothing but abject fear. He was older now, and smarter. Fear was pointless in such a situation, he knew. It stopped you thinking and functioning properly. It only made matters worse.

'If anyone ever takes you captive again,' Mr Mordadson had told him, not long after his brush with the Humanists, 'you take stock, you sit still, you do not panic. You look around you and see if there is anything in the vicinity that you can use to your advantage. You seek a way out. If there isn't one immediately obvious, you bide your time. Co-operate with your captors. Get them to talk as much as you can. Get them to see you as a person, not an object. Meanwhile, use the conversation to search for chinks in their armour. They'll have them. Let's face it, anyone who thinks holding someone else against their will is a good thing, is either desperate or not very clever, or both.'

Az agreed . . . but with reservations.

Desperate and not very clever, after all, could be a dangerous combination. Desperate and not very clever people were apt to do rash and sometimes lethal things.

CHAPTER 28

Les Whitesander, 23, Machinist 2nd Grade

Cassie, Den and Fletcher stood in line, waiting their turn for the Slam-shaft security guard to inspect their passes. Nerves fluttered in Cassie's stomach, but she quelled them with the thought that it was all for *Bertha*. She clung to this notion like a rock in stormy seas. She must keep herself together, not lose her cool. Otherwise, no *Bertha*.

The guard was giving the workers' passes only a cursory look. He was coming to the end of his shift and doubtless thinking about going home and putting his feet up, with a nice cup of tea, maybe, or a beer. That was why Fletcher had chosen this as the time to try and enter the factory. The guard was bored, his concentration wandering. He might not notice, therefore, that the passes the three Grubdollars were carrying had been doctored, the photogravure pictures altered.

At least, that was what they were hoping. Cassie, though, was concerned because the original picture on her pass hadn't looked much like her at all. Not least because the pass's proper owner was a man. A certain Les Whitesander, aged 23, resident at 1205 Cannery Prospect in the First Borough. Employee status: machinist 2nd grade. Sex: M (scratched out and replaced with F). Les Whitesander had a thinner face than hers, and thicker eyebrows, not to mention a pair of jug ears that stuck out like trophy handles. If there was any similarity, it was around the nose and eyes. But it wasn't what you might call close, and even with longer hair added Les Whitesander still looked undeniably masculine.

Toby Nimblenick, however, had said it was the best he could manage at such short notice. Each of the three passes had been pilfered this morning from the pockets of unsuspecting victims who were coming off-shift and were more or less a physical match for each of the Grubdollars. Had Toby had more time, he could have been more selective. In Cassie's case he could have waited for a female Slamshaft employee to come along who resembled her, instead of making do with the first available male near-lookalike. But time was not on his side. The passes had to be used on the same day they were stolen. Tomorrow would be too late. Their owners would report them missing and the guard would be on the lookout for anyone trying to sneak in with them.

A professional forger, a friend of a friend of Toby's who owed him a favour, had carried out the alterations. Technically he had done skilful work with his scalpel, emery board and fine-point pen. It was almost impossible to tell that the pictures had been tampered with. Again, though, time had been a factor. 'You want a perfect job?' he'd said. 'Give me a week. Couple of hours like this, it be'n't going to be anything better than "that'll do". Especially,' he'd added, comparing Cassie's features with Les Whitesander's, 'when you'm trying to make a cabbage out of a turnip.'

'That supposed to be a compliment?' Cassie had growled.

'Take it how you will, darling. Now hold still. It won't be any kind of likeness at all if you keep bobbing around like a monkey with tapeworms.'

As for the Slamshaft overalls the three of them were clad in, these Toby had purloined from the laundry that did all of the company's clothes-cleaning. Unfortunately he'd grabbed them from a hamper load that was about to be washed rather than one that had been washed, so they were grimy and still stank of the body odour of the people who'd previously been wearing them. But this, Cassie supposed, at least made the overalls look and smell authentic. Sort of extra camouflage.

And now the time had come to put the passes and the overalls to the test. Cassie's father was in front of her in the queue, Fletcher behind. Den stepped forward and presented himself to the security guard. He gave the man the kind of smile and nod you would give to a familiar face you saw almost every day.

'Evening,' he said.

Without replying, the guard looked Den over from head to toe, glanced briefly at the pass, then handed it back and jerked a thumb in the direction of the factory. Den walked off without hesitation, heading into the yard. He didn't even look over his shoulder at his daughter and son. It had been agreed that he, Cassie and Fletcher would pretend to have nothing to do with one another for the moment. They were to act as if they were just three ordinary workers, colleagues, insignificant cogs in the gigantic Slamshaft machine, not connected to one another in any way.

The guard turned and beckoned to Cassie. She stepped through the partially opened gateway and approached the guardhouse.

'Hi,' she said.

'Hi,' said the guard. He peered at her, his brow creasing ever so slightly. 'Who be you then? I doesn't recall seeing you before.'

Cassie's heart began to pound.

'That so?' she replied. Her voice came out sounding steadier than she had expected. This surprised her, and also filled her with confidence. 'But I's been through this gate nearly three dozen times already. I mean, I may be a newcomer to the company, but not *that* new.'

'Yeah, but . . .' The guard studied her pass. 'Les, is it?'

'Short for Lesley,' said Cassie. Luckily, the forger had not needed to change the name on the pass.

'I know I sees hundreds of faces every day, Les, but I think I's getting familiar with most of they. And it'm odd because' – here the guard winked, in a manner which he clearly thought charming – 'I's not likely to fail to remember such a pretty face as yours.'

'Well, how kind of you to say so.' Cassie wasn't a natural flirt. Nevertheless, she knew she needed to try and be one now. 'Funny, though. You mayn't recognise I, but I certainly recognises *you*. It'm one of the highlights of my day, as a matter of fact, recognising you.'

The guard had a square head, a piggy nose, crooked teeth, and eyes that were set too close to each other. He was not, by any stretch of the imagination, handsome. He, though, was under the impression that he was, and devastatingly so. The look that came over him in response to Cassie's remark, the glint that entered his eye, suggested he wasn't at all surprised that she found him irresistible.

'I like to think I be pretty recognisable,' he said, making *recognisable* sound like another word for *gorgeous*. 'Mine be the sort of face, once seen, never forgotten.'

'Oh, I wouldn't forget yours in a hurry,' Cassie said, tipping her head to the side coquettishly.

'Don't you,' the guard said, returning the pass to her without further ado.

As she strode into the yard, he called after her, 'See you later, maybe?'

With a smile Cassie replied, 'If I had my way it'd be sooner.'

The guard chuckled, pushing his peaked cap back on his head at a rakish angle.

He let the next dozen people in line, including Fletcher, go through without so much as a quibble.

Dirty old bugger, Fletcher thought during the couple of seconds the guard took to take, inspect and return his bogus pass. *Her's young enough to be your daughter.*

Under any other circumstances, he'd have given the man what-for. Ogling up his little sister like that.

Just be glad I's got bigger fish to fry today.

CHAPTER 29

Plane Parts

The Grubdollars fanned out into the factory, going their separate ways.

Den entered one of the cavernous production-line buildings and was momentarily stunned by the screech and tumult of the work being carried out inside. Everywhere he looked, sheet metal was being shaped, beaten, lathed, planed, stamped, die-cut, drilled, arc-welded. Sparks scattered and bounced. The floor was ankle-deep with flakes, fragments and shavings.

The indoor perspectives were so huge, Den couldn't see the far end of the building. He could barely make out the roof. And swarming all over the place, like ants, were the workers. It was industry on an almost unimaginable scale, frenetic, fast, multifaceted. It made his head spin.

Someone spotted him gawking and gave him a look, as if to say, *What'm you so gobsmacked for?* Immediately, Den snatched up a clipboard that was lying nearby and adopted the air of an inspector. He surveyed the scene loftily, as though noticing countless flaws and faults. The person who'd given him the look sidled off, suddenly keen to appear busy.

Meanwhile Fletcher made a beeline for the engine shed which he had seen *Bertha* go in and out of several times. She wasn't there right now, but a large parking space among the transporter trucks showed where she was kept when she wasn't in use. He noticed a puddle of oil on the concrete floor just below where her motor would be. That crack in her sump casing had opened up again. No wonder she was running rough.

It sickened him that the Slamshaft mechanics were treating *Bertha* with so little respect. They weren't even bothering with basic maintenance. She was being worked to death and they just didn't care. To them, she was only a lumbering, cumbersome murk-comber, outmoded and fit for the scrapheap.

Not much longer, old girl, Fletcher thought. He made himself inconspicuous among the trucks and waited.

As for Cassie, she remained outdoors. Skirting round the main buildings, she made her way towards the rear of the factory. She walked as if she had a purpose, as if some supervisor had sent her on an urgent errand. No one challenged her. Occasionally she sneaked a glance at her watch. They had an hour, from the moment they passed through the gate, to locate and commandeer *Bertha*. An hour from now, Toby and Robert would start their diversion outside.

The minutes slipped by swiftly. Soon quarter of an hour had gone, and still no sign of *Bertha*. Cassie hoped her father and brother were having better luck.

She came to an open-air storage depot, where finished artefacts stood in rows waiting to be hauled by cranes onto trucks and shipped out. She went past the entrance, then halted in her tracks and reversed for another look.

What she saw was an assortment of huge vehicle parts: cylindrical sections that could have been for a tanker lorry, hemispherical pieces that might be an engine cowl or, just possibly, the roof of a cab, and segments of something thin and teardrop-shaped with skeletal cross-bracing inside. Along with these were stacks of tyres that looked too fat and soft for everyday road use, and sets of paddle-like blades which had absolutely no place in any ground-based transport that she knew of.

Cassie understood exactly what she was looking at, of course. Perhaps better than any other Groundling, she was able to identify the individual parts and work out what they could be put together to create.

She understood . . . but it took a while for the implications to sink in.

Aircraft. Massive planes. It could only be. Those cylindrical sections, they were components for a fuselage. The hemispheres, nosecones. The thin, teardrop-shaped slivers, bits of wings. The tyres were undercarriage and the blades propellers.

Slamshaft had moved into the manufacture of airborne vehicles.

And why not? a part of her asked. After all, there were no longer Deacons around to keep aircraft technology out of Groundling hands. More to the point, Airborn and Groundlings were on an equal footing now, supposedly. There seemed no reason why both races shouldn't have flying machines.

But another part of Cassie felt distinctly uneasy about what she was looking at. She wondered if this was because, for most of her life, aeroplanes had been inconceivable, forbidden, beyond the pale. Thanks to the Deacons she had been conditioned – everyone had – to believe it was wrong even to think about them. Planes belonged to the next life, the world above. And here was Slamshaft, openly flouting the taboo and building some.

Or not so openly.

Yes. That, Cassie realised, was what was troubling her. Not so much the aircraft parts' existence – more the fact that she hadn't heard that Slamshaft was making planes. Surely it was the kind of thing that a company like Slamshaft would announce to the world with a whole lot of hype and ballyhoo. And yet no such announcement had been made, at least none that she was aware of. Admittedly Grimvale was off the beaten track, hardly at the hub of events. News was slow to reach there. But news of this magnitude? Even in Grimvale they'd have learned of it by now, if it was public knowledge.

A thought flitted through her mind, a wisp of memory. The two truckers talking at the way-station. *They up there. Training.*

She sensed there was some connection between that and this. She glimpsed the vague outline of a possibility. Something major was going on. And deep down in her bones, she was sure it was something bad.

But now wasn't the time to dwell on these misgivings. First things first. *Bertha.*

Cassie moved on from the storage depot, and shortly arrived at a leavings yard. Here, the vast quantity of excess metal that Slamshaft generated was piled up, ready to be smelted down and re-used. And here was *Bertha*, standing idle, having just added one more trailer-load to a small mountain of steel, iron, chrome and aluminium debris.

The man driving her had stopped for a chat with the leavings yard foreman. The pair of them stood with their backs to her and were bickering, in a more or less friendly fashion, about Slamshaft's management and the amount of overtime everyone on the workforce was being expected to put in.

'All right for Dominic Slamshaft to ask we to work longer hours,' said the driver. 'It be'n't he who has to suffer the blisters and ringing head at the end of a double-shift.'

'I doesn't see you complaining about the extra pay, though,' said the foreman. 'Besides, you'm spending half your time in that murk-comber. Blisters and a ringing head from that? I reckon not.'

'I's speaking up on everyone's behalf, that'm all.'

'Very noble of you, Cedric.'

'And you ever driven a murk-comber? Right bitch to handle, her be.'

Bitch! thought Cassie. *Call my* Bertha *a bitch?*

She was tempted to pick up a metal rod she could see and clout the man with it.

Instead, while the discussion continued, she stole across the patch of open ground between her and *Bertha*. The hatch in *Bertha*'s right flank was wide open. She made for it, keeping low. She tried not to think about the awful slapdash paintjob *Bertha* had been given, or the Slamshaft logo on her side. These would be the first things Cassie would remedy once *Bertha* was home.

She reached the hatch without being seen. She hopped aboard and dived straight into the nearest crawl-duct. Moments later the driver, Cedric, clambered into the loading bay, shut the hatch, and scaled the ladder to the driver's pod. After several false starts, the engine revved into life, and *Bertha* rumbled all around Cassie.

It was the sweetest, snuggest, most welcome sound Cassie had heard in ages. Like the purr of some vast cat, a source and signal of unmitigated pleasure.

CHAPTER 30

At Home And At Peace

Bertha rolled into her parking space and halted with a judder. Switching off her engine, Cedric the driver exited. Cassie overheard him announcing to a mechanic that he was off on his tea break. 'Fuel be running low,' he told the mechanic. 'A top-up would be good, thanks mate.'

Soon Cassie heard a *clunk* as *Bertha's* fuel cap was removed, then the hiss of diesel being poured into her tank. She wriggled up through the crawl-duct to an observation nacelle and peeked out.

The mechanic doing the refuelling was none other than Fletcher.

She tapped on the glass bubble of the nacelle till he noticed her. She gave a little wave and Fletcher nodded back. He looked at his watch, then flashed five fingers at her four times, surreptitiously.

Cassie understood. Twenty minutes left. She slid out of the nacelle and made for the driver's pod.

She eased herself into the seat, whose back still bore the gash left by Deacon Hardscree's knife when he had tried to kill Fletcher. For a while Cassie sat there gently stroking the control sticks and dashboard buttons. She felt at home and at peace.

Someone came aboard, and Cassie stiffened, ready to leap back into hiding if it was Cedric returning from his break.

'It'm I, Cass,' whispered Fletcher. He shinned up the ladder. 'Just been recceing out front. Us has got a clear run to the gate. I's uncoupled *Bertha* from that damn trailer, too.'

'Any sign of Da?'

'No, but that be'n't a problem. Him can make it out under his own steam if needs be.'

'Ten minutes till the diversion,' said Cassie. 'Those two boys better come through for we.'

'Robert and Toby?' Fletcher grinned. 'Us has given they a licence to cause havoc. Them's not likely to waste it.'

CHAPTER 31

Outlaws

Just precisely how they were going to cause a diversion had been left up to Robert and Toby to decide. The aim was to get the guard to leave the guardhouse and come out into the street, so that one of them could then nip in and apply the gate opening mechanism. In order to induce a trained security professional to desert his post, something remarkable was called for, something too loud and dramatic and violent to be ignored.

It was Robert who came up with the idea of fireworks. And it was Toby who was able to supply them. He knew of a shop in the Seventh Borough that sold nothing else. Firecrackers, fountain candles, Catherine wheels, rockets, mortars, screamers, the lot. It was closed today, but that didn't present much of an obstacle to someone with Toby's skills. While Robert waited with the half-tarp in an alley behind the shop, Toby sneaked in through the backyard, broke the lock on the shop's rear door with a carpenter's file, and hey presto, they had the entire stock to pick and choose from. As many fireworks as they wanted.

They started to load up the back of the van. Robert was terrified that someone would turn into the alley and catch them at it, or else spot them from the window of a neighbouring house and run and fetch a constable. Having carried a couple of armfuls out of the shop, he was all for quitting while they were ahead.

'Let's just jump in the van and make our getaway, eh?'

But Toby insisted they should keep at it. 'Us needs as much as us can fit in there,' he said, struggling with a stack of metre-long rockets. 'You want this to be impressive? Then the back of that van better be crammed to bursting.'

His cockiness reassured Robert, although not completely. By the time the van was full the youngest Grubdollar was a trembling mass of nerves.

His fingers were slippery with sweat as he tried to turn the key in the ignition.

'You want I to have a go?' Toby enquired.

'I can do this,' Robert snapped back.

'Only asked.'

The half-tarp started up, and Robert vroomed out of the alley, grinding gears. He couldn't believe they'd done it. They'd pulled it off. Burglary. He was a thief! Officially, he had become a criminal.

He started to laugh, slightly hysterically.

'This were your first time, weren't it?' said Toby. 'Your first time breaking the law.'

'If you doesn't count driving this van under-age.'

'First time breaking a *proper* law.'

'Then yes, it were.'

'It'm fun, no?'

'Not sure I'd call it fun, exactly,' said Robert. 'It certainly got the ticker racing. But I doesn't think I'd want to put myself through that again in a hurry.'

'Ah, you gets used to it,' Toby said, with the jaded tone of experience. 'It becomes easier every time. After a while you doesn't even feel scared. It'm just routine.'

'I be'n't sure I'd *like* to feel that lawbreaking was just routine.'

'You may well have to,' Toby replied, grimly.

'What's that mean?'

'Nothing. Just . . . Well, say you gets your murk-comber back.'

'Which us is going to.'

'Don't assume Slamshaft be going to take it lying down. The moment you steers that thing off the premises, you be outlaws. Your whole family. That'm your future. Slamshaft'll have the police on you, and a big corporation like that? The cops will be under a huge amount of pressure to hunt you down and make an arrest. I doesn't envy you the next few years of your life. You be going to have to go on the run, there'm no two ways about it.'

Robert went quiet. He hadn't thought of things in those terms. He hadn't projected much beyond getting hold of *Bertha* again, and he didn't think anyone else in his family had either.

Finally he shrugged his shoulders. 'Oh well. Come what may.' He let out a thin laugh. 'You sure you'm nine years old, Toby? 'Cause you seem awfully wise for one so young.'

'I's grown up fast,' replied the pickpocket. 'Anyway, I be almost ten.'

'Almost ten,' Robert said, nodding. 'Well then, that explains it.' He consulted the van's dashboard clock. 'Half an hour till us has to be at Slamshaft. How far to the Second Borough?'

'Four kilometres, maybe five. Go left here. Us can take Burners Boulevard down to the Axlegrease Expressway, get to the tunnel that way. That'll shave a few minutes off.'

Robert made the turn. Soon the half-tarp was speeding along the four-lane expressway, and then the crater's rim loomed, a tunnel mouth appeared, and the van was engulfed in roaring darkness.

CHAPTER 32

Fireworks

Twenty-four minutes later Robert stopped the half-tarp at the kerbside, just a few metres along from the factory gate.

'You does realise you's not going to have much of a van left after all this?' said Toby, as Robert applied the handbrake and killed the engine.

'Don't care. Weren't ours in the first place.'

'Fair enough. Just checking. So, you got the matches on you?'

Robert scowled. 'Hold on, Toby. You said *you'd* brought matches.'

'No, it were your job. I definitely remember you saying you had some.'

'No, you told I *you* did. Oh bugger. I don't believe this. You mean to say six minutes to go and neither of we has anything to light these damn fireworks with?'

Toby held up a box of matches, rattling it. 'Hee hee. Just kidding.'

'Little sod,' said Robert, relieved. 'I's a good mind to thump you one. Give I those.'

Toby tossed him the box.

'Now get off with you,' Robert said. 'Go and wait where you be supposed to. Not too close to the van, mind. No telling which way some of these fireworks is going to go off.'

Toby held out a hand. 'Been a pleasure working with you, Robert Grubdollar. You and all your kin.'

'Likewise,' said Robert, shaking the pickpocket's tough little paw.

'Give my regards to they, your sister especially. I's been meaning to ask. Her got a boyfriend?'

'Yup. Him's Airborn, as a matter of fact. Az be his name. You may have heard of he. Him's a pretty cool guy.'

'Oh. Shame. Well, if it don't work out between they, tell she to look I up. I's available.'

'I'll be sure to do that,' Robert said.

'And remember what I said about being outlaws, Robert. That were just a kind of friendly warning, all right? A word to the wise from one who knows.'

'All right, all right. I take the point. Now get going. Time be wasting.'

Toby slipped out of the van and headed along the pavement towards the gate. He drifted past it without drawing a glance from the guard, and halted on the far side.

And then he just sort of faded from view.

It was uncanny. Robert was watching him the whole time, and as soon as Toby started to loiter by the wall, he became hard to spot. Somehow he managed to blend in, merging with the brickwork. One moment he was noticeable, the next not.

Robert shook his head. Fletcher had mentioned something about this talent of Toby's. The kid was quite a piece of work.

The dashboard clock ticked, the minute hand turned, and all at once the hour was up.

Showtime.

Robert twisted round in the driving seat and slid open the little hatch in the back of the cab that gave access to the rear of the van. The gap was just big enough for him to lean through. He eyed the bristling array of fireworks in front of him and selected a chain of firecrackers for use as a fuse. He struck a match, lit the touchpaper on the firecrackers . . . then scrambled out of the half-tarp as fast as he could.

The sizzle of the touchpaper sounded startlingly loud as he sprinted away from the van.

But it wasn't anywhere near as loud as the sound of the first few firecrackers detonating.

And *that* was nothing compared with the ear-splitting cacophony that followed.

CHAPTER 33

Big Bang

A mortar round was the first of the large fireworks to go off. It was a paper-wrapped sphere the size of a grapefruit and was meant to be launched from a cardboard tube and explode a hundred metres in the air, creating a dandelion of sparks ten metres across. But, limited to the confines of the half-tarp, its effect was to blow holes in the canvas awning and ignite several other fireworks.

A fusillade of *bangs*, *thumps* and *booms* followed. The van lurched on its axles and the awning flapped and flailed with each blast, gradually turning to tatters. Now a shower of scarlet flares burst from the back, spraying across the cobblestones. Now three rockets shot out in quick succession, one arcing over the wall into the Slamshaft yard, the other two bouncing off buildings on the opposite side of the street before sailing off towards the clouds. Some Catherine wheels went whizzing off down the road like clumps of blazing razorweed. A few more mortar rounds detonated, deafening as thunderclaps. The half-tarp's windscreen shattered. Its tyres popped. The entire street was lit up in the evening gloom, colours running riot across the building façades, greens and reds and blues and purples and dazzling golds. Windows broke. Passers-by ducked for cover. Robert himself cowered in a gutter some fifty metres from the van with his hands over his head. The ground was shaking beneath him. He'd known the fireworks would make an impact but he had never imagined quite how big it would be. He was laughing to himself and at the same time in fear for his life. One stray fireball and he would be a goner.

Another rocket zoomed over the wall and came down in the factory yard. It rebounded off a crate of rivets and hurtled at waist-height towards a group of administrative workers who had come out from their office to see what the commotion was. The workers scattered in all directions, and the rocket hit the little one-storey administrative block, punching a hole in the side. Within a minute the block was on fire, and a year's worth of Slamshaft paperwork – records, accounts, invoices, correspondence – was turning to cinders.

It was this that galvanised the security guard into action. He had been watching the fireworks through the gate from the shelter of his guard-house, his jaw dropping slightly further with each fresh volley of discharges. When the admin block started to burn, he knew he must do something. Others were rushing to the block with buckets of sand to throw on the fire. The guardhouse itself was equipped with a small, pressurised-water extinguisher. He snatched the canister off its mounting, hit the gate lever to the 'Personnel' setting, and hurried out into the road.

A plume of smoke was billowing from the half-tarp, drifting over the street in a thickening pall. Explosions were still going on in the back of the van, although with decreasing frequency. The air reeked of sulphur and saltpetre. The guard looked at the half-tarp, then at the fire extinguisher in his hands and realised that it wasn't in any way up to the task. The extinguisher was designed for putting out small fires. Fine if the guardhouse should happen to catch alight, but the canister was about the size of a soda siphon, and the entire van was aflame. He had about as much chance of damping down the blaze with it as he did of—

The guard was unable to finish the thought. Next thing he knew, he was flying. Flying backwards through the air. Then landing on his bottom with a bump. Sprawling flat on his back. And the world was one huge *whoomph* of flame, a bright orange mushroom bulging up into the sky.

The half-tarp's fuel tank had gone up. The explosion sent the van somersaulting forwards with an almost athletic grace. It spun end over end, tailpipe over radiator grille, riding the shockwave of its own destruction, to come down finally on its roof, *crunch*, five car-lengths on from where it had started. It rocked a few times then lay still. Fire roared from it. The black skeleton of the upside-down van was enrobed with incandescence, shrouded in an inferno.

The guard lay stunned. He couldn't get up. His limbs wouldn't work. He lolled in the roadway, smelling the stench of singed hair. His own fringe and eyebrows, even the hairs in his nostrils, had been shrivelled to a crisp by the surge of heat from the exploding van.

Toby Nimblenick hadn't been so close to the blast. He was knocked off his feet but was swiftly back on them. His chance had come. He darted in through the partly open gateway and threw the lever from 'Personnel' to 'Vehicle'. The gate rolled further open, all the way, clanging against its endstop. He looked round, and there, right on cue, coming across the yard, floodlights on, was a murk-comber. Toby giggled to himself. Perfect timing.

He saluted as *Bertha* rumbled past. Cassie Grubdollar, looking down from the driver's pod, smiled and saluted back.

'See you again soon, I hope!' Toby yelled, even though he knew she couldn't hear.

He meant it, too. And the remark didn't refer just to Cassie. He was smitten with her, but he thought the Grubdollars in general were a pretty nifty bunch. Fun stuff happened when they were around. Toby, an orphan, had never had a family, but if he did, he'd have wanted it to be one like the Grubdollars.

Then he winced with shame, as he recalled what he planned to do next. How he intended to betray the Grubdollars.

Oh well, a boy couldn't afford to get sentimental.

Not when there was money and a purged police record at stake.

CHAPTER 34

Crazily Spectacular And Spectacularly Crazy

Den emerged from the production-line building in time to see the administrative block go up in smoke. Fireworks were still popping and bursting on the other side of the wall. He groaned, knowing his youngest son and the little street-thief, Toby, were responsible for all this chaos. With hindsight, he could see it had been a mistake to give the two boys free rein in choosing the method by which they would cause a diversion. He recalled them at The Boxes last night, huddling together in a corner and conferring in whispers. When they started to snigger and wouldn't tell anyone what they had just come up with, he should have realised then that it would be a stunt like this, something crazily spectacular and spectacularly crazy.

Mind you, it was doing the trick. Den saw the security guard leave the guardhouse, fire extinguisher in hand, and make for the street. Then, above the racket of conflagration and detonation and the shouts of Slamshaft workers fighting the fire, he heard *Bertha*'s low throbbing cackle. The murk-comber hauled into view, with Cassie at the controls.

Den loped towards *Bertha*. The hatch in her side was wide open. So, now, was the factory gate. Everyone was too preoccupied with the fire to notice either of these two things, let along see that the murk-comber was making a bid for freedom. The plan, which Den had given a fifty-fifty chance of success, had worked. They were stealing *Bertha* back right from under Slamshaft's noses!

He dived into the loading bay, to be greeted by Fletcher, who was grinning from ear to ear. *Bertha* rolled out through the gateway, and moments later Den was helping Robert clamber aboard from the street. The boy looked both shocked and gleeful, his eyes big as saucers.

'You see that?' he breathed. 'Everyone, did you see?'

'Us saw,' replied his father. Framed by the hatchway, the semi-conscious figure of the guard glided past, then the remnants of the half-tarp, still aflame. 'You did good, lad. But if you ever, *ever* tries something like that again, I'll tan ten shades of tar out of you. Get I?'

'I get you,' said a chastened Robert.

'That'm my boy.' Den ruffled his hair.

'Where to?' Cassie asked over the speaker tube system. 'Any suggestions?'

'Home, of course,' said Den, punching the switch to close the hatch.

'Uhh, home mayn't be such a good idea, Da.'

Fletcher frowned at his brother. 'What's you mean, Robert?'

'Well . . .'

Robert relayed the gist of Toby's 'friendly warning'.

'If anyone'd know about living on the wrong side of the law, it'd be he,' said Fletcher.

'True,' said Den. 'I had wondered about this. Fact is, though, no one knows for sure it were we that just took she.'

'Security guard could give a description of we to the cops, maybe.'

'Maybe, Fletch, but maybe not. Us was pretty anonymous once us was decked out to look like Slamshaft workers.'

'Except Cass. The way him were carrying on with she, him'd know her face again if him saw it.'

'Also,' said Robert, 'when us turns up in Grimvale again with *Bertha*, it'm not as though people be'n't going to mark the fact. And our house'll be the first place the police look for she.'

'Anyone care to cut I in on this conversation?' Cassie asked from the driver's pod.

'Sorry, lass,' said her father into the speaker tube. 'Us is just pondering.'

'Well, while you be doing that, might I say something?'

'Go ahead.'

'Before anything else, I reckon us first has to pay a visit to a sky-city.'

'Wha-a-at?' said her father, older brother and younger brother in unison.

CHAPTER 35

Rumours

Cassie continued to steer *Bertha* through the winding streets of Crater-home as Den and Fletcher joined her in the driver's pod. It was a tight squeeze with the three of them, and there was no room for a fourth, so Robert had to perch at the top of the ladder, his head on a level with everyone else's ankles.

'It'm like this,' Cassie said. 'I's prepared to admit I could be imagining things, putting two and two together and coming up with five. But I doesn't think so.'

She repeated the exchange she had overheard between the two truckers, then described the plane parts she had seen at Slamshaft.

'Now you tell I there be'n't something odd about all that. Suspicious-odd.'

'Not necessarily,' said Fletcher. 'Look at it this way. The cat be out of the bag about aircraft. Logically, a big corporation like Slamshaft would see the commercial potential. Planes for Groundlings? Why not?'

'You, of all people, defending Slamshaft, Fletch?'

'I be'n't defending they in the least. All I be saying is, if there'm money to be made out of it, Slamshaft'll have a go. Stands to reason them'd develop planes now that the principles be common knowledge and there'm specimens easy to find and copy from.'

'Anyway,' Robert chimed in, 'who'm to say them's not making they for Airborn, not Groundlings?'

'Yup, good point,' said Fletcher.

'The Airborn doesn't need others to build planes,' Cassie said. 'Them does it perfectly well themselves. And either way, you'd've thought Slamshaft would be keen to trumpet it to the world. "Look, everyone, us is in the aircraft biz now!" But there hasn't been a peep from they on the subject, far as I know. Also, there were something about the way those

100

parts looked. At first glance you'd reckon them was for trucks or the like. You wouldn't straight-off think aircraft. Which leads I to think Slamshaft be keen that no one clocks what them's up to.'

'Now you mention it,' said Fletcher, 'all those trucks I saw leaving the factory, them was covered up pretty tight.'

'Could be that Slamshaft'm worried about industrial espionage,' Robert commented wryly. 'Doesn't want anyone getting a peek at their new stuff.'

'Heh,' said his brother. 'Yeah, scared other people'll nick their ideas.'

'You'm missing the point,' said Cassie. 'That trucker spoke about "fighting" and "they up there", by which I's pretty sure he meant the Airborn. Now, I doesn't deny I could be making a mountain out of a molehill. But my gut feeling be otherwise.'

'Sis, just because us Grubdollars seems to have a knack of getting mixed up in major events,' said Fletcher, 'it don't mean that every time us stumbles onto something, it has to be a war or a conspiracy or a big bad evil out to overturn the world or whatever. I mean, who be us? Us is nobodies. There be'n't a – a law of nature that says every crisis that happens must revolve around the Grubdollars or involve we in some way. There'm certainly an innocent explanation for what you heard and saw.'

'You believe that, Fletch, or you just trying to convince yourself?'

He hesitated. 'Well, I'd like to think it'm true. Last thing us needs now is yet more trouble.'

'Da?' said Cassie, turning to Den. 'You's been pretty quiet. What be your opinion on this?'

Den scratched his chin stubble pensively. At last he said, 'I be with Fletch.'

'Oh,' said Cassie, disappointed.

'The last thing us needs now be yet more trouble. Only, I hate to say it, but I reckon you'm bang on the money, lass.'

'Ah,' said Cassie, a little more brightly.

'See, I's been hearing rumours. Not often, not many. Pub prattle. Street-corner gossip. I's not thought much of it, which'm why I's not felt the need to bring it up before now. But I's been hearing it nevertheless. Talk of jobs available for men and women in good physical condition between the ages of twenty and forty. Talk of well-paid work if you just go to a certain address south of Craterhome and apply. *Suspiciously* well-paid work, for people who be'n't afraid to get their hands dirty and mixing it up a bit. I considered looking it into myself, but . . .'

'But you be'n't forty any more,' said Robert. 'You'm ancient.'

'Oy! I could pass for forty,' Den said, mock-hurt.

'With a bag over your head, maybe.'

'Listen, lad, you'm already on a caution with I. Don't push it.'

'Sorry, Dad. *Of course* you could pass for forty. Thirty, even!'

'My point being,' Den said, struggling to recover some of his dignity, 'I thought it were rubbish. You know, one of those stories that does the rounds. No basis to it. These days, there'm a lot of folk looking for work. The economy got unsettled when the Airborn appeared and it be'n't quite on an even keel again. Companies like Slamshaft might still be raking in the cash, but all over the Territories there be individuals, little people, finding it harder than it used to be to make ends meet. As us ourselves knows only too well. That'm when rumours of this type start – fanciful tales about pots of money being on offer, although nobody can say quite where or what for. But now I be thinking these particular rumours might have a grain of truth in they after all. Question be, what do it all add up to? Do it add up to what Cassie'm thinking, some kind of action against the Airborn, with Slamshaft supplying the transportation?'

'Whether it do or don't,' said Cassie, 'us at least ought to let Az know, and Mr Mordadson. To be on the safe side.'

Her father nodded. 'Spooky old Mordadson probably's already got an inkling. There'm not much that goes on that he don't know about, up there or down here. Still, us'd be doing everyone a disservice if us didn't get word to he.'

'So . . . ?'

'Granite Plains, lass,' Den said, with a smidgeon of a sigh. 'That'm where Pearl Town be planted next to, right? Take we to Granite Plains.'

CHAPTER 36

Ghosts Of Dreams

The cramps came and went, and when they were bad they were agony. But Az did not cry out. He rode the waves of pain, counting his breaths in and out through his nose, one two three, three two one, regularly, focusing on that and nothing else.

The cramps were spasms in muscles which didn't like being trapped in one position and needed to move. They were worst in his legs. At least there was some slack between the bonds on his wrists. He could stretch and turn his arms, albeit in a limited fashion, and ease the muscles that way. But his legs were another story. At times the tendons went as taut as bowstrings, from hip to ankle, and it felt as though the very muscle fibres were tearing apart.

Az rolled and writhed on the floor. His stomach churned. The air hissed through the cloth gagging him.

But he would. Not. Scream.

He refused to give his captors the satisfaction of hearing him scream. Even a whimper, which the gag would surely muffle – he would not allow himself even that.

When the pain receded, he had time to think. These lucid periods were getting shorter and shorter. The cramps were coming thicker and faster.

Mostly he thought about how hungry and thirsty he was. No one had come in to see him. He hadn't even heard voices outside the door to the room. He couldn't help wondering if he'd been abandoned here – left to die in an empty house. Rationally, he knew his death would serve no purpose. He was only valuable to the First!ers alive. Dead, he had no use as a bargaining chip or tool of revenge or whatever it was they wanted him for.

But still, it was hard to shake the image from his head: wasting away in this room, suffering a slow, lingering end, racked by the cramps and by the rigours of starvation. How long would it take? Days? A week?

Evening came. The iridescent lozenges of light on the walls shifted, lengthened and blurred, and finally faded out. Night fell. Az was alone in the dark.

He fell into a stupor. His legs hurt from time to time, but not as severely as before. He knew the pain hadn't lessened. He just wasn't feeling it as much. A kind of inner numbness had set in, his mind saying it had had enough and blanking out the worst of the torment.

He lay on his side and dozed fitfully, snatching scraps of sleep that seemed to last an eye-blink. There were dreams, although they were so brief and fleeting they were more like ghosts of dreams. In one, the Count of Gyre was talking to him. Or at any rate, the Count's lips were moving, his clothes-peg teeth opening and closing, but what emerged was not speech but strings of numbers and mathematical symbols. Az watched them pouring out one after another, forming swirly lines in the air, wreathing themselves around the Count's head, with a few of them breaking off and scattering into corners of the room, where they settled and melted to nothingness.

Then *Cerulean* appeared, and she had an actual voice, unlike the Count. She loomed before Az, and her front propellers were her eyes and the forward viewing windows of her control gondola were her mouth, and she said, 'I'm here. Not far from you.' Her tones were similar to Lady Aanfielsdaughter's, soft, maternal, concerned. 'I'm all better now I've had my refit. My berth is to the east of the city, you know that. I haven't seen you in so long. I miss you. You're so close. You need to come and see me.'

Suddenly she sounded like Cassie. 'I be close, Az.' She *was* Cassie. 'I'd help if I could, but I has other matters to attend to.'

'It's all right, Cassie,' Az said, or thought he said. 'This is my mess. I'll fix it. I hope.'

His girlfriend smiled. 'You do that. I has faith in you. You fix it.'

Except, he couldn't. What could he do? He wasn't able to wriggle out of his bonds. He'd tried. And he was weak, and getting weaker.

Mr Mordadson?

Crimson-shaded eyes regarded Az sorrowfully.

'Whose side are you on?'

'Yours, of course.'

Mr Mordadson shook his head.

Why? Wasn't that the right answer after all?

Then there was blackness.

Just blackness.

Az gazed into it. He had never felt so alone before. Nobody else was there any longer, no dream phantoms visiting him. It was just him and this empty, formless, engulfing blackness.

It was just him, the wingless kid. The boy whom people would point at and whisper about. The boy who'd often been laughed at and shunned by his schoolmates, as if lack of wings was an infection, something you might catch off him.

This still happened. In spite of all he'd done for the Airborn, he still wasn't regarded as an equal by the majority of his race.

Az drifted in the blackness, and noticed it was warm. Comforting. It didn't judge. It didn't condemn. The blackness accepted him as he was. It reflected nothing back. It was pure indifference.

And then there was light.

Searing brightness.

Az winced and screwed up his eyes. The light was like a physical weight pressing on his retinas.

Hands grabbed him roughly and started to loosen his bonds. He tried to peep between his eyelids to see who the hands belonged to, but the brightness was still too intense.

Then a man's voice said, 'I'm going to remove the gag, Gabrielson. But bear in mind that I and my colleagues are carrying knives, and we won't hesitate to use them.' Briefly Az felt an edge of cold, sharp metal against his neck. Proof. 'One chirp out of you and it'll be your last. Do you understand?'

He gave a feeble nod.

'Very well.'

The gag came off, and Az choked and rasped and spluttered.

'Sit up.'

Az did, stiffly, groggily.

'There's food and drink,' said the voice, 'and a bucket for you to, you know, go in. You have ten minutes. No tricks, no funny business.'

Footfalls leaving the room. The door shutting, key turning.

Az prised his eyelids apart, forcing his vision to adjust to the brightness.

On the floor in front of him were a slice of bread, some cheese, an apple, and a cup of water.

Az fell on the meagre meal as though it were a feast.

CHAPTER 37

Interesting Versus *Boring*

As nourishment reached his belly, Az felt his brain start to liven up.

He spent five minutes eating, another minute relieving himself in the bucket.

He used the remaining four minutes to investigate the room. He tested the eye-bolt in the floor. It was firmly screwed in. Finger-strength alone could not make it budge. Then he peeked out through the curtains. Moonlight showed him that the room was at the top of a house that was itself high up, somewhere close to the summit of the city. From the window to the nearest horizontal surface, a patio, was a sheer drop of at least 100 metres. The house was on the outskirts of the city, and not overlooked by any near neighbours. There was no one Az could signal to from the window. He was, though, as he had already deduced, in Prismburg. The few, distant buildings he could see had that distinctive glittery sheen, muted but still visible in the moon's glow.

He tried the window handle carefully. It turned but the window did not open. He looked and found nails driven in between frame and casement.

Still, just a sheet of glass separated him from freedom. He could smash the windowpane, leap out . . .

. . . and fall to that patio where, if he was lucky, he'd break every bone in his body; if he was unlucky, dash his brains out.

He cast a glance over the room again. His captors had left him nothing he could press into service as a weapon. The plate the food had come on was made of waxed paper, the cup likewise. The bucket was enamel, not particularly heavy.

He could fight, of course. When they returned he could hurl himself at them and inflict as much damage as he knew how to.

If only his arm was uninjured. If only his limbs didn't ache from the cramping. If only it wasn't taking every erg of energy he had simply to remain standing.

When the door reopened, Az's captors found him seated meekly in the centre of the room. They approached with knives drawn. The knives were the kind used to skin and gut poultry, short-bladed, half-serrated, curved and cruelly lethal. That settled the question of fighting once and for all, as far as Az was concerned. Unarmed, against people with knives? Not a chance.

The captors numbered three in total. One of them, who appeared to be in charge, motioned to the other two to move behind Az.

'Easy does it, lads,' he said. 'He's pretty tricky.'

'I won't give you any trouble,' Az said. 'I swear.'

'Oh yeah?' The man, who had a very red complexion indeed, did not look convinced. 'Well, after our experience with you in the hospital, forgive me if I don't take any chances. Lie down.' He gestured with his knife. 'Hands behind your back. Feet together.'

'There's no need—'

'Do it.'

Az obeyed, and the two men behind him bent and began tying him up again while the red-faced one held the tip of his knife to Az's throat.

'All right,' the man said, when Az was securely fastened once more. 'Good.' He straightened up, looking relieved.

'See? I'm no threat to you,' Az said. 'I'll go along with whatever you want. If you need me as a hostage, a pawn, ransom material, anything, that's OK. I'm not going to try anything stupid. I want to live.'

'That's handy, because we want you alive. For now.'

'You're Feather First!ers, aren't you?'

A blink, a split-second of startlement, told him he had guessed correctly, and the red-faced man knew his own hesitation meant it was pointless trying to pretend Az was wrong.

'That we are,' he said, with a self-important flourish of his wings. 'You'd have found out soon enough anyway.'

'Well, look,' Az said in a reasonable tone of voice, 'I know a lot of people disagree with your movement and don't like what you stand for, but do you think I'm one of them?'

'Of course you are,' said one of the First!ers behind him. He yanked up a shirtsleeve to show off a tattoo on his biceps the size of medallion. Az recognised the double-feather logo.

'See that?' the man said. 'Know what that means? It means we hate Groundlings. We resent how they've come into our lives and plucked things up for us. In the good old days they knew their place, which was down on the ground, working for us without expecting anything in return. We didn't have to be all concerned about them. We didn't have

107

to worry about their "needs" and "rights". Out of sight, out of mind. And now, thanks to *you*, that's all gone.' He rolled down his sleeve again. 'Why wouldn't you be against us when you're the one responsible for everything we're opposed to?'

'I might have been involved with the plan to open up relations between them and us, but that doesn't mean I'm on the Groundlings' side. I didn't have much choice about going down the first time. Lady Aanfields-daughter used me. And since then, I've had Groundlings try to kill me at least twice. Believe me, I'm no fan of them.'

'Oh yes?' said the red-faced man. 'So how come you have a Groundling girlfriend? Eh? Everyone knows that the great Az Gabrielson is dating some dowdy little trollop from down there. If you're no fan of those ostriches, why go out with one?'

'Because,' said Az, and it was an effort to keep his composure when all he wanted to do was spit a torrent of abuse at the First!er. *Cassie a dowdy little trollop? She's worth a hundred of you, pluck-face!* 'Because, look at me. You think I stand a chance with an Airborn chick, the way I am? Girls up here cross the street to avoid me. Whereas, to a Groundling, I'm more or less normal.' He put on what he hoped was a man-of-the-world expression. 'Got to get some action somehow, haven't I?'

Much though this hurt to say because it was a betrayal of Cassie, it hurt, too, because there was some truth in it.

The red-faced First!er cocked his head to one side. 'No, I'm not buying it. I see what this is. A transparent attempt to get on-side with us. You'll have to be a mite more cunning than that, Gabrielson.'

Az did his best to shrug, in spite of his constricted state. 'Can't blame me for trying. But I can tell you're a smart man. That's why you're the boss of this outfit.'

One of the other two First!ers snorted.

'Oh, he's not?' Az said, craning his head round.

'Him our boss? El El?' said the First!er. 'Hah.'

'Then, don't tell me. Nurse Haatansdaughter's running the show.'

Now it was red-faced El El's turn to snort. 'Wrong again, Gabrielson. Ariella's a sympathiser, and she's been useful to us, no question. We wouldn't have managed to abduct you from the hospital half as easily without her help. But, bossy as she is, she isn't the one we take orders from. We answer to someone much more highly placed. And that,' he went on brusquely, 'is all you need to know. You two? Let's leave our young houseguest to continue to enjoy the, ahem, accommodation.'

El El bent down and knotted the gag back around Az's mouth.

'Comfortable, Gabrielson?'

Az shook his head.

'Good.'

All three First!ers trooped out of the room, El El switching the light off.

Immediately, Az relaxed his limbs. He had tensed them the moment the First!ers started tying him up again. By holding his legs and arms ever so slightly apart from one another, and expanding the muscles, he'd been able to generate some slack in the cords. It wasn't much, certainly not enough to allow him to wriggle loose. But it gave him more freedom of movement than he'd had before, and he would be able to deal with the cramps better.

Thanks, Mr Mordadson.

It was another trick his mentor had taught him. Az found he was learning more from his association with Mr Mordadson than he ever did during the seven hours a day he spent at school. School, indeed, was becoming more and more of an irrelevance in his life. He was falling way behind with his studies and his teachers had begun to despair of him. The principal had even hinted that he should consider dropping out, so abysmal were his exam results, not to mention his attendance record.

'I realise, Azrael, that school can hardly compete with all the numerous, more *interesting* demands on your time,' the principal had said just the other day. 'If these extracurricular activities of yours are where your true focus lies, then perhaps we're fast approaching a parting of the ways, you and I. You're nearing the end of your educational career anyway. I can't see how leaving a few months early will really make much of a difference.'

Right now, however, given the choice, Az would gladly have been at home, in bed, asleep, with the prospect of nothing but another dreary day of lessons ahead of him.

Interesting wasn't always preferable to *boring*.

CHAPTER 38

Treadwell

Detective Inspector Gavin Treadwell of the Craterhome metropolitan police was summoned to the Slamshaft plant at approximately 9.25 p.m.

At first he was led to understand that he was investigating an attack on the factory using some kind of incendiary device or devices. That was the impression he was given by the sergeant who had reported the incident and was supervising the crime scene. The smouldering wreckage of a half-tarp van in the street outside did nothing to dispel the misapprehension. The culprits must have launched the attack from the van, and then either they'd destroyed it to get rid of evidence or, perhaps, it had blown up by accident.

As things turned out, however, the van was of secondary importance. Damage had been done to Slamshaft property, and that was bad, but a theft had taken place also. It didn't take Treadwell long to ascertain that, while the van was exploding and a small part of the factory was burning, a murk-comber had been illegally removed from the premises.

The two events had to be connected. It seemed beyond coincidence that the murk-comber had been driven away just as a series of large, loud detonations were going on outside. Distraction, diversion, whatever you wanted to call it, the incendiary attack had provided cover for the murk-comber heist.

Which left Treadwell with a puzzling question: who would want a murk-comber so badly that they would go to all this trouble pilfering one?

The Slamshaft site manager, a roly-poly fellow by the name of Cuthbert Roundcoring, agreed that it was a head-scratcher all right.

'It's not as if murk-combers are expensive,' Roundcoring said. 'As a matter of fact, these days you can pick one up for a song. The Relic-scavenging industry is all but dead. The bottom's fallen out of that particular market, and murk-comber owners wanting to get shot of them can barely *give* them away.'

'Be that why you was using one here?' Treadwell asked. He was in Roundcoring's office, a room whose plush furnishings and wood-panelled walls were in marked contrast to the busy, utilitarian factory surrounding it. Thanks to soundproofing, the office was an oasis of quiet elegance amid the rumbling hurly-burly of heavy industry.

'Certainly,' said Roundcoring. 'And an absolute bargain it was too. A thousand notes, I think it cost us, if that. Funnily enough, we got it through you lot. Police auction.'

'Oh?' Treadwell jotted in his notebook.

'Yes. Impounded vehicles – usually they're one step up from the scrap-yard, but if you accept that you're just going to work them to death, they're great value.'

'I wouldn't have thought Slamshaft Engineering needed to worry about saving money.'

'You'd be surprised, Inspector. Men like Dominic Slamshaft don't get rich by being spendthrift. As site manager, I'm encouraged to economise wherever possible.'

Treadwell couldn't resist a sly dig. 'That why your product be so unreliable? Cutting corners?'

Roundcoring bristled. 'I resent the accusation. I'll have you know the poor reputation Slamshaft parts have is entirely unfounded. Of course, as we manufacture so extensively, it isn't surprising if faults occur, nor is it surprising if we get more items returned to us than other companies do. It's simple mathematics. We put more stuff out there in the first place. Allowing for the same percentage of defects as our smaller rivals, then—'

'All right, all right,' said Treadwell. 'It were a cheap shot. Sorry.'

'Harrumph,' said Roundcoring, placated.

'So tell I, please, Mr Roundcoring, does you reckon it were an employee who took the murk-comber?'

'I doubt it very much.'

'You sound sure.'

'I am. Who would do such a thing? Stealing from your own company – it'd be madness. Not to mention rank ingratitude.'

'A disgruntled worker maybe? Someone you'd had to fire, getting their own back?'

'That's possible, I grant you. But an ex-employee, stripped of his pass, would not be able to enter the factory.'

'Passes can be faked,' Treadwell observed. 'I just can't help thinking this has the hallmarks of an inside job.'

'But the incendiaries or whatever they were came from outside.'

'Courtesy of an accomplice in the street.'

'You honestly believe someone at Slamshaft did this? Burned down our admin block and stole a virtually worthless vehicle as some kind of . . . of retribution against us?'

'It'm an avenue I'd like to pursue.'

Up till this moment, Roundcoring had been nothing but helpful and accommodating. He'd behaved like a man who couldn't be keener on assisting the police with their enquiries. Suddenly something changed.

'That would mean, I suppose, interviewing the workforce,' he said.

'Undoubtedly,' said Treadwell, noting the guarded look that had come into the site manager's eyes. 'As many of they as I can. Why, be that a problem?'

'It's just . . . we're terribly busy at present. What with one thing and another, I don't feel that we can afford to have our employees leave their machines for any great length of time.'

'I wouldn't need more than five minutes or so with each person.'

'Five minutes is a long time in production-line terms. One man gets pulled off his station, the whole line has to shut down.'

'Surely somebody else could fill in.'

'We're at absolute capacity, Inspector. We don't have spare workers floating around, ready to pitch in at a moment's notice. Everyone here is going flat-out.'

'What about on their lunch breaks? Them could spare five minutes then.'

'It's really quite out of the question, Inspector.'

'This'm a serious matter, Mr Roundcoring, and I needs to get to the bottom of it as best I can.'

'Well now, is it?' said Roundcoring, flashing a smile that was too broad, too congenial. 'Is it really that serious?'

'Destruction of property. Taking a vehicle without owner's consent. Those is first-degree offences in my book. Worth at least ten years in jail each. Fifteen, if the judge trying the case is in a bad mood that day.'

'But, as you yourself pointed out, Slamshaft is a big company, with deep pockets.'

'What I actually said, sir, were that I didn't think you needed to worry about saving money. Not quite the same thing.'

'Essentially the same thing. So what if we've lost a murk-comber? Or our admin block for that matter? We can replace them.'

'You doesn't want me finding and arresting the culprits, then?'

'Have I at any point expressed that wish?'

'Well, no,' Treadwell admitted. 'But you must want that, mustn't you? Why else you be talking to I?'

'Common courtesy. When a police inspector calls, it's only polite to speak to him.'

'You doesn't even want your murk-comber back?'

'Not especially,' said Roundcoring. 'And prosecuting the individuals who stole it wouldn't necessarily be in Slamshaft's best interests, I feel.'

'You want folk thinking Slamshaft be a soft touch? You want they reckoning them can just waltz in and take stuff off you any time them likes? Surely not.'

'I'm prepared to treat this incident as a one-off, Inspector. A hiccup in the otherwise smooth running of this plant. I'd be grateful if you could see your way to treating it similarly. Very grateful, in fact. Remember what I said about deep pockets?'

Roundcoring waggled his eyebrows, and Treadwell knew what was being implied. He brushed the comment aside as if he hadn't heard it. Treadwell was that rarity among Craterhome cops, one who was not susceptible to bribery.

'I have the law to uphold, Mr Roundcoring,' he said coolly and formally.

'And I, Inspector, have a factory to oversee,' said Roundcoring, equally coolly. 'Now, I've been more than co-operative, but I really feel this interview is at an end and I'd like you to vacate the premises if you don't mind.'

Treadwell did mind. But unfortunately, he didn't have a choice. If Roundcoring wasn't willing to pursue the matter any further, there wasn't a lot Treadwell could do about it.

'Don't suppose I could talk to your boss?' he asked, as a parting shot.

'Mr Slamshaft? The likes of you? Talk to him?' Roundcoring barked an arrogant laugh. 'I should say not!'

Treadwell shrugged. 'Just a thought. Goodbye.'

The likes of you.

It was those words that decided him. Crossing the factory yard, making for the gate, Treadwell resolved then and there that the snooty site manager hadn't seen the last of him. There was more to this affair than met the eye. Cuthbert Roundcoring was hiding something. What, Treadwell had no idea. But he was damned if he wasn't going to find out.

CHAPTER 39

A Pipe Man And Proud Of It

Outside the plant, Treadwell stopped and lit up his pipe.

He loved smoking. He loved the taste of tobacco and the stimulating effects, and he loved, too, the whole ritual of taking out the pipe, extracting a thimble-sized clump of Palmwater's Finest Shag (his favourite blend) from his leather pouch, tamping the strands into the bowl of the pipe, then striking a match, letting it flare first in midair so that all the sulphur burned off, then carefully applying it to the tobacco and at the same time inhaling through the stem to make the match flame curl and caress the topmost strands. The soft crackle of burning, the first wisp of smoke rising from the bowl, and then the first proper in-breath, the aromatic fumes sliding coolly over his tongue, down his throat, into his lungs . . .

. . . and then the first cough, because the initial hit of smoke always made him cough.

But after that, it was contented puffing all the way, and his thoughts would sharpen, his mind would grow clearer and see problems in a new light, finding solutions. Whenever Treadwell was perplexed or baffled, a pipe seldom failed to help.

Just as he began to address the issue of the stolen murk-comber and Roundcoring's oddly indifferent reaction to the theft, however, his musings were intruded upon.

'Excuse I,' said a high-pitched voice. 'You'm Inspector Treadwell, right?'

Treadwell glanced down. 'Has us met?'

'Sort of, a couple of times.'

'Wait. Yes, I recognise you,' Treadwell said. 'I's seen you down at the station.'

'Afraid so,' said Toby Nimblenick, not sounding ashamed at all.

114

'You'm a bit of a regular. It'm usually petty larceny, be'n't it?'

'And vagrancy sometimes. I has to sleep rough now and then, and some copper'll come along on his beat and trip over I and then drag I off for a night in the cells.'

'Probably thinking it'll do you some good. Trying to help, even.'

'Oh, I doubt it. More like, him's got an arrest quota to fill and I be an easy collar to make. Plus, most constables know I'm always good for a backhander.'

The kid's cheery cynicism almost made Treadwell laugh. 'You seems to understand how the justice system works in this town, young man. Well, what can I do for you?'

'As it happens,' said Toby, 'I think it'm as much a case of what *I* can do for *you*, Inspector.'

CHAPTER 40

Crossing A Line

A knock at midnight could only mean bad news.

'Az is missing,' said Mr Mordadson.

Lady Aanfielsdaughter wrapped her dressing gown more tightly around her, then enfolded herself with her wings to create an added layer of insulation. Mr Mordadson had let cold night air into her apartment when he entered via the balcony windows, but the chill she felt was as much inner as outward.

'Someone took him from Pearl Town Mercy,' Mr Mordadson went on. 'A receptionist in the lobby thinks she saw him being stretchered out by the main door.'

'Thinks?'

'She can't swear it was him. She saw a pair of porters carrying out a patient who may have been a teenage boy. He was wrapped in blankets and she didn't get a clear look at his face.'

'When?'

'Last night, between one and two. I only found out about it this morning when I went to visit him and he wasn't there. Rest assured, stern words have been had with the hospital administrator. I also got him to put it about that the removal was *our* doing. We've transported Az somewhere else for safekeeping. It's a pretty flimsy cover story but it should hold for the time being.'

'Kidnapped. Az kidnapped,' Lady Aanfielsdaughter breathed. Then, sternly, she said, 'Why didn't you report this till now?'

'Because, milady, I've spent most of today turning Pearl Town upside down looking for him. I stopped at nightfall, then travelled straight here.'

'You should have informed me sooner. A message by carrier dove – how hard would that have been to organise?'

116

'And what would it have achieved?' he sighed.

'Mr Mordadson!' she snapped. 'Do not forget whom you are talking to.'

He arched his wings, startled by her harshness. 'I apologise, milady. As you can imagine, I'm very tired and very anxious. I didn't mean to sound so offhand. I felt it was best to look for Az while the trail was still relatively fresh, not waste a moment. Had I sent a message and then been able to find him, I'd have disturbed you needlessly.'

Lady Aanfielsdaughter conceded the sense in this. 'So if he isn't in Pearl Town, where is he? Who has him?'

'My best guess would be Feather First!'

'You're not serious.'

'Az's relationship with you is well known. My theory is, they didn't succeed in getting at you one way, so now they're trying to get at you another.'

'Through someone close to me.'

'He is, let's face it, your highest-profile friend. Not to mention, he helped foil their assassination bid. He was vulnerable lying there in hospital. That made him the ideal target.' Mr Mordadson clenched a fist. 'Dammit, though, I should have seen it coming. If nothing else I should have posted a Patroller outside his room, just in case.'

'This is not your fault,' Lady Aanfielsdaughter assured him. 'There's no predicting the actions of these fanatics. No telling how low they'll stoop.'

'Even so, I was careless. I knew they'd try something else. In hindsight, it was obvious they'd go for Az.'

'In hindsight, everything is obvious. What we must do is not berate ourselves but formulate an appropriate response to this . . . this . . . *outrage*. The First!ers have crossed a line, Mr Mordadson.' Lady Aanfielsdaughter's voice shook with emotion. 'Attacking me was bad enough, but dragging Az into all this too? I will not stand for it. Do you hear? I will not.'

'Milady, I may say that the whole point of kidnapping him is to provoke you into doing something rash. All the more reason, then, not to take the bait.'

'You may say that,' replied her ladyship with an imperious glare. 'What you may not say is that I should be cool and calm about what's happened. Because I cannot. I've tried calmness, rationality, fairness, and where has it got me? Nowhere. It's simply redoubled the determination of my enemies. Thinking me weak, they've struck at me harder.'

'And I shall strike back at them for you. You know that. It's what I do. I'll find these First!ers and recover Az safe and sound.'

'It's not enough, Mordadson. Not any more.'

The moonlight coming in through the windows caught Lady Aanfields-daughter's eyes and made them blaze. Their usual stratospheric blue became like icy fire.

'Not enough, milady?'

'You are subtle like a stiletto,' she said. 'You get the job done, mostly with stealth and guile. But something else is required here, something louder and larger and heavier. The First!ers must be taught a lesson, one that everyone else will see and learn from.'

'I would strongly caution against—'

'There can't be any finesse,' Lady Aanfieldsdaughter went on, overriding him. 'Sledgehammer-brutal, that's the way to go.'

'What are you suggesting?'

'A crackdown. Arrests. Zero tolerance. Anyone and everyone who has a connection with the Feather First! movement, anyone who is known to be a First!er or who has consorted with one or is related to one, anyone who has ever expressed an opinion remotely sympathetic to the cause – I want them taken into custody. All of them. I want them pulled off the streets and dragged from their homes. We know where they live, don't we?'

'Some of them,' said Mr Mordadson reluctantly. 'We have a little data.'

'We get those ones to give up the rest. Pressure them to name names, inform on their cohorts. We take the entire movement and smash it wide open.'

'What you're proposing is wholly unethical.'

'*You* would lecture me on ethics?' stormed Lady Aanfieldsdaughter.

'At the very least it's against the terms of the Pact of Hegemony.'

'I know full well what the Pact says. I also know that the First!ers' behaviour has gone beyond anything those who drafted it back then could have envisioned.'

'But, milady, taking extreme action against them is playing straight into their hands,' said Mr Mordadson. 'Bad enough they already have one martyr. You would have us create hundreds. Then there's the possible consequences for Az. If it is First!ers who are holding him captive – and I have to stress it's only a theory, I don't know it for sure – then imagine what they might do to him when this crackdown of yours starts.'

'Then it's all the more imperative that you find him, isn't it?' said Lady Aanfieldsdaughter.

'Milady . . .'

'Mordadson! I've given you a task to perform. Perform it.'

'I must counsel against this. Leave it a day or two, I beg you. Canvass opinion in the Sanctum. Take other people's advice if you won't take mine.'

'My mind is made up. I still have some authority. A command from Lady Aanfielsdaughter still counts as an edict from the entire Sanctum. This will be done.'

CHAPTER 41

The Cunning, The Audacity

Mr Mordadson flapped disconsolately past the Patrollers on guard duty outside Lady Aanfielsdaughter's apartment. He was too preoccupied to return their salutes, just as he had been too preoccupied, when arriving, to answer their challenge of 'Who goes there?' with anything more than a weary 'Let me through.'

He flew across the moon-burnished Sanctum, halting every so often to show his silver seal to yet another group of Patrollers on their rounds. Effectively, the Sanctum was under martial law. No one could go anywhere without bumping into Patrollers and having to account for their journey, saying where they were headed and why and supplying proof of identity. Of course it was all about safety and security. The most important people in the realm had to be protected. But at the price of their own liberty?

Not to mention their own sanity.

Mr Mordadson was unable to shake off the mental image of Lady Aanfielsdaughter standing there declaring, 'This will be done.' Looking at her, he'd scarcely recognised her. There had always been steel beneath that benevolent surface, willpower belied by the politeness and grace with which it was wielded. Lady Aanfielsdaughter had always got her way, but through diplomacy and persuasion.

That Lady Aanfielsdaughter, it seemed, was gone. In her stead was a Lady Aanfielsdaughter who had been pushed too far, too hard. She had had enough and wasn't prepared to take any more.

The First!ers might have crossed a line, but her ladyship just had too.

In a certain window a light was twinkling. Mr Mordadson veered down towards Lord Urironson's private quarters.

Something of an insomniac, his lordship was awake, going through correspondence at his desk. He invited Mr Mordadson in and offered him coffee, which the emissary was too sleep-deprived to refuse.

'You've been off on your travels again I see, milord,' Mr Mordadson observed, sipping the coffee.

The doorway to the bedroom was ajar and a small suitcase was lying on the bed, lid open. The untidiness of its contents suggested the suitcase was waiting to be unpacked, rather than had just been packed.

'These disappearances of mine really bother you, don't they?' Lord Urironson replied, with a supercilious little curl of the lip. 'Is it the fact that I won't tell you where I go or the fact that you, who make it your business to know everyone else's business, haven't managed to find out for yourself?'

'Both.'

'Your investigative powers and the range of your contacts are formidable. But even you can't know everything. Your seal can get you a long way, but my seal, coupled with my title, gets me further. I can buy silence and discretion that you haven't a hope of outbidding me for.'

'You said you would reveal all to me in time. I'm content to wait.'

'Are you?' said his lordship dryly.

'But I have something to reveal to you.'

Lord Urironson raised one pendulous eyebrow. 'Something from the Lady Aanfieldsdaughter camp? How is the old girl, by the way? Not liking being under armed guard, I'll bet. The fowl-farmer's daughter, cooped up like one of her dear dead dad's birds. I hope she appreciates the irony.'

'Lost on her, I fear.'

'All the same, she probably—'

He broke off. Echo the mynah, perched in his cage, had begun whistling and chattering.

'Not a trace, *arook!*' the bird said. 'Ground-sickness. Not a trace. *Thweet!*'

Lord Urironson hurried over to the cage.

'Silly creature,' he said. 'What are you going on about?'

'Volatile,' croaked Echo. 'Ordnance.'

His owner snatched up a heavy cloth cover, which he slipped over the cage, shrouding the mynah in darkness. Echo let out a subdued 'Goodnight' and was quiet.

'No idea what got into him,' said Lord Urironson. 'He should be asleep anyway. It's way past his bedtime. You were saying, Mordadson . . . ?'

Mr Mordadson recapped recent events, from Az's kidnapping to Lady Aanfieldsdaughter's decision to take drastic action against the First!ers.

Lord Urironson began chuckling, deep in his throat, a sound like water chasing itself down a drain.

'This is just too perfect!' he exclaimed. 'Mordadson, thank you for this news. So milady has chosen to lash out. It couldn't be better. This will split the race in two.'

'Which is a desirable outcome?'

'Oh yes. I doubt it'll surprise you, Mordadson, when I say I've been waiting for her to make a crucial, fatal misstep, one that will utterly ruin her. This is it. She's finally cracked. That peace-loving façade has crumbled. The dove has shed its plumage and shown itself to be a hawk. No one will forgive her for what she's about to do and the chaos it will unleash. Lady Aanfielsdaughter is finished!' Lord Urironson rubbed his hands in glee. 'And once she's out of the picture, there'll be nothing to prevent me rising up and taking her place. I will become the one every-body admires and adores, the one whose word is law. When the realm descends into chaos, one man will emerge as its master and saviour, and that is me.'

'So it would seem things are panning out as you'd hoped, milord.'

'Hoped? Hope had nothing to do with it. *Planned. Schemed. Intended.* Don't you see? I've been working towards Lady Aanfielsdaughter's down-fall for months. This isn't just some fortuitous falling-together of circum-stances. This is the end-result of meticulous, painstaking preparation and manipulation. I don't mind admitting that to you now, with success so close at hand. You of all people should appreciate the cunning, the audacity of what I've been up to.'

'Tell me,' said Mr Mordadson.

'Tell you? I'll go one better than that. I'll show you. Is that clunky little aeroplane of yours ready for flight?'

'My Wayfarer is on the landing apron being prepped and refuelled even as we speak. I was planning to go and look for Az as soon as I was done here.'

Lord Urironson beamed broadly. 'Then I shall save you a lot of trouble.'

'What do you mean?' said Mr Mordadson, but even as he asked the question he knew what was coming, and the awful obviousness of it hit him like a punch in the gut. Truly, his lordship *had* been cunning and audacious.

'I mean, I'm going to take you directly to him.'

CHAPTER 42

Breakdown At Croaker Gulch

Bertha pounded through the dark, leaving the glow and buzz of Crater-home far behind as she clanked her way towards Granite Plains.

She ran well for a while, but soon her cackle lost its sharpness and became faltering and lugubrious. Then her right front track started to lose traction; a running wheel was slipping. Then the engine temperature gauge on the dashboard began creeping upward till the needle was hovering near the red zone.

'Bless my bum,' Den said softly, shaking his head. 'Her's in poor shape. I doesn't know how much longer her can keep going.'

'It'm those Slamshaft mechanics,' said Cassie. 'Them never looked after she, and all that neglect be taking its toll.'

'How much further?'

Cassie consulted a map. 'Another hundred k or so.'

'Game old girl as her is, her won't make it.'

Sure enough, *Bertha* had to be halted ten kilometres further on. Even at full throttle she was managing no more than 15 kph, and her engine was overheating dangerously. Den pulled off the main road at a town called Croaker Gulch and coasted to a stop in a large market square where, by the first faint grey glimmerings of daybreak, local merchants were setting up their stalls and laying out their wares. *Bertha* gave one last brave, desperate cackle, then fell silent.

All four Grubdollars gathered round the front of the murk-comber. Steam was pouring from under her engine cowl and Den scorched his hand getting it open so that they could diagnose the problem.

A leak in the radiator hose. A worn carburettor valve. Oil sump all but dry.

And as if that wasn't enough, Fletcher slithered under *Bertha* to inspect the dodgy running wheel from behind and saw that the cleaner arm had been worn down to a nub. Without the cleaner arm keeping its sprockets free of mud and stones, the wheel had become clogged up and wasn't driving the track properly.

Fixing all of this was a full morning's work, assuming they could get hold of the parts. As luck would have it, Croaker Gulch boasted an automotive repair shop whose sign claimed there wasn't a single make or model of vehicle the owner couldn't cater for.

'Except murk-combers,' he confessed shamefacedly. 'Us doesn't get many of they around hereabouts. Any of they, to be honest. So no point carrying the parts in stock.'

'Us can make do with generics,' said Den. 'With a bit of bodging and soldering us can make they fit and get she back on the road, even if her won't be running in tip-top condition.'

'What about a cleaner arm?' Fletcher asked.

The repair shop owner shrugged. 'Can't help you there. Unless maybe you can do something with this rocker arm. It'm for a truck camshaft, but it'm about the same size and shape as what you's after, right?'

Fletcher studied the rocker arm and thought he possibly could alter it to fit.

Paying for the parts nearly cleaned the family out. Pooling all the cash they had, they found there was enough left over to buy breakfast and, at a pinch, lunch, but that was it.

As they trudged back to the market square, Fletcher remarked to Cassie, 'This saving-the-world lark don't come cheap, do it? Someone should really give we a salary, or at least an expense account.'

She half smiled. 'Hey, it be'n't a Grubdollar enterprise if it don't almost bankrupt we.'

While the family toiled to get *Bertha* going again, the market grew busy around them. Trading was brisk and the cries of the merchants crowded the air.

'Fresh juicy tomatoes, straight from the Massif, two dozen for a quarter-note!'

'Genuine Airborn artefacts, who'll buy my genuine Airborn artefacts?'

'Hackerjackal-claw necklaces, at these prices I be cutting my own throat!'

It so happened that a local off-duty constable was at the market that morning, grocery-shopping with his wife.

It also so happened that an all-points bulletin had gone out the night before, zipping along the telegraph wires to every police station within a 300-kilometre radius of Craterhome. Officers were told to be on the lookout for a stolen murk-comber emblazoned with Slamshaft livery.

The constable glanced over at the murk-comber that was parked in a corner of the square. One look, and he dropped the melon he was squeezing to test its ripeness, and, without a word to his wife, sprinted off to the station to raise the alarm.

The instructions from Craterhome were not to waylay the murkcomber or its occupants but simply to transmit a report of the sighting to Craterhome police, for the attention of Inspector Gavin Treadwell.

Half an hour later, Treadwell and seven junior policemen were streaking towards Croaker Gulch in two squad cars.

CHAPTER 43

Shades Of Grey

Sunshine filled the room and the iridescent patterns splashed the walls again. Az had been a prisoner for over twenty-four hours, and all things considered he thought he was holding up pretty well. The cords chafed his skin, cramps still plagued him, but he had survived the night. In fact, he had slept soundly and there'd been no more of those weird, feverish dreams. He was beginning to believe that he had got through the worst. If the First!ers were hoping to break his spirit, they had failed. He felt strong, capable of handling anything they did to him. Whatever nasty surprises they might have in store, he could cope.

The key turned in the lock, and Az assumed someone was bringing him breakfast. Good. That meant another ten minutes when he was not tethered, further time to explore escape possibilities. Besides which, he was famished.

But it wasn't one of the First!ers who opened the door and walked in.

Az could hardly believe his eyes.

Mr Mordadson!

In a flash, he knew his ordeal was over. He was saved. Mr Mordadson had come to rescue him.

He struggled into a kneeling position, his heart leaping for joy. He raised his wrists to Mr Mordadson, and although the gag prevented him speaking, the meaning of the gesture was obvious: *untie me.*

Mr Mordadson, oddly, did nothing. He didn't make a move to undo the knots. He just stood stock-still, looking down at Az. His red-shaded eyes were inscrutable.

Az proffered his wrists again. Maybe Mr Mordadson was assessing the cords and felt he needed a cutting implement of some kind. Well, the First!ers had knives, didn't they? Az jerked his head in the direction of the doorway. He pictured the First!ers sprawled in heaps all round the house, unconscious. They'd not even had a chance to pull out those blades of theirs. Mr Mordadson had swept through them like a living jetstream, knocking them flat. He'd shown them no mercy and given them no quarter as he made his way to where Az was being kept.

He wasn't, however, taking Az's hint. Az grunted around the gag, trying to say the word *knife*. No good. His friend continued simply to stare, although Az thought he saw a flicker of emotion. Briefly, almost imperceptibly, he thought he saw something like regret dart across Mr Mordadson's face.

That was when it dawned on him that this was no rescue. He had no idea why Mr Mordadson wasn't lifting a finger to help him, but he had a clear sense of things being awry – horribly, desperately so. He lowered his arms, feeling perplexed and foolish. What was going on? Was it all some sort of prank? Or a test perhaps. Yes. A test. Mr Mordadson had arranged for him to be kidnapped by people posing as Feather First!ers in order to assess Az's resilience and his ability to hold up under pressure.

Az hoped, more than believed, that this was the answer. But the hope, small and frail as it was, was dashed to bits the moment Farris, Lord Urironson strode into the room.

Az looked from Mr Mordadson to Lord Urironson and back again, and understood from the two men's body language that they were in cahoots. The way Mr Mordadson's wings drooped a fraction in his lordship's presence. The way Lord Urironson's wings were partly opened out. The contrast, though slight, spoke volumes.

It was inconceivable. Mr Mordadson had thrown in his lot with Lord Urironson? With Lady Aanfieldsdaughter's chief political foe? Her great rival, the constant thorn in her side?

'Ah, look at the lad,' Lord Urironson crooned. It was hard to tell exactly whom he was speaking to. More than anyone else, he seemed to be addressing the mynah bird that was sitting on his shoulder. 'He's all of a dither. Can't tell up from down. This must come as a shock to you, Azrael, seeing your friend and mentor in *my* company. Not to mention seeing a senior Silver Sanctum resident consorting with Feather First!ers.'

Lord Urironson gestured towards the doorway, where El El and the other two First!ers stood, peering in. They looked to Az like spectators who had arrived at some gala occasion, keen to be entertained.

'We haven't formally met, have we?' Lord Urironson went on. 'But I've long had a hankering to see the famous Az Gabrielson up close and in person. What is it that's so special about you? Why does Lady Aanfields-daughter twitter on about you all the time as though you're some Airborn paragon, the very best of our race? I look at you now and all I see is a wingless juvenile, rendered harmless and indeed helpless. I can't imagine . . . What's that? Hmm?'

Az had growled something through the gag. Lord Urironson reached out and yanked the cloth down from his face.

'I said, get these cords off me and you'll find out how plucking harmless and helpless I am.'

'Oh!' said his lordship, mock-aghast. 'Such language. Such aggression. Echo, did you hear that?'

'Plucking harmless and helpless,' said Echo. The voice the bird used sounded extraordinarily like Az's own.

'Well I never,' Lord Urironson went on. 'Doubtless this is the pent-up frustration of someone who cannot fly. Jealousy that has curdled to anger.'

'I'd rather not be able to fly than have wings and be a pompous old windbag, *milord*,' Az said. The last word sizzled with sarcasm.

One of the First!ers sniggered. Lord Urironson shot the man a withering glare, and he fell silent.

'And d'you know what else?' Az said. 'I don't believe for a moment that Mr Mordadson's joined forces with you. He wouldn't do that. You represent everything he stands against. He wouldn't genuinely betray Lady Aanfieldsdaughter. For *you*, of all people? No way.'

'Your faith in Mordadson's integrity is touching. Isn't it, Mordadson? But what you have to realise, Azrael – what your adolescent brain cannot easily comprehend – is that the adult world is a complicated place. It may not seem so from the outside but it is. Nothing there is cut and dried. How old are you? Sixteen?'

'Seventeen.'

'A seventeen-year-old has a straightforward view of life, everything simple, black and white, no nuances, no shades of grey. Whereas we grown-ups know that such distinctions are illusory and meaningless. There are always grey areas. So, while to you Mordadson's loyalty to Lady Aanfieldsdaughter has always appeared unquestionable and unshakeable, in truth it is anything but. Expediency is the order of the day here. A long word, I realise. It means—'

'I know what it means,' Az intoned coldly.

'Good. I'm glad that our education system continues to develop the minds of our modern youth, as it should. Expediency, flexibility, knowing when to adhere to your principles and when not – this is the mark of a wise, mature person and the talent by which such a person survives and prospers. Mordadson kept allegiance to Lady Aanfieldsdaughter for as long as it was to his advantage to do so. Now, sensible fellow, he has transferred that allegiance to me.'

'Still not convinced,' Az said. He turned to Mr Mordadson. 'Come on, say it. Say it to my face. Suddenly you're on Lord Urironson's side? It's true?'

Mr Mordadson nodded, stiffly.

'This isn't some scam you're pulling?'

Mr Mordadson, again stiffly, shook his head.

'Guano,' said Az, but his voice trembled, bereft of all certainty. Inside, he felt a sense of crumbling and plummeting, as though all the props and supports that held up his world had been snatched away.

'It seems you require proof,' said Lord Urironson. 'You won't take him at his word. And that's fair enough. I myself am not yet a hundred per cent positive that Mordadson is loyal to me and me alone. Let me see, how could I get him to show once and for all that he no longer holds any regard for Lady Aanfielsdaughter and her methods and allies?' He pretended to ponder, then snapped his fingers. 'I've got it. Mordadson?'

'Milord?'

'Hurt the boy.'

'What?'

Lord Urironson pointed to Az. 'You heard me. Hurt him. Consider it your final test. A graduation exam. Do this, and I shall never doubt you again.'

'Hurt . . .'

'Harm him. Beat him up. Bash him around. How many ways do I have to put it? Roll up your sleeves and get stuck in. Go on, man!'

CHAPTER 44

Adrenaline And Anger

For several long seconds Az knelt there and waited for Mr Mordadson to say no. He expected nothing less from Mr Mordadson than outright refusal to go along with Lord Urironson's wishes, and at the back of his mind he was rather hoping that Lord Urironson was the one who would end up getting bashed around. He knew Mr Mordadson. He *had* changed sides, maybe, possibly, but there were certain aspects of his character that were fixed and unalterable. He would never attack a defenceless, innocent victim. It just wasn't his way.

The Silver Sanctum emissary peered at Az, then raised his shoulders and let them fall.

'As you wish,' he said.

Az's jaw dropped.

'But,' Mr Mordadson added, 'I won't do it while he's tied up like that. It wouldn't be right. If I'm going to use my fists on someone, let it be in a fair fight.'

Lord Urironson considered this, then nodded. 'Very well. Give the boy a sporting chance, why not? It's not as if he's going to be much of an opponent, especially with that bad arm.'

'I wouldn't write Az off completely, milord. Remember, I've been training him. I've taught him a trick or two.'

'In that case this ought to be all the more fascinating.'

In no time, Az was untied and on his feet. Lord Urironson and the First!ers retreated to the doorway, where his lordship positioned himself to get the best view, leaving the other three jostling to look over his wing arches. Echo swayed from foot to foot, either anxious or excited. Mr Mordadson was busy warming up in one corner of the room, circling his shoulders and stretching his neck. Az just stood, passive, arms hanging limp.

'I'm not doing this,' he said to Mr Mordadson. 'I'm not taking part in any fight, especially not just to amuse that lot. It's obscene.'

'You have no alternative, Az.'

'Yes, I do. I can stand here and do nothing. You won't attack me if I refuse to hit back.'

'Won't I?' said Mr Mordadson, and with a flap of his wings he sprang.

The room was not large, so he could not build up a great deal of speed and momentum. Nevertheless he hit Az in the midsection with stunning force. Az was propelled backwards, arms and legs flailing, and crashed into the wall. He regained his balance, staggering sideways just as Mr Mordadson followed up his initial assault with a punch. Had the punch connected, it would have broken Az's nose. In the event, Az dodged and it missed him by millimetres. He lunged for a vacant corner of the room and came up in a defensive crouch.

'Not doing this,' he said through gritted teeth. 'Not fighting.'

'Really?' said his one-time mentor. 'Those clenched fists of yours say otherwise.'

Az deliberately relaxed his hands.

'Come on!' shouted one of the First!ers. 'Get the brat! He was a right vicious little bustard at the hospital. Give him one for us!'

Mr Mordadson stalked across the carpet, moving on the balls of his feet, wings outstretched for extra balance. 'Fight,' he told Az. 'You have to.'

'No!' Az yelled. He was shocked to feel tears springing to his eyes. How was it possible to be both furious and miserable at the same time?

Mr Mordadson leapt, both legs extended in a double drop-kick. Again Az dodged, evading the blow by the skin of his teeth. The impact of Mr Mordadson's soles left a dent in the wall. Plaster dust trickled out from cracks in the powder-blue wallpaper.

Az spun, just in time to see Mr Mordadson pirouette in midair and a foot come straight for him. On this occasion he was a fraction too slow. He ducked but the foot still struck him on the side of the head. Next thing he knew, he was flat on the floor. The First!ers were cheering. Echo was emitting a stream of high-pitched whistles. Az could see Lord Urironson's smug face gazing down at him. The world spiralled. The pain was ferocious.

Something snapped.

It was Lord Urironson's expression that did it. How dare he look so pleased with himself, so gloating! How dare he take such joy in other people's misery! He wanted to watch a fight, did he? Well then, Az would give him one worth watching. And while he was at it he would give his lordship's new pal Mr Mordadson a couple of things to think about.

Wings whoomped behind Az, and he barrel-rolled to the side. Mr

Mordadson came thumping down feet-first on the spot where he had been lying a split second earlier. Instantly Az lashed out with a leg, catching his opponent a savage instep shot to the ankle. Mr Mordadson yelped and hopped.

'Hurts, doesn't it?' Az snarled, rising up. 'I learned that from you. Aim for places where there are a lot of nerve endings and the bone's close to the surface.'

'So you *were* paying attention,' Mr Mordadson replied, grimacing. 'And here was I thinking what a useless pupil you'd been and what a waste of time it was trying to drum anything into your thick head.'

He closed in on Az. Az feinted a right hook before delivering a left roundhouse. Mr Mordadson parried with a forearm, then struck at Az's ribs with his left wing. Az instinctively put out his right arm to block. In the heat of the moment he forgot all about his wound. His forearm took the brunt of the wing blow, and there was agony beyond all reckoning.

How he managed to remain upright and conscious, Az had no idea. The pain turned his legs to jelly and he was near fainting. He probably had adrenaline to thank. Adrenaline and anger. Between them these two things kept him on his feet, even as he reeled away from Mr Mordadson, howling his distress. He swore a stream of the foulest language he knew, and then red rage took over and he reeled round and charged at the emissary. His right arm was all but crippled, for now no use, but with his left rained punches at his foe, battered him with hooks and uppercuts, kept the shots coming, did not let up for so much as a second, interspersed the punching with occasional kicks and knee-jabs, expelling a breath with each blow just as he had been taught, and Mr Mordadson defended himself but did not retaliate. Could not. It was all he could do simply to ward off the flurrying assault and wait till Az wore himself out.

Which, eventually, Az did. He fired off a final roundhouse, drawing on all the strength he had left in him. This punch managed to do what all the others hadn't and get past Mr Mordadson's barricade of elbows and wings. It made solid contact with his jaw. His head snapped to one side and his spectacles flew off. They hit the skirting board with a tinkle of breaking glass.

Mr Mordadson looked back round at Az. Az was heaving for breath, sweat trickling off his eyebrows into his eyes. Mr Mordadson blinked myopically at him. Az blinked too, clearing the stinging sweat from his vision.

It was funny how vulnerable Mr Mordadson suddenly looked. Without the spectacles, his face seemed weaker, lessened, incomplete.

And his eyes were grey. Az had never seen them uncovered before. Pale, mushroomy grey, like the underside of the cloud cover on a good day.

'Nice one,' Mr Mordadson said. 'I can manage without my specs, of course. But you've put me at a slight disadvantage all the same. Well done.'

'Sheer luck,' Az replied between gasps.

'Never underestimate the power of luck,' Mr Mordadson said, with the faintest, flintiest glimmer of a smile.

The two of them squared off once more. Az knew that he had given his all and had nothing left. Mr Mordadson's next offensive would be the final one of the fight. After that, it was all over. Az, nonetheless, was determined to go down punching. While breath remained in his body, he would resist. However clumsily, however futilely, he would resist.

A series of loud handclaps sounded from the doorway. Both combatants glanced in that direction.

'Enough,' said Lord Urironson. 'That's enough. I've seen as much as I need to. You've convinced me, Mordadson. You can stop now.'

'Aww,' said a First!er. 'Can't he carry on a bit longer? It was just getting good. Let him finish the kid off.'

'No. This isn't about sating your bloodlust. This is about allaying my doubts, which Mordadson has done to my satisfaction. The fight is at an end. Tie the boy up again.'

The First!ers moved into the room. Az, exhausted, barely able to stand, let them go to work on him once more.

'No, no, not the gag,' Lord Urironson said, wafting a hand. 'You can dispense with that. It's undignified.'

'Undignified,' Echo agreed.

'What if he tries to shout for help?' said El El.

'Who's going to hear? Besides, look at him. The boy's downtrodden. Utterly defeated. Let's leave him with a modicum of self-respect. Call it a reward for the spirited performance he just put on.'

The gag stayed off, even as the cords went back on, tightly as ever.

Meanwhile Mr Mordadson retrieved his spectacles and held them up to inspect the damage. The left lens had shattered. There was a star-shaped hole it and a few tiny shards of crimson glass littered the carpet.

'Luck,' he said, with a sour cluck of the tongue. He picked up all the fragments and slipped them into a pocket.

He bent over Az, slumped on the floor on his side. 'No hard feelings, eh?' he said, patting him on the shoulder. 'Believe me, sore as you think you are about this, you could be sorer.'

Az didn't even favour him with a glance.

The remark, though, lodged in his brain.

Sore as you think you are about this, you could be sorer.

It was a strange turn of phrase.

But then what did he care? Mr Mordadson was a liar and a traitor, a pheasant-plucking scumbag. Nothing the man said had any value any more.

Az curled into a foetal ball and closed his eyes and let misery and despair wash through him. He didn't even hear the door shut or the key turn. He had never felt quite so alone. No, he had never *been* quite so alone. His only real friend above the cloud cover was his friend no longer. The one person he could have counted on to get him out of this fix had, all the time, been part of the plot to kidnap him.

How long? How long had Mr Mordadson been in cahoots with Lord Urironson, conspiring against Lady Aanfielsdaughter?

It didn't matter. All that mattered was that he had played Az for a fool, that Lady Aanfielsdaughter was now exposed and in danger as never before, and that Az was powerless to help. He might as well be dead for all the good he could do anyone.

The ache of sorrow in Az's chest was greater than all his many bodily pains combined.

CHAPTER 45

The Whole Story

'Time, then, to bring you in on the whole scheme,' said Lord Urironson, as he and Mr Mordadson departed from Prismburg in the Wayfarer, with Echo confined to his cage on the back seat. 'Now that we're both clearly dancing to the same tune, I feel it's safe to explain what I've been up to. In a way, it's nice to be talking about this with someone who's on an intellectual par with me. Those First!ers are all very well, they're useful tools, but not exactly what one might call bright.'

'Fanatics seldom are,' Mr Mordadson replied, squinting his left eye in order to see through the broken lens. It took a lot of concentration to pilot the plane with half his field of vision a blur.

'Noaphiel Thothson least of all,' Lord Urironson said. 'A very troubled young man, he was. Product of a broken home. Learning difficulties. Got picked on at school because of that. As an adult, found it hard to hold down a decent job. Fell in with Feather First! last year at the age of twenty-three. Found that their ideology suited him. Those who have been bullied often turn into bullies themselves. They look for someone else to victimise and feel superior to. Thothson decided hating Groundlings would do for him. He took part in a number of raids on Groundling tourists, pelting them with soil. He even advocated using rocks instead of soil, but his First!er colleagues wouldn't go along with it.'

'A nasty piece of work.'

'Oh, he was. Mentally unstable, too. Prone to fits of blinding rage followed by long, sullen silences. As soon as I was introduced to him, I knew I had found the ideal candidate.'

'For assassinating Lady Aanfieldsdaughter.'

'No, no. For *trying* to. I knew he'd never pull it off. Not with you around, her ladyship's human harrier hawk.'

'A compliment?'

'Intended as one. By the way, have you spotted that airbus over there that we're getting rather close to?'

'*Aroops*,' said Echo.

The big, bumbling public-transport plane was looming on the Way-farer's port side. Mr Mordadson calmly made a small correction to their course, as if he had known the airbus was there all along.

'So Thothson and I,' Lord Urironson resumed, 'got together and had a few long talks. I'd already made some solid connections with Feather First! by this time and had reached an understanding with certain members of the more extreme wing of the movement. I, without their ever publicly acknowledging it, would be their figurehead and their inside man at the Sanctum. I would in effect lead them. The remarkable thing is' – here, he chuckled – 'I don't have anything against Ground-lings. I don't particularly like them but neither do I despise them. And yet I was able to persuade the First!ers that I do, with very little difficulty. They wanted to believe they had found a high-placed sympathiser in me, that a senior Sanctum resident was on their side, that they had a rep-resentative with influence. They wanted to believe it so much, they didn't probe deeply. They accepted everything I told them at face value.'

'As you said, not bright.'

'Indeed. So now I recruited Thothson for a special task. I cultivated him carefully, like a rare orchid. I convinced him that Lady Aanfieldsdaughter was not just opposed to Feather First! but was his personal enemy, and that getting rid of her would be a victory not just for the movement but for himself. Then I got him to practise his kite-flying, and practise and practise. The dear simpleton, he spent every spare hour he could at it. He fixated on it as only an educationally subnormal person would. There's probably a clinical term for that kind of obsessive temperament, al-though what it is I have no idea. But he kept at it till flying that kite was second nature. I also coached him in what he had to do if he was caught. I assured him it would be *if*, although I was well aware it would be *when*. He must say nothing, no matter how hard he was pushed to speak. He must do anything and everything he could to prevent himself divulging any information. Whatever it took, he was not to reveal who set him up to kill her ladyship.'

'And in the event, what it took was his life,' said Mr Mordadson. 'That was quite a gamble, milord. What if he hadn't followed your orders? What if he had cracked under interrogation and named you as the instigator of the plot?'

'I'd have denied it. Denied it utterly. And who would have been more plausible? Me or him? Farris, Lord Urironson, or a dull-witted member of the lunatic fringe of an unpopular radical movement? I know who *I'd* have believed more, and the Airborn public likewise.'

'Still a risk.'

'A calculated one, backed up by my reading of Thothson's psychology. Everything about him said that he would be the perfect stooge. And so it proved. Besides, what is life without risk? Nothing that is truly worth gaining comes without a host of potential pitfalls.'

'It would have been good if you'd told me all this sooner. For one thing, I wouldn't have dealt with Thothson in quite the way I did. And for another, I'd have been more careful with the First!ers at the protest in Pearl Town. That El El, for instance.'

'Yes, I noticed him giving you funny looks back at the house. I daresay if I hadn't been there, it wouldn't have stopped at funny looks either. I shan't ask what went on between you two at the protest.'

'It was nothing much. A few harsh words. He got off pretty lightly, all things considered. Him and all the protestors. But we could have done more if we'd known at the time that we were working for the same boss. We could have staged something really theatrical and impressive.'

'Perhaps. But you're forgetting – I didn't fully trust you then. That's partly why I had the Gabrielson boy kidnapped, to force the demonstration of loyalty you just gave me.'

'Partly, but mainly for the disruption it's going to cause.'

'When Lady Aanfielsdaughter bludgeons the First!ers. As she is obligingly going to do.'

'And then, with the Airborn at each other's throats, you step in to heal the breach,' said Mr Mordadson.

'Indeed.'

'Divide and conquer.'

'If you like. And with you securely on my team, Mordadson, I don't see how I can fail.'

Mr Mordadson adjusted his grip on the joystick and checked the compass and altimeter. 'And this is everything?' he said, as the plane banked slightly. 'Everything I need to know? The whole story?'

'The whole story,' Lord Urironson confirmed.

'This accounts for your disappearances?'

'Oh yes.'

'You've held nothing back from me?'

'Not a thing.'

For a moment, the merest moment, it looked as though Mr Mordadson didn't believe him. But then that could have been because of the way he was squinting. The broken spectacles lent his face a very skewed and sceptical cast.

Finally all he said was, 'Thank you for your honesty.'

To which Lord Urironson, with all the sincerity he could muster, replied, 'You're welcome.'

The rest of the flight to the Silver Sanctum was conducted in amenable silence, both men apparently reassured that there were no more secrets between them. Echo seemed forever on the point of saying something, but in the end he, too, stayed silent.

CHAPTER 46

Two Incorrigible Reprobates

On the way to Croaker Gulch, one of the constables in the car with Inspector Treadwell asked why he was so eager to nab the murk-comber thieves. If Slamshaft Engineering wasn't bothered about getting it back, why was he?

'Stealing be stealing,' Treadwell answered, 'and the law'm the law.'

There was more to it than that, though. Treadwell's talk with Cuthbert Roundcoring had left him with the distinct impression that Slamshaft was up to something. His encounter with Toby Nimblenick had added flesh to the bones of that suspicion.

He cast his mind back to his conversation with the little ragamuffin last night. According to Toby, the people who had taken the murk-comber were the vehicle's rightful owners, a family by the name of Grubdollar.

'Them's decent folk, basically,' Toby said. 'None of them be an incorrigible reprobate, not like I.'

'"Incorrigible . . ." Where'd a boy like you pick up language like that?'

'You hang around police stations often enough, Inspector, you gets to hear all sorts of interesting turns of phrase. Those Grubdollars, way I see it them has been hard done by. Their murk-comber should never have been taken from they. What them did, nicking it back, were only right and proper. That be why I helped they. I has a sense of honour, you know.'

'Honour among thieves,' Treadwell remarked. 'Even among short-trousered snatch-purses.'

'Straight up. Having said which, even though I were helping they I had a feeling it'd come in handy, being part of a major felony. So's I could come to the likes of you and turn evidence. You promise my record'll be wiped clean? You wasn't just saying it to get me to agree to tell you what I know?'

'I'll do what I can. You has my word on that as a policeman.'

139

'That be'n't worth much.'

'Best I can offer.'

'Well, it'm better than a poke in the eye, I suppose.'

'Although,' said Treadwell, 'it beats I why you wants your record expunged when you'm only going to go and get caught pickpocketing again in the future.'

'A criminal record be like mud on a tyre, Inspector. The more you gathers, the more it weighs you down. A good scrape-off every so often works wonders, especially if things get bad and you'm up in front of a judge. Frees you up, in a manner of speaking.'

'So what drove this Grubdollar family to such desperate measures?' Treadwell asked. 'What made they take the law into their own hands?'

'Far as I can gather, frustration. And revenge.'

'Revenge?'

'The eldest son, Fletcher, him had a clever idea for some kind of device, and Slamshaft nicked it off he. Or so him said.'

'What sort of device?'

'I be'n't sure. It were all a bit technical, to be honest, and him didn't explain it at length anyway. Something to do with helping the Airborn adjust to the air pressure down here, or we to the pressure up there, or both.' Toby shrugged. 'I be'n't too brilliant at paying attention when I's being lectured at.'

'Maybe if you went to school . . .'

The boy laughed. 'School couldn't teach I anything useful. I's had all the learning I could ever need, out here on the streets.'

Treadwell had rolled his eyes at Toby, and he did so again in the car now, remembering the comment. It would have been a laughable thing to say, had it not been true. For someone who'd led the life Toby Nimblenick had, formal education would be pretty much a waste of time. He knew more about the ways of the world than most children his age could or should know. Going to school would be a backward step.

Treadwell had to admit he saw a lot of himself in Toby, which was why he felt a grudging fondness for the kid. When he had been that age, he too had been a street-roaming tearaway, forever getting into scrapes with the law. While perhaps not as 'incorrigible' a 'reprobate' as Toby was, he had been involved in his share of misbehaviour. At the more harmless end of the scale, he'd sneaked into playhouses via the fire exits to watch variety shows, having a particular penchant for the burlesque revues which were strictly for adults only. But he had been a vandal, too, smashing windows in derelict houses, and he had stolen and torched a few cars in his time.

What had set him on the straight and narrow was being arrested, a week shy of his eleventh birthday, by a policeman called Archerfine.

Sergeant Archerfine had instilled in Treadwell a fear of and respect for the law that he never forgot. He had achieved this by dragging little Gavin round to the home of a man who had been mugged a few months earlier by a gang of teenagers. The man had been badly beaten by the youths, so badly that he would never fully recover. He had been blinded in one eye, his right arm was paralysed, and his speech was slow and slurred. To add to that, a hideous scar circled round his face from the side of his head. He had been left a shattered wreck, and all for the contents of his wallet, which amounted to no more than five notes.

'See?' said Archerfine. 'You carries on the way you'm going, lad, and you'll be responsible for doing something like this soon enough. You mark my words. It'm the way your sort always ends up, running with gangs, hurting others. That what you wants? You really wants to become the kind of kid who could cause somebody so much harm?'

No, the young Treadwell did not want that. In an instant, he knew he wanted the opposite. He would prevent others coming to harm as this poor man had. He would do his utmost to keep tragedies like this from occurring. He resolved on the spot to follow in Archerfine's footsteps and become an officer of the law.

He hadn't known then how unusual it was to come across a copper like Archerfine – one who actually cared about policing and saw the job as more than just a means of lining his own pockets. He hadn't known how lonely it would feel, either, to be that kind of copper himself. His fellow policemen did not admire him because he had integrity. On the contrary, they sneered at him. At best, they acknowledged that it was good to have a few like him on the force, but only because it salved their consciences. It meant *someone* was doing the work the way it was supposed to be done, even if they weren't.

The constable driving the car broke in on Treadwell's reverie. 'Croaker Gulch,' he announced, as the town-limits sign shot past on the left-hand side.

'Now remember, lads,' said Treadwell. 'Easy does it. Let's not make this a whole big song and dance. Us wants these Grubdollars in custody but us also wants they on our side. Them could be very helpful to we.'

141

CHAPTER 47

When Arrests Go Wrong . . .

Treadwell wanted a quick, quiet operation, a clean arrest, no fuss.

In the event, through no fault of his own, what he got was a disaster, with plenty of property damage thrown in.

Before leaving Craterhome, he had instructed that no sirens were to be used. There was no point in alerting the Grubdollars that police were coming, or for that matter alarming them. It might give them a chance to bolt.

The cops in the second car, however, forgot the inspector's warning by the time they reached Croaker Gulch. The excitement of the impending arrest got to them. There was nothing to beat the thrill of turning up at a location with the siren blaring and the bubble lights on the roof whirling. It made heads turn. Everybody looked.

So, while Treadwell's car entered the market square discreetly, the car behind arrived in a sudden tempest of light and noise.

Den had, at that precise moment, just finished inserting the new carburettor valve into its 'seat'. The wail of a police siren made him jump halfway out of his skin. Slamming down the engine cowl, he shouted to his offspring, 'Get inside *Bertha*. Now!'

Fletcher shimmied out from beneath the murk-comber, a soldering iron in his hand, while Robert, who was suspended from the roof erasing the Slamshaft logo with a cloth soaked in paint-thinner, scuttled back up the rope that secured him to the javelin turret.

Cassie was in the driver's pod, running a system check on *Bertha*'s hydraulics. Hearing her father's cry, she hit the switch that opened the iris-like access point in the underside of the pod. Den appeared beneath the short ladder below.

'Fire she up!' he yelled, leaping for the ladder's bottom rung.

Cassie stabbed the ignition button.

Nothing.

'All right, old girl,' she whispered to *Bertha*. 'I know you's been suffering. I know you hasn't been looked after as nicely as you should. Please, though, please, for our sake, start.'

She pressed the button again, holding it down for just the right length of time, meanwhile giving the engine some extra choke.

Hah-koof.

A blurt of engine noise.

Silence again.

'This time,' Cassie begged *Bertha*.

Ignition.

Rumble.

Heh-heh-heghh-heghh-heghh.

'I's in!' Fletcher announced through the speaker tube.

'Where'm Robert?' Cassie asked him.

'On top.'

'Tell he to hang on tight.'

She heard Fletcher relay the instruction, calling up to Robert from the hatchway.

At the same moment, Den hoisted himself into the pod. 'Everybody aboard?'

'Them is now.'

'Then step on it.'

Cassie jammed down the sticks and *Bertha* lurched forward skiddingly, her tracks struggling to gain traction on the paving stones. The market stalls with their multicoloured awnings veered from side to side in the windscreen. Cassie fought with the sticks and finally got the murkcomber's careering fifty-tonne bulk under control. She turned *Bertha* round, aiming her nose towards the entrance they had come in by.

Their exit route was blocked by the two police cars.

'Go over they?' Cassie enquired.

'*Bertha* could manage it all right,' said her father. 'Trouble be, could those coppers get out in time?'

Cassie glanced in the rearview projection mirrors. 'There'm another way out of the square at the other end. But it'll mean driving right through the middle of the market.'

'Us mustn't be arrested. Us has to get you to Pearl Town.'

'Then through the market it be.'

She hauled back on the left stick and rammed forward the right, and *Bertha* swivelled on her axis, 180° anticlockwise. Her swinging rear end sent a table laden with greengroceries flying.

Robert, on the roof, clung to the javelin turret for dear life, while

143

centrifugal force would have hurled Fletcher out through the hatch if he hadn't grabbed the rim with both hands.

Cassie pushed the left stick forward to join the right and gave several loud honks on the horn as *Bertha* gained speed, lumbering towards the main part of the market. To the rear, the policemen ran back to their cars and dived in. Doors slammed as the cars set off in pursuit of the murk-comber.

'Out of the way! Get out of the way!' Cassie yelled, even though she knew nobody outside could hear her. Shoppers and traders looked at the massive machine bearing slowly down on them. They seemed rooted to the spot with fear. She honked the horn some more, and they started to move.

Bertha plunged into a stall that sold second-hand books. She flattened it, grinding pages and dustjackets to shreds beneath her tracks.

'Sorry,' Fletcher said to the stall's owner, leaning out from the hatch. The trader responded with a volley of abuse and lobbed a large hardback in his direction. The book bonged off *Bertha*'s bodywork.

Next she collided with several stacks of wicker cages containing chickens and ducks. The cages smashed open, and suddenly the air was filled with clucking, quacking birds. Feathers flew everywhere. One panic-stricken chicken flapped into the loading bay. Fletcher grabbed it, and for a moment debated whether to keep it. It was a nice plump bird, lunch for everyone. But he was no thief, and the last thing he needed right now was a terrified chicken squawking around the loading bay, leaving feathers and worse all over the place. He hurled it out again.

Then *Bertha* ploughed through a stall of ladies' undergarments. Bras, panties, girdles and stockings were strewn across her engine cowl and driver's pod. Cassie had to put the wipers on the clear the windscreen of lingerie. Something small and frilly landed in Robert's face, and he pulled it off, inspected it, smirked, then flung it over his shoulder. It hit the second of the two police cars behind, hooking itself on one of the bubble lights. None of the policemen realised, and for the next few hours the car would be driving around with a pair of red lacy knickers on top.

People scattered in all directions as *Bertha* continued her steady, inexorable progress through the market. Stall after stall crashed to the ground and was reduced to rags and splinters.

At the very centre of the square lay a large municipal fountain. Cassie didn't spot it until too late. *Bertha* knocked a chunk out of its basin and a wave of water sluiced out across the paving stones.

On she went, trailing destruction and carnage in her wake. It was a miracle nobody got hurt, and there would have been casualties, had she been travelling any faster than a sedate 20 kph.

The police cars navigated around the debris left behind her. Both of them had their sirens on by this point. They slewed through the spilled fountain water and crunched and bumped over the wreckage of stalls and produce.

At last the far end of the square came in sight. Cassie winced as *Bertha* crushed yet another stall, this one peddling handcrafted jewellery. On the way back from the automotive repair shop earlier she had paused to admire the trader's wares. She felt awful about squashing all those beautiful rings and silver pendants.

'How's us ever going to make up for all this?' she asked her father.

He did not have an answer to that.

Then the way ahead was clear, no more stalls.

'That be'n't as wide a street as the one us came in on,' Den observed. 'Better take it a bit easy, lass.'

Cassie decelerated. The street was, in fact, not much broader than *Bertha* herself. There was perhaps half a metre of clearance on either side.

'Parked cars,' Cassie said in dismay, peering ahead.

'No choice. Drive over they.'

'Hang on . . .'

Bertha rode up the bonnet of the first car, tipping at an angle that the roll meter on the dashboard registered as 35 degrees. The car popped beneath her like a bug. Glass sprayed, metal squealed, tyres burst, doors crumpled. *Bertha* came down the other side, jolting as she levelled out. The car was left a mangled, twisted mess, oozing oil onto the road.

Robert only narrowly avoided being shaken off the roof that time. The next time he wasn't so fortunate. The second parked vehicle in line was a hardtop van, taller and sturdier than the average car. *Bertha* thundered up over the rear of it, bouncing high as she mounted its roof. On this occasion the roll meter went to 45 degrees, its maximum reading. Robert felt himself slipping sideways, his hold on the turret weakening. He scrabbled for purchase, but it was no good. As *Bertha's* left-hand set of tracks furrowed through the van, Robert bounced, lost his grip, and slithered off backwards.

CHAPTER 48

Robert's Tumble

The rope around Robert's waist saved him from being dashed against the road.

But instead he ended up dangling off the back of *Bertha*, being thrown around helplessly like a marionette in the hands of a cruel puppeteer. Upside down, back to front, he thumped and bumped repeatedly into *Bertha*'s bodywork as the murk-comber mowed over another innocent parked car. He screamed at Cassie to stop, even though it was useless. She'd never hear.

When *Bertha* was on the flat once more, Robert knew he had to take decisive action. If he didn't release himself before the next car, he would be battered to death against her rear end.

He fumbled at the rope knot with urgent fingers and managed to loosen it in time. He fell to the road, banging his head hard, just as *Bertha* added a fourth vehicle to the tally. Above the rending and tearing of automobile demolition, Robert heard a screech of brakes. He could taste blood on his tongue. He felt faint. He wanted to get up but couldn't. Pain pulsed redly through his skull.

Fletcher had heard Robert yelling and leaned out from the hatchway in time to see him land on the road, then see the frontmost police car halt just a metre away from Robert's supine body.

He grabbed the speaker tube. 'Cass! Da! Robert'm down. I can't be leaving he there. I's going to help he. Us'll be fine. You has to carry on.'

He didn't wait for a response but leaped out. He hit the road, rolled, and came up running. Within seconds he was kneeling at Robert's side. His brother looked OK. He was stunned, blood was trickling from his mouth, but his eyes were open and he was able to focus on Fletcher's face.

'I screwed up, bro,' he said. 'Sorry.'

'Not to worry,' said Fletcher.

He looked up. Policemen had emerged from the first car. The second car had gone past and was continuing to pursue *Bertha*.

A tall, thin man in plainclothes approached. Fletcher knew straight away he was the senior officer here. He also knew, without being quite sure why, that the man was someone he could trust. There was something both stern and kindly about his face, and what was that smell coming off him? A cosy, reassuring aroma. Pipe tobacco.

'My name be Detective Inspector Treadwell,' said the man. 'I could be wrong but I reckon you's Fletcher Grubdollar and this youngster here'm your brother Robert.'

'Be us under arrest?' Fletcher asked.

Treadwell, with a wry grimace, produced two sets of handcuffs and clinked them together in the air. 'Take a wild guess.'

CHAPTER 49

Cloudbusters And Drones

One hundred and fifty kilometres to the south, in a marquee tent on the edge of the Relentless Desert, two men were sword-fighting.

Dressed in padded white clothing, with mesh masks on their heads, they slashed and parried, feinted and lunged. The rapiers in their hands darted with the delicacy of knitting needles, though when they clashed the clang of steel on steel was almost deafening. Their feet kicked up puffs of desert dust.

Dominic Slamshaft, when it came to swordplay, favoured caginess. He would use his rapier to bar vertically and horizontally, creating a protective grid which an opponent found hard to get through. Then, when the other person had grown tired from trying to penetrate his defences, he would seize the opportunity to lash out with a decisive, point-scoring blow.

Brigadier Longnoble-Drumblood, on the other hand, was from what might be called the 'onslaught' school of swordsmanship. He just kept going, attack after attack, thrust upon thrust, battering foes into submission. He was of the belief that, in any theatre of combat, sheer naked aggression would win the day.

The two of them had been friends and sparring partners for so long that each was intimately familiar with the other's technique and tactics. They were evenly matched, and the fight was as much a dance as anything, a matter of rhythm and footwork.

Not that that stopped each from wanting to beat the other soundly.

Now, Slamshaft was attempting to lure Longnoble-Drumblood into making a mistake. He had been deliberately softening his parries on his left, his non weapon side, in the hope that Longnoble-Drumblood would think him weak there. He was waiting for his friend to become

148

overconfident and make a careless thrust, thus leaving himself open for a counterattack.

Longnoble-Drumblood sensed the weakness on Slamshaft's left. He also sensed a trap, and concentrated his efforts on Slamshaft's weapon side in order to show that he would not be tempted.

Trouble was, he couldn't help himself. His attention kept returning to Slamshaft's other side. Through the mesh of his mask he saw how Slamshaft's wrist loosened whenever a strike came from that direction and how Slamshaft's rapier wobbled under each assault.

Maybe, Longnoble-Drumblood thought, *he's not faking it.* An injury, perhaps, that Slamshaft hadn't told him about. A pulled muscle in his shoulder which hurt whenever he put his arm across his body and which now, after a solid half-hour of fighting, was starting to cause him real discomfort.

Like a cat with a wounded bird, Longnoble-Drumblood kept toying and worrying away at Slamshaft's left, till finally he pounced for the kill.

Slamshaft saw it coming. Longnoble-Drumblood check-stepped, pre-tending to retreat then actually making a full advance. Slamshaft, in turn, cross-stepped, twisting his torso round at just the right instant. Longnoble-Drumblood overshot. His chest lay wide open. To Slamshaft it was a target as big as a barn door. With an almost leisurely grace, yet still with some force, he planted the tip of his rapier square in his opponent's sternum.

'Touché,' he said.

Longnoble-Drumblood hissed. Being jabbed by a rapier, even when it had a protective cork stuck on the tip, hurt. His arms dropped to his sides and he groaned. 'Dammit, Dom. I knew you were mucking me about. I *knew* it.'

'Yet still you took the bait. You couldn't resist. Greedy boy.' Slamshaft dug the sword even harder into the padding of Longnoble-Drumblood's jacket.

Longnoble-Drumblood grabbed the flat of the blade with a gauntleted hand and thrust it away. Then he shoved his mask back up over his head. His cheeks were pink and his hair was plastered to his head with sweat. 'How about we call it a day, eh?'

'Have you had enough?' Slamshaft pushed his mask up too. His bald head gleamed glossily.

'More than,' replied his friend.

They faced each other at a distance of two sword lengths and saluted by touching the bell guards of their rapiers to their noses.

Then, with an arm around each other's shoulders, swords in their hands still, the two men walked out of the marquee . . .

. . . to be faced with a scene of military preparation the likes of which had not been witnessed in the Westward Territories since the war with the Axis of Eastern States.

All the way from where they stood to the horizon, the desert teemed with activity. In the foreground, uniformed men were parading in square formation, marching up and down to the shouts of drill instructors. Between hundreds of rows of pup tents, other men were polishing their boots or being taught the proper use of crossbows and timed detonators. Yet more of these soldiers-in-training were learning how to leap from a five-metre-high platform and land safely by tucking their ankles under and rolling with the impact. Every so often a tiny puff of flame and smoke shot upwards from a section of the campsite reserved for explosives practice. A few seconds later the faint, sharp *crack* of the detonation would reach Slamshaft's and Longnoble-Drumblood's ears.

Beyond the camp, further out into the desert, immense aeroplanes were taking shape. Frameworks in various stages of completion were being added to bit by bit, flesh being put on skeletons. Workmen riveted and welded, while cranes swung sections of fuselage and wing into place. Trucks came and went, dropping off aircraft parts.

Further out still, three tarmac runways had been laid on the sand. Each was a couple of kilometres long, and at any given moment each was being used for landing or take-off by a finished version of the planes being put together nearby.

They were giants, those planes, huge roaring things like castles that could fly. Six sets of propellers, each the size of a windmill's sails, adorned their wings and hurled them aloft with a combined thrust of 10,000 gross horsepower. They climbed into the air looking as aerodynamically unfeasible as bumblebees, and yet once they had achieved cruising speed they assumed a gracefulness that totally belied their 60-tonne laden weight. They zigzagged to and fro beneath the cloud cover, every so often disappearing up into it and re-emerging elsewhere several minutes later.

The turbulence and pressure drops within the cloud cover had little effect on planes so sturdy and big. That was why Slamshaft had dubbed them Cloudbusters.

Some of the Cloudbusters practised another kind of manoeuvre. Their tailgates would open and out would pour a swarm of what appeared to be tiny aircraft. On closer inspection, they were actually people strapped to V-shaped wing units, which in turn were attached to motorised propellers. Slamshaft had nicknamed these contraptions Drones and they were, in his view, the pinnacle of his technological genius. Watching the Drones circle in distant clusters now, he was thrilled to the core. The pilots were growing more adept and confident by the day. Steering by means of rudder fins on their bootheels, they could swoop, soar, dart, dive, spin, loop, pivot, all as though flight was second nature.

Slamshaft had given Groundlings wings.

'It's a magnificent sight, don't you think?' he said to Longnoble-Drumblood.

'No argument here, Dom. But while I'd love to stop and marvel, I'm parched, and I know for a fact there's champagne on offer in the pavilion over there. What say we go over and grab some?'

'Yes, why not?' Slamshaft's expression soured. 'That is, if Brickmansworth has left us any.'

CHAPTER 50

Cold Feet, Hot Blood

Slamshaft's syndicate were all present and correct, with the exception of Lord Urironson, who had business of his own to attend to up above the clouds. They were gathered in the shelter of the pavilion, an open-sided tent with an onion-shaped canopy which had been pitched on the brow of a small hill, overlooking the vista of military preparation. The area immediately around it and the marquee had been swept clean of wildlife and enclosed within a wire fence to make sure the dangerous animals, especially the venomous creepy-crawly ones, stayed out.

Chilled champagne sat in ice buckets, alongside platters of canapés. Naturally Harry Brickmansworth had already consumed more than his fair share of the bubbly, and as Slamshaft and Longnoble-Drumblood approached, the construction-industry entrepreneur was delivering a drunken tirade on the subject of armed conflict, its advantages and drawbacks.

'. . . and if you ask me,' he was saying, 'why go to all the trouble of starting a war? I mean, it's all very well, but look at those enormous flying things up there. Amazing! What a feat of ingenuity! A fortune could be made simply by selling them. Same for the . . . the wing harness what-nots those chaps have on their backs. The civil applications for these inventions – the possibilities are endless.'

The others were listening politely but keeping their distance. Apart from anything, Brickmansworth had a tendency to spit when he was pontificating, but also, he was making them feel uncomfortable.

'We've all invested,' he went on, 'and we all stand to gain afterwards, financially. But hang on a moment, eh? Shouldn't we give a thought to the loss of life involved? Shouldn't we at least ask ourselves if profit is really worth the death and destruction that war brings?'

'Of course it isn't, Harry,' said Slamshaft.

152

The other syndicate members were relieved to see the man in charge arrive.

'Profit alone isn't the motive,' he continued. He laid his rapier on the table, then plucked a bottle of champagne from one of the buckets.

'What?' said Brickmansworth, confused. 'What do you mean? You're in this for the money. We all are.'

'Not purely. I don't need any more money. I've already got more than I know what to do with. I'm stinking rich. We all are. And once you're stinking, it doesn't matter how much you stink, you still stink. To put it more delicately, does the ocean need the water from a rainstorm? It doesn't get any fuller after a downpour. It's still the ocean, just as vast and deep. That's how it is with wealth on the scale that we're all dealing with.'

'It's all very well for you,' grumbled Brickmansworth. 'You don't have a wife, an ex-wife and a mistress to support. Not to mention two teenage daughters. I need every damn note I can earn.'

'You have my sympathies. Even so – and I realise what I'm about to say seems like heresy – there's more to life than money. It's taken me a while to realise that, but now that I have, you won't believe what a difference it's made to my outlook. Why do you think I've devoted so much time and energy to this project? Why am I instigating a war when we have elected politicians who are supposed to make such decisions on our behalf? One, because it will prove to the politicians who really runs the show around here – us, the industrialists, the wealth generators, the money people, and not that bunch of jumped-up, timeserving nobodies who sponge off our taxes. And two, because I can. Because I have the power to do something like this and no one can stop me.'

'Our governments would stop you if they knew what you were up to. The Westward Territories Senate would come down on you like a tonne of bricks.'

Slamshaft couldn't resist a jibe. 'What, like one of your shoddily built houses comes down, Harry?'

'Don't talk to me about shoddy, Slamshaft!' Brickmansworth retorted. He glanced at his glass, saw it was empty, and snatched the bottle out of Slamshaft's hand. 'You're the king of shoddy,' he said, taking a swig straight from the bottle, then wiping his mouth with the back of his hand. 'Your name's practically synonymous with dodgy product that breaks down or blows up. Matter of fact, it's a wonder half those aircraft aren't falling out of sky in front of us.'

'There's a difference,' Slamshaft replied, with lethal evenness, 'between product for the masses and product for one's own use. I've made it my personal responsibility that every one of my Cloudbusters and Drones is in perfect working order, right down to the last nut, bolt, rivet and sheer-pin. I may not care about other people's car parts but I care about this. I care about it so much, in fact, that I will not tolerate anyone criticising me on the subject. Do you hear me, Harry?'

'I'm not criticising. I'm simply making a point or two that I feel must be made. If I can't be candid with you, who can? This lot?' Brickmansworth waved in the general direction of the rest of the syndicate. 'These sycophantic sheep? *They're* not going to raise difficult issues. I am.'

The insult caused consternation and dismay. Mrs Graingold snorted, 'Sheep!?', while Paul Copperplate postured, sticking out his chest and challenging Brickmansworth to fisticuffs, safe in the knowledge that an elderly man like him would never be expected to make good on such a threat.

'Harry, Harry, Harry,' said Slamshaft. 'I'm all for people speaking their minds. It's when their minds are full of utter garbage that I get ticked off.'

'It's not utter garbage to suggest there may be downsides to this scheme of yours.'

'It is when what you're really saying is that you're getting cold feet.'

'I am not getting cold feet. I just . . .'

'Just what? You don't have the guts for this, Harry, that's what it boils down to. Indeed, I think you'd be rather pleased if someone in authority got wind of what we're doing and moved to intervene.'

'Not at all. I—'

'And it may well be that you're considering letting someone in authority know. Giving them a tip-off. That'd be the sort of thing you'd do, wouldn't it?'

Brickmansworth looked shifty. 'Of course not.'

'But you've been thinking about it, haven't you? I bet you have, during one of your many bouts of hangover remorse. Thinking how you could pull back from the brink and maybe ease your conscience at the same time.' Slamshaft snatched his rapier off the table, nudging the cork off the end with his thumb.

'N-never. I'd never dream of it,' Brickmansworth said. His eyes, bulging, were fixed on the sword.

'Drunks like you are so unreliable,' Slamshaft sighed. 'Really, I shouldn't have invited you to join us in the first place. It was a mistake, I see that now.'

'Dominic . . .'

'You can't trust a person who has no self-control. That's the lesson I've learned today. You just cannot rely on them.'

'Dominic, please. Please don't. I'll do whatever you want.'

'Fine, because what I want you to do is die.'

So saying, Slamshaft drew back the sword and, almost casually, ran it through Brickmansworth's middle.

The construction entrepreneur looked down at his chest with frank bafflement on his face. The champagne glass in his right hand fell to the sand. The bottle in his other hand quivered and looked as if it was going to go the same way, but Slamshaft reached out and caught it. Then he drove the rapier even deeper into Brickmansworth.

Mrs Graingold let out a horrified gasp. A couple of the other syndicate members looked ashen-faced and close to fainting.

'I said no one can stop me, and I meant it,' Slamshaft hissed to Brickmansworth. The other man's eyes were bulging. His mouth gaped. His body trembled. 'Not any government. Certainly not you. No one.'

He thrust a third time, and the tip of the rapier emerged from the small of Brickmansworth's back. Blood dripped from the end and pattered onto the sand, which sucked it up like blotting paper. More blood gushed from Brickmansworth's lips, pouring down his chin. He gurgled and went limp. Slamshaft snatched the rapier back as Brickmansworth crumpled to the ground, just so much dead weight now.

Slamshaft peered down at the body for a long while. At last he said, 'Oh dear. Poor Harry. He wandered off into the desert and a hackerjackal must have got him. Isn't that so, Jasper?'

Longnoble-Drumblood nodded. 'Leave it with me,' he said, and he picked up the corpse by the wrists and dragged it away.

In a distant voice, Slamshaft continued, 'I always wanted to find out how that feels. You should know what it's like to kill someone, if you're going to send others to do the same. It's only right.'

Suddenly he snapped to attention. 'Well now,' he said, addressing the syndicate, focused again. 'Here I am, totally forgetting my manners. You all look in need of a drink. Who's for a refill? Anyone?'

He held out the bottle from which Brickmansworth had taken his last ever swig of booze. A little of the dead man's saliva glistened on the rim.

Nobody moved.

Then, tentatively, a glass came forward. Then another. Then all of them.

CHAPTER 51

The Crackdown

As Lady Aanfielsdaughter commanded, so it happened. The crackdown on Feather First! began.

Voices rose against her in the Sanctum when her intentions became known. In the halls, plazas and corridors of the city, people spoke out, saying it was madness, it was undemocratic, it flew in the face of everything the Airborn believed in and held dear. Deputations went to her office, demanding an audience with her. Aurora Jukarsdaughter Gabrielson turned them all away, saying her ladyship was not receiving visitors at present. Whatever Aurora's own feelings about Lady Aanfielsdaughter's decision, she was under strict instructions to let no one through, and she did as she was told. There were a few heated arguments in the office antechamber, but Aurora didn't budge and didn't back down. She was a formidable human barrier. Her natural hard-headedness, coupled with the discomfort of being heavily pregnant, left her with little patience for people who wouldn't listen and thought they could browbeat her.

There was support for Lady Aanfielsdaughter in the Sanctum, however, and a lot more of it than she herself might have anticipated. There were those who could not believe her ladyship was capable of putting a foot wrong. If she felt the First!ers needed reining in, then fine, they did.

Other Sanctum residents, less sure of her infallibility, still respected her enough to think that what she was doing was right and necessary. It must be so, given her years of political experience, her hard-won wisdom. Many, even though they were no fans of her, simply agreed with her. It was high time someone showed the First!ers who was boss. Even Lord Urironson was heard to say that at last Lady Aanfielsdaughter was demonstrating some courage, although he qualified the remark by adding, 'I only hope it's not too little too late.'

The debate within the Sanctum reached fever pitch. Squabbles arose. Occasionally brawls broke out, and the Alar Patrollers had to step in and drag the adversaries apart. The Patrollers were there to protect the residents from outside attack; little had they realised they would also have to protect them from one another.

All these disputes were redundant anyway. Outside the Sanctum, throughout the Airborn realm, Lady Aanfieldsdaughter's edict was already being acted upon. In each sky-city's Alar Patrol HQ, the existing intelligence on local First!er groups was gathered and collated. The Patrol had records: names, addresses, the identities of known and suspected sympathisers. It wasn't much, because Feather First! was not an illegal organisation, strictly speaking. Individual members had, however, broken laws now and then – harassing Groundlings, for instance – and their First!er affiliation was noted down on the criminal charges sheets in the section headed Additional Remarks.

Squadrons of Patrollers set out, armed with shields and lances, flocking through the streets in formation. An ever-impressive sight, one that didn't fail to make passers-by stop and stare. Their wings hoops flashing, their helmet visors shining blankly in the sun. The beats of their wings immaculately synchronised. Many bodies but one thought, one aim, one purpose. And now a pair of Patrollers would break off, diving down an avenue to somebody's home, and now another pair, swooping to the entrance of an office block, shop or warehouse. Organised dispersal, triggered by a sequence of peeps from the wing commander's whistle.

'Excuse me but we're looking for . . .'

'Are you . . . ?'

'Does he live here?'

'Then where might we find her?'

Some of the First!ers came quietly. Some put up a fuss to begin with, but soon meekly lowered their wings and allowed themselves to be led away. A few resisted, but they were no match for Patrollers schooled in the art of capture and restraint. In no time they were pinned to the floor, their wings were shackled, and the Patrollers carried them out, hauling them along by the armpits.

All in all, it lasted not much more than a couple of hours. The crackdown was a co-ordinated effort, a pulse of activity that took place more or less simultaneously across the realm.

In a few locations the round-up of First!ers did not proceed straightforwardly.

In Redspire, the Alar Patrol – such as it was – refused point-blank to take part in the crackdown. Their squadron leader tried, albeit half-heartedly, to marshal them and get them to do as they were told. They would not.

They threw down their weapons and went on strike. The squadron leader threw up his hands and went on strike too.

In Prismburg, the job was too large for the local Patrollers to carry out fully. There were just too many First!ers to arrest, so they chose to arrest only the most prominent ones. Even then, they missed El El Blaefson, who was neither at home nor at work. They could not know that he and two other First!ers were occupying an empty house on the city outskirts . . . with a certain wingless youngster as their 'guest'.

The Cumula Collective had no Patrollers within its boundaries. It policed itself. The city was known to harbour a number of female First!ers, but when Patrollers from neighbouring Zenith arrived to take them into custody, they were refused entry. Eventually one Patroller, a woman, was permitted to pass through the main gates and was taken to see the Collective's Mother Major, Tetra Fourth-House. This wizened, imposing creature informed the Patroller that her kind were not welcome there and that, moreover, the Collective had decided to open its doors to any First!ers, female of course, who wished to seek refuge within its walls.

'Collective will not tolerate an abuse of civil rights like this,' Tetra Fourth-House said. She was seated on a wooden chair made to the very simplest specifications, as plain a piece of furniture as could be imagined. Her clothing was sandals and a woollen smock with a hood that covered most of her face. 'Collective stands opposed to the bullying tactics of the Sanctum and to retribution thinly disguised as justice. Collective will maintain this stance until such time as the Sanctum recants its decision. You are dismissed.'

At Gyre, there were no Feather First!ers. It was not a city that paid much attention to political matters, being so wrapped up in mathematical matters instead. Nonetheless, when news of the crackdown reached the Count of Gyre's ears, he ordered a calculation to be performed on the Ultimate Reckoner. How would this event affect the Airborn? The answer came back shortly, and it was grim. The outcome was predicted to be disastrous. Bad for the social fabric of the realm. Bad, too, for the economy, which was what really mattered to Gyre.

In other sky-cities, ones where there existed a reasonable level of anti-First!er sentiment, the crackdown stirred up a surprising amount of public indignation. People who did not like having First!ers in their midst did not like seeing them get dragged off by Patrollers either. To make matters worse, the First!ers weren't even being charged with any crime. By all that's high and bright, they were being arrested just for holding an opinion!

In a short space of time, the Airborn realm went from being a relatively stable world to a world in ferment. That morning, it had woken up secure and contented, feeling there was little that could upset the easy rhythm of life. As the day wore on, this came to seem more and more like an illusion, and there was a sense that, whatever tomorrow brought, it would not be good.

CHAPTER 52

Kratter-klumm-boosh!

Cassie and her father were, of course, unaware of all that was going on above their heads. But then, they had troubles of their own, immediate and pressing concerns.

Such as: the police car that had been following them doggedly since Croaker Gulch.

And: the roadblock that loomed ahead on the highway leading into Granite Plains.

The pursuing police car had kept its distance the entire way. It could have overtaken *Bertha* easily, with barely a nudge on the accelerator, but there would have been little point. Alone, it hadn't a hope of stopping her. The car was shadowing her, that was all. Cassie reckoned the cops inside were counting on *Bertha* running out of fuel before long.

Fat chance of that. Courtesy of Fletcher, *Bertha's* tank was still nicely topped up with Slamshaft diesel.

Then the roadblock appeared.

Six police cars were parked at angles on the road, forming a rough inverted V shape. Cassie estimated that *Bertha* could just about fit through the gap between the first pair of cars, but the second pair were only five metres apart and the third pair were touching bumpers. There was a steep embankment on either side, so no way around the roadblock.

'Well?' she said to her father, hauling gently back on the control sticks. *Bertha* slowed to 20 kph.

Den chewed his lip. 'Them surely doesn't think a bunch of *cars* be going to stop a murk-comber. Must be them's counting on we to pull over like any law-respecting citizen would. And maybe us should. Us could try to reason with they. Tell they about Slamshaft and everything.'

'Yeah,' said Cassie, 'but does you really think that'll work? After all that's happened? "Ooh, us did burn down a bit of the Slamshaft factory and make a mess of that marketplace, yes, but listen, there'm this big bad conspiracy going on, or at any rate us thinks there be, so maybe you could forget what us has done and let we be on our way." I wouldn't put money on it.'

'Me neither,' Den said dourly, nodding. 'There'm nobody actually in those cars, be there?'

Cassie peered through the windscreen. 'Nope, all the coppers be standing behind or up on the roadside.'

Her father sighed. 'OK then, pour on speed, lass.'

'Better find something to hold on to, Da. This'm going to get bumpy.'

The police at the roadblock were confident the murk-comber would halt. The criminals on board must realise their little joyride was over. They were caught in a bottleneck. Surely they wouldn't be so foolhardy as to try to . . .

. . . to accelerate and . . .

. . . steer the murk-comber straight at . . .

'Run!' yelled the senior officer present.

The others didn't need any prompting. There was a mass panic to get off the road. Policemen scurried up the embankments on all fours as *Bertha* gained momentum, closing in on the roadblock. All at once the six police cars looked small and very puny indeed, beetles compared with the raging elephant that was *Bertha*.

Whunch!

One of the first pair of cars was casually butted aside by *Bertha*'s front left track.

Ker-rannnk!

This was the sound of the front ends of the next two cars getting crushed pancake-flat.

Kratter-klumm-boosh!

The final pair of cars presented no obstacle. *Bertha* could climb over hillocks larger than these without any difficulty. She smashed up onto the cars' roofs, teetered briefly on top of them, then thumped down onto the roadway beyond.

Onward she drove, and all the police could do was look on from the embankments and shake their heads in dismay.

The car that had pursued *Bertha* all the way from Croaker Gulch was forced to come to a halt. The Craterhome cops inside leapt out and began shouting and gesticulating at their Granite Plains counterparts. 'Clear the road! Move those cars out of the way!'

But the ruined police cars weren't going anywhere in a hurry, a fact which the local law enforcers pointed out to the Craterhomers with great emphasis and a good deal of anger.

'Us was told by telegram to stop they,' the senior officer said. 'Us did what us could, and look. It'm cost we almost our entire motor pool.'

'And all you managed to do was stop we instead,' said the driver of the Craterhome car. 'Idiot!'

'Don't call I an idiot, idiot!'

'Oh, *I* be an idiot, be I?'

'With that pair of red knickers stuck to your bubble light? I'd say so, yes.'

After that, it nearly came to blows.

CHAPTER 53

Good: The Rockiest Road

Den watched the policemen in *Bertha*'s rearview mirrors. They were getting smaller by the second, but their bickering antics were plain to see.

He smiled. 'You was right, Cass. Trying to reason with that lot? Us'd've been wasting our breath.'

'I's always right, Da. Sooner you gets used to that, the better.'

'I know, I know. You'm your mother's daughter, and no mistake. Her were always right too.'

Granite Plains lay ahead, a tidy little burgh nestled in the midst of a barren, stony landscape. All around, the earth was pockmarked by quarries, and a faint grey mist hung in the air, a miasma of granite dust thrown up by the constant digging and mining.

'You reckon, Da . . .' Cassie began, pensively. She was thinking about the trail of destruction they were leaving behind them and about her brothers being in police custody. 'You reckon that Ma would be pleased with we?'

'What's you mean?'

'With we. What us Grubdollars do. The stuff us gets involved in and the way us deals with it all.'

'Pleased? As in proud?'

'Yeah.'

Den didn't hesitate. 'Her'd be as proud as anything,' he said, placing a hand on Cassie's shoulder. 'Let I tell you something, girl. On her deathbed, you knows what your ma said to I? "Den," her said, "I doesn't care what our kids get up to when them's older, what them grows up to be, as long as them's happy and always knows good from bad." And I said, "That be'n't necessarily easy, Orla." And her, forthright as always, said, "Yes, it be. Happy be'n't hard to come by. It'm what happens when you do good. Even when good hurts, when good gets you in difficulties,

163

when good'm the rockiest road you could ever walk upon, it'll still make you happier than bad ever could. You make sure the four of they understands that, Den. That'm your job from now on."'

His voice began to crack.

'And I's tried to,' he said. 'That'm why I were so cross when Martin and Fletcher fell in with the Humanists. I thought I'd failed. It were obvious the Humanists wasn't anything but a bunch of chancers and troublemakers. I couldn't understand how those boys couldn't see that.'

'Them did eventually, Da. *You* didn't fail. Mart and Fletch did.' Cassie took a turn onto a road that forked off from the main highway. A signpost indicated that this was a bypass route, leading around Granite Plains and off to the base of Pearl Town. The word CHANCEL on the signpost had been painted out and replaced with SKY-CITY ACCESS. 'You raised we just as Ma told you to. Straight up. Hey, if you hadn't, how come us has got barely any money and is on the run from the cops and two of we is probably sitting in prison right now? I mean, if that be'n't "the rockiest road", what be?'

Her father had to laugh. 'Yep, I brought you up to be model citizens all right. Proper pillars of the community. If your ma were alive right now, her'd be dancing with joy at the way you's turned out. Dammit, her'd be so glad, her would be bashing I round the head with her best saucepan.'

'No, her wouldn't.'

'You reckons not?'

'Not her best saucepan. One of old ones, maybe. All burned and sticky with grease and that. But not a decent one. It'd get dented.'

Den laughed again. 'I reckon you be right about that and all.'

'Wasn't you listening, Da?' Cassie said, as Pearl Town's column glimmered into view on the horizon. 'I always be right. I always be.'

CHAPTER 54

A Sliver Of Salvation

Amid Az's many aches and agonies, a single new source of pain wasn't especially noticeable at first.

He had wriggled over onto his front to relieve pressure on his right shoulder and hip, and it wasn't until he had lain in this new position for several minutes that he finally perceived that something sharp was digging into the heel of one palm. The sensation was one of burning, almost – a hot needle jabbing through his skin.

With a grunt, he shifted sideways to see what the cause was.

It twinkled on the carpet, small, no bigger than a moth's wing.

A jagged triangle of red glass.

A sliver of Mr Mordadson's broken spectacles lens.

Az barked a laugh. 'Ha. You missed one,' he whispered, remembering Mr Mordadson gathering up the lens fragments.

He inspected his palm. That piece of glass was sharp. The cut was short but quite deep. Beads of blood had welled along it, like tiny cranberries. Instinctively he raised his hand to suck on the wound, but his bonds prevented him.

A thought occurred. Az looked at the shard, then at the cord around his wrists.

And suddenly Mr Mordadson's parting words came back to him: *Sore as you think you are about this, you could be sorer.*

Frowning, he replayed the sequence of events in his mind. Mr Mordadson picked up the bits of lens, put them in his pocket, came over, patted him, made that curious remark, then walked out.

Patted him patronisingly, just after beating him up. Kind of rubbing salt in the wound.

No.

Az replayed it again, this time as if there was more to Mr Mordadson's actions than met the eye.

Picked up the bits of lens, put them in his pocket . . .

But kept one concealed in his hand. This very one, this sharp sliver here.

Then patted him. Dropped the sliver next to him at the same time, behind him, where Lord Urironson and the First!ers couldn't see it but where Az would find it.

Made that remark.

Sore. Sorer.

Saw. Sawer.

Then walked out.

Walked out, but not before he had provided Az with a means of cutting – sawing – through the cord. Not before he had dropped a big hint, too.

Az wanted to be certain he wasn't making a mistake. He wanted to be quite clear in his own mind that he wasn't giving Mr Mordadson credit for something he had not actually done.

But how else had the sliver got there? The spectacles had got broken all the way over on the other side of the room. The sliver couldn't have ended up right beside Az unless it had been put there deliberately.

Apart from anything else, it proved one thing. Whether or not Mr Mordadson had genuinely joined forces with Lord Urironson, he remained Az's friend.

Breathless with excitement, Az pinched the sliver between thumb and forefinger and twisted his hand over. He was just able to touch the longest edge of the sliver to the length of cord that ran between his wrists.

The key rattled in the door. Az tucked the piece of glass into his cupped hand and curled his fingers around it.

El El and another First!er came in bearing food and water. Briskly they untied Az, then left him alone for ten minutes. Az ate and drank. The First!ers returned and he was soon trussed up once more.

But not for long.

The instant the door was locked, Az uncurled his fingers.

The angle was awkward, but he was able to slide the sliver back and forth across the cord, a few millimetres in each direction.

It was slow, tedious work. The edges of the glass sliver cut into the soft pads of his thumb and forefinger. But it was only pain. Pain didn't matter when freedom was so close.

Fibre by fibre, the cord began to fray.

CHAPTER 55

Time To Face The Music

In the former Chancel, Den and Cassie made their farewells.

'Good luck up there, lass,' Den said, enveloping her in one of his bone-crushing bearhugs. 'You find Az and sort all this out.'

'You'm going to wait here for I?'

'Afraid not.'

'Didn't reckon so. But I's not got any money for a train home.'

'Az'll help you out. Me, I's got to go and see about your brothers. Can't just leave they to the tender mercies of the Craterhome cops, now can I?'

'What'm going to happen, Da? Is us going to be all right?'

'Don't you worry about a thing, Cass. Leave I to handle the stuff down here. Your business be warning the Airborn.'

She rubbed a hand over his bristly cheek. 'You'm the best da in the whole world, Da. You knows that?'

'If you says so, you being the one who'm always right. Now get off with you.'

Cassie climbed into the back seat of a battery-powered cart and was whisked away towards the elevators.

Den meandered back to *Bertha*, discreetly rubbing his eyes. He started the engine up and steered for the exit, thinking all sorts of thoughts. One of them was that he didn't know what this warehouse-like chamber was called any more. Two years ago – was it really only two years? – it was a sorting-house. Simple as that. Now? Nobody had renamed it yet, or renamed anything to do with the Chancels. It was as though people weren't quite willing to let go of the old ways, or else weren't quite prepared to adjust to the new. The same held true for the Deacons. Many of them were still roving the Territories, still preaching their gospel of Ascending, albeit to ever-diminishing audiences in ever more out of the way places. Den had also heard rumours that large numbers of Deacons had recently emigrated to the Axis of Eastern States, among them Archdeacon Corbelgilt of the Grimvale Chancel. What they were up to there was anyone's guess. The Airborn realm did not extend to cover the Axis region, so it wasn't as if there was a ready-made audience for their message. Perhaps they simply wanted to be somewhere else, in a land where nobody had cause to resent them for the systematic and cynical exploitation they had carried out for centuries.

Another of the thoughts Den was thinking, and a much more dominant one, was this: it was time to face the music.

Den had been coming to this conclusion ever since the ruckus in the market square. His family hadn't got away with the theft of *Bertha*, in spite of their best efforts. With Fletcher and Robert in police hands, the game was very definitely over, and Den could think of only one way he was going to be able to save his boys (and Cassie too) from a jail sentence.

He was going to have to turn himself in and take all the blame.

It wouldn't be too hard, he thought. Cassie and Robert were still minors. Technically, he was responsible for whatever they did. Fletcher was an adult, but Den was sure he could make a case for him being impressionable and biddable. Fletcher still lived at home, for one thing. Under his da's roof, under his da's influence.

I be the one, he would say. *I did it. I talked they into committing a crime. Forced they into it, in fact. No one else'm guilty here, only I.*

He wasn't frightened at the prospect of going to prison. He could bear it, as long as he managed to get his kids off the hook.

He drove back along the bypass. A glance in the rearview showed him the sky-city column and the elevators crawling up and down it like ants on a twig. He pictured Cassie beginning the long, rattlesome journey up the column into the clouds, with a breathing apparatus kit in her hands. Fearless girl. Her bravery left him with no excuse not to be brave as well.

Soon enough, a police car appeared in the distance, coming towards him. Its bubble lights came on, confirming that these were 'his' cops and that they had recognised *Bertha*.

Den decelerated. *Bertha* trundled to a halt.

He killed the engine. The police car pulled up alongside.

He slid down the ladder into the loading bay and opened the hatch.

He stepped outside, hands raised. The policemen, four of them in all, leapt out of the car and rushed over to surround him.

'I gives up,' Den said. 'I'll come quietly. You's got I bang to rights.'

The coppers handcuffed him and bundled him into the car. All in all, they were pretty gentle with him. They managed to bang his head against the frame of the car door, but then, oh well, accidents happened. It could have been worse.

One of them took the controls of *Bertha*, and in slow procession, the police car leading, the two vehicles wended their way back to Craterhome.

CHAPTER 56

Ostrich On The Loose

'Hey!'

No answer.

'Hey!'

Finally, a weary 'What?' from the other side of the door.

'I'm bursting for a pee,' Az said.

'Can't you hold it?'

'No.'

'Let him wet himself,' said a second voice from behind the door, El El's. There was laughter.

'Please,' said Az. 'It isn't funny.'

'All right, all right,' said El El. 'Coming.' And the key turned in the lock. In strode El El, followed by the larger of the other two First!ers.

Az lay curled on the floor with his hands between his legs and a pained look on his face.

This time, the First!ers went about the business of untying him casually, almost carelessly. They didn't even bother to wield their knives. That was how confident they were that their captive wasn't going to give them any hassle. As Lord Urironson had said, he was downtrodden, utterly beaten. What harm could he possibly do to them now?

El El received a straight shot to the jaw. He didn't even see it coming. He keeled over onto his back, out cold.

His fellow First!er was flummoxed. The kid's hands were free? But no one had even touched his wrists yet. There was still cord tied around them.

Az took advantage of the man's bafflement. A perfect swinging kick clobbered him on the ear. He went down, but came up again, clutching the side of his head. With a snarl, he reached for Az. Az scuttled back on all fours. The First!er lunged, but Az caught him around the neck with both legs. A scissor hold. He tightened his grip. The First!er choked and spluttered. He flapped his wings to try and pull away. Az flipped over, and the First!er flipped too. On his back, his wings were useless. Az, with everything he had, kept his legs clamped around the man's neck, constricting his airway. The First!er clawed and writhed but could not break free. In the panic of suffocation, he didn't even think about his knife. Gradually his efforts grew feebler. Az held him till he stopped resisting. He let go slowly, wanting to be sure the man wasn't playing possum. No, he wasn't. He had blacked out. He was alive, still breathing, if wheezily. But he was without doubt unconscious.

'What's going on up there?' called a voice from deep in the house. 'I heard noises. Everything OK?'

Az sprang to his feet and made for the doorway. He was on a landing, and coming up the stairs was the third First!er.

'What the—?' said the First!er. He fumbled at his belt, trying to pull out his knife.

Az hurled himself at the man. The First!er spread his wings as Az collided with him. Together, in a jumble of limbs, they rolled down the stairs, feathers flying all around them. They landed in a heap at the bottom. The First!er's wings absorbed the brunt of the impact. Az was on top. He slugged the First!er a dozen times in quick succession, left-handed punches, no let-up. Mercy was a luxury he could not afford right now. This was about escape. Survival. He kept going till the First!er went limp. The man slumped against the wall, his face a bloody pulp. Panting, Az sat back on his haunches and shook out his aching fist.

'Not bad for an ostrich, huh?' he spat.

A snappy(ish) one-liner. If only there'd been someone else around to appreciate it.

Maybe there was.

Relieving the First!er of his knife, Az crept through the house, senses alert. Just because he'd had contact with only the three people, it didn't mean there couldn't be others. Perhaps Lord Urironson himself was still here. And Mr Mordadson.

Az didn't think he was quite ready to face Mr Mordadson again. Either as an enemy or as a friend.

The rest of the house was like the room he had been kept in. Carpets were bare. There were marks on the wallpaper – pale rectangular patches where the pattern hadn't faded as much – indicating where pictures used to hang. There wasn't a stick of furniture to be found, or any sign of occupancy, except in the living room. Here the First!ers had set up camp. Folding chairs, sleeping-bags, bottles of water, food and books littered the floor. A pack of playing cards was laid out on an upturned cardboard box, dealt for a game of three-handed Chicken Scratch.

Az's gaze fell on a long coil of cord, the same stuff that had been used to bind him.

Having assured himself the house was empty apart from him and the three First!ers, he got busy tying them up. He hauled the two in the top room into a sitting position, back to back, and lashed them together like that, crushing their wings flat between them. He tried to lug the one on the staircase up to join his comrades, but couldn't manage it. He had only one good arm and the man was heavy. So instead he attached him securely to the newel post of the banisters.

Just as he was applying the final knot, a groan came from upstairs.

El El was regaining consciousness.

Az squatted down in front of him, poultry knife in hand. He had made sure to take away all of the First!ers' knives and check them for concealed weapons. Now he was the captor and they the captives. He was the one with the blade, the upper hand, all the advantages.

It was a fantastic feeling.

'OK,' he said to El El. 'Let's start at the beginning. Tell me what's going on. What is Lord Urironson after? What's his plan?'

'Pluck you,' said El El. He struggled against his bonds, but he was held fast. As a little bonus, Az had fashioned a kind of double noose to go around the two men's necks. One couldn't pull away from the other without both of them strangling. Az was pretty pleased with that. It was a nice touch. Mr Mordadson would have been impressed.

Az couldn't decide whether Mr Mordadson's opinion was something that mattered to him any more. But on balance, he thought it was.

'I'm in no hurry,' he said. Outside the window, the sunlight was taking on a rosy-golden hue. The refraction patterns on the walls were stretching and growing hazy. 'I've got all night. You can sit there on your tailfeathers and say nothing, if you want. Or you can make life easy for yourself and give me everything I need to know. One of you lot'll co-operate eventually. Might as well be you.'

El El remained tight-lipped. His eyes blazed with humiliation and resentment.

Az toyed with the knife, tossing it up and catching it by the hilt. 'I've killed a man, you know.'

'Guano.'

'No, it's true. He was a pirate, attacking my airship. I shot him with a bolas gun, snarled up his wings, and he fell through the clouds.'

'I don't believe you.'

'Look into my eyes. Go on, look. You'll see I'm not bluffing.'

El El looked.

'It was him or me,' Az went on, holding El El's gaze. 'I barely hesitated before shooting him. That's what I do. I'm Az Gabrielson. That's what I have to do in my life. And the man I killed? I didn't even know him. He'd have stoved my head in with a mace if I'd given him half a chance. But still, I didn't know him. Whereas you' – his voice dropped a few degrees in temperature – 'are someone I know. And someone I don't like at all. So think about it. Think very carefully. Ask yourself this. If he can kill a man he feels nothing for, what would he do to a man he feels a great deal of hatred for? To put it another way: after all I've had to suffer thanks to you, El El, I think I might be looking for a little payback.'

He leaned forward with the knife.

'And here we are, in an abandoned house at the edge of Prismburg, where no one will hear you scream.'

El El swallowed hard, but still refused to talk.

'All right,' Az said. 'I'll leave you to think about it. When you're ready, just give a shout. I'll be downstairs.'

CHAPTER 57

Twin Tines Of A Tuning Fork

Az was not at Pearl Town Mercy. His room was occupied by another patient, and none of the nurses Cassie asked had any idea where he had got to. There was no record of him having been discharged. However, a rumour was going round the hospital that he had been spirited away in the middle of the night to somewhere else, someone less open to the public and less liable to intrusion by the press, possibly the Silver Sanctum. He had connections, you see. He was 'in' with the Sanctum.

Cassie didn't think it was very likely that Az would have gone to the Sanctum. His injury required medical supervision, and where better to get that than here?

Something fishy was going on, but she couldn't for the life of her figure out what.

She was aware, too, that there was a general mood of disquiet, not only at the hospital but all around. Everyone was talking in hushed whispers about an event that had happened earlier that day. Comments were being passed, usually behind a cupped hand or a shielding wing. It was something to do with Feather First! and the Alar Patrol, but Cassie couldn't glean much more than that from her eavesdropping. It felt big but nebulous, a story stitched together from hearsay and half-truths.

In her heart, she couldn't help but feel that if trouble was brewing up here as well as down on the ground, the two things must somehow be linked. The Airborn realm and the world of the Groundlings were more closely interconnected than most people realised. They had always depended on one another, and that was the case more now than ever.

Once, Cassie had watched a mechanic test how well an engine was running by means of a tuning fork. He had touched the base of the Y-shaped implement to various points on the engine and listened to the harmonic vibrations that sounded from the two tines of the fork. If they hummed nicely, he had said, then all was well. If one was slightly out of key, it indicated a fault. The man had claimed he could accurately diagnose any motor problem by this method, although to Cassie it had looked like a piece of flummery. Any halfway decent mechanic could tell if an engine component wasn't working properly, without resorting to a prop purchased from a music shop.

She wondered if her world and Az's weren't like that, however – twin tines of a tuning fork. When one hummed tunefully so did the other, and likewise, when the harmony of one was disturbed so was the harmony of the other.

She didn't have long to dwell on the analogy, because as she was making her way out of the hospital, who should she bump into but Michael.

'Cassie,' he said, embracing her warmly.

'You's heard about Az?'

'Oh yeah. I was here earlier today. Nobody could tell me where he's gone. I've been charging around Pearl Town ever since, looking for him. I've been half out of my mind with worry. I thought I'd come back here and talk to some people on the night shift. It could be that one of *them* can help.'

'Him be'n't at the Sanctum, then?'

'Definitely not. I heard that rumour too. But seeing as that's where I live most of the time, I think I'd know if he'd been brought there.'

'What about Mr Mordadson? Could *him* have gone off with Az somewhere?'

'I don't know, but I doubt it. Old Mordy's been a bit scarce lately. There's all sorts of shenanigans going on with Feather First! and Lady Aanfieldsdaughter, and I think Mordy's in the thick of it. That's where he usually is, in the thick of it.'

'Az too. Which'd suggest them was both off busy on some mission or other, no?'

'Yeah,' Michael conceded. 'Perhaps. Only, Az wasn't supposed to be out of that hospital bed for another couple of days.'

'Common sense be'n't that boy's strong suit.'

'You can say that again.'

'Look, Michael, I be glad I ran into you. I really needs to speak to someone important about something. There'm shenanigans going on down on the ground too, or at least I has a strong suspicion so, and I needs to get word to somebody up here, somebody with clout, because I reckon what I know could be very bad news for the Airborn. If Az and Mr Mordadson be'n't available, what about Lady Aanfieldsdaughter?'

Michael did a sharp intake of breath. 'Her ladyship's . . . What's the word for when no one can get in touch with you?'

'Incommunicado?'

'Yeah. That's her right now. Incommunicado.'

'But her'll surely listen to what I's got to say. Once I—'

'Hold on.' Michael held up a finger. 'Just a tick.' He was looking over her shoulder. 'That's Az's nurse, isn't it?'

Cassie glanced round. The icily beautiful staff nurse, Nurse Haatansdaughter, had just alighted at the main entrance, coming down with a waft of her wings. The setting sun cast a glow around her, turning her blonde hair into a halo and trimming her snowy plumage with gold.

'I bet she knows something,' Michael said. 'If Az got whisked out of here by Mr Mordadson or whoever, she of all people is likely to have seen it.'

He plumped up his wings and wafted towards her across the lobby. Cassie followed, thinking that Michael could try and use his charm on Nurse Haatansdaughter but he wasn't going to get very far. Behind those perfect features lurked a heart of flint.

'Hello,' Michael said in his deepest, sexiest voice. 'It's Ariella, isn't it? I'm Michael, Az Gabrielson's brother. I was wondering . . .'

The nurse looked at him, then looked at Cassie, and her face registered surprise, swiftly followed by alarm.

She turned tail and took off.

'Hey!' said Michael. This wasn't usually the effect he had on women.

'Her knows something all right,' Cassie growled, pushing past him.

Nurse Haatansdaughter flew out through the entrance. Cassie sprinted in pursuit, jettisoning her breathing apparatus along the way.

In front of the hospital there was a narrow concourse just a few metres across, little more than a glorified ledge really. Beyond it lay open space. Nurse Haatansdaughter was almost at the edge of the concourse when Cassie caught up with her. She had broadened her wingspan, ready to propel herself high into the air.

Look before you leap, the saying went, and Cassie often didn't. She was too headstrong. It was both a virtue of hers and a failing.

In this instance, she literally didn't look before she leapt. She hurled herself at Nurse Haatansdaughter, not thinking of the possible cost of her actions, thinking only that she was *not* going to let this woman get away.

She landed on Nurse Haatansdaughter's back. Their combined momentum tipped them over the edge of the concourse.

All at once, they were plummeting.

CHAPTER 58

Solid-boned, All Right?

They fell head-first, plunging away from the hospital and past the building below. Windows flashed by. Nurse Haatansdaughter was screeching, 'Let go! Get off me!' Cassie held on for grim death, her arms locked around the nurse's ribcage. She couldn't have let go if she wanted to.

'I can't fly!' Nurse Haatansdaughter wailed. 'You're too heavy! Let go or we'll both be killed!' Her wings were trailing upwards behind them, flattened together by the force of the descent.

Another building zipped past, and a flock of startled pigeons scattered, and a gyro-cab swerved sharply to avoid colliding with the two falling figures, and Cassie knew she should have thought this stunt through a little better, because now she was going to die. Either she and Nurse Haatansdaughter were going to hit a bridge or a building at high velocity, in which case *splat*, or they were going to shoot clean through the city and into the clouds, in which case also *splat*.

Stupid girl. You's just made your biggest and last mistake.

No.

No! She would not give in that easily.

'Fly, bitch,' she shouted in Nurse Haatansdaughter's ear. 'Spread your wings and fly.'

'I can't. You're too—'

'You can and you will.'

Nurse Haatansdaughter arched her wings, forcing them apart. She managed to brake their progress slightly, but unevenly. One wing was bent out further than the other, and all of a sudden the fall became a spiral. She and Cassie were turning and turning in dizzying circles, as helpless as before.

'Come on, try harder,' Cassie urged.

With a groan of effort Nurse Haatansdaughter stretched out the less extended wing to match its partner. She and Cassie straightened out of the spiral. They were still descending, but at an angle, not vertically down, and not as fast as before.

'Flap. Flap those bloody things like you means it.'

Nurse Haatansdaughter flapped. Cassie could feel the muscles at the roots of the wings straining with every down-sweep and up-sweep. The woman was doing her utmost to keep the two of them aloft. But her utmost wasn't enough. They were still going down.

Cassie cast around for somewhere they could land. She spied the roof of an apartment block ahead. She told Nurse Haatansdaughter to aim for it.

Nurse Haatansdaughter was crying, nearly frantic with fear. They lurched towards the roof, but Cassie had a horrible feeling they weren't going to make it.

'Need a hand?'

Michael appeared alongside them, and without waiting for an answer to his question he grabbed Nurse Haatansdaughter's arm. With his help she was just able to reach the roof. Cassie climbed off her back the moment she set down. Nurse Haatansdaughter then collapsed against a skylight, sobbing and trembling.

Cassie rounded on Michael. 'Where was you?' she demanded. 'What kept you?'

'Whoa, don't thank me or anything. Do you know how hard it is to catch up with someone in freefall? You can't follow at the same speed. You might not be able to pull out of the dive yourself.'

'Yeah, well,' Cassie said, disgruntled. 'Still. You caught Az that time, didn't you, when him had those copper wings on.'

'Only just. And I was ready then. Whereas you took me completely by surprise just now. Are you crazy? Jumping onto her like that?'

'Never mind crazy,' said Nurse Haatansdaughter, pushing herself up into a sitting position. She sniffed wetly and wiped her eyes. Something of a sneer came over her face. 'How can one person weigh so much?'

'You calling I fat?' Cassie snapped. 'You better damn well not be.'

'I'll call you whatever I like, Groundling. You certainly look as though you could do with skipping a meal or two.'

'Now just a moment, you snooty, big-boobed bimbo . . . !'

Cassie stomped towards her, fists clenched. Michael stepped in and restrained her.

'Let I at she,' Cassie said, writhing in his grasp. 'Her needs to be taught some manners.'

'Easy, easy,' said Michael. 'I love watching a hen-fight as much as the next bloke, but hitting her won't solve anything.'

'Yes it will. Anyway, I be'n't fat. Us Groundlings has solid bones, that'm all.'

'Solid bones?' said Nurse Haatansdaughter, her sneer intensifying. 'Is that what they call it down there when you can't do up the top button of your trousers? "Ooh, it be'n't my belly flab, it'm just my solid bones."'

'You – you –!'

'Cassie,' said Michael. 'Leave it. Really. Don't let her rile you.'

Cassie steeled herself with a deep in-breath. 'OK. Yes. I's calm.'

'So I can let go?'

'You can.'

'You're not going to lay into her?'

'Not unless I has to.'

'Not at all. Promise?'

'Fine. I promise.'

Cautiously, Michael released her. Cassie stood for a moment, arms by her sides, looking for all the world like someone who had composed herself and risen above the insults being thrown at her.

Then, too quick for Michael to stop her, she pounced on Nurse Haatansdaughter and fetched her a couple of hard slaps across the face. Nurse Haatansdaughter shrieked.

'Now listen, blondie,' Cassie snarled, hand poised for a third slap. 'Where be Az? Answer I. You turned tail and ran the moment you laid eyes on I and Michael. That were the action of someone with a guilty conscience, someone with something to hide. Tell we where him is, or so help I, I'll—'

By this point Michael managed to wrestle her off Nurse Haatansdaughter, so the threat went unfinished.

'Cassie, what's got into you? Is it lack of oxygen? Is that why you're behaving like a rabid bat?'

'Her knows what went on, Michael. I can tell.'

'You can't be sure about that.'

'Why else did her flee?'

'I fled,' said Nurse Haatansdaughter, clutching her cheek where Cassie had hit her, 'because there was this lunatic Groundling charging at me across the lobby, all hundred and fifty kilogrammes of her.'

'That weren't what happened and you knows it,' Cassie retorted.

'Look, think about it. If I was involved somehow with your friend's disappearance, why would I come back to the hospital? Surely that's the last place I'd dare show my face.'

'She has a point,' said Michael.

'Oh, don't take her side, just because her's pretty and walks around with her chest all sticking out,' Cassie said.

'I'm not taking her side,' he protested.

179

'You is. And *you*,' she said to Nurse Haatansdaughter, 'came back to the hospital because it'd have been suspicious if you hadn't. The one surefire way to look innocent is to act innocent.'

'That really doesn't leave much wriggle room, does it?' Nurse Haatansdaughter replied with a brittle laugh. 'You've decided already. I'm guilty, and my innocence only makes me look guiltier. Next thing I know, you're going to tell me I'm guilty because I'm attractive and have blonde hair – not to mention I watch my figure. Honestly, you Groundlings. You're as dumb as you are ugly. I would have chloroformed that boy even if no one had asked me to, simply because he . . . looks like . . . one of . . .'

Her voice trailed away as she realised what she had just said.

'Oh guano.'

'Ugly us may be,' Cassie said, beaming with triumph. 'But clearly us doesn't have a monopoly on dumb.'

'I think now would be a good time,' Michael said to Nurse Haatansdaughter, folding his arms, 'to come clean.'

CHAPTER 59

A Moral Victory

Wings sagging despondently, Nurse Haatansdaughter did as Michael suggested. She revealed everything she knew about the kidnap plot, including her part in it, and told them where the First!ers had taken Az. Putting a brave face on it, she finished by saying, 'It won't make any difference, now that you know. The damage has been done. First!ers are in prison, and people are up in arms about it. It's a moral victory. Come tomorrow, there'll be more recruits to the cause, more sympathisers than ever. Nothing helps a political movement quite as much as when it's suppressed by the authorities.'

'No one cares that much about Feather First!' said Michael.

'You'd be surprised. People certainly care if their freedoms are being taken away from them. They'll rally round to—'

'Let's save the speechifying for some other time, shall us?' Cassie butted in impatiently. 'What'm important be rescuing Az.'

'True,' said Michael. 'What about her, though? What do you think we should do?'

Cassie peered down at Nurse Haatansdaughter. With her hair dishevelled and her mascara running, not to mention one cheek puffing up into a bruise, she was no longer the lovely creature she had been. She looked a pitiful sight.

'Us ought to turn she over to the Alar Patrol, I suppose, but to be honest? Her's not worth it. Let's just leave she. Every minute us spends dealing with she be a minute us be'n't spending travelling to Prismburg.'

'You want to come to Prismburg?'

'Of course. Why not?'

'Well, don't you need to get back down to the ground? What about altitude sickness?'

'I'll deal with it.'

'And telling everyone about, you know, what you told me about?'

'Finding Az be the same thing.'

Michael knew better than to argue with Cassie when her mind was made up. Az often praised her stubbornness, and just as often complained about it.

He turned to Nurse Haatansdaughter. 'Don't try and warn your First!er pals that we're coming. It won't work. We'll get there faster than any message you can send.'

She shrugged. 'It's too late anyway. The courier services have all closed for the night.'

'Exactly.'

With that, Michael scooped Cassie up in his arms and took off. Nurse Haatansdaughter remained on the rooftop, trying to fix her makeup and put her hair back into some sort of order.

'What a liar that woman was,' Michael said as they rose towards Pearl Town Mercy.

'Tell I about it.'

'No, I mean . . .' He grimaced, his face reddening with exertion. 'You don't weigh a hundred and fifty kilogrammes. A hundred and twenty at most.'

Cassie waited till they were safely on the hospital concourse before giving him the smack he deserved.

CHAPTER 60

Metatron's Wake

Past midnight, it seemed safe to venture out. Lady Aanfielsdaughter took off from her balcony. There was no one else abroad but Patrollers, and they left her alone. Well, she *was* Lady Aanfielsdaughter.

She rose and circled the Silver Sanctum. There were lights on in a number of windows, glowing against the night. Doubtless residents were awake in their beds, unable to sleep, or else were engaged in debate, talking anxiously through the small hours. She continued upwards, spiralling to greater and greater heights. Soon the turrets and pinnacles, bridges and plazas, the Belvedere Vineyard, the Hanging Garden, were so far below that all she had to do was lift a hand and she could blot the whole city out of sight. If only it were that easy to blot out what the Sanctum had come to symbolise for her – the cares, the woes, the antagonism, the remorse.

The stars were bright and profuse, the sky so clear that Lady Aanfields-daughter felt she could ascend for ever, soaring into the universe. She gazed at Metatron's Wake overhead, a band of milky whiteness crossing the firmament, its jagged outline sharply delineated. Metatron – the founding father, the semi-mythical first ruler of the Airborn, he who had travelled to each and every sky-city one after another throughout his life, spending a week at a time in each, listening to its citizens, holding court and dispensing judgement, faultlessly wise. The leader against whom all subsequent leaders were compared and found wanting. Meta-tron the pilot, who had never died, who had simply disappeared on a journey one day, vanishing into the ether, and who was said to be still voyaging, up there among the constellations, going from star to star, looking down on his people, his descendants, benignly, for ever. Meta-tron, bringer of flight, giver of wings. It was even claimed that, thanks to him, the Airborn gained their own wings – a tale which Lady

Aanfielsdaughter and many another senior resident knew better than to dismiss as pure, out-and-out myth.

She felt unworthy, not fit to follow in his footsteps. She knew full well what she had unleashed across the realm. She had had no alternative, however. Her back was against the wall, and whatever she did would have been wrong in some way. Ignore the First!ers' provocation, and it would have given them a licence to continue their crimes. React, and she lost the goodwill of the general populace. The latter, she believed, was the lesser of two evils. Goodwill could be earned back, in time.

Why couldn't Mr Mordadson see that?

She didn't know. Mr Mordadson was not himself these days. Hadn't been since the Redspire pirates business. Evasive. Moody. Self-questioning. She wasn't able to count on him any more, the way she used to. He had rarely argued with her before, if ever, and now it seemed he was disagreeing with her all the time.

She could rely on no one, nothing, except her own instincts, her own intuition. Her own values. That was all she had left.

She began to descend. The Sanctum grew closer, and now she could see the lights were starting to go out, one by one. Here, now here, and over there. Now another one. Now another. The Sanctum was darkening.

Darkening for a fall.

Lady Aanfielsdaughter didn't know where the phrase came from. It just popped into her head. She tried to dismiss it, but there it was, stuck, immoveable.

Truth?

Or simply her own fear?

The lights were going out.

Darkening for a fall.

CHAPTER 61

The Road To War

Lord Urironson's trips to the ground would go something like this.

First, he would fly to Prismburg by gyro-cab. He tipped generously every time, making sure the cabbie understood that the payment was for discretion as well as good service.

Then it was down in an elevator. The supervisor at the supply-arrival depot had become accustomed to his lordship's visits and knew what was required. Lord Urironson always got an elevator to himself and boarded it when there was a lull in the work day and the depot volunteers were off on a break, or else when things were so frantically busy that nobody was paying attention to anything except the unloading and distribution of raw materials from the ground. Again, money changed hands and silence was bought. A Silver Sanctum seal was a useful item to have, but when it came to bribery, nothing could beat cold hard cash.

During the descent, to take his mind off the shaking and buffeting that the elevator was subjected to, Lord Urironson chatted with Echo. This was why the mynah always travelled with him, for companionship. His lordship was deeply attached to the bird. In fact, he preferred Echo to most people. Echo demanded nothing from him except a little bit of food and attention. Echo did not talk back to him or contradict him. Echo was what he was, a simple, faithful, feathered friend.

By prearrangement, a Slamshaft minion would meet Lord Urironson as the elevator arrived and escort him to a private chamber in the former Chancel. Here, Slamshaft's ingenious pressurisation tank awaited. After an hour, his lordship and Echo were ready for the ground.

Such had been the routine over the past few months, since Lord Urironson and Slamshaft first cemented their alliance. It all began with a tentative enquiry from Slamshaft to his lordship, a few carefully couched words in a letter. Without saying anything explicitly, Slamshaft indicated that he was seeking to forge links with the Airborn powers-that-be. He had heard about Lord Urironson thanks to an article in one of Paul Copperplate's more upmarket newspapers, the *Craterhome Messenger*, which had carried an exclusive interview with several senior Sanctum residents. This had been a public relations exercise organised by Lady Aanfieldsdaughter in the wake of the Redspire pirates incident. She'd wanted to show the Groundlings how much the Sanctum deplored the pirates' behaviour and put distance between the Airborn leadership and the actions of a tiny minority of the population. The same went for Feather First!, whose assaults on Groundling tourists were still a source of bitter resentment on the ground, not least in Craterhome.

'It was interesting,' Slamshaft's letter said, 'that of all the Sanctum residents quoted in the article, only you, milord, expressed anything other than unqualified condemnation of the pirates or Feather First!'

In that respect, Lady Aanfieldsdaughter's PR initiative had not been a complete success. Lord Urironson had insisted that the Groundling journalist record *his* opinion too, and the *Messenger*, being a paper that liked to think of itself as balanced and fair, had gladly given his remarks column space.

'You refused to toe the party line,' Slamshaft wrote, 'which in my view is an admirable trait. It suggests individuality and integrity.'

How could Lord Urironson fail to respond positively to such a correct assessment of himself? Soon he and Slamshaft had become regular correspondents, and it wasn't long before they began meeting in person.

Quite when it became clear that Slamshaft's ambitions dovetailed with his own, Lord Urironson could not say. It emerged pretty early on that Slamshaft was aiming high. He had nothing less in mind than all-out war against the Airborn and had gathered a coterie of likeminded types around him to help finance his plan. Lord Urironson was shocked by the idea but not as shocked as he was impressed. He saw a way of turning it to his own advantage, much as Slamshaft had hoped he would.

'If you can help me up there,' Slamshaft said, 'we can both benefit.'

To which Lord Urironson replied, 'I'd be only too happy to be of assistance.' In his mind, he was picturing Lady Aanfieldsdaughter discredited and dethroned, leaving a power vacuum which he would fill. Already he had made overtures towards Feather First!, on the grounds that they stood in ideological opposition to her. Her enemy was his friend, and he knew that by fostering that friendship he could keep up the pressure on her. Voices raised in dissent and protest made her ladyship's position less and less secure by the day.

His decision to collude with Dominic Slamshaft was based on a similar principle and would all but guarantee her overthrow. Lord Urironson would have struck a deal with absolutely anyone, no matter how reprehensible they were, if the end-result was Lady Aanfielsdaughter defeated and himself in her place. Luckily, he found Slamshaft far from reprehensible. They might be from different worlds, the two of them, but they had a surprising amount in common. Slamshaft was refined yet ruthless, and so, Lord Urironson thought, was he himself. He enjoyed their meetings. He even looked forward to them, for all the logistical difficulties involved in getting to them. And dinner the other day with the rest of the syndicate had been delightful. Groundlings might be a dirty, scabby, misshapen race as a whole, but the better ones, the elite, the *crème de la crème*, were almost as good as Airborn. Slap a pair of wings on them, and Lord Urironson would have found it hard to tell them apart from his own kind. Which was high praise indeed.

Now, very early on the morning after Lady Aanfielsdaughter had made a crucial misstep and ordered the crackdown on Feather First!, Lord Urironson was obliged to journey down to the ground once more, only this time he did not go straight from the former Chancel to Slamshaft's mansion. Instead, a hulking black limousine transported him due south, out into countryside that grew ever starker, ever more barren. Fields gave way to scrubby grassland, which in turn gave way to rocky plains and ribbed expanses of sand dune. It was all fascinatingly dreadful to look at, dreary and dry and dim. Someone accustomed to sunshine and cloud-scape could not view these rugged, undulating vistas without experiencing a mild nausea, a claustrophobia almost. There was distance but not the seeming infinity of distance that you found up in Airborn realm. The sky closed down on the earth, like a cupping cauldron. The landscape had too much solidity, too much weight. Lord Urironson stared out at it, challenging himself to endure it, but whenever it got too much he turned to Echo on his shoulder and stroked the little bird's sleek black head and neck, soothing himself.

The limousine's shock absorbers creaked and groaned as it juddered over road surfaces that were increasingly rough and full of potholes. Thankfully, the back seat was thickly padded and well sprung. The drive seemed interminable, but at last a destination appeared. Lord Urironson knew he was out in that region the Groundlings called the Relentless Desert. Ahead lay Slamshaft's base of operations, with its innumerable tents, its runways, its sites for aircraft building and maintenance, just as Slamshaft had described them to him. His lordship felt a keen twinge of anticipation.

Slamshaft was there to greet him as he stepped out of the limousine, along with Brigadier Longnoble-Drumblood. Lord Urironson had got the impression that the relationship between these two ran deeper than mere friendship, although neither, perhaps, was aware that this was so. He had a vague inkling that Longnoble-Drumblood was married, but the wife

187

was so seldom referred to, one could only assume she did not rate high on the brigadier's list of importance. Lord Urironson was not the sort to judge in these matters. The two men enjoyed each other's company; that was enough.

Pleasantries having been dispensed with, Lord Urironson delivered the news that the Airborn were sliding inexorably into disarray.

'According to my sources,' he said, 'a number of huge protest rallies have been organised. They'll be picketing the Alar Patrol HQs today and keeping the Patrollers very busy. Meanwhile the Cumula Collective has opened its doors to female Feather First!ers, and I understand at least twenty have taken refuge there already, with more on the way. It's a highly provocative act from a sky-city that's never been truly comfortable as part of the Airborn community. Meanwhile, Redspire and Prismburg are both discussing the possibility of secession from the realm. If they pull out of the Pact of Hegemony, as seems likely, that's it. The Pact is dead. It's like breaking an egg. The shell, once cracked, can never be whole again. And then, who knows how many other sky-cities could see their example and do the same. The Sanctum will have no control over the realm any more, and anarchy may ensue.'

'Would you say, milord,' said Slamshaft, 'that the deteriorating situation up there might pose a danger to us on the ground?'

Lord Urironson knew what was being asked of him, and gave the appropriate answer. 'I would say, Dominic, that the situation could be very dangerous indeed to you and your kind.'

'So we would be justified in launching a pre-emptive attack on your realm, if only out of self-preservation.'

'It would be a wise action to take. How fortunate' – Lord Urironson waved at the campsite – 'that someone has had the genius to prepare for just such an eventuality. And what better opportunity will you have to attack, when the Airborn are focused inward, preoccupied with their own internal conflicts. The last thing they'll be expecting is for another conflict to be imposed on them from outside.'

'We're clear on this, then,' said Slamshaft, smoothing a hand across his hairless scalp. 'The time's right.'

'If your forces are ready.'

'Oh, absolutely they're ready, milord.'

'Absolutely,' agreed Longnoble-Drumblood.

'And what about the others?' his lordship asked. 'Our collaborators, our co-conspirators? Does their opinion need to be consulted?'

'They've come with us this far,' said Slamshaft. 'They're not going to back out now. Actually, I imagine they're itching to get started. The sooner that happens, the sooner they can begin to recoup on their investment.'

'So they're all safely on side? Zelda Graingold? Copperplate? Even that drunkard, what's his name, Brickmansworth?'

Slamshaft and Longnoble-Drumblood shared a quick glance.

'I wouldn't worry about any of them, milord,' Slamshaft said, with a butter-slick smile.

'Then gentlemen . . .' Lord Urironson spread his wings to touch them both on the shoulder, a generous, inclusive gesture which he would never have deigned to bestow on any other Groundling but these two. 'War.'

'War,' said Longnoble-Drumblood.

'War,' said Slamshaft.

For once, Echo kept his beak shut. Maybe *war* had been repeated often enough already.

CHAPTER 62

Opened Wounds

Towards midday, El El was ready to talk. Az had ignored his complaints throughout the night, and the complaints of the other two First!ers when they, too, had come round. Repeatedly he'd told them he would do nothing for any of them – no food, no water, no toilet breaks – unless one of them gave him the answers he was after. Until then, they could gripe and moan all they liked. He didn't care. He had a pack of cards. He could play endless games of Patience and not get bored.

It was something of a bluff. Az knew he could not stay in the house indefinitely. His arm had begun to bleed. Two of the stitches in the wound had split during his fight with the First!ers, and the blood was flowing, if not rapidly, then consistently. The hospital dressing had become saturated and eventually he'd had to peel it off, revealing a puckered, gory mess beneath that he found hard to look at. Since then, he had fashioned a series of makeshift dressings, using spare shirts he found among the First!ers' belongings. Again and again, with gingerly precision, he'd wrapped a torn strip of shirt around his forearm, leaving it there till it became soaked through and needed to be replaced.

The wound would not stop oozing, though, and he was concerned about blood loss and infection. All in all, he was in rough shape. It had been a gruelling, nightmarish couple of days and he just wanted to get out of this house and have a decent meal and a shower and put the whole experience behind him.

But he needed information from the First!ers. It was his duty to extract it if he could. Grimly he sat downstairs and played the waiting game, determined not to crack before one of the First!ers did.

Then, hurrah, El El finally announced that he would tell Az what he wanted to know. The other two First!ers called him a coward and a traitor, but they did so dispiritedly, their tone suggesting they were secretly relieved that he had caved in.

It was a short conversation and served mainly to confirm what Az already had deduced. Lord Urironson was busy sowing seeds of discontent and conflict, with Feather First!'s assistance. El El was convinced Lord Urironson shared the movement's beliefs and aspirations. Az reckoned his lordship was simply using Feather First! to further his own goals. Either way, the result was the same. With Lady Aanfielsdaughter's unwitting help, Lord Urironson had caused rifts in the Airborn realm. He had opened up wounds long thought healed, and in the long term he would reap the benefits.

'There, that wasn't so hard, was it?' Az said, when El El had finished.

'Will you release us now? Please?' El El implored. 'I swear we won't give you any trouble.'

'Will you agree to testify against Lord Urironson? Sign a confession for the Alar Patrol?'

'Might.'

'Yes or no? Either way, I'm going to go out and find some Patrollers and bring them back here. I can tell them exactly what you've done to me, or I can lie and say you looked after me pretty well. How they treat you will depend on how well they believe you treated me.'

After a lengthy pause, El El nodded. 'All right. I'll testify.'

Before Az could reply, there was a loud thumping at the front door.

He dropped his voice. 'Expecting anybody?'

'No.'

Az felt El El wasn't lying. The sound had surprised him.

Poultry knife in hand, he stole downstairs, stepping around the First!er on the landing. 'Don't say a word,' he told the man in a whisper, the same thing he had just told the other two upstairs. 'Make the slightest noise, shout out a warning, anything, and I'll be back here in a flash and . . .' He mimed slitting a throat.

The First!er nodded meekly.

Az peered from behind the curtain of the living room window but couldn't make out who was at the door. All he could see was the edge of someone's wings. They looked like a young person's wings, the plumage tidy and white, so whoever it was, it wasn't Lord Urironson or Mr Mordadson. Another First!er?

He approached the door on tiptoe.

The thumping came again.

Knife poised, he gripped the handle and levered it down slowly. Then, quick as anything, he whipped the door wide open.

Something heavy swung at his head. Az ducked out of the way, feeling the object whoosh over the top of his crown with millimetres to spare.

Still bent double, he retaliated with a sideways slash of the knife, which his attacker just managed to evade.

A voice shouted, 'No! Stop!'

A very familiar voice.

'Cassie! No! It's Az!'

'Michael?'

Az looked up. Framed in the doorway were his brother, an alarmed expression on his face, and next to him Cassie, with her breathing apparatus cylinder held aloft. She looked like a wild thing, all too keen to bring that metal cylinder crashing down on Az's skull.

They all stared at one another for several startled seconds.

Then an indignant Cassie yelled, 'You – you tried to stab I!'

'You nearly brained *me*,' Az shot back. 'What's the big idea with that?'

'I thought you was one of the First!ers. I were trying to catch you by surprise and knock you out.'

'Well, I'm not one of the First!ers, am I? *Obviously*.'

'But you needn't have tried to stick I with that thing. You could've killed I.'

'I was defending myself. You attacked first.'

'Kids, kids . . .' said Michael with a chuckle. He had got over his shock and was starting to see the funny side of the situation. 'Everyone's all right, yeah? No one hurt?'

'Yeah,' said Az.

'Yeah,' said Cassie.

'Then both of you put down your weapons and, by all that's high and bright, kiss and make up. We're the rescue mission, Az. We've come to save you!'

CHAPTER 63

A Right Royal Skull-splitter

'Some rescue mission,' Az grumbled a short while later. He and Cassie were in the living room, while Michael had gone upstairs to look at the First!ers. He wanted to see it for himself – the three grown men his little brother had turned the tables on and overpowered. His voice was audible from above, mocking and crowing.

'You come a day too late,' Az went on, 'and instead of saving me you try and bounce ten kilogrammes of steel off my head.'

'Hey, give it a rest,' said Cassie. 'I's already apologised for that, and anyway, better late than never, no? Or would you rather us'd not have come at all? Now hold still. This'm going to hurt.'

She had a fresh strip of shirt all ready to wrap around Az's forearm.

'It's hurting now,' Az said.

'Well, I warn you, this'm going to be worse. Honestly, you should never have let it get in such a state. Doesn't you Airborn know anything about first aid? You has to apply pressure to a cut. Then it'll stop bleeding. All you was doing were draping bits of cloth on it, and them was soaking up the blood like a sponge. A scab weren't ever likely to form that way.'

Az faintly recalled Aurora pressing hard on his arm, just after the kite tail slashed it open at the jetball cup final. He'd forgotten that that was what you were supposed to do.

'Look,' he said, 'just get on with it, please. I'd rather have the pain than listen to you nagging.'

'I be'n't nagging. I just be telling you what'm what.'

'Same difference.'

'Does you want I not to help? I'll stop now, if you'd prefer. Let you just bleed to death.'

'No. Go on. Do it, before I *eeeyaghhh*!'

Red pain flashed through Az's body. It was a while before his thoughts

193

were clear enough for him to speak again. By then, Cassie had bound up the whole forearm tightly, from elbow to wrist.

'That was . . . slightly nasty,' he gasped.

'Sorry. Thought I should start while you was distracted.' She inspected the bandaging and was satisfied. 'That'll hold till us can get you to a doctor.'

'No, I'm not going to any doctor. Not while Lord Urironson's out there, running around causing mayhem.'

'I thought you said Mr Mordadson were keeping tabs on he.'

'I don't know that for sure, but whether he is or isn't, I've still got to do something to put a stop to Lord Urironson's plans. And then there are those "shenanigans" you mentioned, the stuff that's going on down on the ground. You yourself said we've got to get a warning to the relevant people.'

'I know, but you won't be getting anything to anyone if you doesn't have that wound looked at properly first.'

'It'll be fine. You've already wasted enough time coming to find me. We need to go to the Sanctum *now*. No more delays.'

'Doctor first.'

'Sanctum.'

'Doctor.'

'You're nagging again. Stop it.'

Cassie bristled. 'I's not nagging! It'm only because I love you that—'

She halted. Her hand flew to her mouth.

They looked at each other. Something had been said that neither of them had said to the other before. Perhaps it should have been said much earlier in their relationship, months ago. Equally, given all the difficulties they faced, all the obstacles that conspired to keep them apart, perhaps both had felt it should never be said, for fear that it would only make matters worse. The frequent separations were easier to bear that way. There was less at stake if no one said, 'I love you.'

Nonetheless, it had been said now, and could not be unsaid.

The awkward silence grew.

At last, Az gave a little cough. 'So, how are you doing?'

'Doing?'

'I mean, erm, altitude-sickness-wise. You've been up here how long? A day?'

'Yup. A day. Best part of.'

'So, you're OK?'

'Well, uh, I's got a bad headache. A right royal skull-splitter of a head-ache, as a matter of fact. But, um, otherwise, can't complain. I borrowed a couple of spare oxygen cylinders off Pearl Town Mercy. Them keeps some there for Groundlings in case of emergency, and Michael and I was able to persuade they that this were an emergency.'

'Headache. So that'll be why you tried to bonk me on the bonce.'

'Eh?'

'Wanted to share the suffering.'

It was a pathetic attempt at humour, scarcely even a joke. Yet both of them laughed long and loud, as though it had been the most hilarious witticism ever uttered.

As Michael walked in, they were still laughing.

'What's so funny?'

'Nothing,' said Az. 'You had to be there.'

'Well, I tell you, the shape those First!ers are in, it's enough to make anyone giggle. I'd almost feel sorry for them if I didn't know what they'd done to you.'

'Mike,' said Cassie, 'I be glad you'm here. Maybe you can talk some sense into Az.'

'I doubt it but I'll try. What's the problem?'

'Him refuses to go and see a doctor about his arm.'

'It's fine. Really,' Az insisted.

'It'm fine if you wants gangrene to set in, Az.'

'That won't happen.'

'Bro,' said Michael, 'if Cassie thinks you need to see a doctor, then you need to see a doctor.'

'But what about—?'

'What about *nothing*. There's no bargaining over this. You're coming with us to the nearest hospital and that's an end of it.'

'You can't make me.'

'I'm your older brother. I know enough embarrassing stories about you to make you do anything.'

Az looked from one of them to the other, and knew they had his best interests at heart, and knew he was defeated.

'All right,' he sighed sullenly. 'All right. Have it your way.'

Michael's open-topped helicopter, a brand spanking new AtmoCorp Vortex V coupé with a forked tail and twin rear rotors, was parked at the far end of the street. They crammed into it, Az and Cassie sharing the passenger seat. The engine whined, the propellers whirled, and soon they were flying.

Az turned round and watched the house where he had been held prisoner slowly recede into the distance. It was an ordinary, nondescript house in an ordinary, nondescript street. Like all the buildings in Prismburg its façade was inset with panels of dazzling, reflective glass, but otherwise there was nothing exceptional about it.

He would send Patrollers there to retrieve the First!ers, as he'd promised, but he had no wish to go back himself. If he ever saw that house again in his life, it would be too soon.

He turned back and looked sideways at Cassie. She knew he was studying her but she couldn't meet his eye. There was still a lurking embarrassment between them, the weight of those words she had uttered, and it was made worse by them being squashed together in the cockpit, body pressing against body.

It was his decision, his move to make.

He clasped her hand in his and said nothing to her.

But the nothing he said, said everything. And as the Vortex V whooshed through Prismburg, Cassie, despite her headache, despite everything, found a ridiculously happy grin was spreading over her face. And so did Az over his.

CHAPTER 64

Monstrous Mechanical Marvels

Someone else had a ridiculously happy grin on his face, and it was Captain Qadoschson, on board *Cerulean*.

Twenty kilometres out from dock, and *Cerulean* was behaving immaculately. It was her third test-flight since the refit. The previous two times, there had been minor hiccups – a leaking gas cell, a propeller drive chain that slipped its cogs – but Chief Engineer Rigzielson had mended these. Now, the captain thought, fingers crossed, it was going to be third time lucky. No more snags, no further niggles. The old girl back on form, good as new.

The moment he laid eyes on *Cerulean* after she limped back to Prismburg following her bruising encounters with *Behemoth* and that airship's pirate crew, Captain Qadoschson had known he had his work cut out. She'd looked so wounded, so helpless, what with the huge, roughly stitched-up tear in her balloon, the damaged propeller mounting that hung down like a broken arm, the jury-rigged rudder cable, and every window in her control gondola shattered. The state of her! So many battle scars! It still made him quite tearful to think about. Nevertheless he and his men had set to work with enthusiasm and determination. The Silver Sanctum had released funds for her to be properly fixed, in gratitude for her services to the realm. The Sanctum had, in fact, been exceedingly generous, and Captain Qadoschson made sure that none of the money was wasted but also that no expense was spared.

The refit had been a long, drawn-out process, but at last it was over. He couldn't remember when *Cerulean* had looked better. And her performance reflected her appearance. To judge by the feedback he was getting from the crew today, she was sailing as smoothly as she had ever done. Not that the captain needed anyone else to tell him that. He could feel it. Through his feet, through his centre of gravity, through all of his ingrained pilot instincts, he could feel how well she was running. The flight was a humming, seamless glide.

The chief engineer also felt it, he could see. Rigzielson was smiling, although there was a wince in the smile. Poor old Rigz, he was still recovering from the injuries he'd received as a result of the propeller being sabotaged and breaking apart violently. His chest ached whenever he moved, though he tried not to let it show. He was fortunate to have survived. Navigator Ra'asielson, wounded in the same incident, hadn't. He had died on the journey home, and in tribute there was now a small brass plaque screwed to the conn wheel, engraved with Ra'asielson's name and rank and the legend, 'HE LOST HIS LIFE BUT NEVER HIS WAY'.

'Chief engineer?' Captain Qadoschson said genially. 'Anything to report?'

'Not as such, sir. I'm not sure if that drive chain isn't pulling slightly out of synch with the—'

'Oh come on, man!'

Rigz gave a wry, reluctant nod. 'No complaints, Captain.'

Coming from the notoriously hard-to-please chief engineer, that was ten out of ten.

Captain Qadoschson suggested a minor course correction and asked the new navigator for a bearing. *Cerulean* hit a jetstream cross-current but rode the turbulence well. Soon they would turn around and head back to Prismburg. Within a day or so, the airship would be taking tourists out on jaunts as before. Captain Qadoschson looked forward to that. Then he would truly know that things were back to normal and all was right with the world.

A frown creased his forehead. Of course, all was *not* right with the world. Prismburg was in uproar after yesterday's string of arrests and the whole Airborn realm was in ferment. His own wife, Muriel, was attending a protest rally today at lunchtime. In fact – the captain glanced at his watch – she was probably on her way to join the rally right now. They'd argued about it last night, Captain Qadoschson saying it wasn't her business and she shouldn't get involved, Muriel saying that on the contrary it was every right-thinking citizen's business and they should all get involved. He hadn't been so foolish as to think he could stop her going. Muriel was still the same headstrong girl he married all those years ago. Her hair and plumage might be greyer and her face might be carrying a few more lines, but inside, that firebrand personality of hers burned as brightly as ever. He'd hoped she might think twice about going but it was, he understood, a slim hope, and in many ways he would have thought less of her if she *didn't* go.

'Sir?'

Lost in his musings, Captain Qadoschson didn't hear the helmsman's query the first time.

'Sir?'

'Mm? Yes, Furlacson, what is it?'

'I think you should take a look at this, sir.'

The helmsman was pointing to the forward viewing windows with a trembling finger. Everyone in the control gondola was staring in that direction. And everyone looked puzzled and not a little frightened.

A kilometre ahead, huge dark shapes were emerging from the cloud cover. There were five of them – no, ten – no, twenty – no, thirty or more – and they rose slowly, at a shallow angle, tearing immense furrows in the whiteness as they came. They were aeroplanes, but like no aeroplanes Captain Qadoschson had seen before. They almost matched *Cerulean* for size, and their fuselages fairly bristled with armaments. Their propellers chopped the cloud-mass into tatters, and now, one after another, the planes broke clear and levelled out. Filling the sky from horizon to horizon, they churned towards the airship with ponderous certainty, and the captain and crew could only stare. Stare at these monstrous mechanical marvels. Stare with awe and fear in their hearts.

Someone in the gondola began murmuring a prayer.

That was what roused Captain Qadoschson from his terrified daze. That was what galvanised him into action.

'Climb!' he ordered. 'They're heading straight for us. We've got to get out of their way. Trim-master, drop ballast. Nose up by twenty degrees. Climb, dammit!'

As *Cerulean* started to lift, Rigz said, 'What are these things? Where did they come from? Who's flying them?'

'No idea,' the captain replied, 'but with that much weaponry on board, I'd hazard a guess their intentions aren't friendly. And even if they are friendly, I'm not taking any chances. We have to put some altitude between us and them. The propeller wash from those things alone could throw us into a tailspin.'

The oncoming planes began to fan out, veering off in various directions. *Cerulean* had gained a couple of hundred metres in height by the time the nearest of them drew level with her. The plane passed below, and she juddered and rocked in its wake but maintained her equilibrium.

The crew breathed sighs of relief. It seemed they'd managed to evade the danger.

Captain Qadoschson wasn't so sure. He peered out of a side porthole at the plane that had gone under them.

It was banking, commencing a turn that would bring it hard about.

He cursed.

'More height!' he shouted. 'Jettison all ballast. Take her up as fast as she'll go.'

The plane was coming for them. *Cerulean* had one chance of getting away from it.

Just one.

And not a very good one, either.

CHAPTER 65

Ceilings

For all aircraft, the sky was the limit, but for some more so than others.

An aeroplane required a certain level of air density in order to stay aloft. The higher in the atmosphere you were, the thinner the air, and if the air became too thin, a plane's propellers had nothing to push against. No propulsion meant no forward motion and no forward motion meant no lift. The plane would stall and plummet.

An airship, by contrast, being in essence just a large balloon, could go up and up without loss of lift. There was no 'ceiling', no operational performance height, except the point at which the atmosphere ended and space began. An airship could skim through the upper stratosphere, riding the winds. In theory, it was possible to go even higher.

You would have to be insane to try, though. Apart from anything else, the decrease in external air pressure would allow the helium gas in the balloon to expand. The gas cells would swell and swell until, eventually, inevitably, at some stage they would burst.

What Captain Qadoschson was hoping, in his desperation, was that *Cerulean* could rise far above the plane's ceiling before reaching her own. She could not outrun that beast of an aircraft, that was for sure. But maybe, just maybe, she could out-climb it.

Tension in the control gondola was wire-taut as *Cerulean* strained upwards. The only crew member speaking was the navigator, calling out altimeter readings. The rate of ascent was breakneck. Every few seconds, the navigator ticked off another ten-metre interval. It seemed just feasible that the captain's tactic was going to succeed. The plane was giving chase but could not match *Cerulean's* precipitous angle of climb. Instead it was circling upwards. Surely, surely, *Cerulean* was going to get away . . .

Then – *boom.*

Something struck her in the stern.
The airship trembled and groaned.
And everyone aboard knew it was all over.

CHAPTER 66

The Downing Of *Cerulean*

What hit *Cerulean* was a metre-long explosive missile fired from a cata-pult mounted on the roof of the pursuing Cloudbuster. The missile speared through her balloon canvas and lodged in the fabric of a gas cell. Backward-pointing steel barbs on its shaft prevented it from falling out. Within its arrowhead-shaped tip, an impact fuse ignited. A few grammes of mercury fulminate sparked and flared, touching off the two kilogrammes of dynamite that was also packed into the tip.

The result: a spherical burst of flame, like an orange bubble suddenly appearing at the rear of the balloon and just as suddenly disappearing.

Cerulean jolted. Smoke and black shreds of debris spilled out from the hole that had been torn in her canvas. Fire flickered at the hole's rim and began spreading outward across her sky-blue skin like a rippling infection.

This alone was devastating enough, a mortal wound, but worse than that, the true fatal blow, was the structural damage the missile caused. The steel ribs which gave shape to the balloon were severely com-promised. The hole swiftly became a dent as, one after another, the ribs gave way. As each crumpled, it pulled down the next one along. The dent deepened and widened. It was a chain reaction. *Cerulean* was imploding.

Helium flooded out of the collapsing balloon. *Cerulean*'s stern was already lower than her bow end, and dipped further with the rapid escape of gas. In no time at all, the airship was almost at vertical, her nosecone pointing at the noontide sun.

For her there was no hope, but for those on board there was still the possibility of survival. Captain Qadoschson gave the order to abandon ship as soon as it became clear that *Cerulean* was beyond saving. He had to shout at the top of his voice so as to be heard above the calamitous shrieks and rending noises coming from aft.

The crew wasted no time in snatching the emergency hammers from their bulkhead cases and smashing out the windows with them. One by one they launched themselves into the open. They were twenty kilometres from the nearest sky-city, a long way to fly under your own steam but it could be done. They set about putting as much distance as they could between them and the doomed *Cerulean.* So frantic were their efforts to flee that they didn't notice, until far too late, that two of their number had not left the airship.

'Well?' said Captain Qadoschson to Rigz, as the deck of the gondola tilted ever more sharply beneath them. 'I know why I'm staying behind. Tradition. Going down with the ship. What about you?'

'Sir,' replied Rigz grimly, 'I'd never forgive myself if I let you do it alone. Besides, I don't much fancy our chances out there. I doubt that plane is going to let anyone fly home scot-free.'

'Me neither. I'd rather die like this. It's been a good life, and may I say, Rigz, it's been a pleasure to serve alongside you.'

'Likewise, Captain.'

Clutching the conn wheel for support, Captain Qadoschson looked upwards, squinting into the sunlight. 'There is one consolation,' he said.

'What's that?'

'We both know of someone who loves this airship as much as we do. Those people out there, whoever they are, won't get away with this. *He'll* see to that.'

Rigz nodded agreement, although it might have been the airship's shuddering death throes that made his head bob up and down.

'Az' was the last word on Rigz's lips as *Cerulean*, with a kind of tormented gracefulness, began to fall from the sky.

CHAPTER 67

Liquid Dynamite

The crew members who had escaped hovered in a cluster, watching numbly as *Cerulean* sank to the clouds. The great airship, the very last of her kind, seemed to take an awfully long time falling, and let out hideous moans and crackles the whole way down. The crushed, mangled thing she had become bore scant resemblance to the buoyant, majestic queen of the skies she had been just minutes ago. It was almost a mercy when the cloud cover swallowed her, stealing her from sight. It was like a shroud being drawn over a mutilated corpse. All that remained to mark her passing was a gouge in the clouds, which soon sealed over, and a pillar of smoke which the wind swiftly set to work dispersing.

Helmsman Furlacson rallied the crew members, saying they had better get going. They couldn't hang around. Mourning the captain and Rigz – and *Cerulean* – could wait. For now, they had to concentrate on getting safely home. The giant plane was flying away, apparently not interested in picking off the survivors. It seemed they had a chance to live.

'Which way?' Furlacson asked the navigator, wings beating hard.

'Prismburg's due north-east,' the navigator replied. 'Which is . . .' He glanced up at the sun for reference.

Then he was gone. In his place there was nothing but a haze of red and a few swirling feathers.

His colleagues gaped in shock and bafflement.

A moment later, a man soared over their heads. He was a Groundling, but he had wings strapped to his back. A leather helmet sheathed his head, smoked-glass goggles covered his eyes, and in his hands was a bulky crossbow. He was busy notching a bolt into its firing groove. This done, he cranked the ratchet handle, then wheeled around and came at the crew members again, pointing the crossbow at them.

The crewmen scattered, like starlings before a falcon. The Groundling

Drone picked on one of them, who happened to be Furlacson, and zoomed in pursuit. He took aim and loosed off his crossbow bolt at the fleeing helmsman. The bolt found its mark, and Furlacson, just as the navigator had, disappeared in a burst of crimson.

The Groundlings' crossbow bolts were compacter versions of the missile that had been used to down *Cerulean*. Their tips contained small, sealed pockets of nitroglycerine, liquid dynamite, a substance so unstable that it only needed a jarring force to set it off. When deployed on a human being, the result was absolute and instantaneous obliteration.

More Drones appeared in the sky, emerging from the tail of the giant plane in a long line. They swooped on the remaining crew members, who darted and dodged frantically as the air became thick with the explosive-tipped crossbow bolts. The crew members were Airborn, flight was innate in them – but the mechanically-powered Groundling intruders had the advantage of greater speed. They pressed hard, matching their quarry manoeuvre for manoeuvre. One by one, bolts struck home. One by one, the crew members were eradicated, vanishing as if they had never existed.

The name for it was *slaughter*, and it carried on till every last crewman had joined his airship in death. There was little to show the men had ever existed except a few tumbling scraps of flesh and feather.

When it was over, the Cloudbuster came back round and scooped all the Drones back into its belly.

Then the plane resumed its journey, much as if nothing had happened.

The encounter with *Cerulean* had been fortuitous. The opportunity to draw first blood against the Airborn had been hard to resist.

But now the plane had its primary mission objective to think about again.

Each Cloudbuster had been assigned a sky-city for attack. This one's was Prismburg, and it would be there in under ten minutes.

CHAPTER 68

Standing Up And Being Counted

The protest rally was well attended and for the most part peaceful.

Still, just to be on the safe side, Group Captain Kfialson put out every Patroller at his disposal. All leave was cancelled, and he would brook no excuses for failure to report for duty. Fully armed and armoured, Primsburg's law enforcers lined the route of the rally from its assembly point in Parakeet Park all the way to its final destination, their own headquarters.

It was anticipated that the turnout would be perhaps a few thousand, but in the event the total was more like twenty thousand. Such were their numbers that the park's permanent residents, the hordes of parakeets who nested in its trees and caged walks, took umbrage. So many people invading their territory, making all that noise! The birds flew off in a huff, finding roosts on nearby eaves and window ledges.

Using megaphones, the rally organisers marshalled everybody on the park's lawns and then gave the order to move out. The protestors took off in a huge flock, to a rippling rumble of wingbeats. They filed along the streets in a phalanx a dozen wide and half a dozen tall. Shouts and chants arose from various quarters, condemning the Alar Patrol and denouncing Lady Aanfielsdaughter. But these were sporadic and out of keeping with the general tone of the rally. The point was not to vent anger. It was to demonstrate, by sheer weight of numbers, how the citizenry felt about the action that had been taken against Feather First! It was about solidarity, ordinary people standing shoulder to shoulder, wing to wing, in opposition to their government. The Sanctum would know how many Airborn were here today. Reports would state that Prismburg, along with every other sky-city, had seen a sizeable proportion of its population take to the streets and make their case in a calm but forthright manner. The message ought to be loud and clear: *we will not put up with this*. And the Sanctum's response would have to be equally loud and clear: *we understand and we bow to your demands*. The desired effect of the rally would be that all the interned First!ers were released within a day or so. Otherwise, further rallies, in all likelihood less civilised ones.

Not to say that this one was completely civilised. There were skirmishes between protestors and Patrollers. Here and there, things got out of hand. A heated word, a scuffle. Using minimum force and maximum self-restraint, the Patrollers brought the malcontents back into line. Kfialson had decreed that no arrests should be made. It would only inflame the situation. So no arrests were made. Anyone responsible for causing an affray was let off with a caution.

The rally wended its way to Patrol HQ. Truly, it was a broad cross-section of the populace. There were children, the elderly, the rich, the not-so-rich, professionals, tradesmen, artists, municipal workers, students, someone from every walk of life. Today social divisions did not exist; the differences between people were erased. What mattered, what unified these disparate souls into a single entity, was the simple fact of being there. Adding oneself to the crowd. Standing up and being counted.

In the early afternoon the vanguard of the rally reached the Patrol HQ plaza. The area was soon teeming with protestors and more were arriving by the minute. This was the part Group Captain Kfialson was tense about, because there was only so much cubic space to be filled. If the plaza and the air above it became overcrowded, the mood might sour, tempers might fray, and there could be an outbreak of violence. Even in the best-case scenario, he foresaw injuries arising as a result of jostling, trampling, the crush of bodies.

His Patrollers, on his instruction, began gently filtering protestors off into side-streets or directing them to higher vantage points – the rooftops of adjacent buildings, open areas overlooking the HQ. For a while it worked, alleviating the pressure in the plaza. But still the protestors came, cramming themselves into the plaza until there was scarcely room to swing a wing.

Kfialson could sense it. Things were going to turn ugly. People were finding it hard to fly. Children wailed in alarm. Grown men and women looked restless and on the brink of panicking. The rally organisers did their best, using their megaphones to advise people to co-operate with the Patrollers and move to higher ground in an orderly fashion.

No good. Nobody could hear above the hubbub of frightened voices and the agitated rustle of wings. Even Kfialson's whistle was next to useless. He blew commands but they were audible only within a thirty-metre radius. On the far corners of the plaza, his Patrollers were leaderless and having to improvise as best they could.

Someone started screaming.

Kfialson knew then that he had a disaster on his hands.

The scream was taken up by others. Senselessly, they screamed too, and the sound grew and grew, a discordant howl of fear that overloaded Kfialson's eardrums to the point of painfulness.

Wincing, he attempted to fly up from the plaza and get an overview of the situation before chaos erupted and he was caught in the middle of it. But the crowd was packed too tightly. He couldn't make any headway.

There was a terrible rumbling, a roaring that shook the city to its very core.

Then came the explosions.

CHAPTER 69

Target: Prismburg

The Cloudbuster's pilots had spied a concentration of people near the centre of Prismburg and made straight for it. In the midsection of the plane's fuselage, on its underside, twin hatches petalled opened. Inside, suspended from rails, lay twin rows of metal spheres. Each was the size of a man's head and bore a short fuse. Each was filled with ball bearings packed tightly around a core of high explosive. Bombs.

It was the task of two men aboard the plane to shunt the bombs along in quick succession, turning crank-handles that operated chains embedded in the rails. Another two men were there to light the fuse on each bomb just before its retaining bolt hit a spar and it detached automatically.

What went through their minds as the order came down from the pilots to bombard the crowd below?

What, for that matter, went through the pilots' minds?

For weeks, months, these Groundlings had been training for this moment. Brigadier Longnoble-Drumblood had schooled them in the need for coolness and maintaining a distance. It should be pointed out that the brigadier himself had seen very little battlefield action. None at all, to be perfectly frank. He'd had the great fortune to join the Westward Territories army at a period when there wasn't any call for that fighting force to go into combat. Nevertheless, his instructors at military academy had prepared him in every way possible for the day he might have to face enemy troops in open conflict, and he had done the same for his friend Dominic's civilian recruits.

In essence, it came down to this. You could not regard those you were about to kill as human. They could not be individuals, people with families and friends and dreams and hopes. They were targets, that was all. *Things.*

That was the Airborn. Not really people, as such. Things. Creepy, too, what with those wings and everything. And they thought themselves better than the rest, a cut above.

Well, now was the time to take them down a peg or two.

So the crank-handles turned, the fuses were lit with tapers, one after another . . . and the bombs dripped from the Cloudbuster's underside in a lethal rain.

And fell onto the crowd.

And detonated.

And reduced people to tangles of flesh.

And splintered their bones.

And sent limbs flying.

And blew brainpans open.

And hurled victims in all directions.

And tore off wings.

And disembowelled.

And blinded.

And maimed.

And killed, and killed, and killed.

CHAPTER 70

Triage

Before zeroing in on the protest rally, the Cloudbuster circled over the city. Its route took it directly above Prismburg General Hospital, where, in a curtained-off cubicle on the second floor, Az was having his arm attended to by a senior resident surgeon.

Dr Ezgadisdaughter-Rusvonson had irrigated the wound with antiseptic and was just putting the second of two new stitches, when the entire building began to quake. Pill bottles clinked and clattered inside cabinets. Stainless steel surgical tools rattled on shelves. Shouts of alarm resounded along the corridors. Dr Ezgadisdaughter-Rusvonson halted work, and both she and Az peered up at the ceiling, alarmed and mystified.

The racket faded, and Az was just about to say, 'What the pluck was *that?*', when Cassie burst into the cubicle.

'I saw,' she said. 'Out of the window. Just now. It were right overhead. It'm an enormous plane, and Michael says him's pretty certain it be'n't Airborn-manufactured.'

'You think this is it?' Az said. 'It's starting?'

'I's afraid so. Dammit, us is too late.'

'This is what?' asked Dr Ezgadisdaughter-Rusvonson. 'What's starting?'

'Finish up with me,' Az told her, 'quickly. I've a horrible feeling you're going to be needed.'

He was right. Not long after the plane flew over, there was a series of distant explosions. Then, a few minutes later, the first casualties from the rally bombing came limping into the hospital. All available doctors and nurses were summoned down to the emergency clinic, which soon was overrun with the wounded and the dying. Every bed and gurney was occupied, then every chair, till finally there was only floorspace. Groans, gasps and howls of distress filled the air as the hospital personnel rushed

212

around trying to cope with the influx of patients. A triage station was set up by the entrance. Each arrival was assessed and given a numbered sticker according to how severe his or her injuries were, ranging from 1 for *superficial* to 5 for *life-threatening*. Every 5 was seen to immediately by the next available member of staff. The 1's were all but ignored.

More casualties came, and yet more, in a seemingly never-ending tide. Those who hadn't been hurt assisted those who had, supporting or carrying them. Sobbing parents entered with broken children in their arms. Two Patrollers brought in a protestor whose legs had been blown off at the knee. Not long afterwards, two protestors brought in a Patroller, half of whose face was a burned, sticky ruin.

There was blood everywhere. The floors became slick with it. Nobody, whether patient or medic, had clothes that weren't piebald with crimson stains. The stench of the blood was overwhelming, as was the stench of charred flesh. The hospital's stocks of swabs, bandages and cotton gauze ran out. Bedsheets were slashed into strips and used as a substitute.

Az, Cassie and Michael asked Dr Ezgadisdaughter-Rusvonson what they could do to help. The answer was brusque and brutal: 'Stay out of the way.'

The three of them felt as though they had been thrown into the heart of a nightmare. Everywhere they looked, someone was writhing in agony or pleading for medical attention or simply sitting there in a stunned stupor. From what the victims were saying, it was clear the plane had attacked without warning and without mercy. One word that kept cropping up was *massacre*.

And the plane was still out there, still bombarding Prismburg. Every so often a dull *crump* could be heard from somewhere on the other side of the city, evoking a wave of flinches and shrieks inside the hospital.

'I could have stopped this,' Cassie said in hollow tones. Her face was as pale as ash. 'This'm my fault. I could have stopped it.'

'No,' Az told her firmly. 'Not so. You came up here to warn us as soon as you could, and it was already too late by then. Whoever planned this had already set the wheels in motion. It would've happened anyway, whether you tried to prevent it or not.'

'But Michael and I spent time looking for you when us could have—'

'Cassie. Listen. Nothing you could have done would have made any difference. Look me in the eye. Know I'm telling you the truth. You weren't even sure there was going to be an attack. You did everything right. You mustn't punish yourself. Save it for whoever's responsible, this Slamshaft Engineering lot, if it's them.'

'Az is right, Cassie,' Michael chipped in. 'No one's to blame except the people in that plane and the people who sent them up here.'

Cassie nodded, not wholly believing what they were saying, but wanting to. 'There'm others like it,' she said. 'There has to be. Amount of stuff that factory were churning out, it were enough to build a whole fleet of those things.'

'Meaning other sky-cities will be getting the same treatment,' said Az.

'If not now, then soon,' said Cassie. 'Prismburg be the first in line, seeing as it'm the closest to Craterhome.'

'Then there's a chance we could get word out to other sky-cities and they could mount a defence.'

'With what?' exclaimed Michael. 'Against a plane that size, armed to the teeth with explosives and who knows what else – we Airborn just don't have the weaponry.'

'We have to try, Mike!' Az snapped. 'We have to do something.'

'I tell you what *I'm* going to do,' Michael said. 'I'm going to fire up my 'copter and fly to the Sanctum as fast as I can. If one of those planes is headed there, I want Aurora and the baby out of the way before it reaches them.'

'What about *Cerulean*?' Cassie said to Az. 'Her's berthed at Prismburg, be'n't her? If anything can take on that plane, it'm she.'

Az slapped his forehead. 'Brilliant! Yes. Why didn't I think of that? Mike, if you need to go to the Sanctum, fine. But first, take us to *Cerulean*.'

CHAPTER 71

Empty Berth

They hurtled away from Prismburg General in Michael's Vortex V, not at all sad to be out of that place of blood-drenched bedlam.

The sky-city's main streets were thronged with people fleeing in all directions, frantic to get away from the giant plane. Some were in aircraft, others went under their own wingpower. In the atmosphere of panic, collisions happened, and several of the main junctions became gridlocked, but Michael zoomed off down side-streets, weaving to and fro, finding shortcuts by instinct rather than through any knowledge of Prismburg's layout. He took the Vortex V down alleys that were signposted TOO NARROW FOR TRAFFIC ACCESS, whisking the helicopter between walls with just centimetres to spare on either side. His steady touch on the joystick and pedals kept the chopper (and those in it) from harm, although there was one heart-stopping moment when he took a turn a fraction too tightly and the rotors clipped the corner of a building. Metal screeched, the helicopter gave a sickening lurch, and both Az and Cassie thought their lives were over. But Michael corrected, and the rotors, miraculously, stayed in one piece. They could so easily have shattered.

Now and then, through the gaps between buildings, Az caught a glimpse of the plane as it continued to savage the city, dropping bombs on houses and workplaces, destroying indiscriminately. It was, as Cassie had said, enormous, and appeared to be just one huge mass of weaponry, an arsenal with wings. *Cerulean* wouldn't stand a chance against a thing like that, and it was foolish to hope that she might.

Still, someone had to fight back somehow.

At last they reached the edge of Prismburg, emerging not far from the main landing apron. Here, normally, *Cerulean* would be tethered at her mooring mast, surrounded by freight aeroplanes and inter-city airbuses.

215

The mast stood proud from the apron, with nothing attached to it except a windsock, bending and straightening as the city-level air currents tugged at it.

Michael set the Vortex V down. Az stared in dismay at the empty mast. He clambered out of the cockpit, Cassie following.

'Where be her?'

'I don't know.' Az scanned the horizon, shading his eyes with both hands. No sign of the airship. 'Out on a run, most likely. She's due back in service soon, and Captain Qadoschson's been keen to make sure she's in top shape after her refit.'

'So her could be coming back any time?'

'Yeah, maybe.'

Misgivings were gnawing away at Az, however. He couldn't escape the feeling that *Cerulean* was not coming back. What if she had run into that plane somewhere out on the blue yonder? The chances were slim, and yet some dreadful gut instinct was telling him it had happened and that his airship had not survived the encounter.

He felt a hollowness in the pit of his stomach, an ache of sorrow. But he refused to give in to it. He couldn't afford to grieve until he knew for certain that there was something to grieve about.

'Uh-oh,' said Michael, who was peering back the other way, towards the city. 'I don't like the look of *that*.'

Az swung round and saw, coming over the rooftops, a small band of people flying. He couldn't make out, at first, what Michael was so leery about. The silhouetted figures were just winged folk gliding down towards the landing apron. Refugees, most likely, in search of an aircraft that could take them out of Prismburg.

Then he realised.

The wings were rigid. They didn't flap, flex and flutter like real wings. These were people using mechanised wing substitutes, powered by propellers.

Groundlings. From the giant plane.

And they were toting the largest portable crossbows he had ever seen.

'Run!' he yelled to Cassie. 'Back in the chopper!'

But it was too late.

One of the winged Groundlings took aim at the Vortex V and let loose a bolt.

CHAPTER 72

A Case Of Mistaken Identity

Michael throttled up and the Vortex V sprang vertically from the landing apron. The crossbow bolt shot beneath it, striking the very spot where its undercarriage had been resting an instant earlier.

The explosion rattled the helicopter and knocked Az and Cassie off their feet.

A smoking crater, one metre across, showed what would have become of Michael and his chopper had he not taken off when he did.

Another of the winged Groundlings fired at the Vortex V, and missed.

Michael put the Vortex V into a hover, looking down at his brother and Cassie. Az, still sprawled on the apron asphalt, could see the anguish etched into his face. He knew what was going through Michael's mind.

He jerked his head, indicating that Michael should leave. No way could Michael swoop back down and pick him and Cassie up. One of the Groundlings would hit the Vortex V for sure. He mustn't risk his life for theirs. He should make for the Sanctum.

Michael nodded, understanding, and swung the helicopter sideways.

A crossbow bolt zinged past his twin tail rotors, arcing out into space.

Then, nose tilting down, the Vortex V sped off. Within seconds it had become a dot on the horizon, no bigger than an insect. A couple of the Groundlings raced after it in pursuit, but soon turned back. It was clear they hadn't a hope of catching it.

The other Groundlings alighted near Az and Cassie, switching off the propellers on their backs by means of control pads mounted on brass wristbands. Pressing another button on the same control pads caused their wings to fold in half, then swivel on hinges to tuck away neatly behind them.

The Groundlings were clad in leather uniforms, padded for warmth and festooned with studs and buckles. In the air, they had been quite graceful. Now, on foot, they waddled, burdened with the weight of their wings, clothing and equipment, not least the crossbows. They stomped towards Az and Cassie, creaking and clanking. Az struggled to his feet and helped Cassie up. Side by side they faced the approaching men warily. With the helmets they were wearing and the tinted goggles, it was impossible to know what the men were thinking, what their intentions were. To be on the safe side Az shifted his weight onto his back foot, not entirely but just enough that he quickly could go into a full defensive stance if necessary. Cassie looked defiant. A knot formed in the skin between her eyebrows, the telltale sign that she was angry and spoiling for a fight.

The Groundlings halted in a semicircle around the two of them.

For a moment no one spoke.

Then one of the Groundlings said, 'Be you OK?'

'Huh?' said Az, with a blink.

'That Airborn. Him in that whirly-rotor thing. Looked like him were giving you grief till us drove he off.'

Groundlings, thought Az. *They think we're both Groundlings.*

'Um, yeah,' he said. 'Him were, sort of, buzzing we in that machine of his.' Az's mimicry of the Groundling dialect wasn't perfect, he knew, but it was passable, he thought. Hoped. 'Him must've reckoned us was with you. Part of the attack, I mean.'

'Thanks for scaring he away,' Cassie chimed in, shooting a quick frown at Az. 'Otherwise him'd've done we a mischief, straight up.'

'Straight up,' Az echoed.

'You be'n't out of danger yet,' said the Groundling. 'As long as this thing be going on, other of the Airborn be'n't going to like seeing you. Us has orders to evacuate all Groundlings us comes across. That applies to you two. You won't be safe unless you'm back on the ground.'

'No, us is fine—' Az began to say, but Cassie broke in.

'You'm right,' she said to the man. 'It'm far too risky up here for the likes of we.'

Now it was Az's turn to frown at *her*. Cassie ignored him.

'You, and you,' the Groundling said, gesturing to two of his cohorts. 'Arthur. Lenny. You's in charge of these two. Take they to the elevators. The rest of you lot, on with business.' He glanced around the landing apron. 'Let's get to doing what us came here to do. All these lovely planes, waiting for the Airborn to use they to get away. Can't have that, now can us?'

The others chortled. No, they certainly couldn't have that.

'Scrap metal time,' said the Groundling.

CHAPTER 73

Scrap Metal Time

As Az and Cassie were escorted away, a programme of systematic aircraft annihilation began. The Groundling Drones went from plane to plane, loosing off bolts at each in turn. The landing apron shuddered underfoot as fuel tanks erupted and the planes went up in flames. An airbus disintegrated, spewing glass and hot metal all around it. A Metatronco Pelican-class goods transporter cracked in two like some vast, brittle egg, shooting a ball of fire into the sky. The Drones whooped and high-fived one another as they claimed each new mechanical victim. Who knew that war could be so much fun?

The two men who had been entrusted with looking after Az and Cassie were resentful that they weren't able to join in.

'Why should them have all the jollies?' grumbled one, as they traipsed off across the apron, back into the city. 'While us gets stuck playing babysitter.'

'Not to worry,' said the other. 'There'll be plenty more stuff to blow up when us is finished with these kids.'

'Let's just ditch they,' said the first. 'You two can find your own way to the elevators, right?'

'Of course us can,' said Az.

'No, Arthur,' said the other Groundling. This one was Lenny, presumably. 'Us has a job to do and us is going to do it. Us can't leave these youngsters to walk through the city unprotected. It be'n't proper.'

'Can't us *fly* them instead? I doesn't know if I can walk much further with all this clobber on. My back be killing I.'

Az tensed. If the men picked him and Cassie up to fly with them, they would immediately realise that he didn't have the correct weight and solidity to be a Groundling.

'The Drone packs doesn't have the power,' replied Lenny. 'Them's – what'm the word? – calibrated for just the weight of one person.'

Az was relieved. Cassie's expression told him the same thoughts had crossed her mind.

'Nope, us is walking and that'm that,' Lenny went on. 'This'm the right way, yes?' he asked Cassie. 'The way you came?'

'As best I can remember.'

Az was curious to know what Cassie's strategy was here. She surely was only pretending to want to go down in the elevators, which was why he was content to follow her lead. She must have some secondary plan. Perhaps, on her signal, they would give the men the slip and run away.

'So, what accent be that of yours?' said Arthur to Az. 'I doesn't recognise it.'

'Him's from the Pale Uplands,' Cassie put in quickly, before Az had a chance to reply. 'A cousin of mine. Him's come to stay for a fortnight, and I thought, you know, let's take a nice trip up to Prismburg, show he what a sky-city looks like. Couldn't have picked a worse day for it, could us?'

'Too true,' said Arthur with a mirthless chuckle. 'Be'n't that so, Lenny?'

Lenny was giving Az a queer, inquisitive look. 'Uplander, eh? Bit of a hunter, then. The outdoorsy type.'

Az shrugged, meanwhile frantically sieving his brain for nuggets of information about the Pale Uplands and the people who lived that remote, mountainous region of the Westward Territories. He recalled that the Grubdollars had had a run-in with an Uplander Deacon while he himself had been tackling Naoutha Nisrocsdaughter, and that that man had been a certifiable lunatic, a savage who'd somehow managed to acquire a veneer of civilisation. Beyond that, he didn't know much about the Uplands at all.

'Don't look very outdoorsy to I, though, I must say,' Lenny continued. The scepticism was clear on his face now.

'It be'n't all wattle huts and caves up there,' Cassie said. 'Them has towns, remember. Big ones. Cragpass. Snowside Halt. Ebbriver Island, which'm a city in all but name. That'm where my cousin be from, actually, Ebbriver Island.'

'Whisky,' Az blurted. He'd remembered that Uplanders liked whisky. A lot. 'My, erm, da works in a distillery. Owns one, actually.'

Lenny said, 'Him must be pretty well-to-do then, by Uplander standards.'

'Oh, him be.'

'That'd explain it, then. Uplanders and their whisky – it'm mother's milk to they. A fellow'd never get poor, brewing that lot's favourite tipple, and his son would never be the sort to have to go out and fend for himself in the wilderness.'

'Don't suppose your da could fix we up with a free bottle or two, hey?' said Arthur with a wink. 'As a reward for, you know, this. We helping you.'

'I'll see what I can do.'

'Send they to Arthur Toothmeat, care of the Unemployment Bureau, Sixth Borough, Craterhome. That'm the sure way them'll get to me, being as I's otherwise what you might call "of no fixed abode".'

'Mental note made,' Az said, tapping his temple with a forefinger.

Phew. They'd pulled that one off. Cassie, though she'd been trying to help him, had dropped him right in it with that remark about him hailing from the Uplands, but between them they'd got Arthur and Lenny believing it was true. It helped that neither man was particularly brimming with brains.

'Your plane's not bombing any more,' Cassie observed. Their little party of four was crossing a footbridge that led down, in zigzag stages, to Prismburg's lower levels. The explosions had ceased and now the city seemed to be holding its breath, waiting for whatever came next.

'First phase, the softening-up process, be over,' said Lenny. 'Now it'm property damage and spreading fear among the population.'

'I reckon you's managed that well enough already. Everyone here be scared out of their wits. What'm the point of all this, may I ask?'

'The point?' said Arthur. 'You means apart from all the lovely loot us is getting paid?'

'Money?' said Az, aghast. 'You're—' He corrected himself. 'You'm waging war against the Airborn for *money*?'

'Us be'n't doing it out of the love of our hearts, that'm for sure. There be a hefty wage on offer for taking part in this. Twenty-five thousand notes. A princely sum. For most of we, that'm a year's salary.'

'More,' said Lenny. 'Although maybe not for your da, boy.'

'To kill people?' said Az.

'I's not personally killed anybody,' Arthur said. 'Though that'm not to say I wouldn't if the conditions was right. If any of the Airborn retaliate and I think my life be in danger, I'll happily use this to defend myself.' He held up his crossbow.

'The point,' Lenny said, with the patient air of a teacher explaining something simple but true to a class of pupils, 'be that someone has decided to take a stand against the Airborn. I's a little less mercenary than Arthur about the whole situation. My take on it be: someone's done what our government'd never have the nerve to do, and that be rise up and learn these snooty so-and-so's up here a lesson. Them's used we and

221

abused we for centuries, and them still think them's in charge even after all the changes that'm happened this past couple of years. Finally someone's had the backbone to get things organised and knock the Airborn off their pedestals.'

'That someone being . . . ?' said Cassie.

'Dominic Slamshaft, of course.'

'Ah.'

'You knows who him be, doesn't you?'

'Who don't? Playboy industrialist, self-made gazillionaire, makes engines parts that doesn't work, bald as a billiard ball.'

'All that and a true visionary,' said Lenny. 'And a true man of the people, I'd say, for all his wealth. Him saw what needed doing and set about doing it, never mind the expense and the logistics. Him knew us Groundlings needed liberating from the tyranny of the Airborn, and took the step that everyone else were too lily-livered to take – except the Humanists.'

'Ah, the Humanists,' said Arthur, with a sly grin. 'Them always come into your conversation, don't them, Lenny? Soon enough it always comes back round to the Humanists.'

'Nothing to be ashamed of, Humanism. I admit it. I'm a Humanist of the old school. I believes in their ideals through and through.'

Az had a hard time masking his disgust. Cassie too. Her lip curled and the knot between her eyebrows was back. Both she and Az, of course, had good reasons to despise the Humanist movement.

'And Dominic Slamshaft,' said Lenny grandly, 'be a Humanist in all but name. You marks my words, when this'm over, him'll be hailed as a hero, a champion of the people, and maybe even the man who single-handedly revived Humanism.'

'By bringing the Airborn to their knees?' said Cassie.

'Yup. That'm what this be about,' said Lenny. 'Simply that.'

'And that be Slamshaft's motivation? That be why him started this?'

'Him may have other reasons, but from what us has been told, him's after Groundling freedom, no more, no less.'

'So, naturally him's up here right now. Leading the charge. Fighting for freedom right alongside all you lot.'

Lenny hesitated. 'No. I doesn't think so.'

'Nope,' Arthur confirmed. 'Him saw we off on our way this morning but stayed on the ground himself.'

'Some freedom fighter,' Cassie said, scornfully enough to raise Az's eyebrows, and Lenny's as well.

'You may scoff, girl,' Lenny said, 'but I still believes he to be a great man. So what if he be'n't with we in person? He be with we in spirit, straight up. Now, how much further to go? Be those elevators close?'

'Not far,' said Cassie.

'Right,' said Lenny, curtly. 'Well, that'm enough jabbering. Let's get there.'

CHAPTER 74

Evacuees

Throughout the rest of the journey to the supply arrival depot Az kept expecting Cassie to make her move. He was all set to back her up in whatever way he could.

The crossbows worried him. Would Arthur and Lenny shoot if their two young charges sprinted away? Maybe not. But even if they didn't shoot, with those wings of theirs they could easily overtake someone on foot, even someone running. The very act of breaking away from them would arouse their suspicions.

Could he and Cassie overpower them instead? Well, it was a possibility. If he'd been with Mr Mordadson rather than Cassie, he'd have felt it was more than a possibility – a dead cert. Cassie, however, scrappy though she was, hadn't had combat training.

What *was* her plan?

Her plan, it turned out, was to let Arthur and Lenny take them all the way to depot and inside. There, they ran into a few more of the winged Groundlings and a group of Groundling tourists who were being evacuated too.

'Couple more here for the elevators,' said Lenny, ushering Az and Cassie towards the huddle of anxious tourists. 'Take they down with you, will you?'

'Yes. Yes, of course,' said a stout, matronly-looking woman. She took charge of the two new arrivals, putting a flabby arm tenderly around each. 'I'll look after them, leave it with I.'

'Don't forget that whisky, eh, mate?' Arthur said to Az.

'I won't,' Az said.

'Come on, let's *all* get out of here,' the matronly woman said, steering him and Cassie towards a staircase. 'What a terrible business this be. Terrible! I's a good mind to complain. Couldn't somebody have warned us in advance? I mean, up us comes, just a plain old sightseeing trip, and next thing us knows, us is in the middle of a war zone. Our own people attacking the Airborn, and no one told we. Somebody's got to take responsibility for this . . .'

On she prattled, as the group of evacuees shuffled hurriedly down the staircase. Az glanced over his shoulder to see all of the winged Ground-lings, Arthur and Lenny included, head out of the depot exit. Outside, they unfolded their wings and powered up their propellers. It seemed they couldn't wait to get up in the air again and start wreaking more havoc. Whether they'd signed up with Slamshaft's army for money or for principles, beneath it all they shared a common thirst for wanton destruction.

As the evacuees neared the elevator chamber, Az and Cassie disengaged themselves from the matronly woman. They drew back slightly from the others, for a quiet conversation.

'I can't believe you tried to speak like a Groundling,' Cassie said.

'I can't believe you told them I was an Uplander,' Az retorted.

'I were trying to save your bacon. You could've just talked ordinary, you know. Us doesn't all speak dialect.'

'It seemed like a good idea at the time. Anyway, it worked. What I want to know is, what now? I've gone along this far. What's the plan? We're not going down in the elevators, are we?' This wasn't a question.

'Matter of fact, us is.'

'Huh? What? But . . . In case you haven't noticed, Cassie. War? Giant plane? Invaders with wings on? City under siege? Hello? Ring a bell, any of that?'

'And how, precisely,' Cassie said, 'does you propose us deal with it? By staying up here and taking on a small army, just the two of we?'

'Well, no. Obviously not. But we could help organise a fight-back. And then there's Mr Mordadson. If we can—'

'You doesn't trust he any more. For all us knows, him could even be behind this whole affair.'

'No!'

'No? If him's on Lord Urironson's side, and Lord Urisonson's been helping to destabilise things up here . . . Join the dots, Az.'

'I just can't believe it of him.'

'But you doesn't *know*, does you? So Mr Mordadson be'n't a safe bet, not for now.'

'All right, then we could get to the Sanctum. Join Michael there. Or . . . my parents! By all that's high and bright, I forgot about my parents. High Haven will be under attack too. That's where we have to go.'

'How? You has a pilot's licence?'

'No. But Michael's taught me the basics. I know my way around a cockpit. We'll grab a plane and—'

'Them's not leaving any planes intact, Az, remember?' Cassie grasped him by the shoulders, turning him square-on to her. 'Listen to I. Just listen. Be realistic. Up here, us can't do any good. This part of the problem be a part us can't fix. If there'm going to be any resistance, if a fight-back happens, the Alar Patrol will organise it, or people'll just do it for themselves.'

'So, what, we just turn tail and scarper?' Az spat out. 'We leave everyone else to get on with it while we slouch away like a pair of right plucking cowards? No way. That's not an option, Cassie.'

'I agree. It be'n't. But what if, instead, us tackles this from another angle? Us can't take on a whole army and win, no. But us could maybe take on the *head* of an army and win. And us knows exactly who that be now.'

It dawned on Az what she was getting at. 'You mean . . .'

'I mean, down there on the ground be the mastermind behind this whole repulsive mess. Dominic Slamshaft. Stop he, and us stops the war.'

CHAPTER 75

Interview Room #2

Inspector Treadwell sat across the table from Den Grubdollar, studying him hard. They were in the confines of Interview Room #2, a white-tiled chamber in the basement of Craterhome police station, not far from the cells where suspects and other offenders were detained. A fanlight window at ceiling height let in some illumination through its grimy panes. An electric bulb on a plaited flex feebly did its bit too.

Treadwell puffed on his pipe, whose smoke contributed to the hazy dimness of the room. He had been talking to Den Grubdollar for an hour. Something niggled him about Den's story. Something did not add up. The more the man insisted he was telling the truth, the more Treadwell became certain that he was lying. He claimed he had coerced his family into helping him recapture their murk-comber. This did not jibe with what the two sons, Fletcher and Robert, had already said. In fact, each of them swore blind that the whole thing had been *his* idea.

So the family members were protecting each other. Treadwell was not surprised. He was touched by their self-sacrificing loyalty to one another.

What he did not understand was why, when fleeing the scene of the crime, the Grubdollars had headed for Granite Plains rather than their hometown of Grimvale. Den Grubdollar insisted it was to throw the cops off the scent. Treadwell was sure there was more to it.

The impression he was forming of the man in front of him was that he was a decent citizen, gruff but fundamentally honest, strong and dependable, a fine father who had suffered his share of setbacks and tragedies but survived. Den had mentioned in passing that he had lost his wife a few years ago and more recently his eldest son. Treadwell had also gleaned, in the course of the interview so far, that Den and his family had frequent dealings with the Airborn. Toby Nimblenick had indicated as much too.

He decided it was a line of enquiry worth pursuing.

'Going back to something you said earlier,' he said, 'you was using your murk-comber to take Airborn visitors on tours of the ground, be that right?'

'Straight up. Till *Bertha* were confiscated from we.'

'So you's got connections with they up there?'

Den looked evasive. 'So to speak. Why'm you asking? Be it relevant? I's told you a dozen times, this'm got nothing to do with anyone but I. I doesn't know why you even be bothering with these questions. I's come clean. You's got I bang to rights. Now drag I before the magistrate, get I sentenced, send I to jail. That'm all there be to it.'

'No, it be'n't,' said Treadwell. 'You drove to Granite Plains, then my men met you coming back and you was alone. I know you had three offspring with you originally, a daughter as well as the two sons us has in custody. You left her at Granite Plains, didn't you? And there'm a sky-city there. So I's reckoning her's gone up above the clouds.'

It was an informed guess, and Den's reaction, a tiny unconscious flinch, told Treadwell he had hit the mark with it.

'With these Airborn connections of yours,' he went on, 'it would make sense that her took the elevator to – which'm be the one above Granite Plains? Pearl Town, that'm it. Her went up there in order to escape arrest. A novel way of going about it, I has to say. You can't get out of police jurisdiction much better than by travelling to a different *world*, now can you? Only trouble be, as us all knows, what goes up must come down. Her can't stay there for ever. Even if she has Airborn friends who'll shelter she, her'll not last much longer than a day or so. It weren't exactly a foolproof plan, eh?'

Den shook his head, appearing rueful. 'That be pretty much how I'd describe everything us has been up to lately. Yes, I were hoping my girl Cassie would find sanctuary above the clouds. But you'm right, it weren't ever going to work.'

Again, Treadwell sensed a hollow ring to Den's words. His policeman's instincts were well honed. After years on the force, exposed to criminals, people who lied as naturally as they breathed, he had an ear for false-hood. He could hear it like a musician with perfect pitch could hear someone singing out of tune.

His pipe had gone out. He made an elaborate fuss of relighting it, taking his time. Silence could be a useful interrogation tool. Often it posed a question more eloquently and forcefully than speech did.

'Do it matter why her went up to Pearl Town?' Den said, jumping into the hole Treadwell had left in the conversation.

'Seeing as you's just asked that,' came the reply, 'then yes. Because, you see, Mr Grubdollar, ever since I got involved in this case yesterday, I's been catching glimpses of something that everyone's been avoiding talking about. It'm as though there be a big gorilla in the corner and nobody's said, "By the way, Inspector, there'm a big gorilla in the corner, did you realise?" In this instance, the gorilla seems to be made up of two parts. One is you leaving your daughter at Granite Plains. I be'n't buying your explanation for that at all. The other is—'

He was interrupted by a sudden loud commotion in the corridor outside. There was scuffling and the sounds of several people grunting, shouting and swearing. He went and knocked on the door. The constable on guard outside opened it. Peering out, Treadwell saw a group of police officers grappling with a large, rowdy man who was evidently very drunk. They were attempting to cram the man through the doorway of a nearby cell and he was resisting with all his might, which seemed quite considerable given that there were seven policemen and only one of him and they were still having trouble getting him where they wanted him to go. As Treadwell watched, the drunkard shrugged off all seven of them with a single flex of his meaty arms and made a bid for freedom. They leapt on him again, a dark blue swarm, and one of them produced a truncheon and coshed him a number of times on the skull. This quietened the drunkard down and, although he continued to fight, his efforts were weaker. The coppers were able to manhandle him into the cell without too much difficulty. Before they slammed the door on him, they took it in turns to give him a few punches and kicks while he lay sprawled on the floor, still stunned from the truncheon blows. Then they gathered outside and compared bruises. One by one they noticed Treadwell glaring at them. Under his scowl of disapproval, they filed off along the corridor sullenly.

'What were all that about?' Den asked as Treadwell re-entered the Interview Room.

Treadwell grimaced. 'The wrong arm of the Law.' He sat back down.

'So, two parts,' said Den.

'Hmm?'

'This gorilla of yours – it were made up of two parts. You's said one. What'm the other?'

'Ah. Right. Well now, I have it on good authority that you and Slamshaft Engineering be'n't exactly the best of pals.'

'That'm so.'

'And with you taking a murk-comber off they, a murk-comber them legitimately bought, even if you still considered it your own – well, them'd be all for prosecuting you for that, no? Wouldn't you say? And also for the property damage you caused.'

'Stands to reason,' said Den. 'Why, has them told you them doesn't want *Bertha*? Us can keep she after all? Everything's forgiven?' He snorted a laugh. 'Yeah, right.'

'As a matter of fact, them *has* said that, all but.'

Den gaped. 'Straight up? You mean it? No, you'm kidding. You's got to be kidding.'

'Do I look like a kidder?'

'The average cop'm got a strange sense of humour.'

'I like to think I be'n't the average cop,' said Treadwell. 'I spoke to the site manager at the Slamshaft plant yesterday and him were quite clear. The company has no interest in taking legal proceedings against you and your family. His precise words was, "It wouldn't be in Slamshaft's best interests, I feel."'

'Huh,' said Den, ponderingly.

'My reaction too. Why would him say that, I wonder, Mr Grubdollar.'

Den looked blank.

But not completely blank.

'You knows, doesn't you?' said Treadwell.

Den raised his gaze, so that he and the inspector were staring levelly into each other's eyes. 'Us may be off the hook here, me and my kids. Be that correct? Be it at least a possibility?'

'It be. Depending on what you can tell I.'

'You'll let my sons go? And you won't arrest my daughter? I has your word on that? If I co-operate?'

'No guarantees. But I's got to say, if you can give me any help on this front, it be very likely that the Grubdollars, all of you, could get off without a mark on your records. I should even be able to swing it that you don't get done for smashing up six police cars.'

'Straight up?'

'Those morons from Granite Plains shouldn't have used them against a murk-comber. Them should've known better. The damage were as much their fault as yours. Or so I could argue.'

For the first time since they'd met, Treadwell saw Den smile. Even with only three teeth, it was a warm, winning grin.

'And us gets *Bertha* to keep?'

'Your murk-comber? Like I said, no guarantees, but I'll see what I can do. So, what does you have for I? What earthly reason would Slamshaft Engineering have for not wanting I to lock you up and throw away the key?'

Den marshalled his thoughts. 'If it'm what I think it be, then—'

There was another interruption, this time in the form of someone hammering on the Interview Room door. Before Treadwell could utter a *come in*, a constable barged into the room.

'Sir!' he gasped, out of breath. 'Sir!'

'What'm up, Kindlebinding?'

'Sir, Chief Superintendent Coldriser needs to see you right away. All senior officers to report to his office immediately.'

'This'm him wanting to share another of his administrative brainwaves with we?'

'No idea, sir. I only know it'm utmost urgency, sir.'

Treadwell gave a hapless, weary shrug. 'Then I'd better go. Can't ignore a summons from the Super. Kindlebinding, see Mr Grubdollar here back to his cell. Apologies, Mr Grubdollar. I'll be back as soon as I can to resume this intriguing chat of ours.'

Den happily allowed himself to be escorted to his cell. As Constable Kindlebinding closed and bolted the door, Den stretched himself out on the hard, narrow bunk where, last night, he had hardly slept a wink. He laced his hands behind his head and let out a relieved, contented sigh.

Free.

Without a mark on your records.

For once, the Grubdollars had caught a break. Their luck had turned. Den couldn't wait to be reunited with Fletcher and Robert, and Cassie too – not forgetting *Bertha*, of course. It would happen soon, he was sure.

Incredibly, it looked as if everything was going to work out all right for them.

CHAPTER 76

A Whole New Kind Of War

The Vortex V probably broke several speed records, and certainly several air traffic laws, on its journey from Prismburg to the Silver Sanctum. Michael pushed the helicopter as hard as it would go, meanwhile watching the needle on the fuel gauge creep steadily round towards Empty. He refused to stop and fill up at a way-station. He couldn't afford a delay of even just a few minutes.

He was flying on fumes by the time the Sanctum appeared on the horizon. The Vortex V's engine was sputtering and the 'TANK EMPTY' light glared from the dashboard.

The engine cut out with less than a hundred metres left to go. A buzzer sounded the alarm. Michael paid it no heed, coasting towards the landing apron on momentum alone, tilting the now-inert rotors in order to use them as a crude kind of rudder. There was a vacant spot between two airbuses. Aiming for it, he yelled out a warning to the airbus drivers who were standing having a natter in the very space where he intended to put down. They leaped clear just in time.

The chopper came down with a bang. Bounced. Slithered. Scraped against one of the airbuses' wings. Skidded to a standstill.

Michael was out of the cockpit in an instant. With the airbus drivers' angry shouts ringing in his ears, he took off and raced towards the tower where Aurora's apartment was.

Halfway there, a thought struck him. He diverted from his course, making for a different tower altogether. It pained him to do this, but he knew it was the right thing. Before Aurora, there was someone else he should see.

Mr Mordadson.

Az had been uncertain as to whether or not Mr Mordadson could be trusted. But, under the circumstances, Michael felt he had a duty to alert

Mr Mordadson about the threat that was on its way. Mr Mordadson could then do with that information as he pleased.

He burst into Mr Mordadson's apartment via the balcony windows, just as the Sanctum emissary was in the middle of taking a shower. Mr Mordadson, hearing someone come noisily in, charged out of the bathroom with a towel around his waist, dripping with soap suds, ready to repel the intruder by force.

'There'd better be a damn good explanation for this,' he growled, when he saw who the intruder was.

'Believe me, there is,' said Michael. 'But first, would you put that down?'

Mr Mordadson lowered the long, wooden-handled scrubbing brush he was brandishing (it was the only weapon that had come to hand in the bathroom).

'So?' he snapped.

'I've just left Az,' Michael began, 'and—'

'Az. He isn't a captive any more. He got free.'

'Yes.'

A hint of a smile played around Mr Mordadson's lips. 'Good lad.'

'You mean you left that shard of glass there on purpose?'

'Did he think that I didn't?'

'He wasn't sure.'

'I don't blame him. How is he?'

'Could be worse. But look, Az isn't the reason I'm here.'

Briefly Michael outlined recent events at Prismburg. When he was finished, a scowling Mr Mordadson swore loudly. 'Of course,' he said. 'Pluck it, of course.'

'You knew this was going to happen?'

'No. But in the light of it, certain other facts make sense. That conniving old buzzard. Damn him. I thought he was just playing one game, but oh no . . . Two at once, and one of them nothing more than a ruse. He tricked me. Idiot that I am, he tricked *me.*'

'Sorry?' said Michael. 'Who are we talking about?'

'Never mind. Let me get dried off and dressed, and then tell me more. Tell me everything you saw. I want to know about the Groundlings' numbers, weaponry, equipment, anything you can recall, anything.'

Minutes later, Michael was describing the bombs that had hit Prismburg, and the planes that had dropped them, and the flying Groundlings with their back-mounted wings and their explosive crossbow bolts. As he spoke, the set of Mr Mordadson's jaw grew tighter and grimmer. A tendon twitched in his cheek. His wings quivered.

'We don't stand a chance,' Mr Mordadson said eventually. 'Whoever organised this knew exactly our level of strategic defensive capability and knew what was needed to outmatch it. We've waged wars in our own way in the past, fighting our own kind with our own methods, but this is a whole new kind of war. Resisting *this* enemy would be like a pigeon trying to resist an eagle.'

'You're saying we should just roll over and let them win?'

'On the contrary.' Mr Mordadson's eyes blazed behind the lenses of his spectacles, an older pair which he kept for spare. 'I'd say it was imperative that we do everything in our power *not* to let them win. Now, you're sure one of those planes is on its way here?'

'I spotted a couple of them in the distance when I was about five kilometres out of Prismburg. I gave them a wide berth, but it looked to me like they were on the same bearing as I was. There's no other sky-city in this direction except Azuropolis.'

'One plane for Azuropolis, one for the Sanctum.'

'I'd imagine so.'

'OK. The good news is, owing to our heightened security situation we have nearly three whole squadrons of Patrollers billeted here right now. The bad news is, this is a small city and the majority of its inhabitants are somewhat on the elderly side. We don't have that many able-bodied young men and women to augment the Patrol's numbers. Nor do we have weapons that are in any way comparable to the Groundlings'. Our main advantage, perhaps our only advantage, is that thanks to you, Michael, we have advance notice of the attack. How long do you reckon before one of the planes you saw reaches us?'

'At the rate they were going, we've at least an hour. Closer on two. They're not what you might call nippy.'

'It's not much but it's something. All right, here's what I want you to do . . .'

'Whoa,' said Michael, stopping him. 'I'm not doing anything except making sure Aurora and the baby are out of harm's way.'

'No, Michael, wrong.' There was iron in Mr Mordadson's voice, sheer implacable command. 'You're going to do precisely as I tell you. You're going to round up the seniormost residents, along with the more vulnerable juniors, in which category I definitely include your wife in her present condition. You're going to get them to take refuge in the refectory and you're going to see to it that that place is barricaded thoroughly on the inside. The refectory has the fewest windows of any large enclosed space in this city, and thus the fewest vulnerable points. It's where they'll be safest.'

'Can't we just ship them out of the city?'

'To where? The entire realm is under assault, and we can't have people just circling around in airbuses with nowhere to go, nowhere to land.'

'Send them down to the ground then.'

'There isn't time. Besides, it's possible the Groundlings could go for them while they're in the elevators, before they even reach the cloud cover. No, everyone stays, and we defend the Silver Sanctum with everything we've got. If there's one sky-city that must be protected at all costs, it's this one.'

CHAPTER 77

Redspire's Expiry

Prismburg was the first sky-city hit by the Cloudbusters and Drones, by virtue of its proximity to Slamshaft's base of operations in the Relentless Desert. After the initial bombardment, and while Az and Cassie were descending in one of the elevators with the other evacuees, the Drones combed the streets, wreaking havoc wherever they went. They were under orders to keep loss of life to a minimum but few of them found this much of a restriction. The mass murder that had taken place outside the Alar Patrol HQ seemed to have opened up a void in their souls. They unleashed their crossbow bolts indiscriminately, laughing as Airborn scattered in panic and died in annihilating bursts of nitroglycerine.

Prismburg Patrollers, those who had escaped the bombing, launched a series of counter-offensives across the city. Incensed civilians did as well. It was a fierce and spirited retaliation, if disorganised and sporadic. Casualties were inflicted on the Groundlings. Many a Drone met his end on the point of a Patroller's lance or was run down and maimed by an Airborn piloting a private plane. But these were small victories in a generally one-sided conflict. The battle's outcome – Prismburg subjugated by Slamshaft's forces – was never really in doubt.

Second on the attack list was Redspire. Although a far-flung outpost of the Airborn realm, from the Groundling invaders' point of view Redspire wasn't actually that remote. One Cloudbuster set off on a trajectory completely opposite from that of the others, sailed above the rugged wastes of the Relentless Desert, and shortly was homing in on the rebel sky-city. On board, there was a keen sense of anticipation. The deeds of Redspire's pirates had been an affront to all Groundlings. These were Airborn who had openly plundered Groundling industrial sites and openly killed innocent, hard-working Groundling men. Among the Drones on the planes there were several Westward Oil Enterprises roughnecks who had lost friends and colleagues in the pirates' raids. Were they harbouring a grudge? Were they looking for some kind of revenge? No question, they were. Where Redspire was concerned, the motive for attack wasn't so much invasion as reprisal.

At Redspire it had started out as a typical day. After a slow wake-up the city had shaken off its collective hangover and was, in a bleary manner, getting down to work. Shops were open. So were bars. People flew from place to place with slow, desultory flaps of their wings, many still wishing they hadn't had that last glass of wine the night before and had got to bed a little bit earlier. Redspirians seldom regretted anything except their own self-indulgences. They certainly did not regret the achievements of those local buccaneer heroes, Naoutha Nisrocsdaughter and the crew of *Behemoth*.

The Cloudbuster would soon give them cause to revise that opinion.

Bombs.

Bombs fell in waves.

Fell incessantly.

Redspire's red spires shattered and burst. Debris rained down onto plazas. Bridges quaked and cracked apart. Buildings caught fire. Smoke unfurled into the sky.

The pounding onslaught went on and on, till Redspire was a burning ruin. Whole sections of the city broke off and went tumbling through the clouds, smashing into the plain below with a titanic impact. Smouldering chunks of rubble collected around the base of its column, embedded in the desert surface. The column itself shuddered and groaned. Fine fissures began to appear in its reinforced concrete, widening and spreading like wrinkles in skin.

Finally the Cloudbuster withdrew, its fuselage emptied of ordnance, its work done. Now it was the Drones' turn. They buzzed over the shattered sky-city. Everywhere, there were scenes of confusion. Panicking Airborn flocked this way and that. A few of the more level-headed ones were attempting to put out the fires, fetching water from municipal fountains to hurl onto the flames – a noble but vain effort. Others were combing the wreckage of buildings, doing their best to rescue people trapped inside. The great majority, however, charged about frantically. Amid the devastation they were looking for leadership, someone they could unite around, someone who would tell them what to do. This being Redspire, no such person existed. Even the Alar Patrol wasn't able to muster itself to take action.

The Drones savoured the moment. It was almost a pleasure, taking potshots at the milling winged rabble. These Airborn, they weren't so high-and-mighty after all, were they? Look at them scatter! Look at the abject fear on their faces!

And all the while, the cracks in the column were deepening and multiplying. Fatal harm had been done to the integrity of Redspire's structure. The city had just minutes left.

The Drones swirled and harried. The Redspirians dodged and died.

Then – a shivering in the air. The fires guttered. The pillars of smoke hiccupped in their flow.

There was a shriek, an immense, grinding, unnatural sound.

Redspire, what remained of Redspire, tilted a fraction of a degree from true. More debris was dislodged from the damaged buildings and came crashing down onto people's heads.

The shriek came again.

This was the death cry of a sky-city, and it was echoed by a thousand Airborn throats. They could sense it. Everyone who lived in Redspire knew, even in the midst of all this madness and murder, that a deeper and more awful disaster was on its way. The entire city shifted again beneath them, around them, and the sheer *wrongness* of this sent a chill right through to their bones.

At the apex of the column, where it intersected with the city's underside, a slab of concrete the size of a house sheared off and fell. Another, smaller slab came loose. Then another, and another.

Then, all at once, the entire top segment of the column crumbled and gave way, and with it went Redspire.

A torturously laborious falling.

Vast outward billowings of dust.

Spire tipping against spire.

Vertical becoming angled then horizontal.

Like a gigantic flower blooming, but in reverse.

Sucking down people with it.

No escape, either for Redspirian or for Drone.

A clenching fist dragging down countless victims into the clouds.

Louder than earthquakes.

A cataclysm to match anything the Great Cataclysm had had to offer.

Redspire collapsed and plunged to the ground, and the only survivors, the only witnesses of its demise, were those who were also the architects of its doom, the Cloudbuster crew, who stared in frank astonishment at the apocalypse they had helped bring about.

CHAPTER 78

Residents In The Refectory

The refectory was a bustle of anxious bodies. Michael had done his best in the time available. Aurora performed a quick head-count and estimated the tally of senior Sanctum residents at just under two hundred, give or take. Added to that total were several members of the serving staff, old retainers who had worked at the Sanctum all their lives, along with three junior female residents – four, counting Aurora – who were at various stages of pregnancy, and one junior male resident, a skilled harpist who had been blind since birth. Two hundred voices now burbled worriedly. Two hundred pairs of wings flickered and flashed in agitation.

In accordance with Mr Mordadson's orders, Michael set about barricading the room. He enlisted the help of several of the more robust-looking lords and ladies in raising several of the refectory's large, heavy oak tables to the windows. They held the tables flat against the window frames while he used a hammer and some ten-centimetre carpentry nails to fix them in place. One by one the windows were blocked up, and the refectory, normally dazzling with all its myriad of candles and mirror-like metallic surfaces, grew dark.

More tables were secured across the passageway that gave access to and from the kitchens. This left just one way in or out of the refectory, the main entrance, a pair of huge, sturdy steel doors which could be fastened by a hinged locking bar. The doors stood ajar for the time being.

The dimming of the light and the sense of being enclosed had a subduing effect on everyone. A hush fell over the room, the rumble of disquiet muting to murmurs and whispers.

That was when Lady Aanfieldsdaughter spoke up.

'Michael,' she said, 'I think perhaps that now is the time to tell us what's going on. You said Mr Mordadson wants us all in here, you said you're acting on his authority and it's for our own good, and we've all gone along with that – but we deserve an explanation, at the very least.'

There were echoes of assent around the room.

'Is it Feather First!?' said another senior resident. 'Another assassination attempt?'

'Erm, not quite,' said Michael. 'It's like this . . .'

'War,' said Mr Mordadson, who at that moment came gliding in through the main entrance. He alighted atop one of the few remaining tables that hadn't been used to seal the room. 'The Groundlings have declared war on us, and an assault on this city is imminent.'

Consternation reigned. Everybody seemed to be shouting at once. Lady Aanfielsdaughter had to shout to make herself heard above the hullabaloo.

'Is this some kind of joke, Mr Mordadson? War? You can't surely be serious. Relations with the Groundlings have been improving steadily since—'

'This comes as a surprise to me as much as anyone, milady. According to Michael, there *is* someone who knew something about it. Cassie Grubdollar. She came up to warn us. Unfortunately, in the time it took her to locate Az to share the information with him, events overtook her.'

'Az?' said Lady Aanfielsdaughter. 'Az has been found?'

'He has.'

'Michael, you didn't mention this.'

'Sorry, milady,' Michael replied. 'I was in a hurry and had other things to think about. It didn't occur to me that you didn't know.'

'And he's all right?'

'Generally speaking, yes.' Michael didn't add that the last time he had seen Az, a group of Groundlings had been closing in menacingly on him and Cassie. He trusted that his little brother had survived the encounter. Az had faced worse threats in the past and come out on top.

The tension in Lady Aanfielsdaughter's face eased just a fraction. 'I am so glad to hear it.' She turned back to her emissary. 'But why, Mr Mordadson? Why are the Groundlings attacking us? What could we possibly have done to provoke them?'

'I was hoping,' said Mr Mordadson, scanning the crowd, 'that there'd a certain person here who might be able to supply answers to those questions. Except, I don't see him. Michael – Lord Urironson? Did you manage to round him up?'

Michael shook his head. 'Afraid not. I didn't come across him. I tried his quarters but he wasn't there.'

Mr Mordadson's expression suggested this wasn't wholly unexpected. 'Never mind. He'll keep.'

'Lord Urironson?' said Lady Aanfielsdaughter. 'How is Lord Urironson connected . . . with . . . ?'

The words trailed off. A deep, resonant vibration had become audible. Rapidly it grew in volume until the entire refectory seemed to tremble with it. The stained-glass windowpanes rattled behind the tables. The golden candelabra quivered.

'This is it,' said Michael, tautly. 'The plane. They're coming.'

CHAPTER 79

Foreboding

Aurora knew what Michael was going to say next. He turned to her with anguish in his eyes and a grim tightness to his mouth, and she just *knew* what he was planning to do. They'd known each other for the best part of two years and been married for a quarter of that time. Not long, in the grand scheme of things, but long enough for Aurora to have gained an intimate understanding of the mind of this man she loved, this father of her baby-to-be, this dashingly handsome charmer whom she had captivated and made hers. For all that Michael came across as cocksure and flighty, he was actually one of the most caring and responsible people Aurora had ever met. He had a sure sense of what was right and what was wrong and always strove to do the former not the latter. In that respect he was just like Az. The Gabrielson boys – they had the stuff of heroism in them.

So she could have spoken Michael's next few sentences for him, or else simply told him to be quiet and just go. But she didn't. She let him stumble through what he had to say, and with each syllable her heart swelled with pride and pain.

'Aurora,' he began. 'I can't stay here with you. I have to . . . I have to go out there and help Mr Mordadson and the Patrollers. This Groundling plane, you've never seen anything like it. It's – it's beautiful and awful at the same time, and somehow we've got to stop it because if we don't it'll smash this city to smithereens. I'm a pilot. That's what I do, and I happen to be plucking amazing at it. They need me, and . . . and . . . that's it. That's all. I have to help. For your sake. For the baby's. For everyone's.'

His wings drooped plaintively. She knew he would have given anything not to leave her, but duty – what was right – was like a gale inside him. When it blew, he couldn't help but be swept along by it.

She refused to cry. Tears would only add to his pain.

'Yes,' she said, in a voice as clear and steady as she could make it. 'Of course. I wouldn't have expected anything less. We've been here before, haven't we? When you decided to help the roughnecks tackle *Behemoth*.'

'Yeah. Yeah! And we made mincemeat of that airship, and it'll be the same this time. You can count on it.'

He looked into her eyes. This wasn't, he realised, a time for bragging.

'Aurora,' he said softly, 'I swear it's going to be all right. I won't be reckless. Why would I? I have everything to live for. I have you. I have our son.'

'Or daughter.'

'Or daughter. The two of you are my future. My world. My life. I'm not about to throw that all away, now am I?'

Aren't you? she nearly asked. Aurora was aware of a feeling in the pit of her stomach, a gnawing ache. It wasn't merely fear for her husband's safety. It was a dreadful foreboding – a certainty, almost, that something bad was going to happen to him. The baby writhed and stretched inside her, picking up on her distress. Or maybe it, too, through some kind of foetal intuition, sensed dark things in store for its father.

Don't go, Aurora nearly said. But she couldn't say it. She couldn't sow doubt in Michael's mind. He had made a difficult choice, and he would stick with it come what may. She had to be unselfish. She must not make things any harder for him than they already were.

So finally, all she did was say, 'I love you,' and hold him tight, pressing her face against his neck and smelling his skin, a smell she adored, a smell that spoke of strength and security, a smell that, if it had a name, would be called *home*.

Then she wheeled away, turning her back so that he wouldn't see her face crumple and her eyes spill.

Lady Aanfielsdaughter placed an arm and a wing tenderly around her shoulders.

When Aurora looked back, the refectory door had been shut. The locking bar was firmly in place. Mr Mordadson wasn't anywhere to be seen. Neither was Michael.

CHAPTER 80

The Small Constable

The cell door clanked open and a constable brought in lunch for Den. Glumly Den eyed the contents of the tin tray – thin soup, a crust of bread, a sorry-looking apple – and asked, 'Where'm the stuffed pheasant I were promised?'

The constable failed to appreciate his humour.

'You's lucky to get anything at all,' he said. 'What with everything else that'm going on right now.'

'Oh yeah? And what be "everything else"?'

The constable was a small man who thought his uniform made him tall. 'Well, it'm none of your business, but all hell's broken loose upstairs.'

'Upstairs? Be that why Inspector Treadwell had to hare off and see the chief superintendent? There'm some crisis among the top brass here?'

'No, upstairs as in above the clouds.'

'Oh,' said Den. Then: 'Ohhh.'

'Yes,' said the constable. 'Us has been getting reports of these loud bangs coming from the sky-cities and things falling into the Shadow Zones, you know, plane wreckage and that. Bodies too, dead Airborn. It'm happening all across the Territories, far as us can tell. Nobody be sure what'm going on. Details is sketchy. But it'm serious enough to warrant a whole bunch of emergency planning sessions and every off-duty copper has been drafted in, just in case. Including I,' he added grumpily. 'I got dragged out of home, and I'd only clocked off from the night shift three hours ago. Barely had my pyjamas on, and back I had to come.'

So there it was, thought Den. Cassie's gut feeling about the Slamshaft plane parts had been on the money. He hoped she'd got the message to Az in time. He also hoped, fervently, that wherever she was right now, it was somewhere down on the ground.

'Listen,' he said to the constable. 'I need to see Treadwell. Straight away. I think I has a pretty good idea what all this is about.'

'Oh really? Be that so?' The constable's voice oozed scepticism. 'Well, *I* think the inspector'm too busy at the moment to be bothered by the likes of you.'

'But I can help he.'

The constable, with one hand on the door, gave an officious little sniff. 'I seriously doubt that. Why doesn't you instead just sit tight, eat your food and not cause we any fuss. Us has enough on our plate without having to deal with people in cells who'll come up with any old excuse to try and get a bit of attention.'

'I be'n't—!'

But the door whumped shut before Den could finish his objection. He leaped up and pounded on it with his fist, telling the constable he was serious, he *did* know what was going on up in the sky-cities.

No good. The constable, evidently, had decided to ignore him.

Den slumped back onto the bunk.

'Bless my bum,' he sighed. 'Rotten timing or what? I were just about to tell Treadwell everything when him got called away. And now I be'n't in a position to tell he anything at all.' He shook his head. 'And now I be talking to myself! Den old chap, it may well be that you'm starting to lose it. Your kids better start looking for a nice, clean nursing home to dump you in. You'm soon going to need it.'

Next moment, he heard a sudden, loud thump, followed by a yelp and another thump. The sounds echoed along the corridor outside. Then, a long silence.

Curious, he got up and put his ear to the cell door.

The silence continued. Then somebody yelled out, 'Grubdollars? The Grubdollar family? Be you here, any of you?'

For several seconds Den was too startled to speak.

He couldn't believe it.

He knew that voice.

But it wasn't possible. He must be imagining it. Surely.

'Colin?' he said. 'Colin Amblescrut?'

CHAPTER 81

Colin Amblescrut's Literally Gobsmacking
Idea For A Jailbreak

'So you see,' said Colin, 'my conscience wouldn't let I alone. Nag, nag, nag, it went. "Colin, you did your pal Fletcher wrong. Colin, it weren't your fault but you still made a big mistake. Colin, you's no choice but to go and try and fix things." All day long, and all night too, and not even beer would get it to shut up. So eventually I upped and followed you down to Craterhome, 'cause that'm where general opinion in Grimvale reckoned you'd gone, and for two days I were busy scouring the city for you. I just wanted to say sorry, mainly to Fletch. Fletch!' he shouted. 'Give a yell again. I can't quite get a fix on you.'

'In here!' came the reply from a nearby cell.

Colin located the correct door and unbolted it.

Out walked Fletcher, looking nonplussed and wary. 'What be *you* doing here?' he shot at Colin.

'I were just explaining to your da. I's come to say sorry. Sorry, Fletch. I know it don't change what I did, but, for what it'm worth, I mean it.'

'Yeah, well,' said Fletcher. 'You'm right. It don't change what you did.'

'And,' Colin added brightly, 'now I be breaking all three of you out of here. That'm how I's making amends. Robert? Robert!'

A faint reply came from a cell at the other end of the corridor. Colin backtracked, stepping over the unconscious form of the small constable.

The occupant of the first cell Colin tried was not Robert.

'Oops,' he said, shutting the door swiftly.

'Don't leave I in here,' protested the person in the cell.

'You be'n't a Grubdollar. I be freeing only Grubdollars today.'

The next door along was the right one. Robert stepped blinking into the corridor.

'Da! Fletch!'

He ran to join them.

'How come Colin'm helping we?' he asked.

'It'm one of the mysteries of the universe,' said Fletcher.

'Him's making up for the Fletcher Tank fiasco,' said Den. 'I don't know the full story yet, but I be guessing him knew us had been taken into police custody and so deliberately went and got himself arrested. Something like that, Colin?'

'Straight up, Den,' said Colin, smiling. ' "Drunk and disorderly in a public place" be the charge. I went to a boozer not far from here and picked a fight with some of the locals. Quite a ruckus! There'm some tough nuts in this city, and no mistake. Anyway, police was called, I got hauled away, and them shoved I in here with you, just like I'd hoped. Them thought them'd got I all meek and docile after a few clonks with a truncheon.' He rubbed his head proudly. 'Them hadn't reckoned on the quality of the bonce them was dealing with. I just pretended to be dazed and lay quiet for a while, till the next time somebody came into my cell.'

Den recalled the scuffle in the corridor during his interview with Treadwell. 'But how'd you know us was here in this station?'

'I heard about the trouble at Slamshaft Engineering and a murk-comber getting stolen, and I said to myself, "That reeks of Grubdollar through and through." And I knew – don't take this the wrong way or anything – but I just knew it were likelier than not that you wouldn't make a clean getaway. Some folks is built for lawbreaking and some be'n't, and you lot'm in the "be'n't" camp. Nothing to be ashamed of. That'm anything but a criticism. But I were willing to lay good money the cops'd catch up with you and be feeling your collars in no time, so I hung around outside this police station waiting for you to turn up, and lo and behold, you did, and *Bertha* too. And that were when I came up with my literally gobsmacking idea for a jailbreak.'

'And this'm it,' said Fletcher frostily. 'And now us just strolls out of here, through a station full of policemen, and none of they's going to so much as look twice at we?' He sneered. 'Yeah, *great* plan, Colin. Really going to work – I don't think.'

'A-ha,' replied Colin, 'that'm where part two of my absolutely stunning idea comes in. Only question be, which of we be going dress up in *his* clothes?' He indicated the constable on the floor. The policeman had entered Colin's cell with his lunch, and Colin had taken him by surprise and knocked him cold. A big bruise swelled his mouth and jaw. 'Given the size of he, I reckon there'm only one person it can be.'

He looked at Robert.

'Me?' said Robert.

'Him's a right old titch,' said Colin, 'and you'm by far the smallest of we.'

'But – but I be'n't nearly old enough to be a cop.'

247

'I know, but beggars can't be choosers. Now come on, help I get this stuff of he.'

Colin bent and started unbuttoning the constable's tunic. The constable groaned and stirred. Colin casually thwacked him on the chin, knocking him insensible again.

Robert looked to his father for guidance, but Den was sunk deep in thought.

Common sense was telling Den they should not go along with Colin's plan. To the best of his knowledge, he and his children did not stand accused of any crime. Sooner or later they would be released anyway, and therefore, logically, they ought to stay put for now. Breaking out from the police station would only put them back on the wrong side of the law.

On the other hand, Den thought, what if Slamshaft Engineering had a change of heart and decided to prosecute after all? And what if Inspector Treadwell was unable to follow through on his assurance that the Grubdollars were off the hook? He'd said, 'No guarantees.' And although Treadwell struck Den as honest and fair, Den didn't altogether trust him. He didn't altogether trust any cop. No wise person did.

Moreover, there was a war in the Airborn realm, and Den had no idea whether Cassie was up there, down here, or somewhere in between, but wherever she was he hated the thought that she was without him and her brothers. Of course she was a big girl now, more than capable of looking after herself. But she was also his only daughter, and she carried the face of her mother, his beloved Orla, which made him cherish her all the more, and if anything happened to her he would never forgive himself. As long as there was the slimmest possibility that Cassie was in danger, he simply could not sit on his backside and do nothing. Who knew when Treadwell would get round to officially setting the Grubdollars free? With all that was going on, it might be days. He might even forget about them.

Soon the constable had been stripped to his underpants, and Robert, since his father hadn't told him not to, began taking off his own clothes and putting the man's uniform on. Meanwhile, Colin dragged the constable into the cell in which he himself had been shut up. He locked the door with a satisfied air.

'Best place for his kind,' Colin muttered, brushing his palms together.

'This'm insane,' said Fletcher. 'Lunacy. You'll never be able to pass for a copper, Robert. Look at you.'

'I don't know,' said Robert, settling the constable's peaked cap on his head. 'I's beginning to feel the part already.'

'Yeah,' agreed Colin. 'So what if him's a bit fresh-faced? What'm it everyone says about policemen looking younger every year?'

'Not *that* young,' snorted Fletcher.

Robert stiffened his neck and said in a gruff voice, 'All right, you horrible lot, move along. Let's be having you.' He grinned. 'How were that? That sound OK?'

Fletcher clapped a hand over his face. 'Awful,' he said. 'Da, you tell they. This'm never going to work.'

'Probably not,' said Den, 'but unless you can think of a better idea, I's afraid it'm all us has got.'

Fletcher sighed.

Colin beamed from ear to ear, his smile like a slash cut in a watermelon.

'The old team, back together,' he said. 'Hurrah!'

They set off down the corridor, Robert leading the way, Colin following, Fletcher trudging in Colin's wake.

Den, at the rear, remained full of misgivings, but he believed that they might just be able to pull this off, if luck was on their side.

CHAPTER 82

The Virtue Of Simplicity

Luck *was* on their side. The police station was in uproar. Officers were charging about, barking queries and commands at one another. With all the extra hands that had been drafted in, the chaos was even greater than it might have been. Nobody had a clear idea what they were supposed to be doing, but since everybody else was rushing madly around the place, shouting at the tops of their voices, the sensible thing seemed to be to join in.

Amid the hurly-burly, not much attention was paid to a single constable moving through the station with three civilians in tow. Three men who looked in need of sleep and a shave being escorted somewhere by a junior officer – it wasn't that remarkable a sight. Now and then somebody would give Robert a second glance, and the first few times this happened he was petrified that he would be rumbled as an impostor. But, although his face might not fit, it seemed that all anyone really saw was the uniform. After a while he started saluting, getting into the role. He stopped when Fletcher hissed, 'Don't get cocky.'

A sign appeared, pointing the way to the main entrance. The three Grubdollars began to think that they were actually going to make it. As for Colin, there had never been a shred of doubt in his mind on the subject. His jailbreak idea had the virtue of simplicity, and he'd long believed that the simpler a thing was, the less likely it was to go awry. If the Amblescruts had a family motto, that would be it: Simple Is Best.

Then . . .

'Oh bugger,' Den groaned under his breath.

Just in front of the police station doors, the doors that led to the world outside and freedom, stood Inspector Treadwell.

The inspector was deep in dialogue with a tall, sleek-haired, distinguished-looking man whose uniform marked him out as the chief superintendent. No one could have epaulettes that extravagantly bulky or that much gold braid on his cap and not be the chief superintendent.

'Pull back, pull back,' Den growled, just loud enough to be heard by the others.

The four of them regrouped around a corner and Den explained to Colin why they couldn't proceed.

'Treadwell knows my, Fletch's and Robert's faces,' he said. 'Yours too, probably. And him's no fool. There'm no way us can just troop past he without he recognising we.'

'Colin's dumb idea falls apart,' said Fletcher. 'Told you so.'

'Hey,' said Colin, looking hurt.

'Yeah, Fletch,' said Den, 'that weren't wholly fair. It got we this far, didn't it?'

Fletcher folded his arms and *hmph*ed.

'Reckon there'm a back entrance to this place?' said Robert. 'Or, like, a fire exit or something?'

Den grinned. 'Now why didn't I think of that?'

They set off again, but hadn't gone more than ten paces when a stern voice from behind halted them in their tracks.

'Hold on a moment, you four.'

The voice was Treadwell's, and it cut through the air with such clean, crisp precision that Den knew Treadwell had spotted them as they were withdrawing around the corner and had gone chasing after them. They hadn't pulled out of his sightline fast enough, and now the game was up.

Den turned wearily round, and sure enough, here came the inspector, bearing down on them at a fair lick.

'Stop right there,' Treadwell said, jabbing a finger in their direction. 'Don't you move a muscle.'

Den weighed up the options.

'Scram!' he said to the other three. 'Every man for himself. He can't nab all three of we. Whoever gets out, go find Cass.'

Immediately, Fletcher, Robert and Colin sprinted off, and Den himself broke into as fast a run as his middle-aged legs could manage. Treadwell accelerated, meanwhile calling out to every police officer within earshot, 'Prisoners on the loose! Us has prisoners on the loose, one of they impersonating a constable!'

The uproar that had prevailed beforehand was nothing compared with the uproar that ensued. All at once the station was clotted with police. Every corridor and staircase was a teeming mass of blue-clad bodies. Whichever way the fugitives turned, there were cops blocking their path, and more cops in hot pursuit behind them. They jinked and zig-zagged through the building, but increasingly there were fewer routes open to them, fewer ways to go, until finally they found themselves

251

trapped on a landing in a stairwell, with a score of policemen advancing on them from below and another score descending from above.

Treadwell was among the latter group. He was flushed and out of breath. A man with a pipe habit like his found that any kind of physical exertion was hard on the heart and lungs.

'Den . . . Grubdollar,' he rasped out between gasps.

'Yes,' said Den, with profound resignation. 'I know, I know. Us is under arrest.' He held up his hands, ready for the handcuffs.

'I be'n't going down without a fight,' said Colin. He too was holding up his hands, but his were clenched into fists.

'No, Colin, leave it be,' Den told him. 'Us gave it a decent shot, but it'm over now.'

Unwillingly, Colin let his hands drop to his sides.

Treadwell had more to say, but needed to get his wind back first. He bent double, grasping the banister for support and waving his other arm in a gesture that begged everyone to wait.

Everyone waited. The police officers seethed, eager to get on with the business of apprehending these miscreants and dishing out some Craterhome-cop justice.

Finally Treadwell raised his head, his face looking less unhealthily ruddy now.

What he said next came as a surprise to everyone.

CHAPTER 83

For The Sanctum! For The Realm!

The Patrollers flew out to meet the Cloudbuster in three lines a couple of hundred metres apart. The first two lines constituted the bulk of the defence force and were arranged in arrowhead formations, while the third was made up of a few pairs of Patrollers, each lugging between them one of several ten-metre lengths of chain which Mr Mordadson had scrounged from the Sanctum's supply-arrival depot. To the ends of the thick chains he had attached rocks taken from an ornamental garden, for extra weight and stability. Dropped through the air onto the plane's propellers in just the right way, these makeshift bolases could do some serious damage – perhaps even terminal damage.

But Mr Mordadson, who was flying with the third line of Patrollers, was counting on this battle not turning into a direct conflict between people and aircraft. If all went according to plan, the Patrollers would not have to get anywhere near the plane, with its lethal-looking array of armaments.

He threw a glance in the direction of the Sanctum's landing apron, where, right on schedule, a commandeered airbus was taking off, with Michael at the controls. The stubby multi-passenger vehicle was a dwarf compared with that Groundling monstrosity. In terms of size, speed and power it was hopelessly outclassed. What it had in its favour was the fact that it was being flown by one of the finest Airborn pilots around . . . and the fact that it had been deemed expendable.

Turning back to the Cloudbuster, Mr Mordadson saw, emerging from it, a horde of those artificially winged men Michael had described.

Good, he thought.

Organised resistance from a sky city was not, perhaps, a contingency that the Groundlings were prepared for. But however unexpected the threat was, they were now responding to it in completely the right way, the way Mr Mordadson had been hoping they would. Meeting it head-on, like for like, man to man.

The Patroller squadron leaders peeped on their whistles. *Maintain tight formation. Weapons ready.*

For his part, Mr Mordadson shouted encouragement to anyone who could hear him: 'These motherpluckers don't know the first thing about aerial combat. Let's show them how it's done. For the Sanctum! For the realm!'

His cry was taken up, spreading from line to line, from Patroller to Patroller.

'For the Sanctum! For the realm!' they chanted at the tops of their voices.

The Drones circled and swarmed.

The Patrollers closed in.

The first clash, when it came, was abrupt and brutal.

A line of Drones loosed off their crossbows at the first line of Patrollers. There were screams as men burst open like popped blood-blisters, but the Patrollers kept going. Nobody broke rank, except to move up to fill the gap left in a formation by a fallen comrade. All of them had lances in their hands.

The Groundlings veered off to the right and left, leaving room for a second wave of their own kind to come forward and shoot. As they did so, however, a series of whistle peeps gave the order to abandon formation. The Patroller arrowheads almost magically dispersed, and the crossbow bolts whisked harmlessly through empty air.

So now there were two sets of Drones who were taking evasive action while trying to reload their crossbows at the same time. The lance-bearing Patrollers swooped after them, wings whirring. Flying flat-out, a fit young Airborn could just about reach the speeds that the Groundlings could achieve with their motorised backpacks. No Airborn could maintain such a pace for more than a minute at a time.

But a minute was enough.

The Patrollers gained on the Drones, and each selected a target and lofted his lance and threw.

The lances spiked, speared and skewered. Now it was the Drones' turn to scream. Some were killed instantly, and fell. Some flew on with the lance tips protruding from their torsos, blood gushing out. Mr Mordadson saw one Drone whose belly had been ripped right open. His guts bulged out and he was desperately trying to press them back in with both hands. Hurtling out of control, he slammed sideways into another Drone. Their backpacks exploded and they disappeared in a billow of flame.

Another Drone had suffered a near-miss. The lance hadn't struck his body but it had wrecked one of his wings. He was whirling downwards in a death-spiral. His limbs flailed, as if he hoped by flapping them hard enough he could defy gravity and stay aloft.

A cruel, crooked smile skewed Mr Mordadson's face. *Not so easy, is it, chum?* he thought. *Flying unaided. You should leave it to the pros, the ones born with the proper equipment.*

The Patrollers fell back, exhausted from the effort of catching up with the Drones. The second line came forward to take their place. These Patrollers all bore short-handled maces and were ready for some hand-to-hand combat.

Mr Mordadson's battle strategy, which he had agreed upon with the squadron leaders, was that the lance attacks would leave the enemy wary. The Groundlings, having learned that their Airborn foes could bite back, would adopt a cautious approach. But when they saw that the next group of Patrollers *weren't* carrying lances, caution would give way to over-confidence. In the heat of the moment, the Groundlings would snap from one extreme to the other.

Sure enough, the Drones kept their distance for a while, then suddenly coalesced into a ball and came zooming at the Patrollers in a single, buzzing, furious surge. Crossbows twanged, Patrollers died, but the Drones couldn't scatter in time. They'd put to much faith in their superior firepower and poured on too much speed. They struck the Patrollers head-on, crashing into the human arrowheads, their own rough formation disintegrating.

Now, at close quarters, the advantage belonged to the Airborn. Mr Mordadson watched as the maces swung in a frenzy of hammering and battering. Skulls cracked, jaws snapped, teeth splintered, bones broke. The Patrollers were relentless and remorseless. The Drones dropped like flies.

While all this was going on, the Cloudbuster continued its steady, inexorable approach to the Sanctum.

And out of the corner of his eye, Mr Mordadson saw the airbus creeping round towards the giant plane's starboard flank.

He estimated the Groundling plane would reach the Sanctum in less than a minute.

Michael was going to get once chance, and one chance only, to do what he had to do.

And he had better do it quickly. Time was running out.

255

CHAPTER 84

Long Odds

What Michael was relying on, what this entire semi-suicidal scheme hinged on, was that the Groundling plane wouldn't see him coming. Its pilots would be focused on the battle between their own propeller-powered troops and the Sanctum's winged defenders. So intently would they be following that, they'd fail to notice the airbus coming at them from the side, or if they did notice, not until it was too late.

This was what the Alar Patrollers were fighting and dying for. They were providing a distraction, buying Michael time so that he could do his bit.

Michael was determined not to let their sacrifice go to waste.

He completed his turn and levelled the airbus out, lining the giant plane up in his windscreen. The airbus was an absolute pain in the tailfeathers to fly. It had the aerodynamics of a brick and the power-to-weight ratio of a turkey. As far as control-responsiveness went, you'd have been better off ripping the joystick off its mounting and holding it out of the window as a rudder. It was almost funny: he, Michael Gabrielson, test pilot extraordinaire, in the cockpit of a common-or-garden airbus! The guys back at the Aerodyne hangar would be wetting themselves with laughter if they knew.

Michael allowed himself a quick, grim grin at this thought, before returning his attention to the task at hand.

The Groundling plane loomed. By all that's high and bright, it was a vast thing! He made a tiny course correction. He was aiming amidships, at a spot just below and behind the starboard wing. Structurally this was an aircraft's weak point. It had more joins and rivets there than anywhere else in its fuselage; the airframe was under the greatest strain, and therefore at its most fragile. Ramming the plane there with the airbus should – *should* – deal a catastrophic and fatal blow. And it had to be an airbus rather than some smaller, more manoeuvrable vehicle. Anything else would be too light to deliver enough of an impact.

He recalled Magnus Clockweight, the man who had led the Groundling oil workers in their brave assault on *Behemoth*. Clockweight had delivered the fatal blow to the pirate airship by ramming it with a plane, with himself still inside. Michael was about to carry out much the same manoeuvre, the difference being that Clockweight had not had the option of baling out at the last moment.

Holding the joystick steady, Michael slid open the cockpit's side window. Wind pounded in. The aperture wasn't large but it was large enough. He had practised on the landing apron. With his wings as tightly furled as he could make them, he could just squeeze himself through.

His mouth had gone so dry, he could hardly move his tongue.

He thought of Aurora, and of their unborn child.

Azrael if it was a boy. They were both in firm agreement on that. The kid could do a lot worse than take after his namesake Uncle Az. And if it was a girl? Michael was keen on calling her Ramona, after his mother, but Aurora preferred Serena, after the woman who had been a substitute for her own late mother for many years, Lady Aanfieldsdaughter. They'd argued gently about this, on and off for several weeks, and Michael had a feeling he was being won round to Aurora's choice. Or worn down, which amounted to the same thing.

Whichever name it ended up with, Ramona or Serena or Azrael, Michael didn't really mind, so long as the baby was born healthy. He was vaguely concerned that it might not develop wings, but doctors had reassured him and Aurora that the chances of their child inheriting Az's condition were a million to one.

Long odds.

Somewhat like the odds on him emerging from this insane stunt unscathed.

The Groundling plane was now less than 500 metres away. It filled Michael's entire field of vision.

And his survival odds suddenly and sharply lengthened, as, before his very eyes, the weapons on the plane's hull were turned on him.

He had been spotted.

One by one the missile launchers, or whatever they were, swivelled round, locking on to the airbus.

Michael gritted his teeth and gripped the joystick ferociously tight as the Groundlings opened fire.

CHAPTER 85

A Clodhopping Thing Dancing Like A Ballerina

There was nothing Mr Mordadson could do but look on in helpless, horrified dismay. The diversionary tactic hadn't succeeded, and now Michael was in mortal danger.

The weapons that festooned the plane were, as far as Mr Mordadson could tell, catapults of some kind – glorified crossbows, in effect – each mounted on gimbals and manned by a Groundling. He had no doubt that the projectiles they were loaded with had explosive heads. Every other weapon in the Groundlings' armoury used explosives. Why not these ones too?

Mentally he begged Michael to abort the attack run. But he knew it wasn't going to happen. Michael was the Sanctum's only real hope of survival. If he failed, it was all over. Chickening out was not an option.

And the bumbling, ungainly airbus was such an easy target, too. So slow and large, it might as well be hovering stationary in the sky with a big bull's-eye painted on it.

The Groundlings trained their sights on it and started firing at will. Clusters of projectiles darted towards the airbus.

What happened next made Mr Mordadson gape and blink in astonishment.

The airbus dodged.

With as much elegance as if it were a top-of-the-range sports plane, it weaved through the cloud of missiles. It rolled on its axis, then righted itself, then went into a steep, banking turn, seemed to pivot on one wingtip, flattened out once more, shimmied, dived, pulled up, and one after another the missiles shot past it, all of them missing their mark.

More missiles came, and the airbus's ailerons flapped in complicated configurations and its rear end wagged like a wagtail's tail, and again it avoided everything the Groundlings were throwing at it, albeit on several occasions by the slenderest of margins.

Mr Mordadson had never seen quite such a miraculous display of precision flying. Everyone knew what clodhopping things airbuses were, but somehow Michael was managing to make this one dance like a ballerina.

For several breathtaking seconds it looked as though Michael was going to make it safely through the missile barrage.

Then either he got unlucky or one of the Groundlings got lucky.

It was only a glancing blow, but it was sufficient. The airbus's tailfin went up in a burst of flame. The stubby plane sheared and corkscrewed. Mr Mordadson had visions of it going into a nosedive from which even Michael would not be able to pull out. He couldn't bear to watch. At the same time, he couldn't turn away.

Michael kept control.

How, Mr Mordadson had no idea, but he did it. The airbus resumed its original flightpath. Tail afire, trailing smoke, it continued to race towards the giant plane, swerving, shuddering, but still on target.

Get out! Mr Mordadson yelled inside his head. *Bail! Now!*

He didn't realise he wasn't just thinking the words, he was shouting them aloud.

'Get out of there, Michael!'

The airbus disappeared behind the Cloudbuster.

KA-BOOM!

CHAPTER 86

Wings On Fire

The Cloudbuster quaked. Then, with startling suddenness, it was in halves. Struck by the airbus, the plane snapped in two as easily as a wishbone, and all at once the rear portion of it was plummeting, while the front portion, which still had the wings, lumbered on, slowly canting forwards onto its nose.

The bombs were in the rear half, and swiftly detonated. A ripple of explosions reduced the massive, falling cylinder of metal to mangled shreds. In amongst the debris could be seen torn Groundling bodies, falling too.

Meanwhile the rest of the Cloudbuster lurched through space towards the Sanctum. Mr Mordadson was close enough to get a glimpse inside the cockpit. The pilots were wrestling futilely with the controls, their faces contorted in terror. The Groundlings in charge of the missile launchers were letting out senseless screams, the sound of men who knew that the life remaining to them could be measured in seconds. The half-plane was now pointing vertically down, forming an immense T-shape. It was going to hit the Sanctum full-on.

No, not quite.

Momentum dwindled. Gravity began to take hold. The front end of the Cloudbuster only clipped the Sanctum, losing one wing in the process.

Several of the towers on the sky-city's edge trembled. Stained-glass windows shattered, dissolving into a myriad of rainbow shards. Chunks of silvery fascia-work fell.

The broken Cloudbuster rebounded and sailed off downward to the cloud cover, spinning lazily. The severed wing went with it.

Mr Mordadson felt no sense of triumph as he watched it go. It was a victory, no question. The Airborn had won, the Sanctum was saved. But at such a cost. So many lives. Including—

'Sir?' said one of the nearby chain-bearing Patrollers. 'Look.'

The man was pointing towards the midair battle, which was still going on, even though the Groundlings were defeated and they knew it. Patrollers were wheeling around them, picking them off one by one. Having lost their plane, the Groundlings had lost heart too. A courageous few fought back, but the great majority seemed resigned to their fate. The Patrollers hit them and destroyed their backpacks, and they fell.

'Yes, we've beaten them,' Mr Mordadson intoned tiredly. 'Well done us.'

'No,' said the Patroller. 'Look past. Down near the clouds. Isn't that . . . ?'

Mr Mordadson squinted.

A distant, tiny figure.

Struggling.

Wings on fire.

Fighting to stay aloft.

Michael.

Mr Mordadson flapped his wings and flew as he had never flown before. Arms straight out in front, he knifed through the air, with his gaze fixed on Michael and nothing else.

Michael's wings were smouldering, giving off wafts of black smoke. Charred tatters came off with every frantic downstroke and upstroke. He was straining with all his might, but in vain. Feathers were appallingly flammable. His wings were disintegrating and he was sinking. Already the misty upper layer of the clouds was wreathed around him. Within moments he would be lost from sight.

Faster! Mr Mordadson ordered himself. *Faster, you creaky old fool, faster!*

He glimpsed Michael's face, riven with fear and agony. He could see ripples of bright orange snaking through his wings. There were holes in the plumage. The wings were becoming shredded black skeletons of themselves.

Then Michael was gone, swallowed by the cloud cover.

Without hesitation Mr Mordadson plunged in after him. The world went white; or rather, opaque pink. He was flying blind. He didn't care. He plummeted through the vapour, following the faint, ember-like glow of the burning wings. He groped. His hand brushed a wing-edge. A singe of pain, and a palmful of black ash. He clutched. More singeing, more ash, the brittle remnants of burnt feathers. Then his fingers located a hand, a wrist. He clamped on. Wings outstretched, he slowed his and Michael's descent as smoothly as he could. Then he flapped down, and flapped down, struggling to lift Michael's weight as well as his own, and he began to climb. Gradually. Agonisingly. Arms aching. Wing roots throbbing. Began to rise from the cloud cover, hauling Michael with him.

The stench of scorched feathers was strong and repugnant. Michael, barely conscious, whimpered and sobbed.

Up they went, out of the cloud shade, into blueness and brilliance.

CHAPTER 87

Az-And-Cassie

The matronly woman proved to be a useful source of information. By the time they reached the ground, Az and Cassie knew where to look for Dominic Slamshaft. The woman, a native Craterhomer, admiringly described the Slamshaft mansion in the Fifth Borough, cooing over its twenty bedrooms and its lavish collection of priceless artworks. She could even furnish an address: Traction Boulevard. This was thanks to her love of lifestyle magazines, the kind that revelled in stories about the rich and famous and recorded these celebrities' every word and deed for the benefit of the less fortunate. Slamshaft was often profiled in such periodicals. Flattering photogravure portraits of him accompanied articles that were sometimes serious ('The Sharpest Business Brain In The Westward Territories') but more often silly ('Why Not Try A Toupee, Mr Slamshaft?').

'Him's the most eligible bachelor in the city,' said the woman. 'Him really ought to settle down and find himself a wife. It'm criminal that a man like he be still single.' She sounded a little wistful, as though thinking, *If only I were younger . . . !*

Cassie had steered the conversation around to the subject of Slamshaft with great care, so that neither the woman nor any of the other passengers in the elevator guessed why she was enquiring about him. They all thought Cassie was just making small talk, trying to while away the journey and keep her mind off the scary events taking place above. It was an artful performance, and Az congratulated her on it as they exited the former Chancel and joined the queue for the shuttle bus that would take them into Craterhome.

'You're quite an actress,' he said.

Cassie bobbed a curtsey. 'Why, thank you, kind sir.'

'And very devious.'

'I do my best.'

While the bus rolled through the Shadow Zone, they hunkered together on the back seat and talked tactics.

It wasn't enough simply to have good reason to believe that Slamshaft was behind the war, Az said. Hard evidence of some kind was needed, and to obtain it they would have to break into his home. There would be something there they could use, surely. A letter, a document, something incriminating, something that linked him inextricably to the attack on the sky-cities.

'What, and then us takes that to the police?'

'Of course. Why not? That's what they're there for, isn't it?'

'Maybe in your world. Maybe your Patrollers does their job like them's supposed to. Down here, though, it'm a bit different.'

'Even so, with something as major as this, they'll have to sit up and take notice. Won't they?'

Cassie screwed up her face in a *perhaps* expression. 'Truth be told, with all the trouble my family's got itself in, I doubt anybody'm going to listen twice to what I has to tell they.'

'Then it's a good thing I'm with you,' Az said. 'I'm Az Gabrielson. They've got to have heard of me and know what I represent. If *I* go to the authorities with proof that Slamshaft is the bad guy here . . .' He waved a hand. *Simple as that.*

'All my hard work, and that big head of yours be'n't getting any smaller,' Cassie teased. ' "Ay'm Az Gabrielson. Ay'm famous, dontcha know." '

'Your Airborn accent's as bad as my Groundling one.'

' "Ay have a prophecy about me and everything." '

'Oh, give it a rest. All I'm doing is stating a fact. I can even drop Lady Aanfielsdaughter's name, if it comes to that.'

'Well, I hope you'm right,' Cassie said. 'I hope that'll work.'

'It will.' Az paused, then said in a rush, 'Cassie, you know that thing you said up in Prismburg when you were bandaging my hand?'

'Yup.' She looked anxious. 'Why?'

'Don't worry. It's just . . . I wish I'd said it first.'

'I wish I'd said it properly, not let it come out by mistake.'

He took her hand in his. 'Because, here we are, the whole world's gone mad, but I've never felt safer or truer than I do right now, with you. You're what makes me feel important, not working for the Sanctum or any stupid old prophecy or anything like that. You and me – what we have – is why I do what I do, why I fight and struggle on and try and be the best person I can be and do what I'm meant to. Don't get me wrong, I'm guano-scared about what's happening up above. Michael, my

264

parents, everything I know and hold dear is under threat. But you're still OK, and somehow that's all that really matters. What?'

She was looking at him in a funny way.

'What?' he said again. 'Am I blabbering on? Have I said too much? Is it "shut up, Az" time?'

'No,' said Cassie softly. 'No, you's said exactly the right amount. Now, kiss I.'

They kissed.

They kissed, with their hearts alive with joy.

They kissed so hard and passionately, it felt as though they were falling into each other.

They kissed, and there was no more Az and Cassie. It was Az-and-Cassie, a single fused entity. Their love was a place of its own, distinct from the Airborn realm and the ground, a country which only they two occupied and which had closed its borders to the rest of creation.

The bus emerged from the Shadow Zone, and not far away a hunk of debris came crashing down from Prismburg, thudding into the roadside dirt and kicking up a plume of grit and earth. The driver swerved. Everyone aboard the bus jumped and gasped.

Except Az-and-Cassie, who didn't even notice.

CHAPTER 88

An Exclusive Enclave

And then, a while later, they were plain Az and Cassie once more, and they were casing the Slamshaft mansion from across the road, looking for a way in.

'Those walls are high,' Az observed.

'Yeah, well spotted, eagle-eye.'

'That gate too. We'll never climb over it.'

'You mean that gate that'm six metres tall and made of straight iron bars with spikes on top? Us'll never climb over that? Whatever gave you such an idea?'

'Hey, enough of the sarcasm, smarty-pants. What about security? Do you think Slamshaft has bodyguards patrolling the grounds?'

'I honestly don't know. Super-rich types often does, but I's not seen anyone in the time that us has been standing here. You'd think somebody'd go past the gate quite regularly if there *was* bodyguards on site. There might be dogs, of course.'

'Dogs?' Az said, frowning. 'Oh yeah. Those large furry animals with the teeth that make that barky sound.'

'It be'n't the *teeth* that make that barky sound.'

'You know what I meant.'

'But if there'm dogs,' Cassie went on, 'there'm usually a warning sign posted outside.'

'So no dogs.'

'But not everyone puts up a sign.'

The mansion itself was just visible through the gateway, nestling impressively amidst the foliage of dark, abundant trees at the far end of a gravel drive. It was late afternoon and the sky's grey was deepening, nudging towards black. The house looked empty, the windows blank.

Then a light came on.

'That answers that question,' Cassie said. 'Somebody be in.'

'Doesn't make much difference if we can't physically get onto the premises,' said Az. 'All it means is . . . Wuhhh.'

'You all right? You'm a bit pale.'

'Just a ground-sickness wobble. I'll be fine. I'm hardened to it. If this were two years ago, I'd be flat on my back. Remember?'

'Oh, I remember. Us has both come a long way since then.'

'A long way,' Az agreed. 'And that makes me think that it's not so impossible that you and your family could come and live up . . ."

Cassie wasn't listening. A noise had caught her attention.

A vehicle had come around a far corner and was approaching slowly along the road. Az and Cassie shrank back behind the tree trunk they were using for cover. Traction Boulevard was a long, broad street lined with cedars and sequoias, and it didn't seem to be the kind of thoroughfare you drove along unless you lived there or had business in one of the properties. The whole of the Fifth Borough was like that, not welcoming to outsiders and passing traffic. It was an exclusive enclave, a city-within-a-city to which only wealth could grant you the right to belong, and it was so tranquil that you could forget you were in the heart of a huge metropolis – so tranquil, indeed, that the drone of a four-stroke engine was a startling intrusion.

The engine belonged to a maroon van with the words FLANNEL-WHITE'S LAUNDRY SERVICES emblazoned on the side in bronze-effect lettering. It went past the Slamshaft mansion and halted outside the next gate along. A man got out, dressed in overalls the same colour as the van, with the same inscription embroidered across the back. He fetched a stack of pressed, folded bedlinen from the rear of the vehicle and tugged the handle of the bell-rope beside the gate. Somewhere, a faint clanging could be heard. He waited for a couple of minutes then tried again. No one came. With an irritable *tsk*, he put the bedlinen back in the van and drove off.

'You thinking what I be thinking?' said Cassie.

'Don't know. What are you thinking?'

She nodded towards the house the laundry man had just tried to get into. 'No one be home there, and that gate'm a far sight lower than the other one. All those decorations on it too. Them'd make good handholds and toeholds.'

The gate was indeed half the height of Slamshaft's, and had been fashioned to resemble a line of sheet-music, with a treble clef on the left and various notes, sharps and flats dotted along an undulating stave. The owner of the house was doubtless a musician of some sort, and the gate wasn't so much a barrier as a mark of vanity.

'I reckon us could scale it without too much trouble, then try to get into Slamshaft's place from the side. Maybe at the back there'm fence rather than wall, or even better, hedge.'

It sounded sensible enough to Az. A doubt flitted across his mind, a vague uneasiness about the gate's lack of height. If everyone in this borough was so paranoid about privacy and security, why install a gate that was clearly not much of an obstacle to intruders?

Cassie was already off across the road before he could voice his concern. And anyway, he thought, his fears were most likely unfounded.

CHAPTER 89

Unfounded? Unfortunately Not
(Or: What Could Be Worse Than A Guard Dog?)

Alighting on the other side of the gate, Cassie stole off into the grounds of the house without a backward glance. Az, hampered by his injured arm, took longer getting over than she did. She was almost out of sight by the time his feet touched the driveway.

'Cassie,' he hissed, hurrying after her. 'Cassie, wait for me.'

She didn't hear. She plunged on into the tree-shaded gloom, disappearing round the side of the mansion. Az sprinted to catch up. She obviously assumed he was right behind her. Sometimes that girl just didn't stop to think!

Every window on the house was tightly shuttered. Weeds had sprung up on the stone steps leading up to the front porch, and the porch itself had not been swept clean of last autumn's leaves.

No one home for sure. The owner had not been here for quite a while.

The garden at the rear consisted of an expanse of springy lawn, bracketed by towering privet hedgerows which ran parallel to the walls on either side. At the far end lay a small, dense patch of woodland with a jumble of undergrowth. Cassie was nowhere to be seen, but her footprints left a clear trail across the damp grass, leading to the forest. Az followed them. As he neared the other side of the lawn he spied a second line of footprints that came towards Cassie's at an angle then converged with them. These looked as fresh as hers, but whatever had made them had slightly smaller feet than she did.

No, not feet.

Whatever made them had paws.

Az halted in his tracks. All at once his scalp was prickling and his stomach felt like it was full of nettles.

Guard dog.

Had to be.

Then he heard a low, menacing growl from the forest.

The growl changed his fear, shifting it from emotion to motivation. He charged into the forest, heading along a packed-mud path, calling out Cassie's name as he went.

In reply he got a querulous cry from up ahead.

'Az. Go back. Get out of here now, fast as you can.'

As if he was going to obey *that* instruction. He ran on, till he came to a small clearing.

There, on one side of the clearing, stood Cassie, keeping very still and looking very, very frightened.

Opposite her, less than five metres away, crouched a large, yellow-eyed, brown-pelted beast with a ridge of bristling black spikes of fur all along its spine. Its teeth were bared in a scimitar-like grin. Huge white talons dug into the soil as the animal gathered itself. It quivered all over, every muscle in its body tensed, ready to pounce.

Az's mind went blank.

Then a memory surfaced in his thoughts.

He had seen creatures like this once before, from far above, through the windows of *Cerulean*'s control gondola. He had never been so close to one, though, close enough to see the drool that was leaking from its chops and smell its rank, sour odour, like a mixture of mushrooms and old vinegar.

And then its name came to him, the name the Groundlings had given it, a name that was redolent of teeth gnashing and bones crunching.

Hackerjackal.

CHAPTER 90

Marigold

Some people would claim that you could never tame a hackerjackal.

Some people would be right. And also wrong.

Certainly you could never keep one as a pet, but then you'd be mad to want to. A hackerjackal wouldn't fetch your slippers and curl up next to you beside the hearth. Most likely it would eat your slippers, with your feet inside them, then go on to gulp down the rest of you. *Then* it would curl up beside the hearth, alone, to sleep off its dinner.

But a hackerjackal that had been captured when a cub, taken from its pack, raised by man according to a brutal regime, caged, trained, starved, regularly beaten, taught to obey commands or suffer painful punishment, might – just might – eventually have its will broken and become domesticated. Superficially domesticated. Domesticated enough, at least, to be put into service as a security measure for someone's private residence.

Dominic Slamshaft's next-door neighbour was a wildly popular soprano, Lorelei Lovesharp, whose concerts were a sell-out wherever she went. She spent half of the year on tour, travelling around the Westward Territories *and* the Eastern States, and sometimes even going overseas to the Low Lands. Every night, she performed to packed houses, earning herself more money than even she, who never wore the same outfit twice, could spend.

Offstage she was a nightmare, a stroppy, demanding diva who got through managers and orchestra conductors the way most people got through loaves of bread, chopping away at them slice by slice till there was nothing left. Onstage, though, she trilled as beautifully as a lark, and audiences adored her.

To protect her house while she was absent for these long periods, Miss Lovesharp would settle for nothing less than the ultimate in burglar deterrents. She had hired the hackerjackal from a company called 'Sure Fang' Property Protection. Their slogan ran: *Once Bitten . . . That's It.*

She had been scheduled to return home tonight, hence the attempted delivery of clean, fresh bedlinen. However, her tour had been delayed halfway through owing to a throat infection, and new dates had been added at the end to make up for the ones she had missed. (Naturally, when the illness struck, she had sacked her then-current manager, who was obviously to blame, and had replaced him with another.) The message that she would not be back at her house for another week had filtered through to everyone in Craterhome who needed to know, except Flannelwhite's Laundry Services, which had accidentally been left off the list.

Hence the hackerjackal continued to roam the grounds of the mansion, which it had come to regard as its own territory. Only one other creature was permitted to share this space with it and live, and that was its handler. He visited twice a day to make sure that everything was well and to drop off a live patchrabbit or two for the hackerjackal to catch, kill and consume. Which it did with speed and relish, trotting up to its handler afterwards and begging for more.

'No,' he would say. 'Us has got to keep you hungry, Marigold.'

For Marigold was the name he had given the hackerjackal, who was a bitch. Marigold was also the name of the handler's ex-wife, to whom he believed the same description applied.

Marigold the hackerjackal, being hungry, was in a perpetually foul mood and, being female, was a deadlier and far more skilled hunter than any male of her species.

This was what faced Cassie now across the clearing.

Snarling.

Ravenous.

Luminous-eyed.

Lethal.

This was the animal that would, in the next few seconds, rend Cassie limb from limb, unless she or Az did something.

But what?

CHAPTER 91

What

Three things happened at once.

The hackerjackal sprang.

Cassie threw herself sideways.

Az lunged.

Simultaneously, he hit the hackerjackal, the hackerjackal hit the ground, and Cassie hit her head against a rock.

The hackerjackal tried to get up. Az tried to stop it from doing so. Cassie clambered to her knees and tried to prise the rock out of the earth.

With a shrug, the hackerjackal shook Az off its back. Az went flailing away and tripped on a tree root. Cassie hauled the rock free with both hands.

Az was lying on his back in the undergrowth. The hackerjackal bounded towards him. Cassie lumbered after it, her head reeling.

Az kicked out at the beast, catching it a glancing blow on the muzzle. The hackerjackal snapped angrily at the air, then leapt on him, sinking talons into his flesh. Az screamed. Teeth the size of table knives loomed in his vision. A gust of foul meaty breath made him retch.

He knew he was staring death in the face. *His* death.

Then a yip.

A howl.

Blood spattering in his eyes.

It was Cassie, hammering the rock down on the hackerjackal's head.

'Get!'

Crack.

'Your!'

Crunch.

'Filthy!'

Scrunch.

'Paws!'
Scrussh.
'Off!'
Squoosh.
'My!'
Skloodge.
'Boyfriend!'
Smoossshhh.

The thuds of impact got wetter and wetter. Scraps of fur, shreds of scalp flesh, slivers of bone flew with each blow.

The light faded in the animal's sulphur-glow eyes.

And still Cassie went on hitting it with the rock. The hackerjackal lay sprawled on the earth, and Cassie straddled it, pounding, sobbing, snot pouring from her nostrils, and she knew the animal was dead but she just could not stop. It needed to be more than dead. Deader than dead. It needed to be obliterated from existence. Wiped off the face of the planet.

Finally the rock, slick with gore, slipped from her grasp.

Cassie knelt back on her haunches.

'I hate those things,' she said.

She got shakily to her feet, then helped Az up.

'You OK?' She examined the wounds in his chest, the gouges put there by the hackerjackal's talons. There was so much blood around – all over his front, all over her hands – that it was hard to tell how much of it had come from where. But, blessedly, it seemed that most of the blood was the hackerjackal's. Az wasn't hurt too badly. The talons had left holes rather than furrows. His shirt was a write-off but he himself had escaped serious damage.

'But if you'd been a fraction slower . . .' Az said, wincing at the thought.

'I don't even want to think about it. Now, you reckons you'm all right to carry on? I wouldn't blame you if you said you wanted to quit.'

'I'm not quitting,' he said flatly. 'Not on your life. We've come this far, might as well go the rest of the way.

The hackerjackal's legs gave a sudden twitch. Both Az and Cassie stared at it in alarm. But the creature didn't move again. The twitch must have been some final spark of life passing through its nervous system, a last galvanic death spasm.

'Time to go,' said Az.

'Definitely.'

CHAPTER 92

Burglary In All But Name

The wall dividing the Slamshaft and Lovesharp estates ended at the woodland, giving way to a yew hedge. This was a different kind of border but no less tall and thick. It also seemed no less impenetrable, but anyone who was determined enough, anyone prepared to get down on their belly and crawl and thrust and wriggle, even burrow, could get through.

There was more forest on the other side, and through the trees Az and Cassie could see Slamshaft's ornamental lake and the willows around it and, beyond, the back of the mansion. The fountain in the centre of the lake spurted a jet of green water that rattled down onto the lily pads and duckweed. The air at its shore was dense with gnats and midges. Frogs croaked a dusk chorus.

Lights blazed in a number of windows, but the house did not give off the impression of a great deal of activity within. Moving closer to it, Az and Cassie glimpsed a solitary figure in one of the ground-floor rooms. He stood briefly to help himself to a drink at a drinks cabinet, then sat down again, out of sight.

'That him?' Az asked in a whisper.

'No. Whoever that were had hair. Slamshaft'm a slaphead, remember?'

They sneaked up onto the terrace, ducked past the lit windows, and arrived at a pair of glassed doors. Cassie tentatively tried the knob on one of them. It turned.

Seconds later, they were in the house.

The matronly woman hadn't lied about Slamshaft's penchant for artworks and artefacts. The room Az and Cassie found themselves in, a library, was packed with sculptures, paintings, antiques and curios, not to mention the hundreds of leather-bound books which lined the walls, their tooled-gilt inscriptions glinting in the twilight dimness.

There was no time to stop and stare, however.

'A study,' Cassie suggested. 'That'd be where him keeps his correspondence and such.'

They tried one of the doors leading off from the library. By a stroke of good fortune, it connected to a study.

'Jackpot!' Cassie whispered.

Dominating the room was a desk not much smaller than a king-size bed. A whole tree must have gone into its making. Cassie hurried over and started going through the drawers. They slid out as smoothly as tongues, and each had its cargo of paperwork and stationery. While she rifled through the desk, Az kept lookout, standing with his ear pressed to the door. He still couldn't quite get over the fact that they had illegally entered a house. This was burglary in all but name. A crime! But a crime in a good cause, the ends justifying the means.

The unreality of it all kept threatening to overwhelm him. That and his mild dose of ground-sickness made him woozy. But then there was the pain from his wounds, old and new. Their sharp throbbing helped keep him focused and steady.

Cassie came to a drawer that would not open. Locked.

'A-ha.'

A locked drawer meant something valuable inside, something worth looking at. She grabbed a letter-opener off the desktop, a long slim knife with a sterling silver blade and a jade hilt. With it, she set to work trying to jimmy the drawer open.

The lock was strong and the letter-opener not quite up to the job. Its blade began to bend.

Then a voice spoke from the corner of the room.

'Who's there?' it said.

CHAPTER 93

Living Proof

Cassie froze. The hairs on the nape of Az's neck stood up.

'Who's there?' the voice said again.

It was a strange sound, a cross between a croak and a peep, hardly human at all.

Cassie turned. Az turned. Both of them peered into the gloom. There was no one in the corner, they were certain of that. All they could see was a small table with a cloth-covered, dome-shaped object on it. This looked like just another of Slamshaft's many ornaments . . .

. . . yet it was the source of the voice. The sound could not have come from anywhere else.

Neither of them moved. Or even dared breathe.

Once more the voice piped up.

'Good evening, milord.'

Az frowned. There was a tiny click of recognition in his head.

'Hold on a second,' he said softly.

Crossing the room, he whisked the cloth off the thing it was draped over.

The dome-shaped object was a cage, which was home to a perky little mynah bird. The mynah hopped along its perch, eyed Az quizzically, then let out a faint squawk, followed by a two-tone whistle.

'I's not seen one of they before,' said Cassie. 'What kind of bird be it?'

'It's a mynah. People keep them as pets.'

'Your people maybe. And it . . . talks?'

'No, it parrots. Like, er, a parrot. You know, mimics what you say.'

'What you say,' said the mynah, obligingly proving Az's point.

'The question is,' he said, 'why's it here?'

Cassie shrugged. 'Probably it'm just one of Slamshaft's possessions.'

'Well, yeah, but you just told me you don't have mynahs down here.'

'So it were a gift from someone Airborn.'

'But you heard. It said "milord". That's not an expression you Ground-lings use.'

'OK. So it'm a mystery, straight up. Now help I get this damn drawer open.'

Az leaned close to the wire-thin bars of the cage.

'You know,' he said, 'I'm pretty sure I know this bird.'

The mynah looked back at him beadily, almost as if it recognised him too.

'Are you . . . Echo?'

In answer, the mynah chirped, 'Pompous old windbag, milord.'

Az blinked; then a smile flirted with his lips.

'That's me. I said that. To Lord Urironson. When he turned up at the house where the First!ers were holding me.'

'Roll up your sleeves, *thweet!*' said the mynah. 'Get stuck in.'

'And that's Lord Urironson telling Mr Mordadson to start a fight with me. This is definitely Echo. Lord Urironson's mynah.'

'Echo,' said Echo, putting the matter beyond doubt.

'So?' said Cassie.

'So, what in the name of all that's high and bright is it doing in Dominic Slamshaft's house? Unless . . .'

A series of connections fizzed through Az's brain, idea knocking against idea like a row of dominoes.

Lord Urironson. Mr Mordadson. Dominic Slamshaft. Feather First!. War.

In a flash, it all became clear.

Mr Mordadson had been keeping close tabs on Lord Urironson but wasn't in league with him. His lordship, meanwhile, had used Feather First! to provide a diversion, enabling another ally, Slamshaft, to launch his war while the Airborn's attention was elsewhere. Mr Mordadson hadn't known about this. How could he? Otherwise he'd have made moves to prevent the war happening, or at least prepared a defence against the attacks.

Az was sure of all this, as sure as he'd even been of anything. It confirmed his belief that Mr Mordadson had not betrayed him. Mr Mordadson had been undercover at the First!er house in Prismburg, so had had to demonstrate his supposed loyalty to Lord Urironson by agreeing to fight with Az. But, being Mr Mordadson, he had used the fight as an opportunity to surreptitiously provide Az with a means of escape.

The only traitor in this whole affair was Lord Urironson. He had betrayed the entire Airborn race. And Az could only think the reason was so that he could take charge once the war was over. Power – it was what Lord Urironson had long been hankering after. Greater power, along with Lady Aanfielsdaughter's downfall, and he would stop at nothing to get either.

'Echo,' Az said to the mynah. He felt slightly foolish, but he knew how intelligent this type of bird could be. There was no harm in asking it a question. It just might give him the answer he wanted. 'Lord Urironson and Slamshaft, they're in this together, correct?'

Echo studied him for a moment. So did Cassie. It was impossible to tell what the mynah was thinking, but Cassie's expression made her thoughts plain: *Has you gone mad?*

Then Echo said, '*Arook!* It's going to be a pleasure. *Awk!* Turning the world upside down with you.'

'That was him,' Az said excitedly. 'That was definitely Lord Urironson. Sounded uncannily like him.'

'I'll take your word for it,' Cassie said, dubious.

'I would say, Dominic,' said Echo. 'Very dangerous indeed.'

'And again,' Az exclaimed. 'That clinches it. Lord Urironson is involved in instigating the war, just like Slamshaft. Forget that drawer, Cassie. You want proof?' He gestured at Echo. 'I've got your proof right here. Living proof. An eyewitness, even.'

'All right, all right,' Cassie hissed. 'Clip it down, would you? Does you want everyone to know us is here?'

'No, of course not. But all we have to do is take this cage and sneak out the way we came, and go straight to the police. Even if what the mynah says can't be used as evidence, the fact that we found it here is pretty incriminating for—'

The door from the library burst open.

Light flooded in.

Framed in the doorway was the man whom Az and Cassie had seen in the window earlier.

He stared at them.

Then he snarled, 'I *thought* I heard talking. I assumed it was that stupid bird. So who the hell are you two?'

Paralysed, Az and Cassie had no idea what to do.

CHAPTER 94

Twenty-one Ways To Kill –
And One Way To Wound

The man advanced into the study. As he did so, Cassie remembered the letter-opener she was still holding. She slipped the slightly bent implement behind her back. The man didn't appear to have seen.

'You're just a pair of children,' he said, bemusedly. 'A rather scruffy pair as well. And you're here to steal something, is that right? Are you two of these street urchins one's always hearing about? If so, you picked the wrong place to burgle, let me tell you. Do you know who I am?'

Nonplussed, Az and Cassie shook their heads.

'I'm Jasper Longnoble-Drumblood, and I'm Dominic Slamshaft's best friend. That's whose house you're in – *the* Dominic Slamshaft. I'm also a serving military officer, a brigadier no less, and I know twenty-one ways to kill a man with my bare hands. How does it make you feel, hearing that? Not too happy, I'd imagine. And here's the thing. You've broken into someone's house. You are on another person's premises without their permission. That means you have no protection under the law. Whatever happens to you is your own fault. If I were to use force on you, and you were to be injured horribly as a result, or even die, I wouldn't be to blame. Amusing, no?'

His smile was cold.

'Us doesn't want any trouble,' said Cassie.

'Oh, doesn't *us*?' sneered Longnoble-Drumblood. 'I think it's a little late for that. If you're lucky I might just leave you capable of walking out of here unaided. *If* you're lucky.'

'Wait,' said Az.

Longnoble-Drumblood flicked a testy glance at him. 'What?'

Az thought fast. There must be some way he could wrongfoot this man, confuse him for a moment. A moment was all they would need. Given an opening, they could rush past him and escape through the library. At any rate they could try.

'You're Slamshaft's best friend, you say?'

'I am, and proud of it.'

'And he's gone to war against the Airborn.'

'He has.' The man's eyes narrowed. 'How d'you know about that?'

Az pressed on. 'And I bet you're the military brains behind the operation, you being a brigadier and all.'

'As a matter of fact that's true. But you'd better explain how a nobody like you knows Dom's responsible for the war.'

'Isn't it a little convenient?'

'What do you mean?'

'Put it this way. Your pal Dominic decides he's going to launch an attack on the sky-cities, and it just so happens he's got a friend who's a professional soldier. Which came first I wonder? The friendship, or the idea for an attack?'

'Now just a minute,' said Longnoble-Drumblood. 'Don't you call him Dominic. You have no right. Only people like me get to call him that. His equals. His peers.'

'But it were pretty handy for he, having you around,' said Cassie. She had cottoned on to Az's ploy. At the same time, in case it didn't work, she kept a tight grip on the letter-opener behind her.

'No,' Longnoble-Drumblood said firmly. 'Dom and I have known each other for ages. He'd never use me like that.'

'Really?' said Cassie. 'Rich people, them tends to be out for whatever them can get from others. Even from their mates. Not much in the way of a conscience, them has. It be'n't in their natures.'

'Dominic is one of the finest men to walk this planet.'

'But do you trust him?' said Az.

'Implicitly.' Longnoble-Drumblood snorted. 'This is ridiculous. I've no idea why I'm even having this conversation. I don't have to justify myself to the likes of you.'

'And yet here you be, doing just that,' said Cassie.

'All right!' he snapped. 'That's enough! Whoever you two are, you've just guaranteed yourselves the thrashing of a lifetime. And you, you common little trollop, are going to get it first.'

Arms outstretched, he skirted the desk and made a lunge for Cassie.

Az leapt to intervene but didn't get there quite in time. Longnoble-Drumblood managed to clamp his hands on Cassie's shoulders and was all set to start knocking her around.

Then, oddly, he loosened his grasp. He gave a startled little choke. His hands fell. It was as though, having been hellbent on hurting Cassie, he had had an abrupt change of heart.

He tottered away, looking down at his left leg.

There, standing proud from his thigh, was the letter-opener. Its blade was fully buried in his flesh, and blood was spilling out over the jade hilt and his trouser leg.

'You . . . you . . .' he spluttered. 'You . . . ghastly child. What have you done?'

'What'm it look like?' Cassie replied. 'What any common little trollop would do when a snooty git gets it into his head to try and beat she up.'

Longnoble-Drumblood lurched towards her in a rage, but his leg gave way under him and he toppled to the floor. He let out a cry that was half pain, half sheer infuriation.

'Come on,' Cassie said to Az. 'Grab that bird and let's scram.'

Echo let out a squawk of protest as Az grabbed the cage. Together, Az and Cassie fled the room with their prize.

'Stop!' Longnoble-Drumblood yelled at them. 'Stop right there!'

He hauled himself part-way upright, clinging to the desk for support.

'STOP!' he roared. 'That is an order, dammit.'

It didn't even occur to Az and Cassie to obey. They sped through the library towards the doors to the terrace. Cassie thrust one of the doors open.

Outside was a glitter of fangs. A pair of lambent, egg-yolk eyes.

The hackerjackal.

With a snarl, it sprang.

CHAPTER 95

A Better, Truer Kind Of World

'Fifth century pre-Cataclysm,' said Slamshaft, indicating the suit of armour with a proud wave of his hand.

Lord Urironson nodded appreciatively.

'You'll note the filigree work on the cuirass,' Slamshaft went on, 'and the decoration on the greaves. See? Those brass flames curling up from the ankles? There was a saying among knights in those days, apparently. "I can run so fast, my feet are alight." '

'It's hard to imagine anyone wearing that much metal being able even to walk, let alone run.'

'Exactly!' Slamshaft laughed. 'It was a joke, and a boast. And that's why the armour-maker put the flames there, as a splendid piece of sales-manship. You might even call it early advertising. "Wear this armour and fleetness of foot *will* be yours!" '

Lord Urironson chuckled politely and stifled a yawn. He was beginning to regret having asked to be given a tour of the mansion. Slamshaft owned so many artefacts, and had such a lot to say about each, that progress from room to room was achingly slow. At first his enthusiasm for his collection had been charming. Now Lord Urironson was finding it somewhat tedious.

'A complete suit like this,' Slamshaft said, 'in such good condition, is almost impossibly rare. It's funny, our race used to treasure the Relics your race deposited on us, yet the true relics, that hardest-to-find and most valuable items, are those from our own history, dating from before the Great Cataclysm.'

'Yes, funny.'

'But the truly beautiful aspect of this armour is the broadsword. Take a look at that. The coat of arms engraved on the pommel – a tiny detail, something only its owner would see. I did consider having my company logo put there instead, but it would be vulgar, an act of desecration. I couldn't do it. The blade itself is hundred-times-folded steel, and still as sharp as a razor. Go on, touch it.'

'I'll take your word for it.'

'No, really. Go on.'

'No.'

'Well, it's lethal, believe me. A cutting edge that sharp, with such a weight of sword behind it, makes any stroke a potentially killing one. I'm a bit of a swordsman myself, you know. I fence regularly with Jasper.'

'Yes,' said Lord Urironson, 'I was aware that the two of you enjoy thrusting your weapons at each other.'

Slamshaft shot him a look, sensing mockery. Lord Urironson's expression, however, was blankly neutral. The remark, it appeared, had been nothing but innocent.

'The rapier is my preferred choice,' he continued. 'It's neat and precise, whereas a broadsword is for bludgeoning. It's as much cosh as blade. Nevertheless, one like this . . .'

Slamshaft regarded the sword dreamily.

'Sometimes,' he said, 'I feel that I don't belong in this age, milord. You ever feel like that? Born out of time? Things are too safe and civilised these days. Hand-to-hand combat is the only true measure of a man's mettle. I suppose I've used business dealings as an outlet for my aggression – you know, fought my battles in the boardroom and on the shop-floor, tested myself that way. But it isn't the same. And I know what you're going to say. You're going to say, "If you feel that way, then why aren't you up there above the clouds, fighting alongside your troops?" Well, it may seem hypocritical to you, but I don't consider what they're doing fighting. It certainly isn't an evenly-matched battle. What I'm talking about is traditional combat, the kind where you look your foe in the eye and he has the same chance of beating you as you do of beating him. Whereas what's going on up there is . . .' He searched for the appropriate phrase.

'A hostile takeover?'

'Yes. Yes! Well put. Not wholly accurate, but well put. But there's more to it than that. All my life, you see, milord, I've been fending off boredom. I've been grappling with the sense that the world is just a bit too unchallenging. I can't stand stagnation, and that, I fear, is what our society has lapsed into.'

'Your society and ours too,' Lord Urironson said, livening up. Slamshaft had hit on a topic that was interesting to him. 'The Airborn have known peace for so long, we've lost purpose and direction. We've grown complacent, soft. We've needed shaking up for quite some time, which is why this war of yours was such a good idea. It's the shock that'll bring us to our senses again. It'll wake us up out of our contented doze.'

'Indeed. And the same for us, especially when your lot retaliate, as they're bound to. When the dust settles and the smoke clears and the rebuilding begins, everyone will be invigorated. Oh, there'll be moaning and grieving, no question. I'm not saying people will be happy about what's happened. But as memories of the conflict fade, I predict a general knuckling-down, a new mood of resolve, possibly even a cheerful one. Something that has been missing in this debased era, a proper understanding of the fragility and preciousness of life, will have been brought back to us, and we'll all be the better for it. Struggle will be the catalyst for a better, truer kind of world. How does the phrase go? "You can't make an omelette without . . ."'

'Sir? Please, sir, excuse I, sir.'

A scullery maid had come bustling into the hallway. She bobbed her head to Slamshaft, then to Lord Urironson.

'I be so sorry to interrupt, sir,' she said, wringing her apron in her hands, 'but cook says she just saw something out of the kitchen window.'

Her employer frowned. 'Something? What do you mean? Spit it out, girl.'

'I don't believe it myself, sir, but cook insists it were . . . Well, she looked out, sir, and there were a . . . a hackerjackal.'

'What!'

'I know, sir. Cook says it were running across the garden towards the house, sir. Only, how could it be? A hackerjackal? Not here in the middle of Craterhome.'

Slamshaft's lips tightened. 'Oh, it could be,' he said grimly. 'It definitely could be.'

'How so, sir?'

'Don't you know? That silly singer woman next door has one. It's meant to be trained so that it doesn't leave the grounds, but . . .'

He left the sentence unfinished, the implication being that you could no more train a hackerjackal than you could command rain to fall upwards. It was madness, having a creature like that as a guard dog. Only a temperamental, highly-strung loon like Lorelei Lovesharp would ever have thought it a good idea.

At that moment, shouting came from the other end of the mansion. A voice bellowed in anger and distress.

'Jasper!' said Slamshaft.

Lord Urironson peered worriedly in the direction the sound was coming from. Wasn't that the part of the building where he had left Echo?

There was more shouting and a clatter of running feet.

Lord Urironson took flight.

Slamshaft, meanwhile, turned and reached out to the suit of armour.

CHAPTER 96

A Dead End

Cassie reacted on reflex. She backpedalled, pulling the door shut with her. The hackerjackal slammed into the door with an almighty *whump*, the impact cracking several of the panes. It recoiled, then launched itself a second time. Both doors shuddered. A splinter flew off one of them at the hinge.

The hackerjackal withdrew, looking as if it was going to make a third assault on the doors. It decided against, and instead began prowling back and forth along the terrace in a figure of eight, its tail lashing. Every so often it put its nose to one of the door panes, clouding the glass with a huff of breath. Then, with a surly snarl, it started prowling again. The gaping gash in the top of its head seemed not to be bothering it. It was beyond feeling pain, too severely injured even to realise it was injured. In the addled frenzy that was its mind, all the hackerjackal knew was that it dearly wished to dismember and disembowel the two young humans. Every instinct it had screamed for bloody revenge. That was why it had pursued them through the hedge, out of its own territory, following their scent across unfamiliar ground. Nothing else mattered to it but their deaths.

But now, there was a barrier between it and them. They were visible, tantalisingly close, but the hackerjackal just could not get at them.

'I thought that thing was dead,' said a shaken Az. 'It ought to be with such a huge great hole in its head. I can even see brain. How come it's still going?'

'What, I's a hackerjackal expert all of a sudden? It be a tough bugger, that'm all I can tell you. Maybe there'm some Amblescrut in its family tree.'

Az let out a thin laugh. 'So how are we supposed to get out of here now?'

'The front door maybe?'

'Or maybe,' said a low, silky voice which Az recognised all too well, 'you don't get out of here at all.'

They turned.

Another of the doors leading out of the library stood wide open, and filling its frame was an imposing, grey-winged figure.

Lord Urironson slowly, resignedly shook his head.

'Azrael Gabrielson,' he said. 'I wish I could say I'm surprised, but somehow I'm not. You freed yourself?'

Az glared at him with pure contempt. 'What do *you* think, pluckhead?' he said acidly.

His lordship brushed aside the insult. 'Well, it was inevitable I suppose. Those First!ers were solid and dependable but anyone with half a brain could have outwitted them. They served their purpose, anyway. And now here you are with . . . your Groundling girlfriend, yes? Miss Grotduller? Grabdollar? Something along those lines.'

'Grubdollar,' Cassie snapped. 'So this be the bloke who had you kidnapped, Az. This'm that Lord Urineson.'

Az smirked and nodded.

'All right, very clever,' said Lord Urironson. 'So we've both made fun of each other's names. Congratulations us. Now, in all seriousness – my mynah, Gabrielson. Hand him over. Right now.' This was said in a tone of voice that suggested he had no doubt Az would comply.

'*Arook!*' said a rather ruffled Echo. 'Hand him over. *Thweet!*'

'Or what?' said Az.

'No, you're looking at this the wrong way,' said Lord Urironson. 'There's no "or" about it. Consider your situation. You've come to steal my bird, for who knows what bizarre reason. Doubtless you've deduced that Slamshaft and I are involved in the events taking place up in the sky-cities and you think that by taking Echo you can – what? Blackmail me? Is that it? Threaten to harm him unless I persuade Slamshaft to call off the attack?'

'Not a bad idea,' Az said. 'Wish I'd thought of that, actually.'

'Or it could be this is just tit-for-tat revenge. I kidnap you, you kidnap my mynah. Well, either way, you've failed. And now that frightful creature out there, that hackerjackal, has cut off that particular means of egress for you. And here am I, blocking another exit route. And look, here's Brigadier Longnoble-Drumblood.'

The aforesaid had just appeared in the study doorway. He hobbled a few steps into the library, ashen-faced, clenching his teeth.

'Are you all right, Jasper?'

'Do I *look* all right?' Longnoble-Drumblood gestured at the protruding letter-opener. From thigh to shin his left trouser-leg was soaked with blood. 'But, I tell you, I'll be feeling a whole lot better in a couple of minutes' time when that little slut who stabbed me gets what's coming to her. Where's Dom?'

'Right behind me. In fact . . .' Lord Urironson glanced over his shoulder, then moved aside from the doorway.

In strode Slamshaft.

He was younger than Az had expected, or at any rate younger-looking. The shaven head somehow smoothed out his features, making his true age hard to estimate. Az had pictured him as a corpulent corporate type, one boozy lunch away from his first heart attack. But this man was sharp and lithe and evidently dangerous.

Not least because he came in bearing a broadsword and a shield. They were both venerable-looking items, burnished and brass-trimmed, and Slamshaft held them with a confident deftness, the sword at an angle, the shield screening his left flank. It wasn't hard to see that he knew how to use them properly.

'Right, what's going on here?' Slamshaft barked. 'What's all this . . .' His face fell as he laid eyes on Az and Cassie. 'Kids?'

'Don't underestimate them,' warned Lord Urironson. 'These two may be young but they're trouble. Especially the boy. That's Az Gabrielson.'

'Oh. Oh yes, you mentioned him. What's he doing here?'

'Absconding with my mynah, by the looks of things.'

'The girl's trouble too,' said Longnoble-Drumblood.

'Really?' said Slamshaft. 'She doesn't look like it to me.'

'Trust me. Look.'

'Your leg! Jasper, are you—'

'Yes, yes, fine, I'll live. It hurts like blazes, but it's a flesh wound. She missed the artery. Just get on with it, Dom. Kill the brats, then I can go and find a doctor.'

Slamshaft swivelled back round to face Az and Cassie.

'So let me see if I can work out what's going on here,' he said, in a brisk, summing-up kind of way. 'You've broken into my home to steal his lordship's mynah, my friend caught you in the act and tried to stop you so you stuck a letter-opener in him, and out there' – he glanced past them – 'is next-door's hackerjackal, whose presence in my garden is a fact not unconnected with your presence in my house. Would those be correct assumptions? My my, you two *are* trouble, aren't you?'

'I just want my mynah,' Lord Urironson said. 'I've already told them to give him back and they refused. But so help me, if they harm so much as one feather on his head . . .'

That, for Slamshaft, clinched it.

'You'd better do as his lordship asks,' he said, closing in on Az and Cassie with the sword levelled. 'This is a weapon that hasn't tasted blood

289

in several centuries. Do you really want to be the ones who help bring an end to its drought?'

There wasn't much you could say in answer to a remark like that. Az and Cassie simply exchanged looks. Both knew they'd managed to get themselves cornered. They were in a dead end – a literal dead end. In each other's eyes they saw a hopelessness and desperation that acknowledged this fact.

But they also saw a shared resolve, a refusal to go down without a fight.

They smiled at each other, fatalistically.

Then, in unison, they acted.

CHAPTER 97

Man Versus Hackerjackal In Single Combat

Cassie grasped the doorknob and turned it.

Az swung the birdcage and threw it.

Two different kinds of howl erupted. One was a howl of triumph from the hackerjackal, as it saw that it was being allowed access to the place where all the humans were. The other was a howl of horror from Lord Urironson, as he saw his precious Echo being hurled violently through space.

Az and Cassie flung themselves in opposite directions as the hackerjackal shot through the open door in a blur of pelt and sinew. Meanwhile Lord Urironson took to the air, reaching out to catch the cage.

The hackerjackal's full-tilt leap carried it past the two young humans, the ones it was so keen on sinking its teeth into and tearing apart. Momentum propelled it straight towards the human in the middle of the room, the male with the pink head and the bits of metal in his hands. As it landed the hackerjackal debated whether to turn around but decided to keep on going. All five humans in the room were going to die, it was certain about that. The wild animal in it demanded nothing less than total slaughter. The male with the metal in his hands was as good a place to start as any.

Slamshaft, of course, had other ideas.

He rushed at the hackerjackal, broadsword aloft. There was a ferocious glint in his eye, a matching smile on his lips. This was precisely the sort of challenge he had been speaking about to Lord Urironson. Man versus hackerjackal in single combat. He just couldn't pass up such an opportunity. Besides, he was the only person in the room who was armed, and the only person who stood a hope of halting the beast in its tracks.

The hackerjackal struck at him with a forepaw. Its talons raked along the shield, screeching and leaving scratch-marks in the steel. Slamshaft responded with a slash of his sword. The hackerjackal shrank back, the tip of the blade whirring past its muzzle, missing by millimetres.

At the same instant Lord Urironson came back down, alighting on the floor with Echo's cage in cradled in his arms. He cooed and murmured to the bird, trying to soothe it, while Echo flustered against the bars and shrilled in indignation.

Cassie scrambled to her feet and beelined for the open doorway to the terrace. Az began following her but then spun on his heel.

'What'm you doing? Us should scarper while us can!'

'I'm not leaving without the mynah. If we don't have it, then all this has been pointless.'

'But you just chucked it away.'

'I didn't want to run from the hackerjackal carrying it. But things have changed and I've got a chance of getting it back.'

He darted around a small side-table, picking up a spherical crystal paperweight as he went. He jumped onto a sofa and, using the cushions as a springboard, launched himself through the air at Lord Urironson.

Meanwhile the snarling, seething hackerjackal was subjecting Slamshaft to a barrage of bites and slashes. He deflected each with the shield, but the animal's onslaught was driving him backwards, step by step. His sword blows were finding their mark, a nick on an ear, a jab to a shoulder, but the hackerjackal shrugged these off as though they were pinpricks. Still, Slamshaft's face was a mask of glee. The thrill of the fight and the deadliness of his foe made him feel alive. Not since running Harry Brickmansworth through with his rapier had he experienced such a heart-pounding rush of *purpose*. But that was nothing compared with this. Doling out death to an unarmed victim was one thing, confronting death was quite another. Facing a savage beast, with only his wits and swordsmanship to save him – *this* was what living was truly about.

He found himself pressed up against a wall, and the hackerjackal reared on its hind legs and landed on him with its full weight. If he hadn't put the shield between him and it in time, its talons would now be rending his chest to ribbons.

The hackerjackal snapped at his face. Strings of bloody drool flew from its jowls. Its breath was the stench of the slaughterhouse. Its eyes were fire.

Every muscle in Slamshaft's body strained to hold the hackerjackal at bay. Every erg of energy he had went on keeping those fangs from tearing his face off.

Longnoble-Drumblood observed that his friend was in difficulties. The hackerjackal had the better of him. Slamshaft was in a position where he couldn't even raise the sword to counterattack with. The thing was squashing him against the wall.

With a grimace, Longnoble-Drumblood realised what he must do.

He grasped the hilt of the letter-opener and began working the blade free. He gritted his teeth but eventually the pain was too great and he couldn't contain his scream any more. He let it out, howling as the letter-opener twisted through thigh muscle and gradually emerged. With a final wrench it came out, dripping blood and gobbets of flesh and skin.

Longnoble-Drumblood hissed with relief. Then, letter-opener in hand, he limped grimly towards Slamshaft and the hackerjackal.

Az would have caught Lord Urironson unawares, if Echo hadn't spotted him coming and chirped a warning.

'Milord!' it croaked.

Lord Urironson half-turned, just in time to see Az bounding off the sofa, brandishing the paperweight. Instinctively, he brought up a wing. It struck Az on the chin and he was volleyed sideways, straight into a bookcase. He ricocheted off, the paperweight flying from his grasp. As he hit the floor, dozens of voluminous tomes tumbled from their shelves onto him, swamping him in a landslide of paper and leather.

Cassie knew she had no choice but to go to his aid. Az was struggling to get up, and Lord Urironson, having set aside the birdcage, was standing over him with a triumphant gleam in his eyes.

'Loathsome boy,' he said, snatching up the paperweight which Az had been intending to use on *him*. 'Lady Aanfieldsdaughter's special little cripple. You disgust me. I should have had my First!ers kill you. It would have saved everyone a lot of bother. Ah well, if you want a job done properly . . .' He hoisted the paperweight above his head. 'It'll be doing our entire race a favour, eliminating a wingless abortion of nature like you.'

'Put that down, your lordship,' said Cassie. 'Put it down or the bird gets it.'

She had Echo clasped firmly in her fist. Lord Urironson's gaze flicked to the cage, whose little door stood open. It was as if he'd been hoping Cassie had somehow got hold of another mynah, conjured one out of thin air perhaps.

The bird could move only its head. Its beak gaped and its eyes glittered with panic.

'I'll crush it,' she said. 'Don't think I won't because I will. Us Groundlings doesn't make such a fuss as you Airborn over things with wings. Now put the damn paperweight down.'

Lord Urironson hesitated, then lowered his arm.

'Please,' he said softly. 'Please don't hurt him. He's my only friend in the world.'

Az pushed himself up onto all fours, shaking off the books that had half buried him.

'Owww,' he said.

'Please,' Lord Urironson begged again, holding out his free hand to Cassie.

At that moment, Longnoble-Drumblood reached Slamshaft and, without a pause, jammed the letter-opener into the hackerjackal's eye. The beast recoiled, keening in distress. The popped eyeball oozed a slick of yellow jelly down the side of its face. The hackerjackal swiped at the letter-opener with its paw and managed to dislodge it. With its single remaining eye it glared balefully at Longnoble-Drumblood.

Then it charged, fangs bared.

Longnoble-Drumblood tried to get out of the way but his injured leg twisted under him and he stumbled.

Slamshaft unthinkingly threw himself into the hackerjackal's path.

Its jaws fastened around his hairless head. At the same time, the broadsword slid between two of the hackerjackal's ribs. The animal's forward motion made this a perfect killing blow. The sword impaled the length of its body, the tip emerging somewhere in the region of its hindquarters.

But in the throes of death, the hackerjackal's jaws clamped shut like a vice.

Slamshaft managed a half-second's scream, which was cut off by a horrendous cracking sound, like rocks breaking or a thick tree branch being wrenched in half.

They toppled to the floor, locked together, the business magnate and the mangled beast, both of them utterly and incontrovertibly dead.

CHAPTER 98

Just Deserts

There was silence then, a shocked, ghastly silence, ultimately broken by a wail of anguish from Longnoble-Drumblood. He crawled over to Slamshaft, struggled to free his friend's head from the hackerjackal's maw, succeeded, then cradled the corpse in his lap. Rocking Slamshaft to and fro, he wept and babbled. He talked of the good times they had had together, all the things they'd done and the places they'd visited, jokes they'd shared. The words came out in a torrent, and the tears likewise.

Az and Cassie looked on. Az veered between pity and indifference. He couldn't forget that Longnoble-Drumblood had manhandled Cassie and that he was complicit in the war. Equally, the man's agony was terrible to behold.

Cassie was much harder-hearted. Slamshaft had got his just deserts, and Longnoble-Drumblood could cry himself dry for all she cared.

As for Lord Urironson, his principal response was self-interest: he saw that he had one last chance to retrieve Echo. He sidled towards Cassie, the crystal paperweight still in his fist. With Longnoble-Drumblood's grief providing a distraction, he thought he would be able to sneak up on the girl from behind, knock her cold and get his beloved pet back. He quite liked the idea of ramming the paperweight into Cassie's skull. In fact, he looked forward to it. Despicable, bird-hating child.

A loud, crashing *clang* from outside put paid to his lordship's plans.

Cassie jerked her head round at the noise. She spotted Lord Urironson, instantly clocked what he was up to, and raised the mynah in front of her.

'Uh-uh,' she said, putting her other hand around Echo's head. 'I'll wring its neck. Straight up I will.'

Immediately in the wake of the clang came a whoop of police sirens.

Lord Urironson sensed defeat. Numbly he let the paperweight drop. It clunked to the floor and rolled beneath a lacquered-wood display cabinet. His glance strayed to the wide-open terrace door, and Az could see him weighing up the alternatives: whether to flee and leave Echo behind, or remain where he was to ensure the mynah's continued safety.

'Don't,' Az said. 'Don't even think about ducking out of here. I beat your First!er henchmen, remember? Three of them weren't a match for me. What makes you think a clapped-out old buzzard like you will do any better? Now just sit down, shut up, and wait.'

Fuming but resigned, Lord Urironson did as told.

Moments later, the mansion was invaded by dozens of police officers. They were everywhere, indoors, outdoors, swarming all over the place, and with them came . . .

'Da! Fletch! Robert!'

Cassie ran to greet her family. By this time Echo was back in his cage and had been entrusted to Az for safekeeping. Cassie was engulfed in a massive Grubdollar group-hug.

A plainclothes policeman appeared, puffing on a pipe. He surveyed the bloody scene in the library, and gave orders to the uniformed coppers, telling them to cordon off the area around the bodies of Slamshaft and the hackerjackal and find something to cover them up with. Then he tapped out the dottle from his pipe into the fireplace and strode over to Lord Urironson. Having introduced himself as Inspector Treadwell, the detective in charge of this investigation, he confessed to mild surprise that there was a member of the Airborn race present.

'You need to be talking to me, not him,' Az said.

'I does?' said Treadwell.

Az pointed at the sulky Lord Urironson. 'That man there is an accomplice of Dominic Slamshaft. Just as that man there' – he gestured at Longnoble-Drumblood, who was being persuaded to let go of Slamshaft – 'is also. *Him* I'll leave you to deal with, but his lordship here, he's my race's responsibility, and I aim to see he's punished to the fullest extent of our laws.'

Treadwell raised an eyebrow. 'And just who might you be?'

Az told him.

Much to his gratification, Inspector Treadwell had heard of Az Gabrielson. Even more gratifyingly, he deferred to Az's judgement when it came to dealing with Lord Urironson.

Meanwhile, outside on the mansion driveway, *Cackling Bertha* stood at the head of a long queue of parked police cars. She had been used to ram the gates, one of which now hung open and askew, the other of which had been knocked off its hinges completely and lay buckled on the ground.

Inside *Bertha*, Colin Amblescrut and a constable were keeping an eye on Cuthbert Roundcoring, the site manager at the Slamshaft plant. Roundcoring looked exceedingly glum. Treadwell had gone to him and persuaded him that it would be in his best interests to rat on his boss. He'd told him the game was up. The police had evidence of the company's involvement in the war on the Airborn, and only by agreeing to testify against Slamshaft could Roundcoring save his own neck. In exchange, he would receive immunity from prosecution. He might never hold down a decent job again, his days of well-paid white-collar employment were over, but at least he wouldn't be going to prison.

Faced with such a choice, the podgy site manager had agreed to do as Treadwell asked, which then gave Treadwell grounds to be able to obtain a warrant for Slamshaft's arrest from Chief Superintendent Coldriser.

Roundcoring realised he had aroused the inspector's suspicions earlier by saying he didn't want to take legal action against the people who had attacked the factory with fireworks and taken the murk-comber. What else could he have done, though? The war plans had been at a delicate stage and the last thing anyone needed was a bunch of policemen poking around at the factory, sticking their noses everywhere.

In a sense, Slamshaft only had himself to blame. Roundcoring was oddly relieved that it was all over and he wouldn't have to go lying to the authorities again.

He was aware that he was seated in the very same murk-comber that had helped bring Slamshaft Engineering's shady activities to the police's attention in the first place. The irony, painful as it was, was not lost on him.

After an hour, police officers began emerging from the mansion. Something was up. Car after car pulled out into the street and drove away into the night. Roundcoring had no way of knowing where they were all headed . . . but he had a pretty strong suspicion that it was to the Relentless Desert.

CHAPTER 99

Desert Justice

The last of the Cloudbusters came in to land, zeroing in on the runway lights, then taxiing to a halt beside its fellow planes.

Celebrations were well under way in the camp. Crates of beer had been broached. A massive barbecue was roasting away. Comrades had been lost, and it was rumoured that the Airborn had managed to down one of the Cloudbusters. But in general, the mood was victorious. The raids had been a great success, and there was the prospect of more tomorrow.

Across the encampment, everyone thought of themselves as heroes. And why not? There was cheering and the occasional drunken outburst of song. Jubilation rang to the clouds.

Then: a flicker of red lights on the horizon.

A squall of sirens, rapidly getting louder.

A long line of police vehicles came into view. It was seemingly endless. Nobody had ever seen so many of them at once. It was as if all the cop cars in the Westward Territories were driving across the desert. And not just cars either; there were vans as well, the kind that had no passenger windows, the kind that were used to transport prisoners from A to B.

The vehicles encircled the camp. The party atmosphere rapidly cooled. All at once the 'heroes' felt horribly sober.

Many of them took to their heels, racing off into the dark wilderness. This being the Relentless Desert, they were never heard from again. *Missing, Presumed Dead* was how they would be described in the police case-files.

Others ran to the Cloudbusters, but the planes were too low on fuel to risk flying.

Some went for their crossbows, but they had run out of bolts and the armoury was locked.

The police moved in. There were countless scuffles. Hundreds of arrests were made.

For the Craterhome Metropolitan Police Force it was the busiest night in living memory, but also one of the most satisfying. By morning, the job was done. The troops in Slamshaft's illegal war had been rounded up and cuffed and were on their way to the city. A few would manage to bribe or wheedle their way out of trouble. The Craterhome legal system was far from flawless. But the vast majority would face arraignment and sentencing, followed by lengthy prison terms, because with an operation this size, even normally unprincipled lawmen could see that justice came first, above all other considerations; and also, given the circumstances, public scrutiny of their actions would be that much more intense, so they couldn't afford to be seen bending the rules.

Sometimes honesty wasn't just the best policy, it was the only policy available.

CHAPTER 100

And Then . . .

En route from the elevators to his house, Az saw for himself the destruction that had been visited on High Haven. Large portions of his hometown were a smoking ruin. Some of the main thoroughfares had been bombed so extensively as to be all but unrecognisable. Sunbeam Boulevard, for instance, existed now in name alone, a mark on a street map. Collapsed buildings on either side had filled it in, and there was nothing to prove it had once been the city's main four-lane artery except the odd traffic sign and half-buried aircraft sticking up from the rubble.

Everywhere, Az saw people putting boards over hollowed-out windows and sweeping up dust and broken glass. They moved slowly, mechanically, their eyes glazed with shock.

It was bad, but he drew comfort from the thought that, without his and Cassie's efforts, it could have been so much worse.

Luckily, his own neighbourhood had escaped bombardment. The worst any of the houses in his street had suffered was a few cracked roof shingles.

He wasn't expecting a rousing reception as he entered the house. He had, however, thought his parents would show how glad they were to see him alive and well, even if in a subdued way. In the event, his mother just hugged him silently, then started sobbing.

That was when he had his first inkling that something was very wrong.

'Come into the living room, Az,' his father said, solemnly. 'Sit down. I have some news.'

It wasn't good news, either. Az knew that. His father's tone of voice told him so; the redness and swollenness of his mother's eyes confirmed it.

'It's Michael . . .' Gabriel Enochson began.

'He's dead?' said Az, scarcely able to believe he was uttering the words.

'No. No, no. Michael is alive. But . . .'

A few hours later, Az was at Michael's bedside in Aurora's apartment at the Sanctum.

Michael's entire torso was swathed in bandages. His eyes were ringed with purple circles, while the rest of his face was pallid, almost bleached in its whiteness. Clumps of his hair, and one eyebrow, were missing, singed off. There were a few minor burns elsewhere on his body. He barely acknowledged Az's presence. He stared up at the ceiling, his head shifting listlessly from time to time, his gaze unfocused, as if he was contemplating far horizons of sorrow.

It was shocking to see him without wings. Their absence disfigured him, dehumanised him. It was hard to remember that this was Michael. He looked like someone else, someone Az vaguely recognised but didn't know.

According to Az's father, Michael's wings had been burned so badly that the doctors had had no alternative but to amputate. The damage certainly could not be repaired. Better to remove what was left of the wings, so as to prevent infection. In a three-hour operation, surgeons had cut them off clean down to the sockets.

Az tried to put a brave face on it. He joked gently with his brother, telling him that he had it on good authority that Michael Gabrielson was a hero who had saved hundreds of lives. Well, that put the two of them on an even footing, didn't it? At last Michael was catching up with his kid brother in the derring-do stakes.

It wasn't very convincing. That kind of teasing worked only if your voice didn't crack and your heart wasn't breaking.

Az tried another tack. 'It's . . . it's not so bad, Mike. Not having wings. Honestly. I've managed without all this time. It hasn't stopped me, has it?'

Finally Michael found his voice. 'Az?'

'Yeah?'

'Just pluck off, will you?'

The abuse was delivered so feebly, Az couldn't take offence. Michael was too lost in his misery even to be angry properly. His words had no sting.

'He shouldn't have saved me,' Michael went on, in a dull monotone. 'Mordadson. He should just have let me fall. It would have been better. Anything would have been better than . . . this.'

'Mike, I—'

With a wince, Michael rolled over, turning his back on Az and putting his face to the wall. He didn't want to hear any more from his brother, or from anyone.

'Right then,' Az snapped. 'If you're going to be like that . . . Pluck you.'

He went to the sitting room, commiserated with Aurora for a while, then left the apartment.

In the gyro-cab back to High Haven, soaring through the blue, he felt once more the pull of the void inside him, the inner darkness he had glimpsed during his time as the First!ers' captive. He felt its weight and gravity. Its evenness. Its certainty.

Everything else was an illusion, he realised. The moments of exquisite happiness he and Cassie had recently shared – an illusion. The achievement of bringing Slamshaft's war to an end almost as soon as it had begun – an illusion. All the good works he had done in his life – an illusion. Nothing meant anything, not in a world like this, a world that could allow an event as awful as Michael's wings getting burnt off. The one confirmed truth was the black emptiness in his own soul. Believing in anything else was just fooling himself.

The long journey gave Az plenty of time to dwell on these thoughts.

The person who stepped out of the gyro-cab at the other end was not the same Az who had got on board.

CHAPTER 101

And Then . . .

Cassie assumed that a visit from Inspector Treadwell could only mean that a few loose ends needed to be tied up, a few legal formalities needed to be sorted out. That was all. When she invited him into the house, she even thought the smile he gave her was a reassuring one, not just a polite one.

How wrong could a girl be?

'I know I told you there'd be no repercussions from anything you did at the Slamshaft factory,' Treadwell said to the assembled family as he sat down in their lounge. 'The assistance you gave we in fingering Slamshaft as the culprit behind the war puts you firmly in the clear as far as the law be concerned. Likewise the assistance you gave we in our effort to arrest he, even if that didn't work out quite as planned.'

'Well, that'm good news, right?' said Den, slapping his hands on his thighs in a positive, hearty kind of way.

'It be,' Treadwell confirmed. 'There'm also some good news for you in the fact that Slamshaft Engineering Incorporated has gone into receivership. Basically, the firm's been obliged to fold and all its assets has been seized by the state, along with Slamshaft's personal fortune. The money'll be going towards war reparations. In other words, compensating the Airborn for what Slamshaft did to they. It won't even begin to cover the cost of fixing the damage, and it won't make up for the lives that has been lost, but it'm a gesture in the right direction.'

'How be that good news for we?' asked Robert. 'Don't get I wrong, I's pleased for the Airborn and everything, but . . .'

'How it affects you be that any design patents owned by Slamshaft Engineering be now up for grabs.'

Fletcher perked up. 'Meaning my Fletcher Tank . . .'

'. . . could be yours again,' said Treadwell with a nod.

'Yes!' Fletcher cried, punching the air. 'Wahoo!'

'Except,' Treadwell went on, 'there'm a dozen major corporations all circling Slamshaft's company like vultures round a carcass, keen to pick off all the tasty bits for themselves. Them has more money and better legal representation than you, so if you wanted the patents, you'm going to have a fight on your hands, and I suspect you won't win.'

'Oh,' said Fletcher.

Treadwell took out his pipe and tobacco from his pocket. 'Anyone mind?'

'Go right ahead,' said Den.

Filling and lighting the pipe gave Treadwell a minute or so in which to compose his thoughts and allow the Grubdollars to settle down again. Eventually Fletcher stopped whooping and shouting about how rich the family was going to be and how, even though they were going to be gazillionaires, they weren't going to be loony warmongering gazillionaires like Slamshaft.

'That aside, there'm one really big problem, however,' Treadwell said, exhaling blue plumes of Palmwater's Finest Shag.

'Yeah,' said Den, 'I were beginning to get the feeling there must be.'

'What sort of hitch?' said Cassie.

'For one thing,' said Treadwell, 'us has good reason to believe that there was other folk involved in Slamshaft's scheme. According to his domestic staff, over the past few months Slamshaft'd been having regular, secretive meetings with a dozen or so very important men and women. Us even has a few of their names. The likelihood, though, of we being able to pin anything on they – well, given who us is talking about, it'm going to be pretty slim. These is the highest of the high-ranking, the wealthiest of the wealthy. Probably them was there to help finance the whole operation, but there'm no money trail us has been able to follow. And without absolute, definite, cast-iron proof that them was in on it, trying to get they to court would be futile. Us'd be on a hiding to nothing.'

'So?' said Cassie. 'It'm a shame, but I don't see how it'm relevant to we. Somebodies like they won't give a hoot about nobodies like we.'

Treadwell disagreed. 'Them just may, at that. You's responsible for bringing down their friend and colleague, after all, and that way putting they in jeopardy to a certain extent. Them may well take that amiss. I's not saying them will, but it'm a possibility worth bearing in mind. You's made yourselves some powerful enemies.'

Den grinned his three-tooth grin. 'Powerful enemies? Pah! Bring it on, I say. Mess with the Grubdollars and you's messing with trouble.'

'I admire your bravado. But there'm more, I's afraid. Jasper Longnoble-Drumblood . . .'

Cassie snorted. 'That scumbag.'

'Quite. But unfortunately, him's a very posh scumbag from a family with good connections. Him's also, at present, a scumbag who'm out on bail. Us has him on charges of assault on a minor – that'm you, Cassie – and of conspiracy to commit mass murder. But he being who him be, I don't know if us is going to be able to make the charges stick, even the assault one. Not only that but it'm reported that him's been going around making threats against the people who killed his friend Slamshaft.'

'That'm I again,' said Cassie.

'Along with your boyfriend from up there. Now, these is threats that I would take seriously if I was you. Very seriously. Them's not bluster at all. Longnoble-Drumblood be out for revenge and be just about reckless and grief-crazed enough to try and take it, too. Him's in trouble already and might think it don't make much difference if him gets into deeper trouble.'

'You's saying us should take care,' said Den. 'Watch our backs. That type of thing.'

'More than that, Den,' Treadwell replied gravely. 'I be advising you to go into hiding for a while.'

'What?' said Robert.

'Hiding?' said Fletcher.

'Come again?' said Den.

'Only till it all blows over. Longnoble-Drumblood could end up in jail. Slamshaft's rich pals could decide it'd be better to leave you alone rather than stir up any more hassle for themselves by going after you. I's proposing a temporary exile, that'm all. Somewhere far away where nobody knows you. Just to be on the safe side.'

He stood up to go.

'I'll leave you to think about it. But if you does decide to follow my suggestion, do it soon and don't tell anyone where you be going. Not a single person. Not even I. Understood?'

The family debated the issue long into the night, but in the end there could be only one decision, and it was unanimous.

The next morning, their house was empty and *Bertha* was gone from the courtyard. No one in Grimvale, not even Colin Amblescrut, had any clue why the family had departed so abruptly or where they'd disappeared to. Nor would anyone in Grimvale see them again for many a month.

CHAPTER 102

And Then . . .

'Ah, there you are. I was hoping I'd bump into you.'

Az frowned at Mr Mordadson. 'Bump into me? You were looking for me, more like.'

Mr Mordadson acknowledged this with one of his thin smiles and a slight shake of his wings. 'All right, you got me. Yes, I was looking for you. I went to your house but your parents said you were out and about in town, they didn't know where, although apparently you did mumble something about shops as the front door closed behind you. In High Haven, "shops" basically means the Seven Dreams Mall. So here I am, and here you are.'

'Here we are,' said Az.

Around him and Mr Mordadson, streams of people flowed along the main concourse of the Seven Dreams. A week after the bombing, High Haven's premier retail destination was in business once more. Some areas remained cordoned off, with notices warning NO ENTRY – UNSAFE STRUCTURE. But the majority of the mall stood more or less intact, and where there had been superficial damage in its interior, the concession holders had tidied up, re-glazed their display windows, dusted down their stock, and proudly turned the little signs on their doors from Closed to Open. It was an indication that things were getting back to normal, or at any rate that everyone was trying hard to get things back to normal. Whether life in the Airborn realm would ever be truly normal again was a matter of debate.

'Your mum and dad are worried about you,' Mr Mordadson said. 'They told me you've not been yourself these past few days. You barely talk to them, they have no idea where you are half the time . . .'

'Yeah, well, I'm old enough that I don't have to give them hourly updates on my movements.'

'But as a courtesy, you could at least say when you might be home again. You can see why they might be concerned, can't you? What with Michael being—'

'Look,' Az cut in, 'have you come all this way just to give me a lecture on how to be a good son? Because if you have, save it. Not interested.'

'No,' said Mr Mordadson. 'No, actually I . . . Would you like to go and get a coffee?'

'Not particularly.'

'I'd appreciate it if you said yes. We need to talk, you and I.'

'Do we?'

'The fact that you just said that, and the way you said it, means we definitely do.'

Az allowed himself to be coaxed into joining Mr Mordadson for a beverage at the Skyline Café, up on the roof of the mall.

From here, there was a panoramic view of High Haven, and you could see the full extent of the devastation wrought by the Groundlings, and also the scale of the rebuilding programme that was already well under way. Cranes towered above the cityscape, hauling girders and pallets of bricks and timber into place and shifting debris into hover-skips for disposal. Workmen flocked around the less badly hit buildings, layering plaster onto façades and shoring up tumbledown walls. It was like seeing flesh put back on skeletons, the dead restored to life.

'Gives you cause for hope, doesn't it?' said Mr Mordadson, looking out across the city. He took a sip of his coffee, which he took strong and black.

'Yeah, whatever,' said Az. He had opted for a glass of carbonated water with a twist of lime – sharp and bitter on his tongue.

'Listen, Az,' said Mr Mordadson, setting down his cup, 'I know I should have told you what I was up to with Lord Urironson, and I'm sorry I didn't, and if you want to be angry with me about that, then fine, be my guest. You have to understand, I simply couldn't take the risk of letting anyone else in on the plan. It took me ages to cultivate Urironson's trust, making him believe I was working for him and only pretending to work for Lady Aanfieldsdaughter, and he's such a wily old owl. The whole act was delicately poised and a careless word from the wrong person could have brought it all crashing down.'

'What it boils down to is you didn't have faith in me. You didn't think it was safe to share your secret with me.'

'No, what it boils down to is I had to make it look convincing. I had to leave him in no doubt that my old allies, mainly you and her ladyship, meant nothing to me, and the best way to do that, the *only* way, was to keep you both in the dark. Or so I thought. Let's say I had clued you in. If Lord Urironson then saw me with one or other of you, there was a chance you might give the game away. Not deliberately, not consciously, but still, something you did or said might tip him off that you knew I was only faking my loyalty to him. The safest subterfuge is the one nobody else knows about. If it's any consolation, Lady Aanfielsdaughter is pretty peeved with me as well. She appreciates that what I did was for the best, but it'll be a while before she forgives me, I fear. Assuming she ever forgives me.'

'And how is her ladyship?'

It sounded like Az couldn't care less.

'She's understandably upset about everything that's happened,' Mr Mordadson said. 'She blames herself, first and foremost, and I've tried hard as I can to convince her she's wrong but without success. She's at a very low ebb. Between you and me, I have a horrible feeling she might be about to pack it all in and retire. Worse than that – she was asking me about the Cumula Collective the other day, wondering what it would be like to live there.'

Az was genuinely surprised. 'Lady Aanfielsdaughter, joining the Collective?'

'Maybe it was just talk, I don't know. But she's depressed, and depressed people are apt to take dramatic steps, are they not? Do things that are completely out of character.'

'How would I know?' Az shrugged, and the gesture led to a tiny wince of discomfort.

'You all right?' Mr Mordadson asked. 'Is your wound still bothering you?'

Az glanced down at his right forearm. 'The stitches are out. It's mending. So, Lord Urironson? What's likely to happen to him?'

'He's due to face a Special Tribunal of senior Sanctum residents, although no date's been set for that as yet. Trial by twelve of his peers. If it goes the way it ought to, he'll be stripped of his rank and put away for life.'

'It might *not* go as it ought to?'

'Afraid so. We could certainly get him on the lesser charge of kidnap. Your three First!er friends were pretty sore when they discovered he didn't really support their cause, he'd just been using them. They'll testify against him, no question. But the main charge is treason against the realm. That's the one he should really go down for, but that's also the one that's going to be hard to make stick.'

'But it's clearly an open and shut case. I mean, Cassie and I caught him in Slamshaft's house. They were allies. What more do you need to convict him?'

'Lord Urironson still has friends in the Sanctum, people who'll back him however overwhelming the evidence against him is. That's why there's no trial date. Putting together an *impartial* Special Tribunal is proving next to impossible. Lots of his lordship's cronies want to be on it and have put their names down for the lottery. Which means there's every chance one or more of them will have their names drawn out of the hat and end up in the final twelve, and that'll make it almost impossible for there to be the unanimous verdict needed. And,' he added, 'even if a trial does go ahead, there's a huge question mark hanging over the validity of the star witness.'

'Star witness? You mean . . .'

'Lord Urironson's mynah. That damn bird has got everything we need, lodged up there in its little brain.' Mr Mordadson tapped his temple. 'I've been . . . interviewing it, if that's the right word. All you have to do is supply a leading question, prompt it just a little, and it'll blurt out a snatch of conversation, something Lord Urironson said to Slamshaft or vice versa. Word perfect. It even does the voices.'

'I know.'

'Amazing, really. You'd almost think it knows what it's doing, that this isn't a camouflage skill evolved by nature to allow its species to encroach on other birds' territories. And what it has to say is incriminating stuff, no question. The trouble is, I'm not sure any of it will be legally admissible. There's no precedent in Airborn law for proof by avian testimony.'

Az let out a hollow, cynical laugh. 'So it's likely his lordship will get off with a slap on the wrist, if that.'

'Not if I can help it,' said Mr Mordadson adamantly. 'I can't forget how that man played me. *Used* me. He had me so busy chasing around trying to prove his First!er connections that I didn't even glimpse his wider scheme. Believe me, Az, I want Lord Urironson to rot behind bars for ever for what he did, and I'll do everything in my power to make sure he does.'

'But there's a chance he might not. And wouldn't that be just plucking typical. Nobody ever gets punished for anything, not if they're grand enough, high enough up in the pecking order. Nobody with power is ever accountable for the rotten things they do.'

'Az, I realise that you—'

'No,' Az snapped. 'You don't realise anything, Mr Mordadson. Take my brother. You've seen the state he's in.'

'Michael pulled off one of the most incredible feats of daring I have ever had the privilege to see.'

'And where did it get him? Crippled for life! He's a broken shell of himself. And *Cerulean* was brought down by one of those planes. Did you hear about that?"

'I did.'

'I had a feeling that the Groundlings must have got her, but I kept hoping they hadn't. And then, yesterday, there it was in the papers. The wreckage had been discovered in farmland not far from Craterhome. Along with the bodies of her entire crew. Captain Qadoschson, Rigz, Furlacson, the lot of them – dead. The most beautiful aircraft in existence – gone. And then there's Redspire . . .'

'Some might say not a great loss to the Airborn race.'

'But an entire sky-city wiped out. Obliterated. There were children there. Innocents. And somehow' – Az's voice was rising, and other people at the café were turning to look – '*somehow* no one is to blame. Somehow we're supposed to sweep it all under the carpet, behave as if none of it matters.'

'Nobody's saying that, Az,' said Mr Mordadson.

'But that's what's going to happen, isn't it? I bet at the Sanctum they're talking about diplomacy with the Groundlings. Mending fences. Let bygones be bygones and all that. No good inflaming the situation, eh? Mustn't point the finger and name names. I bet there hasn't even been any mention of retaliating.'

'There has, as a matter of fact. Several important senior residents are lobbying for us to do just that. But, what, would you really have us go to war with the Groundlings? With Cassie's people? Is that what you want?'

'No. No, of course not. It's the . . . the spinelessness I can't stand. Terrible things have been done to us, awful things, and I look around and all I see is people getting on with their lives, cleaning up the mess, trying to act as if none of it happened.'

'That's what you see but that isn't how it is. Yes, we have to get on with our lives. What else are we going to do? Stew in our own misery and rage? Not really very productive.'

'But it's right, isn't it? It's what we ought to do. If we don't, if we just sort of heave a sigh and soldier on, aren't we in denial? And aren't we laying ourselves open for something like this to happen again?'

Mr Mordadson studied Az carefully through his crimson lenses. 'It'll pass Az,' he said. 'These feelings you have – they'll fade in time. I know you're angry, and I understand it, but being angry is useless, especially if the anger isn't directed at anything in particular. There are other ways of showing you're upset, other purposes you can put that energy to.'

'Oh, don't patronise me!' Az stood up, shunting back his chair noisily. 'You short-sighted pluckwit. You're as bad as the rest of them.' He swung round, addressing the whole of the Skyline Café. 'You're idiots, the lot of you!' he shouted. 'You know that? Swanning around the shops, buying stuff, thinking this makes you good citizens somehow because it shows you're not beaten, you're not giving in. Guano! All it shows is how ignorant you are, how blinkered. You're sparrows. A bunch of twittering sparrows. Nondescript, drab, not a brain cell between you.'

'Az,' said Mr Mordadson, 'that's enough. Sit down.'

'No, it's not enough! These people need to be told what's wrong with them.'

'Really,' urged Mr Mordadson. 'Sit down.'

He grabbed Az by the wrist.

Az hissed with pain.

Mr Mordadson frowned. His hand was nowhere near the kite-tail injury. Indeed, he was holding Az's left arm, not his right. What, then, was causing the pain?

Still holding the wrist, he undid Az's shirtcuff and rolled up the sleeve. Az tried tugging his arm away but Mr Mordadson would not let go.

On Az's left biceps there was a piece of sticking plaster, securing a large pad of cotton wool.

Mr Mordadson peeled back the plaster and pad, to expose . . .

A tattoo.

The tattoo had been done recently, within the past hour. It was so fresh, in fact, that the skin around it was puffy and the ink lines smeared with blood.

'What *have* you done to yourself?' he murmured.

Az twisted his mouth and said nothing.

Mr Mordadson recognised the tattooed image, or, to be accurate, *half* recognised it:

It was the lower half of the double arrow from the Ultimate Reckoner's prophecy. On the original there had been a question mark at the midpoint. Here there was none at all, just the downward-pointing, gradually darkening arrow.

Now that he thought about it, Mr Mordadson recalled that when he first spotted Az on the mall's main concourse, there had been a tattoo parlour close by.

'Well, that's not coming off in a hurry, is it?' he said. 'So what does it mean? What's it supposed to represent?'

'That's for me to know,' Az replied, snatching his arm away.

Without another word, without even a goodbye, Az strode off through the café, rolling his sleeve back down. Patrons and waiting staff watched him go, their expressions either puzzled or resentful, or both.

Mr Mordadson watched him go as well. He could have taken off and caught up with him – but why? What would it achieve?

This was no mere adolescent tantrum, he thought. The tattoo showed that. You'd never do something that permanent to yourself, just out of a fit of petulance.

Az was lost. He was embroiled in a seething morass of emotions – rage, loathing, self-pity, regret, guilt. Mr Mordadson was aware that he himself was partly responsible, but the world, too, had just given Az a thorough kicking, and it wasn't surprising that he had reacted in just this way. Above all else, he was the victim of a crushing sense of unfairness. And Mr Mordadson knew there was very little he could say or do that would jolt Az out of this mood and bring him to his senses.

The boy would just have to find his own way back from this. He would have to fight and conquer the demons within him by himself, if he could. No one else could do it for him.

And if he couldn't conquer them?

Mr Mordadson regarded that possibility with sorrow . . . and not a small amount of alarm.

EMPIRE OF CHAOS

CHAPTER 1

Storm Over The Steel Sea

Olaf Haarfret, owner-captain of the midwater trawler *Merry Narwhal*, stood at the prow of his boat and scanned the eastern horizon. He didn't like what he saw.

Haarfret's eyes were bloodshot with age and sunk in wrinkled, nut-brown pouches of skin. They mightn't be quite as sharp as they used to be, but they were eyes that knew what to look for. They recognised certain signs. The deepening texture of the cloud cover. The shape and pattern of the sea swell. The colour of the water itself, which was turning from its usual light grey to a darker shade, closer to iron than steel.

He sniffed the air, tasting the wind in the back of his throat. That confirmed it.

'Men!' Haarfret called out to his crew. 'And lady,' he added. 'Finish you haulint in this there catch, and then are I-and-you headint for home.'

'But it yet ain't ten o'clock, Cap'n,' said one of the pair of trawlermen working the windlass that was slowly reeling the net in. 'I-and-you have got plenty of hours left to be fishint.'

The other trawlermen – and one trawlergirl – looked at Haarfret too, frowning. They were assisting the men who were at the windlass, heaving the net by hand to help get it aboard. The catch was a good, heavy load. Aft of the boat, where the net had gathered in a huge teardrop shape, the sea seethed with fish. Fins and bodies flashed brightly, thousands of silverjacks and ripplesprats and the like wrestling in a frantic mass, barely contained by the waxed-twine mesh. Gulls that had followed the *Merry Narwhal* all the way from harbour dive-bombed the trapped fish. Each bird would tug a wriggling prize from the net, then soar into the air with its gorge bulging, wheel round, caw greedily, and come back down for more.

'Just do you as I say,' Haarfret snapped. 'No arguint.'

He strode to the wheelhouse, started up the motor and began bringing the trawler about. This made his crew's lives harder. Now, as well as the weight of the catch, they were having to fight the drag on the net caused by the boat's motion. Still, it couldn't be helped. Haarfret knew he had to get the *Merry Narwhal* to port as quickly as possible.

There was a storm coming, and it was going to be a bad one.

Haarfret had spent most of his long life out on the Steel Sea. He was intimately familiar with its moods and changes. He knew this body of water almost better than he knew himself. Out to the east a ferocious squall was brewing, and it would be on top of the boat sooner than he dared think about. He wasn't sure if they could make it to land in time. They certainly weren't going to reach Scaler's Cliff before the storm hit. But there were a couple of other ports where they could put in, closer along the shoreline. Failing that, Haarfret knew of a few sheltered bays where the *Merry Narwhal* could drop anchor and ride out the tempest.

The crew picked up on their skipper's sense of urgency. One or two of them even had an inkling what had spooked Haarfret, but they said nothing so as not to alarm the others. Everyone kept working, lugging on the net with all their might.

Eventually they brought it up the stern chute and onto the boat. The two men at the windlass bent double for one last effort, toiling at the handles and raising the net till it finally hung clear of the deck. They locked the cable and swung the boom so that the net was directly above the cargo hatch. Then a crewman opened the pursed end of the net and a gleaming torrent of fish vomited out, pouring into the hold. Thanks to the swaying of the boat, large numbers of the fish missed the hatch and went skidding across the deck timbers. The crew found themselves ankle deep in a flip-flopping frenzy of suffocating marine life. The gulls pounced, snaffling up as much of this easy prey as they could while the crew raced around scooping up and shovelling armfuls of spilled fish into the hold.

By the time the deck was cleared and the cargo hatch had been battened down, it was now obvious to everyone why Captain Haarfret had cut short the morning's activity. Winds were gusting hard at the trawler's stern. The sea was being whipped up into choppy points. But worst of all, most worrying, was the darkness of the clouds to the east. A black pall was draped across the horizon there, stretching from north to south. The line between sea and sky had become gloomily blurred, as though someone had smeared their thumb across a charcoal sketch.

'I mayn't be much of a seadog, Cass,' said Fletcher Grubdollar to his sister, 'but even I can tell that don't look good.'

Cassie had to agree. 'And it'm coming up on we fast,' she said. 'Faster maybe than this rustbucket can sail.'

She glanced towards the wheelhouse, where Haarfret stood like a statue, one hand on the helm, the other on the throttle. His gaze was fixed dead ahead, focused on some point of land which he knew was there but which could not yet be seen. The *Merry Narwhal* was chugging stolidly through the lurch and dip of the waves. Her engine was going flat out at ten knots. Diesel fumes spouted from her smokestack.

'If anyone can get we to safety, it'm Haarfret,' Cassie said. 'Even so . . .'

Fletcher shivered and nodded.

The two siblings had been crewing on the *Merry Narwhal* for more than three months. In that time they had learned many things. They had learned to understand the Easterntip dialect, with its odd plural pronouns like 'I-and-you' and its '-int' endings and its sometimes confusing word order. They had learned how to get up at three in the morning, snatch some breakfast, put on their overalls and oilskins and be ready at the dockside for work by three thirty. They had learned that Captain Haarfret was a harsh taskmaster, not willing to forgive or overlook mistakes, but that he needed to be that way because trawler fishing was a dangerous, precarious trade and carelessness could cause loss of livelihood, not to mention loss of life.

Above all else they had learned to trust Haarfret and be grateful to him. He, after all, had taken the risk of employing them as deckhands, two 'drylanders', outsiders who hadn't the first clue about shipcraft. They knew that the best way to repay the favour was to shut up, listen to what he told them to do, do it well, and have faith that he would look after them.

So far nothing had happened to make them doubt Haarfret. Even now, Cassie was convinced the captain would do everything in his power to keep his crew and boat from coming to harm. Of course he would.

But the storm was closing in with horrible speed, and all the seamanship in the world would count for nothing if nature decided to visit her full fury on them.

The bo'sun, Benny Spinnereel, approached Cassie and Fletcher. He had some coils of rope on his hand.

'Tie you these 'uns to the rail,' he advised, 'and around your waists. It's goint to get rocky and wants nobody to be washed overboard.'

'Definitely wants nobody *that*,' said Fletcher, taking the ropes off him. 'No point in we going belowdecks, d'you reckon?'

'Where belowdecks?' came the reply. 'There's only the cargo hold, with our catch sloppint around inside. Take you your chances down there if you like and be buried alive 'neath a couple of tonnes of fresh fish. Me, stayint I'm right here.'

'Benny, you's weathered storms in the past, no?' said Cassie. 'I mean, you's been on this boat nearly as long as the skipper has. There'm been worse than this one that be coming, right?'

Spinnereel cast a swift glance at the sky, then shot her a smile. 'Don't be you troublint yourself, missy. Bit of a waltz with Molly Wetbones, that there's all this is.' He staggered off along the swaying, bucking deck.

Cassie was far from reassured. 'I don't think even him believed that.'

'Yeah,' said Fletcher grimly, 'and when someone starts mentioning Molly Wetbones it'm really time to be afraid. You'd think them could've come up with a nicer nickname for the spirit of the sea. What be wrong with, I don't know, Mrs Fluffykins, or the Friendly Lass Who Wouldn't Hurt A Fly, something like that? Molly Wetbones! Might as well call her the Watery Grave and have done with it.'

'Clip it, Fletch,' said his sister. 'Less talk, more tying.'

'Um, Cass, I don't suppose you'd . . .'

Cassie sighed. Fletcher was attempting to attach one of the ropes to the rail with a reef knot and was making a mess of even that simple procedure. One of the aspects of nautical life he just couldn't get to grips with was knots.

She undid his botched effort and started again with a double bowline. Looping the other end of the rope around Fletcher's waist, she tied it to itself with a rolling hitch, which she tightened until her brother let out a yelp.

Securing herself the same way, she mused on the fact that the *Merry Narwhal* had no cabin or other place of shelter for the crew. The boat was essentially a large, hollow container for fish, so purely functional that there were just two pieces of superstructure, the wheelhouse and the boom, and no space belowdecks for anything but the engine and the hold. There wasn't even a toilet. You were expected to relieve yourself over the side.

The lack of facilities was bearable except at a moment like this. It would have been good to have somewhere to take cover in, out of the elements – although if the boat were to sink, it wouldn't make any difference whether you were above deck or below. Either way you were going to drown, or 'kiss Molly Wetbones' as the sailors termed it.

Cassie told herself not to think like that. Nobody was kissing any mythical figures, not today. She and Fletcher and the whole crew were going to survive this. She couldn't die. For her da's sake, for Robert's, she couldn't.

For Az's sake too.

Immediately, she banished Az from her mind. It hurt too much to think about him.

Then, like some gigantic sweeping fist, the storm struck.

CHAPTER 2

The Castle In The Waves

The first flurries of rain stung. It was like being bombarded by a swarm of hornets.

But that was nothing compared with the driving, hammering vicious-ness of what came next. The rain slammed in horizontally, hard enough to knock a couple of crew members off their feet. There wasn't a thing any of them could do to defend against it. They could only put up their hoods, turn their faces away, and let the rain pummel their backs. After a while the pain faded. Their bodies were beaten numb.

And the wind was a howling monstrosity, a solid force that tore the wavetops to shreds and screeched across the deck. It sent the sea over the gunwales and up through the sluices. The trawler was soon awash, and Cassie could see water sloshing around the cargo hatch, seeping under the wooden cover.

And the Steel Sea itself was a broken field of pyramidal peaks and wallowing troughs. The *Merry Narwhal* pitched upwards, yawed sideways, lolled alarmingly, ducked and pivoted. There was no regularity to its motion. It went any way and every way.

In glimpses through the sheeting rain Cassie saw Haarfret struggling with the helm, battling to keep the boat's stern to the wind and maintain a landward course. His upper body was rigid, while his feet were firmly planted on the wheelhouse floor and his legs were braced, knees bent, like shock absorbers, flexing however was necessary in order to keep him upright and balanced. She copied him, clutching the rail behind her for extra stability. She glanced sidelong at Fletcher. His face, half hidden by the hood of his oilskins, was taut and pale. He caught her eye and tried to offer her a game grin. It looked more like the rictus smile of a skull.

And on the storm came, battering the trawler, which seemed small and pitiful beneath its power, as capable of withstanding this onslaught as an

319

egg under a steamroller. Soon it became apparent that the *Merry Narwhal* was taking on water. The hold was filling up quicker than the bilge pumps could empty it. The boat was riding lower and lower in the waves, and now and then her bow would submerge altogether, although each time it always resurfaced, cresting back up, shedding surf. But she was starting to founder, without doubt. It was a question of how long she could continue to stay afloat and how much longer the storm was going to last. If the storm blew itself out shortly, there was a possibility that the *Merry Narwhal* might survive. She'd remain just seaworthy enough to limp to shore.

The storm, though, didn't seem like it had any plans to die down just yet. If anything, it was strengthening. It was just getting going.

The waves were mountains. The rain was unremitting. The toss and churn of the trawler was sickening. And minute by minute the *Merry Narwhal* was losing freeboard; settling ever deeper into the sea. Whenever her bow went under, it took a little longer to lift itself out again.

Then, finally, it didn't lift out at all.

The boat was nose down in the sea. She wasn't making headway any more. She was doomed.

Cassie saw the other crew members unfastening their ropes. They were bellowing at one another, and she couldn't hear what they were saying above the storm but it could only be 'Abandon ship!' She followed their example, yanking loose the free end of the rolling hitch at her waist. Her feet slithered on the canted deck. She scrambled to maintain purchase. A deep groan issued from somewhere low in the bowels of the boat, the *Merry Narwhal* sadly acknowledging her fate. Suddenly the sea was rushing up the angled trawler, swamping her. No, the sea wasn't rising, it was the boat sinking. Crewmen were hurling themselves off the sides. Cassie looked over at Haarfret in the wheelhouse, expecting he would do the same. He just stood there, however, watching the grey coldness of the Steel Sea loom in the window. He seemed almost calm, to judge by his posture. Accepting.

Cassie turned to Fletcher, hoping that he was as ready to throw himself overboard as she was.

To her horror she saw that he was still tethered to the rail. He'd pulled the free end of the rolling hitch the wrong way. Rather than loosening the knot, he had tangled it.

Idiot! she yelled inside her head.

The trawler's descent was accelerating. They had seconds before the stern went under.

Cassie dived for the double bowline that was holding Fletcher's rope to the rail. It was a harder knot to release than the rolling hitch, and her fingers were numb with cold and the gloves she was wearing made them clumsier still. She managed to tug the first loop free. She barely felt the sea as it swept over her boots and up her legs. Freezing water engulfed her but she kept working at the second part of the knot. A panicking Fletcher tried to help but she swatted his hands aside. The water reached her waist, and suddenly she could no longer see the rail or the knot. Fletcher was going to be dragged under if she didn't untie him. The sea was at her shoulders, her neck, her chin . . . She gulped in a breath. She had the second loop of the knot in her hands. She had to hope that whichever way she pulled the free end was the right way.

'Cassie!' Fletcher's voice was a rising, quavering wail.

Both their heads went under.

Cassie pulled on the knot.

Then she was floating. A surging wave hauled her upwards, free from the plummeting boat. She broke clear of the surface and heaved air into her lungs. Splashing desperately, she looked around for Fletcher. Another wave crashed over her face. She spluttered, blinked salt water out of her eyes, and screamed her brother's name. Her overalls and oilskins hung heavy on her, weighed down with sea. She flailed her arms and kicked her legs, fighting to remain above the surface. It felt as though there were bricks in her pockets and her boots were made of lead.

Suddenly, a few metres away, Fletcher's head bobbed into view.

'Fletch!'

Cassie thrashed towards him. Her brother looked half drowned, barely conscious. Just as she reached him, he slipped back under the waves. She grabbed him by the armpits and heaved him up. With one arm around his chest, she trod water as best she could, keeping his body afloat and his face upturned.

She knew it was futile. How long could she hold out like this, keeping them both alive? A few minutes at best. Already she could feel the cold – the shocking, appalling iciness of the water – seeping into her muscles. Her limbs were tiring, her movements growing weak and cumbersome. Her breathing was a series of rapid, shallow gasps. All around, waves towered and pounded.

This was it. This was the end.

Az.

Now at last she could speak his name in her thoughts. Now she could picture his face, which she had not seen in months – his well-shaped, sometimes kind, sometimes melancholy face, which she loved, and missed, and yearned to see again, one more time. She could rue the recent spell of separation from him, and wish it hadn't had to be, and long to explain the situation to him and beg his forgiveness. She could allow herself, in her final moments of life, to feel all the emotions she had denied herself and had clamped down on since her family fled Grimvale.

Before she gave up struggling and vanished beneath the sea for ever, and Fletcher with her, she could indulge in remorse and misery and wishful thinking.

Molly Wetbones was waiting below. Cassie imagined a scaly, half-human creature, pallid green complexion, kelp for hair, webbed fingers. Arms extended wide in a welcoming embrace. Barnacled lips pursed for that final, fatal kiss. Molly Wetbones in the depths, the fear that lurked in every seaman's dreams, the threat of death that haunted every sailor who ever put to sea.

Cassie was only dimly aware of the water starting to froth and bubble around her. Her senses were fading, shutting down. She had an impression of something massive in the sea, something lumbering up towards the surface. She could feel huge pressures at work around her, amid the waves. She glimpsed hard, shiny contours, ascending.

Maybe she'd been wrong about Molly Wetbones. Not human-like at all. A structure. An enormous *thing*.

Towers pierced the surface. Roofs reared towards the sky. Cassie saw portholes, rivets, pitted metal walls, domes, sealed circular apertures . . .

And it carried on rising, bursting upwards from a welter of turbulence.

Like – like some sort of castle.

A metallic castle, coming up out of the Steel Sea.

And Cassie realised she was mad. She realised this was a dying person's hallucination.

But she kept a firm grip on Fletcher and watched anyway, as right in front of her more and more of the castle emerged into view, water gushing from its summits and sides.

Until she could watch no more.

And she let go of her brother.

And closed her eyes.

And submitted, succumbed, surrendered to the sea.

CHAPTER 3

Detainee Transfer

Farris, Lord Urironson, shuffled towards the prisoner transport plane. His wrists were manacled, his legs were shackled and his wings were fastened flat against his back with leather straps. An Alar Patroller walked either side of him, each with a steadying hand on his elbow.

It was, all in all, not the most dignified position to be in, but his lordship was determined not to appear downcast or humiliated. He kept his head high and his expression serene. He wanted it to look as if he was just out for a pleasant morning stroll and the Patrollers flanking him merely happened to be there, he had no idea why.

A gaggle of onlookers had collected outside the Azimuth City Patrol HQ. It was common knowledge that Lord Urironson was being taken to the Silver Sanctum today. The newspapers had been full of little else this past week, especially here in his lordship's home town, where one tabloid in particular, the *Azimuth Gazette*, was celebrating the fall from grace of this notorious local son with glee. The *Az Gaz* had been running a spoof prison diary, allegedly penned by his lordship, along with a series of articles claiming to be interviews with Lord Urironson's beloved pet mynah, Echo.

After months of delays, during which his lordship's team of lawyers had wrangled and haggled and prevaricated and come up with a million and one reasons why their client should *not* be subject to justice, he was finally going to be so. A Special Tribunal was due to be convened at the Sanctum tomorrow. Twelve of Lord Urironson's fellow senior residents were ready to hear the evidence for and against him and decide whether or not he had committed the crime of treason against the realm. If the verdict was guilty, he would have his rank and title stripped from him and would spend the next twenty-five years behind bars, which,

323

considering his age, was tantamount to a life sentence. Or indeed a death sentence.

The crowd jeered as Lord Urironson crossed the landing apron to the waiting plane. Many of these people had travelled all the way from Prismburg just for this glimpse of the prisoner. They'd lost loved ones and friends during the Groundling attack on their sky-city. They wanted Lord Urironson to know that they held him personally responsible for the deaths.

'Plucker!'

'They should clip your wings and chuck you into the clouds!'

'I hope you rot in jail for ever!'

'You betrayed your own race, you emu lover!'

Lord Urironson remained impassive, although a hint of a smile could be detected on his face, as though he found the insults and anger being hurled his way faintly amusing.

There were also a number of journalists present, who clamoured for a comment from his lordship. They too were ignored. It was obviously beneath Lord Urironson to engage in conversation with members of the press.

The two Patrollers accompanied him up the ramp at the rear of the plane. There they were met by a couple more Patrollers, these ones from the specialist Detainee Transfer Corps. They helped Lord Urironson aboard, placed him in a seat and padlocked his leg shackles to an eye-bolt in the floor. Documents were signed, keys were passed on, the handover was formalised with an exchange of salutes, and the Azimuth City Patrollers headed back down the ramp to the landing apron. Moments later the pot-bellied little plane taxied onto the HQ's runway and, twin propellers roaring, leapt into the air. Next stop, several hours hence, the Sanctum.

On board the plane the two Detainee Transfer Patrollers shared a cramped, sealed compartment with Lord Urironson. He studied their uniforms, then their faces through their helmet visors. They stared back at him blankly. Nothing was said, but after a while Lord Urironson seemed to reach a conclusion, deducing some kind of significant fact. His brow furrowed somewhat, and for the first time that morning he looked like a man who had something to worry about. Then, with a fatalistic grimace, he leaned his head back against the bulkhead behind him and partly closed his eyes. You might have thought he was dozing – but between his eyelids his gaze remained bright and watchful and cautious.

An hour into the journey, one of the Patrollers got up and knocked on the narrow door that connected the rear compartment to the cockpit.

'Hello, up front.'

A slot slid open and the co-pilot peered in.

'Yes?'

'How's it going? Everything OK?'

'Fine. Should be a smooth flight the whole way.'

'Don't suppose you've got something to drink? A flask of tea maybe? I'm parched.'

The co-pilot's eyes narrowed. 'Didn't you bring your own re-freshments?'

'It's like I told you earlier. Me and him' – the Patroller indicated his colleague – 'we got called in at the very last minute. Neither of the blokes who were meant to be doing this job turned up, so our group captain just sort of dragged out the first two people he saw, us, and told us we'd been volunteered. We didn't have time to prepare. It was like "You and you, get your helmets on, I've got a VIP for you to babysit." '

'Well . . .' The co-pilot sounded doubtful. 'Strictly speaking we're not meant to open the door unless it's an emergency. Transit regulations. You know.'

'I understand. But look, you and the pilot are civilian contractees, right? The Patrol's paying you to fly this plane for us.'

'Right.'

'Then that pretty much makes you one of us, doesn't it?' said the Patroller with a chummy chuckle. 'An honorary Patroller.'

The co-pilot was clearly flattered. 'I suppose so, yeah. You could look at it like that.'

'So, as one Patroller to another, can you spare a cup of tea?'

It was a reasonable request. The co-pilot decided it was, at any rate. He unbolted the door and let the Patroller through.

Lord Urironson raised an eyebrow in anticipation. Now was when he discovered whether his fears were baseless or well founded.

Murmurs of conversation drifted through the doorway. There was the gurgle of liquid being poured.

The Patroller still in the rear compartment with Lord Urironson slipped a hand behind his back to grasp something there.

Then a scream.

A shrill, ghastly, gargling cry.

The co-pilot tumbled into the rear compartment, clutching his throat. Blood was spurting through his fingers.

Shouts in the cockpit.

The plane lurched abruptly.

The Patroller opposite Lord Urironson drew a knife from the back of his belt. He leapt over the prone form of the co-pilot, who was shuddering on the floor, blood spreading around his head in a vermilion halo. He lunged into the cockpit to join his colleague. There was the noise of a struggle. The plane rocked and see-sawed all over the place. Lord Uri-ronson gripped his seat so that he wouldn't slide off. The noise of struggle diminished. The plane's course evened out.

The pilot's body was flung through the doorway, landing in an ungainly sprawl on top of the co-pilot. His throat too had been cut, and his hands and wings bore slash marks, showing that he had put up a fight.

The first Patroller returned to the rear compartment, wiping the blade of a bloodied knife on a cloth. Lord Urironson braced himself, certain that he was next in line for death.

'Apologies for that, milord,' the Patroller said, stowing away the knife. 'Not quite as straightforward as I'd hoped.'

Lord Urironson tried not to look startled. *Apologies? Milord?* 'Um, no. A spot of turbulence, once might say. But it's results that matter, not how one achieves them. Tell me, who are you? You're not Feather First!ers. Are you?'

'No,' said the Patroller. He produced keys and knelt to unlock Lord Urironson's chains.

'Good. I was concerned about that. Feather First! and I aren't on the best of terms any more. And you're not Patrollers, that much I know. Their uniforms are always a good fit, and yours aren't. That's what tipped me off that something funny was going on here. I suppose the real owners of those uniforms are . . .'

'Best not think about them.'

The plane banked steeply, starting to perform a sharp turn.

'So what is this? Why have you freed me? Where are you taking me?' Lord Urironson asked as the last of the chains was removed. He rubbed his wrists and flexed the cramps out his wings. 'Obviously we're not going to the Sanctum any more.'

'A minor detour, milord,' the man said. 'There's someone who's very keen to meet you.'

'Who?'

'You'll just have to wait and see.'

CHAPTER 4

A Not So Minor Detour

The 'minor detour' turned out to be a trip lasting the rest of the day, through the night and well into the following day. There were two stops at way-stations en route, where Lord Urironson's liberators, still in Patroller uniform, bought food and fuel. At a later stage, during darkness, the corpses of the pilot and co-pilot were jettisoned out of the back of the plane.

Finally, more than twenty-four hours after departure from Azimuth City, journey's end came in sight.

It was Redspire.

Or rather, what was left of Redspire.

The sky-city had suffered the worst of any during the attacks launched by Dominic Slamshaft. Most of the sky-cities had been damaged, some severely, but only one had been demolished – Redspire.

Like a beheaded flower, all that remained of Redspire was its stem. The city itself, with its homes and plazas and shops and offices, was now just so much charred, tumbled rubble in the Relentless Desert below. The column's jagged apex jutted above the cloud cover. Twisted spars of sewage duct stuck out in all directions like the prongs of some strange crown.

Peering from the cockpit, Lord Urironson couldn't help but gasp. 'I never imagined,' he said. 'What a sight. Makes you sick to the stomach. To see a sky-city that's been *obliterated* like that . . .'

'It was your friends that did it,' said the man piloting the plane, his tone matter-of-fact.

'I know, but even so. Such destruction. Such finality.' Lord Urironson wanted to turn away but the vision of the topless column exerted a horrible fascination. 'So why are we here? Why bring me to Redspire? I've been very patient but I think I have a right to some answers now.'

'You'll need to be patient just a little longer, milord. Quiet, also. I have to concentrate here.'

The man circled the column a couple of times, getting his bearings. Then he guided the plane downwards, aiming for a point just adjacent to the column. He hit the lever to lower the undercarriage.

'The lookouts ought to have spotted us by now,' he said, mainly to himself. 'They're expecting us, so the beacons'll be coming on . . . any moment . . . there!'

Within the clouds, two parallel rows of lights appeared and began flashing in unison at slow intervals. The pilot adjusted course, lining the lights up in the windscreen so that they formed the two angled sides of an imaginary trapezoid.

'A runway,' breathed Lord Urironson. 'A runway in the cloud cover.'

'Please, milord, no talking. This really is very tricky.'

As the plane bumped down through the surface layer of the clouds, the runway itself came into view. It was an iron platform that had been built onto the side of the column, resting atop a fan of cantilevering girders. It looked, to Lord Urironson, rather fragile . . . and rather short. He bit his lip and trusted that the pilot was skilled enough and had had sufficient practice at this manoeuvre to pull it off successfully.

With the plane less than fifty metres from the start of the platform, the man killed the engines. The propellers fell silent and the plane coasted towards the runway. All three wheels hit, tyres screeched, the plane bounced, the wheels touched down again, and then the iron plates of the platform were rumbling and clanging beneath them. The pilot put the flaps full on, but the plane was still racing along, using up the runway at what seemed to Lord Urironson an alarming rate. He was certain that they weren't going to stop in time. The plane was going to go shooting off the far end.

Then, with perhaps twenty metres of runway left, a huge, spring-mounted rope net leapt up, spanning the platform. The plane plunged into it. The net stretched, absorbing the last of the plane's momentum.

With its net-gripped nose-cone poking over the tip of the platform, the plane finally came to a halt.

'Phew.' The pilot looked distinctly relieved, but not as relieved as Lord Urironson felt. His lordship had begun to wonder if his unexpected liberation was worth it. Yes, he had his freedom back, which was undoubtedly a good thing, but it was clear there was some kind of price involved. This perilous landing was only the start of it.

The fake Patrollers escorted him out of the plane. A group of men and women were alighting nearby on the platform. Lord Urironson noted that they were armed to the teeth with traditional Airborn weapons –

knives, swords and maces. Some, though, were also carrying Groundling weapons, namely the Slamshaft-designed crossbows with explosive bolts.

A reception committee.

One of the Patrollers hailed them. 'This is him. We have his lordship.'

A man in the group, the eldest among them, with light brown skin and a lush beard, nodded. 'So you do.' He instructed two of the people with him to take care of the plane. 'Stow it below with the rest.' Then the bearded man turned and addressed Lord Urironson. 'Milord, if you'd follow me . . .'

They all took off in a flock and crossed through the swirling cloud to a large hole that had been blowtorched out of the side of the column. As they passed through this, a dropcloth was lowered into place behind them, shutting out the chilly vapour. They entered the column's interior, which was brightly illuminated by a shaft of sunlight coming from the gaping hole at the top. Hovering, Lord Urironson looked down, and what he saw amazed him.

Below were buildings. Crude, slipshod buildings, to be sure, but buildings nonetheless. Partly made of brick, mostly of wood, they nestled against the inner wall of the column, although a few were suspended further out, hanging from struts or perching on enormous brackets. They descended as far as the eye could see, becoming lost in gloom a good kilometre down. It was a small, makeshift, vertical city clustering around the column's rim.

Who had constructed it? Who *were* these people?

Lord Urironson sensed that enlightenment was coming soon. He was led downwards, past several levels of buildings. Quite a few of them were open-sided or had broad doorless entrances, and he received glimpses of activity inside. In one, a dozen or so Airborn were being given combat training. Their teacher, evidently a skilled fighter, was demonstrating sword thrusts, which his pupils dutifully copied. Another, much bigger structure contained what looked like some sort of laboratory, or perhaps factory. Inside, men and women wearing masks over their mouths and noses worked on a production line. Vats gurgled and bubbled, and their vapour was collected through pipes and passed through various pieces of distillation and filtration equipment, ending up as a clear liquid which was then decanted into a series of glass jars.

Eventually the reception committee and his lordship arrived at a building that had the appearance of a meeting hall. It was bare within, unfurnished, apart from a dais at one end. Light and some warmth came from a couple of blazing braziers.

On the dais stood a wheelchair, and in the wheelchair, propped up on cushions, sat a bent, misshapen figure, more scarecrow than human. The bearded man invited Lord Urironson to approach this person, which he did, circumspectly. As he got nearer, he was able to make out that it was a woman. He saw that one of her legs was lumpy and crooked and the other was absent below the knee. Her left arm lay across her lap, withered-looking and, if he didn't miss his guess, paralysed. Her face was swathed in bandages that left a nose and a lipless gash of a mouth exposed but covered one eye. And her wings . . .

Her wings were tattered, broken things. One scarcely had a feather on it. It was a skeletal armature, an outline of skin and bone. Waxy scar tissue suggested it had been badly burnt.

The other wing, though . . .

The other still bore most of its plumage.

And the feathers on it were black. Black as a raven's. Black as night.

The woman in the wheelchair fixed Lord Urironson with her single glittering eye, and spoke.

Her voice was a cracked, rasping whisper, but somehow it still carried authority and commanded attention.

'Milord,' she said, 'good of you to come. How nice to meet you. Please allow me to introduce myself.'

'No need,' said his lordship, his own voice dry with disbelief. 'I know who you are. But – but you're dead. Aren't you?'

'Apparently not,' said the shattered remnants of Naoutha Nisrocsdaughter.

CHAPTER 5

Chronicle Of A Death Forgone

Naoutha Nisrocsdaughter was once the leader of a band of drug-addict sky pirates, based at Redspire. They'd carried out raids on the ground in an airship called *Behemoth*, stealing supplies and causing deaths. The gang were routed by Az Gabrielson in his airship, *Cerulean*, and Naoutha was presumed to have been killed when *Behemoth*, with her aboard, crashed into the mouth of a cavern. The airship had disintegrated in a massive explosion and been buried beneath tonnes of rock and earth.

Everyone who had witnessed this event agreed: there was no way she could have survived.

Yet here she was, right before Lord Urironson's very eyes. It was indisputably her. Black plumage like that was a rarity, a one-in-a-million freak of nature. Add that to the damage her body had suffered and there could be no doubt.

'I love to see. Bafflement on someone's face,' Naoutha croaked. Every word she said seemed to come out only with a great effort. Her sentences were irregularly punctuated with gasps. 'Especially a man like you, milord, who I imagine. Isn't often baffled.'

Lord Urironson fought to regain his self-composure. 'It isn't often,' he said, 'that I'm ushered into the presence of a person widely believed to be no longer among the living. Perhaps I should congratulate you on cheating what was by all accounts a pretty conclusive death.'

'I'm not sure I did. Cheat death.' Naoutha gestured at herself with her functioning arm. 'Not completely. Death took. A large bite out of me. But I'm still here in spirit. If not so much in the flesh. So I suppose we can call that. A victory.'

'You jumped clear of your airship at the last second? I take it that's what happened.'

Naoutha let out a low rattling, choking sound which Lord Urironson just about recognised as a laugh. 'If only,' she said. 'No, I was in the. Control gondola all the way to the end. I was there, flames all around me. Rocks crashing down on me. I remember every. Moment of it. With perfect clarity. The pain of burning. The roar of the cave-in. Louder than you could ever believe. Metal grinding and grating. The sudden, suffocating darkness. My legs in agony. The sound of my own screaming.'

Her eye rolled in its socket, writhing with the memory.

'But you don't. Want to hear about any of this,' she said at last.

'Why not?' said his lordship. 'I'd be fascinated.' He meant it too, but there also seemed no harm in letting her talk. It would buy him time to try and fathom what she wanted from him.

'Very well,' said Naoutha. 'The story of my survival. Well. After I stopped screaming, there was silence. The absolute. Worst kind of silence. Muffled and empty. A silence that told me I was alive. Trapped. Helpless. Beyond rescue. A silence that said I'd be listening to it. For a frighteningly long time. The control gondola saved me, you see. It got crushed. But not completely. The hull and bulkheads were. Just rigid enough. To create a pocket of space around me. I couldn't move. My legs were pinned. Under a section of the gondola's ceiling. My arm was stuck too, beneath. The conn wheel capstan, which was lying on its side. But I hadn't been squashed flat. Only. Buried alive.'

She gave another of those laughs, reminiscent of a magpie's chatter.

'And then there was. The pterine shot that that old buzzard Mordadson. Injected me with,' she said. 'Pterine *shots*, actually. A multiple. Dose. Enough of the drug to. Kill a normal person. But not me. I'd built up a tolerance over the years. Habitual user. I needed more and more of the stuff. To get a hit. The amount Mordadson put in me gave me. A serious head-rush. But my system could cope. And in fact, that's how I managed. To get through the whole ordeal. The pterine. Once it got to work properly. It numbed my pain. Lent me strength and endurance. Lent me the ability to. Wrench my arm and one leg free and the nerve to do. What had to be done to release. The other leg.'

Lord Urironson's gaze went to the stump of her right leg.

'You mean . . . ?' he said.

Naoutha nodded. 'It was. Partly severed already. Halfway down the shin. I clawed it. All the way loose. Literally tore apart my own flesh and bone. With my own fingers. I managed to stem the bleeding. Used my belt as a tourniquet. So now I was free. But still trapped. In the gondola. No way out. I was stuck. In a space about two metres long. Metre wide. Half a metre high. Entombed. I was going to die there. No doubt about it. If the burns and the blood loss didn't finish me off. Lack of air would. I estimated I had an hour left. The longest, and last, hour. Of my life.'

'But then?'

Naoutha paused. 'You could describe. What happened next. As a miracle. Or just dumb luck. All of a sudden. The ground gave way under me. There was a smaller cavern. Directly below the entrance to the main cavern. The layer of rock between. Got damaged by. The impact of *Behemoth* and the cave-in. A crevice opened up and I fell through. Along with a heap of debris from the airship. Turns out. There was a whole network of tunnels. Just under the surface of the desert there. I dropped into one of them. It was large enough to stand up in. Not that I was in a fit state to do any standing up. But I could kneel, and crawl. I had enough control over. My body for that. More importantly. I had the *will*. Once I realised I was in a tunnel. I knew I'd been granted a. Reprieve. A second chance. And I was determined. To make the most of it. I was going to get out of there. Whatever it took. I would *live*.'

'I'm impressed,' said Lord Urironson. It didn't hurt to pay Naoutha a compliment, as he seemed to be her captive and she had the upper hand. But he was, besides, genuinely impressed. The grit and tenacity of the woman were remarkable. In a situation so desperate it would have left most people gibbering wrecks, she had refused to give in. 'How long did it take to find your way out?'

'I have no idea. An hour, a day. Can't say. It felt like. For ever. It was pitch black. I couldn't see. A thing. I made my way by touch alone. Groping like a blind person. I slithered through gaps. Hauling myself with one arm. Kept bumping into stalactites. Stalagmites. Or whatever. I had no idea where I was. Going. I didn't even know if I wasn't just. Going round in circles. I only knew that I had to *keep* going. As long as I could. To stop would be to die. The pterine helped, I'm sure. Prevented me from collapsing with shock. But also blotted out. Every unnecessary emotion. Left me with. The one emotion I needed to stay focused.'

'Which was?'

'Hatred. Pure, undiluted hatred. For the people who'd done this to me. That was what eventually. Got me to the surface. Hatred drove me on until finally. I glimpsed a sliver of light. Daylight. I wormed my way out. Through a crack in the ground. I lay in the open air, beneath the clouds. It was evening. I looked up. It was only then that. I realised I couldn't see properly out of. One eye. Everything was a haze. On that side of my vision. I've since lost the sight. In that eye completely. But I was alive! That's all I was thinking then. Been given a second chance. And I vowed I would use that. To some purpose.'

'Revenge.'

'Partly, yes. There are certain persons. I'd gladly see suffer. For what happened to me.'

'Az Gabrielson. Mordadson. That's who you mean. The ones responsible for . . . for the condition you're now in.'

'The ones who crippled me, yes. Them and the rest. Of the Airborn establishment. The high and mighty of the realm. I lay there on the desert sand and vowed I would. Find a way of bringing them down. But more than that. Vowed I would change things. So that the high and mighty wouldn't be able to ruin. Anyone else's lives. The way they had mine.'

'Well,' said Lord Urironson. 'I see. And how do I fit in with all of this? Don't get me wrong, I appreciate your sending some men to rescue me and spare me from facing a Tribunal. But I'm a pragmatist, Miss Nisrocsdaughter. I know that nothing in life comes for free. Not even, ha ha, freedom. So now that you've made me a fugitive from justice, I'm assuming you wish me to join you on this quest for revenge, this vendetta of yours. Is that right?'

'I think – I hope – that we share. Certain enemies in common, milord,' replied Naoutha. 'I had the feeling you might want. To see them destroyed as much as I do. The Airborn establishment was going. To punish you, after all. They were going to lock you away. For good.'

'They were going to try. I still have friends and sympathisers at the Sanctum. There's a reasonable chance I might have been let off, or at least been awarded a token sentence. The Sanctum is always reluctant to censure its own residents, particularly senior ones. If they admit that one of their number has gone bad, it implies that any of them can go bad at any time. They'd rather give the impression that they're all perfect and infallible, even if it means lying to the public.'

'Equally, they might have chosen to make an. Example of you. In order to distance them from you and. You from them.'

'I suppose it's possible. Either way, I'm now quite definitely a criminal, thanks to you.'

'All the more reason,' said Naoutha, 'for you and me to form a. Partnership. I could do with someone like you. By my side.'

'You seem to have managed well enough on your own,' said Lord Urironson. 'What are your plans, anyway? Why this secret lair? If I were to guess, I'd say you're putting together an army to take over the realm.'

'Not even close, milord. These people you've seen. Aren't an army. I call them my Regulars, and yes. They're learning a thing or two about combat. For self-defence purposes. But otherwise they're just. Ordinary Airborn. Citizens of the realm like you and me. This is no mere vendetta, milord. It's much, much more. But I'm not about to reveal my plans. Unless I have a commitment from you that you'll. Help.'

'My dear girl, I can't possibly commit to something without first knowing what it is.' He chuckled, as if the very notion was absurd. The chuckle echoed hollowly, emptily, in the large open space of the meeting hall. 'That would go against every instinct I have.'

'Including the instinct for self-preservation?' said Naoutha.

Lord Urironson fluffed his wings. 'You're not giving me any choice, then? Join you or else.'

'That's pretty much it.' So saying, Naoutha pressed a switch on her wheelchair and a device sprang up from the arm. It was tube-shaped, with a handle and trigger, and was mounted on a ball-and-socket joint, so that it could be swivelled to point in almost any direction.

Naoutha grasped the handle and trained the device on Lord Urironson, taking aim at the centre of his chest.

'Spring-loaded,' she said. 'Fires crossbow bolts.'

His lordship flattened his wings and raised his hands with the palms facing out. 'Really, there's no call for that, Miss Nisrocsdaughter. Put that thing away. I haven't said I won't help you. I just need some idea of what's—'

'For pluck's sake. Stop jabbering,' Naoutha said. 'It's simple enough. With me or not? Yes or no?'

Lord Urironson stared at the wheelchair-arm weapon. He could just make out the sharp iron tip of the crossbow bolt inside the tube, glinting goldenly in the brazier light. The woman was bluffing. Why go to the bother of springing him from Patroller custody, only to shoot him dead within minutes of his arrival? Talk about counter-productive. No, she was trying to scare him, that was all. This was how a pirate queen got her way, by brandishing weapons and making threats.

And Farris, Lord Urironson was not the type to respond well to intimidation.

'I refuse to be treated like this,' he snorted. 'How can you expect me to give you a firm answer when I don't have half the necessary facts?'

Naoutha sighed.

And pulled the trigger.

His lordship continued speaking, even after the crossbow bolt pierced his torso. 'In order for me . . . to make an . . . informed . . . decision . . . I'd . . .'

He looked down at his chest. A few centimetres of ash-wood shaft protruded from just below his breastbone. He touched the end of it with a tremulous hand, brushing one of the three partridge-feather flights. Blood was seeping over his shirt, blossoming like a poppy's petals around the bolt.

'What . . .' he gasped. 'What . . . why . . .'

Suddenly the whole of his shirtfront was red.

Lord Urironson looked at Naoutha.

'Oh, you witch . . .'

Then his eyes rolled up till only the whites showed, and he keeled over. Dead.

CHAPTER 6

A Message, Of Sorts

Naoutha stowed the weapon away. It clicked back neatly into its housing, flush with the arm of the chair. The action of pressing it down automatically loaded a fresh bolt into the tube from a magazine secreted in the side of the wheelchair.

'Take him, Af Bri,' she told the leader of the reception committee. 'Get rid of him. Toss him into the bottom of. The column with the rest of the. Garbage.'

The bearded man did as ordered, dragging Lord Urironson's corpse to the edge of the room then flying out with it to the centre of the column. There he let go. The body plummeted like a lead weight into the darkness below. A few loose feathers drifted down slowly in its wake. Almost as an afterthought Af Bri summoned some saliva to his mouth and spat. The gobbet of liquid joined Lord Urironson, vanishing into the column's depths.

Af Bri rejoined Naoutha, who seemed satisfied with the way the encounter had gone.

'Pity his lordship couldn't. See his way to enlisting with us,' she said. 'Not that he'd have been much practical use. But it would have been nice and. Ironic. Having him on the team. A disgraced member of the elite. Symbol of all that's wrong with. The Airborn government. Corrupt, self-serving, uncaring . . .'

'We can manage without,' said Af Bri. 'I doubt he'd have been much good at taking orders anyway. His kind only like to give them.'

'You're right. We'd never have been able to trust him. Crafty, slippery old coot like that. Sooner or later we'd have had to. Dispose of him. Might as well be sooner. No, you're much more the type I need, Af Bri. Loyal, bright. With a genuine reason for wanting to help me. I'd much rather have a dozen. Regulars like you than—'

Naoutha's voice dissolved into a bout of fierce, racking coughs. Her entire body twisted and convulsed, her useless arm leaping up and down in her lap. Her eye streamed tears, and each cough seemed as much a shout of pain as anything.

Af Bri bent and comforted her, holding her shoulders till the coughing fit subsided. Then he took a cotton handkerchief from his back pocket and wiped her mouth through the hole in her mask of bandages. Pink foam flecked Naoutha's lips and stained the handkerchief.

'You must rest,' he said. 'You'll never recover fully if you keep exerting yourself like this.'

'Recover fully?' said Naoutha with a hoarse bark of a laugh. 'Doctor Mumiahson, you know as well as I do. That I'm never going to recover. Not fully. Not even partly. Frankly it's a miracle. I've lasted till now. The most I can hope for is to hold death off. For a little while longer.'

'I've seen patients get over seemingly terminal illnesses,' said Af Bri. 'Men and women who come right back from the brink and go on to live for years.'

'But me? Shattered like this? Straitjacketed inside my own body? I don't think so. And you don't really. Either.'

'The healing power of the human will should not be underestimated.'

Naoutha seemed almost touched by his optimism, his faith in her. 'Well, I'll try. I'll do my best. I have something. To live for, after all. We all do.'

'Thanks to you, Naoutha.' Af Bri hesitated. 'You – you will make good on your promise to me, won't you?'

'Of course I will. The wheels are already in motion. Lord Urironson was just the start. He may not have been willing to help us in one way. But he's helped us in another. Without knowing it. His abduction is a message. An invitation. And if the right person comes to answer it, and I'm sure he will. Then you'll get your wish, Af Bri. I swear it.'

Af Bri, Dr Mumiahson, bowed to her. 'Thank you, Naoutha. That's all I could hope for.'

CHAPTER 7

The Wingless Brothers

There was a knock at the front door of the Enochson/Gabrielson house in High Haven. Michael went to answer it. Halfway along the hall, he poised to take flight. He would cover the short distance much more quickly that way. He went up on tiptoes, ready for the shoulder-muscle surge that would raise him off the floor.

Then he remembered.

There was to be no lift-off, no flapping up into the air. Not any more. Not ever.

Not for a man whose wings had been amputated.

Michael slumped and slouched to the door on feet that felt like two concrete blocks.

The caller was a man he had not seen in a while.

Mr Mordadson.

The two of them eyed each other warily across the threshold.

'Michael,' said Mr Mordadson, in a neutral tone. 'How are you?'

'How do you think? Just fine. Super-duper. Couldn't be better.'

'I was told you were staying at your parents' – you and Aurora. While you recuperated.'

'Yeah, well, it seemed sensible. Aurora's too pregnant to be rushing around looking after me, and my parents can help look after *her*.'

'Baby's due any day now.'

'I know. I'm so excited, I could jump into the air and turn cartwheels. Oh no, wait, I can't.'

There was no humour in Michael's expression, only bitterness. He looked thin and gaunt, a sketch of the person he used to be.

'Michael,' said Mr Mordadson, 'you didn't deserve this. It's awful, and I can't tell you how sorry I am.'

'Then don't try.'

'But you're a hero, never forget that. You saved the Sanctum.'

'Yeah, I've got a lovely big medal to prove it and all. The Order of the Realm, Second Grade. Do you want me to show it to you? I think it's in my sock drawer.'

'Michael . . .'

'You shouldn't have dived after me,' Michael said with sudden savageness. 'You shouldn't have pulled me out of the clouds. My wings were burned off. You should have just let me fall.'

Mr Mordadson shook his head. 'If I had the chance all over again, I'd do exactly the same. I know it's difficult but you can get through this. You have so much to live for. A wife, a child . . . And consider Az. He's never had wings, and he doesn't let that stop him.'

'The wingless brothers, yeah, that's us. We're quite a pair. The freak and the cripple.'

'And you can still be a test pilot. Lack of wings doesn't change that.'

'Funny thing, though,' said Michael. 'Aerodyne Aeronauticals don't seem any too keen to have me back. They've told me I can take as long a sick leave as I want. And when I do go back to work, they've told me I'll be starting out in admin. Just till I get my bearings again.'

'Seems reasonable.'

'A desk job! I doubt they'll ever let me near another prototype. I'll be stuck in an office, shuffling paper, and Aerodyne will keep coming up with excuses why I can't fly. Basically, I think they think I'll creep the other test pilots out. The guys won't like to be reminded what can happen when an aerial manoeuvre goes wrong.'

'There are other aircraft manufacturers. Surely one of them would—'

'Oh, spare me the pep talk, Mordy!' Michael growled. 'That's not what you're here for anyway, is it? You're here to see Az.'

With a shrug of his wings, Mr Mordadson said, 'Is he in?'

Michael disappeared into the house, leaving Mr Mordadson on the doorstep. A few planes whirred along the street. It was early evening, and commuters were alighting outside their homes, back from the day's work. Some small children screeched and fluttered in a fenced-in play area, chasing after a helium-filled ball. Pigeons crooned in the eaves of the house next door to the Gabrielsons', and swifts and martins darted between the roof of one building and the base of the building above.

An ordinary street-scene, and yet just four months ago the city had been bombed and hundreds of its inhabitants killed. Was everything really back to normal already? Could people get over a trauma like that so quickly? Or was this appearance of calm and order no more than an illusion, disguising wounds that were far from healed? If so, what did that mean for the collective well-being of the Airborn?

It was Mr Mordadson's job to fear the worst and prepare for it, and right now what he saw at High Haven and had seen in other sky-cities, this heads-down return to routine, troubled him deeply. He sensed – or thought he sensed – the tension of a potential backlash, quivering below the surface.

But perhaps that was just him. Too old, too paranoid, to believe that people could simply forgive and forget and carry on with their lives.

'Oh. It's you.'

Mr Mordadson snapped out of his musing.

Az stood in the doorway.

Only, he hardly looked like Az any more.

CHAPTER 8

Dark Az

The Gabrielsons' lounge was where Mr Mordadson had first introduced himself properly to Az. It was in this very room that he'd engaged the wingless boy as a spy, to be sent down to the ground to find out why the supply of raw materials was being interrupted. That event took place a little under two years ago. No time at all, and yet so much had happened since, to him and to Az. So much wind had blown through their lives during that period, so much change.

Mr Mordadson was not the same man he had been then. Older, wiser, somewhat more careworn and beaten at the edges.

But Az . . .

Mr Mordadson pictured him as he had been, sitting across from him like now. Just sixteen. Absence of wings aside, an ordinary kid from an ordinary home.

He had got taller, naturally. His face had elongated and was much more as it would look when he was a full-grown adult. His limbs had become tough and rangy.

His eyes, though, were harder. Mr Mordadson remembered them from that first time as wary, but still soft and hopeful. Two years on, they flashed flint and ice.

Since the Groundling attacks earlier in the year, Az had grown his hair. It was collar-length now, and he had dyed it black. He had also sprouted a goatee, although it was more a patch of scrubby fluff than a true beard. That was dyed black to match.

Then there was the scar on his right forearm, an ugly white twisting pucker of hard tissue. That Az had earned saving Lady Aanfieldsdaughter from a would-be assassin at the jetball cup final.

Last but not least there was the tattoo on his left biceps. Az's sleeveless shirt showed it off clearly, proudly. The downward-pointing, darkening arrow seemed to sum up everything he felt about the world and his place in it.

He glared across the lounge at Mr Mordadson, his elbows on his knees. Cagey, defiant. The two of them were alone in the room. The rest of the Gabrielson family were in other parts of the house, maintaining a discreet distance. Mr Mordadson had not been offered tea or any other kind of refreshment.

'So,' Az said, 'long time no see.'

'Too long,' replied Mr Mordadson. 'You stopped coming to the Sanctum for combat training. I thought you'd keep that up. I enjoyed our sessions, and you were making great strides. I even sent you a couple of letters, just enquiring how things were. I assume you got them.'

'Yep. Got 'em, read 'em.' Az jerked his shoulders up and down dismissively.

'But you have other priorities.'

'Family,' Az said, with a nod. 'That comes first. Helping Mike get on his feet again. Helping Mum and Dad as well. They're doing their best but this has really hit them hard. Having me was one thing. They've had eighteen years to get used to be me being the way I am. But then to see Mike end up the same way . . . You can't blame them for thinking fate's really got it in for them.'

'Family does matter,' said Mr Mordadson. 'I won't dispute that.'

'How do *you* know?' Az shot back. 'You don't have any. Or do you? If you have, you've never mentioned them.'

'No, I don't have family. Well, one cousin about a hundred times removed, but that's it. All my close relatives are dead. But I know what family signifies, and I know it's important to have them around you when things get rocky.'

'Right. So you'll understand that they're my priority now.'

'I'd think less of you if they weren't.'

'They're what I care about. Not the Sanctum. Not the realm. Not Airborn-Groundling relations. None of that guano.'

Mr Mordadson chose to disregard the last remark. 'Of course, but—'

Az overrode him. 'But nothing. You're here because you want my help, yes? Some new crisis is brewing. It's another thrilling mission for Mr Mordadson and his youthful sidekick. Off they go to save the world from the forces of chaos yet again. Except: no. Not this time.'

'Az, hear me out.'

'It's Lord Urironson, isn't it? I bet it is. I read about it in the papers. He was on his way to the Sanctum in Patroller custody but never arrived. And don't tell me, you reckon he's been snatched by allies of his, or else by Feather First!, one or the other.'

'Correct.'

'And we should go after him and try to find him.'

'Yes. The trail points southwards, and I was hoping that you'd—'

'Why should I care?' Az said, interrupting again. 'Why should I give even one hoot where Lord Urironson is? If he's in Feather First!'s clutches, then I imagine they won't exactly be showering him with gifts and flowers. They want some payback for the way he used and abused them? Good luck, I say. Let them have him. And if it's friends of his who've spirited him away, so what? It's not as if he's ever going to have any influence again among the Airborn. The public despises him for what he did. He'll spend the rest of his days in exile, hiding, relying on the charity of his pals. Not much of a life. Not much better than jail.'

'I'd've thought you'd be eager to see him brought to justice.'

'Justice? *Justice?*' Az's voice began to rise. Then, all at once, it lowered again. He sounded resigned, too tired for strong emotion. 'There's no justice, Mr Mordadson. Of any kind. Anywhere. There's just bad people getting away with bad deeds and good people being left to suffer the consequences.'

'That may be so,' said Mr Mordadson, 'but don't you think you can make a difference? You can redress the balance slightly? You have before.'

'No. I don't think it's even worth trying. Besides, I won't be any practical help to you. There's no airship for me to captain any more. *Cerulean*'s come a cropper too, just like everything else.'

'I wouldn't want you with me just because of *Cerulean*. I'd want you with me because . . .'

'Because?'

Mr Mordadson spread out his palms. 'Because, Az, when my tail-feathers are on the line, there's no one I'd rather have by my side. I can't put it any plainer than that.'

Az huffed. 'You didn't trust me enough to tell me you hadn't really sold out and joined forces with Lord Urironson.'

'Those were special circumstances. I explained why I did what I did.'

'Still and all. It showed disrespect.'

'It showed misjudgement, perhaps. Nothing more. But if you want to make a big thing out of it . . .'

'No,' said Az wearily. 'No, I don't want to make anything out of anything. Ever.'

The cuckoo clock on the mantelshelf ticked sonorously, twenty times.

'So your mind's made up,' said Mr Mordadson.

Az nodded.

'But if you ever have a change of heart . . .'

'Unlikely.'

'Fair enough. I shan't bother you again.' Mr Mordadson stood to go. 'Oh, how's Cassie, by the way?'

'How should I know?' was the bleak reply. 'How's Lady Aanfields-daughter?'

Mr Mordadson would have laughed, if the throb of sorrow in his chest hadn't been so painful. 'How should I know? She's vanished into the Cumula Collective. It's unlikely I'll ever see her again.'

'Snap,' said Az.

Stiffly Mr Mordadson extended a hand to his former protégé. 'It's been nice working with you, Az.'

The handshake was tight but short-lived.

Outside the house, Mr Mordadson had to remove his crimson spectacles. Just briefly. There was a speck of dust on one of the lenses, it seemed. He held the spectacles up to the sky and examined them and blinked. Blinked again. Then he put them back on and everything was once more as it should be. No problems. Not a one.

CHAPTER 9

Penetrating The Cumula Collective

Overnight Mr Mordadson flew his Metatronco Wayfarer due east. He combated tiredness with stops for coffee at way-stations, but it was harder to combat a mounting sense of futility. With every kilometre that passed, more and more he felt that this would be a wasted trip. Why was he even bothering? He should be devoting his energies to locating and capturing Lord Urironson. The trail was growing colder by the hour. Taking time out to pay Lady Aanfielsdaughter a visit was a delay he could ill afford. And that was assuming he could convince the Cumula Collective to let him into their city, which, given how seriously they took their privacy, was far from likely.

The moment Az had mentioned her name, however, Mr Mordadson had realised that he sorely needed to see Lady Aanfielsdaughter. He wanted to consult her about Lord Urironson, but more than that, simpler than that, he missed her. Since she quit the Sanctum he had been uncommonly unsure of himself and his place in the world. All the certainties in his life had fallen away. Visiting her might, he hoped, bring some of them back.

'You're a weak, sentimental old fool,' he told himself several times during the course of the night, and each time he said it, it seemed less of a joke.

Long journeys did not agree with the Wayfarer any more. It puttered and sputtered on its final approach to the Cumula Collective. A few tufts of smoke began to spout from the radial cylinders, mounted just behind the propeller, and the engine temperature gauge was nudging uncomfortably close to the red. Mr Mordadson found it hard to accept that this unassuming, boxy little plane of his might be nearing the end of its useful life – but then nothing lasted for ever, did it?

He set down on the Cumula Collective's civic landing apron and stepped out. High walls reared before him. The place was less a city, more a stronghold. It presented few windows to the outside world, and those it did were either archery slits or glazed casements too small for even a child to squeeze through. Watchtowers were positioned at intervals around the city perimeter, with runs of battlement in between.

Mr Mordadson knew better than just to stroll up to the main entrance, which was blockaded with a huge, oaken, bolt-studded gate. He'd get an arrow through the neck before he came within ten paces of it. He stood beside his plane, hands at his sides and wings lowered, looking as unthreatening as he could.

He didn't have to wait long. A horde of guards came swooping out from the watchtowers. Some landed next to him, swords unsheathed. Others hovered at a distance, arrows nocked in their bows. Mr Mordadson found himself surrounded by a dome-formation of armed and armoured women, with enough lethal weaponry aimed at him to kill him a dozen times over.

He looked around to see which of the guards was in charge. The stoutest of them also had the greatest number of coin-like emblems embossed onto her bronze breastplate.

He bowed carefully to her.

'State your business,' the woman said.

'My name is Mordadson, Silver Sanctum emissary. I crave permission to enter your city and visit a certain Cumulan.'

'Out of the question. A ridiculous request. Leave immediately.'

'I realise my gender makes me unwelcome here,' Mr Mordadson said. 'However, I am, as I said, a Sanctum official, and I can prove it. Please allow me to reach inside my jacket pocket. I promise, no tricks.'

The chief guard, who was as tall as him and broader in the shoulder and hip, puffed out her cheeks. 'All right,' she said, placing the edge of her blade against his Adam's apple. 'But one false move and you'll be breathing though a new hole.'

With exquisite slowness Mr Mordadson produced his silver seal and showed it to the Cumulans.

'I don't think you can deny that this grants me access anywhere in the realm.'

'Anywhere but here,' said one of the guards with a snort.

Her senior officer appeared to agree. 'We're not subject to the Sanctum's rule,' she said. 'Your laws are not ours. That little piece of tin means nothing to us.'

Mr Mordadson picked his words judiciously. 'With the greatest of respect, is that *your* decision to make? Isn't it the sort of thing your Mother Major ought to be consulted about? Does she not judge and speak on behalf of the whole Collective?'

The woman tilted her head, studying him. 'Are you telling me what to do, cockerel?' she said. 'And while my sword is at your throat, too?'

Then she gave a deep, guttural laugh.

'Stone the crows, you certainly have a pair on you!'

'Would it be wrong of me to return the compliment?' said Mr Mordadson with a wry look.

'I was talking about your wings.'

'So was I.'

The chief guard laughed again, although whether from admiration or disbelief, it wasn't clear. 'Wait here,' she said, and took to the air, carrying the seal with her.

Mr Mordadson stood stock still for a good ten minutes. The guards kept their swordpoints and arrowheads trained on him, unwaveringly. An itch developed on his nose but he resisted the urge to scratch it. By and by the senior-ranking guard returned.

'The Mother Major is in a benevolent mood this morning,' she said, sounding more than a little surprised. She handed Mr Mordadson his seal. 'Come with me.'

CHAPTER 10

Mother Major

The Mother Major perched on a plain wooden chair in a large chamber with bare floorboards and no curtains or soft furnishings of any kind. In fact the only decoration to be found in the room was the series of twelve friezes that hung around the walls. Each was fashioned austerely from unburnished copper and each depicted one of the Twelve Virtues, the code the Cumulans lived by. *Modesty* was represented by a woman in a simple, all-covering dress, *Chastity* by a woman with her wings folded around her naked body, *Co-operation* by several women embracing in a circle, *Compassion* by one woman hugging another, and so on. The most striking of the friezes were *Aggression* and *Vigour*. The most appealing, at least as far as Mr Mordadson was concerned, was *Grace*.

Behind the Mother Major, a dozen of her handmaidens sat on a semi-circular bench. Like her they wore woollen smocks with hoods, which were drawn down to hide most of the face. The Mother Major had pulled her hood back, as a courtesy to her guest.

She had tightly braided hair and stern, wily features. Amid a myriad of wrinkles her eyes peered out bright and clear, while her purse-lipped mouth suggested pensiveness and high moral standards. Mr Mordadson reckoned this was a crone who was hard to please and who never missed a trick. She reminded him of an older and less kindly Lady Aanfielsdaughter.

He offered her an elaborate downward splay of the wings, not quite grovelling but close.

'Tetra Fourth-House,' he said, 'I'm aware that this is a rare boon, a man being allowed to set foot inside the Collective's walls. I shall endeavour not to prove unworthy of the honour.'

'What a fine and flowery speaker you are, Mr Mordadson,' the Mother

Major replied. 'Quite the fancy-man. Tell me, are they all as silver-tongued at the Silver Sanctum as you?'

'I'm sure many of them wish they were.'

'Well, Collective values directness in all things. Life must be lived at its essence or not at all.'

'I beg your pardon. I meant no disrespect.'

'I'm sure you didn't. I'm just letting you know that Collective does not hold with artfulness and artifice. Collective regards those as cardinal sins, a source of worldly woes.'

'Then in that spirit, I'll get straight to the point. I'm here to see—'

'Oh, I know who you're here to see,' said the Mother Major with a waft of one grey wing. 'It's obvious. There's only one Cumulan who'd be of any interest to the notorious Mr Mordadson.'

'Notorious?'

'You sound hurt, Mr Mordadson.' The old woman's mouth tightened, a kind of smile. 'Can it be that I've pricked your masculine pride?'

'No, it's merely that all my life I've strived to keep a low profile. The fewer people who know about me, the better I can do my job. If I'm "notorious", it implies fame, and fame I can do without.'

'You have a reputation, though. Collective is aware of your deeds, and admires most, though not all, of them.'

'Ah, of course, the Collective's *notorious* Invisible Web,' said Mr Mordadson. 'Your network of gossips, passing tittle-tattle from backyard to backyard across the realm till it ends up here. That's how you know about me.'

The Mother Major's many wrinkles gathered into a scowl. 'Be careful not to use such a patronising tone with us, cockerel. Considering where you are, you're on shaky ground.'

'Forgive me, I was letting envy get the better of me,' Mr Mordadson said, deadpan. 'Your Invisible Web is the kind of efficient, realm-wide information-gathering system a man like me would give several pin-feathers to have.'

'Collective, insular as it is, needs to know what's going on around it. Though we try to remain independent from affairs of the realm, affairs of the realm can sometimes affect us. It helps if we're forewarned.'

'You didn't manage to remain independent when it came to Feather First!, did you? You opened your doors to them when the Sanctum was rounding them up and interning them. What sort of insularity do you call that?'

Mr Mordadson knew he shouldn't be saying this. It wasn't going to help his cause one iota. But if the Mother Major wanted directness, then directness she would have.

'A special case,' the Mother Major replied. 'Collective couldn't sit idly by and watch a monumental injustice take place. Innocents were being persecuted. The Sanctum was behaving in a manner we felt was harmful, to both itself and the Airborn. Harbouring a number of female First!er refugees was Collective's way of lodging a protest. They've all returned to their homes since, now that the furore has died down. But a point had to be made, and was.'

'All I'm saying is you can't have it both ways, Mother Major. Either you Cumulans are part of society or you're not. You can't just pick and choose which aspects of Airborn life you want to involve yourselves in and discard the rest. That's not how it works. That's not what the Pact of Hegemony was invented for. You have a jetball team that's kicking everyone else's tailfeathers right now. The Harpies are at the top of the league. How is it OK for you to join in at jetball and not anything else? Isn't that double standards, to say the least?'

'Our prowess at jetball demonstrates the superiority of our lifestyle. Besides, we're women. We can have things any way we want.'

'Oh don't! Don't play the "fickle female" card. It insults both of us.'

Out of the corner of his eye Mr Mordadson noticed one of the Mother Major's handmaidens stifling a smile with her hand. Clearly she felt he was arguing his way out of any chance of getting to see Lady Aanfields-daughter, and she was probably right. But really! The Mother Major couldn't expect him to let these remarks of hers go unchallenged, could she?

'The Collective,' he went on, 'trades with the rest of the realm. It needs the rest of the realm to survive, as does any sky-city. Why not submit to the laws of the realm then, like everyone else?'

'Laws laid down by an unelected body,' said the Mother Major, 'by a self-important, so-called intellectual elite who aren't accountable in any meaningful way to the people they rule. No one votes to place someone in the Sanctum. The residents aren't put there by the democratic will of the Airborn race. It's an arrogant and repellent system of government, and Collective will not bow down to it.'

'But anybody can go to the Sanctum and gain patronage and work their way to the top. It's open to all.'

'But somehow seems to attract only the vainest and the most self-serving – the type who rather fancy earning the title of lord or lady for no good reason. And the rest of us have to deal with the consequences of the decisions these stuck-up popinjays make. Consequences such as our sky-cities being attacked by Groundlings, for example.'

'As I understand it, the Collective was lucky. The Groundlings didn't actually get this far east. You escaped unscathed.'

'Still and all, a terrible toll was paid by others, thanks largely to a senior Sanctum resident.'

'Lord Urironson will be held to answer for what he did.'

'If you find him.'

'No, when.' Mr Mordadson felt a sudden yawn rising inside him. He fought it down but it came out anyway. Lack of sleep was making his head swim.

'Are we boring you, Mr Mordadson?'

'No. But, to be blunt, I've not much time and my patience is wearing thin. Just tell me, can I see Lady Aanfielsdaughter? If not, fine. Say so and I'll leave.'

'In as much as seeing her goes,' said the Mother Major, 'you already have.' She swivelled in her seat and gestured to one of the handmaidens. 'Serena Second-House?'

The handmaiden stood. It was the same one who Mr Mordadson had seen smiling earlier. She lowered her hood, and there was the long, tapering nose and the stratospheric blue eyes he knew so well.

'As to whether you may talk with her,' the Mother Major continued, 'I think on balance that I'm going to say yes. Serena has spoken highly of you, and it's a mark of your character that you, a man, have served so faithfully and for so long under a woman. You may have quarter of an hour together, no more.' She nodded to the sturdy, senior-ranking guard. 'Protectrix Esme will accompany you and escort you off the premises the minute your quarter-hour is up. Serena? You are temporarily released from your vow of silence.'

'Thank you, Mother Major,' said Lady Aanfielsdaughter.

'Use your time wisely, Mr Mordadson,' the Mother Major told him. 'I doubt you'll have an opportunity like this again.'

CHAPTER 11

The Fowl Farmer Formerly Known
as Lady Aanfielsdaughter

'Milady . . .' said Mr Mordadson, as they circled above the pitched roofs of the Collective.

'Just Serena, Mordadson. There's no Lady Aanfielsdaughter, not any more. I've renounced my title and all that goes with it.'

'Does that mean you've also renounced being a – how did the Mother Major put it? A "stuck-up popinjay"?'

'I don't blindly subscribe to everything the Collective stands for,' said Serena Second-House. 'I think their opinion of the Sanctum is wrong. But having said that, one has to wonder *how* wrong, given the mess that we – I – have made of things lately.'

'And . . . a vow of silence?' said Mr Mordadson, just a hint of incredulity in his voice.

'What's so surprising? That I should have taken one at all, or that I've stuck to it?' She said this with a teasing laugh. 'The vow is a sign of good intent, Mordadson. It shows I'm serious about being part of the Collective and also creates a symbolic break with the past, a gap between what I used to be and what I'd like to become. Every novice does it. And it's not absolute. It only operates between sunrise and sunset. After dark I can talk all I want.'

'I'm just – just having a bit of difficulty with it all,' he admitted. 'You as a handmaiden as well. An attendant. It doesn't seem right, you playing second fiddle to someone.'

'Oh, but to be chosen as a Mother Major's handmaiden is a great honour. Not every novice gets the chance.'

Sitting in the background while the Mother Major holds court? That's an honour? Mr Mordadson thought.

'You disagree,' said the former Lady Aanfielsdaughter. 'I know you so well, Mordadson. You think I'm demeaning myself. But that's not so. I'm starting again. Near the bottom, yes, but it's preferable to remaining at the top and being unhappy, or not getting to start again at all. Joining the Collective is the best decision I've made in years. I'd reached the end of my time at the Sanctum. I was flapping around, not doing anyone any good. I'd lost sight of what it meant to be in charge, what it means to be *me*. Cracking down on the First!ers – that was my final misstep, the one that told me it was definitely time to go.' Her gaze turned wistful. 'I do miss the place, though, and the people there. Most of them. How are things? Ticking over nicely without me, I imagine.'

'To be honest, milady . . .'

'I said. Serena.'

'Milady,' Mr Mordadson countered, firmly. 'And, to answer your question, the Sanctum is carrying on much as it used to. But it isn't the same. Not without you. Not the same at all.'

'What have you been up to? Who are you working for now?'

'Nobody in particular. I pick up odd jobs here and there. Lady Jeduthunsdaughter-Ochson seems to have taken me under her wing. I run errands for her but, you know, messenger stuff, nothing important.'

'She's always had a soft spot for you, has Faith.'

'She's organising a programme of building defences, anti-aircraft batteries and the like, as well as strengthening security around the supply arrival depots, just in case the Groundlings get it in their heads to attack us again.'

'Might that happen?'

'I doubt it, but it's wise to be prepared, just in case. So I've been helping her out with that. I've also been lobbying with her for funding to construct a new airship to replace *Cerulean*. The Sanctum as a whole doesn't seem very sold on the idea but a few influential figures are coming round to it.'

'The public was always very fond of *Cerulean*. A romantic attachment rather than a practical one, although there's nothing wrong with that.'

'Mostly, though,' Mr Mordadson said, 'I've been concentrating on the Lord Urironson tribunal. Conferring with prosecution lawyers, extracting testimony from disgruntled Feather First!ers . . . Basically, dealing with scum.'

'The lawyers or the First!ers?'

'Take your pick. But at least our star witness has been helpful.'

'The mynah?'

'Quite the blabbermouth, that bird. I've collected several notepads' worth of transcribed evidence from it. A lot of what it says is irrelevant, and if it's not that then it's gibberish, but where it damns Lord Urironson, it damns him utterly. All we need now is his lordship in the dock, and there'll be an end of it.'

'Except, he's disappeared.'

'Yes,' said Mr Mordadson through gritted teeth. 'Somewhere between Azimuth City and the Sanctum the plane transporting him was hijacked. The two Patrollers on board were ringers. They killed the real Patrollers for their uniforms. The bodies were discovered yesterday stashed in a cleaning closet in the basement of the Detainee Transfer Corps HQ. Not a pretty sight.'

'And the pilot and co-pilot? Do you think they were in on it?'

'Hard to say. Maybe, but if not, I fear for their wellbeing. The plane headed south, that much I have been able to glean. Two separate way-stations on a southward heading reported a Detainee Transfer plane stopping off, and since no other DTC flights were scheduled in that direction we have to assume it was Lord Urironson's.'

'Friends got him, or foes?'

'No idea.'

'Do you think it's significant that they allowed themselves to be spotted at the way-stations? It wasn't very discreet.'

'I catch your drift,' said Mr Mordadson. 'It does seem slightly suspicious, but then a plane that size would have to stop somewhere for refuelling. It doesn't have the range for much more than an inter-city hop.'

'So you don't think they wanted to be followed.'

'Whatever for? I just think their plan, such as it was, didn't allow them to make as clean a getaway as they might have liked.'

A sudden updraught caught both of them, and for a while they rode it wordlessly, wings arched, relishing the feel of the sharp, cool wind ruffling their plumage. Protectrix Esme followed at a distance, just out of earshot, unless her hearing was more than normally acute. The towers and battlements of the Cumula Collective sank below.

'It is good to see you again, Serena,' said Mr Mordadson, still stumbling over the unfamiliar form of address.

'You too. I'm sorry that I had to leave. You no doubt feel I abandoned you, but I simply couldn't stay on. It wouldn't have been good for either of us. My career was over, and I wouldn't have wanted to drag you down with me.'

'I'm managing. I'm nothing if not adaptable.'

'Indeed. Any word on Aurora and the baby?'

'Nothing yet.'

Serena raised an eyebrow. 'And Az?'

'It's . . .' Mr Mordadson looked down. 'Awkward. I just came from High Haven, as a matter of fact. Got very short shrift there.'

'You two haven't made up after your falling-out?'

'I'm not sure we even had a falling-out. Az has got a lot on his mind, what with Michael losing his wings and Cassie disappearing and everything. He's in a bleak, black place, and I don't know if he'll be able to find his way out.'

'He will. He's Az.'

'I wish I shared your confidence.' Mr Mordadson hesitated, then said, 'It isn't too late, Serena. You could always return to the Sanctum. They'd have you back, no questions asked. Reinstate your title, everything. I know this.'

Sombrely she held his gaze. 'No, Mordadson. I can't. You know I can't. I've closed that door in my life, and it would cost me too much to reopen it. Besides' – she brightened – 'I'm happy here. You may not believe it, but I am. Do you know what they've got me doing? When I'm not serving as a handmaiden, I'm looking after the eagles.'

'*The* eagles? The Aquila Flight eagles?'

'None other. The present keeper's getting a bit old for the job, so I'm taking over. Not that I'm that much younger, but she, poor thing, is suffering from arthritis and her eyesight's going, and you need a turn of speed and your wits about you with *those* birds. So here's me, the fowl farmer's daughter, fowl farming once more. And I've got the talon marks to prove it.'

She rolled up her sleeve to show off a set of deep, slashing scars in her forearm. Each of the three parallel gouges was as long and thick as a forefinger.

Mr Mordadson winced. 'Ouch.'

'First day in the cage. My fault. I forgot that you don't just walk up to an eagle on the perch and put the jesses on. Especially not a trained attack eagle. You have to let it know first of all that you're boss. Stare it down. I didn't, or didn't do it well enough, and the eagle let me know that *it* was boss. But hey-ho, live and learn.'

'Quarter-hour's nearly up,' Protectrix Esme called out.

'That was quick,' said Serena.

'Time flies,' said Mr Mordadson, 'and so must I.'

The two of them looked at each other, no longer senior resident and emissary, just two old friends who had done a great deal and shared a great deal in their many years together.

'Do what you do, Mordadson,' she said, softly. A blessing. 'As well as you can. As long as you can. That's all I can say.'

'I'll try.'

'And catch that bustard Urironson. That's my final ever order to you.'

Mr Mordadson saluted. 'Consider the bustard caught, milady.'

He turned to go, then remembered something and turned back.

'I nearly forgot.' He rummaged in a pocket and produced a small, somewhat creased envelope, which he passed to her.

'Who's this for?' Serena asked. The envelope was unmarked.

'Az.'

'And why are you writing to him?'

'Because there are some things that need to be said. But not right now,' Mr Mordadson added. 'Just make sure it gets to him, please.'

'I'll do what I can.'

'But only if.'

'If?'

'You know.' Mr Mordadson shot her a dark, sad look. 'As with any mission. If. Just in case.'

Serena held his gaze, then nodded, understanding.

'If,' she said.

CHAPTER 12

Professor Eric Emeritus (And His Cat Adam)

Be this the afterlife?

That was Cassie's first, fuddled thought as she parted her eyelids and squinted around.

She'd never put much store in the Deacons' talk of Ascension, even back in the days when that had seemed to have had some value. For centuries the Deacons had just been running an elaborate scam, building up a mythology around the sky-cities and using it as an excuse to feather their own nests. No, when you died, Cassie believed, you died. You winked out, end of story. There was no second chance at life for anyone.

She was so convinced she'd drowned, however, that it seemed nothing short of a miracle to come awake and find herself safe, warm and dry somewhere. It seemed, in fact, as though she must have been transported to some kind of heaven. She was a soul and this was eternity.

If so, then heaven was a surprisingly solid and mechanical-looking place. It had walls of sheet metal, ribbed with ducts and wiring. It had electric lights, recessed into the ceiling. It had hammocks, several of them, including the one she was lying in. It smelled of real things: salt, iron, rust, damp, decay. It thrummed, too. Cassie was aware of a constant lurching vibration in the background, a sound that reminded her of *Cackling Bertha*'s engine, a distant hubbub of powerful propulsion and motion.

She tried to climb out of the hammock. She was weak and the sling of knotted cord seemed unwilling to let her go. She struggled, and all at once the hammock flipped over and tipped her out face-first onto the floor.

She swore, and a familiar voice nearby grunted sleepily, 'Hmm? What'm that?'

'Fletch?'

Cassie whirled round. Her brother was berthed in another of the hammocks. She ran to him and hugged him hard – so hard that she accidentally managed to up-end his hammock as well. He tumbled out, and Cassie tried to catch him but he was too heavy and they crashed to the floor together in a heap.

Fletcher blinked at his sister beneath him.

'Er, wakey-wakey?' said Cassie apologetically.

Soon they were sitting up side by side and trying to fathom what had happened to them.

'Where is us?' Fletcher said. 'Last thing I remember were the *Narwhal* going down and we on it.'

'Last thing *I* remember were . . .' Cassie had a dim recollection of the castle that had arisen from the sea. It must have been some fantastic delusion, that was all.

And yet . . . what if it wasn't?

'Come on,' she said, jumping to her feet. 'Let's take a look around.'

'Fine by I,' said Fletcher. 'Wherever us is, I hope it'm got a kitchen. I be famished.'

Cassie was very hungry too. But more than that, she was very curious.

'Maybe us can find the rest of the crew,' Fletcher added. 'I mean, us drylanders has survived, so likely as not them must've. Haarfret especially. Hoary old seadog like he, him's got to know how to keep his head above water long enough, no?'

'Perhaps,' said Cassie. Fletcher had clearly forgotten, or not seen, that the captain had stayed in the wheelhouse as the *Merry Narwhal* went down. As for the rest of the trawler's crew, her feeling was that if they weren't here now, in this room with all the hammocks, then there was a very good chance that Molly Wetbones had claimed them. Just two people had lived to tell the tale of the sinking of the *Narwhal*: Cassie and Fletcher Grubdollar.

The door to the room was more hatch than anything, a metal rectangle with rounded corners, secured by a locking wheel. As she spun the wheel Cassie thought of boats she knew, ones unlike the *Narwhal* that had cabins belowdecks, compartments that needed to be kept watertight.

She and Fletcher were on some type of ocean-going vessel, that much she was certain of.

But: the castle?

Outside lay a narrow, curving corridor. The two Grubdollars hadn't gone more than a few metres along it when they heard a deep, sonorous yowl behind them. The noise was so loud and unexpected, it stopped them in their tracks and set the hairs on the back of their necks prickling.

They turned and saw a black cat padding towards them along the corridor. The cat yowled again, its green eyes flashing as they caught the glow of an overhead light. It was a sleek little creature, and as it got closer Cassie noticed there was something odd about its paws, although she couldn't work out what. They were misshapen in some way.

The cat halted in front of them and yowled a third time. Its tail curled into a question mark, then straightened.

'Hello there, puss,' said Cassie, bending to stroke its head.

The cat nuzzled her fingers briefly, then leaped around and strode off. It paused and looked over its shoulder, yowling yet again.

'Cass,' said Fletcher, 'call I crazy, but does you reckon kitty here be asking we to go with he?'

'Cats doesn't do that,' Cassie replied. 'Dogs maybe. But not cats. Does them?'

This cat certainly did appear to want them to follow. It switched its tail to and fro, head held expectantly high. Fletcher took a step towards it and the cat sprang into action, trotting off down the corridor, slender legs flickering. Fletcher stopped, and the cat, noticing this, stopped as well. The moment Fletcher moved again, so did the cat.

'Definitely,' he said. 'Him's come to take we somewhere.'

'Never trust a cat,' said Cassie. 'Them be'n't after anything but what serves they best. Still,' she added with a shrug, 'us could do worse than see where him's going. Could be him'll lead we to where there'm people.'

The black cat walked purposefully along several snaky twists and turns of corridor, always staying a few paces ahead of Cassie and Fletcher. Now and then it meowed, as if reminding them to keep up and not fall behind. They arrived at a steel ladder, and the cat scrambled smartly up the rungs, hanging on with its forepaws, propelling itself with its rear paws. It vanished into the aperture at the top. A moment later it poked its head down through the hole, making sure that the two humans understood the function of ladders. Then, with a terse *mrrow*, it disappeared from view again.

One level up, Cassie and Fletcher found themselves in a low-head-roomed dining area. There were tables bolted to the floor, and chairs with tubular frames and thinly padded seats. It was all arranged tidily enough but a distinct air of neglect hung over everything. The upholstery on many of the chairs was torn and mildewed. On a sideboard Cassie spied a stack of dishes that had a layer of mould bulging between each, like the fillings in a multi-tier cake. In one corner of the ceiling a drip of water had formed a small pale stalactite and left a pancake of sediment on the floor below.

The cat was waiting patiently for them in the middle of the room, grooming itself.

'Great! Grub!' exclaimed Fletcher. He made a beeline for the entrance to a galley kitchen, rubbing his hands.

But that wasn't the direction the cat wished to go. With a sharp cry, much like a reprimand, it chose a different exit from the dining area, one that led to a kind of lounge-cum-library. Cassie obediently went after the cat, and Fletcher, with a grumble of annoyance, diverted away from the galley and did the same.

In the lounge/library they threaded between armchairs and low circular tables, with the sweet peppery smell of ancient paper filling their nostrils. Leather-bound books were everywhere, on shelves, on the floor in piles, strewn across the tabletops. Many had whiskery growths of fungus on their covers and spines. Open pages showed technical drawings and close-printed text.

It was hard to escape the impression – the eerie impression – that the ship, or whatever it was, was deserted. There was nobody here but the cat. But Cassie dismissed the notion. *Someone* had hauled her and Fletcher aboard and left them in the hammocks to dry out. Then again, if there were passengers and crew, where were they? And why did it look like hardly anyone ever ventured into this section of the ship?

A tunnel-like staircase, a companionway, brought them up one more deck . . .

. . . and into a space the size of a theatre auditorium.

It was vast and open and it resonated echoingly to the hum of the engines. There were platforms at a number of different levels, linked to one another by steps and walkways. Control consoles sprouted everywhere, bristling with levers and knobs, lights, dials and other instrumentation. Everything was fitted out with trimmings of brass and bronze. And dominating it all was a massive window at the front, a half-dome made up of perhaps two hundred individual panes, each at least a metre square, inset into a gridlike metal framework.

Impressive as the window itself was, what was truly amazing about it – what stopped Cassie and Fletcher in their tracks and took their breath away – was the scene it showed.

Outside lay a world of gloom, pierced by the beams of several searchlights. A plain of mud and rock stretched ahead into the distance, rippled and undulating. Here and there, clumps of vegetation waved their fronds. To that extent, the view reminded Cassie very much of the Grimvale Shadow Zone.

But above the pitted, uneven landscape, a million shreds and fragments of *stuff* swarmed and swirled. And in amongst this weird blizzard of particles swam fish. Some were tiny, others large. Some darted, others moved with ponderous slowness. Some clustered in schools, others were solo. Silvery scales flashed in the searchlights' cones of brightness. Fins twitched and tails flicked.

'Underwater,' Fletcher breathed. 'That'm the sea out there. Us is travelling underwater.'

Cassie didn't even look at him as she nodded. At the right and left peripheries of the window she could see the rims of immense wheels. Their deep-grooved, cog-like treads rolled slowly across the seabed, churning up billows of silt on either side.

This wasn't a ship, then. Nor was it a castle. It was a huge vehicle, like a murk-comber but a hundred times bigger. Plying the bottom of the sea.

While Cassie and Fletcher stood and stared, the black cat skipped briskly from platform to platform till it reached the highest and centremost one. A man was seated there in a command chair, facing the window. His hands were pressed together, his chin resting on the fingertips, and his brow was furrowed – a picture of profound contemplation. The cat had to miaow several times to get his attention. At last the man snapped out of his reverie and acknowledged the cat with a smile.

'They've regained consciousness then?' he said. 'You've fetched them?'

The cat blinked serenely: a yes.

The man swivelled his chair round and located Cassie and Fletcher, down at the head of the companionway.

'There you are,' he said. 'Greetings. Welcome aboard Bathylab Four. I'm Professor Eric Emeritus. My furry feline friend here is Adam. We're running along the seabed at a depth of sixty fathoms, our groundspeed is approximately ten kilometres per hour, autopilot is engaged, and I do believe it's time for tea. Anyone fancy a scone?'

Cassie remained tongue-tied, still stunned by what she was seeing. Fletcher, though, had no trouble answering the question.

'Scone? Straight up!'

CHAPTER 13

Tea At 60 Fathoms

Down in the dining area, Professor Emeritus produced a dish of lumpy, greenish, half-burnt things that bore only a vague resemblance to scones. They tasted even less scone-like than they looked and were hard work to chew. Fletcher nonetheless polished off three of them, while the professor and Cassie managed a more modest one apiece. A cup of tea helped Cassie wash down each sludgy mouthful. Although there was a briny tang to the drink, it was hot and wet and had at least roughly the right flavour.

She was struck by how odd it was to be doing something as mundane as taking tea inside an enormous vehicle that was crawling along more than 100 metres below the surface of the Steel Sea. She tried not to think of all that water above and around them, pressing in. It made her feel quite claustrophobic.

To distract herself she focused on Emeritus, studying him as he played mother with the teapot and refreshed everyone's cups. He was in his sixties and shabbily dressed. Both he and his clothes looked as if they could do with a good scrub. He had last shaved two or three days ago and had done a less than thorough job, judging by the way some patches of his grey stubble were thicker than others. As for his hair, it seemed not to have grown from his head so much as exploded, its dramatic, sticking-out state not helped by the fact that its owner was evidently a stranger to the use of a comb. His eyes blazed intently, and in general his manner was courteous but distracted, that of a man with a manic, restless mind that he was doing his best to keep in check. Cassie didn't get any sense of unfriendliness or threat from him. All the same, some intuition told her to be wary.

'By the way, I be Cassie, and this'm my brother Fletcher,' she said, conscious that Emeritus had introduced himself to them but neglected to ask their names in return. 'Thanks for rescuing we.'

'Oh, it was nothing,' said the professor. 'I could hardly leave you out there to drown, now could I?'

'Us was on a trawler. Did you find anyone else in the water?'

'Only you two, I'm afraid, and that was down to sheer chance. If I hadn't decided to surface when I did, where I did, you'd have been goners. It was a pretty nasty storm you'd got yourselves into, worst I've seen in ages. I needed to come up to refill the Bathylab's air tanks. I checked through the periscope to see what the conditions were like up top, and there you were, the two of you, struggling in the waves. Damn lucky I spotted you, and even luckier that I managed to get out to you in a motor launch in the nick of time. There were other crew then? I didn't see anyone else, but I have to admit I didn't spend a great deal of time searching. It was as much as I could do to get you two aboard the launch. After that I turned about and headed straight back here to safety. The launch was shipping water and, sorry, call me a coward, but I do rather value my life.' He frowned. 'Damn, though. I really should have looked a bit harder.'

'No, you did all that you could,' Cassie reassured him. 'You wasn't to know there was more of we.' She thought of Benny Spinnereel and the others with a pang of sorrow. They hadn't been the warmest-hearted bunch of men she'd ever met, but they were brave and hard-working and she had come to respect them, and they her. Now they were lost to the sea, the death they'd always feared and expected would be theirs. Perhaps there was some kind of contentment for them in that. Captain Haarfret, certainly, had accepted his fate calmly enough. Maybe the others had too.

'Still, better two lives saved than none at all,' said Emeritus.

'Straight up,' said Fletcher.

' "Straight up",' Emeritus echoed. 'Hmm. Tell me, am I wrong or is that a Westward Territories dialect? It is, isn't it? And from the accent I'd say . . . hmmm . . . somewhere to the north-east of the Massif. One of the coalmining regions, although I daren't hazard which. Oh all right, I will. Grimvale.'

Fletcher's jaw dropped, exposing a gobbet of partly munched scone. 'How on earth did you do that!?'

'Little party trick of mine,' Emeritus replied with a shy tilt of the head. 'Ethnolinguistics is one of my specialities. Grimvale . . . You two are certainly a long way from home.'

'And it'm a long story why,' said Fletcher.

'Go on. I like long stories.'

'Well . . .' Fletcher began, but Cassie nudged him. 'What?'

'I'm sure the professor be'n't interested in how us ended up at Scaler's Cliff, Fletch,' she said. 'It'm not particularly fascinating.'

Her brother frowned at her. Not fascinating? The Grubdollar family was on the run, having managed to earn the undying hatred of an aristocratic military man, Brigadier Jasper Longnoble-Drumblood. He had vowed to avenge the death of his close friend Dominic Slamshaft, which he blamed on Cassie even though her role in it had been marginal at best. On the advice of a policeman, Inspector Treadwell, the Grubdollars had upped stakes and relocated to one of the remotest, most desolate spots in the whole of the Territories. There they were lying low, biding their time till it seemed safe to return home. And that *wasn't* a fascinating tale?

Cassie shook her head fractionally. The professor didn't need to know any of it. To be in hiding, whatever the cause, wasn't something you really wanted to advertise, and besides, they hardly knew this man. Just because he'd saved their lives didn't mean they should go blabbing their secrets to him.

'Fair enough,' Emeritus said. 'You don't have to tell me. I respect your right to privacy. I, by contrast, am only too happy to talk about myself and answer any questions you might have. It's been a good while since I've had company. Human company, I mean,' he added, with a nod at the cat, who was perched on the next table, head down, tail tucked around paws, apparently fast asleep. 'Adam and I understand each other well enough, but he's no great shakes in the conversation department.'

'So you'm all alone,' Cassie said. 'On this great big . . . whatever it be.'

'Roving amphibious hermetic research installation, is the correct term. And yes, I'm alone here.'

'But there be room for hundreds in a thing this size, I'd reckon.'

'Bathylab Four can accommodate a full personnel complement of three hundred and fourteen. That's its optimal operating capacity.'

'So where be them all, these other three-hundred-odd? What's become of they?'

'Gone. All gone. Long gone.' It came out as a sigh, not sad but not wholly matter-of-fact either.

'Them left?' said Fletcher.

'No. No, they're dead. I'm the last of us. The last of the Keepers of Knowledge. Generation after generation of my kind have lived and worked aboard this and the other Bathylabs. But through natural causes our numbers have dwindled, and I'm all that remains. The end of the line.'

'Keepers of Knowledge?' Cassie said.

'A grandiose title, granted, but as close to the truth as one can get. You haven't heard of us. Not surprising. Our order was established a long, long time ago, and since then we've not exactly made our presence felt in the world. Quite the opposite. We've chosen to keep a low profile, and profiles don't come much lower than the ocean floor, do they?' Emeritus laughed. 'Down here in the depths one is never disturbed and one doesn't disturb anybody, except the odd passing whale, and we've ways of dealing with *them* if they get too curious. It's the perfect place to carry out our labours.'

'So what do you actually *do*?'

'Me personally? Not a lot. My working days are behind me. Mostly I just travel, and dabble now and then in whatever discipline takes my fancy. But that's not how it used to be. Way back when, the Bathylabs were hives of industry. In this one alone, the concentrated brainpower – connect that up to the electricity grid and it could have lit an entire city! My forebears, you see, dedicated themselves to lives of pure study. That, nothing more, nothing less, was their reason for being. That was why they constructed and launched the Bathylabs. Would you be at all curious to hear about it? It wouldn't bore you?'

'No,' said Cassie, and she was being polite but she also meant it.

'Some of this you'll already know . . .' said the professor.

CHAPTER 14

A Brief History Of The Keepers of Knowledge

The Great Cataclysm. When fire fell from the sky.

That (said Professor Emeritus) was how the event was remembered in the popular imagination: *when fire fell from the sky*. But it was only half the truth. It wasn't fire that fell, it was rocks from outer space. Meteors. Burning up as they hit the atmosphere. Scorched by friction, their immense speed superheating the air around them till they caught alight.

The meteors had been out there in the vastness of the universe, in the cold and distant reaches of the void, a mass of them hurtling along on the same trajectory for millions of years, untouched, untroubled, until eventually, as was bound to happen, they collided with something. This planet. It was just plain bad luck. A few hundred kilometres either way and they'd have shot past – a near-miss in astronomical terms, but a miss nonetheless. As it was, they struck dead-on, and struck hard.

Some of the meteors weren't much bigger than pebbles. Some were as large as boulders, some as large as houses, and a few even as large as city blocks. The pebble-sized ones never reached the ground. They just disintegrated in midair, blazing a trail through the sky before blinking out. As for the rest . . .

The ground groaned. The world wobbled. The meteors pounded like gigantic fists, gouging a series of deep holes in the earth's crust. Cities were flattened, pulverised, reduced to smoking ruins. Forests and grassland were set aflame, and the fires were fanned by cyclonic winds whipped up by the impact explosions. Where the meteors plunged into sea rather than land, they sent vast waves rippling out in all directions to devastate coastlines. It all happened in the space of an hour. In that brief span of time, a civilisation that had grown and flourished over the course of centuries was all but destroyed.

The bombardment wiped out half the population of the planet, literally in a flash. But it was what came next that nearly obliterated humankind for good.

The meteors – strictly speaking, since they'd landed, meteor*ites* – kicked up immense quantities of dust. The firestorms that raged across the continents filled the air with soot and ash. Seas where the furnace-hot space rocks had come to rest bubbled and boiled, producing fogbanks of steam. All of this rose and mingled together to generate a layer of cloud, and the cloud thickened and spread till it enveloped the earth and blotted out the sun.

Deprived of sunlight, plants began dying. Then the animals that relied on the plants for sustenance began dying too. And these two facts spelled disaster for the species right at the top of the food chain, the human race, what was left of it.

They were dark days, in more ways than one. The world was engulfed in perpetual night. Famine came, and with it disease and war. Death was everywhere. Death became an everyday fact of life. People fought savagely over scraps of food, and murdered at the slightest provocation. You could be killed, for instance, simply for sneezing – because the sneeze might mean you were carrying plague and were a health hazard, although equally it might just mean you had an itch in your nose. You could also be killed by someone who was especially hungry. Cannibalism was commonplace. Starving men and women didn't much care how they filled their aching bellies, so long as they filled them.

Sheer, blind panic afflicted everyone. Well, not quite everyone. Some heads remained level. A few people kept their cool and dedicated themselves to coming up with a solution to the crisis.

Their answer, of course, was a sky-city.

It took guts and determination to marshal an army of terrified survivors and put them to work building the first of the sky-cities. It was a feat of leadership and organisation, planning and engineering, unprecedented in history. There were many who doubted it would succeed. But once the job was under way and the foundations had been laid, even the sceptics realised that this was no mere pipe-dream. It was genuinely a way out of the nightmare. It was hope. And so the doubters and the naysayers bent their backs and joined in, helping to assemble the column, lofting the enormous structure higher and higher till its summit pierced the clouds.

Ten years it took, from start to finish. No time at all, given the colossal scale of the project. And when it was done, the new city stood as a shining beacon, a symbol of the possibility of life continuing.

Then, it had no name. It was just 'the sky-city'.

Nowadays it's called the Silver Sanctum.

It was meant to be temporary, somewhere for people to perch only until the clouds cleared and sunlight touched the ground again.

As time went by, however, it became apparent that the clouds were not going to clear. Not soon, maybe not ever. And so, in nearby regions, other groups of people banded together and began erecting sky-cities of their own. Using the first one as a template, they raised columns and built living accommodation on top. It was like flowers blooming all across the planet, shoots poking into the sunlight, then heads budding and unfurling outwards. Within a couple of dozen years, the job was done. Now there were places available for at least half the population to live, free from the darkness and blight below.

The plan was that the people above the clouds would develop their own forms of agriculture, fowl farming and the like, so as to make their civilisation self-sufficient. In the meantime, they would receive supplies from the ground, sent up by those who volunteered to remain behind. Those who remained behind, for their part, would get busy arranging for the supply process to be automated. Once this was achieved and the sky-cities could manage on their own, unaided, everyone down below would move up into them.

Somewhere along the line, this failed to happen. It seems that the sky-citizens failed to crack the self-sufficiency problem. They stopped trying. They got used to living off the supplies from the ground. Generations passed, and the sky-citizens grew ever more comfortable with their lot and ever more forgetful. After a while they came to assume that the supply chain *had* become automated, that people on the ground had indeed succeeded in their task and come up to join them. This wasn't so, but how were they to know any different? More to the point, they no longer cared enough to check. The notion that there was anyone left on the ground became a trace memory, a piece of folklore, and who worries about folklore?

On the ground, meanwhile, certain individuals had taken charge of the supply lines. They saw a situation they could exploit. They appointed themselves to oversee the gathering and despatching of raw materials, and charged a fee for doing so. Wherever goods are being trafficked, there'll always be someone wanting to take a percentage. These people, these middlemen, were the forerunners of what everyone now knows as the Deacons. The robes, Ascending, tithes on the deceased, the promise of an afterlife above the clouds – all that came later. In the beginning, Deacons weren't a religious order, they were merely businessmen. Some might say that they never really changed.

But let us go back in time a little bit, to just after the first sky-city arose and the others were at the drawing board stage. It was around then that a group of eminent scientists banded together and applied their brains to a different task. These sky-cities were all very well, they thought, but it wasn't enough that the human race should physically carry on. What about the learning that had been accumulated over millennia? The knowledge and expertise that had been gathered? The discoveries and breakthroughs made by the great thinkers and pioneers? There was a danger that it could all get lost in the scramble to reach above the cloud layer. No provision had been made to preserve the scholarship of the past or create an environment where it could be furthered in the future. The builders of the sky-cities had accounted for everything in their plans except that. Their goal was the short-term one of simply keeping people alive. The scientists had a more abstract but no less worthy concern: keeping alive the culture. They feared that the inhabitants of the sky-cities would move into their new homes and then, concentrating on survival to the exclusion of all else, might gradually and inexorably slide into ignorance and barbarism. The world's intellectual achievements must be safeguarded, just in case.

While most gazes were turned upwards to the swiftly rising columns, the scientists turned theirs in the opposite direction. The oceans, they decided, would be their refuge. Blueprints were drawn up, and the Bathylab project commenced.

The Bathylabs had to be large and they had to be self-contained and self-sustaining. For a power source, the scientists looked no further than the sea itself. They devised multiple turbine arrays that generated electricity from the force of the ocean currents. To recharge its batteries, a Bathylab simply had to sit still for a while and let the tides and temperature differentials within the ocean do their work. Desalination plants would provide fresh water for drinking and washing, and for food what else was there but fish and kelp? These could be harvested using remote-controlled external nets and scoops. The sea would be the Bathylabs' inexhaustible larder.

Five of them were constructed in all. Their libraries were stocked with every important technical and literary tome ever published. Their laboratories were kitted out with the best equipment that could be found. Volunteers came from far and wide to staff them. Biologists, chemists, engineers, physicists, historians, university lecturers – the finest minds the world had left to offer. Collectively they dubbed themselves the Keepers of Knowledge. They brought their families with them. It was understood that the Bathylabs weren't some temporary thing, a stopgap measure; their function would be ongoing. For years, decades, centuries even, they would roam the seabed and play host to successive generations of researchers and experimenters. They would be undersea academies. Submarine arks of wisdom.

They were launched without fanfare. They rolled out of dry-dock and down the slipway, one after another, and vanished beneath the waves. No crowds gathered to see them off, and that was how their creators wished it. The Keepers of Knowledge didn't want anyone supposing that they lacked faith in the sky-city effort. On the contrary, they whole-heartedly endorsed it. They hoped the sky-cities would thrive and prosper. The Bathylabs were, in essence, there for back-up, a contingency plan, in the event that something went awry.

They dispersed across the oceans, going their separate ways. It had been agreed that each Bathylab should send out scouts at regular intervals to monitor the situation on the ground and above the clouds. It had also been agreed that once a year the Bathylabs would rendezvous at a prearranged set of co-ordinates. There would be an exchange of data and the scouts' reports would be compiled and assessed. If it looked as though humankind was in dire need of the Keepers' help, it would be given. If not, the Bathylabs would return to the sea for another year.

These annual meetings, known as Grand Congresses, were still going on when Emeritus was a boy. By then there were just three Bathylabs left. Shortly before Emeritus was born, Bathylab Two had met with an unfortunate accident while making a close study of an erupting volcanic island. Of Bathylab Five, nothing had been heard for at least a century. It was assumed that a warning sensor had failed and Five drove over the edge of a deep-sea trench. During the professor's lifetime, both One and Three also went offline. Three's engine expired, despite strenuous efforts to patch it up and keep it running, and the personnel amalgamated with that of One. This led to difficulties of another sort aboard One. The conditions were too cramped for that many people. All sorts of arguments and squabbles arose, and finally One's inhabitants divided into two opposing factions that were permanently at loggerheads. The initial bone of contention was some fine point of laboratory etiquette to do with titration burettes – should one rinse out the burette for the next person or expect to have to clean it oneself before use? In the enclosed environment of a Bathylab, such small matters could take on great significance, and soon the dispute escalated into a kind of war. At the Grand Congresses, One's people would put on a united front, but the loathing and disharmony behind the scenes became harder and harder to hide. It got so bad that the two factions withdrew into separate territories within the Bathylab. They started brawling with one another, then came tit-for-tat killings, and ultimately, perhaps inevitably, one or other of the two sides committed an act of suicidal sabotage. Bathylab Four came across the wreck of Bathylab One quite by chance, somewhere not far from Half-Moon Reef in the Southern Ocean. It was a broken shell, blown open from the inside out. Marine creatures flitted through its chambers and corridors. Coral had already begun to accumulate on its wheels.

Four, the last remaining Bathylab, continued on its way, but by now a sense of purposelessness had settled over those aboard. The rest of humankind had coped pretty well without help from the Keepers of Knowledge, it seemed. There had been a single instance of intervention a long, long time back, a few decades after the Cataclysm. Since then, nothing. The Keepers had not been needed after all.

Bathylab One's demise was the final straw. On Four, there was a collective collapse of will, a giving in to redundancy. The urge to procreate faded. Emeritus was among the last few children born within the Bathylab's confines. One by one Four's personnel died and weren't replaced by the next wave of offspring. The numbers aboard kept shrinking. There was constant fine talk of 'forging on with the mission' and 'keeping the flame of intellect alive' but deep down everyone knew it was futile. Hearts weren't in it any more. Bathylab Four travelled around, and research still went on but in a perfunctory fashion – a case of going through the motions while going through the oceans.

Emeritus had jettisoned the corpse of the last of his colleagues only a few months ago. Professor Victoria Valedictorian, a lovely old girl and an expert on the mating habits of bivalves. Quite without peer in that field.

Now he was alone. Apart from Adam, of course, himself the last of a dynasty of Bathylab Four cats.

All alone.

CHAPTER 15

A Telltale Yawn

'Couldn't have been much fun,' Fletcher said with sympathy. 'Growing up with everybody dying off around you. What a life.'

Emeritus looked sanguine. 'You accept as normal whatever situation you're born into. I didn't know any different. Bathylab Four was in decline and I had no reason to believe I was anything but part of the entropy.'

'But didn't you want sons and daughters? Couldn't you have hooked up with Professor What's-her-name, perhaps? When you was both younger, I mean. Sounds to I like you fancied her.'

'Victoria was certainly a hell of a lady, and a hell of a biologist too. What she didn't know about molluscan gonopores wasn't worth knowing. But no, we never got round to "hooking up", as you put it. Our relationship remained purely at the intellectual level, and my experiments were my children, just as hers were hers. It never really occurred to us, any of us, to think otherwise.' Emeritus's shoulders rose and fell. 'Anyway, it's too late now. I'm happy. I have no regrets. I was raised to live a life of the mind, and I've lived it.'

Cassie said, 'It were interesting to hear about all that stuff that happened in the Cataclysm. Rocks from space. Firestorms. Cannibals. I mean, I'd heard stories that it was bad during and after, but I never realised how bad. I suppose most folk nowadays doesn't want to dwell on it. That'm why it be'n't spoken of much or written about in books much either. People'd rather ignore it and concentrate on the now instead.'

'It was and it wasn't the human race's finest hour,' said Emeritus. 'Yes, it was a hellish experience and brought out the worst in people, but it also brought out the best. From the crucible of chaos came beauty and a new order. There's always an upside.'

'For the Airborn maybe,' said Fletcher. 'Them got to live in bright shiny new cities in the sunlight. There weren't so much of an upside for the poor buggers who was left on the ground to look after they.'

Cassie flashed a glance at her brother. What he'd said was perfectly reasonable and true, but she was always on the lookout for a resurgence of his Humanist tendencies. If he ever got that way again, she was ready to clip down on it hard.

'Not saying it were out-and-out wrong,' he added, catching her glance. 'Just, you know, not very fair.'

'On that I agree with you,' Cassie said. 'Those folk pretty much got shafted, didn't them?'

'One might argue, though, that Groundlings benefited from the creation of the sky-cities as much as the Airborn did,' said Emeritus. 'The situation obliged them to develop methods for supplying the Airborn's daily needs. New strains of crops that needed less sunlight, for example. Without that, *everyone* would have starved. There's no question the Groundlings got the rough end of the deal, but at least they got a deal. And let's not forget, the first of them remained behind willingly. No one forced them to. They didn't know how long they might have to stay down there. Some of them probably suspected they mightn't ever get to join the people above the clouds. They stayed all the same. Brave souls.'

'You mentioned,' said Cassie, 'what were it? Something about the Keepers intervening one time. Deciding them was needed for some reason, a few decades after the Cataclysm. What for? What did them do?'

Emeritus's eyes twitched in their sockets. His gaze darted to Adam, then back to Cassie.

'Oh that. It wasn't all of them, as a matter of fact. Just one. Professor Metier. His big project. Metier was one of the first Keepers and quite the scientist, but he was also undisciplined and vainglorious. He interfered more than intervened, actually, and he did so for fame and glory, which is against our principles, and I'd rather not talk about it any further.'

'Go on,' Cassie joshed. 'It were ages ago. You can tell we.'

'No.' The professor scrubbed a hand through his wild hair, as though trying to rid his head of a thought the way he might a flea. 'It's in the past. And it wasn't that great an achievement anyway. I mean, I'm as smart as Metier ever was. Smarter, perhaps.'

'It were nothing to do with the Airborn getting their wings, then?'

Emeritus looked surprised, then said quickly, 'No. Oh no. Dear me, no. Why ever would you say that?'

'I just thought, those first people who moved into the sky-cities, them was Groundlings like we, right? To start with. That'm what you just told we.'

'Yeah,' said Fletcher. 'Good point. Them didn't have wings when them went up there. How did it happen? What made they start sprouting feathers?'

'Evolutionary adaptation,' said Emeritus. 'That's all. A necessary response to the pressures and demands of the environment. They had begun living in the sky, therefore nature had to arrange for them to develop a suitable means of getting around up there.'

'Them got a bit frisky with the local bird life,' said Fletcher. 'That'm my theory.'

Cassie rolled her eyes. 'That *would* be your theory, Fletch. But Professor, not to argue or anything, but from what I know about evolution, it be'n't something that takes place over just years. Centuries, more like. Eons.'

'Really, my girl?' said Emeritus sharply. 'You're an expert on the subject then?'

'No, of course not.'

'Well, I am a scientist. This is the sort of thing I know about. Take it from me, it was evolution, nothing more, nothing less. Think of the Relentless Desert and some of the creatures that live there, scorpipedes, hackerjackals and the like. Or think closer to home, the verms that infest the Shadow Zones. They weren't around in that form before the Cataclysm. Their ancestors were some kind of mole or other burrowing mammal, and in order to survive in the world after the Cataclysm they changed. Over several generations, the traits that helped them thrive, such as sharp teeth, greater size and good hearing, improved. The traits they didn't need, such as eyes and fur, got weeded out. It had to happen quickly as well, otherwise the outcome would have been extinction. Same thing in the sky-cities. Evolution can happen fast, if the correct stimuli are there.'

Cassie was sceptical but chose not to press him further on the subject.

'Anyway,' Emeritus went on, 'none of this has any relevance to Professor Metier, and that's that.'

'But what *did* Metier do?' Cassie asked. 'How did him "interfere"?'

'It's not important.'

All right, she thought, *be like that*. Whatever Professor Metier's 'big project' had been, it was obviously a source of professional jealousy for Emeritus and he felt peeved about it. If he really didn't want to discuss it, then fine. He had allowed her and Fletcher the liberty of not telling him how they came to be at Scaler's Cliff. It was only right to return the favour and let him keep a secret.

'So,' she said, in an obvious, changing-the-subject kind of way, 'I be looking forward to getting back to dry land. Be'n't you, Fletch? I reckon our da and Robert'll be starting to worry about we, when the *Narwhal* don't return to harbour.'

Emeritus picked up on her hint. 'Yes, I'll gladly take you to the coast.

374

Not a problem. We'll surface near land and I'll take you the rest of the way in one of the motor launches. I may have to drop you somewhere a bit off the beaten track, though, and at night as well, if that's all right.'

'You doesn't want anyone seeing the Bathylab.'

'I prefer it that way. I rather like my anonymity. It's what I'm used to. And, on that front, I can trust you two to keep mum, can't I?'

'Of course you can,' said Cassie.

'Straight up,' said Fletcher, with a lip-pinching gesture. 'When us gets back to civilisation, us'll just say us clung on to some large bit of driftwood and floated ashore. Us won't tell a soul about you.'

'Thank you,' said Emeritus. 'Much appreciated. Bear in mind, the journey'll take us a couple of days. Bathylabs aren't noted for their speed.'

'Fine by we,' said Cassie. 'Our da and brother will fret but them'll get over it. Meantime, us'll enjoy the ride.'

'Yes, why not?' Emeritus grinned – briskly and, it seemed to Cassie, falsely. He got to his feet and headed off to the command deck. Adam snapped awake and made to leap off the table top after him.

Before doing so, however, the cat yawned and performed a long, back-arching stretch, flattening his ears, closing his eyes, and reaching both forelegs forward, then shaking out each hindleg in turn while his tail quivered erect.

Cassie watched his paws splay and saw clearly now what was odd about them. Between each toe there was a flap of skin, a whitish-grey membrane that attached right at the root of the claw. When the paws were spread out, the extended skin flaps became so thin you could almost see through them. When the paws returned to normal, the flaps shrank to the size of rice grains, only just visible between the toes' fur.

Adam had webbed feet, much like a duck.

Was this a feature that Bathylab cats had evolved after so many generations of them had spent their lives under the water? Or was it just a freak of birth, unique to Adam?

Cassie had a feeling that if she asked Emeritus, he would know the answer . . . and wouldn't share it with her.

There was something definitely off-kilter about Bathylab Four and the last surviving Keeper of Knowledge.

And Cassie being Cassie, she trusted she'd be able to winkle out what it was, before they made landfall.

CHAPTER 16

Vertigo

Michael teetered on the edge of the strip of pavement outside the house. Below him he could see three streets stacked on top of one another. The lowest was traversed by a diamond-shaped plaza, beneath which lay another couple of streets and then nothing but open air. Either side of the plaza there was a sliver of whiteness – the clouds. It wasn't a busy time of day. The sun was high. Traffic was thin.

Michael shuffled forward till the toecaps of his shoes poked out over the edge. He felt his belly knot. An uncomfortable, giddy sensation rushed up through him. The soles of his feet prickled.

This, he thought, *must be vertigo.*

He'd learned the expression from Cassie. Some Groundlings had a fear of heights, or rather a fear of falling from heights. Michael knew now how that felt.

Falling.

It would be so easy. So easy. All he had to do was take a step. Topple forwards. Let gravity do the rest.

He would have to time it right, make sure there was a lull in the traffic flow and nobody below was crossing the street. He didn't want to kill someone on the way down. Just himself.

He spread out his arms. Moments ticked by. His heartbeat hammered in his ears. Part of him knew that he didn't have the nerve to go through with what he planned. Another part of him was certain that he did. He closed his eyes and listened to the inner voice that was telling him (as it had been telling him for days, weeks, months) that his life was worthless, there was no point in carrying on, without wings he was no use to anyone, he was a burden, a waste of space, ugly, deformed, he'd be better off dead.

So easy.

Just one step forward.

'Go ahead,' said a voice behind him. 'Go on. Do it. I dare you.'

Eyes still shut, Michael said, 'Pluck off, Az. Leave me alone.'

'No,' said Az, 'I'm staying. I want to see this. Come on, jump. I know that's what you'd like to do. Do it.'

Michael wavered. Why not? Yes. He could jump. That'd show Az. That'd show all of them. It wasn't as if Az could prevent him. He couldn't swoop after him and catch him in midair. One wingless freak couldn't save another.

But with Az watching, the idea of suicide all at once seemed selfish and shameful. Michael's goading inner voice now sounded more like a whine than a command.

'Arrgh!' he grunted, and he stepped back from the edge and rounded on Az. 'You had to stop me, didn't you? You had to stick your beak in. You couldn't just let me get on with it.'

His brother's face was impassive. 'I told you to do it. I dared you. Not my fault you chickened out.'

'Yes, but – but you knew! You knew it'd be impossible with you standing there.'

Az strode up to the edge and glanced over. 'D'you remember, Mike, when Dad made those copper wings for me? And he strapped them on me and you picked me up and chucked me off here. Right here. This very spot. I was, what, fourteen?'

'Yeah, I remember. Of course I remember.'

'Twice my own bodyweight of metal on my back. Like that was going to work. Like that was going to allow me to fly. What was the old geezer thinking?'

'He was thinking he was granting you your deepest wish.'

'And you? What were you thinking?'

'Much the same,' said Michael. 'I was pretty sure the wings wouldn't work, so I was all set to leap off after you. But I was also wondering, what if they did work? Even for just a few seconds. Then you'd know what it was like for the rest of us. You'd feel Airborn. You wouldn't feel such an outsider any more.'

'Outlier,' Az said, half to himself.

'What?'

'Nothing. What I'm getting at is, you almost killed me, you and Dad. With the best of intentions, but still. And of course I'm glad you didn't, but there'll always be that nagging doubt inside me. "Maybe they should have let me fall. Maybe, for everyone's sake, it would have been better if I'd died that day." I have to deal with that thought every day. Every single day. I could have been put out of my misery at the age of fourteen. I'd never have to look in the mirror again and see Az Gabrielson, the kid with no wings. I'd never have to walk around a sky-city knowing that I'm just a sidestep away from plummeting to my doom. I'd never have to catch all those pitying looks I get. I'd never have to think, like I do most days, "It just isn't *fair!*" '

'But things have changed, Az. You've got Cassie. You're a big hero now.'

'Yeah, right. My girlfriend's vanished without a trace, and I'm such a big hero that I can't even protect my own family from getting hurt. All said and done, I'm still just that useless wingless boy I've always been.'

'Guano.'

'But it doesn't matter, Mike,' Az said, scratching his goatee beard, still peering down towards the clouds. 'Really it doesn't. Life's not that important. Nothing's worth caring about that much. Wings. No wings. Wife. Girlfriend. Baby. Family. Future. Any of it. I could jump now. It wouldn't make any difference. You could too. We could go together. Keep each company on the way down. I promise I won't scream if you won't.'

Michael peered at his brother. He couldn't make up his mind whether Az was bluffing or not. He had a scary feeling the answer was *not*.

'Today, tomorrow,' Az went on, with an eerie kind of calmness. 'Whenever you're ready. The wingless Gabrielsons' suicide pact. What do you reckon?'

'I reckon,' said Michael with a hollow chuckle, 'that it's not the worst idea you've ever had but it's not the best either. I'll say maybe, for now. But I tell you this, I'm not getting any dumb tattoo. If that's a condition for joining you in your pact, you can forget it.'

'Afraid of a little pain? Is that it?'

'No. Afraid of making a fool of myself, that's all. Only sad pluckers get tattoos.'

'Only cowards don't.'

'I don't feel the urge to make some big statement about myself to the world. I'm not that insecure.' Michael checked himself. 'Well, not about most things.'

A gleam of triumph flared in Az's eyes, there then gone in an instant. 'We could always ask Dad to build us both a new pair of copper wings. How about that? Then we could launch ourselves off here and pretend we believe we're actually going to fly. That way it wouldn't be suicide. More like sudden disappointment.'

Michael chuckled again, and this time it wasn't so hollow-sounding. 'You have a warped mind, little brother.'

'Maybe,' said Az, 'or maybe I'm sane and it's everyone else that's warped.'

The front door opened behind them, and out came Aurora. She eyed the two brothers curiously and somewhat grumpily. One hand was slung beneath her bulging belly, supporting it; the other hand was on the door jamb, supporting her. At this late stage in the pregnancy, she looked very uncomfortable indeed.

'What are you two up to?' Aurora enquired.

Michael and Az exchanged glances.

'Just chatting,' said Az.

'Yeah,' said Michael, 'chatting. That's all.'

'Well, the cot is waiting to be assembled,' Aurora said, adding, 'as it has been for the past five days since it was delivered. Perhaps you can both tear yourselves away from your chatting and have a go at that.'

'What do you say, Mike?' said Az. 'Nothing better to do? Fancy a spot of cot assembling?'

Michael glanced over his shoulder – his wingless shoulder – at the long, sheer drop behind him.

'Today, tomorrow,' he murmured. 'Whenever I'm ready.'

He turned back towards his wife. 'The cot it is.'

They went indoors.

CHAPTER 17

A Hard Day's Flight

The Wayfarer was sputtering and coughing like someone with bronchitis. Mr Mordadson had pushed the ageing aircraft to its limits. A hard day's flight, averaging 110 kph the whole way, had got him to Acme Empyrean at the border between the eastern and southern quadrants, but now just about every warning light on the dashboard was blinking and he knew his little plane wasn't going to take him any further without a thorough overhaul.

He set down at the city's main landing apron and engaged the services of a mechanic, who looked at the engine, sucked his teeth, fluffed his wings, and sighed and said something about not being a miracle-worker.

'But you can keep her going?' said Mr Mordadson.

'If you insist. But it's going to cost.'

Mr Mordadson flashed his Silver Sanctum seal, and the mechanic's expression became even more pained.

'You have a problem?' Mr Mordadson demanded. 'The seal not good enough for you?'

'Well, no, you see, it's not that.'

But it was. Mr Mordadson could tell. The Sanctum had lost much of its lustre lately. It could no longer lay claim to the wholehearted endorsement of the people. All across the realm there were feelings of resentment and ill-will towards it for the poor decisions it had made in the past couple of years. It had become devalued currency, and so had its seal.

'I'll pay half cash, then,' Mr Mordadson said. 'A compromise. How about that?' It irked him to do this. The mechanic had a duty, as a citizen of the realm, to honour the seal. But Mr Mordadson just didn't feel like getting into an argument about it.

Reluctantly the mechanic agreed to his offer.

While the Wayfarer was being repaired, Mr Mordadson killed time by visiting an aircraft dealership and taking a brand new Aerodyne Glimmer out of the showroom for a test-flight. The Glimmer was a twin-tailed, rear-fan thing with rather more detailing and bodywork sculpting than was strictly necessary. He chose it because Michael Gabrielson had raved about it some time back, during the research and development phase. Michael had said it was vulture-ugly but flew like a dream.

And he was right. Rear-mounted propulsion took some getting used to. It made the Glimmer aft-heavy and you had to give the nose more lift than you expected, although this was counterbalanced to some extent by the rear spoiler that bridged the gap between the two tails. Once aloft, however, the plane seemed to be gliding rather than pushing itself through the air. The ride was all but silent and vibration-free, thanks to the propeller being set well apart from the main body of the machine. Mr Mordadson settled back in his seat and put the plane through its paces, circling and looping. Compared with this, his Wayfarer was a fussy, bumbling old rattletrap. He really ought to consider getting rid of it and upgrading. The Glimmer was a young person's plane, certainly, but no harm in that. He could see himself buying one. He had the money. He seldom splurged on anything new for himself. It was about time he did.

When he came back in to land, the salesman asked if he was interested in making a purchase. Mr Mordadson said he would think about it. Back in the cockpit of his Wayfarer, however, he immediately felt at home. The mechanic had done a decent job. The plane would keep going for a little while longer. Mr Mordadson was by nature a conservative man, and piloting the Wayfarer was like slipping into a pair of comfortable old shoes. He decided he would stick with it for now. Maybe there was only so much change a man like him could put up with, only so many new beginnings he could handle at one time.

Throughout the rest of the day and into the evening, as he traversed the southern quadrant, his mood remained elevated. He had a mission again. He was doing what he did best, serving as the physical embodiment of the Silver Sanctum's will. The period of aimlessness and uncertainty was over. The visit to Lady Aanfielsdaughter had rekindled his sense of purpose. He was a hawk with the hood taken off, searching beadily for prey.

Crossing the border into the western quadrant, he rested that night at the very same way-station where the Detainee Transfer Corps plane had last been sighted. Next day he interviewed the staff. Their descriptions of the pilot and co-pilot matched those he had gleaned elsewhere. He established which bearing the DTC plane had taken off in. Due south. A total of three sky-cities lay southward of this point: Goldenfast, Hope's Summit, and Gyre. Four if you counted Redspire – but Redspire was no more.

Such a loss to the realm, Mr Mordadson thought. But then he scolded himself. There'd been good people in Redspire. Naoutha Nisrocsdaughter and her cronies may have come from there but that didn't mean he should tar the entire city with the same brush. Children had perished too. Innocents. How could he be so hard-hearted?

Turning his attention to the other three sky-cities, he asked himself which one would Lord Urironson have been taken to. None of them was noted for its Feather First! sympathies, assuming that it was First!ers who'd spirited his lordship away. Nor was any of them particularly rebellious. Mr Mordadson had a theory that Lord Urironson might be regarded by some people as a heroic figure. He was a maverick, out-spoken, never afraid to take a stance against the consensus opinion at the Sanctum. The fact that he had collaborated in the Groundling attacks, and the fact that he was facing trial for treason, might in some people's view lend him a perverse glamour. He still had supporters in the Sanc-tum, in spite of all he'd done. It was perfectly possible he had supporters in the wider realm as well. To a rebellious sky-city he might appear a martyr, a victim of establishment bullying tactics, and worth rescuing for that reason alone.

Had Redspire still been standing, that was where Mr Mordadson would have gone first. Instead, he set a course for Goldenfast, it being the nearest city to his present location.

'Glorious Goldenfast, aureate queen of the south', as the celebrated poet Phoenix Raduerielson once put it. And there were plenty of poets living there now, along with painters, sculptors, novelists, jewellers, musicians, artists of every stripe. The place drew them to it. Almost every week Goldenfast seemed to be hosting some sort of creative arts event or other. When Mr Mordadson arrived, a drama festival was in full swing. The streets were thronged with swaggering, wing-fluffing actors. On every plaza a play was being performed on a makeshift stage, and with so much theatre to choose from the citizens didn't quite know which way to turn. Comedy and tragedy vied for their attention. Should they go and see *The Azimuth Barber's Seven Wives* and laugh themselves silly, or *A Wake For Metatron The Wing Giver* and feel improved afterwards if also a little depressed? Judging by how the plays' casts often out-numbered their audiences, the answer seemed to be neither.

Mr Mordadson made enquiries at the local transport office, where records were kept of every aircraft that arrived and departed from the city. The log showed no DTC plane had visited in more than two months.

He drew a similar blank at Hope's Summit. This sky-city was unique in that it was the only one to have been built over water rather than on land. The former Chancel at its base was a floating edifice, a set of lightweight steel structures erected on pontoons and anchored to the column. Barges ferried in supplies, and the Relic hunters who had once scoured the city's Shadow Zone had done so not in murk-combers but in glass-bottomed boats, from which they would free-dive, sometimes as much as six fathoms down, to retrieve items off the sea floor. To the Airborn living above none of this had any relevance, even now, except that the raw material that came their way often bore a faint salty odour.

Having overnighted at Hope's Summit, Mr Mordadson left the next morning for Gyre. It struck him as very unlikely that Lord Urironson would be there. The accountants and other number-crunchers who made up Gyre's population were hardly the sort to harbour a known fugitive from justice. They were too narrow-visioned, too limited in their outlook, for that. Nothing interested them except mathematics. Still, he felt he ought at least cross the city off his list. And who knew, even if the DTC plane hadn't landed at Gyre, perhaps someone had spotted it flying by. At this stage in the hunt, Mr Mordadson was becoming desperate for a lead, any lead, however slim.

CHAPTER 18

Out For The Count

The Count of Gyre, with his shaven head, emaciated frame and clothes-peg teeth, welcomed Mr Mordadson into the Temple of Totality. Inviting his guest to make himself comfortable on one of the many plush quilted cushions that littered the floor, he sent a young novice actuary off to fetch refreshments. With a flap of wings and toga, the novice disappeared down through the trapdoor which was the room's only direct link with the rest of Gyre. The Temple of Totality was situated at the very apex of the spiral-shaped city, a conical chamber with large, slanting plate-glass windows that gave views in all directions and drenched the interior with sunlight. The only higher point Gyre could boast was the airship mooring mast where Az had once, disastrously, attempted to dock *Cerulean*.

'This is indeed an unexpected honour,' the Count said.

Mr Mordadson impishly raised an eyebrow. 'Really? With your Ultimate Reckoner, I thought nothing was unexpected here.'

The Count gave a thin smile. 'No, true, we did receive an evaluation yesterday concerning your visit, the result of one of our regular data input sessions. But given how sceptical most people are about the Reckoner's capabilities, we're in the habit of pretending that events come as a surprise.'

'Not good to look too clever.'

'It rubs feathers up the wrong way.' Absently the Count fingered the oversized platinum abacus that sat on a small altar in the epicentre of the room. The abacus, which had gold beads and a solid, plinth-like base, was Gyre's most sacred object, symbol of everything the city held dear – wealth and mathematics. The Count, as the city's elected-for-life ruler, was permitted to touch it. All other Gyrians were allowed only to look at it and meditate on what it stood for.

'So if you've had a Reckoner evaluation telling you I'd be coming, then you probably know *why* I've come, too,' Mr Mordadson said wryly.

'You've come,' said the Count, 'on a mission of great importance.'

Mr Mordadson ruffled his wings. That was pretty self-evident. He was a Sanctum emissary. He wouldn't be here on some trivial matter.

'You're seeking someone,' the Count went on. Aware that Gyre's ultra-sophisticated adding machine was being put to the test, he seemed to relish the opportunity to prove its worth. 'One of your own, by which I mean a Sanctum official.'

'Go on.'

'Lord Urironson.'

'I wouldn't call that a prediction,' Mr Mordadson snorted. 'I wouldn't even call it a lucky guess. Lord Urironson's disappearance has been headline news for days. Who else would be looking for him except me?'

'Then I can't win, can I?' said the Count. 'I reveal that I knew in advance what you're after, and you tell me it's obvious. Here.' He drew a rolled-up slip of paper from a fold in his toga and passed it across the desk. 'Take a look for yourself. This is what the Reckoner offered us vis-à-vis you.'

Mr Mordadson uncurled the paper, which was a strip of tickertape from the Reckoner's printer. On it was a series of symbols:

$$1 \ 2 \ 3$$
$$\Downarrow$$
$$!$$
$$\mathrm{III}$$

He scanned the strip of paper cursorily, then gave it back, saying, 'Beats me. You're the one who's a dab hand at reading these things. You tell me what it's supposed to be saying.'

'The top line,' said the Count, 'the numbers, that's myself. The Count. And by extension Gyre, since I am the city's figurehead. The next symbol, the downward arrow, implies a visit – someone descending on us, as it were. The exclamation mark conveys importance. The final symbol, that kind of squared-off W, is one we've come to interpret over the years as a crown. It denotes rank, nobility, status. Put them all together and you get me greeting an important visitor who has come for reasons to do with an ennobled person.' He spread his hands and wings, indicating himself, Mr Mordadson and their present circumstances. 'QED,' he said.

'Fascinating,' his guest replied. 'To get all that from a few marks on a piece of paper.'

'Though,' the Count added, 'it might not be the only way of deciphering that particular evaluation.'

'Yes?'

'Yes. Often the Reckoner's evaluations carry a dual meaning.'

'Because they're so vague?'

'Because,' the Count said patiently, 'that's how destiny works. It's never clear cut. There's always a subtext, a hidden agenda. Nothing is ever straightforward, nothing set in stone. It all comes down to choice.' He stroked the platinum abacus again. 'But I'm bashing you over the head with this. You'd probably prefer it if I didn't.'

Bashing you over the head? An odd turn of phrase, but Mr Mordadson took it in his stride. The Count was an odd man, after all. 'Probably,' he said, smothering the word in a laugh.

'It could be that you'd rather leave than continue to listen to me go on about the Reckoner and its amazing attributes.'

Something in the Count's tone gave Mr Mordadson the impression that this was more than a humorous, self-deprecating remark – that he was actually being invited to depart. He was tempted to. He knew he was wasting his time here, time he could be spending looking for Lord Urironson elsewhere.

Just then the novice actuary reappeared, bearing a tray laden with canapés, sweetmeats and a jug of ortanique juice. It all looked delicious, and Mr Mordadson felt he ought not to turn down hospitality. For the sake of politeness, and his stomach, he decided to stay a little while longer.

The apprentice poured two glasses of the juice, handed them out, then exited, shutting the trapdoor after him. Mr Mordadson and the Count sipped the cloudy, orange-coloured drink and helped themselves to the snacks.

'I take it you have no idea of his lordship's whereabouts, then?' the Count said.

'I wish I did. What about you?'

'There'd be no profit in us giving refuge to him here, if that's what you're implying. It just wouldn't add up. Gyre has a reputation for honesty and reliability that we'd be foolish to put at risk.'

'I don't suppose anyone here has seen a DTC plane passing this way recently?'

'I'm sure if someone had, Mr Mordadson, I'd have been told about it.'

Mr Mordadson's instincts told him the Count wasn't lying. So where did that leave his search? He was right at the edge of Airborn territory. He had run out of realm to explore. Beyond Gyre, it was ruined Redspire then nothingness. His only hope now was that Lord Urironson's abductors had been laying a false trail and had doubled back after their stop at the second way-station.

'Your quarry has eluded you,' the Count said.

'So it seems. But not for long. I'll find him.'

'I don't doubt it.' The Count gulped down a small, sticky almond pastry and licked his long thin fingers elaborately. 'And what of our young friend Az Gabrielson? The crasher of airships. How is he faring?'

'Up and down.'

'As the Reckoner foresaw.'

Mr Mordadson gave a rueful grimace, recalling the two-way arrow on Az's prophecy, the one Az had tattooed just half of onto his arm. He should have been more careful with his choice of words.

'A teenager with mood swings, now there's a surprise,' he said. 'Fact is, Az is far more down than up these days.'

'He'll recover. His evaluation suggests balance, a resolution of opposites.'

'I'm sure it does. I'm sure it suggests a great deal of things.'

'You have no idea.' The Count aimed a glance past Mr Mordadson's head. Mr Mordadson followed the direction of the glance and saw nothing of any interest. The view from the windows was just as it had been, a vista of overarching blue and undulating white.

He felt a faint tingle of disquiet. Something was not quite right here.

Maybe he was starting to get paranoid in his old age. This was Gyre. Nothing happened at Gyre.

All the same, the urge to get up and go – *now* – was strong. And paranoia had served him well in the past. He wouldn't have survived to be an old man without it.

'I shan't take up any more of your time,' he told the Count, rising. 'Time is money to you people, I know.'

The Count gave an understanding nod and bade him farewell. Mr Mordadson turned and bent to open the trapdoor.

Just as he did so, moving shadows crossed the floor, accompanied by the sound of multiple wingbeats. Mr Mordadson looked up and saw that people had appeared outside the room, rising from below, nearly twenty of them, one for every window and more. They weren't Gyrians. They weren't shaven-headed and wearing togas. They were dressed ordinarily, if a little shabbily . . . and they were toting weapons.

Ambush!

'Come on!' he yelled to the Count. 'This way! It's our only chance.'

He yanked on the trapdoor's ring-handle. Outnumbered, surrounded – the only option was to flee. Get out as quickly as possible. Fine a more easily defensible position.

The trapdoor came up slowly. Very heavy.

He glanced round to see where the Count had got to.

The Count was directly behind him, hovering. In his hands, which were raised up high, was the platinum abacus. His face was a mask of grim purpose.

Mr Mordadson was too startled to get his guard up in time.

Down came the abacus onto the crown of his head.

Thunk.

Down fell Mr Mordadson, crumpling to the floor. With a groan he tried to get back to his feet. The Count coshed him again, even harder. The pain was a searing scarlet flash that abruptly faded to black.

Standing over the unconscious emissary, the Count let out a sigh that was resigned and wistful.

'I tried to warn you, really I did,' he said. 'I gave you every chance. But some things, alas, are inevitable.'

Then he set down the counting device and went to open the windows.

CHAPTER 19

The World Below The World Below

Cassie stole out of the cabin, leaving Fletcher snoring raucously in his hammock. She made her way up to the main chamber, the bridge, where they'd first encountered Professor Emeritus. He wasn't there. Bathylab Four was at rest, squatting on the sea floor, recharging. Cassie could hear a distant, rising-and-falling whirr, the noise of the turbine arrays being galvanised by the suck and push of the currents. It sounded uncannily like breathing.

For a time she simply stood in front of the half-dome window and gazed out at the indigo ocean depths. Was it still night? Or was it morning now? She couldn't tell. A dim glow from above that could have been moon-glimmer or early dawn revealed faint shapes moving in the water, the merest outline of things, hints of fish. Down below, on the muddy sand, large crabs scuttled like footstools with too many legs. Then a parade of ghostly blue lights glided past the window, a school of squid travelling in formation, each illuminated by its own phosphorescence. They were just centimetres from the glass, so that Cassie could make out every detail of their tentacles, their soft bodies, their rippling frills of fin, their ancient black eyes. She was mesmerised. She'd seen creatures like these fished up in deep-water nets. Out of the sea they were just lumps of pale, pulpy flesh, writhing slimily, but down here, alive and in their element, they were graceful and gorgeous.

Cassie had been born into a life of limitations. The boundaries of her existence were the ground underfoot and the roof of cloud overhead that separated her from the true sky. Airborn above, Groundlings beneath – that was how it had been till not so long ago, and how it still remained, essentially. Two distinct yet mutually reliant worlds, each defined by the other, by what it was not.

But here before her was a third world, a world below the world below. A world that belonged to neither people with wings nor people without. A world untouched, untainted, by human conflicts and prejudices. What Cassie saw as she looked out into the teeming darkness was a strange, alien place, but a place, also, that was independent and pure and free.

She could have stood there for ever, staring, wondering. But she'd set herself a mission. Bathylab Four must be explored and investigated. She tore herself away from the window and got going.

Everywhere she went she found mess and dilapidation. Emeritus simply wasn't up to the task of keeping so many rooms and corridors tidy or repairing every bit of damage, every tiny leak, every fused electrical circuit. Maintaining a vehicle this size was more than one person could cope with. Large parts of Bathylab Four were completely dark, the light switches useless, and Cassie lost count of the number of times a trickle of cold water pattered onto her head.

She could easily have got lost in the vessel's maze of decks and ladders and companionways, except that each junction and hatch carried a sign that told her whether she was fore or aft, port or starboard, on an upper level or lower, in a living area or a working area. A logical, scientific way of ordering things. She roamed, groping her way through the unlit sections, clambering up and down long shafts, and peeking into rooms. Most were bare and empty or else so jam-packed with trash and debris she could barely get the door open to take a look in. In some she saw tattered photographs attached to the walls, faded family snapshots, plus other signs of past domesticity such as a mildewed rag doll or a shelf of mould-furred novels. One room looked like it had been a schoolroom, with stacked-up desks and a chalkboard still showing vague, cloudy traces of maths problems and chemical formulae.

Gradually she began to build up a three-dimensional mental map of the Bathylab's layout. Now and then she would pause in her tracks and listen. She had no idea where Emeritus was, but it didn't seem wise to bump into him or have him bump into her unexpectedly. She didn't want to look as if she was sneaking around being nosy – although that, of course, was exactly what she was doing.

Somewhere in Bathylab Four's bowels, not far from the engine room, Cassie came to a hatch whose markings made her stop in curiosity. Just above the locking wheel there was a painted symbol, three intersecting crescents picked out in yellow paint. Above that, the words BIOLOGICAL CONTAINMENT UNIT, also yellow.

She tried the wheel but it wouldn't turn. The reason for this was that, at its hub, there was a knurled steel knob with numbers on it. A combination lock, as on a safe or a bank vault.

She thought of the Craterhome pickpocket, Toby Nimblenick. Were he here, he'd have had the hatch open in next to no time, she was sure. Never a boy criminal around when you needed one!

She retreated from the hatch, thinking that she didn't have to know what lay on the other side. Probably it wasn't anything important anyway. 'Biological Containment' could mean a number of things. Perhaps it was even a posh term for septic tank, in which case she should count herself lucky she couldn't get in.

Just as she reached the ladder that would take her back to a higher, less dingy level, Cassie heard footsteps.

They were coming from the direction of the engine room, further along the corridor, past the locked hatch.

Swiftly she shinned up the ladder, nipping through the hole at the top.

The footsteps got louder, and Cassie braced herself, ready to scoot off if Emeritus (for it could only be him) halted below and started to climb after her.

But the footsteps stopped some distance from the ladder, and in the silence that followed Cassie heard a sequence of soft, rapid metallic clicks. The sound of a combination lock being operated.

She poked her head over the lip of the hole, inching it down till she had a view of the hatch.

There was the professor, dialling the knob clockwise then anti-clockwise. A loud *clunk* of bolts withdrawing, and Emeritus spun the wheel and ducked in through the hatchway. He closed the hatch behind him but the wheel did not turn, suggesting to Cassie that he hadn't bothered to shut it properly.

She contemplated returning to her and Fletcher's cabin. Settling down in her hammock. Drifting off back to sleep.

That would have been the cautious thing to do, the sensible thing to do.

On the other hand . . .

CHAPTER 20

An Undrowned Rat

Cassie crept down the ladder. She padded stealthily up to the hatch. She grasped the wheel and pushed as gently as she could, opening the hatch millimetre by millimetre, degree by degree. She winced, anticipating a tell-tale squeak of hinge, a giveaway scrape of metal edge against jamb. None came. Soon there was a gap wide enough to squeeze through. She peered in. No sign of Professor Emeritus, just a forest of laboratory apparatus on workbenches: retort stands, test tubes, flasks, condensers, a microscope, a set of fine calibrated scales and more. She eased herself into the room, her movements fluid, lizard-slow, and scanned around. Where had Emeritus gone?

A half-glassed partition screened off one end of the room, creating a smaller secondary space that was accessible by a door. She glimpsed Emeritus in there, looking busy and preoccupied. Tiptoeing between the workbenches to the partition, she crouched down and peeked through the window.

Emeritus was surrounded by aquariums and steel cages. Most were empty but several held animals of various kinds. In one cage a half-dozen mice skittered around agitatedly. In another a small, alarmed-looking monkey crouched with its knees drawn up to its chest, rocking to and fro. As for the aquariums, their murky water was home to placid fish and to other, larger marine creatures that Cassie didn't recognise.

The professor was bent over a stainless steel table with his back to her. She couldn't see what he was scrutinising on the table but, whatever it was, it fascinated him. She shuffled sideways to get a better angle.

In his hands Emeritus had a rat. An ordinary-looking white rat with red eyes. He alternated between stroking it soothingly and inspecting its neck just behind the ears. Cassie could make out what appeared to be two extra flaps of skin there, one on either side. The rat didn't much enjoy having these prodded. Its squeals of protest were just audible through the thick glass.

Now Emeritus drew a large, transparent jar towards him. It was filled to the brim with water, and came with a lid. He picked up the rat by the tail and dropped it head-first into the jar. Then he slammed the lid on tight, splashing water across the tabletop.

Cassie gasped. There was no gap between the lid and the surface of the water. The rat was going to drown!

The rat seemed to think so too. It thrashed and scrabbled in the water, clawing at the inside of the jar as if trying to burrow its way out of danger. Its frenzy was in stark contrast to the calmness of the man who was killing it. Emeritus looked completely unperturbed by the rat's plight.

Cassie was torn. She wanted to storm in there and save the rat, but at the same time knew it was none of her business. This was Emeritus's home and he was entitled to do as liked here. Besides, she felt she mustn't risk antagonising him. She and Fletcher were counting on him to get them to shore.

The rat's panic began to subside. It appeared to accept its fate. Its thrashing turned to feeble twitches, and then it was just floating acquiescently in the water, strings of tiny bubbles rising from its pelt and nostrils.

Then, to Cassie's surprise and horror, the rat began to move again. This time, though, it wasn't struggling frantically to survive.

It was swimming.

She, and the professor, watched the white rodent paddle round and round inside the jar, propelling itself with kicks of its paws and lashes of its tail. It looked utterly at home underwater, as though all its life it had never known any medium but this one. Minutes passed, and the rat didn't once show that it needed to come up for air.

Looking closely, Cassie saw that the two flaps of skin on its neck were extended outwards and pulsing, and she realised what their function was, what they were.

Gills.

Her next thought was that Emeritus had discovered a new breed of rat, one that could exist in both air and water, like a frog. An amphibious rat. She'd never heard of such a thing, but the world was a big place and Emeritus had ventured far and wide in it. Who was to say what weird beasts might be found in the remoter regions of the planet?

But then she recalled how frightened the rat had been when it was first submerged in the water.

And then she knew.

The rat was something the professor had made. Somehow he had given it gills, and what she'd just witnessed was a tryout, the submarine rat's maiden voyage.

For several moments Cassie's mind was a blank. She didn't know whether to be amazed or appalled. Half of her wanted to rush in and congratulate Emeritus on his achievement. The other half wanted to run screaming from the room.

As her thoughts settled, she directed her gaze to the aquariums. She understood now why she hadn't been able to identify some of the creatures inside. In one, a little reptilian-type thing that might have been a baby crocodile was actually, she saw now, a mouse covered in hard scales. In another, what appeared to be a turtle or a terrapin turned out to be a small dog, or perhaps a patchrabbit, with a crablike shell on its back. Fully half of the aquariums contained hybrids like these, fusions of mammal and non-mammal, air breathers transformed into water breathers.

Adam the cat's webbed feet suddenly didn't seem so extraordinary any more. Compared with what she was looking at, they were positively normal.

And it was at that precise instant, as Cassie thought of Adam, that a loud, irate yowl arose behind her. It was so sudden and piercing, she almost jumped out of her skin.

Adam was standing on the nearest workbench, tail brushed, spine arched, hackles raised. Green eyes blazed accusingly at her as the yowl continued to emerge from his mouth, rising in pitch and volume.

'Scat!' Cassie hissed, flapping an arm. 'Skedaddle! Get out of here!'

But Adam wasn't budging. She tried to shove him off the workbench, and he retaliated by slashing at her hand with one paw, narrowly missing her fingertips.

Cassie glanced over her shoulder, and saw that she had been rumbled. Professor Emeritus had turned and was glaring at her through the partition window. Adam had alerted him to her presence.

'Snitch,' she growled at the cat, and she straightened up and started to run, just as Emeritus lunged for the door.

'Cassie! Stop! Come back!' he called out.

But Cassie had no intention of stopping.

The fury she had seen in Emeritus's eyes as he'd glared at her, the cold, horrified indignation, told her she wasn't meant to have witnessed what she did.

CHAPTER 21

Paralysis

'Fletch! Fletch!'

Fletcher was one of life's deep sleepers. It took a full thirty seconds for Cassie to wake him. It took another couple of minutes for him to come round completely. During that time she recounted her experiences in the Biological Containment Unit. Then she had to go over it again because Fletcher had been too bleary to take it all in the first time.

'So him's not just some daffy professor,' he said, yawning, 'him's your actual, genuine, bonafide mad scientist?'

'Yes. No. Sort of. Him's been doing bad things to animals, that'm for sure.'

'Like many a shepherd I know,' Fletcher said with a smirk.

'This be'n't a joking matter, Fletch. You hasn't seen them, the what-nots in those aquariums. Monsters be the only word for they. Just plain . . . *wrong*. Makes your skin crawl to look at they.'

'Well, what'm us supposed to do about it, girl? Go beat up the old boy, just because him's been tampering with nature? I reckon not.'

'But us can't possibly trust he now,' Cassie said. 'You should've seen the look on his face when him caught sight of I. Him looked all set to kill I. Straight up.'

'I's sure it be'n't that bad, Cass. Him were probably more embarrassed than anything. Look, why doesn't us go and—'

'Cassie? Fletcher?' Emeritus's voice echoed along the corridor outside the cabin. He was panting slightly. 'I know you're there. I must have a word with you.'

Cassie hurried to the hatch and closed it, turning the wheel firmly.

'Oh, there's no need for that,' said Emeritus. He sounded quite genial, like a head teacher who wasn't going to dish out the harsh punishment everyone expected, only a mild ticking-off. He halted outside the hatch and knocked. 'Come on, let me in. We really ought to have a chat.'

'Let's chat like this,' said Cassie, gripping the locking wheel tight. She nodded to Fletcher, indicating she wanted help. With a sigh Fletcher sidled over and grasped the wheel with one hand.

'I'd prefer face to face,' said Emeritus.

'I wouldn't.'

'Very well then. Why did you run like that, Cassie? That's all I want to know.'

'Why did you invent a rat that can breathe underwater?' Cassie retorted.

'Ah. Yes. Well, the glib answer would be "because I can". Come to think of it, that's also the non-glib answer. I'm a scientist, Cassie. Researching, enquiring, delving into things, seeing how I can change them and make them better – that's what I do. Such is my vocation. The universe has set us many conundrums, mysteries that demand to be solved. It's my job to solve them.'

'What do turning a rat into a fish solve?'

'You'd be surprised. Although, if I'm going to be perfectly honest, I can't claim all the credit for that little trick. I'm not the first to have carried out genomorphic mutation. We were doing stuff like that ages ago, right back at the beginning. By Bathylab standards it's old hat. Professor Metier himself figured out the basic principles. I've built on his notes and the work he performed, adding a few new wrinkles of my own. Improvements, definitely.'

'You must be very pleased with yourself.'

'Unlike that old glory-hound Metier, I feel that success in an experiment is its own reward,' said Emeritus, although he did sound pleased with himself. 'Now, shall we end this nonsense? Open the door. You have nothing to fear from me. I'm an old man who enjoys tinkering in the lab, that's all. I'd rather you hadn't seen what I was up to, but only because I was afraid it might give rise to precisely this sort of misunderstanding.'

Cassie mouthed the word *Tinkering?* to Fletcher. He mouthed back *Misunderstanding*, making it clear that that was what he thought this was.

'Come on, give he a break,' Fletcher added in a whisper. 'Him may have a slightly dodgy hobby but otherwise him's just a harmless old geezer. What can him do to we? Nothing. And even if him tried, I could take he, easy. Reckon you could too. All said and done, you be making a huge fuss over very little, lass.'

Was she? Cassie felt not. She couldn't shake the impression that there was more to Emeritus's behaviour than simple egghead eccentricity, that at his heart lay something calculating and dangerously cruel.

But she had to admit that her brother had a point. Physically the professor wasn't a match for either of them. If he gave them any trouble, they'd have no difficulty slapping him down.

'Cassie?' said Emeritus. 'How about it? Why don't you open the hatch and we can sit down and discuss this like civilised people?'

Fletcher raised his eyebrows at her, asking the same question.

Cassie, though riddled with misgiving, relented. 'All right then.'

'Wise girl,' said Emeritus.

Fletcher agreed. Cassie let go of the locking wheel and he began turning it, the look on his face telling her that there was nothing to worry about, this would all be easily sorted out, she'd see.

He tugged the hatch halfway open.

A hand snaked through from outside. It was holding a small, tubular device made of chrome and glass, some kind of hypodermic syringe with a handle and a yellowish liquid inside. Cassie tried to shout out a warning – too late. The tip of the device pressed against Fletcher's neck. A *pffft!* of compressed air. Fletcher yelped. He reeled sideways, clutching his neck. Cassie grabbed the wheel and shoved. The hand withdrew smartly just as the hatch slammed shut. She spun the wheel and looked over at Fletcher. He had fallen to the floor. His eyes were rolling and his body was in spasm.

'A paralysing toxin!' Emeritus yelled from the other side of the hatch. 'Derived from the liver of *Lagocephalus lagocephalus*, the oceanic puffer fish. Your brother's muscles are stiffening, going rigid, and he has less than a minute to live. If I don't administer the antidote in time, his diaphragm seizes up and his lungs stop working. You have to let me in now, Cassie.'

Cassie clung to the locking wheel, staring at Fletcher. His lips had started to turn blue. He was gagging and choking horribly, while his limbs were going through ghastly contortions, hand twisting against biceps, legs bending inwards. She wanted to go to his side but couldn't without releasing the wheel, and if she did that, there was nothing to prevent Emeritus barging straight into the cabin.

'Let me in, young lady, or he dies. It's a simple as that.'

And supposing she did let Emeritus in. Who was to say he wouldn't just inject her with the toxin too?

'Your choice. Fletcher has half a minute left, if that.'

Cassie had no idea what to do.

CHAPTER 22

Doctor, No!

It was a small room, meagrely furnished, no windows. Above the thin-mattressed bed a motto had been painted on the wall in neat letters:

Never Let The Sun Set On An Unbalanced Equation

The creed of Gyre. This must be the living quarters of some middle-ranking bookkeeper, one of the Count's countless accountant minions.

But the dark-complexioned man standing in front of Mr Mordadson was not from Gyre. His clothing and beard marked him as an outsider, an ordinary Airborn. He stared down at Mr Mordadson, wings twitching with impatience, as the Sanctum emissary stirred from unconsciousness.

Mr Mordadson was not surprised to discover that he was hanging from the ceiling by ropes attached to his wing roots, with his wrists and ankles tightly bound and a thick strip of sticky tape covering his mouth. Nor was he surprised by the pain that pulsed sickeningly down through his head. It felt as though his skull had been cracked in two and the halves were grinding against each other. Maybe this was actually so. The Count had hit him hard.

None of it came as a shock because this wasn't the first time Mr Mordadson had been knocked out and come round to find himself tied up and at someone's mercy. It wasn't so very long ago, after all, that he'd been taken captive by Naoutha Nisrocsdaughter and held prisoner aboard her airship, to be beaten and tortured there. In spite of the pain and grogginess, his present situation filled him with an almost wearying sense of déjà vu.

He comforted himself with the thought that, just as he'd got away then, he would do so again. He started to focus on how he would escape, even as the bearded man opened his mouth to speak.

'My name is Af Bri Mumiahson,' he said. 'I don't expect you to have heard of me. There's no reason why you should. I'm no one special, just a solid, average citizen of the realm. I've never done anything particularly remarkable with my life. A doctor, a husband, a father, a man just trying to make his way in the world, help a few people, provide for his family, that's all. The kind of fellow you'd flutter past in the street and not even notice.'

His voice was restrained, neutral. Unnaturally neutral, it seemed to Mr Mordadson. The voice of a man keeping very strong emotions in check.

Who was he? What did he want?

These were questions which Mr Mordadson could not, of course, ask out loud.

'I live in Prismburg,' Af Bri went on. 'I should say *lived*. I haven't been back there in a while, though I'll always think of myself as a Prismburger. I'm sure you've visited that city. A big, important Silver Sanctum official like you gets around. It's a beautiful place. Now that they've repaired the damage, I mean. It wasn't such a beautiful place straight after the Groundlings bombed it and massacred all those people. No, on the contrary, it was one of the ugliest places imaginable then. Half ruined. Awash with blood. I assume you know the statistics. The death toll.'

Mr Mordadson nodded. It hurt to hold his head up in order to maintain eye contact with the other man, and nodding only made matters worse, but he had no choice. A basic rule of captivity was not to show fear. You had to engage with your captors. They wanted to dehumanise you, to regard you as inferior. It made their role easier. But by not letting yourself be belittled, you could counteract that. You could remind them, if they had a conscience, that over and above anything else you and they were just people. Equals. The same.

'Seven hundred and ninety-two. That was the total, Mr Mordadson. No other sky-city took as many casualties. Seven hundred and ninety-two lives were snuffed out that day. It's difficult to get that figure out of your head once it's lodged in there. They were slaughtered like chickens on the Feast of Metatron.'

Af Bri started walking slowly back and forth, hands behind back, pacing like a lecturer.

'Most of those killed were taking part in the protest rally. Remember? It was a day of action across the entire realm, folk voicing their objection to the Sanctum's crackdown on Feather First! In every sky-city they marched on the Alar Patrol HQ and chanted slogans and waved placards. A noisy but peaceful demonstration. I would have joined the one in Prismburg but I had to work. I had a shift at the hospital and couldn't get out of it. Just my luck, eh?'

He stopped pacing.

'Only thing was, my wife and children did go on the march. My wife's name was Liwet. My son was called Tariel, and he was eleven. My daughter was called Coré, and she was nine. They all three were keen to make their feelings known. They wanted to send a message to our so-called leaders: *we will not tolerate this.*'

He took a deep breath. Swallowed hard. His voice was beginning to quiver. His restraint was in danger of crumbling.

'It was shortly after lunchtime that the first of the injured were brought in to Prismburg General. At the hospital we'd heard the explosions. Some of us had seen the massive aeroplane fly over. All of a sudden the trickle of wounded arriving became a flood. Every doctor was summoned to the A and E department. We had to drop everything and go.'

Mr Mordadson knew, with a gut-wrenching sense of inevitability, what was coming.

'So there I was,' said Af Bri, 'up to my elbows in blood and gore, splinting shattered limbs and pulling shards of glass from stomachs and stemming the bleeding from severed arteries, and trying all the while not to think about my family and how they'd been on the same rally as all these maimed and dying people, trying to keep alive the hope that somehow they'd managed to escape the carnage. And then an intern came up to me, young chap, promising doctor, and his face was absolutely grey, and I told myself it was grey from the horror of what he was seeing, grey because he'd never witnessed anything on such a scale before. Who had? But deep down I knew. I knew from his expression – the pity on his face – what he was about to tell me.'

A bitter, trembling sigh.

'I won't forget what happened next. It's engraved in my memory for ever. It's the last thing I think of before I go to sleep every night. It'll be the last thing I think of on my deathbed. The intern led me to a ward. There I found my wife, cradling our son in her arms. Our daughter was lying beside them. Coré was dead. I could tell that at a glance. Tariel was barely alive and not likely to stay that way long. Half his guts were outside his body. My wife was trying to keep them in with her hands. She was literally trying to hold our boy together. The front of her dress was drenched in blood. His blood, I assumed. Her eyes were empty, faraway. She said nothing as I took Tariel from her and did my best to return his entrails where they belonged. Even as I did, I realised it was futile. The trauma alone was going to kill him. He was out cold, slipping away second by second. All at once, just like that, he was gone. His heart stopped. I felt like screaming but couldn't get a sound out. I turned to Liwet to break the news. My tongue wouldn't work so I tried to tell her with my eyes alone. But it wasn't any use.'

A single tear rolled down his cheek, disappearing into his beard.

'Liwet was dead too. Just sitting there, gone. With all the blood on her dress, I simply hadn't noticed. She'd been injured as badly as our children but she hadn't said a word. She'd wanted me to concentrate on saving Tariel, not to worry about her.'

He steeled himself, an immense, almost superhuman effort.

'I died too, that moment. At a stroke my life was over. My family, wiped out, and nothing I could do to help them. And do you know who I blame for it? I should blame the Groundlings, shouldn't I? I should blame Dominic Slamshaft or whatever his name is, and all the mindless brutes he employed to do his bidding. I should blame Lord Urironson too, for conniving with them. But I don't. It's the weirdest thing but I can't find it in me to hold any of them responsible. To me, the guilty ones are the people who got us into this whole mess in the first place. The Silver Sanctum. The politicians who we trusted to steer us right and who've let us down so badly. The intelligence-gathering operatives who showed us that day how truly incompetent they were. You, Mr Mordadson. Basically, you.'

Af Bri knelt and started unlacing Mr Mordadson's left shoe.

'I've been waiting for this,' he said. 'I have never wanted anything as much as I've wanted this. I've been looking forward to it for months. One of my conditions for agreeing to help the lady I now work for was that, once you'd wandered into our trap, I should have first dibs. She guaranteed me that. All I had to give her in return was my undying loyalty. A small price to pay. A bargain, really.'

The shoe came off, then the sock.

'Do you know which are the most painful bones to break, Mr Mordadson? Funnily enough it's not the large ones, it's the smaller ones. There's a greater concentration of nerve endings around them. I know these things, thanks to my medical training.'

Mr Mordadson clamped his teeth together. There was no point resisting, trying to break free. He was too firmly fastened, and with his wings incapacitated and his feet barely touching the floor he had no leverage. Af Bri Mumiahson could do as he wished and Mr Mordadson could only brace himself and endure.

'This bone, for instance.' He grasped the base of Mr Mordadson's little toe. 'Proximal phalange. Tiny. One of the smallest in the body.'

Questions swirled through Mr Mordadson's head. Why had the Count betrayed him? Who was the woman Af Bri Mumiahson had referred to? What was she after? Did she have anything to do with Lord Urironson's disappearance?

He forced himself to focus. There must be a connection, some factor that linked all these unknowns. He channelled all his brainpower into the mystery, in an effort to close off his mind to all other thoughts.

'This may sting a little,' said Af Bri.

He began to bend the toe backwards against Mr Mordadson's foot.

'Trust me, I'm a doctor.'

Snap.

CHAPTER 23

Prime Consideration

The Count of Gyre was more than a little troubled, so he did what he normally did in times of stress. He began mentally listing happy primes.

7, 13, 19, 23, 31, 79, 97 . . .

A happy prime was a beautiful number. Simply being a prime, divisible only by 1 and itself, made it special enough, but if you added up the squares of its digits, then added up the squares of the digits of that total, and so on, eventually the result was 1.

Happy primes were orchids of the mathematical world, rare and exotic, and when ranked in order showed a delicate kind of symmetry. Reciting them should have soothed the Count, but not today. Not with his city overrun by outsiders. Not with the gruesome, mummy-like husk of Naoutha Nisrocsdaughter sitting across from him in his office, flanked by two of her accomplices and fixing him with a baleful, triumphant eye. Above all, not with the guilt that writhed inside him like a worm.

103, 109, 139, 167, 193, 239, 263, 293, 313, 331 . . .

No, it just wasn't working. The happy primes had lost their power to divert and console. What had he done? What had he *done*?

'You've done the right thing, Count,' said Naoutha, as though reading his thoughts. 'It would have been a mistake. To disobey me or renege. On our agreement. The kind of mistake. You wouldn't live to regret.'

'But Mr Mordadson . . .'

'Don't worry yourself about him. Don't give him another moment's thought. He's getting what. He deserves.'

'But he suspected nothing, right up until I hit him. It never even crossed his mind that I might be his enemy.'

'Then you performed your role well. Besides, didn't the Ultimate Reckoner predict that you. Would do what you did? Just as it predicted that you and I. Would form an alliance.'

'Yes,' the Count said doubtfully.

'So what are you. In such a flap about? His fate was a foregone. Conclusion. You had no choice.'

Didn't I? thought the Count.

'And in exchange for your help. In capturing Mr Mordadson. Not one single citizen of Gyre will be killed,' Naoutha continued. 'You people are all about numbers. And transactions. Right? Well, it seems to me that one life. In return for the lives of hundreds. Is a pretty reasonable deal. A whole lot of credit against. One small debit.'

'That's not really how the principles of accountancy work,' the Count felt obliged to point out. 'In double-entry bookkeeping we—'

Naoutha hitched up her one good shoulder, the nearest she could manage to a shrug. 'I was never into all that stuff anyway. Maths? Figures? Waste of time. What's the use? Life isn't a sum. It doesn't follow a. Set of given rules. It isn't something you can add up. And round off neatly.'

To the Count's ears this was tantamount to blasphemy, but he said nothing. She was trying to get a rise out of him, and he'd already compromised himself enough. Naoutha had taken his integrity. She wouldn't have his dignity as well.

Just then, a scream sounded from below.

Even though it came from several storeys down, it could be heard clearly because the rest of Gyre was quiet and still. Work had been suspended and the city's residents were confined to the dormitories and common areas. Naoutha's armed footsoldiers – her Regulars, as she called them – had taken charge of the place, rounding people up. Naoutha had said this was for the Gyrians' own good, and the Count had gone along with it, giving the order that nobody should put up any resistance. Naoutha claimed she didn't want anyone accidentally getting hurt.

Someone *was* getting hurt, though, and the Count had no doubt who. Another scream followed the first, and then there were more screams. Protracted, roaring, muffled and yet still terrible, one after another they echoed up through Gyre's spiralling corridors and narrow concourses.

Mr Mordadson had seemed to view the Count as a friend, somebody he could trust. And this was how the Count repaid him?

His stomach lurched. He tried the happy primes again, but it didn't quell the nausea or blot out Mr Mordadson's cries of agony.

Naoutha, by contrast, looked as though she was listening to the sweetest song ever composed. The two Regulars, taking their cue from her, shared a grin.

After a while, to the Count's great relief, the screaming abated.

'So what now?' he asked. His mouth felt parchment-dry. 'I've done what you wanted. My city has complied with your every demand. It's over, isn't it? You'll move on and leave us be?'

Naoutha's rasp of a voice sounded regretful, almost sincerely so. 'Would that we could, Count. But you see, my plans call. For more than just submission. From Gyre.'

'What do you mean?'

'Gyrians have a vital part to. Play in the next phase of. My scheme.'

The Count was aghast. 'But . . . we had an agreement! You get Mr Mordadson, my citizens are safe, that's it.'

'No,' said Naoutha, 'the deal was that none of them. Would be killed. I never said anything about. Safe.'

'It was implicit.'

'Like pluck it was.' Naoutha emitted a brutal cackle. 'You ought to be more careful how. You strike your bargains, Count. Just because you're a slave to. Rules doesn't mean we. All are.'

The Count struggled to find words to express his outrage and anguish. In the end what burst out of him was the worst insult anyone could use in Gyre.

'You *cheat!*'

It was water off a duck's back to Naoutha. Turning to her accomplices she said, 'Time to try out the formula. We'll probably need. What do you think? Five test subjects? To begin with.'

'Test subjects?' the Count mumbled numbly.

'Yes. And you can come with us. And watch,' said Naoutha. 'You might as well see for yourself what you get. When you do a deal with the. Non-mathematically-minded.'

CHAPTER 24

Ultrapterine

Five Gyre residents, selected at random, were herded onto a curving terrace at the city's rim. They huddled together, their wings drooping. Several of Naoutha's Regulars hovered above, crossbows and maces at the ready. Naoutha herself was wheeled out onto a colonnaded balcony overlooking the terrace, and the Count was made to stand beside her.

The five Gyrians looked bare and vulnerable in their togas. They turned their faces up to the Count, beseeching their leader for an explanation, reassurance, *something*.

He avoided their gazes.

At Naoutha's command, a Regular descended and handed each of the five a small, stoppered phial with a clear liquid inside.

'Drink,' she told them.

They hesitated.

'What is it?' asked one. The green hem of his toga marked him out as a Calculator Savant, one of those rare, gifted individuals who was able to carry out incredibly complicated arithmetical processes in his head, with no need for paper and pen or mechanical assistance.

Naoutha nodded to her Regulars, and one of them fired his crossbow, shooting the Calculator Savant in the thigh. The Calculator Savant crumpled to his knees, sobbing and groaning.

'It's something that prevents you. Getting a crossbow bolt through the leg,' Naoutha said. 'Or through some. Even more sensitive part of. Your anatomy. But only if you swallow it down. *Right now*.'

The four other Gyre residents nervously pulled the stoppers from the phials. One of them helped the Savant do the same. Then, in unison, the five raised the little glass bottles to their lips. A couple of them glanced up at the Count again, and saw no hope of a reprieve there. They all drank.

The contents of the phials tasted foully bitter. All five grimaced. One of them retched.

A minute passed. Naoutha levered herself forward to get a better look, pushing herself off the wheelchair armrest with her good elbow. Down below on the terrace the five residents peered at one another, curious to know which of them was going to be first to show any ill effects. It began to look as if none of them was. Another minute went by, and five furrowed brows eased. Even the injured Savant braved a smile of relief.

The Count sneaked a sidelong peek at Naoutha. It was impossible to read her true mood with her face swathed in bandages like that, but he fancied he saw thwarted anger in her eye, and was glad. Her 'formula', whatever it was, wasn't working. She had failed.

Then someone on the terrace complained of feeling faint. Another said everything had started spinning. A third began to tremble violently, then all at once doubled over and fell onto the flagstone floor, frothing at the mouth.

Naoutha let out a croak of glee. 'This is it!' she said.

'What's going on?' the Count demanded. 'What's that stuff doing to them?'

'Keep looking. You'll see.'

The Count had no desire to keep looking, but neither could he *not* look. The five Gyrians were now all of them on the floor, bent over and shaking and writhing. Saliva foamed from their lips. Their eyes bulged. Three of them clutched at their chests and bellies. The other two raked the air with clawed hands. Choking, gurgling noises came from all five throats, while five pairs of wings snapped open and shut rapidly, shedding small clouds of feathers.

'They're dying,' said the Count. 'You've poisoned them!'

'No, not dying,' Naoutha replied. 'Being reborn. Transformed. Transformed into. Harbingers of a new age.'

Gripping the balcony balustrade, the Count continued to stare down at the five. These were colleagues. Subjects of his. He knew them, liked them, and for one of them, the Calculator Savant, even felt a kind of reverence. This, what was happening to them, was an abomination. He prayed it would stop soon.

The whites of their eyes flooded with red. The wet sounds coming from their throats grew dry and crackly, turning into grunts, snarls, screeches, gibbering. Then, as if in answer to the Count's prayer, the shudders and tremors halted. The five Gyrians appeared to regain control of themselves, as though some shared fit of madness had passed and sanity had returned. One by one they picked themselves up, shook out their wings, cricked their necks, settled their shoulders and straightened their spines. The sounds they were making dwindled to low moans and grumbles.

They stood on the terrace, swaying a little, seemingly dazed by what they had just been through.

For a fleeting instant the Count dared to believe that all was well.

Then he saw their faces.

There was nothing there. No life, no animation. They were blank. Devoid of expression. Inhuman. The faces of people that were no longer people. Bloodshot-eyed *things*.

Even the Savant, possessor of that amazing brain, now gazed vacantly around him with drool dribbling down his chin. He clacked his teeth a few times. Then, noticing the crossbow bolt that protruded from his thigh, he grasped the shaft and slowly worked it free. This ought to have been agony but his face showed no sign of it. He spent the best part of a minute studying the blood-dripping bolt, holding it up to his nose and turning it this way and that as though he had no idea what this object could be or how it had come to be stuck in him. He sniffed it, licked it, then casually, obliviously, tossed it aside.

The other four were behaving in a similar fashion. They milled around on the terrace like sleepwalkers, sometimes stopping to peer down at themselves or up at the sun in frank bafflement, all the while muttering strings of nonsense words. It wasn't that they didn't appear to know where they were. They didn't appear to know *who* they were.

'Pterine,' said Naoutha to the Count. 'That's what they drank. An extreme form of the drug. Enhanced and refined. All impurities removed. Ultrapterine, I'm calling it. The effects are permanent. Not temporary like the original. Thickened muscle fibre. Enlarged heart. Increased endurance. Decreased sensitivity to pain. And almost complete obliteration of. The higher brain functions. A mind-blowing concoction. Literally. Those aren't the people you knew, Count. Not any more. They're both more and. Less than they were. Empty shells, but what shells! Tougher, faster, hardier . . .'

Two of the five inadvertently bumped into each other. The collision confused them, and their confusion blossomed into rage. Suddenly they fell on each other, growling and brawling. They scratched, kicked, punched, pulled hair, wing-battered, even bit. It was like a schoolyard scuffle, except infinitely fiercer and more savage.

'Oh yes, and uninhibited. Aggression too,' said Naoutha. 'That's the other effect of. Ultrapterine. A tripwire temper.'

The fight carried on. Blood flew. Small chunks of flesh were torn off. Togas got ripped. Then, as abruptly as it started, it ended. The two combatants broke apart and wandered off in different directions. Aside from the fresh wounds on their bodies and the togas hanging off them in tatters, there was no indication they'd just been engaged in a ferocious struggle. Neither of them acknowledged the other's presence. They'd been trying to kill each other. Now they weren't. No lingering resentment, just a return to the meandering mindlessness of before.

The Count was beyond shock, beyond horror. Beyond any kind of emotion.

'You'd – you'd inflict *this* on the Airborn realm?' he said, in husky, hollow tones.

'Of course I would,' said Naoutha. 'And will. Starting here. Spreading outward. Why ever not?'

'Because . . . Because it's monstrous, that's why! Hideous!'

'Hideous?' said Naoutha, gazing down on the five shambling creatures below. 'Well, endings. *Are* hideous, I suppose. Beginnings sometimes, too.'

CHAPTER 25

The Eyes Of Someone Not To Be Messed With

'There,' said Professor Emeritus, crouching over Fletcher. He'd administered a second injection, using a conventional syringe. The shaking had
subsided and Fletcher's limbs were no longer going through contortions.
He lay limp, his breath coming in shallow gasps. 'Your brother will be
fine, but we should get him to the sick bay, just to be on the safe side.
Will you give me a hand? He's too heavy to manage on my own.'

Cassie had a good mind to give Emeritus more than a hand. How about
a fist instead? Right up the hooter.

But she said, 'OK,' and helped him hoist Fletcher up to a sitting
position. Then, either side of him, each with an arm yoked over their
shoulders, they lugged him out of the cabin. *First things first*, Cassie
thought. *Make sure Fletch be comfortable,* then *give the professor what-for.*

They laid him out on a bed in the sick bay. Emeritus inserted a saline
drip into his forearm and checked his pulse. Adam the cat poked a head
round the door, saw nothing that interested him, and left.

Fletcher's face was sallow and sweaty, and his eyelids fluttered. Cassie
was appalled to think how close her brother had come to dying. In the
end, there'd been no alternative. She had had to let Emeritus into the
cabin. But now that the emergency appeared to be past and Fletcher was
safe, Emeritus was about to find out what happened when you hurt a
Grubdollar. The twisted old bastard would pay.

'So what did you do that for?' Cassie began, grabbing him by the lapel
and swinging him round to face her. 'Pumping he full of venom. There
were no call for it!'

Emeritus raised a hand in surrender. 'Please, Cassie. Let's take this
somewhere else, where we won't disturb Fletcher. He needs rest and
quiet.'

Cassie hauled the professor out of the sick bay. She was shorter than

410

him by a head but what she lacked in height she made up in strength and sturdiness. She strode through the Bathylab, Emeritus stumbling along behind her, tripping over his own feet. Finally they reached the dining area, where Cassie shoved him into a chair.

'Right. Talk.'

'What can I tell you?' said Emeritus, smoothing out his rumpled jacket. 'I'm sorry. Truly I am. I couldn't see any way of us reaching an amicable settlement, you on one side of that door, me on the other. So I persuaded you to open up, and then used the compressed-air hypodermic on Fletcher to . . . well, to get your attention, really.'

'What!?' exploded Cassie.

'Drastic, I appreciate. But it levelled the playing field, and now you and I can have a reasoned, serious discussion, just the two of us. No disrespect to your brother, but he's not quite on the same intellectual plane as we are, Cassie. Without him hanging over me, breathing down my neck, I feel I can—'

'Clip it down!' Cassie snapped, banging a table with her fist. Emeritus flinched. 'Be you even listening to yourself? You nearly kill Fletch, and all because you want a private little chat with I? You's been down here on your own too long, old man. You's completely lost all sense of pro-portion. People be'n't like those animals in your lab, for you to mess around with as you please.'

'No, of course not. And I've apologised, haven't I? I realise I got things wrong, and I'm going to do everything I can to ensure that Fletcher comes to no further harm. I don't know how else I can make amends.'

Minutes ago Emeritus had put Fletcher's life on the line, and now he was calmly justifying it on the grounds that it had been the only way he could get Cassie to listen to him. Either he was so incredibly smart that he could rationalise his own extremes of behaviour – or he was a total nutter. Maybe, Cassie thought, the two things weren't that different.

'Look,' she said, voice thunderously low and threatening, 'it'm very simple. You be going to get we to land as promised, and in the meantime you also be going to take care of Fletch and see him makes a full recovery. Use all your science on he and whatever else. If him be'n't back to his old self by the time us is at the coast, you'm going to rue the day you ever met a Grubdollar. Be I making myself clear?'

'Abundantly.'

'Look into my eyes,' she went on. 'Look hard. I's seen death. I's hurt people, when I's had to. These'm the eyes of someone you doesn't want to mess with.'

Emeritus gulped and nodded. He didn't doubt her for a moment. And that was fine, because she was telling the truth.

411

'Good,' she said. 'Now up you get. Start up Bathylab and let's be on our way.'

'Yes,' said Emeritus, rising from the chair. 'The batteries should be at full charge by now. With autopilot on, I can tend to Fletcher while we're on the move.'

He made to walk past her, then a sudden frown flickered across his face. He began patting his pockets.

'What'm up?' said Cassie. 'Lost something?'

'I'm sure I . . .' He hummed distractedly. 'It ought to be . . .'

Cassie tutted. Daft old fool. 'Don't tell I, you can't find the keys to get this vehicle going.'

'No, no, a Bathylab doesn't need keys. Now where . . . ? Ah!'

Quick as a flash, Emeritus pulled an object from his pocket, a sort of slim plastic box with two metal prongs at one end. In the same swift action he thrust the prongs against Cassie's midriff and pressed a button with his thumb. She had a microsecond to realise she had been tricked.

But the knowledge didn't save her. There was a sharp *zap*, and Cassie collapsed as though every bone had been removed from her body, and she heard the clang of her head hitting the floor, and she knew she had been electrocuted, the object in Emeritus's hand was a miniature version of the high-voltage defence system on *Cackling Bertha*, and she was stunned and she was helpless, everything felt like jelly, and now she was sliding, no, she was being dragged by the ankles, the ceiling rolling overhead, she was being pulled through a doorway, along a corridor, down a companionway, bump bump bump, then more dragging, into another room, dumped unceremoniously in there, Emeritus saying, 'Stay put, child, I have work to do,' followed by a *slam* and a series of heavy clunking sounds, then footfalls disappearing, and then nothing but the deep, bassy thrum of Bathylab Four's turbines reverberating through her supine form, the in-and-out of the tides, for a long time this was the only sensation Cassie was aware of, pulsing into her, in her, with her, the sea, the slow eternal heartbeat of the sea.

CHAPTER 26

Hot And Cold Water

By the time she was able to move again Cassie had stoked up a fierce inner blaze of anger, most of it directed at herself. Numbskull! Moron! Sucker! She'd let herself be lulled by Emeritus's show of meekness and absentmindedness. As he'd jolted her with his portable electric shock device, the weird, cold light had been back in his eyes. That was the real Professor Emeritus, the same one she'd seen at the Biological Containment Unit. The only Professor Emeritus. Everything else was an act.

Simply clambering to her knees made her head reel. Standing upright, she felt the world seesaw beneath her as though she was back aboard the *Merry Narwhal* on a high wave-swell. Bile burned her throat. She clung to the wall for support till, eventually, the nausea passed.

Emeritus had hauled her into a lower-level maintenance storeroom. One end of it was taken up by a pipe that was as broad in diameter as she was tall. The rest was shelves full of tools and diagnostic equipment, mostly old and corroded. She tried the door but Emeritus had, naturally, secured it, probably by jamming something into the locking wheel outside. She threw herself against the door a few times, just to see if this made any difference. It didn't. She found a crowbar and tried that. The door would not budge. Finally she resorted to hammering on it with both fists and shouting, calling Emeritus every bad name she could think of. This didn't affect the door in the slightest but it did make her feel a little better.

At last she admitted defeat and stepped back from the door. There had to be some other way out of the storeroom. Certainly she had no intention of cooling her heels in here while she waited for Emeritus to come back and let her out. That wasn't likely to happen any time soon. Emeritus had shut her away for a reason.

Stay put, child, I have work to do, the professor had said.

413

In itself it was an innocent enough remark, but not the way he had said it. Cassie's gut instinct was that he'd been referring to Fletcher. Her brother was still unconscious in the sick bay as far as she knew. It was vital that she escape and save him. Somehow.

But how?

She scanned the storeroom again, and her eye fell on the pipe at the far end. From her earlier explorations of the Bathylab she recognised it as part of the tidal-powered recharging system. It was clammily cold to the touch, and through her fingers she could feel the susurrant vibration of the seawater flowing within.

At the top, accessible by rungs bolted into the side of the pipe, was a glass inspection panel. Cassie climbed up and peered in. Black water sluiced below the glass, its movement detectable only by the jiggling dance of bubbles around the inside of the panel's frame.

The panel was a rectangle perhaps forty centimetres by sixty. That was an aperture a person could fit in through, just.

Cassie's mental map of Bathylab Four told her that the pipe ran the length of this section of the vessel. If she judged the flow of the water correctly, roughly twenty metres downstream from here lay the wet dock, where the motor launches were berthed. An idea was forming in her mind, and its success hinged on whether there was a similar inspection panel fitted into the pipe at the wet dock. She had a feeling there was. If memory served, she'd seen a set of rungs like these ones attached to the wet-dock portion of the pipe.

The inspection panel here in the storeroom could be removed easily enough. It was held in place by eight wingnuts, and most of them were done up only finger-tight, although for a couple of the stiffer, rustier ones Cassie had to use an adjustable spanner she found on a shelf. A strong odour of brine hit her as she pulled the panel free. A few stray trickles splashed over the rim. She dipped her hand experimentally in the water. It was so cold her fingertips went numb immediately, and then started to tingle in an exquisitely painful way. She shook her hand dry, and knew it was crazy even to contemplate doing what she intended to do.

But there was no alternative. There was no other way out of the storeroom, and she couldn't leave Fletcher at Emeritus's mercy. She had no idea what, if anything, the professor had in mind for her brother. Might he even try and experiment on Fletcher, as he had on those animals? It seemed unthinkable, but Cassie wouldn't put anything past the man.

Trapped in the storeroom, she was no use to anyone. If her escape plan failed, and it was likely it would, she'd be dead and therefore still no use to anyone. But at least she'd have tried.

She looked around for a length of rope she could secure herself with, but there wasn't any. What she did find was a stubby claw-hammer. She tucked it into her belt. Then she clambered back up onto the pipe, straddling it just next to the inspection panel.

When faced with very cold water there were two possible approaches: immerse yourself bit by bit, or plunge straight in. It was the same amount of torture, either spread out over a long period or compressed into a couple of seconds.

If she opted for the slower of the two, she'd have plenty of time to think better of her plan and back out.

Cassie raised her legs, ankles together. She took a deep breath and thrust herself down through the panel aperture.

She screamed and gasped simultaneously. The water wasn't just cold, it was *freezing*. And she wasn't even all the way in. Only her legs were submerged. She'd got stuck. Her bottom was wedged in the aperture. Her damn fat bum!

She pulled with both hands on the rim of the hole, squeezing herself deeper in, centimetre by wriggling centimetre. She didn't want to do this. Already her legs were throbbing with the cold and she couldn't feel her toes any more.

Then her hips were through, and the rest of her swiftly followed. She found herself clinging onto the aperture, her head still out of the water, the rest of her being pulled nearly horizontal by the current in the pipe. She peered down and could see nothing of her body. It was as though she'd lowered herself into ink. Icy black ink.

Her breath was coming in rapid, shallow huffs. Now was her very last chance to give up on this idea. She could still haul herself out of the pipe. Her escape plan was beyond stupid. Beyond desperate. It was downright suicidal.

She thought of Fletcher, held her breath, and let go.

CHAPTER 27

In The Pipeline

Cassie swam on her back, propelling herself along with sweeping backward arcs of her arms. Now and then she used the interior of the pipe to push off against. The current helped, giving her added impetus.

The initial shock of the cold water on her body had given way to a kind of low, pulsing, all-over ache. She hurt, but bluntly, no longer sharply, and the pain had the benefit of keeping her focused. It distracted her from the terror of her situation. She was in a water-flooded pipe, she couldn't see a thing, she was being swept along towards a place where she hoped there was another inspection panel, and if there was no such panel, if her memory had misled her, then she would drown, plain as that. She wouldn't be able to swim back to the storeroom. She'd run out of air before she made it. The pain kept her in the here and now, forcing her to concentrate on every movement she made, every second as it passed. It reminded her of the simple urgency of staying alive.

After a while she wasn't certain she was on her back any more. She was still in contact with the inside of the pipe, but it was hard to tell up from down in the blind-blackness of the water, and the current kept buffeting her about. For all she knew she might have rotated and now be clawing her way along the side of the pipe or even the base, and then wouldn't see the inspection panel as she passed it. She made sure to look around her, swivelling her gaze in all directions. The water stung her eyes horribly. She could almost feel the jelly in her eyeballs starting to congeal with the cold.

Then, in the blackness, a glimpse of light. A vague, fuzzy rectangle, up and to her left.

She struggled towards it. Her limbs were beginning to feel heavy, sluggish. The cold was getting to her, penetrating to her bones. She remembered this from the sinking of the *Merry Narwhal*. She knew what it meant. She had very little time left before her numbed muscles stopped obeying her. At the back of her throat she could feel a cramping sensation, something else that told her she didn't have much time left. Her lungs were wanting to know when they were next going to be allowed some oxygen.

She caught onto the rim of the panel with her fingernails. She held herself in place, one-handed, while groping with her other hand for the hammer. She couldn't find it. It wasn't in her belt any more. It must have dropped out!

She started to panic. She ordered herself to stay calm. She searched again, and there the hammer was, where she'd left it. Her fingers felt the curved shape of the hammer's head. They'd missed it the first time round, that was all.

She drew the hammer out and attempted to get a grip on its handle. The simple act of closing her fingers into a fist took an extraordinary amount of effort. It was as though the water was resisting her, and even when she did finally clasp the handle it seemed to be encased in a thick cylinder of solid ice. She couldn't be fully certain she was even holding it.

She raised the hammer to the panel and hit the glass.

Nothing. Not even a crack.

Despair surged through her.

She tried again, swinging the hammer up through the water as hard and as fast as she could.

Through her blurred vision, a tiny white line appeared in the glass.

That was enough. That was all the encouragement she needed.

She whacked and whacked and whacked at the panel, and every blow seemed to require more exertion than the last, even though the glass was now snowflaked with impact points and clearly weakening. She couldn't feel her arm any more, or any of her limbs, and her lungs were crying out for air, but she kept bringing the hammer up against the panel because that was all she could do. That was what she *must* do. It was her only hope.

Suddenly the glass shattered. A large central segment of it fell away and was whisked off by the water. Its jagged tip swept past Cassie's nose, just missing it. She raised her face to the gap and sucked in air. Then she set about quickly knocking out the remaining shards from the panel frame. Within moments the aperture was clear of glass. She chucked the hammer out through the hole, then pulled herself after it. She hooked her elbows over the rim, then wriggled and struggled to get her torso up and over. Her bum jammed in the aperture, as before, but this time her sodden clothing provided some lubrication. She slithered out, and before she could stop herself went sliding headfirst down the side of the pipe, onto the floor. She lay there in a heap, shivering, shuddering, spluttering, weak as a baby.

Cassie had never felt so exhausted in her life. She could quite happily have gone to sleep. But she knew that if she did hypothermia would set in and she would probably die. She must keep going, for her own sake now as well as Fletcher's.

She forced herself to stand and began wringing the water out her clothes.

She was in the wet dock, as she'd expected. A pair of motor launches bobbed side by side at their moorings in a long, narrow pool that had a sluice gate at one end. Beyond was a watertight door that led to a sea lock which in turn gave access to the outside. Cassie allowed herself a moment of self-congratulation. When Emeritus shut her in the store-room he'd had no idea how well she knew the internal layout of the Bathylab. It was thanks to that and her own foolhardy bravery that she had managed to get out.

And now: Fletcher.

Cassie picked up the hammer and, with her soaking-wet clothes squelching around her, made for the exit.

CHAPTER 28

Sick

The sick bay door had a small porthole inset at eye level. Cassie padded up to it and peered in. There was her brother, flat out on the bed, insensible. She couldn't see anyone else in the room, but she observed that a small trolley had been stationed at the bedside . . . and what lay on the trolley sent a jolt of horror through her.

It was a set of surgical instruments. There were several scalpels of different sizes, a small saw, a couple of pairs of scissors, a sort of retractor device with a ratchet and a turning handle, a long double-clawed thing that resembled ice-cube tongs, and a number of other bizarre, intrusive-looking items whose function she could only guess at. All gleamed and glinted wickedly.

So Emeritus *was* insane enough to experiment on Fletcher.

It gave Cassie no satisfaction to have her worst fears confirmed. Hammer at the ready, she stole into the sick bay, leaving the door ajar. Reaching Fletcher, she saw that his wrists and ankles had been bound to the bed frame with leather straps. This was possibly more alarming than the sight of all those surgical instruments. If Emeritus needed Fletcher restrained while he did what he was going to do to him, then clearly he was anticipating resistance from his 'patient'.

Vivisection. Carrying out operations on live specimens.

Emeritus was worse than mad. He was downright sick.

Shivering, and not just from the cold of her sodden clothing, Cassie reached down and shook her brother, trying to rouse him. He just rolled his head, burbled, and lapsed back into unconsciousness.

Setting down the hammer, she undid the buckle on one of the wrist straps. She would free Fletcher first, then figure out what she was going to do. Getting him out of the sick bay and finding somewhere to hide seemed like a good idea. If she had to carry him piggyback, she would.

419

'Ah.'

She spun round.

Emeritus had entered the room without her hearing him. He had put on a surgical smock and rubber gloves, with a paper mask over his nose and mouth. In his hand was a tall aluminium flask speckled with condensation. Adam the cat was at his ankles.

Cassie and he stared at each other for several seconds.

Then she lunged for the hammer.

He lunged for the trolley at the same time, setting down the flask and snatching up a scalpel.

Cassie didn't hesitate. She threw herself at him, lashing out with the hammer. Emeritus recoiled, surprisingly fast for a man his age. Her weapon swung through empty air. His much smaller and sharper weapon flickered out, catching her shirt. She thought he'd missed cutting her arm. Then blood came oozing through the slit in her sleeve, soaking the material.

She hissed with pain, and swung the hammer at him again. This time the head struck home, somewhere near his belly, but its impact was diluted by the folds of his smock. Cassie grunted in annoyance.

Staggering backwards, Emeritus knocked against the trolley, and the aluminium flask toppled over. A viscous red fluid poured out, giving off twists of frosty vapour as it oozed over the surgical implements and dripped onto the floor.

'Dammit!' he snarled. 'Do you know how difficult that was to make?'

'No idea,' said Cassie. 'What be it?'

'Genomorph serum. A week's work down the drain. Don't worry, I have more. But even so . . . !'

Glittering-eyed, Emeritus lashed out with the scalpel once more. Cassie managed to evade the blow this time, but before she could bring the hammer up she found herself attacked on a second front. Adam the cat launched himself at her, landing squarely on her chest. More through surprise than anything she stumbled backwards. Her heel caught against Fletcher's bedstead, and she fell down with the cat on top of her, dropping the hammer as she did so.

Ears flattened, hackles raised, Adam was a fury of snarling and spitting. His claws raked Cassie's face and chest. When she put up an arm to protect herself, he sank his teeth into her finger.

Eventually she was able to close both hands around the cat's midsection. She prised the writhing, squirming creature off her and flung. Adam somersaulted across the sick bay, thumping against a cupboard and fetching up on the floor, dazed.

Cassie sprang upright, to find Emeritus poised over her, now with a scalpel in both hands. Her hammer lay under the bed, out of reach.

Emeritus jabbed at her repeatedly with the two blades, driving her backward. She retreated till she butted up against a worktop. He closed in, the scalpels now aimed straight at her face.

'Cassie, Cassie, Cassie . . .' he intoned. The paper mask puffed outward with each syllable. 'This has all got hopelessly, tragically out of hand. I've no desire to hurt you. My intentions are nothing but noble. I want to give Fletcher, and you too if you'll let me, an opportunity like no other. That's all I'm after. I want to offer you a gift of a kind that no human has been offered before.'

'Gift?' said Cassie.

'Yes, I had a feeling that might surprise you. When I pulled the two of you from the sea, it was serendipity itself. I couldn't believe my good fortune. I'd long been wondering whether I could apply my own particular extrapolation of Professor Metier's genomorphic treatments to human subjects. I'd done mice, rats, cats, all the lower-order mammals, starting simple and working my way up the ladder of complexity, as a good scientist should. The next logical step, after primates, was people. And then you happened along, almost literally falling into my lap. The only survivors of a shipwreck. I could try out my procedures on you, and in the unlikely event that something went wrong, there wouldn't be a problem. Everyone would assume you're dead anyway. You wouldn't be missed.'

Cassie held his gaze, even though she would have preferred to look anywhere but those sparkling, mad eyes. Meanwhile her hand began exploring the worktop behind her.

'And your gift,' she said, 'that'd be turning Fletch and I into fish-people, no? With gills and webbed feet and suchlike?'

'Very astute, Cassie. Yes.'

'Might I ask what for? I mean, us is very happy as us is, with the lungs that breathe air and the not living underwater and everything. What'm the point of making Groundlings . . . oceanlings?'

'The point,' said Emeritus, 'is mainly to prove it can be done. Science for science's sake. The purest motive there is. However, more broadly speaking, have you seen the state of the world these days? I'm not that cut off from civilisation down here. I keep up with current events, on the rare occasions that I visit the surface for field research and the like. I know about the conflicts the Airborn and the Groundlings have been having, and the tensions that are mounting within each race as well, and it makes me very pessimistic about the future. I foresee the Bilateral Covenant falling apart and the start of an all-out war, leading to the destruction of one or perhaps both of the races. It's my role as a Keeper of Knowledge to help when help is called for, and the way I can do that is by providing an alternative – creating a third race, one that can live more or less independently of the other two.'

'In the sea.' Cassie's hand had come across something cold and metallic. Her fingers explored its contours. It was an enamel dish, one of those bean-shaped ones used in hospitals for countless different purposes.

'Where better?' said Emeritus. 'It's an environment that can sustain all manner of life. It's self-sufficient. Everything you could want is there for the taking. Bathylab Four has managed down here quite nicely for hundreds and hundreds of years. There's no reason why a race of under-water-adapted beings couldn't exist in similar vehicles, larger ones even, Bathylabs the size of cities. As amphibians they could venture out into the sea any time they liked, to forage and hunt. Their Bathylabs would simply be convenient places to gather and sleep.'

'Um, excuse I, but would that really work?' Cassie's hand closed over the enamel dish. It might not weigh much but, banged hard against Emeritus's head, it would stun him long enough for her to make a dash for the hammer. 'To build new Bathylabs, for instance, people'd have to be on land, wouldn't them? And there'm loads of other stuff you can't do under the water. Like, anything involving fire. So, not so self-sufficient after all. And the Bathylabs themselves wasn't exactly a great success story, was them?'

'Oh, I'm sure any problems could be overcome with a modicum of ingenuity. My goal is only the short-term one of proving that I can make humans amphibious. Think big, start small. The wider practicalities can wait. And Cassie,' he added, 'if you think I haven't noticed you oh-so-subtly picking up that kidney dish, you're sorely mistaken.'

The scalpels hovered unwaveringly in front of her face.

'You'd better put it down,' he said. 'It's not going to help you. You and your brother are going to be my patients whether you like it or not. Nothing is going to alter that fact.'

'Oh yeah?' said Cassie.

Emeritus blinked. She sounded very confident all of a sudden. What did she know that he didn't?

She was looking past him, over his shoulder.

Emeritus turned.

And Fletcher punched him in the face.

CHAPTER 29

Everlasting Renown

Emeritus reeled, staggering round and crashing into the same worktop Cassie was standing against. He rebounded, then slumped to the floor with a groan. Lying there on his side, he looked down his body, and his face wrinkled in curiosity.

Both scalpels were lodged deep in his chest. Barely a centimetre of each handle protruded from the front of his smock.

'Oh,' he said. 'Oh dear, that is not good.'

Cassie skirted around him to join Fletcher. Her brother looked perplexed by the situation. He still didn't have all his wits about him.

'Why were I tied to that bed?' he asked. 'Why were the prof pointing those scalpels at you? And look at the state of you, girl! Why be you in such a mess? You look like you's been taking a shower with all your clothes on.'

'I'll tell you all about it in a minute.' She knelt down beside Emeritus. 'That'm fatal, be'n't it?'

Emeritus gently prodded one of the scalpel handles. 'Yes. Yes, I believe so. Both of them right through the intercostal wall. What are the chances?' He coughed. A fine spatter-pattern of blood darkened his paper mask. 'Bronchial tube's been pierced. The pulmonary artery too, I think. So this is what it feels like.'

'I be'n't going to pretend I's sorry,' Cassie said. 'This'm no more than you deserve. But because I know what compassion is and you doesn't, I'll ask if there'm anything I can do to make you more comfortable.'

'Ha! You're just loving the irony of this, aren't you?'

'It'm a sincere offer. Should I pull the scalpels out?'

'No! Don't. That'll only speed things along. Honestly, there's nothing I want you to do for me.' Emeritus coughed again, moistly. 'I feel quite relaxed, as a matter of fact. It hurts but it's also . . . also peaceful.'

Adam came over, mewling plaintively. Emeritus let him sniff at the scalpel handles. He touched the cat's head with fond fingers.

"Bye, old puss,' he said.

He sank back, supine on the floor. His breath was coming in wheezes now, each shallower and wetter than the last.

'Interesting,' he gasped. 'So calm. That's . . . oxygen deprivation for you. Mild narcosis. Bit like being drunk.'

In spite of herself Cassie clasped his hand.

'You've really missed out, you know,' Emeritus said to her. 'You two could have been . . . pioneers. The first of a new race. Instead of . . . plain old Groundlings. A chance for glory. For all of us. I'd have outshone even . . . Professor Metier. Him and his . . . "everlasting renown". That's . . . what he was after. And I suppose he did achieve . . . it. Would they have . . . remembered me too . . . the same way? Like old Met . . . Met . . . Met a . . .'

One final cough. Blood came out of his mouth with such a gush, Cassie had to look away.

Then Emeritus was silent, and the coldness in his eyes was no longer the coldness of insanity.

CHAPTER 30

A Talent For Machinery

'Phew,' said Fletcher, peering down at the corpse. 'Him were a scientist right to the end. Analysing even as him died.'

'I know,' said Cassie. 'And before you start feeling guilty, Fletch, it weren't your fault. You didn't mean to kill he when you clocked he one.'

'Yeah, well, I weren't thinking about anything except stopping he from stabbing my little sis. It were a good thing I came to when I did. Good thing one of those straps were unbuckled as well. Otherwise it'd have been you there on the floor, not he.'

He teetered slightly, rubbing his head.

'Bless my bum, I doesn't feel too brilliant at all, I'll tell you that, Cass.'

'You'd be feeling a lot worse if Emeritus had had his way. Take it from I.' And she explained what the professor's plans had been.

'Bastard!' Fletcher exclaimed. 'You think him could actually have managed it? Turned we into fish-folk?'

'Doesn't matter. Either way it wouldn't've been much fun.'

'Good point. Well, I certainly doesn't feel the least bit guilty now. So, what next?'

Cassie twisted her lips wryly. 'You said "bless my bum" a moment ago. That'm your answer.'

'Da?'

'Straight up. Us has got to get ourselves back to Scaler's Cliff, soon as possible. Put Da and Robert out of their misery.'

'All fine and well,' said Fletcher, looking around him, 'but how'm us going to do that? You any idea how to drive this thing?'

She shook her head. 'Not the foggiest. Us'll just have to try and work it out. Doesn't want to be stuck here on the seabed for ever, does us?'

'What about old Professor Chop-'em-up?' Fletcher said, jerking a thumb at the corpse.

'Him's not in a state to be much help.'

'No, I mean, what'm us to do with he?'

'I dunno. A snack for the sharks? Let's deal with that later.'

They made their way to the bridge. Adam trotted along in their wake, seemingly at a loss what to do with himself now that Emeritus was dead. Several times Cassie told him to shoo, and even aimed a kick at him. The bitten finger and the scratch marks he had given her throbbed nastily. But the cat refused to be deterred and continued to dog them.

At the bridge, Fletcher went round inspecting the various control consoles. 'Emeritus could do it single-handed,' he mused. 'Can't be that hard, can it?'

Finally he settled down in the command chair.

'Reckon this be the master unit,' he said. 'Those other consoles are slaved to it. Easier to run the vehicle if there'm a team effort going on, but one person can manage if necessary. That looks like the override switch, and it'm activated. OK. And that lever be probably a throttle. Yeah, it'm got graduated markings next to it. Hmm. So there'm separate power output to the front, middle and back wheels. Makes sense. Separate transmissions too then, probably. Meaning this'm six-wheel drive. Good for when the terrain be rough. Now, that says "Ballast". That says "Depressurise". "Focused Sonic Amplification Unit"? No idea what that be. Best avoided for now. Yep, it'm all starting to become clear . . .'

Cassie watched admiringly as her brother familiarised himself with Bathylab Four's controls. All the Grubdollars had a talent for machinery but Fletcher more than any of them.

Nearby, Adam the cat watched too, glancing up idly between bouts of self-grooming.

At last Fletcher thought he was ready.

'Sit down, strap yourself in, girl,' he said, grasping the controls. 'Here goes nothing!'

A moment later, Bathylab began to rumble and thrum.

CHAPTER 31

Search For Her

Five days had passed since Mr Mordadson's visit to the Enochson/ Gabrielson house. Two days had passed since Az and Michael had – only half jokingly – discussed a wingless Gabrielsons' suicide pact.

Time moved slowly at the house in High Haven. Hours had no momentum. They came, they went, one not that much different from another. All was drift.

Michael moped and pined. Aurora was irritable, and napped a lot. Gabriel Enochson spent longer and longer periods in his basement work-shop. No sounds of activity came from down there, no invention or creation, just a fruitless silence.

His wife felt it was her duty to keep things ticking along. Mrs Enochson fussed and fluttered, more manic than ever, as though she thought, if she was a bustle of movement and noise, it might make up for the lack of movement and noise elsewhere. She was trying to fill the gloomy empti-ness in the house with herself. She cooked, cleaned, tidied, organised shopping expeditions, rearranged furniture. But the effort left her drained. By the evening of each day she had become brittle and snappish.

Az lived in the midst of this stagnation, helping his mother when it could not be avoided, otherwise whiling away his free time with books and jetball magazines. His last ever term at school was coming up, and exams with it, but he wasn't bothered. He wasn't going back. Az and education had come to a parting of the ways. Occasionally his mother might mutter something about getting qualifications, perhaps attending university. He'd learned to tune her out. She couldn't make him do anything. No one could.

It had been a lie when he'd told Mr Mordadson that families came first. The truth was, Az would have loved to be anywhere but here, stuck in the house with Michael, Aurora, his mum and his dad, all of them suffocating in misery. If he could have thought of some legitimate way of escaping, he'd have done it. He wanted to be shot of them all. But that wasn't something he could admit to anyone, hardly even to himself. It was unthinkable to abandon his family just now, when everyone was at their lowest ebb. It would be callous and cowardly. Unforgivable.

He was imprisoned here, shackled by a weight of responsibility.

Besides, where could he go? What would he do?

Search for Cassie.

Countless times every day this thought occurred to him. Cassie's disappearance obsessed him. The more he tried not to dwell on it, the harder it became to ignore. Why had she gone? Where? Why had she not told him she was leaving? Why no note, no warning, nothing?

Grimvale, three months ago. The Grubdollars' house: empty. *Cackling Bertha*: not there. Clothing was absent from drawers. The kitchen cupboards had been raided for every last scrap of food. A days-old cobweb stretched between the shade and the bulb of Cassie's bedside lamp, dotted with husks of dead flies.

Az roamed the town, asking passers-by for help, pumping them for information, getting none. Nobody had a clue what had happened to the Grubdollars. They'd vanished, that was all anyone could say.

He went to the Hole and Shovel, looking for Colin Amblescrut. The publican told him Colin hadn't been in recently. Which was not like Colin. The Grubdollars' friend had vanished too, it seemed.

Riding the elevator back up to Heliotropia, Az felt anger mounting in him. In the decompression chamber and on the airbus to High Haven, it worsened. As he made his way through the city, still rebuilding itself after the Groundling onslaught, the anger curdled into contempt.

So that was what she felt about him, eh? That was how highly she thought of him. So highly, she could just pack up and disappear along with her family, and not even have the courtesy to drop him a line and say she was off.

Bitch.

Search for her.

She had dumped him. That was what it came down to. Even if there was some other reason why the entire family had left Grimvale, that was just a convenient pretext. Or maybe they were all in on it. It was a Grubdollar conspiracy. Den, Fletcher and Robert were giving him the cold shoulder, while Cassie was giving him the elbow.

Az's mother seemed to believe that he had been jilted, and she hinted as much every now and then. 'I can't imagine why a person would just *go* like that,' Mrs Enochson said, 'unless it was to make some sort of point.' There was disapproval in her voice, and something more. A note of vindication, as if some private doubt she'd had was now confirmed. She could have added, 'That girl wasn't good enough for you.' She might as well have. All along, Az thought, his mother had never been wholly happy with her son dating a Groundling. She did a good job of pretending she was all right with it. To her friends she was never anything less than enthusiastic about Cassie. 'So *novel* to have a girl like that around,' she would say. 'So refreshing. She has such an unusually frank way of looking at things.' But Az was sure his mother secretly hoped the relationship would fizzle out sooner or later.

Perhaps she was right. Perhaps it was never meant to last. Perhaps they'd been fools to believe it would.

Search for her.

And suppose he did search for her, and found her. What then? What if he scoured the Westward Territories, tracked Cassie down, only to have her turn round and reject him? 'I were in hiding,' she might say. 'And who does you reckon I were hiding from? You, you great moron!'

Sometimes the tattoo on his arm would catch his eye. Az still wasn't used to it being there. He would think he must have rubbed against some fresh paint or spilled some ink, stained the arm somehow. Then he'd remember.

The downward, darkening arrow – symbol of every negative feeling he had ever had. Symbol of his world. Of what he knew to be true.

But sometimes, not often, it struck him differently. The arrow seemed almost to be . . . an instruction.

Search for her.

He chose to disregard it.

Time crawled on. Drift and stagnation.

Az continued to resist the impulse to do what he knew ought to be done.

Then the parcel from Gyre arrived.

CHAPTER 32

The Parcel From Gyre

It was a cardboard box, 20cm long, 10cm square at the ends. The delivery address was simply *Az Gabrielson, High Haven*, but the local sorting office had no difficulty with that. They knew which street this particular celebrity lived on. As for a return address, there was just *Gyre*. The parcel did, though, come with the official stamp of the Count on it.

Az groaned when he saw that. What was this, another evaluation from the Ultimate Reckoner? Just what he didn't need.

He unsealed the box. Aurora happened to be with him at the time. They were in the living room, which had become Aurora's semi-permanent bedroom, since the only position she could sleep at all comfortably in was sitting upright in an armchair.

Inside there was a small, thin object wrapped in white cotton, along with a covering note.

The note, from the Count, read:

> Azrael,
> IN A WOFUL RUT I HAIL AZ. I FOIST YOU
> THE 'EYES' OF ROGUE!
> – the Count of Gyre

Az couldn't make head or tail of it. Aurora didn't have much luck either.

'Why the capitals?' she wondered. 'And surely the Count knows how to spell "woeful", doesn't he?'

'He's barmy,' Az opined. 'Several strings short of a harp. I wouldn't waste much time puzzling over it. We should think ourselves lucky it's words and not a series of random numbers. That'd be much more his style.'

He turned his attention to the cotton-wreathed object. He began unwinding the fabric, which turned out to be a single, very long strip. As it unspooled he noticed a few brown splotches here and there on it. Some kind of liquid had seeped through from within, staining the cotton. The closer he got to the object at the centre, the more splotches there were. They were getting progressively bigger and darker.

He started to have a horrible thought. The brown stains had a reddish tinge, one he was familiar with.

There was no colour quite like the colour of dried blood.

Finally the strip of cotton was coming to an end. Az could make out the shape of the thing it was wrapped around.

Aurora, looking over his shoulder, said, 'Is that . . . ?'

The cotton, completely blood-covered now, stiff with the stuff, ran out. What was inside plopped into Az's open palm.

He was holding a pair of spectacles. They were smeared all over with sticky blobs of blood. They had crimson-tinted lenses. One of the lenses, the left, was cracked – a tiny fissure running from top to bottom, like a lightning bolt.

Az felt a coldness in his gut. Aurora stifled a small cry.

Together they stared at the spectacles, in silence, because neither was willing just yet to say what they were both thinking.

Mr Mordadson was dead.

CHAPTER 33

The Call Of Duty

'What if he isn't?' Az said. 'What if this is, I don't know, a ransom demand? You know, like when kidnappers cut off their victim's finger and post it to his relatives, to prove they've got him.'

'The Count's note doesn't make much sense but one thing it isn't is a ransom demand,' Aurora pointed out. 'Besides, why send the spectacles to *you*, Az? It would be more logical to send them to the Sanctum. If someone does have Mr Mordadson and they're after money, the Sanctum's the place to go. Its pockets are deep. Yours aren't.'

'Point taken. I just thought . . . I was hoping . . .' Az could feel a terrible, howling anguish inside him, threatening to burst out. He wanted to believe that the bloodied spectacles meant anything other than the obvious. Mr Mordadson *must* be alive. The man was all but indestructible. He could take a lot of punishment but he always survived. That was one of the central laws of Az's universe.

Mr Mordadson had more lives than a phoenix. But what if the wily old bustard's luck had finally run out?

'Why would the spectacles have come from Gyre, of all places?' Aurora mused. 'Why there?'

'He was heading that way,' Az said, 'on his hunt for Lord Urironson. Maybe he had an accident at Gyre. A plane crash. And the Count mailed the spectacles to me as evidence.'

'If that's the case, why not say so in the note? Why all that stuff about 'foist' and 'rogue'? I wouldn't describe Mr Mordadson as a rogue, would you? Why would the Count be so damn cryptic?'

'I don't know!' Az said hotly. 'How should I know? I don't have all the answers. You're the Sanctum resident with the brilliant brain and the bright prospects, Aurora. You damn well work it out.'

432

'Az, there's no need for that. I know you're upset, but getting snitty with me won't help.'

'I'm not upset,' Az said, with firmness. 'What I am is annoyed. Really plucking annoyed. And do you want to know why? It's because nothing's straightforward, is it? Questions. Mysteries. Is Mordy dead? What's the Count's note all about? I wish someone would just once come out with some plain, honest facts. I wish people would pull their heads out of their tailfeathers and stop expecting me to somehow psychically know what they want. I'd just like – I'd just like some *normality* in the world!'

He flung the spectacles onto the low table in the middle of the room. They landed with a satisfyingly loud *clack* but didn't, as he'd hoped, shatter.

'Is that too much to ask for?' he went on. 'Some normality? Instead of all this danger, intrigue, subterfuge, what have you – just a bit of ordinariness? Because I tell you, I've had it up to here with war and death and the Sanctum and politicians who lie and politicians who don't lie but still feel free to treat you like a pawn in a chess game. I'm fed up of everyone using me and looking to me to save the day. I don't want to be that kid any more. I don't want to be "Az Gabrielson". I want things to be simple, like they used to be. I want Michael with wings again, and I want a life where no one sends me a friend's blood-spattered glasses in the post, and most of all I want . . .'

His words petered out. Aurora looked at him, eyebrows raised.

'Want what?' she prompted.

But Az's tirade was at an end.

'It doesn't matter,' he said, calm again now. 'I've decided what I'm going to do.'

'Good,' said Aurora. 'So you're travelling to Gyre, yes? To learn what's happened to Mr Mordadson. I'll get together the money you'll need and book a gyro-cab for you, and sort out anything else. Leave the arrangements to me. This is a good idea, Az. You need to get out of the house and do something. If Mr Mordadson's still alive, you're the best person to find him and help him.'

'No,' Az said.

'What?'

'No, there's every chance Mr Mordadson isn't alive, and I'm not going to Gyre.'

'But . . .' Aurora was flummoxed. 'You can't ignore this.' She gestured at the spectacles with one wingtip. 'You can't *not* go and find out why the Count sent you those. It's your job, Az. It's your duty!'

'Weren't you listening to a word I said?' said Az. 'My duty, my only duty, is to myself. And for that reason, I'm going to do what I should have done three months ago.'

His tone was soft but unyielding, like a scabbard sheathing a dagger.

'I'm going down to the ground and I'm going to look for my girlfriend and I'm not going to stop looking until I've found her, even if it takes for ever.'

CHAPTER 34

Necessary Things

Aurora called him heartless. She called him shameful. She even called him selfish. She said Mr Mordadson was his priority. The problem of Cassie's disappearance had waited three months. It could wait a little longer.

Az replied that she wasn't the boss of him. She was just his sister-in-law. She couldn't order him to go after Mr Mordadson.

Aurora said, by the authority of the Sanctum, she could.

Az laughed in her face. The only Sanctum resident he took orders from, he said, wasn't even a resident of the Sanctum any more. She'd joined those 'birds of a feather' at the Cumula Collective. Aurora was welcome to waddle over there and get a directive from Lady Aanfieldsdaughter if she wanted. Then he'd obey her. Otherwise . . .

' "Waddle"!' Aurora exclaimed.

That was when Michael entered the living room, drawn by the sound of raised voices. He took in the situation at a glance. He didn't know why hostilities had broken out between Az and Aurora, but he did know that he needed to take sides, and quickly. It wasn't even a choice. Aurora was giving him that look, the one that said *Back me up or else.*

'OK, OK, what's all this then?' Michael said. He went and stood by his heavily pregnant wife. 'Az, are you having a go at Aurora? Because if you are, I don't care why. Just back down. Now. She's days away from giving birth. What are you *thinking*? The last thing she needs is someone stressing her out.'

'*Thwee-eet!*' Az made the sound of a hawker's whistle. 'Boy, she's got you well trained, Mike, hasn't she? Clipped those wings of yours good and proper.'

Michael bristled, his face flooding red. 'That's not even close to funny, little bro. You take that back.'

'I'd love to, only I can't. I'm far too busy looking for the jesses on your ankles.'

Michael took a step towards him, fists raised. 'I'm telling you, Az, right now, I don't know what's put you in this mood, but you'd better snap out of it or else.'

'Or else you'll hit me?' Az sneered. 'Come on, big bro. Try.' He raised his fists too. 'I can kick seven shades of guano out of you. You know I can. I could do it when you had wings. It'll be even easier now.'

Az feinted, jabbing a punch. Michael flinched and took a step back. The scars from his surgery had healed, but they'd been tender and delicate for so long that he was still sensitive to any shocks or sudden movements.

'See?' Az said. 'I'm big bad Az Gabrielson, defender of the realm. You're just Mike the chicken.'

'Chicken!?' roared Michael. That was it. Surgery scars be damned. He lunged at Az.

Aurora grabbed him by the sleeve and held him back. 'No,' she said. 'Stop it. Stop it the pair of you. I won't have this. You're brothers, for pluck's sake. I know we've all been cooped up in this house together for what seems like ages, I know we're all rubbing each other up the wrong way, but no fighting. Let's keep our tempers under control. No lashing out at each other. Do I make myself clear?'

'Let go, Aurora,' Michael said out of the side of his mouth. 'I'm going to teach that mardy little pipsqueak a lesson.'

'No, Mike. Absolutely not.'

'Quite right, Aurora,' Az said. 'Mike couldn't teach anyone anything – unless it's how to be a professional whiner.'

'Az!' snapped Aurora.

' "Ooh, look at me," ' said Az. ' "I'm Michael. I've lost my wings. Boo hoo. I'm feeling so sorry for myself." '

Growling with rage, Michael tore his sleeve out of Aurora's grasp and hurled himself across the room.

Thanks to Mr Mordadson, Az knew at least eight ways he could bring Michael down with a single blow. A straight-finger jab to the throat, a right hook to the midsection, knee to the groin, elbow to the nose . . . The list went on.

But he couldn't use any of them. Even now, in the madness of the moment, he couldn't bring himself to harm his brother. Many of the combat techniques Mr Mordadson had schooled him in were designed to cause severe, perhaps permanent injury. And all said and done, Michael was still Michael. Az wasn't going to do something to him that they would both regret.

So the fight – and Az and Michael *did* fight – was a brawl more than anything. It was a succession of loosely aimed punches interspersed with a lot of grabbing and shoving and clothes-pulling. There was a bit of kicking. Some furniture was overturned. A floor lamp went flying.

Aurora looked on with a mixture of anxiety and exasperation. For the baby's sake she didn't try to get involved and break up the fight. One or other of the brothers might accidentally hit her, perhaps in the stomach, and she just couldn't risk that. The baby's safety came first, before all else.

Mrs Enochson, however, had no reason to prevent her from intervening. The hefty bangs and crashes coming from the living room brought her storming down the stairs, across the hallway and through the door. One look at her sons knocking each other about, and she took off and crossed the room in a wingbeat. Next thing they knew, Az and Michael found themselves being seized by the ear. Mrs Enochson pinched hard enough to make the two of them yelp. She had never been so furious before in her life, or so appalled. Her voice trembled and there were tears in her eyes as she said, 'You . . . two. You . . . two . . . animals! What are you doing? Just what? Behaving like – like *louts*. Common louts. And in our home as well. How dare you! How dare you, under my roof, go walloping one another as though this is your personal boxing ring. Well? What have you got to say for yourselves?'

Az and Michael glared at each other. They were panting, and there were rough pink swellings on their faces that would soon be full-blown bruises, and Michael had a cut lip and one of Az's nostrils was leaking blood.

'He started it,' Az said.

'Oh for –! How old are you?' Michael exclaimed.

'Well, you did. You—'

'I don't care who started it,' their mother cut in. 'I just want to know why. You've never done anything like this in the past. You've always been the best of friends. What's got into you?'

The glaring match continued. Neither Michael nor Az spoke. Finally Az dropped his gaze, batted Mrs Enochson's hand away from his ear, and stalked sullenly out of the room.

A bubble had burst. The tension that had been building up in the household for weeks had finally come to a head. Pressure had been released.

It had been necessary. But like so many necessary things, it had been painful too.

Az went to his room, cleaned the blood off his face, packed a bag, and went outside to hail a passing gyro-cab.

His father came out after him.

Gabriel Enochson stood with his younger son at the pavement's edge in silence. His face was etched with sorrow and concern.

'I heard all about it,' he said at last. 'Talk to me, son.'

Az said nothing.

'Please,' his father went on. 'Tell me what's eating you. I can help. I'll understand. Whatever the matter is, I'm sure we can work it out.'

'If you don't know what the matter is, Dad,' Az said, coldly, cruelly, 'then you'll never know.'

The old man's eyes narrowed and hardened, which told Az he'd scored a hit. Yet another hit. Az had managed to bullseye both Aurora and Michael with some lethally accurate one-liners. Now he'd added his father to the tally. Hooray for him.

Gabriel Enochson tried one last time. 'The world doesn't hate you,' he said to Az. 'It only hates you if you hate it. Life may not always be fair but it's never vindictive. That's only in your head. The measure of a man isn't how hard he fights back when things go wrong for him. It's how he learns to accept and adapt.'

Az turned and looked straight at him. 'Oh,' he said. 'You still here, Dad?'

That did it. Something broke. You could almost hear the snap.

Gabriel Enochson turned away. His lifted one wing to cover his face and trudged back towards the house. He moved stiffly. His shoulders were stooped. He looked very, very old.

Az resisted the urge to run after him, apologise, beg his forgiveness. It took every ounce of willpower he had just to stay put.

A gyro-cab appeared. Az held up a hand. The cab slowed, at the same time accelerating its top rotor to go into hover mode.

Az stepped aboard.

CHAPTER 35

A Smile Like Butchery In Progress

Gently Af Bri Mumiahson changed the dressings on Naoutha's face. Even he, a doctor, someone who had beheld more than his fair share of laceration and disfigurement, couldn't help wincing at the sight of the ruin that lay beneath the bandages. These were not the kind of injuries anyone could get used to looking at. Glints of bone showed through the mangled flesh. Sores oozed pus. The place where her lost eye had been was a crisscross mesh of scar tissue and flaps of skin. The tear duct was exposed and still functioned, a tiny puckered orifice that wept continuously. Af Bri couldn't begin to imagine how much pain Naoutha was in. The agony must be constant and overwhelming. And yet somehow she bore it. She even seemed to thrive on it.

'Tell me, Dr Mumiahson,' she rasped. 'How bad is it? Will I live?'

Af Bri laughed. 'Frankly, you should have been dead long ago, Naoutha. If you were in my hospital right now, I'd be calling for a porter to take you down to the morgue.'

'Then let's be grateful I'm. Not in your hospital.' Naoutha tried to smile. It was like watching butchery in progress. Exposed tendons stretched and flexed wetly. 'And how is your. Other patient?' she asked.

'Convalescing,' came the curt reply. 'Recovering for the next round of treatment.' Af Bri grimaced uneasily.

'Don't feel guilty, Doctor. If that's a concern. Put it from your mind. Mordadson isn't worth. A moment of your compassion. The things that man has done. This is a. Long-overdue comeuppance.'

'I'm . . .' Af Bri hesitated. 'I'm just not sure if it's making any difference.'

'I've heard him. We all have. Trust me. It's making a difference.'

'Not to him. To me. I don't feel any better for what I've done to him. It's strange. I was expecting it to stop hurting – the ache inside me, the memory of my wife and kids. I keep thinking it should be going away now, like when your stomach's growling and you feed it and the hunger's gone. That's not happening. Maybe the ache wasn't a hunger after all.'

Naoutha fixed him with her good eye. 'Keep at it,' she said. 'You'll see. You'll start to feel the benefit. Soon. Just give it time.'

Af Bri made a noncommittal gesture with his wings. 'What about the Gabrielson boy?' he said. 'He'll have received the spectacles by now. Do you think he's coming?'

'Possibly,' said Naoutha. 'To be honest, I was surprised he. Wasn't with Mordadson in the first place. Joined at the hip, those two. But maybe he had other. Commitments. Or maybe they've fallen out. I gather from some of our Feather First! friends. That Mordadson posed as Lord Uriron-son's. Ally for a while. He and the boy even had a fight. So it could be that the bond. Isn't as strong as it was. Also, I used Mordadson as bait for. Gabrielson once before.'

'Meaning he's not going to fall for the same trick twice.'

'Indeed. I'm not bothered, though. If he doesn't come, he doesn't come. We'll get him at a. Later date.'

'I still think it was a mistake to take the Count up on his offer to write a covering note.'

'Do you? I'm fine with it. It lent an extra layer. Of intrigue to the package. It'll pique Gabrielson's curiosity.'

'But the Count probably was trying to warn him away.'

'Probably? Almost certainly, I'd say. If I don't miss my guess, the Count. Inserted some fiendishly cunning. Code into his message. There was something about the phrasing. Something that suggests there's more to it. Than meets the eye. Oh, poor old Count. Thinking he's been so wily. Poor scrawny old Count.'

'Nothing troubles you, does it?' said Af Bri with admiration. 'You take everything into account. You plan for every contingency.'

'I've had a long time to work on this,' Naoutha replied. 'I've thought about it. Every waking hour I've had. And believe me, the state I'm in, *all* my hours. Are waking hours. I've—'

A tap at the door interrupted her.

'Wait!' she rasped.

Af Bri finished applying the bandages. He secured them at the back of her head with a safety pin. Once more, her mutilated features were hidden.

'Come in.'

They were in the Count's office. Naoutha had commandeered the room for herself. It was by far the nicest and best appointed chamber in Gyre. Everywhere else in the city was a bit too plain for her liking.

In came another member of her team, a chemist and university lecturer by the name of Sarafinah Yahelsdaughter.

'Sarafinah,' said Naoutha. 'How are the test subjects? Everything all right?'

'Not really.' Sarafinah looked ashen-faced and more than a little disconcerted. 'Something's happened. There's been an accident. I think you should come and see.'

CHAPTER 36

Gnaw Recruit

Between them Af Bri and Sarafinah carried Naoutha down through the city. Gyre was in lockdown. All its citizens, including the Count, were under guard in various communal rooms. Breezes twisted along the empty, winding corridors and across the deserted plazas. In the massive bookkeeping halls, the adding machines sat silent. Even the Ultimate Reckoner had been switched to idle. Its ongoing quest to calculate π to a trillion decimal places was in hiatus, and who knew when it would be resumed again?

The test subjects had been sequestered in a large pantry on the lowest level of Gyre, not far from the elevator arrival depot. Behind a barred door, they shuffled about amid crates of dried goods and shelves of fresh produce. One of them carried an apple in his hand and was puzzling over it, turning it to and fro, as though he vaguely recognised this piece of fruit but couldn't remember what to do with it. Another two were squabbling stupidly over a packet of desiccated haricot beans, snatching it back from each other with irritable flaps of their wings. Low, meaningless moans accompanied the test subjects' listless activity.

Naoutha peered into the pantry, supported by her two colleagues. 'I don't see anything unusual,' she said. 'They look exactly as they did. Nothing's . . .'

Her voice trailed off.

Af Bri noticed the anomaly too. 'Correct me if I'm wrong, but weren't there five of them?' he said. 'So how come I count six?'

One of the test subjects was not a Gyrian. He had a full head of lank blond hair, and a Feather First! tattoo was plainly visible on his neck.

'It's Jazar,' Naoutha exclaimed. 'He's supposed be guarding them. What's he doing. In there with them? Why is he one of them?'

She swivelled her head to look at Sarafinah.

'What is this?' she demanded. 'Jazar surely didn't drink. Ultrapterine, did he? He wouldn't be that idiotic.'

'No,' said Sarafinah. 'No, he was just standing watch over them, like you told him to. We both were. Well, as a matter of fact, that's not quite true. Jazar had got bored and he was sort of – sort of teasing the test subjects. You know, prodding them through the bars with a broom handle. He thought it was funny. He'd jab them in the stomach, make them snarl at him. Then they'd forget he did it, and he'd do it again. He was laughing himself silly. I told him to stop it but he wouldn't. One of them came close to the door, and Jazar thought it would be even funnier to flick him on the nose. So he reached in, and then the test subject suddenly . . .'

'Suddenly what?' said Naoutha.

'I didn't really see it happen. It was very quick. I just heard Jazar go "ow!", and then he was holding his hand, waving it in the air. It was bleeding. He'd been bitten.'

'Bitten,' said Af Bri.

'Yes. Nasty. You could see teeth marks and everything. And now, I'll admit, *I* laughed. Served him right, I thought. Only, then he began to feel unwell. He complained of being dizzy and short of breath. In actual truth, he looked sick as a parrot. He sat down. He started shaking and sweating. I don't know how long it went on, five minutes maybe. Looking at him I thought, He's doing exactly what the test subjects did. Same symptoms. Same reaction. That was what made me open up the pantry door and bundle him inside. It was just so similar, what was happening to him, and instinct was telling me I should get Jazar under lock and key while I still could, before his condition got . . . worse.'

Sarafinah had acted out of self-preservation, and knew she'd done the right thing but wished she hadn't had to.

'I was only just in time,' she went on. 'I slammed the door, turned the key, and the next second Jazar was up and growling. He'd changed. He'd changed into one of them. As you can see. The red eyes, the lack of awareness, the reduced intellect – exactly like the others.'

'Yes,' said Naoutha. 'I can see. This. From a bite. Hmmm.'

'I'm sorry, Naoutha,' Sarafinah said. 'It wasn't my fault. Please don't be cross with me.'

'There's no need. To apologise, Sarafinah. You did everything you should. And I'm not cross. Anything but.'

'Really?'

'This is a welcome. Turn of events.'

'It is?' said Af Bri. 'But Jazar's one of us.'

'Was,' said Naoutha. 'And I regret losing him. But in losing him we've gained. Something else. Knowledge. I did have an inkling that the effect

443

of ultrapterine. Might be communicable. That it could be passed on from one person. To the next. Like a disease. Jazar has proved it.'

'Bodily fluids,' said Af Bri. 'Of course. The bite transferred saliva from the test subject's mouth into Jazar's bloodstream, and with the saliva came traces of the formula.'

'Because it's organic, ultrapterine has self-replicating qualities,' Sarafinah chimed in, nodding. With her knowledge of chemistry, she had been instrumental in the development of the drug. 'It propagates itself inside the host body. It binds with the white blood cells and uses them to carry it through the cardiovascular system. As they reproduce, so does it. That's how we designed it.'

'Indeed,' said Naoutha. 'We manufactured a very cunning weapon. But it turns out to be even more cunning. Than we realised.'

'The propagation continues even when it's transferred to another host body.'

'Right. Which is going to make. Our lives a whole lot easier.'

'How?' asked Af Bri.

'Isn't it obvious?' said Naoutha, smiling beneath her bandages. 'We'll still introduce ultrapterine. Into the sky-cities' water supplies. As planned. But now we don't have to cart. Huge amounts of the stuff around. And try and get it into the main storage reservoirs. They're not easily accessible. And there's always a chance of the ultrapterine. Becoming over-diluted and losing. Its potency. *This* way, all we have to do is contaminate. A few of the secondary cisterns. Then sit back and let events. Take their course. Citizens will do our work for us. Much more efficiently than we ever could. Plus, the ultrapterine has a life beyond. The initial first-stage dose. It's more effective than ever. It's all but. Unstoppable. Don't you see?'

'I do,' said Sarafinah. 'What we've made isn't just a poison any more. It's a *plague*.'

CHAPTER 37

A Welcoming Bash

The portcullis gate at the Grubdollars' house was raised wide open, like a yawning mouth. Az took this as a good sign. No *Cackling Bertha* in the yard, but perhaps she'd been driven in and then out again. Someone was home, at any rate, or had been recently.

'Hello?'

He trod boldly up the spiral staircase, listening out for a reply. There was only silence. But the lounge was strewn with clothing. Dirty dishes were piled up seesaw-fashion in the kitchen sink. The mouldering smell of a vacant house was gone. They were back. The Grubdollars were back!

Az's pleasure was tempered by anxiety. Now, at last, he would discover why Cassie had abandoned him. It was a conversation he was both looking forward to and dreading. As he exited the kitchen, heading back into the hallway, he wondered if she would—

Wham!

The fist came out of nowhere. Az glimpsed it at the corner of his eye, sensed the rush of displaced air, and his reflexes were fast enough for him to raise an arm to parry the punch, but not fully. The fist drove his own hand hard into his face. The impact shivered through him like an axe blow through a tree.

His training was there, though. All the combat lessons he'd had with Mr Mordadson were embedded in him, part of his nervous system almost, a reservoir of skills he could draw on with scarcely a thought.

Instant retaliation.

A sidelong stamp at his assailant's knee.

Followed by a straight-arm jab to the solar plexus.

Both blows found their mark. Az had known his attacker's exact position and stance without having to look. He had an impression of a man of considerable bulk, which was confirmed by the solid feel of the leg and the stomach as he hit them.

'Oooch!' said the man.

Oooch! wasn't bad, but it wasn't the cry of abject agony that Az had been hoping for. It wasn't the sound of somebody who'd been temporarily crippled by a devastating one-two combo.

Az went for the head. He swung a high instep kick at the man's temple.

This had no effect whatsoever, other than to send a sharp jolt of pain shooting up Az's foot.

Then he saw two large, meaty hands reaching for him. He was propelled backwards against the wall. Skull met woodwork with stunning, teeth-jarring force.

He kept his wits, however. He was up against an opponent who was clearly far stronger than him, and who seemed impervious to being hurt by any of the conventional methods.

Fine.

When you're physically outclassed, Mr Mordadson would say, *don't panic. Cheat.*

Az raised his hands flat, ready to slam them onto his opponent's ears. Popping the eardrums was excruciating for the victim. It could stop even the most boneheaded of thugs in their tracks. Reputedly it was like having knitting needles jabbed into your brain.

'Az?'

Az's hands faltered, just centimetres from their target. He blinked to clear his vision.

'Az!'

All of a sudden Az found himself being enveloped in a hug that wasn't much less violent than the fight preceding it. He felt his ribs being crushed, his spine creaking. It was hard to breathe. What his assailant had failed to do with aggression, he might just achieve through sheer exuberance.

'Whoa, whoa,' Az said. 'Easy there. I need to . . . let some air in.'

'Sure. Sorry.' The hug relaxed. 'Just pleased to see you, that'm all. How be things, Az? How'm life with my Groundling-lookalike Airborn pal?'

'Reasonable, Colin,' Az said wheezily to Colin Amblescrut. 'And how's life with you?'

CHAPTER 38

Colin The Hero

Colin prepared Az the most disgusting cup of tea he had ever tasted. It was stewed and the milk was slightly off. Colin glugged his own cup down with relish, while Az nursed his, taking very occasional, very tiny sips, then smacking his lips as though it was delicious. A short while ago he'd been trying to do maximum damage to this man whom he'd taken for an enemy. Now he was scared of hurting a friend's feelings.

'You look so different.' Colin said. 'I honestly didn't recognise you, what with the dyed hair and the whole bum-fluff beard thing going on.'

'Bum-fluff beard?'

'No offence, Az, mate, but it'm hardly the most impressive display of face fungus I's ever seen.'

'Oh. OK. Don't hold back now, Colin. Say what you really think.'

'Always do,' Colin said breezily. 'But that'm why I laid into you, anyway. I came in and took you for some stranger, trespassing. I thought you might even be—'

He broke off.

'Who?'

'No one.'

'Who did you think I was, Colin?'

'I be'n't supposed to say. I be'n't supposed to talk about it at all. Not to anybody. Still,' Colin went on, brightening, 'you'm a tough little tyke, I'll give you that. Quite a barney us just had, eh?' He rubbed his knee. 'It even smarts here still. A little.'

'I should've known it was you when I kicked you in the head and it didn't even faze you.'

'Heh! Yeah. There'm nothing quite as thick as an Amblescrut noggin.'

'Too true,' said Az. 'So you're housesitting for the Grubdollars, is that it? Minding the place till they get back?'

447

'Well . . .' Colin shifted in his seat. 'In one sense, yes. But in another sense, not really. I mean, I be minding the place, but it mayn't exactly be with the Grubdollars' permission. Or even knowledge. You see, I became sort of homeless recently owing to me and my landlord having a bit of a disagreement about the rent.'

'Disagreement?'

'Yeah. I didn't pay it for a couple of months and my landlord disagreed with that. So him chucked out all my stuff onto the street and changed the locks. Of course I's got loads of family I could bunk with if I wanted to, but you know I, Az. Footloose, fancy-free bachelor, that'm I. Can't be tied down by someone else's house rules. Can't come and go as I please if I be kipping on the couch in someone's front room. And I knew the Grubdollars' house were empty right now, and it seemed a waste, decent place like this with no one in it. And security, that'm important. It be doing they a favour, having a bloke like I here, keeping an eye on things for they. Them'd be grateful if them knew. What if there were a fire, eh? And there'm some bad folks out there. Vacant house like this, why, it'm a burglary waiting to happen.'

'Some people just don't have a conscience.'

'Straight up! One of my own half-cousins, in fact, said something the other day about casing the joint, seeing if there were anything worth nicking. That were what made my mind up. Think how bad it'd be if the Grubdollars came back and found the place burgled, and it turned out to be an Amblescrut that did it. Den'd never forgive I, I reckon, if I didn't put a stop to that.'

'You're nothing short of a hero, Colin.'

'You said it, Az old pal. So, you's dropped by to see Cass, right?'

Az nodded. 'But she's not back, is she, from wherever she's been.'

'Nope.' Colin looked awkward, and that clinched it for Az. The Grubdollars' self-appointed housesitter knew exactly where the family was. Now Az's problem was how to extract that knowledge from him. Colin was a lot smarter than most people gave him credit for. Sober, at least, he was hard to bamboozle. Az debated whether to take him down to the Hole and Shovel and get him drunk. He put that idea on the back burner and decided to try the direct approach first.

'Where is she, Colin?'

'I were hoping you wasn't going to ask.'

'Well, I have.'

'This'm tricky, though,' Colin said. 'I just can't tell you. I swore a vow. On the life of all my family, which'm a pretty big vow for anyone but especially for an Amblescrut. But I *want* to tell you. But I can't.'

Confusion rippled across his face in waves.

'I's been there with they, you see,' he went on. 'It'm a long way from here. Them's gone into hiding and I went with they, for moral support and because I fancied a change of scenery. Only, after a few weeks I found I didn't much like it where us was. Too boring. Nothing happening, and the only job going were one I couldn't do on account of all the bumping up and down meant I kept throwing up.' He shook his head, annoyed at himself. 'Shouldn't even have said what I just said. No clues. Mustn't give *anything* away. And it don't help that I took another vow that I wouldn't drink while the Grubdollars be away. Den made I swear that too, after I told he I wanted to go back to Grimvale. Him remembered the last time, when I gave away a little bit too much about Fletcher's pressurisation tank to that man at the pub. So I be'n't touching a drop right now, more'm the pity. But it be hard. Sometimes, without alcohol, it'm difficult to think straight.'

Az's pub plan would have been a non-starter, then. He pressed on with the direct approach.

'Come on, Colin. This is me. Az. Look at it from my perspective. It's been three months. Cassie disappeared without a trace. I've been half going out of my mind. You can tell *me*.'

'I know, I know. That be what I's having such a tussle with. I mean, if I can't trust you with the secret, who can I trust?'

Colin wrung his massive, meaty hands together. His brow knitted into a set of deep, V-shaped grooves. Az had never seen quite such a display of agonising. He almost felt sorry for the man. At the same time, he wanted to bludgeon him with a blunt implement till the truth came out.

'All right!' Colin said, slapping his thigh. 'I know. I's got it.'

'You'll tell me where she is? And why she's gone there?'

'No. But it wouldn't be breaking my vow if I *took* you there.'

449

CHAPTER 39

The Final Passenger

And so, within the hour, Az and Colin were standing on the platform at Grimvale's railway station, waiting for the next northbound train to pull in. Colin had stuffed a small rucksack with belongings. It was going to be at least a three-day trip, he had said. Four if the connections didn't work out quite right. But on the plus side, he'd added, they would have each other for company. The time would fly by. And Az was going to have the opportunity to see some of the most spectacular landscapes the Westward Territories had to offer.

'We're heading for the coast, aren't we?' Az said, peering along the tracks to where they met at a point on the horizon, below the dark grey rim of the clouds.

'Um, how'd you know?'

'A guess. My ground geography isn't perfect but if we're travelling that far, we're going to run out of land eventually. And you said something about the only job available being one with a lot of bumping up and down that makes you feel unwell. That would be out at sea, wouldn't it? Working on boats. Cassie told me about seasickness once. It's the same as airsickness, when you're flying through turbulence in a plane. Some people aren't affected by it, others just can't cope.'

'And it turns out I be among the can't cope,' said Colin ruefully. 'Ten minutes on the water and I were spewing my guts up. Never felt so poorly in my life. I wanted to die, that'm how bad it felt.' He wagged a finger at Az. 'But that be all you's getting out of I, Azrael Gabrielson. Not another word about where us is going, not till us gets there. Uh-uh.' He mimed buttoning up his mouth. 'My lips is clipped.'

Az half smiled. It was good to be doing something at last. It was good to have an objective and the prospect of a resolution to his troubles. He glanced round the platform. Crowds were gathering in advance of the train's arrival. Mothers marshalled children. A group of young soldiers – fresh cadets by the look of them, off to camp for basic training – lounged on their kitbags, smoking and joking. Porters shouted and bustled. Peddlers paraded up and down with racks of newssheets and trays of snacks and bottled drinks, trying to outdo one another with their sales pitches. He viewed them all with a tourist's eye, aloof but fascinated. He was hardly a stranger to the ground, but this was the first time he'd ever gone journeying any great distance there. He felt a keen edge of expectation. This might even be fun.

Then the train came humming in. The locomotive was a diesel/electric hybrid, capable of drawing power from overhead cables or, where there were none, travelling under its own steam, so to speak. It was flat-fronted and imperturbable-looking, designed to give the impression that nothing could stand in its way. It would shoulder forth along those rails come hell or high water.

Colin leapt into the nearest carriage before the train had come to a complete rest. He barged past passengers trying to get off, in his haste to find some decent seats.

Az remained on the platform till the exodus from the carriages had finished. Then he clambered aboard and joined Colin.

He didn't see a tall man embark a minute later, the very last passenger to get onto the train.

The man, who had been loitering in the doorway to the ticketing hall, crossed the platform in a few swift strides and jumped on just as the conductor blew his whistle. He was wearing a long coat and a slouch-brimmed hat which hid most of his face, and he moved with considerable grace and agility, despite being hampered by a slight limp. He plumped himself down in the nearest available seat, nodded politely to the rather portly lady next to him, then drew his hat brim even further down over his face, folded his arms, and appeared to go to sleep.

Beneath the hat the man's features were sleek and faintly foxlike. He had a strong jawline and a neat moustache which looked like some sort of small, furry creature that had been impaled on the end of his sharp, narrow nose.

Had Az seen this face, he would have recognised it instantly. And he would have had good reason to be alarmed.

Brigadier Jasper Longnoble-Drumblood had waited three long months for a lead on the whereabouts of Cassie Grubdollar. Patiently, doggedly, he had staked out the Grubdollars' house, watching it at all hours, in all weathers, from a number of different vantage points, using a number of different disguises. Thanks to his army training he knew about concealment and surveillance. He knew how to observe a place, unobserved.

Week after week had passed, and Longnoble-Drumblood had not abandoned his vigil, nor even once thought of doing so.

Now, finally, his persistence had paid off. He had caught a break. And better yet, the break had come courtesy of Azrael Gabrielson, the only other person Longnoble-Drumblood loathed as much as Cassie Grubdollar. Gabrielson was down here looking for the girl. The Grubdollars' friend, the inbred giant who had taken up residence in the house, was escorting him to her.

It couldn't have been better for Longnoble-Drumblood. Now he could get them both together. Satisfaction for the death of Dominic Slamshaft was going to be his at last. Both murderers at once. Two birds with one stone.

The train rolled out of Grimvale station. Behind his closed eyes, Longnoble-Drumblood's mind churned with thoughts of bloody vengeance.

CHAPTER 40

First Strike: Goldenfast

The curtain was coming down on the drama festival. Goldenfast had had its fill of all things theatrical, for now. Final performances were taking place all across the city. Everywhere, tonight was a last night.

The hot ticket this evening was a special, one-off appearance by the Greatest Actor of His Generation, Janiel Boelson, in his own staging of the classic tragedy *Framoch's Kin*. Officially Boelson had retired, so it was a rare treat to have a chance to see this venerable thespian in the flesh, doing what he did best. The play itself wasn't perhaps the subtlest or most psychologically intricate piece of theatre ever written, but what its revenge plot lacked in telling human insight was compensated for by sheer bloodiness. Come the final scene, almost every major character was lying dead on stage, murdered by the Framoch of the title, who held them all responsible for the deaths of his family and who, having settled his scores, then took his own life. It started with a bloodbath and ended with a bloodbath, with lots of passionate emoting in between as Framoch debated whether killing killers solved anything or simply perpetuated the cycle of violence. It took him two hours of soliloquising to reach the conclusion which the audience already knew he would, but then the role was as much about the journey as the destination, and Framoch's lengthy, brow-furrowing, breast-beating speeches were a gift to any actor who loved the sound of his own voice and relished the spotlight. In other words, any actor.

Towards the end of the play, Framoch had to spend several minutes in the wings while the other characters gathered onstage for the showdown. They had been summoned to the spot where Framoch's family died, little suspecting that this was to be the site of their own gruesome demises. While they tried to fathom their reason for being there, the leading man was able to take a rest and collect his strength for the dénouement.

453

Backstage, Janiel Boelson slaked his thirst with a glass of water. His throat was parched from declaiming all those speeches. He felt utterly drained, but that was all right because he knew that the performance had gone well so far and he had given it his all. At sixty, he was at least twenty years too old to play Framoch, but such was the vigour he brought to the role that he didn't think anyone in the audience either noticed or cared. Beyond the footlights, all he had seen were rapt faces and shiningly admiring eyes. And so many of them! The auditorium was fuller than full. The theatre manager had sold dozens of extra tickets to punters who'd agreed to hover near the ceiling for the duration of the play. The house was literally packed to the rafters.

His moment to return onstage was nearly here. Boelson took a last sip of water, shook off a fleeting feeling of wooziness, then strode to the sightlines to await his cue.

His fellow actors went through their dialogue, paving the way for Framoch's climactic, tumultuous reappearance. Such mumblers, this lot, Boelson thought. Especially the younger ones. However hard he'd drilled them, they still couldn't seem to grasp the concept of diction – projecting every word so that it might be heard by a deaf old granny in the back row of the cheap seats. Alas, the craft of acting was not what it had been in *his* day. Not for the first time, he wondered if he was not perhaps the last of a dying breed.

The wooziness came again. Boelson found he was feeling distinctly odd. The voices onstage were getting thicker, even harder to understand. Everyone was talking as though with a mouthful of syrup.

This made Boelson very annoyed. They were ruining his play! Was it sabotage? He thought so. He knew for a fact that a couple of the junior males in the cast were deeply envious of him. Of his talent. Hardly surprising, then, that they should wish to make a fool of him in public.

Now nobody was speaking at all. A silence had fallen. Then a voice hissed at Boelson. It was the prompter, repeating his entry line, which he had failed to hear the first time.

'But lo, here comes Framoch himself.'

Everyone onstage was looking upwards. Boelson was meant to come on flying. He'd always been proud of his ability to make a dramatic entrance on the wing. He knew how to act with his entire body, all the way to the tips of his feathers.

He trudged on instead, wings drooping. He looked slowly round him, squinting against the stage lights. The other actors peered at him, in tableau, puzzled. They waited for his next line. When he said nothing, one of them improvised: 'So you've made it, Framoch. As I was just saying to everyone, the unravelling of this tangled mystery will be short work for such nimble wits as yours. Eh?'

It had no effect. Boelson remained silent. Bewildered.

In the auditorium, people began to cough and shift their feet.

Then all at once, unprovoked, Boelson threw himself at an actress nearby. He grabbed her by the wing root, held her down and started to beat her. When other cast members tried to pull him off, he lashed out at them too, savagely.

There was pandemonium onstage. Boelson bit, clawed, kicked, scratched, pulled hair, snarling all the while. He was a lethal whirlwind. He could not be restrained. No matter how many actors jumped on him, he shook them off and continued his rampage, attacking and wounding anyone who came within reach. Blood flowed, and for a time the audience took this as all part of the show. Somehow, using fake gore and clever makeup, the actors were managing to make it look as if the violence was real. There was even a smattering of applause. Very impressive. No one had seen the ending of *Framoch's Kin* performed with quite such a visceral intensity before. This wasn't the scene as the playwright had written it, but even so, bravo! A bold re-imagining.

The claps and cheers soon faded, however.

To be replaced by screams.

CHAPTER 41

Hidden Within

Pregnancy was not beautiful, or serene, or a magical experience, or any of those sorts of things. Aurora had no idea where it had got this reputation. Before falling pregnant herself, she'd only heard stories about how fulfilling it was to be a mum-to-be, how the act of carrying a baby to term made you understand yourself as a woman in a way that nothing else could. Your body rejoiced at the life growing inside it. You bloomed. You glowed.

Complete guano. Were these women mad or liars or what? Aurora had never felt worse than she had these past few months, and especially during the final trimester of the pregnancy. She ached all over. She slept in fits and starts. She could never get comfortable. She could take in only small amounts of food before she felt like vomiting. She needed to pee at least once an hour. She could barely get aloft under her own wingpower with the extra weight, and when she did fly she seemed to have all the airworthiness of a bumble-bee, and a clumsy bumble-bee at that. Worst of all was when the baby stretched and kicked. This was not a sweet, lovely tickling sensation inside her belly. Oh no. It was like having her innards rummaged through and rearranged, brutally, sickeningly.

'Oh look, a future jetball star,' Michael had said the other day, watching the baby writhe under Aurora's abdominal muscles.

It was a rare moment of cuteness from him, following the loss of his wings. That was the only reason she hadn't smacked him in the face.

Sleeplessness being such a problem, Aurora found that all she could do at night was sit up in an armchair in her in-laws' living room and read books. She'd doze for a couple of hours here and there, then resume reading, or else stare wakefully into the darkness and think. Thinking was the one activity left to her that she could carry out with as much agility as before. Her brain could still dance even if her body had become this vast, ungainly, baby-housing dollop that might possibly never dance again.

There was now plenty of stuff, more than ever, to occupy her night-time thoughts. The spat between Michael and Az. Az's surly walk-out. The atmosphere of tension in the house that was on its way to becoming one long, suppressed scream of anguish.

Michael had withdrawn deep into himself. He hadn't been so depressed since straight after the amputation. Aurora was terrified he might do something stupid – something irrevocably stupid.

Meanwhile Mr and Mrs Enochson had begun bickering almost constantly. They were a couple who'd always seemed happily entrenched in their roles. With three decades of marriage behind them, they had settled into a pattern where they didn't have to talk much to each other while still being secure in their mutual support and affection. But now, the way they were arguing, it was as though they'd rediscovered each other afresh and found they didn't like what they saw.

Aurora knew she was watching a family tear itself apart. And there was very little she could think of to do to help.

Adding to her worries was the unknown fate of Mr Mordadson. She'd sent a letter via carrier dove to the Sanctum, for the attention of Lady Aanfieldsdaughter's old friend and colleague Pendroz, Lord Luelson, who was now perhaps Aurora's staunchest ally. In it she expressed her concern about the missing emissary. She hadn't yet received a reply, and if one didn't come soon she would travel to the Sanctum and demand action in person.

Mr Mordadson's blood-spattered spectacles still sat on the living room table, in their winding sheet of cotton. The Count's note lay next to them.

Aurora had pored over that note countless times, night and day. There was something there in those two upper-case sentences, she was sure. Something lurked within that awkward phrasing, some hidden meaning, a clue Az had been meant to find. A code of some sort. But she had tried turning the words into anagrams and come up with nothing that made any sense. She had tried using a straightforward substitution cipher, each letter of the alphabet representing another, again without success. An acrostic of the first letters of the two sentences yielded gibberish.

At 3 a.m., by the lonely light of a standard lamp, Aurora sat in her chair and perused the note yet again. What was she missing? What had she overlooked? If the note *was* a code, there must be some obvious key to it.

She glanced up as the living room clock struck three with a soft and sonorous chime. Several other clocks in the house dinged and donged more or less simultaneously, near and far. Gabriel Enochson, former clockmaker by trade, took pride in his horology. Even now, with his household in disarray, he kept every timepiece he owned meticulously wound and accurate.

Aurora looked at the clock face. At the numerals around the dial.

Then she had it.

Numbers.

All the codes she'd been looking for in the Count's note were language-based. But Gyre was a place where they worshipped numbers and figures above all else. If the Count was going to encrypt a message, he would do it mathematically rather than alphabetically.

Excited, Aurora grabbed a pencil and a pad of paper. Her first idea was to assign each letter of the alphabet a number according to its position: A = 1, B = 2, and so on. She wrote the corresponding number above each letter of the note and studied the result. Map co-ordinates? Dates? The time and location of Mr Mordadson's possible accident?

Hmm. Maybe. But she didn't think so.

The sequence of apparently random digits sparked off another idea. She erased the numbers she had just written, then jotted 1 – 41 above the forty-one capitalised characters of the note, ignoring the punctuation marks. Perhaps she should be looking at the odd-numbered letters only, or the even-numbered ones, or every third letter, or . . .

Or . . .

Primes.

Oh, how the arithmetically-inclined loved their primes. Couldn't get enough of them. Primes were their pride and joy, their clever pets, their darlings.

Now, what *were* the first few prime numbers?

Aurora scratched her head over that. Fortunately a nearby bookcase held a twenty-volume encyclopaedia set, and she was able to groan her way over to it, fist braced against the base of her spine, locate the relevant volume, and flick through to the entry on primes.

Then, sighing back down into the armchair, she underlined each letter of the Count's note that had a prime number above it, not counting 1.

The note now looked like this.

> Azrael,
> IN <u>A</u> W<u>O</u>F<u>U</u>L RU<u>T</u> I <u>H</u>AIL <u>A</u>Z. <u>I</u> FOI<u>S</u>T YOU
> TH<u>E</u> '<u>E</u>YES' OF <u>R</u>OG<u>UE</u>!
>
>   – the Count of Gyre

Aurora read the underlined letters in order.

And her blood ran cold.

CHAPTER 42

Second Strike: Azuropolis

Azuropolis, the Blue City, nearest neighbour of the Silver Sanctum.
  Daybreak.

The air crisp and sharp over the dome of the Cobalt Citadel and the huddled towers of Sapphire Mansions. The sun's rays creeping westward to gild the junipers and hydrangeas of Cyan Park and add glitter to the pools of the Aquamarine Water Gardens. The dawn chorus rising from the throats of grosbeaks and indigo buntings, filling the empty spaces between the slumberous buildings with a shimmer of song.

Itmon Penatson's favourite time of day.

Which was just as well since, being a postman, Penatson saw an awful lot of dawns.

Winging his way along Periwinkle Street, Penatson counted himself lucky that he had a job so suited to his temperament. He was a natural early riser, and he enjoyed solitude. That wasn't to say he disliked other people. He was a pretty sociable fellow, he felt. But equally, he was happy in his own company, content with the sound of his own thoughts. And delivering the mail was honest, necessary work that benefited everybody. He had nothing to complain about, really. Life was good.

His sack of letters was halfway emptied when he came across the group of people at the junction of Periwinkle Street and Royal Avenue. There were eight of them, and Penatson took them to be revellers who were heading home after some all-night party. He'd seen their type before, many a time. This lot trudged along the pavement with the stiff, bleary gait common to drunks. The fact that they were walking rather than flying said it all. They didn't trust themselves in the air.

Penatson alighted near them in order to distribute a sheaf of letters among the boxes outside the main entrance of an apartment block on the corner. Busy doing this, he didn't notice the revellers homing in on him, until all at once he realised they had surrounded him in a rough semicircle.

A trusting sort, Penatson turned and saluted them, tapping a wingtip to the peak of his postman's cap.

'Morning, all,' he said. 'Is this where you live? Keen to get to your beds, I should imag—'

Eight pairs of scarlet-flooded eyes surveyed him curiously. Eight mouths issued low, papery moans.

Penatson was suddenly very afraid. These people weren't partygoers. In fact, whatever they were, he wasn't sure they were even people any more.

His mistake was to shout at them. Had he simply taken to the air and flitted over their heads, he might have escaped. But instead he yelled, 'Go away! Leave me alone! I've done nothing to you!' adding, perhaps absurdly, 'I'm a postman!'

The sound of his voice startled the eight and somehow, in some obscure way, annoyed them. They charged at him, as one, hands out-stretched, teeth bared. Within instants Penatson was overwhelmed, the weight of eight bodies shoving him down onto his back. His wings were squashed beneath him. He writhed futilely.

Then the biting began. And the screaming.

Some time later he stopped squirming and screaming, and the eight lost interest and wandered away. Penatson had been correct in assuming that their behaviour could be blamed on something they'd drunk. But it wasn't alcohol, of course. It was just tap water. Tap water laced with ultrapterine.

Penatson himself was soon back on his feet. Bleeding profusely from a number of wounds, he continued on his round. His sack hung forgotten at his side as he went from one door to the next, walking the route he normally flew. At each door he paused. Sometimes, as if he had some parcel too big for a letterbox, he knocked.

From now on his fate was to deliver nothing but fear and misery.

CHAPTER 43

Sleeping Like A Baby

Aurora let Michael sleep through the night, needing him to be fully rested for the day ahead. Before she woke him she sat beside the bed and watched him for a while. He lay flat on his back, a position that was inconceivable for any other full-grown Airborn, except Az. Babies slept that way, and toddlers too, until they started to fledge. At that moment Michael looked much like a baby to her – as peaceful, as helpless.

Her eye strayed to the cot in the corner of the room. Soon – but not soon enough for her liking – there would be a new little life lying there. For a moment she almost felt excited. Then anxiety came and swept the excitement flat. Aurora wasn't concerned about motherhood itself or the pain of giving birth. She knew she could cope. Her anxiety was broader than that, and its source was the coded message in the Count's note.

Naoutha is here.

How? Why? Was it even possible? Was the Count lying? Deluded?

She wanted to think so. She hoped there'd been no code at all; it was just some ghastly coincidence, a happenstance pattern of letters. She'd seen a message where none existed.

Deep down in her gut, however, she knew it did exist. The bloodied spectacles confirmed the truth of it. Naoutha Nisrocsdaughter was alive, back from the dead, and obviously out for revenge. Which meant Az wasn't safe and those close to Az probably weren't safe either.

So Aurora had more than one reason for wishing to travel to the Sanctum today.

As the house clocks struck six she roused Michael. He snuffled and grumbled while she was explaining what she wanted him to do. It was the word Naoutha that got him sitting bolt upright, wide awake.

'You're kidding, right?'

'I wish I were.'

'Naoutha. Pluck me! But . . . how's it possible?'

'Don't ask me. I have no idea.'

'Just as well Az decided not to go to Gyre.'

'Absolutely. The best place for him right now is where he is, on the ground. And the best place for us is the Sanctum. We'll alert the senior residents to what's going on, then stay there while the Alar Patrol move in on Gyre at full strength and sort everything out.'

'Mum and Dad should come with us.'

'To be frank, Mike, no. They should stay put. Your helicopter is the fastest means of transport we have, and it's only a two-seater. If we all go by plane it'll take twice as long, and speed is of the essence. Your parents will be fine here for the time it takes us to get to the Sanctum and raise the alarm. And after that they won't be in any danger because Naoutha will have her hands full dealing with every damn Patroller in the realm coming down on her in force.'

Michael saw the logic in this. 'We should at least warn them.'

'The less they know, the better. Why worry them needlessly?'

'I suppose. But they're not stupid. They already know something's up. Mr Mordadson's specs . . .'

'And that's our pretext for rushing off to the Sanctum. I still haven't heard back from Lord Luelson, and I'm genuinely not pleased about that. Mr Mordadson might not have the clout he used to back in Lady Aanfieldsdaughter's day but he's still a major player, and his lordship ought to acknowledge that and be concerned about him. I'm going to have stern words with the old boy, I promise you, and that'll be the purpose of our journey – or at least so we'll tell your parents.'

'You sure you're up to the trip?'

Aurora grimaced. 'No. I can't imagine anything worse than sitting cooped up in your Vortex V for several hours. There'll be no stopping for pee breaks. I'll have to go in a cup.'

It was Michael's turn to grimace. 'Just keep it off the upholstery, that's all I ask.'

They looked at each other, and abruptly burst out laughing. It seemed absurd to laugh, given the deadly seriousness of the situation, but it felt right somehow. And good. They hadn't laughed together in . . . neither could remember how long.

'Aurora . . .' said Michael.

'I know. Same here. Now put some clothes on and go get the chopper prepped. I'm going to speak to your parents.'

'Be advised, Dad's usually pretty grumpy when he's just woken up.'

'Like father, like son. Go!'

CHAPTER 44

Third Strike: High Haven

Even as Michael's Vortex V lifted off from outside the house, trouble was stirring in another part of High Haven.

The Seven Dreams shopping mall hadn't yet opened its doors to customers but already a small knot of people had gathered outside the main entrance, loitering there as if impatient, keen for the day's retail adventures to begin.

To nightwatchman Gergot Rorexson and his partner Sarga Phulsdaughter, it was somewhat puzzling.

'There a sale on today?' Rorexson wondered, peering out at the crowd. 'If so, nobody told me.'

'Nobody tells us anything,' said Phulsdaughter. 'We're only the ones who keep this place safe at night, stop the burglars breaking in and patrol every nook and cranny till our feet and wings are sore. Why would anyone think *we're* important?'

'So young and yet so cynical,' said Rorexson, who was Phulsdaughter's senior by some three decades and was due to retire in a couple of months' time. 'I've taught you well.'

He looked out again through the glass doors at the shambling, milling crowd.

'It's funny. That lot just aren't acting the way bargain hunters normally do. I'd expect them to be forming a queue, maybe chatting to one another, maybe checking to-buy lists. I'm not seeing any of that.'

Phulsdaughter suppressed a small shiver. 'Now that you mention it, it is kind of creepy, how they're moving around. I'd call it . . . "aimless", I suppose. They look like they've lost their way and don't know where they are.'

'I'm going out there,' her partner said, with resolve. He produced a huge set of keys and began unlocking one of the doors. 'I'll see them off. I

463

don't think they're here for shopping. I think they're troublemakers. Feather First!ers, more than likely. I thought we'd seen the last of *them*, but obviously I was wrong. This'll be another of their protest rallies, and I'm not having that in front of my mall.'

He swung the door outward, clanking the handle noisily to get attention. The people outside all turned at once and started shuffling towards the entrance.

Rorexson went out to greet them with much fluffing of his wings and brandishing of his keys.

'All right, everyone,' he said. 'Listen up. I'm giving you one chance. Clear off now or I'm fetching the Patrol. Go and assert your Airborn rights somewhere else. This is private property, and the owners and shareholders of the Seven Dreams Mall have no interest . . . in . . .'

The words trailed off. The authority in Rorexson's voice and posture vanished. He seemed suddenly limp and deflated, like a kite with no wind to buoy it up.

Eyes wide, jaw sagging, he took two steps back. He reached for the baton that hung from his belt.

He wasn't able to unclip it in time.

Nor was Phulsdaughter able to slam the door shut in time.

Both of them succumbed to the ultrapterine-poisoned people. The attack was swift and brutal, and then the red-eyed creatures were inside the mall, free to roam its many arcades and concourses.

Later, shopkeepers arrived.

Then shoppers.

And High Haven's Seven Dreams Mall became the venue for innumerable nightmares.

CHAPTER 45

Righting Wrongs

Af Bri Mumiahson recognised the smell from his hospital days. He knew it all too well. It was the stench of pain and humiliation. The whole room reeked of it, and it emanated from the bound, black-clad figure.

Mr Mordadson hung from his ropes, his face slack, his eyes half open. His head twitched as Af Bri walked in – an involuntary spasm, a dim anticipation of further suffering to come. Then he went still once more, as a sparrow might when it knew it was mortally injured and all it could do was wait for the bird of prey to deliver the final, killing stroke.

Af Bri stood in front of his victim. His expression was sombre.

'Mordadson?'

All he got in response were a few burbled syllables, nothing he could make any sense of, although it sounded like a curse, or a threat. The man's body was wracked with torment, he could barely talk, and yet his mind somehow remained unbroken. Such inner resilience, Af Bri thought, was nothing sort of amazing.

'Perhaps it would be best if you didn't try to speak, for now,' he said. 'Just listen to me. I told you about my family, didn't I? Before I got started on you. I told you how they died at Prismburg and I couldn't save them. I – I wanted so much to believe that by hurting you I could somehow make up for losing them. Your suffering would cancel my suffering. It seemed so straightforward, like balancing a set of scales.'

He paused.

'But there's that old saying, isn't there?' he said. ' "Two wrongs don't make a right." I've never thought much of it before. It just seemed a trite moral aphorism, nothing more. But then until my family were killed I didn't really know what a wrong was. Now I do. I also know what it's like to be on the giving rather than the receiving end of a wrong.'

He rubbed his face wearily.

'The pain I've caused you – *this* is a wrong. And I'm hoping to make amends. At the very least, undo the damage I've done.'

He reached for a small, soft leather holdall, a doctor's medical bag. From inside it he took out a syringe, some ampoules, a roll of bandage and a jar of ointment.

'Because I'm a healer,' he went on. 'I forgot that for a while but I remember now. I make people better. My wife, if she were here, would be telling me to do everything in my power to get you on your feet again. I've realised that torturing you was never going to bring her or my children back. Instead it was dishonouring their memory. Liwet wouldn't have wanted it. Neither would Tariel or Coré. Saving you is what they'd want.'

He gripped Mr Mordadson around the waist and, taking his full body-weight, he unhooked him from the ceiling and lowered him gently to the floor. Then he started to fill the syringe from one of the ampoules.

'I warn you,' he said, 'the next hour or so isn't going to be pleasant.'

And he was right.

CHAPTER 46

An Empty Feast

Injections of local anaesthetic in various places helped dull the pain. Bones were reset. Wounds were stitched. Splints and salves were applied. Plugs of cotton wool were inserted.

Af Bri worked methodically but quickly. Outside, dawn was breaking. Late last night Naoutha had expressed the desire to come down and see Mr Mordadson today. After all, the ultrapterine had been sent out. Her Regulars were distributing it across the realm. Its first impact was probably already being felt. Now at last she could turn her attention to other matters, specifically her captive, her hated enemy. Her final words to Af Bri, as he made her comfortable in her wheelchair yesterday evening before retiring to bed, had been: 'You've had your fun with Mordadson. Tomorrow it's my turn.'

All night Af Bri had tossed and turned, hounded by doubt and remorse. What had he got himself into? What had he *become*? In a kind of waking dream he had relived the moment of seeing his family at the hospital, his futile efforts to save Tariel, Liwet dying even as he did so, Coré beyond recovery to begin with. The small hours had rolled past with ghastly insomniac slowness, until ultimately he had understood that he couldn't carry on inflicting torment on Mr Mordadson any longer. Enough was enough. He couldn't keep dwelling on the deaths of his family for ever and using grief to justify his actions. Grief was an empty feast. You could keep feeding off it but it never brought contentment. Somehow it only left you hollower inside.

As the sun rose clear of the clouds, Af Bri pulled Mr Mordadson up into a sitting position and gave him a drink of water, followed by a combined shot of painkiller, stimulant and vitamins. Mr Mordadson's complexion was sickly-sallow, but once the drugs got to work some of the colour returned to his cheeks and the spark was rekindled in his eyes.

Af Bri had left in place a couple of the ropes binding him, just to be on the safe side. Naoutha had warned him how dangerous a customer Mr Mordadson could be.

Now he grasped the knot that was securing Mr Mordadson's wrists together.

'Before I untie this,' he said, 'do I have your word that you won't attack me?'

The other man's mouth arched into a listless grin. 'I don't think I have the strength,' he rasped. 'And anyway, have you seen what you did to my right hand? I'm not going to be hitting anyone with that for a while.'

'But I need to know I can trust you before I free you.'

'Can I trust *you*?' Mr Mordadson replied. 'This could all be a trick. You pretend to release me, I have a whiff of liberty, then I get recaptured. Psychological torture, as a change from physical.'

'I've gone to a lot of trouble to fix you up,' Af Bri said. 'I want to get you out of here. If you're half the man I'm told you are, the realm needs you right now, probably more than it's ever needed you. You have to believe that I'm being straight with you. And for my part, I have to be reassured that you're not going to kill me at the first opportunity.'

'You want absolute mutual honesty? We've hardly got off on the right footing for that.'

'I'd say sorry for what I've done, except that wouldn't even begin to cover it. What I'm doing now – this is my apology.'

Mr Mordadson regarded him balefully for several seconds. Then, with heavy resignation, he nodded.

'Very well,' he said. 'You have my word.'

Af Bri undid the knot. He helped Mr Mordadson to his feet. Supporting his weight on one shoulder, he led him towards the door. He peered out warily into the corridor. The coast was clear.

'We don't have long,' he said. 'Someone's bound to come down here sooner or later, looking for me. She'll be needing me to tend to her. She always does first thing in the morning.'

'She,' said Mr Mordadson as they headed off down the corridor, Af Bri setting a fast pace, himself hop-hobbling alongside. 'I've been trying to think who this "she" is who you work for. When I've been capable of thought, that is. I can only name one woman who'd want me dealt with in the way I have been – and she's dead.'

'No, she isn't.'

The reply stunned Mr Mordadson into silence, and at the same time answered almost every question he had.

Finally he said, 'Then I have to kill her. Take me to her. Now.'

'You're in no fit state to kill anyone,' said Af Bri, marvelling again at Mr Mordadson's grit and tenacity. Barely able to walk, and he was still

468

determined to take the fight to his enemy when a lesser man would be thinking only of fleeing. 'And even if you were, I owe her enough loyalty that I wouldn't let you.'

'Come on!' exclaimed Mr Mordadson. 'Naoutha Nisrocsdaughter? Loyalty? To her the world's divided into people she can use and people she can't.'

'Maybe,' Af Bri said. 'But it makes no difference. I'm betraying her by releasing you, but that's as far as I'm prepared to go.'

'What are you going to say to her when she finds out I'm gone? She's not going to be pleased, is she?'

'I'll tell her you managed to wriggle out of the ropes somehow, then when I entered the room you overpowered me and escaped.'

'I hope you're a good liar. Because otherwise she'll see through you in an instant. I wouldn't want to be in your shoes when that happens.'

'I'll take my chances.'

'Get me to her,' Mr Mordadson urged. 'Please. She has to die.'

Af Bri laughed mirthlessly. 'She's all but dead already, Mordadson. There isn't much left of her to kill. She has a few weeks, if that. It's a wonder she's alive at all. Leave her be. Nature will take its course soon enough and do the job for you.'

They turned a corner and descended a flight of stairs. Mr Mordadson winced with every step.

'Then at least explain to me who you are and what you're up to,' he said, as they set off down another corridor. This one was curved and followed a gentle downward gradient. 'What's become of Lord Urironson? Where are all of Gyre's citizens? Why did you take my spectacles away? What does Naoutha want, other than getting her own back on me? You just said the realm needs me. Why?'

Briefly Af Bri sketched out Naoutha's plans. He said that Lord Urironson had merely been bait to lure Mr Mordadson, and now, having served his usefulness, was dead. The spectacles had been mailed to Az Gabrielson for the same reason: bait. That part of Naoutha's scheme was personal. The rest of it involved ultrapterine, the effects of which he described in grim detail.

'This stuff is going to be spread throughout the realm?' Mr Mordadson gasped. 'Every sky-city?'

'Just about.'

'But . . .' Mr Mordadson was finding it impossible to fathom Naoutha's motives. '*Why?* Why do such a monstrous thing? What will it achieve? Nothing but misery. Suffering. Pandemonium. On a colossal scale.'

'That's more or less it.'

'She's trying to destroy the Airborn? So this is all just some sick revenge fantasy of hers. She's going to die soon and wants everybody else to as well.'

'Oh no. On the contrary.'

'What do you mean?'

'Mordadson, Naoutha wants to save us.'

CHAPTER 47

Empire Of Chaos

Mr Mordadson stared long and hard at the man beside him. The doctor's tone and expression were sincere. He wasn't joking. He was wholly convinced about what he had just said. No irony, no indication that he found his own statement in any way absurd.

'Save us,' Mr Mordadson said, 'by obliterating us?'

'By confronting us with danger. By giving us a challenge we can rise to. Like pruning a shrub to make it grow back thicker than before, or tempering steel to make it stronger.'

'At what cost? What if the plan doesn't succeed like you hope? What if we fail to meet the challenge?'

Af Bri made a vague noise with his mouth, a verbal shrug. 'Kill or cure,' he said.

'And what's wrong with the race anyway, that it needs this "pruning", this "tempering"?'

'We're soft. We're vulnerable and divided. Life has been too easy, we take too much for granted, and we don't know how to defend ourselves or fend for ourselves. We need to be tested – truly tested. We need to have a pressing common cause to unite against. We need to rediscover some of the vim and vigour we used to have.'

'When we had "vim and vigour", back before the Pact of Hegemony, all we did was wage war. City against city. You'd like us to return to that? The way we were?'

'The wars were also symptoms of the malaise,' Af Bri said. 'Civil strife is a form of decadence. The aim of the ultrapterine plague is to sweep away the past, not bring it back. It's intended to provoke a crisis. Do you know the precise, literal meaning of that word, crisis? In medical terms a crisis isn't just an emergency. It's a turning point. And that's our objective, to use the ultrapterine to bring the Airborn to a turning point. What's going to happen will draw a very firm line under what has gone before and will usher in a new age of co-operation and collective purpose.'

'Do you honestly believe that?' said Mr Mordadson. 'Or are you just parroting Naoutha?'

'I'm an intelligent, independent-minded man,' said Af Bri, somewhat affronted. 'I am no one's parrot. I'm also a man who has lost everything. All of us are, all of us Regulars. We've all been deprived of family, livelihoods, hope, as a consequence of the recent disasters that have befallen the Airborn and the bad political decisions that have caused them. There are First!ers among us who've seen their beliefs discredited and belittled. There are those, like me, who've had loved ones taken from them in the Groundling attacks. There are Redspirians, some of the few who survived when their hometown was reduced to rubble. There are shopkeepers who've been forced to go out of business thanks to the levies we now pay on supplies from the ground. Plain, ordinary folk who are sickened by their own leadership's lack of backbone and by the harm it has brought. Courtesy of Naoutha, we shall see an end to that. The old era will give way to a new one – a braver one, a prouder one. A new Airborn empire will arise. An empire of strength and order.'

'Or, if it all goes bad, an empire of chaos.'

Af Bri nodded gravely. 'If so, then the race won't have been worthy of the prize it's being offered.'

'I'm going to try and put a stop to all this, you know,' Mr Mordadson said. 'You can dress it up however you like, but what you're doing is terrorism, plain and simple.'

'That's what we're counting on,' said Af Bri. 'You and others like you, responding to the crisis, fighting back, leading the way. You'll be the vanguard of the improved, toughened Airborn.'

The corridor led to the outer edge of Gyre, almost at the lowest level of the city. The two men arrived at a balcony overlooking the landing apron. Mr Mordadson saw his Wayfarer parked down there, not far from the civic runway.

'Can you fly?' Af Bri asked.

'Myself? Or a plane?'

'Both.'

'The way I'm feeling, I'm not sure. But I'm just going to have to, aren't I?'

'You are. This is where we part company. I've helped you as far as I dare. I need to go up and report your absence to Naoutha now.'

'I think your cover story about my escape is going to need some added authenticity,' said Mr Mordadson.

'I don't see what—'

Mr Mordadson swung at Af Bri with a hard left hook, catching his face between beard and eye. The punch took everything he had but was highly satisfying nonetheless. Af Bri went down like a felled tree. He struggled onto his knees, clutching his cheek and hissing in pain.

'*Now* you look like someone who's been overpowered,' said Mr Mordadson.

'You gave your word you wouldn't attack me,' Af Bri said thickly. 'I think you've fractured my cheekbone.'

Mr Mordadson gave a cold smile. 'I'm trying to save you,' he said, 'same way Naoutha's trying to save the Airborn.'

And with a grunt of effort, he spread his wings and launched himself over the balcony balustrade.

CHAPTER 48

Stayyy Sharrrp

It was far from being a textbook take-off. The Wayfarer clipped a couple of other planes while taxiing to the runway, and Mr Mordadson almost ran out of landing apron before managing to get aloft. His right hand was next to useless. He had to operate both joystick and throttle with his left only, switching between the two.

But he made it into the air, and that was what counted. With the Wayfarer seesawing slipperily from side to side, he soared. A glance in the rearview mirror showed Gyre, receding swiftly into the distance. He would be long out of sight before the alarm was raised and anyone could give chase.

Everything hurt. The slightest movement of his body brought a crackle of grinding pain from somewhere or other. But the cocktail of medications his ex-torturer had given him was still working. He was alert, he had energy, and the pain could have been a lot more severe. He prayed the effects of the drugs would last until he got to Hope's Summit. That was all he asked for: to be able to reach that city and despatch a carrier dove to the Sanctum with a warning message.

He kept the Wayfarer on a north-northeast heading, and as he flew he reviewed the chain of events that had brought him to Gyre and delivered him into the clutches of Naoutha Nisrocsdaughter. With hindsight he could see how neatly he had been suckered. He'd been rash, over-confident. He ought to have realised that Lord Urironson's kidnapping was more than it appeared to be. He ought to have known he was being played. The whole thing fairly screamed *trap*. But he had let pride and anger cloud his judgement. His personal feelings about Lord Urironson had got in the way of his professionalism.

He'd paid a heavy price for that. But he was determined that everyone involved in his capture and torture – Naoutha, her Regulars, even that traitor the Count – would pay a heavy price in turn.

Once he got to Hope's Summit/

/

/Mr Mordadson blinked. That was odd. The sun was in the wrong position in the sky. He checked his instrumentation and saw that the Wayfarer had somehow drifted off-course. The compass bearing was now due east. He corrected, noticing at the same time that he had lost altitude.

Pluck it, he must have fallen asleep! Dozed off at the controls!

Idiot!

He was horribly tired, though. Exhausted. He could feel the strength was leaking out of him, draining away like water down a plughole. His limbs had become heavy. Even keeping his head upright was/

/

/no!

He snapped himself awake.

'Stay with it,' he muttered. 'You can't afford to black out now. Focus. Stay sharp.'

He widened his eyes owlishly and tightened his grip on the joystick.

'You've just been put through the wringer for a few days, that's all, ha ha. Don't be weak. Honestly, you're starting to show your age, old man. This journey is a piece of cake. Couple more hours. You can do it.'

He squinted at the dashboard, reading every dial and meter carefully, then re-reading them. He had to keep his mind occupied. He'd be all right, as long as he didn't let his concentration wander and/

/

/so tired. So tired. His brutalised body was crying out for rest. Sleep. Oblivion.

Concentrate, Mr Mordadson ordered himself. Take those readings. Keep taking them.

But a small voice deep inside him was saying that he could surely close his eyes, just for a moment or two. What was the worst that could happen? If the plane stalled and went into a nosedive, warning lights would flash and buzzers would buzz loud enough to rouse him. He'd have time to pull out of/

/

/what? What was happening?

The instrumentation swam blurrily in his vision. Numbers were superimposed over other numbers, dials over dials. Was that the altimeter or the airspeed indicator? The turn co-ordinator or the artificial horizon?

'Stayyy . . .'

His eyelids felt like steel shutters.

'Sharrrp . . .'/
/
/
/

With Mr Mordadson slumped in the pilot's seat, insensible, the Wayfarer skewed off-course again.

Then gradually, almost gracefully, it began to follow a long, slow arc of
descent into the cloud cover.

CHAPTER 49

A Spot Of Bother At The Potted Shrimp

The only pub in Scaler's Cliff was a dingy, low-ceilinged establishment on the waterfront. It jutted over the sea on stilts, like the mooring jetties on either side of it, and inside it reeked of body odour, brine and fish guts.

The décor was what an interior designer might call 'distressed nautical'. Shreds of rigging hung in corners like ropey cobwebs, the tables were upturned wooden fish crates, and windows and doorways were shrouded with lengths of frayed sailcloth. Candles in hurricane lanterns cast a sickly glow over everything, including the rather badly painted murals that showed lusty sailors grappling with busty mermaids.

The name of this less than salubrious watering-hole was The Potted Shrimp, and since there was nowhere else to go of an evening, everybody in Scaler's Cliff gathered here religiously to drink, and swap sea stories, and drink, and sing shanties, and drink, and tell raucous jokes, and drink some more. The landlord of the pub was, consequently, the wealthiest man in town by far. His clientele all scraped a living in the fishing industry, sold their wares for meagre profits at markets up and down the coast, then deposited most of those profits nightly into his till. While they drowned their sorrows – and they had a great many that needed drowning – the landlord counted his blessings, and his takings.

Tonight, a week after the great storm, the people of Scaler's Cliff were holding a wake, an event which always swelled the landlord's coffers even further. When a boat was lost at sea, a period of seven days was allowed before the crewmen were officially considered dead. During that time survivors of the sinking might be found and rescued, or else bodies might wash up somewhere along the shoreline. Until a missing sailor showed up either alive or otherwise, he was regarded as being in limbo, his status uncertain. Once the week was up, if he had not returned to land either safe and well or as a corpse, he was deemed drowned and could then be mourned. Very few sailors came back after seven days' absence. In fact it was unheard of, apart from in the celebrated local ditty 'The Man Who Proposed A Toast To Himself'.

During the storm two Scaler's Cliff boats had failed to make it back to harbour. One was the *Ray*, a small inshore fishing smack owned by one Valentin Catchpurse. The other was Olaf Haarfret's *Merry Narwhal*. All of the town's other vessels had been accounted for.

Glasses were raised again and again to the souls lost at sea. Curses were spat at Molly Wetbones, that grasping oceanic whore, may she one day have her fill of fisherfolk. Somebody played a screeching dirge on a fiddle.

In one very, very dark corner of the pub Den Grubdollar sat by himself clutching a shot-glass and a bottle of bladderwreck, the local rotgut, which was distilled from fermented seaweed and tasted like it. The glass kept being filled and emptied. The bottle just got emptier.

When, for about the ninetieth time, it was suggested that everyone should take a drink in memory of the friends and relations who were now lying on the seabed, food for fish, Den couldn't bear it any more. He rose to his feet with a deep growl, overturning the crate table in front of him. Bottle and glass shattered on the sawdust-covered floor.

'Enough!' he bellowed. 'That'm enough!'

The pub went suddenly, echoingly quiet.

'I's had enough of your singsongs and your "let's have another round" and your prattling on about Molly Wishbones or whatever her name be.'

'Pipe down, drylander,' someone said.

There was a general low cheer of assent.

'No. No, I won't pipe down,' Den said. 'You lot pipe down and listen. Them's not dead. I be sure of it, surer than I's ever been of anything. My boy Fletcher, my girl Cassie, them's still alive. I know it, and I'll tell you why. My kids be fighters, that'm why. Them's faced far worse than storms in the past and come through, and I won't have you writing they off as gone. Them be'n't gone. I know deep down in my heart of hearts them be'n't.'

'Then why're you so drunk?' someone called out. 'Only reason for gettint as drunk as are you is because someone you love isn't here any more.'

'Someone I love *be'n't* here any more!' Den snapped. 'Two people, as a matter of fact. My wife and my eldest boy. I buried they both at different times, and the pain I feel for they – it never really goes away. But Cass and Fletch, that'm another story. Them's coming back. I know them is.'

'Yeah, yeah,' said a sarcastic voice, 'and I've got wings.'

People chortled.

A kindlier voice, this one belonging to a leathery old salt with mutton chop whiskers and a threadbare peaked cap, said, 'Drylander Grubdollar, doesn't you understand the Steel Sea like I-and-they here do. The sea takint and takint is, and hardly ever givint back. Swallowed by the waves all the time, boats are, and not a spar, not a sheet, not so much as a patch of oil left behind. I-and-they are willint to pay this price to the sea for the fish it provides. A bargain of sorts this is, and I-and-they are used to it. Were you born into this kind of life, you'd be used to it too.'

'I doesn't accept them's dead,' Den said, grimly, bleakly.

'No, you don't *want* to,' said the ancient mariner. 'Not the same thing is that.'

'So shut up you and let us get on with our wake,' said one of the locals.

'Or why not go back home,' jeered another, 'like that halfwit ape friend of yours, the one who couldn't even paddle in a puddle without chuckint up!'

As laughter pealed across the pub, Den rounded on the person who'd last spoken. 'Halfwit . . . ? How dare you! Colin Amblescrut mayn't be the brightest diamond in the mine but him's still worth a dozen of you, you – you pig-ignorant Easterntip yokel!'

A chair scraped back as the man Den had just insulted got to his feet. He was well over two metres tall and built like a wine barrel. He had a scar on his face where it had been torn open once by a longline fish-hook, and was missing two fingers on his right hand, bitten off by a dogfish.

'Yokel!?' he roared, his cheeks turning as red as his nose.

'Yes, yokel!' Den shot back, unafraid. 'Ignorant, hairy-palmed, anchovy-breathed—'

He didn't get any further with the abuse. The man lunged for him. Den, though inflamed with alcohol, still had his wits about him. He sidestepped his attacker and snatched a pewter tankard off a nearby table. As the man lumbered past, Den slammed the tankard down on the crown of his head. Beer sprayed everywhere. The man sprawled unconscious. The tankard was dented beyond repair.

'Hoy, my pint!' cried the pub patron who'd been enjoying the tankard's contents before Den unceremoniously relieved him of it. He reared up. 'C'mere, drylander.'

Den grabbed the man's outstretched wrists, stepped inside his reach, and headbutted him on the bridge of his nose. The man went down wailing and bleeding a river.

A half-dozen other locals now weighed in. Vociferous in their indignation, they converged on Den. It took them a while, and they suffered for it, but eventually they managed to subdue him. He wound up pinned prone on the floor, shouting threats and spitting sawdust, with a split lip and the beginnings of a black eye. The landlord personally oversaw his eviction from the premises. Den was carried out by four men, one at each limb, and tossed from the entrance of The Potted Shrimp onto the shingle beach below.

It was a drop of some four metres and it knocked the wind clean out of him. He lay on the pebbles, bruised and battered, listening to the waves seething close by and feeling very sorry for himself. Above, in the pub, the wake resumed as if nothing had happened.

Then, for a time, all sounds faded, and so did Den's thoughts.

CHAPTER 50

The Art Of Not Outstaying Your Welcome

Much later, when a tiny crab began exploring the tip of his nose with its pincers, Den stirred. He struggled to his knees and shortly after that to his feet. He trod groggily up the beach, clambered up onto the boardwalk and continued along the waterfront till he reached the steps that led to the main part of the town.

Scaler's Cliff was a vertical community, perched on the side of a cliff face that ran in a kilometre-long curve between the two horns of a crescent-shaped bay. The houses were crude, bulbous dwellings made of poured concrete and they clung hugger-mugger to the sheer precipitous rock like a host of giant limpets. Each had a rounded roof, low doorways and slit-like windows, and was anchored in place by embedded stone beams.

The main flight of steps was made of concrete too and rose the full height of the cliff, doubling back on itself in a series of hairpin turns. Several narrow catwalks branched off from it, leading to shorter, even steeper flights of steps and yet more catwalks. These twisting and often precarious foot-thoroughfares were more suitable for a mountain goat than a person. Den threaded his way along them, clutching the guide-ropes for support and reassurance. He passed door after door, each ornamented with shells and with the surname of the resident carved out on a segment of whalebone that hung above the lintel.

More by luck than memory he found his way to the Grubdollar abode, whose door had no distinguishing features because it was a rented home. He banged his head when entering, as he usually did, forgetting to bend low enough. His hissed 'oww!' awoke Robert, who'd been sleeping in a bundle of blankets in the corner of the larger of the house's two rooms.

'Da? That you?'

'It'm I. Go back to sleep, Robert.'

Robert lit a fish-oil lamp. 'The state of you! What happened?'

'Fell over on the way back.'

'Onto a bunch of people's fists, I'd say. You's been drinking, hasn't you, Da?'

'And if I has?'

'You swore off the booze,' Robert said accusingly. 'When Martin died and you spent all those months drowning in beer, you swore after then that you'd be more careful. And now look at you.'

Den was overcome with shame. 'I promised myself I'd only have a glass or two, but that damn bladderwreck . . . Terrible stuff. It gets you without you knowing.'

He sat down at the small kitchen table and sank his face into his hands, sighing heavily. He stayed like this for a while, and Robert went to the stove and put the coffee pot on.

As the coffee began to bubble, Den said, 'Them's definitely alive, son. Your brother and sister. I know them is, because otherwise I'd feel it. Not wishing to sound all airy-fairy and everything, but if them was dead there'd be an emptiness' – he thumped his chest – 'right here. And there be'n't. But nobody around here'll believe I. Them's all so resigned about death, like it'm part of their everyday lives. Which I suppose it be. But it bothers I how them can be so . . . unbothered. I mean, you'd've thought them'd be organising search parties the moment those two boats didn't come in. But oh no, all them did were sort of shrug and say, "Let's wait and see". I tried to pay a captain to take I out to where the *Narwhal* might last have been. None of they would take my money. I tried but them just didn't seem to care.'

'I know, Da,' said Robert. 'And for what it'm worth, *I* believe you. Cass and Fletch, them has to be OK. Until I see two dead bodies looking very much like they, I won't think anything else.'

'You'm a good lad,' Den told his youngest. His eyes shone with pride, even the one that was red and puffy and slowly closing up.

'Tell you what, though,' Robert said, placing a cup of reheated black coffee in front of his father. 'It be'n't helping we any, staying at this place.'

'What's you mean?'

'Well, our money be running low. You barely has a job.'

'I mend boat engines.'

'When anybody lets you. Mostly them hasn't got the money spare to pay someone else to do what them can do themselves. Basically, us has been scraping by on what Cass and Fletch could pull in. It'm not even as I be being any help, seeing as you insist I go to school rather than work.'

'And rightly so. I doesn't have many rules in my household but one of they be that my children stays in school till them's at least fifteen.'

'But Da, all us ever seems to get taught about is the weather and how to use a sextant, and it's damp in that poxy little schoolhouse, and half the local kids can barely read or write. Even that dumpy old biddy Miss Sandygill, *her* can't spell properly.'

'Still and all, you has to go,' Den said sternly, sipping the coffee.

'I doesn't disagree. Only, that'm not really my point. Us be'n't achieving anything here.'

'In Scaler's Cliff? Us is hiding from Longnoble-Drumblood, that be what us is achieving.'

'Him's probably long since given up looking for we.'

'Who knows? Maybe so. But a few more weeks won't hurt.'

'A few more weeks. Us be'n't going to last that long. You's nothing to do and it'm driving you potty, and I be bored stupid at school and it'm driving *I* potty. Even Colin couldn't hack it here, and you know what him's like. Him can put up with most things.'

'Us can't leave. It'm simple as that. When Cass and Fletch return—'

'Da,' Robert cut in, 'us didn't get much of a welcome here to start with, but such as us did, us has outstayed. Your face proves it. And us can hang on, moping around, if us wants. Or . . .'

'Or?'

Robert said, 'What if Cass and Fletch be already back on land, somewhere further along the coast? One of the things I did learn in class recently was about the prevailing currents round here. The Middle Ocean be kind of this great big anticlockwise swirl. So the currents goes southward mostly, down from the Deep Banks towards the warmer latitudes, then round up again towards the shores of the Axis of Eastern States. So anything adrift in the Steel Sea gets swept down towards places like Pinchport and the Humpback Shoals.'

'Anything adrift . . .'

'As in a boat whose engine has been put out of action, or a section of broken decking with people clinging onto it like a life-raft.'

Den sat lost in thought, while a draught whistled under the door and the waves boomed hollowly below.

'Robert,' he said at last, 'your education at Miss Sandygill's hasn't been a complete waste of time.'

'You mean . . . ?'

'Pack your things. And Cass and Fletch's. Let's fire up *Bertha* and be on our way.'

'Us is quitting town? Right now?'

'No time like the present.'

Robert was so delighted, he whooped.

In no time he and his father had collected two large bags full of belongings. They took one last look round the primitive little house that had been their lodging for half a year. Neither felt any remorse about leaving it. Dingy, cramped, uncomfortable – it would never evoke any cherished memories.

Together, by moonlight, they negotiated their way along the tributary staircases and catwalks to the main flight of steps, took this up to the clifftop, then followed a gorse-fringed track to a barren clearing. There, various vehicles were parked, mainly pick-up trucks and vans with trailers, all of them with bodywork so corroded by the salty air that they were on the verge of disintegration.

Hulking in their midst, like a rhinoceros surrounded by armadillos, was *Cackling Bertha*.

She needed some coaxing to get going. Although Den had maintained her scrupulously, and turned over her motor for half an hour at least once a week, her ignition kept failing to catch. The engine whined flatly each time.

'I know, old girl, I know,' Den said. 'Can't blame you, either. Sitting here with all these rusting jalopies for company, nothing to do all day except stare out to sea . . . you's every right to be narked.'

He tried the ignition once more, with the choke out as far as it would go, and this time success. *Bertha* roared into glorious, chugging, cackling life. She'd made her point. All was forgiven. Raring to go.

'Robert?' Den rose out of the driving seat. 'Controls is all yours. I be in no fit state to be in charge of a moving vehicle.'

Robert leapt eagerly into the seat, and *Bertha* swivelled round, aimed for the coast road and rumbled off into the night.

CHAPTER 51

Old Soldiers' Reunion

From eastbound train to eastbound train, Longnoble-Drumblood kept up with his quarry. At every station he would lean out and check to see if the Gabrielson boy and his giant friend were disembarking. If they did, so did he. He'd then immediately take cover, moving with haste but stealthily too, unobtrusively. Shadows, doorways and, later on in the journey, billows of steam were his camouflage.

He altered his appearance frequently, too. He bought a new coat and shirt, he wore his hat any number of different ways, and he even donned a pair of spectacles someone had accidentally left behind on their seat, although the prescription lenses gave him eyestrain. For a while he exaggerated his limp, hobbling along as though his left leg barely worked at all. Although the injury had healed as well as could be expected, the muscles in his thigh hadn't worked properly since. Some mornings, the wound ached horribly, as though the blade of the letter-opener which the Grubdollar girl had stabbed him with was still dug in there.

There was one occasion, during the second day of travel, when he thought Gabrielson might have spotted him. A carriage door jammed as he was trying to exit, and he only managed to get it open after the train had begun pulling out. He jumped out from the moving carriage, lost his footing on the platform and went stumbling into a travelling sales rep. The sales rep was carrying two sample cases, each filled with ladies' underwear. The impact knocked them from his hands, one of them burst open, bras and knickers everywhere, the rep understandably upset, his stock getting all dirty on the floor, bit of a fracas – and the boy and his gigantic friend were among the many people on the platform who turned to stare.

Keeping his head low, Longnoble-Drumblood put on his plummiest voice, apologised profusely to the rep and played the upper-class nitwit for as long as it took to convince the man that he was dealing with a clumsy but harmless fool. By the time it was all over and the rep had been mollified, Gabrielson and chum were nowhere in sight, and Longnoble-Drumblood had to sprint to find out where they'd gone, cursing his misfortune every step of the way.

In the event, they'd got only as far as the other end of the station concourse to study the timetables, and judging by their behaviour they were still unaware that they were being tailed. They had a snack at a café, Gabrielson loitered at a bookstall, the giant snoozed on a bench, then both of them ambled to the relevant platform when their train was called over the tannoy system.

Longnoble-Drumblood departed on the same train, of course, and resolved to be more careful than ever from now on.

On the third day he was nearly scuppered by a stroke of abysmally bad luck. By this stage he'd begun to wonder where on earth this pursuit was taking him. He was far from any of the civilised places he knew, passing through regions he'd never heard of and cities many of whose names he could scarcely read, let alone recognise. He'd been on trains that meandered through mountain passes, trains that arrowed across vast empty plains, trains that clattered through towns that looked abandoned, trains that circumnavigated crater-lakes like vast round mirrors silverily reflecting the sky. The deeper they got into the fringes of the Westward Territories, the slower the journey became. Electrification extended only so far. Then the rail network was reduced to diesel, then steam – ancient puffing locomotives that belonged in a museum, hauling rattletrap rolling stock that belonged in a scrapyard.

The stroke of bad luck came as Longnoble-Drumblood was being bounced along in the last-but-one carriage of a train on a narrow-gauge track that cleaved through a series of hills. The tender-engine pulling it was named *Lightninglike* and was anything but. Not only was it slow, it was desperately unsteady. Its wheels kept slipping on the rails, and each lurch made the carriages cannon against one another with a shriek of couplings and a shudder of woodwork.

It was late in the afternoon and, jolted and exhausted, Longnoble-Drumblood craved sleep.

Then a voice said, 'Brigadier? Is that you?'

Longnoble-Drumblood's eyes snapped open. His first thought was that the Gabrielson boy had found him. He tensed, ready to attack.

But the face before him was a middle-aged man's, and it bore the marks of hard living. It was haggard, ravaged by time and despair.

He didn't recognise the fellow. Then he did.

'Colonel Makethrill?'

'None other.' Without being invited to, Makethrill plumped himself down in the seat opposite. 'Bizarre, eh? Us meeting up like this in the middle of nowhere. What are the chances? I saw you from across the aisle, thought to myself, "No, it can't be." But it is. How are you? How long has it been since we last saw each other?'

'I don't know. A while.' Longnoble-Drumblood glanced past the other man. Gabrielson was in the next carriage along. There was no way he could have overheard Makethrill use the word brigadier. Still, Longnoble-Drumblood was not happy.

'Yes, when we were both serving out at Fort Yellowsands, keeping an eye on the Axis across the Roaring Strait. I heard you took a desk job after that tour of duty. Went administrative on us. Had enough of bunks, wanted to sleep in a proper bed at night, ha ha!'

'A change of perspective. My priorities shifted.'

'I also heard you were involved in that business with the Airborn not so long ago, launching the attacks on them. I don't suppose there's any substance to that story, is there?'

'Colonel, please,' Longnoble-Drumblood said, laying emphasis on Makethrill's lesser rank. 'Voice down. Even if you're only repeating a rumour.'

Especially a rumour that happened to be true.

'Yes, sir,' said Makethrill, perhaps a little sarcastically. 'Sorry, sir.'

'Look, I don't mean to be rude, but—'

'I quit the service myself three years ago,' Makethrill went on. 'Well, let's be honest, got thrown out actually. Dishonourable discharge. I was stealing supplies from the quartermaster's store to sell to civilians. Had a bit of a debt problem, you see. Gambling.'

He continued in this vein for several minutes, spinning a hard-luck tale about card sharps and loan sharks, and no amount of cajoling or subject-changing from Longnoble-Drumblood would divert him. The man had evidently had some kind of mental breakdown after leaving the army in disgrace. This chance meeting with his former commanding officer was an opportunity to share his woes and confess his sins. Perhaps he was looking for forgiveness, or maybe a handout. Either way he was speaking loudly, too loudly, and others in the carriage were listening in. The conversation had to be ended, and soon. It was drawing unwelcome attention.

'I'm sorry,' said Longnoble-Drumblood, abruptly getting up. 'All this bumping about . . . making me rather queasy.'

He headed for the rear carriage and locked himself in the toilet for quarter of an hour. When he emerged, he didn't return to his original seat but took the first vacant spot he found in the rear carriage.

Dusk fell. The train lumbered on through the hills, trundling over trestle bridges and ploughing through tunnels. Every so often it paused with a sigh at some tiny, single-platform halt where no one got on and no one got off.

Eventually, well into the night, Makethrill reappeared.

'There you are,' he said, yawning. 'I nodded off after you went. Woke up and was wondering where you'd got to.'

It was then that Longnoble-Drumblood knew he would have to kill this man.

The two ex-soldiers chatted in low voices for a while. Around them sleeping passengers snored and snuffled. Longnoble-Drumblood pretended he was now eager to chat about the old days and learn about Makethrill's plans for the future. Makethrill was heading for the Pale Uplands because he'd heard a man could live there on very little money, far removed from vice and temptation. It would be a fresh start for him and he was excited about it.

'And you?' he asked Longnoble-Drumblood, narrowing his gaze. 'What brings *you* here?'

Avoiding the question, Longnoble-Drumblood proposed they should take a breath of fresh air on the balcony at the back of the carriage.

They passed the guard, hunkered in his little cubicle, chin on chest, dead to the world. The night air was filled with smoke and sparks. The clouds were silver. The rails clattered beneath the wheels, curving off into the distance like twin strands of spider web. Makethrill offered Longnoble-Drumblood a cigarette. The offer was politely declined. Makethrill lit one for himself. Longnoble-Drumblood let him smoke it down to the filter. Then, as Makethrill flicked the stub away into the dark, Longnoble-Drumblood grabbed him from behind in a chokehold, left arm around his neck, right arm braced against the back of his head, pushing it sideways and compressing his carotid artery. Makethrill struggled futilely as the blood supply to his brain was slowly cut off and he lost consciousness. Longnoble-Drumblood kept the pressure up for a while longer, till there was no pulse. Then he shoved Makethrill's inert form over the balcony railing. The body bounced heavily off the track and over the side of the bridge they were crossing. It plummeted without a sound into the black ravine below.

Back inside the carriage, Longnoble-Drumblood settled down in a seat.

He had just ended a human life. His first ever killing. And it had been easy, so easy. Nothing to it. Like throwing a switch from on to off.

That boded well for the future and the two specific murders he had in mind.

He was soon fast asleep.

CHAPTER 52

Inaction At The Sanctum

Aurora could have screamed with frustration.

No one would listen to her, not even Pendroz, Lord Luelson, even though he was supposed to be her new mentor, filling Lady Aanfieldsdaughter's shoes. When her ladyship had quit the Silver Sanctum she'd made Lord Luelson promise that he would take on her role and ensure Aurora's career continued to progress smoothly and rapidly. He had declared it would be more than simply doing an old friend a favour; it would be his pleasure.

But neither he nor any of the other senior residents would believe Aurora about Naoutha. She showed Mr Mordadson's spectacles to a small gathering of them, and also the accompanying note from the Count of Gyre. She pointed out the prime number code that spelled out NAOUTHA IS HERE.

'That's quite a feat of ingenuity,' Lord Luelson said, peering through pince-nez glasses at the message. '*Your* ingenuity, though, not the Count's. To my mind, it's just a trick of the letters. Mere happenstance. After all, Naoutha Nisrocsdaughter cannot be alive. Mr Mordadson himself told me so. He saw *Behemoth* destroyed and her with it.'

'I saw it too, milord,' said Aurora. 'And I agree, it's hard to believe anyone could have lived through that. But no one actually found a body.'

'Because it was burned to a crisp and buried under a huge pile of rubble.'

'Without a body, though, without tangible proof that she's dead, isn't it just conceivable she did survive? And now Mr Mordadson is missing and here are his spectacles, covered in blood, and I advocate that we send Alar Patrollers to Gyre to at least investigate the possibility that she is there and so is he.'

'Mr Mordadson is hunting for Lord Urironson,' said Faith, Lady Jeduthunsdaughter-Ochson.

'Have you heard from him lately? Has he reported in?'

'No, but that doesn't mean anything. I gather he often goes incommunicado when he's on a mission.'

'But the spectacles!' Aurora insisted, waving them in the air and wondering how she could be dealing with people so blinkered, so shortsighted.

'They mightn't be his,' said Lord Luelson. 'You know how this strikes me? It's an elaborate practical joke. Someone, maybe Feather First!, has dreamed up a nasty hoax. They sent the package to your brother-in-law in order to get your attention, which in turn would get *our* attention. They're hoping to lure us into precipitate action and then publicly mock us for falling for it. In which case we should treat it with the contempt and indifference it merits.'

'Yes,' said Lady Jeduthunsdaughter-Ochson, 'and my dear, not wishing to sound patronising, but really, is it wise for a woman in your condition to get so agitated?'

Several of the other seniors present agreed.

'Can't have the girl giving birth on the spot, now can we?' said one.

'I hear the latter stages of pregnancy can provoke all sorts of strange whims and fancies,' said another.

'Hormones, you know,' said a third.

Aurora just about managed to keep her temper in check.

'Listen to me,' she said. 'Listen well. I have no doubt in my mind that the message is genuine and Naoutha is alive and poses a threat to us all even as we speak. Why won't you believe me? I know Lady Aanfielsdaughter would.'

She realised, the moment she said this, that she shouldn't have. She had just handed them another stick to beat her with.

'Well, why don't you go and tell *her* then?' sneered Alimon, Lord Yurkemison. 'Oh no, wait. You can't, because she doesn't work here any more.'

'And we're well rid of her,' said Lady Jeduthunsdaughter-Ochson. 'I'd be the first to admit that Serena was a vital force in her time, but she was getting on. She'd started to outlive her usefulness.'

'But— but—'

'Really, dear,' Lady Jeduthunsdaughter-Ochson went on, 'you must try and calm down. Think of your blood pressure, and the baby. I remember when I was pregnant and in my third trimester, I—'

Aurora stormed out of the meeting before she could hear the rest of her ladyship's anecdote and before she herself said something that might permanently damage her prospects at the Sanctum.

For the rest of the day she spoke to other, not so senior residents. She canvassed views. She tried to get people on her side, in the hope of creating a groundswell of opinion, a consensus that the seniors would then *have* to pay attention to. It was exhausting, aggravating and, in the end, futile.

'It's like they just don't care,' she told Michael in her apartment that evening, leaning against him in despair. 'They're snug here in their ivory tower, snug and smug, and nothing out there matters. Lady Aanfields-daughter was the only sensible one among them. I think she might even have been the glue that was holding this place together. I know she wasn't perfect, but without her they don't seem to have the first inkling what to do any more. They say people get the leadership they deserve. Do we really deserve this lot?'

'I don't know, Aurora,' was all her husband could think of by way of a reply. 'I don't know if anybody gets anything they deserve any more.'

That night, reports started filtering in from various corners of the realm. They spoke of violence. Deaths. A strange kind of rioting.

The reports were confused, and confusing. They didn't really build a coherent picture. The only common thread was that people – groups of people – seemed to have gone collectively mad. Local Alar Patrols said they were trying to contain the situation, with moderate success, but some form of official policy directive from the Silver Sanctum would be welcome.

The Sanctum was abuzz with the news the next morning, and when Aurora learned about it, she knew all her efforts had been in vain. It was too late. Naoutha had already made her next move.

CHAPTER 53

The Invisible Man

After three days Az had lost track of time. Morning, afternoon, evening, night, all had become one shapeless grey mass. Life was a succession of stations and train carriages that all seemed essentially the same. The only thing that changed was the landscape outside, growing ever more jagged and unpopulated and stark.

Colin remained an upbeat presence beside him. He never appeared to get bored, or tired, or uninterested in the world around him. There was always something to see, some new sight that caught his eye: that distant line of mountains whose summits were lost in the cloud cover, that limestone gorge whose sheer sides shone like polished marble, that herd of wild ghostponies galloping through marshes alongside the tracks . . . He nudged Az repeatedly to alert him to some fresh vista, an item of vegetation, an animal. He was like the world's most overenthusiastic tour guide.

When he slept, he slept suddenly and hard, like a child, and Az was grateful for the reprieve from his chatter. Az himself barely slept at all. He snatched an hour here and there but even in an upholstered seat he couldn't get truly comfortable, and anyway a thought kept nagging at him and wouldn't let him rest.

They were being followed.

At first he felt he was imagining it. Then he was sure of it. Then he only imagined he was sure.

The notion had entered his head when he'd happened to glance over his shoulder while they were changing trains at Fallowdyke Station and had spotted a man skulking by the ticket office. It was the same man – he could have sworn it – who'd collided with a travelling sales rep at Nine-trees Cross Station the previous day, two train connections ago. Both times he saw him only at a distance, but the hat was the same, the coat was the same, the build, the posture. The first time, the man had looked understandably embarrassed. The second time, he looked like he just didn't want to be seen, and indeed Az caught only a glimpse of him before he abruptly vanished from view. A large, noisy family arrived at the ticket office, and the man just seemed to melt away at the same moment. He was there then gone in the blink of an eye, his disappearance so swift that Az was left wondering if he had actually seen anyone at all.

A coincidence? Possibly. There were plenty of other fellow-travellers who became familiar faces over the course of a few hours, sharing two, three, perhaps even four trains in a row with Az and Colin.

Something about the man in the hat spooked Az, however, and he recalled what Mr Mordadson had once told him, that you knew if someone was tailing you because you wouldn't see them.

'Sounds like a paradox, I know,' Mr Mordadson had said, 'but it's hard to put it any other way. If whoever-it-is is doing their job well, they'll stay out of your direct line of vision. The eye, though, always perceives more than you're aware of. The brain notices things at the periphery and logs them without your realising. That's when you feel something as an instinct. What your brain won't tell you consciously it'll tell you as a hunch, a gut feeling, intuition. Heed it. It might just save your life.'

And an instinct was tingling away inside Az, faintly, like an alarm bell in another building. The man in the hat hadn't reappeared since Nine-trees Cross. Rationally Az had no cause to think he was still with them, this invisible presence dogging their tracks. Nevertheless he remained convinced the man was there.

Had he been one hundred per cent certain, he would have informed Colin. As it was, he reckoned his companion was better off not knowing unless or until the man chose to take overt action. There was no point voicing his concern if, after everything, it turned out that his instinct was wrong and Hat Man was simply someone whose path happened to have intersected with theirs twice. He didn't want to look flighty or paranoid.

He stayed on his guard, though, all the way to the end of the line.

CHAPTER 54

The End Of The Line

'Easterntip Branch Terminus!' the guard announced. 'Next stop is Easterntip Branch Terminus! All change!'

It was a tiny station, little more than a corrugated iron shack and beyond that a turntable where the locomotive could be reversed in order to shunt its carriages back the way they came. A dozen or so bleary passengers alighted into a shivering-cold dawn wind. They collected themselves, then marched off in various directions. Some headed for the largish nearby town, Oxbow Bank. Others set off into the surrounding countryside, which was bleak and apparently uninhabited but they seemed to know where they were going. Perhaps a hamlet or an isolated croft awaited them, somewhere amid the grassland and the low folds of hill.

For Colin and Az there was nothing to do but stand beside the road that ran past the station and wait for the daily bus to the coast to come by. Which, according to the couldn't-care-less stationmaster, wouldn't be for another three hours.

'If comint it be at all,' he added helpfully, before disappearing into the shack and shutting the door.

'So here's where you fetched up,' Az said to Colin. 'The edge of the world.'

'More or less. It'm still a few kilometres to the actual edge of the world, but us is almost there.'

'And you still can't tell me why you and the Grubdollars came here? Even though we're almost there?'

'Not my place to. If Den or Cassie or whoever thinks it be OK to explain everything, then them can.'

'It didn't . . . didn't have anything to do with me, did it?'

Colin turned and peered at him. 'You? Why on earth would it have anything to do with you, Az?'

'I dunno. No reason really. Just being silly.'

'I'll say. Be that why you's been so twitchy this past couple of days?'

'Twitchy?'

'Sure! You know, on edge. Like a dog with a flea. Oh mate, you doesn't think all this were Cassie's idea, does you? Her were running away from you somehow?'

'No. Oh no. Not a bit.'

'I should hope not,' Colin chortled. 'You'd be daft if you did. Broke her heart to have to take off like that. Honest it did. Her hated to go without telling you, but her had to. It were for the best.'

The words fell on Az like a warm shower of reassurance. He'd been wrong. He'd been so wrong. How could he have doubted her? What an idiot! All these months he had let the worst-case scenario run rampant inside his head. He'd tortured himself with mistrust of Cassie's motives. He hadn't had faith in her, that was what it boiled down to. And he should have.

He started laughing.

'What'm so funny?'

'Nothing, Colin,' he said, still laughing. 'That's what's so funny. It was all . . . *nothing*.'

When the bus finally arrived, they got on board. Just them, no one else. No man in a hat. Az hadn't spied their stalker among the crowd that had got off the train. He, too, was nothing, it seemed. Just a shadow.

CHAPTER 55

An Absence And A New Arrival

And so to Scaler's Cliff.

The bus deposited them on a windswept rise overlooking the sea. Az, who had never before beheld so much water in one place, was awestruck and dizzied by the view. The sea went on for ever, an expanse of white-flecked grey so massive he thought that nothing could contain it. Why didn't it overspill its boundaries? Why didn't it blanket the entire planet? He could hear its far-off tumultuous crash and roar. The wind carried its moistness – he could feel it on his skin, taste it. He was almost scared that such a thing existed, so immense, so self-evidently powerful. He wanted to back away. The ground felt shaky beneath his feet.

'Hmm, that be odd,' said Colin.

'What?' said Az, a little more sharply than he'd intended.

Colin was peering towards a collection of vehicles parked in a clearing near the point where the land gave out and the sea began.

'I doesn't see *Bertha*.'

'No offence, but we are in the right spot, aren't we? I don't see any houses anywhere.'

'Oh, there'm houses here all right. But no *Bertha*. Well, perhaps them's taken she out for a spin. Let's press on. Last push. Shame if this were a wasted journey but I doesn't reckon it will be.'

They walked down to the clearing and on along a track right to the very edge of the continent.

Az looked down, and there lay the houses Colin had promised. They were stuck to the cliffside like so many swifts' nests, and he thought to himself, *So this is where the Grubdollars have been hiding*. It was certainly an out-of-the-way place. You weren't even likely find it till you were almost on top of it.

And then the question came: what exactly were they hiding from, that

496

they'd come here to get away from it? What was so awful that it could have driven them to hole up in a community as remote and inaccessible as this?

'Huh?'

This from Colin, who was looking not at the town below but at something a couple of hundred metres out from shore.

'*That* weren't there last time,' he added, puzzled.

It appeared to Az to be some kind of manmade metallic island, a citadel maybe. He'd assumed at first glance that it belonged to the town, but obviously not, if Colin hadn't seen it before. The sea swelled and seethed around it, and large grey-and-white birds were wheeling above it in a squawking flock, as though shocked by its presence. A couple of small boats had been tethered near it, and all along the beach below there were knots of people standing and staring at it.

He made out some letters and a number painted on its side in faded, rust-streaked white:

BATHYLAB 4

That, though, left him none the wiser.

Colin, beside himself with curiosity, set off down the steps that zigzagged perpendicularly through the centre of the town.

Az followed.

CHAPTER 56

An Epidemic Of Madness

The reports continued to flood into the Sanctum from across the realm, and the news just got more perplexing and alarming.

Large numbers of Airborn had fallen victim to the sickness, mania, whatever it was. Outbreaks had occurred in at least eleven separate sky-cities, and in every case the symptoms were the same. Ordinary civilians had been transformed into blank-faced, mindless, drooling, red-eyed creatures who were docile unless provoked or startled, at which point they became bloodthirsty savages, attacking anything that moved. The victims they didn't kill became like them. It appeared the disease could be passed on by means of bites.

The Alar Patrol found that there was no easy way to round up the affected people and imprison them. It was too risky. One group captain watched three of his men get torn apart – literally, to pieces – by a group of elderly folk at a retirement home. After that he pulled his forces back and set up a barricade around the home. No one was allowed in, and anyone who came out would be shot dead by sniper archers positioned in the surrounding buildings.

This tactic was adopted, on a larger scale, by Patrollers in all of the cities touched by the epidemic of madness. Areas that experienced an outbreak were cordoned off. Anyone within those areas who seemed healthy was evacuated. The rest were left where they were, guarded by Patrollers who were under specific orders not to interact with them or antagonise them in any way, and to use all means necessary, up to and including lethal force, to prevent them leaving.

So far, it was working. The outbreaks were confined and apparently not spreading. But that was the most the Patrol could do until somebody came up with an explanation for the phenomenon and a method for preventing it happening anywhere else.

Another, perhaps more severe problem was fear.

Realm-wide, people were panicking. Some were taking to their planes and flying off into the blue. Some were flocking to the elevators and travelling to the ground. Many were simply taking refuge in their own homes, locking the doors and boarding up the windows, prepared to defend themselves with whatever utensils from around the house they could press into service as weapons. There'd been instances of looting, and shopkeepers had been hurt as they tried to prevent the looters from helping themselves to their merchandise.

The panic took hold even in the cities where no outbreaks had been recorded as yet. In Northernheights, for example, a stampede at the supply-arrival depot led to a number of people being trampled to death as they were queuing for a down elevator, while in Acme Empyrean a case of mistaken identity meant that a somewhat drunk but otherwise normal man was set upon by a vigilante mob and beaten to death.

Everywhere, the Patrol was appealing for calm, but few were listening. In a population still jittery after the Groundling attacks, terror lay only just below the surface, like a parasitic worm in its host, eating away from the inside. The madness might not have infected everyone, but fear of it certainly had.

The Patrollers could only give thanks that the Maddened (as they were soon nicknamed) showed themselves incapable of flying. If they rediscovered the use of their wings, it would be immeasurably harder to keep them in one place.

Without doubt the worst hit sky-city was Azuropolis. There, an entire sector had had to be shut off and abandoned to the red-eyed crazies, whose massed moans could be heard echoing above the rooftops and along the empty streets, night and day. Patrollers were stationed at various chokepoints between this no-go zone and the rest of the city. As instructed, they killed anyone who wandered into their line of sight. By all accounts it could take up to ten arrows to bring down one of the Maddened. Even then, festooned with arrows like a living pincushion, the Maddened person might haul himself along on all fours for several metres before finally shuddering his last and lying still.

Of the countless Azuropolitans who fled their city, a great many fetched up on the doorstep of its nearest neighbour, the Silver Sanctum. They brought with them chilling eyewitness accounts of the epidemic, and also extra anxiety for the Sanctum residents. The more the residents learned about the madness – and particularly about the fact that it was spread by biting – the less they liked the idea of having these refugees in their midst. The Azuropolitans had been exposed to the contagion, even if only by watching it take effect on others. What if they themselves were carrying it, unknowingly? It might be the kind of condition that could be caught at a distance as well as through direct, skin-penetrating contact. Maybe the Azuropolitan refugees only *looked* normal. The sickness was latent within them. They were Maddened waiting to happen.

Since the Sanctum had so far escaped the epidemic, it quickly, quietly, politely but very firmly invited the new arrivals to leave. It was the Sanctum, after all, not a sanctuary. The Azuropolitans objected and refused to budge, but as a compromise allowed themselves to be corralled in a couple of buildings on the Sanctum's perimeter. These places were then shunned by the residents.

The presence of the Azuropolitans ought to have focused the residents' minds and made them concentrate all the more diligently on the Airborn's predicament. Instead it seemed to have the opposite result. They argued about little else but the refugees – how long they were going to stay, how much food should be shared with them, how to deal with any others who might turn up, what to do if any or all of them suddenly went Maddened. It seemed that the wider emergency was too huge, too overwhelming a problem to be tackled. The refugee issue, on the other hand, was something manageably straightforward that the residents could debate and dicker over to their hearts' content.

Not everyone at the Sanctum was paralysed with indecision. A number of residents set out theories to account for the madness epidemic, along with solutions for dealing with it. They ranged from the credible to the crackpot.

'It's a Groundling plot,' said one. 'A follow-up to the attacks. They've developed some device that can unbalance the brain at long range, probably using sound waves. Or maybe some kind of gas. Whatever it is, there's no doubt we must retaliate. Air superiority is ours. Let's build firebombs and drop them on all their major cities.'

'It's a rerun of the Sinking Cities Panic,' said another. 'That was mass hysteria, none of the city columns was really about to collapse. Same thing here. As we did then, we'll print leaflets explaining that there's nothing to worry about and airdrop them over the affected areas. That'll clear it up in no time.'

'No question, this is some new strain of disease,' said a third. 'Probably one we've picked up from below the clouds. All that trafficking to and fro between here and the ground – it was bound to happen. We don't have the immune systems to cope with the germs from down there. My answer? Immediate quarantine. It's the only way. Nothing comes up, nothing goes down, until the epidemic has run its course.'

These and other views were aired, but failed to gain any traction. Not enough residents could be found to back any of them, which meant they withered and died through lack of popularity, as a plant might through lack of watering. The Sanctum approach to policy-making was being tested to its limits by the crisis – and was falling apart. It would have helped if there had been a single, imposing, charismatic figure who would listen to all the different opinions and nudge the residents gently but persistently towards accepting one of them and putting it into action. There was no such person at the Sanctum any more, however. There hadn't been for three months. There were only . . .

'Headless chickens!' Aurora exploded. 'Running around clucking stupidly at one another, achieving absolutely pluck-all!'

Michael bit his lip, reluctant to point out to his wife that chickens without heads had no beaks and therefore couldn't cluck. He let her rage on, knowing she needed to get this anger out. She could barely walk, yet she stomped round the apartment anyway, pausing every so often to yell abuse out of the window at the gleaming towers that lay outside.

Aurora was certain that the origins of the madness epidemic lay with Naoutha Nisrocsdaughter, and she had put all her energies into persuading the Sanctum of this. But since no one would believe Naoutha was alive, the possibility that she was to blame for the crisis was not even worth considering. Aurora got short shrift wherever she went, until in the end she gave up trying and was left with nothing to do but fume and curse.

And when, finally, she was done with *that*, Michael said, 'So what now, love?'

Aurora slumped into a chair, looking spent, utterly exhausted. 'I don't know. I just don't know. I don't even think I care.'

'All right. Well, I reckon you could do with something to perk you up. Let me go and get you a drink. Juice? Some tea?'

'Don't want any. Not thirsty. Oh, what am I saying? The baby's kicking like mad. Could you find me a cup of peppermint tea? That usually settles him down. Oh, and a cake maybe. Actually, I fancy a plate of fruit. Can you get that too?'

Michael went down to one of the refectories and loaded a tray with everything Aurora wanted. On his way back to the apartment he passed a small group of residents in a corridor. They were huddled together, talking in low, urgent tones, discussing the latest developments. As Michael went by he caught the words 'High Haven'. He halted and leaned close, to hear more.

'. . . apparently the cordon's been broken there,' said the resident who was speaking. 'The Patrol had them cooped up in the Seven Dreams Mall but they managed to get out somehow.'

'I heard there was a back entrance the Patrollers forgot to cover,' said another of the residents.

'I heard some of the Patrollers themselves got bitten and Maddened,' said yet another.

'Well,' said the first, 'they're out in the city now, at any rate. Most of the upper sector is overrun, and the Patrol's stretched to breaking point. There's talk of them abandoning High Haven altogether, leaving it to fend for itself.'

'They wouldn't do that!'

'Yes. Abandon the place, and take as many non-Maddened people as they can with them.'

'But not all?'

'I doubt it's possible. Consider the practicalities. If—'

CRASH!

This was the sound of Michael hurling the tray of food and drink onto the floor as he sprinted off down the corridor. Startled, the residents watched him go, wondering who he was and what had got into him. Then one of them recognised him as that wingless man who was married to that girl who'd been peddling that ludicrous story about Naoutha Nisrocsdaughter. He was from High Haven, wasn't he?

'I wouldn't be in a rush to get home, then, if I was him,' someone remarked.

But that, of course, was precisely Michael's intention.

CHAPTER 57

Invisible Cannonball

From the people on the beach below Scaler's Cliff, Az and Colin quickly gleaned that the huge metal *thing* out to sea had appeared less than quarter of an hour ago. It had loomed up out of the water, sending a violent wave crashing onto the shingles. Since then it has just sat there, silent and ominous, as though waiting for something. A couple of lobstermen had ventured in for a closer look in their dinghies. They'd weighed anchor nearby but still hadn't summoned up the nerve to go aboard. And who could blame them?

'Never seen the likes of it in all my born days, I haven't,' said one woman, gnawing worriedly on a yellowed thumbnail. 'A vehicle, is it? A ship? A buildint? Right it isn't, that's for sure.'

Az peered at the various small windows that dotted the thing's superstructure, looking for signs of life within. Nothing. Bathylab Four? What sort of name was that anyway?

Then, with a deep resonant creak, a large panel opened up in one of its upper surfaces. There was a gasp of surprise from the people on the beach, followed by worried muttering as an object emerged from within.

It consisted of a saucer-like dish with three arms sticking out from it tripod formation, although they did not quite meet at the apex. Each arm was as long as five men laid end to end, and was split down the middle like a tuning fork. The device stuck out at an angle, pointing towards land.

As everyone watched, the arms began to quiver and hum. The noise rapidly grew louder until it made your bones feel as though they were vibrating. Clamping hands over your ears, which everyone did, made no difference. It couldn't shut the sound out.

The air around the device warped and shimmered, like the air above the spout of a steam kettle in the moments before boiling. Then, all at once, with a great trumpeting blare, a beam of this warping, shimmering air leapt out from the apex of the arms. It shot towards the cliff, striking it near one of the promontories, just past the edge of the town.

The cliff face sagged inwards. A perfectly circular depression appeared in the rock, riddled with splits and cracks. It was as though a gigantic, invisible cannonball had caromed into it. Shards and slivers of broken rock rained down onto the beach, followed by a fall of larger chunks, a rumbling, slithering avalanche of boulders and jagged rubble. It poured onto the shingles and into the sea with an almighty roar, sending up a billowing cloud of dust and a tremendous splash of water.

People shrieked. Many of the townsfolk retreated up the beach, seeking shelter under the boardwalk. Others just stood and stared, appalled.

As the dust settled and the sea spray subsided, the mood turned from shock to outrage.

'What *was* that?'

'Attackint me-and-you it is!'

'Grab the young 'uns! Get 'em indoors!'

'Run!'

'Some new type of Axis man-o'-war. Has to be. They're invadint!'

All at once everyone was charging around. Some headed for the cliff-face houses. Others grabbed boathooks and took up position on the jetties, aware that there wasn't much they could do to defend their town against a vessel as large and technologically powerful as this one, but willing to give it a try nonetheless.

'Us should get out of here too!' Colin urged Az. 'Them's found their range. All them has to do is cook up another of those . . . big noisy whatevers, aim it this way, and us is toast!'

'Wait,' said Az. 'Look.'

The tripod-like weapon was being retracted, drawing back into the metal leviathan's hull. The panel slid shut, and shortly another, larger aperture appeared, this one in the side of the vessel, at water level.

A motor launch came out and scudded across the waves in the direction of the beach. There was just one person aboard, not very tall and not dressed in military uniform. If this was the vanguard of an invading army, Az didn't think much of it.

Closer to shore, the person at the helm of the motor launch started waving.

Closer still, the person started shouting.

'Sorry! Sorry! Us is so sorry! Didn't mean to scare you. It were a mistake.'

Az's jaw dropped.

Cassie?

'Cassie!' he yelled.

'Az?' said Cassie, throttling back at the boat reached the shallows. 'Az!'

Az lunged into the sea. It was shockingly, shrivellingly cold but he didn't notice.

Cassie vaulted off the side of the boat.

They waded towards each other, waist-deep in the water.

Az stretched out his arms.

And stumbled, plunging under.

Cassie caught him and pulled him spluttering up.

Soaked through, freezing, laughing, they clung together and kissed in the foam and sway of the sea.

Colin on the beach clapped his hands with delight. The young lovers were reunited, largely thanks to him. A small tear welled in one eye.

And crouching up on the clifftop, someone else looked on with a different kind of delight.

The Gabrielson boy. The Grubdollar girl. Together.

Longnoble-Drumblood grinned.

CHAPTER 58

Full Pub, Empty House

The people of Scaler's Cliff took some pacifying. On the beach, Fletcher apologised and apologised, saying he'd switched on something called a 'Focused Sonic Amplification Unit' on the Bathylab's master console without really knowing what it was.

'I assumed it were a loud hailer of some kind,' he said. 'Thought I'd use it to announce us was friendly. Only, turned out it were an industrial-scale noisemaker instead, probably used for scaring off whales. Which didn't really send the "us is friendly" message at all. But I didn't hit anything, now did I? Lucky fluke there. Blasted a section of cliff but not any people. So, let's let bygones be bygones, eh? What d'you say?'

He looked at the irate faces all around him, and the gutting knives and the boathooks that were levelled point-first at him, and he put on the most winsome smile he could manage.

'The storm,' growled one of the locals. 'Caught up in it weren't you?'

'Certainly were. There'm something I doesn't want ever to have to live through again.'

'So why aren't you and you sister kissint Molly Wetbones right now? And Haarfret and the rest of the *Narwhal*'s crew, to them what's happened?'

Fletcher explained as truthfully as he could. The only part of the story he skated over was how Professor Emeritus had met his end. He said that he had died 'in an accident'. He didn't think it would help the situation if he revealed that he himself had in effect killed the professor, even though it was in self-defence. The townspeople were already feeling threatened by him, and he didn't want to make himself look any more dangerous in their eyes.

'Had you down as drowned, we did,' a woman said. 'Held a wake for you and everything.'

'Well, for my part, I be glad you held it in vain,' said Fletcher. An idea occurred to him. 'But since you mention it, how about us has another kind of celebration? To mark the fact that Miss Wetbones *didn't* get her hooks into Cass and I?'

Several in the crowd seemed to think this was a good suggestion. The landlord of The Potted Shrimp, who was present, seemed to think it was an especially good suggestion.

'Tell you what,' Fletcher added, 'I'll even buy all the drinks.'

That got everyone on his side and cheering. The knives and boathooks were put away and the townspeople trooped off eagerly to the pub, to begin running up an enormous bar tab in Fletcher's name.

Az and Cassie, meanwhile, had gone to the Grubdollars' rented house in order to dry themselves off and get reacquainted. Along the way Cassie sketched out her family's reasons for fleeing Grimvale and not telling anyone, even Az, why.

'Inspector Treadwell said us didn't have a choice,' she said. 'Him didn't even want to know himself where us was going, in case Longnoble-Drumblood paid he a visit and tried to get it out of he by bribery or worse. Da looked at a map and picked out the furthest, remotest spot him could find, a place where no one would have heard of we or even of Grimvale. At first it were going to be the Pale Uplands, but Da associates that with Deacon Hardscree, so no. The Easterntip coast were chosen, and that'm where us went. And you, Az . . .' She was shivering from her dunk in the water, but her brown eyes were warm. 'You came all this way to find I.'

'It took me a while to get my act together,' Az said, 'but yeah.'

'Well, when us gets indoors, I be going to show you how much I appreciate that and how glad I be to see you again.'

'Sounds OK to me.'

'Liking the new look, by the way,' Cassie said. They had reached the house. 'The beard, the hair – nice. Mean and moody, but in a good way.'

'Really?' said Az. 'Colin wasn't that impressed.'

'What's his opinion matter? Colin be'n't the one who'm about to . . .'

Cassie's voice trailed off. She had opened the door, only to find that the place was bare inside. The family's belongings were gone.

'Da? Robert?' she called. She'd been hoping they weren't home, but not like this. She went in, calling their names again.

'Home sweet hovel,' Az murmured to himself, giving the interior of the house a wry once-over. It was more animal burrow than human habitation.

'Them's left,' Cassie said, returning from the back room, which had been cleared out too. 'Moved out. Vamoosed. Not even a note saying where to.'

'Colin said *Bertha* wasn't where she was supposed to be, up top, but he thought they'd just taken her out for a day-trip.'

Cassie looked desolate. 'But why would them go?'

'At the risk of stating the obvious, maybe, I don't know, because they thought you were dead? After all, you and Fletcher were missing for over a week, presumed drowned.'

'Dammit, yes! Poor Da, poor Robert. Them had no way of knowing us is OK. But then where's them gone *to*?'

'Back to Grimvale?' Az suggested. 'That'd be my guess.'

'Far as us knows, it be'n't safe to return home yet.'

'But maybe your dad's not thinking straight, or maybe he doesn't care about Longnoble-Drumblood any more.'

'True, and I can't off the top of my head think of anywhere else him'd go, so Grimvale be probably the best place to start.' Cassie strode towards the door.

'Hold on a mo,' said Az. 'Aren't you forgetting something?'

'What?'

'The whole getting dry scenario. And removing our wet clothes first. And the, er, the naked bit in between.'

'Hate to be practical at a time like this, Az, but us has no towels and no fresh clothes to get into.'

'Yes, but . . .'

'Let's go to the Bathylab. There'm pretty much everything you could need there. Including,' she added with a wink, 'hammocks.'

'Hammocks?' said Az. Then he thought about it and said, 'Oh yeah, hammocks. Hammocks could be interesting. I could definitely see a use for hammocks.'

'Thought you might,' said Cassie, leading him out of the house.

CHAPTER 59

A Missed Opportunity And An Unavoidable Dip

At Easterntip Branch Terminus, Longnoble-Drumblood had stayed on the train while everybody else got off. Hiding on the rear-carriage balcony, he'd waited till the locomotive had been turned and the train was about to move off. Then, alighting, he'd found cover behind the station building, out of sight of Gabrielson and the giant.

He had overheard their brief exchange of words with the stationmaster. Scaler's Cliff was the name of their final destination, then, was it? Fine. Longnoble-Drumblood had set off cross-country towards Oxbow Bank, keeping low and taking a circuitous route. In the town he'd located a taxi service, or what passed for one around these parts: a man with a battered old jalopy who didn't mind giving lifts to strangers for cash. Longnoble-Drumblood had offered him a sheaf of notes, probably more money than the bumpkin normally saw in a month.

'For that much, sir, takint you to Craterhome I'd be,' the man had said. 'And back.'

'Scaler's Cliff will do fine. Just stick to the back roads, that's all I ask. Whichever way the bus isn't going, go.'

He'd arrived there well ahead of the bus. Lurking in a gorse thicket, he'd watched what followed with great interest. He had no idea where that enormous seagoing craft could have come from or why the Grub-dollar girl was on it. What he did know was that he had never seen anything like it, and that the fearsome device which came out from it was an extraordinary piece of armament. A weapon that used sound to destroy things? Longnoble-Drumblood had no idea if that was what it was, but he knew Dominic Slamshaft would have figured it out in moments. He knew, too, what his friend would have said.

'Just let me get my hands on that, Jasper, and I'll copy it and improve on it and make a mint!'

A true entrepreneur, Slamshaft had never been one to let scruples get in the way of profit. Money was money, and it hadn't bothered him whether he earned it through someone else's inventiveness or his own.

Longnoble-Drumblood smiled ruefully as he remembered his good friend. He felt a cold satisfaction that now, at last, he had both of Slamshaft's murderers within his grasp. He was going to take his time killing them. He would have them pleading for mercy long before he granted it by finishing them off.

As luck would have it, he missed his first opportunity to begin enacting his revenge. He glimpsed the boy and the girl making their way up through Scaler's Cliff, but by the time he'd left his vantage point and scrambled down to intercept them, they were already returning to the beach. Whatever they'd come up to do, it hadn't detained them long.

A little dismayed, he followed them down. On the beach they met up with the giant and another young man whom Longnoble-Drumblood swiftly gathered was one of the Grubdollar brothers. Crouching behind a jetty piling, he eavesdropped on their conversation. The gist of it was that the girl wanted to head home, and the other three seemed happy to go along with that. The brother, in particular, was keen to make a quick getaway, preferably starting now, since he hadn't a clue how he was going to pay for all the drinks that the people of Scaler's Cliff were currently quaffing in his name.

They debated whether to make the journey by train, but the girl pointed out that they already had transportation. She gestured at the massive vessel out to sea. It was all theirs, she said, to do with as they pleased. It was comfortable, it was reasonably fast, it had plenty of room inside, and best of all, since money was an issue, it wouldn't cost them a thing. They could travel south along the coast, pass through the Roaring Strait and put ashore near Blackcrab Lee, the port closest to Grimvale.

All of them agreed to this, and they moved off down the beach towards a waiting motor launch. Longnoble-Drumblood cursed under his breath. He was tempted to attack them now, but, at four to one, the odds were not in his favour. Besides, he didn't rate his chances against the giant. Alone, man to man, he reckoned he could take him, but he wouldn't have been able to deal with the other three at the same time.

No, the best course of action open to him – the only course of action – was to join them aboard the Bathylab thing before it departed.

The motor launch churned into life, and the foursome set out across the waves.

Longnoble-Drumblood looked around, and his eye fell on a nearby skiff with an outboard engine. As far as he could tell its owner was nowhere in sight. In fact, everyone in the town seemed to be in the pub.

A rain-slicker jacket and a sou'wester hat lay bundled in the skiff's bows. Longnoble-Drumblood pulled these on, then yanked the engine ripcord and steered away from the jetty. As long as he kept his distance from the motor launch, it wouldn't matter if any of the four on that boat glanced his way. They would just take him for a local sailor, heading off on some fish-related errand.

The moment the motor launch disappeared inside the Bathylab, Longnoble-Drumblood halted the skiff, then stripped down to his vest and pants and dived over the side. He was a strong swimmer and cut through the icy water with long, easy strokes and kicks. Pausing only a couple of times to check his bearings and make sure he was on course, he soon covered the distance to the vessel. He swam around it to the opening where the motor launch had entered. There was a wet dock within, and the outer door was just starting to close. Taking in a lungful of air, Longnoble-Drumblood ducked under the surface and powered beneath the outer door and then the inner one as they came down. Having reached the sluice gate that led to the pool where the motor launch was now berthed, he raised his head slowly out of the water, expelling air silently through his nostrils before sucking in a fresh breath through his mouth.

At the other end of the wet dock a door clanged shut. The Gabrielson boy, the two Grubdollars and the giant had exited, heading into the bowels of the Bathylab. Longnoble-Drumblood was alone.

He slid over the sluice gate, swam across the pool, and hauled himself out. He felt a surge of elation. He'd done it! He was a stowaway on the Bathylab. No one had any idea he was here.

He clamped his teeth together to stop them chattering.

First things first: find something dry to wear and a place to hole up.

Then, at his leisure, take revenge.

CHAPTER 60

The Invisible Web

The Invisible Web was tingling.

Information flowed from mouth to ear, mouth to ear, all across the Airborn realm. Woman whispered to woman, passing on news and knowledge. Every strand of the Web led to another, and all the strands led ultimately towards their epicentre, the Cumula Collective. And the spider at the very heart of the Web, the Mother Major, received the information and grew grim.

Her immediate, instinctive response was to order the city to be isolated. A message went out: any Cumulan at present not within Collective's boundaries was to return straight away. The shutters were coming down, and once they were down nobody would enter and nobody would leave. The madness that was afflicting others would not find a foothold here.

The Mother Major's next decree was that every Cumulan of arms-bearing age must put on uniform and stand guard at the city's perimeter. Unlike last time during the Feather First! persecution, there would be no open door for refugees. Any outsiders arriving would be given one warning to turn back. Failure to comply meant death.

To reinforce this measure, the Aquila Flight took to the sky on emergency practice manoeuvres. Each woman flew up accompanied by her own personal eagle. These were birds that had been bred for size, speed and aggression, and they were bonded with their handlers from the moment of hatching. No Aquila Flight eagle answered to any mistress but its own. Such was the closeness of the relationship that if a handler passed away, the bird was put down; otherwise it would simply refuse food and pine away in misery till it died of its own accord. Similarly, if the eagle died, its handler would more often than not succumb to some terminal illness soon after, or else take her own life. What existed between the two creatures was more than just a working partnership. It was like a marriage. It was love.

Serena Aanfieldsdaughter looked on from the battlements of Second House as the Flight soared and swooped above. She marvelled at the eagles' agility and responsiveness. In each instance all it took was a word from a handler, a short sequence of whistles, perhaps just a twitch of her wings, and the bird would obey. It came close, it circled around her, it stood off at a distance hovering, it returned to her leather-sleeved arm to perch – whatever she instructed, it did. When she gave the attack command, the bird dived straight for its target, which could either be a fake bird being whirled on a string by an assistant, or else a static marker on a rooftop. It would have been amazing enough to see just a single woman-and-eagle pair at work, but to see scores of them at once, all operating with the same precision, in unison, no one getting in anyone else's way, was downright mind-boggling. Serena could have watched them at it all day.

But she had business elsewhere. She had craved an audience with the Mother Major and been granted it. The time scheduled for the appointment was drawing near. She went to the Chamber of the Twelve Virtues and was ushered in by one of her fellow handmaidens.

The Mother Major greeted her warmly, if wearily. 'You have permission to speak, Serena Second-House.'

'Speak freely?'

'Of course. Although I have a feeling I know what you're about to say.'

'The situation out there is grave.'

'You think I'm unaware of that? The Invisible Web positively reeks of doom and dread.'

'And yet Collective has closed itself off to the rest of the realm.'

'Naturally. Like a snail withdrawing into its shell.'

'Snails may still be crushed underfoot, shell notwithstanding.'

'A bad analogy,' said the Mother Major with a dry smile. 'Shall we use up all of the time allotted for your audience trying to find a better one?'

Serena took the point. If she had something to say, get on and say it. 'Mother Major, from what I understand, the Alar Patrol in every sky-city is overburdened. The madness epidemic is barely checked and in some places has broken loose. There's a mass exodus down to the ground, and that isn't sitting too well with the Groundlings, since they fear our people are carrying the contagion with them. All in all—'

'Let me stop you there,' said the Mother Major, raising one bony hand. 'You say "our people". *These* are our people, Serena.' She waved the hand, indicating the Collective. 'This city's concerns and interests extend no further than its outer walls. Anything that happens beyond them is none of our business. There is no madness epidemic within Collective.

Therefore Collective has nothing to worry about, and certainly has no reason to get involved in what's going on.'

Serena fluffed up her wings indignantly then, remembering herself, lowered them.

'If events go from bad to worse,' she said evenly, 'the entire realm faces calamity, perhaps even extinction. What if every sky-city falls to the Maddened? What if the survivors are forced to remain on the ground, having no safe place to go back to? And as far as Collective goes, if there's no realm around us any more, if we're the only non-Maddened Airborn left up here, what good will that be? Who will we trade with? Who will we exchange supplies with? Who will we, by all that's high and bright, play jetball with?'

Briefly, just briefly, the Mother Major blinked. It was a lizardly flicker of the eyelids, and it told Serena her argument had struck home.

Then the Mother Major put her calm, all-wise face back on and said, 'It won't come to that. The matter will be resolved. Such disasters have been confronted in the past and equilibrium has been maintained – without intervention from Collective.'

'Never a disaster on this scale,' Serena said. 'Even the Groundling attacks were nothing compared to this. It just seems to me that Collective has the power to do something, to make a difference, but would rather sit on its tailfeathers doing nothing.'

'But what would you have Collective *do*, Serena? That's what I fail to understand. The entire realm is affected and we're just one city.'

'The Aquila Flight.'

'What about them?'

'We could send them out.'

'Where? To every city? Stretch their forces so thin as to render them virtually useless?'

'No, to a single city. High Haven. That's where the epidemic is at its worst. The whole place is on a knife edge. The Patrol there can't cope and are about to pull out. The presence of the Flight could tip the balance back in their favour.'

'Ah,' said the Mother Major. 'Now tell me, does the fact that you have friends in High Haven have any bearing on your desire to see it saved?'

'I'd like to see every sky-city saved,' Serena replied, 'but if you want an honest answer, yes, it has some bearing. Az Gabrielson and his family have done a great deal for the realm over the past couple of years, and it appals me to think that they could fall victim to the Maddened – that's if they haven't done so already. However, I like to believe that I'd have suggested High Haven even if they didn't happen to live there. If there's any one sky-city that needs all the help it can get right now, High Haven is it.'

'Really? And not Azuropolis, say?'

'No one's given up on Azuropolis yet. Whereas High Haven . . .'

'No, Serena.' This was said with finality. 'Collective will not hear of it. Collective refuses to risk the lives of Cumulans, and its own inviolate independence, by sending the Aquila Flight *anywhere*. The Flight is our last and most important line of defence. It stays here.'

Serena knew that was the end of it. No further discussion. The Mother Major's mind was made up.

'Before I resume my vow of silence,' she said, 'remember these friezes that adorn your walls, Mother Major. Remember the Twelve Virtues, and in particular' – she gestured with a wingtip at *Compassion* – 'that one.'

She bowed and left the chamber, knowing she'd done her best. The rest was up to the Mother Major and her conscience.

Assuming the old bat had one.

CHAPTER 61

Happy, Unhappy

Af Bri Mumiahson couldn't quite believe he had got away with it.

Naoutha had received the news of Mr Mordadson's escape calmly. Af Bri had anticipated an explosion of rage, a torrent of curses and bile. He'd been braced for it, and also for the possibility of some kind of reprisal against himself.

But her wheelchair-arm weapon had stayed where it was. To his surprise – a surprise he'd hoped he hid well – all Naoutha did was sigh.

'He's a. Slippery one, that Mordadson,' she said. 'This is the second time. He's done this to me. But it's too late to make any. Difference.'

'Won't he bring the Patrol down on our heads?' Af Bri asked, slurring his words somewhat. His cheek was swollen stiff where Mr Mordadson had punched him.

'He might, but again, if he does. Too late. The ultrapterine's gone out. Whatever the authorities do to us. We've won. I just hope you're not too badly hurt, Af Bri. He got you a good. One, didn't he?'

'I'll live, Naoutha.'

'I should hope so. I can't manage without you.'

She hadn't been suspicious. She hadn't cross-examined him. She'd taken his story at face value, and not once in the time since had she asked him about it again.

But then, a new mood had come over her lately. There was a kind of blissfulness about her, a serenity, as though nothing much bothered her any more. Af Bri thought he recognised this from his doctoring days. He'd watched terminally ill patients enter a similar phase. Near the end, with death hovering close by on its dark wings, they all at once relaxed. They accepted. Anguish was over. They found inner peace.

Naoutha was there, he thought.

But perhaps she was so content, too, because everything was going swimmingly. Mr Mordadson aside, her plans were a success. A couple of Regulars had been making brief forays into neighbouring sky-cities to pick up the latest news and keep Naoutha abreast of what was happening. Ultrapterine had sown terror and confusion throughout the realm. The Silver Sanctum was in a shambles. It was all working out as she'd hoped. No wonder she was happy.

Af Bri wished he could say the same about himself.

Guilt had compelled him to take a huge risk and liberate his captive. Now the same guilt continued to churn away inside him. Freeing Mr Mordadson hadn't alleviated it. Instead, it grew and deepened with every passing hour. Sky-cities were becoming bloodbaths, and *he* was partly responsible. Months ago, when he'd first been taken to a secret meeting with Naoutha, Af Bri had been entranced by her vision of the Airborn race being broken down and rebuilding itself, stronger, better. He'd also felt a furtive relish at the prospect of others suffering, just as he was suffering. It had struck him as just and necessary.

Faced with the reality of it, however, he was feeling differently. The theory was one thing, the actual, horrible outcome another.

He fancied he could see it in the eyes of some of the other Regulars: the same dawning sense of doubt, the same hollow, haunted look of *What have we done?*

There were whispers, too. People saying, 'It's getting out of hand.' People saying, 'I never thought it would be quite this bad. This isn't what I signed up for.'

In hindsight, Af Bri wished he had got Mr Mordadson out of Gyre sooner. He even wished the ultrapterine had never been unleashed on the realm.

Nothing could change that now, though. They'd done what they'd done, and they would just have to live with the consequences.

CHAPTER 62

Two Copies Of The Same Book

Mr Mordadson awoke to the rumble of an engine and a none too gentle rocking motion.

He was lying on the back seat of a Groundling vehicle, a car. Looking up through a grimy side-window he could see the underbelly of the cloud cover, a rectangle of grey that jolted up, down, around. He felt sick and dizzy and achey and stiff, and was aware that these sensations were just the upper surface of something larger and far worse. It was as though his mind was allowing him a restricted peek into the state of his body, since it knew he couldn't bear the full truth.

He tried to think. Last thing he could remember? Arriving at Gyre. Being met by the Count. There had been events since then, he was sure. How come he had ended up down on the ground? What had happened between then and now?

A vague inkling of unpleasantness, like a bad taste lingering in the mouth. Betrayal. Suffering. Escape.

Naoutha.

Naoutha!

Mr Mordadson struggled to speak. He needed to tell whoever was driving the car that he was a Silver Sanctum emissary and had urgent information to pass on to his superiors. All that came out, however, was a groan.

'Ma,' said a voice. 'I think him's coming round.'

'Be his eyes open?'

'Sort of. Not really.'

'Well, it'm not far now. Another five minutes to the camp. Us'll drop he off there and then him's his own kind's problem, not ours.'

Mr Mordadson shifted his gaze and saw the face of a girl. She was leaning over the back of the passenger seat, staring down at him. She was perhaps eight years old, with a mop of stringy hair and a large scabby sore in the corner of her mouth. She didn't look unfriendly. She didn't look friendly either. Her eyes held mainly just a blank, childish curiosity.

'I like your wings,' she said.

Mr Mordadson tried again to frame a sentence, but without success. Tongue and lips seemed to belong to a part of him he could no longer gain access to.

Shortly, the car lurched to a halt and the driver got out. The door beside Mr Mordadson's head opened and the face of a chunky, coarse-complexioned woman appeared in his field of vision. She and the girl were mother and daughter, of that there could be no doubt. They were like two copies of the same book, the one battered and thumbed and creased, the other yet to be read.

The woman lugged him out of the car by the armpits. She let his heels drop onto the ground, then the rest of him. He felt the impact as though it was happening to someone else.

'Mary-Jane,' she said. 'Check his pockets.'

'Why, Ma?' said the girl.

'Because I's telling you to. And because if you doesn't do as I say, my hand and your backside be going to have a sharp exchange of views.'

Small hands rifled through Mr Mordadson's clothes. Feebly he reached up and tried to stop her. His arm was swatted aside by the mother.

'Found this, Ma. What'm it?'

A glint of light on silver. His Sanctum seal.

'Dunno. Looks worth a bit, though. Us'll take that. Payment for our trouble.'

'I thought Da said the bits of his crashed plane ought to fetch us something.'

'You know my opinion on your father, my girl. Him's an idiot. A few broken pieces of metal, even if they come from above, be'n't worth much to anyone. Him should be grateful if Scrapheap Pete gives he more than ten notes for they. This, on the other hand . . .'

His seal. They couldn't take his seal!

But Mr Mordadson had no more luck protesting than he'd had with any of his other attempts at communication.

The seal vanished.

And so too, soon, did Mary-Jane and her mother. The car pulled away, leaving a cloud of fumes and gritty dust that slowly thinned and settled.

Some time later, Mr Mordadson heard voices. These weren't Ground-lings. Their accents marked them out as Airborn.

'Look!'

'Who's that?'

'Why's he lying there?'

'He doesn't look at all well.'

'Quick. Somebody fetch something to carry him with.'

'What if he's . . . one of *them*?'

'Down here? I doubt it.'

'I'm not touching him. I'm not going anywhere near him.'

'Don't be stupid. He needs help. Let's get him under cover.'

Mr Mordadson was picked up. He was carried. He was laid down.

He was on a rough-woven blanket. There was a canvas roof above him. Around him was the bustle and flap of wings, perhaps a dozen pairs, perhaps more.

Airborn on the ground? In numbers?

He knew then that the ultrapterine had been used. Up above the clouds, Naoutha's campaign of terror was under way. Her empire of chaos had begun.

And for a while afterwards, as oblivion claimed him once again, Mr Mordadson knew nothing more.

CHAPTER 63

A Landlady Of The Deep?

'This is just incredible,' said Az.

'I know!' said Cassie.

Az's face was pressed up against the glass of Bathylab Four's half-dome viewing window, so close to it he could see lines of tiny bubbles dancing at the edges of the panes. Outside, the seabed world loomed in the corona of the searchlights. Marine creatures scuttled and swam.

'Not to mention a bit spooky. It's like something out of a dream.'

'Yeah, you think it can't be real, but it be.'

'And this ship, or whatever you call it . . .'

'I be wanting to go with "submersible murk-comber",' said Fletcher in the command chair. 'But Cass thinks that'm too much of a mouthful and us needs something snappier.'

'But it's seriously old, isn't it?'

'Dates back to the time of the Cataclysm,' said Cassie. 'So us was told.'

'And it's yours now.'

'Suppose. Hadn't really thought about it.'

'But the mad professor, the Keeper of Knowledge, he's dead, right?'

'As a doornail. Us buried him at sea the day before yesterday, with as much dignity as us could manage, and more than him deserved.'

'And he was the last of his kind, so it can't belong to anyone else now. It must be yours,' said Az.

'Yeah,' said Cassie. 'It just doesn't feel like us owns it, because us didn't come by it legitimately. Us didn't *earn* it.'

'Oh, I think you did. You paid for it with your lives, almost. Several times.'

'Still . . .'

'It works for I, Cass,' said Fletcher. 'Az be making sense. And it'm about time the Grubdollars caught a break. Past few years, it'm been one piece of bad luck after another for we. If I were the superstitious type – which I be'n't, touch wood – I'd have said our family were cursed. But for once it looks like fate might actually have smiled on we for a change. Us has been handed the keys to our very own Bathylab.'

'But what'm us going to do with it, Fletch? Us be'n't scientists. Us be'n't going to travel the oceans doing research or what-have-you. No, when us has finished with the Bathylab us should just hand it over to the authorities.'

'Hand it over to . . . !?' Her brother snorted. 'Has you gone soft in the head, girl? Those buggers would only go and do something ridiculous with it, like turn it into a warship or a casino, or else sell it to someone else and keep the profit for themselves.'

'Tours,' said Az.

'What?' said Cassie.

'You've been in the tour business before. You could do the same with this, only on a much grander scale.'

'Hey, yeah, now you'm talking,' said Fletcher. 'Undersea tours. Brilliant, Az. Us sets ourselves up as an adventure holiday business. Can you imagine? This thing could be made into a roving undersea hotel. Us'll take people exploring. Do you know how much us could charge in fees?'

'No,' said Cassie.

'Exactly! There'm no telling how much. A fortune. Rich folk'd stump up plenty to spend a few nights in this and see what us is seeing now. And us could offer cheaper, steerage-class accommodate as well. Subsidise that by getting the rich folk to pay through the nose. Airborn, of course, would be welcome.' Fletcher was brimming with excitement. 'Girl, this could be the making of us. Really it could. Straight up.'

Cassie looked at Az. 'Does *you* think so? Would it work?'

'Don't see why not,' Az replied.

'It'd take quite a bit of start-up money. Us'd need to refit the whole place, for one thing. You know, make it cosier.'

'So find investors. People would surely be queuing up to back you.'

'And what about—'

'A cat!'

Colin appeared on the bridge, with Adam draped contentedly around his neck like a mink stole.

'You didn't mention there were a cat on board,' he went on. 'I love cats. What'm this one called? No, don't tell I. Sooty? No. Blackie? Midnight?'

'Adam,' said Cassie.

'Oh no, that be'n't right,' Colin said, scratching the cat under the chin. 'Him's not an Adam. Let I think. I's got it! With those webbed feet of his, him's a bit like one of those funny-looking animals with the face like a duck. What'm it called? A platypus. Hey, platy*puss*! That'm, like, a pun. That be his name.'

'That'm pretty clever, Colin,' said Cassie.

'Platypuss. Suits he.' Colin went off, stroking the newly rechristened cat.

'Well, them's both found a friend,' said Fletcher.

'Good,' said his sister. 'That bloody animal were getting on my nerves. Maybe now him's got Colin to fuss over he, him'll leave the rest of we alone.'

'Funny how Colin doesn't think it be at all strange, a cat having webbed feet. I wonder if—'

'Don't, Fletch. Don't be unkind.'

'What?'

'You were going make some joke about Amblescruts and webbed feet and cousins marrying.'

'No, I weren't.'

'Yes, you was and you know it.'

Fletcher smirked.

'So?' Az said to Cassie, resuming the earlier topic of conversation. 'What do you think? Fancy yourself as a moving underwater hotel proprietor? Think you have a future as a landlady of the deep? Eh?'

'Well . . . It'm not a wholly hopeless idea.'

Cassie laced her fingers through Az's, and turned back to look at the prospect from the window. She was smiling a little, and secretly, on the inside, smiling a lot.

It almost, almost seemed possible that everything was going to work out all right.

CHAPTER 64

A Dream Of Killing

Elsewhere on the Bathylab, Longnoble-Drumblood emerged from a deep and troubled slumber. He was lying curled up under a weight of jumbled clothing in the corner of a furniture-cluttered room somewhere on the vessel's lower levels. The effort of swimming to the Bathylab had left him depleted of energy. The cold of the water had chilled him to the core. He'd had enough stamina left to find this room, strip naked and haul his makeshift bedlinen over him. Then, shuddering, exhausted, he'd passed out.

In his sleep he had dreamed of Dominic Slamshaft. The moment of his friend's death. The hackerjackal leaping. Dominic thrusting a broadsword through the creature's ribs. The hackerjackal clamping its jaws around his head.

But in the dream Dominic did not die instantly. Pressed beneath the lifeless predator, blood pouring down his face, he rolled his eyes and fixed his gaze on Longnoble-Drumblood.

'Why didn't you save me, Jasper?' he pleaded. 'You're my best friend. Why did you let this happen?'

'I couldn't stop it.' Longnoble-Drumblood was close to weeping. 'I didn't have a chance to. You were saving *me*.'

'But I relied on you. I thought I could always count on you. I thought you'd never let me down, Jasper,' said the blood-drenched face. 'You have to make it right.'

'I will, Dom, I swear. Those children are dead, do you hear me? Dead, dead, dead.'

'Make sure of it.'

In the background, the Gabrielson boy and the Grubdollar girl were laughing. The girl was laughing especially hard. That was because she was the one who had let the hackerjackal into the house. She, more than anyone, bore responsibility for Dominic's death.

In the dream, Longnoble-Drumblood staggered towards the two murderers. They continued to laugh, mockingly. He reached out with both hands to throttle them. They vanished. Their laughter dwindled to an echo. Longnoble-Drumblood was awake.

Refreshed.

Ready to get on his with mission.

He kitted himself out in whichever items of clothing he could find that were his size. Then he sneaked out of the room on a reconnaissance sortie. First priority was to establish where everyone was aboard the vessel. Then he had to figure out how he might neutralise the giant and the Grubdollar brother, so that he could have uninterrupted time alone with his intended victims. If the giant and the brother had to die too, so be it. In fact, Longnoble-Drumblood could think of few ways his revenge scenario could pan out that didn't involve all four of them – Gabrielson, giant, two Grubdollars – winding up dead. There could be no witnesses, after all. Nobody could be left alive to give him trouble at a later date.

The Bathylab was in motion. Longnoble-Drumblood felt it vibrating around him. He moved along its corridors and companionways with the utmost stealth, treading toe-to-heel just as he had been trained. At every turn and junction he paused, listened, peered round, moved on.

Then: heavy footfalls. The sound of someone humming tunelessly. Up ahead.

Longnoble-Drumblood backtracked, found an open door, sneaked inside, left the door open a crack, watched from within, waited.

The giant came sauntering by, carrying a black cat on his shoulder. He had an air of aimlessness about him. He was just taking a look around the place, seeing what was what.

As he passed the room where Longnoble-Drumblood was hiding, the cat gave a sudden start and began to hiss.

'Oww, Platypuss!' said the giant. 'You'm digging your claws into I.'

The cat stared at the door, still hissing. Its hackles were up, its tail fluffed like a feather duster.

'What'm going on, puss? What'm got into you?'

The giant prised it off his shoulder and held it at arm's length. The cat spat and swiped at the air with one paw.

The giant turned to look at the doorway. Scowling, he set the cat down and pushed the door open. Leaning in, he turned on a light and scanned the room.

Empty.

'No one there, Platypuss,' he said to the cat. 'Just a room. No need for all that fussing. Hey, be you hungry? I know I be. Let's go and find that galley again and see what us can rustle up. Yeah? How about it?'

Plucking the still agitated cat off the floor, the giant strode away.

Pressed against the wall behind the door, Longnoble-Drumblood let out the breath he'd been holding.

Close one. He wasn't ready just yet to tackle the giant. He needed some kind of weapon first, something that would put the outcome of a fight between the two of them beyond all doubt. He was glad to hear that the Bathylab had a kitchen. That was always a good place to look. Kitchens had knives, forks, cleavers, pokers, even mallets – they were regular domestic arsenals. He would wait a bit, then head the way the giant had gone and see if he could stock up on implements that one cut and carved and battered with.

The room he found himself in certainly didn't look as if it was going to be much help in that respect. It was a laboratory, not the first that Longnoble-Drumblood had come across so far on his explorations, and like the others bristling with apparatus and equipment for conducting experiments. The only thing unusual here was that one of the work-benches was strewn with papers, files and journals. Somebody had been sitting and reading lately, doing some homework.

Idly curious, Longnoble-Drumblood went over to have a look. He sifted through sheet after sheet of paper covered in chemical formulae and equations. The sight of them sent a small chill through him as he recalled his days at boarding school and the masters who beat him savagely because he couldn't make head or tail of what they were trying to teach him. No great shakes in the scholastic department, was Jasper Longnoble-Drumblood. It was one of the many reasons he'd admired Dominic Slamshaft so much: his brains. Sometimes he'd felt honoured that so smart a man could be friends with a duffer like him.

His eye fell on a journal that was lying open, bookmarked with a red pencil laid in the cleft between the pages. He glanced at the cover, where was written:

PROFESSOR ROGER METIER

HIS JOURNAL

(COMMENCING YEAR OF CATACLYSM +5)

*

BEQUEATHED TO BATHYLAB FOUR

He began to flick through. The journal took the form of handwritten diary entries. The paper was brittle and old, the ink faded in places almost to invisibility. At first Longnoble-Drumblood skimmed. Then he started to peruse the text more thoroughly, his eyes growing wider and wider.

CHAPTER 65

Selected Extracts From The Journal of Professor Metier

An early passage from the journal read:

My ongoing researches into genomorphic compounds have shown me that it is possible to manipulate DNA at base-pair level in order to achieve instantaneous and permanent effects. The primary characteristics will be physical alterations. The secondary characteristics will be hereditary traits that may be passed down through the generations, manifesting as the primary characteristics.

In essence, the changes will be now and for ever. I have it in my power to institute modifications which evolution may (or may not) generate of its own accord. What can take millennia, eons even, I may do in a day.

The question is, should I?

A few pages further on the journal read:

I have become convinced there is no real moral dilemma here. An animal must be perfectly adapted to its environment, otherwise it will not thrive and may not survive – and this applies to the human animal as much as any other. Since with the Cataclysm's meteor strikes nature has radically altered our environment, necessitating a massive and irrevocable upheaval in mankind's mode of living, the logical response is to engineer a similarly radical alteration in mankind itself, or at least in those who have been obliged to adopt a habitat utterly different from the one to which our species has become fitted and accustomed over the millennia. If people are to live in the skies, then they must be given the wherewithal to flourish in the skies.

Such is the argument I have set out before the Keeper of Knowledge ethics and standards committee at this year's Grand Congress, and I expect them to come back with an answer soon. I also expect – indeed am in no doubt – that their answer will be a positive one.

And a page or two after that:

I have, to my surprise, failed to obtain the endorsement of my peers. Evidently these are not peers at all, as I thought, but rather a group of fussbudgets and ditherers who take the title of Keeper of Knowledge too literally and would prefer to cling on to their science for themselves rather than share it, like little children hoarding sweets. I have been told that what I am proposing comes dangerously close to tampering with the natural order of things, which is overstating the case horrendously. Permission has been granted, in rather grudging terms, for me to continue my work, but only on a purely theoretical basis. No practical application is allowed.

Absurd! The short-sighted idiots! They would deny the denizens of the sky-cities their one and perhaps only opportunity to become truly at home in the skies – to *belong*. Honestly, these men and women, these so-called scientists, wouldn't know progress if it came up and bit them on their moribund backsides.

I am resolved to forge on regardless, and to hell with the committee and my colleagues. To that end, I am now engaged in the business of isolating and extracting the genes relating to the specific avian qualities I wish to replicate and propagate. A light skeleton is, of course, a must. Otherwise the size of the wings relative to the body would be disproportionately and impractically huge. The wings themselves must of course be extraneous, i.e. not forelimb adaptations as they are in birds but an unrelated addition, complete with their own musculature and bone structure. I believe this will be achievable by means of cellular stimulation in the relevant (upper dorsal) areas, but the trick will be ensuring the stimulation occurs in subsequent generations. The relevant nucleotide insertions and deletions will have to be inferred after the event, but given that this is an art at which I have grown highly proficient over the course of my life's work, I do not foresee it as posing much of a problem.

Then, further on:

The genomorph serum has performed well so far when tested on various small mammals. The results have been so beautiful to behold that it pains me to have to euthanase and incinerate the creatures immediately afterwards. But I must destroy them, in order to continue my work undiscovered and uninterrupted. If anyone aboard Bathylab Four were to learn what I am up to, I would be barred from access to the laboratories and perhaps even evicted. Besides, I can always re-create them at a later date if I so desire.

One final crucial test remains, and that is gauging the serum's effects on a human subject. But how can I do that without giving the game away once and for all?

And then:

I have no choice. I cannot take my research any further without submitting it to the ultimate test. Besides, suspicion is already rife among my colleagues. Most of Bathylab Four seems aware that I have defied the ethics and standards committee's edict, and my recent furtive behaviour has offered scant argument to the contrary. Therefore I have nothing left to lose.

I have decided to 'volunteer' myself for the role of human guinea pig, and indeed have already administered the serum to myself intravenously, ten minutes ago as of writing. Thus far the only symptoms I have experienced are a numbness in the upper back and a mild but unpleasant itching deep within. The latter would appear to be happening at the osteal level, and I can only assume this signifies porosity setting in.

30 minutes after dosage. The itching has become grotesquely uncomfortable, almost painful, and the numbness between my shoulderblades is now a pulsing ache. I have urinated, and what came out was chalk white, very much like milk. This would be a by-product of the bone decalcification.

I have a scalpel at the ready for what I fear may come next.

2 hours after dosage. It has happened. I cannot describe the agony I had to go through in order to relieve the pressure at my back and allow out that which needed to emerge. But now it is done. Visible in the mirror are pair of small, raw, bloody growths either side of my spine. The worst, I suspect, is over, and now it is merely a matter of time and patience.

There were a few spatters and smears of dried blood on this page, crusty and brown. The next page was cleaner:

24 hours after dosage. I cannot help but marvel at them. They are broad, gleaming white, magnificent. It hurts to move them, but

530

decreasingly with every moment. I feel wretchedly tired, wrung out, utterly drained, but the adrenaline engendered by success is a welcome antidote to that. My reflection in the mirror shows a man who is still clearly me, still recognisably Roger Metier, but changed out of all proportion. I feel lighter, greater. I feel – and this is no mere simile any more – like I could fly.

CHAPTER 66

Further Extracts From The Journal of Professor Metier

Longnoble-Drumblood felt an urge to glance over his shoulder.

The room was empty apart from him. He had known it would be.

But still he couldn't help thinking that someone had to be watching him. Because this was a practical joke. A hoax. The journal was a fake. It must be. It had been planted here on the workbench in the hope that somebody like him would come across it and read it. And why play a practical joke if you weren't there to see its effect on the victim?

There was no such person as Professor Metier. Never had been. No scientist had devised a process that could give you a pair of wings. The Airborn had come by their wings naturally, over the course of centuries, via evolution. That was the truth. No one had helped them grow them. It had just happened of its own accord.

Hadn't it?

On the other hand, the journal was a genuinely old artefact. The creak of the binding and the fragility of the paper said so. The style that Professor Metier wrote in, with his slightly archaic turn of phrase, came from the right period. The scientific jargon he used seemed authentic too. Longnoble-Drumblood understood very little of it, and had to skip several long passages that described biological techniques and experiment protocols in head-achingly dense detail. It reeked, nonetheless, of the kind of knowledge that had been lost during the Great Cataclysm and the years of the turmoil after. It was like a forgotten foreign language. It read right, even if much of it was unintelligible.

If the journal was the real deal – and despite his misgivings Longnoble-Drumblood thought it was – then what he had in his hands was a vitally significant document. In a few faint pen strokes, it rewrote history.

He turned a page and read on:

I have been told that I am to be excluded from our undersea community, and this comes as no surprise. There is no getting round the fact that I have done that which I was expressly forbidden to do. The proof is plain to see. It measures three metres at full span, from tip to tip, and is dazzlingly plumaged. It enables me to hover and flit, in as much as one can within the limited confines of a Bathylab.

My notes have been confiscated, but I have managed to keep this journal hidden and in it lies all the information I need. I have taken care to jot down the serum's precise composition and every step of the transformative procedure, so that these may be reproduced at a later date. My colleagues can hinder me but they cannot stop me. I am ready now to go out into the world, with my journal secreted upon my person, and take my gift of flight to the residents of the sky-cities. For the hope and joy I am going to bring to the people above the clouds, exile from the Bathylab is a small price to pay.

It will be a long, arduous task, dosing every man, woman and child up there and providing surgical assistance with the development of their wings. However, I anticipate that once I have demonstrated the technique successfully on perhaps fifty individuals within each city, the others will be able to emulate it for themselves and there will be no further need for my direct involvement.

I am prepared for some initial resistance to what I am offering. People are squeamish when it comes to intimate bodily intervention of an artificial nature. Not only that but the experience is far from pleasant, although the worst effects may be counteracted by the judicious use of pain-relief medication.

However, the benefits will surely be self-evident, as I myself can amply show. In point of fact, I feel somewhat as though I am a living advertisement for the serum and its effects. Here aboard Bathylab Four I have met with nothing but looks of horror and expressions of disgust at what I have done to myself. People shun me and these new appendages of mine. They shrink aside when I walk past, not daring to let so much as one of my feathers touch them, as though I were infected with some virulent disease. To them, I am a freakish abomination.

But up in the sky-cities I am confident I will have a very different reception. I seriously doubt I shall have any trouble when it comes to 'peddling my wares' there.

And, several pages on, this turned out to be the case:

These sky-city people are almost inordinately grateful! They talk of the genomorphic procedure in terms so breathless and glowing, I can hardly avoid blushing. They speak of 'gifts' and 'miracles', and everywhere I go I am feted, adulated, treated with a reverence that would not shame a king or, for that matter, a god. I do my best to disregard their awe and shrug off their veneration with a humble smile and nod, but it is hard not to feel that at least some of the praise, the tiniest smidgeon of it, is my due.

To see them try out their newfound powers of flight, to watch them tremblingly take to the air for the first time, to hear their nervous murmurs turn to hoots of confident delight – this is satisfying, without question. I never cease to be gratified by the experience. I know now how a father must feel as each of his infants in turn takes its first toddling steps. It is a fresh thrill every time. It does not pall with repetition.

But I am finding that the sky-citizens' effusive appreciation is equally as great a reward. Who would not wish to be a hero to so many? Who would not wish to be held in the esteem that has commonly been considered as the province solely of the royal, the divine?

In the margin next to this paragraph, a comment had been scrawled with a red pencil:

Who? Certainly not you, Metier, you conceited old blowhard!

Longnoble-Drumblood checked. It was almost certainly the same pencil that had been used to bookmark the journal.

Other, similar comments had been added to later pages. Whoever had last been reading the journal had a lot of things to say about its author, few of them complimentary. The general tone of the remarks implied a fellow-scientist, steeped in professional spite.

The next set of entries saw Professor Metier becoming increasingly comfortable with the role of wing-giving quasi-deity, so much so that he decided to change his name:

'Professor Roger Metier' is altogether too ordinary-sounding. It doesn't jibe with the status I have attained in the sky-cities. People look at me and see a saviour, someone with the power to transform their lives for the better, immeasurably so. It is without doubt a disappointment to them that such an exalted figure should have a name no different from any of theirs, and I feel it demeans me to continue trading under that sobriquet, and demeans them too. To play the part as fully as they expect me to, I must adopt a suitable alias.

534

The one I have chosen stems from the upper reaches of the cosmological hierarchy enshrined in a certain religion. It is also, ahem, a slight pun on my surname.

From now on I am to be known as Metatron.

CHAPTER 67

A Final Few Extracts From The Journal,
With Additional Comments

Metatron? Longnoble-Drumblood almost laughed out loud. He didn't know much about Airborn society but he'd heard of Metatron. They revered him as their 'wing-giver', a legendary figure from the past. Most of them didn't really believe he existed.

But it seemed he *had* existed, and he'd been just a man, a Groundling scientist.

Longnoble-Drumblood read on:

A great number of sky-citizens have asked me if I would stay on after my work is completed and be their ruler. I cannot say the offer is not a tempting one. This fledgling offshoot of the human race is in need of sound leadership. They are nervous in their new, towering eyries. They have acclimatised to the high altitude but not to the sense of dislocation they feel up here. All that they used to know is gone. The ground is a devastated, nightmarish place to which they would be mad to return and yet which they still miss and mourn. I suspect future generations will feel no great attachment to what lies below the clouds and will probably cease to give it much thought. For now, however, these uprooted people require guidance and shepherding. They need a wise head to see them through a difficult period of transition and adjustment.

And perhaps that wise head should be mine.

The words 'wise head' in the last sentence were underlined in red, with an arrow leading to a remark in the margin:

Wise head? Swollen head, more like.

As Metatron, Professor Metier began supplying the Airborn with wings of another kind:

Little thought was ever given as to the matter of travelling across the distances between the sky-cities. One assumes it was not a high priority during their construction. Simply getting the things built was uppermost in people's minds.

Planes are the logical solution, and hence I have been helping various mechanically-minded types develop and manufacture aircraft. Neither physics nor engineering is my forte, but nonetheless my friends and I, together, have taken great strides and made many breakthroughs.

This is life. Not hiding away in a Bathylab, losing oneself in abstract ideas, adrift in theory and experimentation. *This* – making things, helping others, getting one's hands dirty. This is what it's all about.

And a few pages later:

I attended a birth this morning. It was the first child to be born up here to genomorphically altered parents. It was delivered safely, a healthy girl. I was permitted to inspect the infant and I noted her lightness – she was a goodly size but weighed a mere two or three kilos. I noted, too, the presence of a pair of hard protuberances beneath the skin of her back. These are the buds from which her wings will sprout.

In keeping with my choice of alias, her parents have elected to call her Raphaella, another name from the same cosmology. It is a mark of respect for me. I feel honoured. I am a lucky man.

Further on:

I travel. From sky-city to sky-city, I fly by plane, surveying my realm, visiting my people. Beneath the vast blue of the firmament, above the pristine white blanket of cloud, I go from place to place, and everywhere I land I am Metatron. Metatron the pilot. Metatron the wing-giver.

I am cordially welcomed. I am treated with great hospitality. I am looked after and loved. And in exchange I offer advice and assistance. People come to me with disputes and I settle them as best I can. I am shown newborn babies and asked to give them my blessing (which of course I do). I am consulted for such wisdom as I may lay claim to, and dispense it as liberally as I can.

I do not consider myself anyone's superior. I do, however, feel a paternal duty of care here. I am shaping this race to cope with the future. I have proposed, for instance, that one sky-city be designated the home of a central ruling body, where laws are formed by agreement instead of through the usual democratic farrago of two sides arguing then trying to reach a compromise. I am convinced this will result in a new kind of politics, one where leaders strive for the very best solution, not settle for the least harmful.

I make these and other suggestions to my people because I am not a young man, far from it, and I will not be here for ever. One day I will be gone, and then my winged progeny will have to find their own way through life, without my help. I am preparing them for that.

Metatron/Metier's final entry in the journal went:

I have almost run out of room in these pages, and anyway have very little left to add. I am happy. I have found my calling. I no longer need a journal in which to summarise my research and unburden myself of my intimate thoughts. My life is no longer one of questing and examining. It's simply one of existing and enjoying existence.

I have decided to parcel this journal up and send it to my erstwhile colleagues below the waves. This is a long but not impossibly long shot. There are certain places where Bathylab representatives put to shore from time to time in motor launches, and certain merchants there who supply them with goods and materials. If I get this to one of *them*, chances are it will be passed on.

The plan may not work. The journal may never reach Bathylab Four. But I would like this to happen. I would like the journal to be read, simply so that those reading it will know how I have triumphed. I did what they tried to prevent me from doing. I succeeded where they feared I would bring disaster. I had the foresight and courage to bring change where they wished only to maintain the status quo. I had vision where they had self-imposed blindness.

This is my legacy, and through it I will be remembered for ever, while they in their subaquatic 'ivory towers' will soon slip from memory and vanish.

The next section was entirely in red pencil. Professor Metier had left the last two pages of his journal blank, and its recent reader had filled them with his own musings:

Metier may have been a sentimental, meddling old fool, but he did some good science, there's no question of that.

So can his achievement be improved upon?

I've always believed so. And now I'm going to prove it.

Metier laid the groundwork for adapting a species to live in a different element from the one to which it has been habituated. I've studied and recreated his serum and, knowing I can take things a step further, have devised a serum of my own.

After all, from living on the ground to living in the air isn't that giant a leap. The fundamental physiological requirements stay much the same.

But to take a species into an environment that is actively hostile to its existence – to change its living-medium from air to water – that truly would be an achievement!

And today I am ready to give it a go. Two test subjects have fortuitously come my way. They are expendable. I rescued them from the water and saved their lives. Hence any life they have left to them is mine by right – mine to do with as I please. Being young and healthy, these two teenage siblings are likely to withstand the rigours of the transformative process.

If successful, I will be opening up a whole new world to them, and to all people. I, Professor Eric Emeritus, last of the Keepers, will have undoubtedly proved my worth, and for noble reasons too, not in order to improve my standing with my peers, for I have none left, nor to garner renown and acclaim, but simply for the common good and in the name of Science.

My motives are pure. My ambition is selfless. In that way will *my* legacy be assured.

It didn't take Longnoble-Drumblood long to deduce that the two test subjects must have been the Grubdollar brother and sister. Clearly, then, this Professor Emeritus had not been able to put his serum to work. The Grubdollars had got the better of him.

For his own sake, Longnoble-Drumblood was glad of that, but he also felt a kind of sympathy for the professor, who he guessed must be dead now – otherwise, how come his Bathylab had been commandeered? Emeritus had fallen foul of the Grubdollars' ruthless peasant savagery, just as Dominic Slamshaft had.

Longnoble-Drumblood was beginning to think that getting rid of Cassie Grubdollar wouldn't just be a personal accomplishment, it would be a public service as well. Like exterminating a rabid dog.

And now an idea had begun to form in his mind. He scanned the room, noting the glass-fronted freezer cabinet whirring gently to itself in a corner. Inside were a quantity of aluminium flasks. Each was labelled in Professor Emeritus's handwriting.

Seeing these, Longnoble-Drumblood knew he had found what he needed, the thing that would give him an edge over his opponents.

Dare he use it? That was the question.

CHAPTER 68

Coasting

On the road south along the coast, *Cackling Bertha* pulled in at every sea port and fishing village. She stayed as long as it took for Den and Robert to ask the locals if any shipwrecked sailors had washed ashore lately. When the answer came back no, she moved on.

After a couple of days of this, Robert began to feel discouraged.

'Maybe I were wrong about the tides and that, Da,' he said. 'Maybe us should turn back to Scaler's Cliff and carry on waiting.'

'Us presses on, lad,' said his father determinedly. 'Keeping going be the best way. The only way. Fletch and Cass could be just around the next corner. I's not giving up on they. Did you kids give up on I when I were off gallivanting in the Relentless Desert?'

'No.'

'No, exactly. You kept on looking. And the same here. Once us has scoured the entire length of the coast, then and only then does us think about turning back.'

Den's face said he was certain they were doing the right thing – and if Robert had any doubts, he didn't want to hear them.

It was hard work speaking to stranger after stranger about Fletcher and Cassie, and getting blank looks every time, along with the occasional sigh of sympathy. It was harder still because everyone seemed keen to talk about another subject.

The Airborn were having a spot of bother up in their sky-cities. A disease was on the loose. It drove you crazy, turned you into a raging monster. The Airborn were fleeing in their thousands, coming down to the ground to find safety. Nobody knew what to do with them or where to put them, so the Westward Territories government had set up make-shift camps. The camps were getting fuller by the hour, and more over-crowded, because there were only so many tents to go round. The government was saying it was glad to be able to offer the Airborn assistance in their time of need and hoped this show of charity would prove there were no hard feelings between the two races after recent clashes and misunderstandings. A number of politicians, however, were grumbling loudly that the problem wasn't a Groundling problem and the Airborn were not welcome down here. There was a risk that they had brought their disease with them and it might spill over into the Groundling population.

The further south Den and Robert went, the more they learned about the situation, and the more they learned, the graver it sounded.

One person told them that soldiers had been drafted in to stand guard around the camps, to stop anyone leaving, although it was hard to see how people who could fly could be kept in one place if they didn't want to be. Another said that food handouts to the Airborn were limited and some of them were beginning to go hungry. Den spotted a newspaper headline which read 'Angry Airborn Refugees Riot Over Lack Of Fresh Water', although in the article underneath it was admitted that this was, at the time of going to press, a rumour that had yet to be confirmed.

Den remarked to Robert, 'What'm the odds that our friend Az be up there right now, sorting the whole thing out?'

'Him and Mr Mordadson,' said Robert. 'And I bet us'd have got dragged into it too somehow, if everything had been normal.'

'Heh! Yes. The Grubdollars has a knack of getting involved in Airborn doings. Blame your sister and her taste in boyfriends.'

Robert gave a slightly sombre nod. 'Cass were missing Az badly, weren't her? Him'll need to be told if her be . . .' The words petered out.

'What was you about to say, Robert?'

'Him and her'll be able to get back together soon. Once us is back in Grimvale, all four of we. That'm what I were going to say.'

'That'm what I thought.'

Bertha rolled on, with the sea always to her left. On and on.

CHAPTER 69

The Forbidden City

From afar, High Haven looked normal, no different from the city Michael and Aurora had left the best part of a week ago. Closer to, they could see that the outer streets were empty of traffic. There were also a number of helicopters circling the outskirts like bees around a hive. They bore Alar Patrol markings.

One of them intercepted Michael's Vortex V on its approach. The pilot made emphatic hand gestures, indicating that Michael should put down at one of the municipal landing aprons on the perimeter. When Michael tried to jink around him, the pilot countered the manoeuvre expertly, placing his aircraft once again between the Vortex V and the sky-city.

'This guy's not bad,' Michael muttered. 'Almost as good as me.'

'He's also got a bolas gun on his 'copter,' Aurora said, 'and orders to use it if he has to. Do as he says, Mike.'

Grumbling, Michael did.

Within seconds of the Vortex V touching down, it was surrounded by Patrollers. Their faces were almost entirely hidden by their helmet visors but the set of their jaws looked implacable.

'What's your business here?' one said. 'Come to gawp?'

'My business here,' replied Michael hotly, 'is none of your business.'

'Then for your own safety,' the Patroller said, aiming his lance at Michael, 'I suggest you jump right back in your chopper and go. We've enough on our plate without having mouthy loons like you to deal with.' He cocked his head quizzically. 'Where are your wings, anyway? You a Groundling?'

'That definitely is none of your business. Just get out of my face, you tin-hatted turkey. I'm going into High Haven even if I have to walk in.'

The lance tip jabbed into Michael's solar plexus.

'One more step,' said the Patroller, 'and I run you through. High Haven is off-limits. End of story.'

By now Aurora had made it round from the other side of the Vortex V. She rolled her eyes. Typical Michael, starting an argument when tact and persuasion were called for.

'Excuse me,' she said. 'My name is Aurora Jukarsdaughter-Gabrielson. And the senior officer here is . . . ?'

'Me, of course,' said the Patroller with his lance levelled at Michael. His triple-grooved wing hoops marked him out as a squadron leader.

'Well, Squadron Leader,' Aurora said, 'we're here because my husband's parents are High Haven residents and we're very concerned about their welfare.'

'You're not the first,' said the squadron leader. 'And I can only tell you what I've told everyone else who's turned up worried about friends and relatives. We've evacuated at least half the population, either to other sky-cities or down to the ground. The rest are still here. Some won't leave. They're barricaded inside their homes, too scared to come out. Others *can't* leave for one reason or another. So we've just had to abandon them. The Maddened are absolutely plucking everywhere. The city's infested with them. We couldn't save everyone. There's only so much we can do.'

'I don't suppose you have a list of the names of the people you did manage to get out?'

'Keeping records wasn't uppermost in our minds at the time, ma'am,' the squadron leader replied dryly. 'We were a little busy with, you know, fending off red-eyed lunatics trying to bite big chunks out of us and turn us into the same as them.'

'I heard that the upper section of the city's where most of them are.'

'That's completely true. We couldn't even get in there.' The squadron leader wearily rubbed his chin, which was shaded with at least three days' worth of stubble. 'Didn't dare. Maddened on every street corner.'

'That's where my parents live!' Michael snarled, pushing the man's lance aside. 'And that's where I'm going right now, whether you like it or not.'

Aurora restrained him with a wing across his chest. 'Wait, Mike.' She spoke to the Patroller again: 'You can understand my husband's concern, Squadron Leader. His mother and father are both elderly. There's a very good chance they haven't made it out of the city. We just need to fly in, check out their house, airlift them out if we can. You can let us do that, surely.'

The squadron leader gave a firm shake of the head. 'No, I can't. It's out of the question. If I let you go in I'd have to let everyone, and then this would turn into an even bigger clusterpluck than it already is.'

Aurora produced her Silver Sanctum seal. She had been hoping she wouldn't have to resort to this. Equally, she'd known she probably would.

'Squadron Leader,' she said, 'by the power vested in me as a resident of the Silver Sanctum, I am overriding your existing orders. You're going to have to make an exception for my husband and me. Tell you men they are not to stop us.'

The squadron leader eyed the seal, at first with resentment, then with resignation.

'All right,' he said. 'Doesn't look as if I have a choice, does it? You're mad, both of you. Especially you, ma'am, with a baby on the way. Enter that city and it's as good as committing suicide. But' – he shrugged – 'can't argue with the seal.'

'Thank you, Squadron Leader,' said Aurora.

'Yeah, thanks a bunch,' said Michael.

The Patroller bristled. 'If you had a pair, I'd smack you in the face for that.'

'If *you* had a pair . . .'

'Mike!' Aurora snapped. 'That's enough. In the chopper. Now.'

CHAPTER 70

An Absence Of Birds

They took one of the vertical routes into High Haven, descending from above the city, down through the Clearway Shaft. It led to Hub Junction, where Michael turned onto Sunbeam Boulevard, which he followed west, through the main commercial district, towards the suburbs. The broad street was eerily empty. The doors to many of the shops, offices and restaurants stood wide open. Here and there, piles of abandoned shopping lay strewn, and litter, and scraps of takeaway meals. Here and there, too, bodies lay.

Aurora gnawed her knuckle. Michael piloted the Vortex V grimly on.

At the corner of Sunbeam Boulevard and Four Winds Avenue they got their first sight of a Maddened. It was a man, and he emerged from a building as the helicopter flew past. He stumbled in pursuit, as though he believed he could catch up with them. He halted only when he ran out of pavement, some instinct preventing him from stepping off the edge. Then he just stood there, clawing the air, raving wildly.

'They can't fly,' Aurora murmured, 'but imagine if they could. Imagine if they remembered how. We'd never be able to contain them. They'd be *everywhere.*'

Swivelling in her seat, she watched the man scream and howl at the helicopter, until he was lost from view.

Other Maddened reacted similarly. The roar of the Vortex V's rotors and engine roused them into a frenzy. They came out into the open, singly and in packs, sometimes knocking one another down in their eagerness to get at the aircraft. Many had blood around their mouths or staining their clothes.

Each one she saw made Aurora shudder. Her stomach knotted. She felt repulsed. She also felt, beneath the fear and disgust, extremely sad. These people hadn't asked for this thing to happen to them. They were as innocent as they were abhorrent.

Now the Vortex V was nearing the district where Michael's parents lived, and the clenching in Aurora's belly just wouldn't go away. There were fewer Maddened out and about here. But a feeling of nausea was coursing through her nevertheless. Her stomach was actually starting to hurt.

Then she realised.

Oh no.

Not now.

It couldn't be.

'Aurora?'

'Yes, Mike?' She kept her voice steady. No need to alarm him. This was just the early stages. There was plenty of time before it got serious.

'This is the plan. I'm going to land as close to Mum and Dad's as I can. I'm going to run into the house and look for them. You are going to stay with the 'copter. I won't be gone more than a couple of minutes. I'll either come back with them or without them, and if it's with, they can squeeze in the back of the cockpit behind our seats. It'll be tight, but they'll only have to put up with it for as long as it takes us to fly out of the city. OK?'

A rippling spasm of pain passed through Aurora.

'Aurora? I said is that OK?'

'Fine, Mike. It's fine.'

Michael set the Vortex V down in a landing space about a hundred metres from the house. He clambered out, ducking under the downwash from the rotors.

'Keep the doors latched shut,' he shouted above the engine roar.

'Don't worry, I will.'

She watched him lope off towards the house. The street was deserted. There weren't even the usual flocks of swifts and swallows darting between the rooftops. In fact, now that she thought about it, Aurora couldn't recall having seen a single bird on the way through the city. They must either have taken to their roosts or scattered to other cities. It was the Maddened. The birds had fled from them, just as people had.

Michael reached the front door and tried the handle. She could see him calling for his parents at the same time. The door appeared to be locked but still wouldn't open even when he used his key. It must be secured on the inside somehow. Michael pounded with his fist, calling out again. No use. Possibly, if his parents were there, they couldn't hear him above the ruckus from the Vortex V.

The shutters on every downstairs window were firmly closed. Michael took a step back, eyeing the upper storey. Aurora saw him brace himself as though to take off, then remember that he couldn't. It would be a long time, she thought, before the instinct for flying finally left him, if it ever did.

Another wrench of pain in her belly, like someone yanking her innards upwards. A contraction, definitely. The baby was announcing its wish to be born. The timing could not have been worse.

Michael had resumed pounding on the front door. He paused, canting his head, listening. Then he shouted something.

His parents were home, then.

Michael looked over at Aurora and gave her the thumbs-up. Then he raised an index finger, to tell her he'd be a moment.

Just past him, a movement caught Aurora's eye.

One of the Maddened was sidling purposefully along the pavement towards Michael.

There was another right behind.

Michael had no idea they were there.

CHAPTER 71

Crowbars And Craniums

It was the noise of the helicopter – the shrill whine of the engine, the heavy *whup-whup-whup* of the rotors. It was drawing them like a beacon. Sound aggravated the Maddened. Here they came, homing in on the source.

Now Aurora could see three of them – no, make that four – and still Michael was oblivious. He was concentrating on the front door, waiting for it to open.

Aurora had no choice. She had to warn him. She climbed out of the cockpit, into the deafening, buffeting cyclone of the downwash. Crouching, she lumbered away from the helicopter, knowing she would have to get much closer to Michael to make herself heard. She gesticulated, but he still wasn't looking in her direction. The front door hadn't yet opened. What was keeping Mr and Mrs Enochson? Why were they taking so long?

Another contraction came, this one almost cripplingly painful. Aurora stumbled to her knees. She felt a sudden gush of dampness between her thighs. Oh great. Just great. Her waters had broken.

She cried out to her husband at the top of her voice. She wasn't even sure what she said. It was a scream more than anything.

Michael heard. Turned. Saw her outside the helicopter.

Saw, too, something that Aurora could not.

There were Maddened shambling along the pavement behind her, nearing the Vortex V. These in addition to the four coming from the other direction.

He sprinted over to her. He grabbed her and helped her up.

At that moment the front door finally came open and Gabriel Enochson peered out. He was holding a crowbar, which he had just used to pry off planks he had nailed up inside the door.

On the pavement, Michael took in their predicament. Maddened ahead, Maddened behind. He could still get to the helicopter if he ran, but Aurora couldn't because she was in no fit state to run. She shouldn't even be moving. She had gone into labour. She needed somewhere to sit down and stay seated.

He saw his father at the door. A spur-of-the-moment decision. The only logical option. He started to move towards the house, half pushing Aurora, half dragging her.

His father held the door wide open. He understood at a glance what was happening, why Aurora was bent double and having trouble walking. He yelled at her and Michael to hurry. Behind him, his wife asked fretfully what the matter was. Why weren't they all going to the helicopter?

One of the Maddened, the first Aurora had caught sight of, was nearly at the front of the house now, just a few paces from her and Michael.

Gabriel Enochson spotted this. Without hesitation he launched himself out of the house, crowbar raised. He whanged it down on the head of the Maddened, who crumpled and fell as though all the bones had been removed from his body. The same treatment was dished out on the next Maddened in line. Michael's father was taking no chances.

Michael and Aurora made it to the house, with Michael's mother ushering them urgently inside. Gabriel Enochson retreated, flying backwards, high enough to be out of the Maddened's reach. He landed on the threshold and scuttled in, slamming the door shut. Without hesitation he picked up a hammer and began nailing the planks back in place.

Outside, some of the Maddened continued heading for the house, stepping over the static forms of the two that had been coshed by Gabriel Enochson. They congregated at the door and pounded on it, to match the sound of hammering coming from within. They groaned and wailed, a chorus of vexation and horrible eagerness.

The rest gathered around the Vortex V, whose rotors were still spinning remorselessly. They clawed at the aircraft's hull. They pummelled it. Some even tried to bite it. The noise was driving them into a fury. If the Vortex V had been a person, they would have torn it to pieces.

In the house, Mrs Enochson helped Aurora to the living room sofa. She spoke soothing words to her, telling her everything was going to be all right.

Aurora might have begged to differ.

She was having her baby, not in hospital, but in her parents-in-law's house.

Outside, there was a horde of crazed people wanting to get in.

The only means of escape was Michael's helicopter, and Maddened were swarming around it.

Everything was going to be all right?

Aurora would have laughed if she hadn't felt so much like crying.

CHAPTER 72

People Who Can Be Used,
And People Who Can't

A summons from Naoutha could not be ignored. Af Bri flew up through Gyre's spiralling corridors, and with every wingbeat his heart raced faster, although whether the cause was hope or dread he couldn't say. Both, maybe.

She was very near death. He had tended to her just a couple of hours ago and noted then how weak her vital signs were. Her pulse had been thready, her breathing shallow and coarse. Her temperature was dropping. Her one good eye had tracked slowly and looked dull.

Perhaps this was it, the end of the road for Naoutha Nisrocsdaughter.

When she died, would he be glad or sad?

He didn't know.

All the Regulars had been called. Af Bri joined a group of them not far from their destination, the Count's office. Naoutha wanted everyone present. Clearly, if she *was* in the final throes of life, she wanted to go out in company.

Af Bri and the others crammed into the room. He went straight to Naoutha's side, and a quick examination showed him he was right. This was a woman with minutes remaining.

And yet, when Naoutha addressed her Regulars, her voice sounded remarkably strong. It wasn't loud but it was clear, and it had force.

'You've done well, all of you,' she said. 'You've achieved. Everything I asked of you. I remember how you gathered around me. A ragtag band of ordinary men and women. All of you nursing a grievance. Against the realm. None of you with any firm idea. What to do about it. I offered you a focus. A purpose. You responded. I moulded you into a force for change. You accepted. I placed a heavy burden of responsibility on. Your shoulders. You bore it. You should be congratulating yourselves.'

There were murmurs of assent around the room. The Regulars had been having some misgivings lately, Af Bri in particular. The rightness of their cause was never in doubt, but they'd found the methods they were using harder and harder to stomach. At this moment, however, with their leader breathing her last, it didn't seem fitting to dwell on that. They should take a positive view instead. That, after all, was why she had had them come here, wasn't it? So that she could rally them one last time. Remind them that the end did justify the means. Urge them to stick to the course even after she was no longer around to guide them.

'All I have to say to you now,' Naoutha went on, 'is this.'

She started to cough violently, and all at once blood spewed from her mouth. Af Bri rushed over with a cloth and mopped up the mess.

'Thank you,' she said, wheezing wetly. 'All I have to say is . . .'

Her gaze fixed them all. The Regulars were ready to be encouraged. Naoutha was going to steady their nerves, stiffen their sinews.

'What a bunch of chumps you are.'

Silence in the room.

'Prize chumps.'

Dumbstruck silence.

Naoutha laughed, and it sounded like drowning.

'Did you really think I was trying. To *save* the Airborn?' she said, the sneer in her voice blatant. 'Did you honestly believe. I give a hoot about a race that has rejected me. Criminalised me. Done its level best to destroy me? Of course I don't! Only a simpleton would think that. I loathe the Airborn. I loathe everything they represent. Since I crawled out of the ground. In the Relentless Desert. All I've ever wanted is revenge. I've wanted the Airborn driven from their homes. I've wanted them humbled. Humiliated. I've wanted bloodshed in the streets. Terror in every heart. I've wanted wholesale slaughter. Genocide has been my only goal. My hope is that. After all this is over. Every sky-city will lie abandoned. A monument to arrogance and. Complacency. And thanks to you, my loyal underlings. My Regulars. That's coming about. That dream of vengeance is becoming. Reality.'

Someone let out a gasp of shock. Someone else barked, 'This is a joke!'

'Oh, it's surely not,' Naoutha said. 'Or if it is. The joke's on you. Look at yourselves. What are you? Radicals? Terrorists? Anarchists? I don't think so. You're thrilled to imagine you are. You've enjoyed the idea. Of rebelling against the old order and forging. A new society. Trouble is, your hearts aren't. In it. Especially now, as you realise what's involved. What the cost of that new society is. Now, when it comes to the crunch. That's when you discover what you're made of. And you, my friends, have learned. That you're conformists after all. Much to your own disappointment. I've been watching. I've had my beady eye on you. You're troubled. You're uneasy. You're regretting becoming involved in all this. Well, too late!'

She smacked the armrest of her wheelchair. People flinched.

'It's too late for any of you. Yes, I misled you. Yes, I duped you and tricked you. Bamboozled you. You can resent me for that. But what you'll have to live with. For the rest of your lives. Is the fact that you let it happen. You were willing, you were only too eager. To pool your knowledge and resources to. Help me. You followed me unthinkingly. Blindly. You with all your sob stories. "Boo hoo, I lost my job." "Boo hoo, someone I loved died." "Boo hoo, they cracked down on my protest group." Your tears were preventing you. From seeing clearly. You came to me in pain. I turned your pain into a weapon I could use. A lethal weapon. Yes, lethal. Don't believe for one moment that the Airborn. Are going to survive the ultrapterine plague. It isn't going to be the. Making of the race. It's going to be the *breaking*. It's going to. Destroy them. The Airborn are weak and this is the blow. That'll finish them off. And you played a part in that, all of you. You fooled yourselves into thinking. That your motives were noble. You got it into your heads that you were. Helping your fellow men. In fact all you were doing was. Lashing out. Like peevish children. No real thought for the consequences. And I led you along. Your wicked den-mother.' She laughed again. 'I knew full well what I was up to. You only thought you did. You—'

A voice cut her off sharply.

'Naoutha.'

Af Bri growled the word, as though it was broken glass stuck in his throat.

'Ah, dear Dr Mumiahson. The biggest. Chump of the lot.'

'Mr Mordadson was right about you,' Af Bri said. 'He told me that for you the world is divided into people you can use and people you can't. I should have listened to him more closely.'

'What, when you helped him escape? Oh, don't look like that. I knew you helped him get away. Soon as you told me. The bruise on your cheek was a nice touch but. Didn't quite swing it for me. Seemed a bit too neat. A bit too *arranged*. Besides, you're a useless liar. I toyed with the idea of killing you then and there. On the spot. But I needed you alive a little longer. To help keep *me* alive a little longer. I wasn't even that bothered about. Mordadson. Much though I'd like to have finished him off personally. It pleases me to imagine him out there. In the realm. Witnessing for himself the havoc I've caused. All his life he's fought for order. Stability. Now it's all crashing down around. His ears.'

'He could still stop it. He could still turn things around.'

'You think so? *I* think if he was going to. He'd have done so by now. No, more than likely Mordadson is feeling. Hopeless and helpless right now. For a man like him that's an agony. Far greater than any of the physical. Agonies you inflicted, Doctor. By the way, you made a very good. Torturer, didn't you? You took to it well. I hardly had to persuade you. You showed an instinct for it. An aptitude. How does that make you feel? That you're as good at harming. As healing?'

'I . . .' Af Bri looked down at his hands.

'No real answer to that, is there? Like everyone else in this room, you're finding yourself. Appalled and ashamed. You had no idea how low you could stoop. Or how good it would make you feel.'

'I don't feel good.'

'Not now. But at the time?'

'No. Maybe. But now, I feel just hatred.'

'Of yourself?'

'Yes!' Af Bri snarled. 'Hatred of myself. But of you too.'

A rumble of agreement went around the room. He wasn't the only one.

'Naturally you hate me,' said Naoutha. 'I pulled the wool over your eyes. Now I'm pulling the rug from. Under your feet. The real tragedy is. There's nothing you can. Do about it. Why do you think I left it till now. To tell you all of this? Why do you think I'm telling you at all? Because I'm fading fast. Every heartbeat, every breath, feels like. There isn't going to be another one. And what's making the experience bearable. Enjoyable even. Is the sight of your faces. Looking at you, I know I haven't merely. Destroyed the Airborn. I've done it by distorting the race's own. Dearly held values. I've crushed souls. I've killed hope. There's never been a victory so perfect. So complete.'

Af Bri took a step towards her. Black despair was surging sickeningly inside him. Naoutha was right. She had exposed him to the evil within himself, and done the same to the others. It hadn't taken much, just a few fine-sounding words and they'd given in to their basest impulses. Revenge. Destruction. Torture. Murder. On the flimsiest of pretexts, the Regulars had shrugged off their consciences and *wallowed*.

'Ah-ah-ah,' said Naoutha, as though Af Bri were some naughty schoolboy.

Her bolt-firing weapon snapped up from the wheelchair arm.

That blasted thing.

'When I die,' she said, 'I die in my own way. No one else gets to dictate. How it happens. Only me.'

Af Bri eyed the weapon. Eyed her. This creature whose life he'd helped sustain. This mutilated monster of a woman.

He took another step closer.

'I mean it.'

The wheelchair weapon wavered in front of him. Naoutha could barely hold it steady, but pulling the trigger would require very little effort.

'Just stand there, Af Bri,' she said. 'It won't be. For long.'

She was starting to shudder. Convulsions were passing through her. Everything was shutting down. Heart, lungs, other organs – the whole of her tormented, pain-wracked body was doing what it ought to have done long ago and giving in.

Her final victory would be dying of her own accord.

Af Bri refused to grant her that.

He lunged.

The weapon twanged.

There was an impact, a ripping sensation in his abdomen, but he scarcely felt it. In his rage, his sheer detestation of Naoutha, Af Bri thought only of grabbing her by the neck.

Throttling her.

Squeezing what was left of her life out of her.

She choked. She gargled. Her eye glared at him, and she knew she had been thwarted. In the very final seconds, she had lost.

But when Af Bri fell away from her, bleeding from his stomach and back, it was clear she had won too.

CHAPTER 73

A Casual Luxury

Deep in the bowels of Bathylab Four, Az heard screaming.

Or thought he did.

The sound was distorted by distance and echoes, and was only just audible above the rumble and hum of the Bathylab itself. At first Az wasn't sure if what seemed to be screams weren't actually high-pitched machine noises, but they were too irregular for that, and too varied. The way they rose and fell, they could only be coming from the throat of a living being.

He went to investigate.

The screams led him into the vessel's lowest levels. Down here it was all laboratories and storage. The air was clammy and the lighting dim. As Az padded along and the screams continued, fitfully, keeningly, he began to feel very unnerved. There were only the four of them on board, right? Him, Cassie, Fletcher and Colin. And the other three were all on the upper levels. He'd left them there to go and explore. There couldn't be anybody else here.

Or could there? Someone who'd been on the Bathylab all along maybe, someone Professor Emeritus hadn't mentioned and Cassie and Fletcher hadn't encountered since they took over the vessel. This was a big place, after all, with all sorts of nooks and crannies. What if Emeritus had taken another captive before Cassie and Fletcher? Perhaps they weren't his very first test subjects. Perhaps he'd started his experiments on humans before he hauled the two Grubdollars aboard.

Thinking about this, Az began to get seriously creeped out. He had an urge to rush back to the upper levels and fetch reinforcements. He was no coward but this was the kind of situation where a little moral support – in the shape of, say, a hulking great Amblescrut – would come in handy.

He told himself not to be silly. If someone was screaming, it meant they were in pain and therefore unlikely to pose much of a threat.

The screaming stopped. Az stopped too, listening hard.

Then it started again, a little louder. Now he was able to pinpoint which direction it was coming from. The source was close by.

Az called out, 'Hey! Hello? Who's that?'

No reply. No more screaming either.

He moved on, his whole body on tenterhooks. Although the screams had not resumed, he was pretty sure they'd been coming from the next corridor. He reached the junction, turned the corner, took a step forward –

– and fell flat on his face.

Something small, warm and dark had got tangled up in his ankles. It yowled and hissed as Az tripped over it. Sprawled on the floor, Az looked up and found himself face to face with a very disgruntled-looking Platypuss. The cat was standing with legs splayed, tail stiff, every strand of fur on his body erect. In the dull light he was an almost perfect silhouette, all black except for his flashing eyes.

He hissed at Az again, revealing pin-sharp white fangs. Az, piqued, hissed back. Picking himself up off the floor, he called the cat several choice names.

'You could've broken my neck, you mangy fleabag,' was the nicest thing he said.

Platypuss yowled irritably at him, then flicked his tail and trotted off. Az brushed himself down and returned to the upper levels feeling somewhat foolish. Passing the galley, he saw Colin frying fish in a skillet.

'Your plucking cat,' he said. 'He was making an awful din downstairs. Howling away – sounded human, almost.'

'Platypuss? So that'm where him's got to,' said Colin. He shook his head. 'Something down there really irritates he. No idea what it be. Day before yesterday, him got a right steam up outside one of the labs. But there were nothing in there. I looked.'

'Yeah, well, whatever his problem is, I wish he wouldn't skulk in the shadows like that. He's too well disguised. I nearly broke my neck falling over him.'

'Them's tricky creatures, cats,' Colin said fondly. 'A law unto themselves. Doesn't do anything them's told to. That'm why I like they.'

Az carried on up to the bridge, where he found Cassie occupying the command chair and Fletcher at the periscope.

'Hi, Az,' said Cassie. 'Had a nice wander? Discover anything interesting?'

'Only that gravity still works.'

'Huh?'

'Nothing.' He stood behind her, leaned over the back of the chair and began massaging her neck and shoulders.

'Ooh, that feels great,' she crooned.

'Good.' Az relished the fact that he could be near Cassie like this, touch her any time, talk to her whenever he felt like it. These were ordinary pleasures, things most couples took for granted, but for him and Cassie they were a novelty. After months of separation, and sporadic get-togethers before that, it seemed almost incredible to now be spending twenty-four hours a day with his girlfriend. In fact, he didn't think they'd ever been in each other's company for a stretch as long as this – was it three whole days now? It felt weird, in a good way. Like a treat that just went on and on. Sometimes he didn't even want to sleep. He would lie there in the hammock next to Cassie's, staring at her while she slumbered. Because he could. Because neither he nor she had to go back home in a few hours' time. Because this casual luxury was available to him.

Not for that much longer, though. Every journey had to end, and after this one he had a job to carry out. Something he hadn't done and should have.

'Little bit harder on the right shoulder there,' Cassie instructed.

'Your wish is my command, milady.'

Fletcher slapped the periscope handles shut and hit the switch that retracted the device into a recessed shaft above.

'Does you two mind?' he said, turning round with mock grimace. 'It'm great that you be all loved up and that, but some of we has stomachs and food us'd like to keep down in they.'

'Oh, you'm just jealous,' said Cassie.

'Yeah, I be. Come on over here and give I a massage too, please, Az.'

They laughed.

'So where's us now, Fletch?' Cassie asked.

'Best as I can reckon, about to enter the Roaring Strait. I can see coastline both ways, and the water be rough up there. It'm rough down here as well. Look.'

The viewing window showed clouds of sand and silt, swirling and eddying. The seabed, just visible, was smoothly grooved, as though scraped flat by a giant's rake. Immense forces were at work out there. The Bathylab shuddered and trembled in their grip, in a way that reminded Az of piloting *Cerulean* through the cloud cover.

'What's the Roaring Strait?' he asked.

'It'm where the Middle Ocean feeds into the Southern,' Fletcher explained, 'and the point where the Westward Territories be closest to the Eastern States. The two landmasses be almost touching each other, in fact. The strait'm no more than six kilometres across at its narrowest, and the currents here get fierce. All that sea, being channelled through a kind of bottleneck – it goes at quite a pace. Not much fun for shipping. For we, on the other hand, it'm great. Bathylab Four be going downstream, with the flow, which'm giving we a helping hand. What'm our groundspeed, Cass?'

'Pushing thirty.'

'There. Not bad at all, seeing as us has been averaging twenty-five up till now. Likely as not us'll hit forty in the narrows. Which, at a rough estimate, means reaching Blackcrab Lee by midnight, I'd say. No later than the small hours, at any rate.'

'Blackcrab Lee,' said Az. 'That's quite far south down the continent, isn't it?'

'Yep.'

'Do you happen to know how near it is to Greyview Pass?'

'Greyview Pass? No such place. Does you mean Greylook Pass?'

'Probably.'

'No more than a hundred k or so. Train'll get you from one to the other in a couple of hours. Why's you ask?'

'Greylook Pass?' said Cassie, craning round to look at Az. 'What's you after there?'

'Nothing really,' said Az. 'Fletcher? Do you mind doing us a favour?'

'Sure.'

'Could you take the controls for a spell? I'd like to go and have a chat with Cassie in our cabin.'

'A chat . . .' Fletcher rolled his eyes. 'Fine. Off you go. Just try to keep the noise down. Some of your "chats" lately has been keeping the rest of we awake.'

They did talk – eventually. Lying together in a hammock, naked, Az told Cassie why he wanted to go to Greylook Pass.

'Gyre's above there,' he said.

'And what'm so fascinating at Gyre that you's all of a sudden got to pay a visit?' She tapped the tattoo on his arm. 'Be it anything to do with this?'

'With . . . ? No. Oh no.'

She started stroking the tattoo, running her finger around the contours of the downward arrow 'You had this done because, what were it you said? Because "that's how life is". That be what you told I, right?'

'Yes.'

'All darkness and downwardness.'

'Yes.' Az shifted, a little embarrassed. He didn't feel that way any more. Not completely.

'Well, here us is, down in the darkness. Not so bad, be it?'

Az had to admit, lying there with Cassie, pressed against her, warm bare skin to warm bare skin, that it wasn't so bad at all.

'But then going to Gyre be'n't anything to do with the Count or the prophecy or any of that,' she said. 'Yeah?

'Yeah.'

'So why?'

'Mr Mordadson.'

Az explained briefly about Mr Mordadson's disappearance and the parcel containing the bloodied spectacles.

'And you didn't go to find out what had happened to he?' Cassie said, aghast. 'Az!'

'I wanted to come and find you more.'

'Even so. Him's your friend.'

'Things were different then. *I* was different then. And – and I realise now I got my priorities back to front.'

'I'll say. Don't get I wrong, I love you for coming to find I. But it weren't exactly life or death. Whereas with Mr Mordadson . . .'

'We don't know for sure that he's in trouble. In any case, I'm making him my priority now. It's all worked out pretty well, as a matter of fact. I doubt I could have got to Greylook Pass any more quickly if I'd travelled overland. Going with you on Bathylab Four turns out to have been the right decision.'

'Well, I suppose I'd have to agree,' Cassie said, 'for selfish reasons if nothing else. So. Tomorrow, us parts.'

'Again.'

'Again.' Her hand moved down his arm to his elbow, to his hand, and then across. 'Us'd better make the most of the time us has left, then.'

'I'm not sure that I can . . . Oh.'

'Not sure you can . . . ?'

'Forget it. I've changed my mind. I am sure.'

'So I sees. In fact, from this angle, I'd say you looks more than sure. Cocksure.'

Az smiled. 'Straight up?'

Cassie smiled back. 'Or straight down. It'm your choice.'

CHAPTER 74

Scrapheap Pete

Hehhh hehhh hehhh, cackled *Bertha*.

Hugghh hehh hugghh, she continued.

Hugghh hakk huhh, she went on.

Then: *hakk hakk hucchhhh ahhh squeeeeeeeee*.

Den engaged neutral and let *Bertha* roll to the roadside. He and Robert got out to check the engine. Wisps of steam were curling out from under the cowling. Den knew pretty much what the problem was even before he lifted the cowling and looked.

'Drive belt be gone,' he predicted, and he was right. Shreds of high-tensile cord and rubber were strewn across the engine. He picked up one lump of belt with a disgusted look and tossed it over his shoulder. 'These long journeys, them just doesn't agree with the old girl.'

Luckily the breakdown had happened close to a large town. They set off on foot and soon came to the outskirts of Rivermouth Quay. Not far away was the column of a sky-city, rising not from the land but from the sea. Den knew of only one sky-city that had its foot in the ocean. Hope's Peak was it called? Something like that.

It didn't take them long to find a motor factor, but he didn't keep murk-comber parts in stock.

'You'm wanting a three-centimetre serpentine belt,' he said. 'I could order one in, but it'll take at least a week.'

'Can't sit here cooling our heels for a week,' Den said.

'Then what about Scrapheap Pete? Down on Turnpike Lane. Him's a right pack-rat, got all kinds of odds and sods. Chances be him'll have what you be after.'

Scrapheap Pete was a squat, round-headed man whose overalls were covered in splotches of grease and oil, like a butcher's apron might be covered in bloodstains. He smoked a stubby cigar and talked gruffly and choppily as if angry with everything, although it didn't take Den long to work out that beneath all the bluster he was a reasonable enough fellow.

'Murk-comber,' said Pete. 'Who drives a murk-comber these days? I'll tell you. No one. Murk-combers? Thing of the past. Myself, though, I love they. What'm not to love? Beautiful great hunk of purpose-built engineering. Designed for nothing except what them's supposed to do. Of course, round here us uses boats in our Shadow Zone. Or did, at any rate. Everything changes, right? Everything changes. Now, I reckon I's got a drive belt for you somewhere. No, I be sure I has. Give me a few moments.'

He waddled off to search among the vast piles of rusting wrecks and broken-down machinery that filled his yard. Den let his gaze rove around. The place had alleys and avenues, like a small city – a city built from teetering stacks of junk. There was every make and model of vehicle imaginable, some so damaged or so cannibalised for parts that they were hard to identify. There were also farming implements, heavy-industry tools, old stoves and cookers . . . Essentially, if it was made of metal and it no longer worked, Scrapheap Pete would take it.

There was even an aeroplane, or rather the crashed remnants of an aeroplane.

'Look at that, Da,' said Robert, pointing to it.

'Bless my bum,' said Den, 'that'm a . . . whatchemacall. Mr Mordadson has one. A Wayfarer. Az says Michael says it's rubbish.'

'This one ended up in the right place then, didn't it?'

Den went in for a closer look. The plane's nose was crumpled, one wing had sheared off, and the tailfin assembly was barely hanging on. The main section of the fuselage, however, was more or less intact. The inside of the cockpit was a mess of shattered windscreen glass but the seat, the joystick, the dashboard, everything was still where it should be.

'A bad landing,' Den mused, 'but one you could walk away from.'

Scrapheap Pete reappeared, carrying a drive belt. 'Be you interested in that?' he asked, stabbing his cigar in the direction of the plane. 'I came by it just the other day. A bit of soldering here and there, and I reckon you could have it airworthy again.'

'Take a damn sight more than "a bit of soldering",' Den said.

'Well, true, but look on it as a project. Could be fun. Tell you what, a hundred notes and it'm yours.'

'Nope, I doesn't need a plane.'

'Why not? Fifty.'

'Really.'

'Thirty. Final offer. Everyone wants to fly, doesn't them?'

Den shook his head firmly. 'Were there someone in it when it came down?'

'Why's you ask?'

'Just curious.'

'Ah yes. Professionally curious. A murk-comber owner. Bet you's come across a few downed aircraft in your time, back when them was called Relics.'

'It be'n't that. It'm more . . . personal. I knows a man who has one of these. I'd like to tell he I's seen one that dropped out of the sky and the pilot were OK afterwards. Or maybe him weren't?'

'Well,' said Pete, 'far as I can gather, there were a pilot. But as to how him be, I's no idea. You'd be better off speaking to the folks that found the plane and sold it to I.'

'And them is?'

'The Tilthtillers. Them lives off Saltmarsh Road. Them's farmers and them's got a few hectares out there. Head for the river, follow the road inland, over the first bridge you come to, left at the junction after that, and down a dirt track. It'm signposted. You can't miss it. Word of advice, though. Fred Tilthtiller be nice enough, but his missus, her's a tough old boot. Don't get on the wrong side of she.'

'Thanks.' Den paid for the drive belt, and he and Robert made their way back to *Bertha*.

'Da, us be'n't going to visit these Tilthtillers, be us?' Robert said as Den got busy with a spanner and a torque wrench, fitting the new belt in place.

'Yep.'

'What for?'

Den frowned. 'I's not wholly sure. I just feel as though us should.'

'What about Cass and Fletch?'

'This'm only going to be a brief diversion.'

'You doesn't think that were actually Mr Mordadson's plane? There'm loads of Metatronco Wayfarers buzzing around up there. Hundreds of they, probably.'

'You'm right. It'm unlikely that one be his. But I'd like to know for certain that it be'n't. I can't put it any plainer than that.'

CHAPTER 75

The Tilthtillers

The dirt track to the Tilthtiller farm was too narrow for *Bertha*, so they left her at the main road and walked. The land on either side of the track was swampy and criss-crossed with drainage ditches. Now and then there was a field of sickly-looking wheat or a small orchard of blighted apple trees. Some skinny goats cropped coarse grass in a pasture.

Nearing the farm they passed hand-painted signs that read NO TRES-PESSERS! and PRIVIT PROPERTY. As they reached the main gate they were greeted by a pair of dogs, who came scuttering out from a kennel and charged at them, snarling savagely. Den and Robert stood stock still while the dogs leapt and barked around them. Teeth snapped. Saliva few. These were mad, scarred hounds whose only job and pleasure in life was scaring away visitors.

'Da . . .'

'Give it a minute, Robert. If them was trained to bite, them'd have done it already.'

From the farmhouse, a ramshackle two-storey clapboard building, a man emerged. He shouted at the dogs to go back to their kennel. The dogs ignored him, so he strode over and booted both of them hard in the ribs. Whimpering, they retreated.

'Yes?' the man said, regarding the two Grubdollars warily. He was sallow-skinned and thin as a reed, with a nervous tic that made his mouth move even when he wasn't speaking.

'Mr Tilthtiller?' said Den.

'Who wants to know? Be you from the Revenue?'

'Does us look like taxmen?'

'No.'

'There you goes then. All us is be a pair of ordinary folk wanting to ask you a couple of questions.'

'About?'

'A plane that crashed on your land.'

Tilthtiller's mouth worked uneasily. 'A plane?'

'Which you sold to Scrapheap Pete.'

'I's no idea what you—'

'Fred!' A woman had appeared on the farmhouse veranda. She was sturdily built, a formidable figure. This had to be the Mrs Tilthtiller whom Scrapheap Pete had mentioned. From behind her skirts a small girl peeped. She was a dead ringer for her mother, except that Mrs Tilthtiller's face resembled a clenched fist while hers was more of an open hand.

'Who be them?' Mrs Tilthtiller demanded.

'No one,' said her husband.

'Then tell they to clear off.'

'Mrs Tilthtiller?' Den called out. He could see who was the driver and who was the passenger in this partnership. 'Your husband's been telling we about a plane wreck him discovered.'

'Fred! What did you say about a plane?'

'N-nothing, dear,' Tilthtiller stammered. 'I didn't say a word about it. Straight up.'

Mrs Tilthtiller came down off the porch like a juggernaut, the girl trailing in her slipstream. One of the dogs strayed into Mrs Tilthtiller's path and she barged it aside like it wasn't there.

'That plane belonged to we fair and square,' she said, thrusting herself into Den's face. 'It came down on our property, meaning by the laws of claim and recovery it were ours to do with as us pleased. I know my rights, Mister whoever-you-are. Of course in the old days it'd've gone straight to the Deacons and us would have earned a tidy sum for it. Instead, us had to make do with a pathetic amount from Scrapheap Pete. But us has done nothing wrong!' She jabbed a pudgy finger at Den. 'So if you's come here thinking to arrest we for selling goods that wasn't ours to sell, you can ruddy well think again.'

'I be'n't a taxman and I certainly be'n't a cop,' Den growled. 'All I wants to know about that plane be, were there anyone on board?'

Mrs Tilthtiller blinked. She glanced at her husband.

'What if there were?' she said.

'A man, maybe?' said Den. 'Middle-aged. Short dark hair. About my height. Probably wearing a dark suit. Winged, of course.'

'Crimson spectacles,' Robert added.

'No, no spectacles,' said Mrs Tilthtiller.

'But there *were* a man matching that description,' said Den.

Mrs Tilthtiller realised, to her dismay, that she had backed herself into a corner. 'Him were . . . well, yes, dark hair. Oldish. In bad shape, too.'

'But alive?'

'Yes. Just. Us didn't know what else to do with he, so us took he to where us knew others of his kind was.'

'The camp,' said Tilthtiller. 'There'm a refugee camp just south of Rivermouth Quay, in the dunes there. That be where my wife took he. I suggested the hospital in town, but her insisted—'

'Him's Airborn!' Mrs Tilthtiller snapped. 'His own kind would know what to do with he, better than our doctors.'

'But a human body be a human body, dear. Wings aside, the Airborn be'n't much different from we.'

'Fred, I said at the time, us could do without the hassle of explaining where him had come from. So dump him at the camp, sell the plane, end of story. No complications that way. *Your* way, us wouldn't have had a plane to sell because rightfully it were his. Besides, doctors and hospitals cost money.'

'But the decent thing to do . . .'

'Oh, bugger your "decent"! Where'm "decent" ever got we? Toiling on this useless plot of land you inherited from your useless da, scratching a living, barely making ends meet.'

'Farming be an honourable trade. And some make money out of it.'

'Only the agro-businesses on the Massif, with all the lamp arrays and other equipment to make the crops grow better.'

'Us can't afford lamp arrays.'

'Us can't afford anything!' Mrs Tilthtiller shrilled. 'That'm just it. Not even nice clothes for Mary-Jane. Us can barely even eat properly.'

Den felt that couldn't be completely true. Mrs Tilthtiller was not a woman who looked like she skimped on her portions.

'Here I be,' she went on, 'trying to come up with ways of earning an extra note or two, and you keep trying to undermine I. Straight up, I doesn't know why I bother.'

'There'm this, Ma,' said the girl. She produced something from a pocket of her dress and held it up. 'Don't forget. Us is going to sell this and pull in some cash, be'n't us?'

What she had in her hands was a disc-shaped, medallion-like object. It was made of silver and had a feather motif embossed on it.

'Put that away, Mary-Jane!'

'But it'm pretty, Ma,' Mary-Jane said. 'You said I could play with it.'

'Play with it indoors. I didn't say you could take it outside with you and wave it around in front of strangers.' Her mother snatched the silver object from her and slipped it into one of her own pockets.

All this happened fast, but not so fast that Den and Robert couldn't tell what the object was.

Den's scalp prickled all over. A Silver Sanctum seal. That clinched it. The Wayfarer was Mr Mordadson's.

'Listen,' he said. 'Thanks for your time. Us shan't trouble you any further.'

'You'm going to report we to the authorities?' said Mrs Tilthtiller. Her tone was aggressive but underneath that there was fear.

I ought to, Den thought. *Ten to one old Mordy didn't just hand over that seal.*

'Nope,' he said. 'Why should I? If you feels you's done nothing wrong, then you's done nothing wrong.'

Mrs Tilthtiller's large chest sank with relief. 'Then I be glad us was able to help you. This man, the Airborn in the plane, him's somebody you knows?'

'A friend. Friend of a friend, really.'

'Well, I hope him's going to be all right.'

'So does I, Mrs Tilthtiller,' said Den. 'So does I.'

CHAPTER 76

The Camp

Khaki army tents dotted the dunes. There looked to be several hundred of them, pitched in clusters, all straining and billowing in the onshore wind. Above, a few solitary Airborn could be seen, hovering on the spot or flying in listless circles.

Lorries delivering supplies had carved a route between the dunes. Den and Robert followed the overlapping tyre tracks in *Bertha* till they came to the entrance to the camp, which was nothing more than an improvised barrier consisting of a long plank of wood suspended between two oildrums. They drew up beside a group of soldiers who were squatting in the lee of one of the larger dunes, out of the wind. If these men were meant to be performing some kind of sentry duty, they didn't look it.

One of them rose to his feet and ambled over to meet *Bertha*. He was a private, barely a couple of years older than Robert, with a bad dose of acne.

Den opened a side window in the driver's pod and leaned out. 'Be you the boss around here?' he called down, trying to keep a note of scepticism out of his voice.

The private looked round at the others, then back. They were all the same rank as him. He'd drawn the short straw and been put in charge. ''Spose,' he said.

'Us'd like to go in.' Den gestured towards the tents. 'Be that OK? Us is looking for someone us knows.'

'In there? With the Airborn?'

'Yep.'

'Well, I be'n't sure about that.' The private screwed up his face, ineffably perplexed. 'Our orders is to oversee the lorries dropping stuff off and make sure it gets distributed properly. Nobody said anything about visitors. Or murk-combers, for that matter.'

'Meaning you can let we through.'

'No, meaning I can't. Surely you can see my point of view? Unless something be mentioned specifically, us has to assume it be'n't allowed.'

The wind was flinging particles of sand into Den's eyes, making them sting. 'That'm how the army works, eh?'

'Pretty much. I could get into all sorts of trouble if you go in and then I find out you wasn't supposed to.'

Den's patience, never in great supply at the best of times, was running low. 'Come on, it'm just the two of we, and us has reason to think there'm a fellow in there who needs our help.'

The private shrugged. 'Orders be orders.'

'Except if those orders doesn't even exist!' Den spat. 'All right, here'm the options. You wave we through, or else us takes this whacking great murk-comber and drives it right over your poxy little gate, and you too if us has to. Then explain *that* to your commanding officer or whoever you has to report to.'

'Us could stop you.'

'Yeah? How?'

'Erm . . .' The private gulped. He couldn't think of a way a handful of lightly armed soldiers could prevent a murk-comber from going anywhere.

'Exactly,' said Den, and engaged gear. *Bertha* let out a purposeful growl.

The private rubbed his face agitatedly, then heaved a sigh and jogged over to the barrier. He slid the plank aside and Den drove through. In the rearview mirror Den saw the private replace the plank, before rejoining his friends beneath the dune. He was trying to look as if he had chosen to let the murk-comber into the camp rather then been forced to, but they just jeered at him and bombarded him with their berets. In the end, all dignity gone, he kicked sand at them and stomped away.

'Just a bunch of kids,' Den said to Robert. 'It'm a babysitting job. They army be'n't going to waste anyone with brains and initiative on a babysitting job.'

They parked out of sight of the soldiers and continued on foot. The first tents they came to were packed with Airborn, as many as twelve of them huddled inside a space designed for four, if that. Their wings left them with even less room to spare. They stared out through the open flaps with haggard, hollow eyes. Many of them were clutching personal effects – pictures, books, valuables – items they'd brought with them from their homes and now clung to for comfort.

Further into the camp, there were cooking fires that smouldered feebly. People were stoking them with driftwood and clumps of dry brush, but the wind and the sand seemed intent on snuffing them out. There were open latrines that reeked horribly, and discarded food cartons littered the ground. Again, eyes followed Den and Robert as they went by, watchful, sullen, mistrustful.

They passed two Airborn children who were squabbling over a toy toucan. It belonged to one of them, the other wanted it. The fight turned vicious, but none of the adults stirred themselves to break it up. Den stepped in and pulled the biting, kicking, wing-grabbing opponents apart. He handed the toucan back to its owner and sent both children on their way with a glare and a growl.

He and Robert walked on, with mounting disbelief. The refugees looked grubby and forlorn, not like Airborn at all. Never had they seen so many pairs of wings that drooped so low, like sails with no breeze to fill them. Everywhere in the camp there was squalor and shabbiness. Was this really the best that Westward Territories government could do for these people? Apparently so.

Then one of the Airborn yelled out: 'Who are you? Are you here to gloat?'

Another Airborn joined in. 'Nice to look *down* on us for a change, isn't it?'

The cry was taken up by a man flying overhead. 'Come and see the Ascended Ones living in misery. Come and laugh. Bring your emu friends.'

All around Den and Robert, the discontent simmered and boiled.

'Them thinks us is some sort of . . . of ghoulish tourists,' Robert murmured to his father.

'Don't let it get to you, son. It be'n't personal. Them's hungry and scared and just lashing out.'

'But what if them gets physical?'

'I doubt it'll come to that, and if it does, us'll be more than a match for they.'

'If you say so.'

'I does.'

In the most densely populated part of the camp Den came to a halt. Raising his hands and his voice, he addressed the Airborn around him.

'Everybody, please, listen to I. My son and I is here on business, no other reason than that. Us is looking for a fellow name of Mordadson. Him were brought here a day or two ago, injured from a plane crash. You must know who I's talking about. One of you? Someone? Anyone?'

Surly muttering followed. Finally a young woman spoke up. 'He's not far from here. What do you want with him?'

'To help he.'

The young woman studied Den's face and judged that he was sincere. 'I'll take you.'

She led the two Grubdollars down through the dunes. The ground levelled out, the dunes flattened, and soon they were at the shore. Here, above the high tide mark, several tents had been hung out flat on top of poles made of driftwood, forming shelters without sides. The wind was stronger here but the beach was damp from the receding tide so there was less loose sand flying about.

These shelters were plainly being used as a makeshift hospital, and the reason for their open sides became clear to Den and Robert as soon as they got close. Beneath the flapping canvas, pallid-looking people were laid out on blankets, head to foot. Some were groaning and shaking, others lying insensible and still. The stench of vomit and diarrhoea coming off them made Den and Robert gag. It would have been much worse, suffocatingly awful, had they been in an enclosed space.

'So many of us are getting ill,' the woman said. 'It isn't ground-sickness. Perhaps it's a Groundling bug that we don't have immunity to, or the unsanitary conditions we're having to live in. Or perhaps it's simply the shock of being displaced like this. They get put here because we don't know what else to do with them. There's maybe three doctors who got out from Hope's Summit, no more than that, and they're run ragged trying to treat everyone. We've asked the soldiers for medicine but nothing seems to be coming. If we don't get any soon, there'll be deaths.'

'No wonder you lot be so unhappy,' said Den. 'I wish us Groundlings was doing more for you.'

The woman shrugged sadly. 'Me too. He's over there, anyway, the man you're looking for.'

She led them the last shelter in line. In the corner, a dark-clad figure lay curled up in a ball. The two Grubdollars went to him. Den hunkered down beside him.

'Mordadson?' he said softly. 'Mr Mordadson?'

Eyelids flickered. Opened. Eyes peered from an almost unrecognisably swollen and bruised face.

'Den?' It was barely a whisper.

'None other.'

'What . . . what are you doing here?'

'I could ask the same of you.'

Mr Mordadson offered a thin sketch of a smile that faded fast.

'It's the end of the world,' he said, 'and I couldn't stop it. I didn't even get close.'

'None of that now,' said Den. 'Us has come to get you out of here.'

'No. Leave me. There's no point.'

'Sorry,' said Den, 'but you doesn't get much say in the matter.' He slid

572

his hands under Mr Mordadson and lifted him up. Mr Mordadson was barely conscious, but even as dead weight, to Den he was no more effort to carry than a child.

The walk back to *Bertha* turned into a kind of procession. Den strode along with the limp form of Mr Mordadson in his arms. Behind him came Robert and the young Airborn woman. Behind them, other Airborn began to fall in line. The sight of a Groundling carrying one of their own drew them in. They were intrigued. Where was the man taking him? Why? They were touched as well. A Groundling who was concerned for the welfare of one of them? Who seemed to care? Remarkable.

By the time Den reached *Bertha*, he had a large crowd following him. Having deposited Mr Mordadson on a bench in the loading bay, he turned round to the refugees. The mood among them had changed. They were looking at him not with resentment any more but with respect.

'Take us with you!' one of them implored.

'Get us out of here!' cried another.

Others joined in the chorus.

Den held up his hands to quieten them. 'I wish I could take you all somewhere else,' he said, 'but *Bertha* be'n't big enough – and where would us go? I promise, though, that whatever I can do to improve your situation, I'll do. I know people – people who knows people. I be'n't a big wheel but I be a useful cog that helps turns the big wheels. Just hang in there, be patient. This be'n't going to last for ever. You has my word on that.'

The refugees watched *Bertha* rumble off. They had come down from Hope's Summit. Now, in the depths of their despair, they felt a tingle of something like hope again.

In the driver's pod, Robert asked, 'Where to next, Da?'

'The nearest telegraph bureau. I needs to send a message.'

'Us is getting involved in Airborn doings again, be'n't us?'

Den chuckled. 'Let's face it, with our track record it'd be surprising if us wasn't.'

CHAPTER 77

Miss Rampelsdaughter's Attitude
Towards Helicopters

Michael watched from an upstairs window as more and more of the Maddened encircled the Vortex V. He recognised several faces, twisted in hate though they were. There were the Kokavielsons from next door, whom he'd never thought of as anything but a sweet old couple. There was Mr Samandirielson from across the way, whose daughter Pancia he had dated when they were in their teens. There was Miss Rampelsdaughter from a few houses along, a crabby, neurotic spinster who was forever complaining to the authorities about the traffic on the street and particularly about the noise of helicopters landing and taking off. For years she'd been trying to get all non-fixed-wing aircraft banned from the neighbourhood, a campaign which Michael took as a personal attack, with some justification. Miss Rampelsdaughter had never liked him, not since the time he and Az, as kids, had leant an open bottle against her front door, knocked and run away. It had been a harmless enough prank – except that the bottle had been filled with water and had drenched Miss Rampelsdaughter's shoes when she opened the door. She'd been unable to find out who the culprits were but she'd had her suspicions and had regarded the Gabrielson boys, the elder one especially, with sniffy contempt ever since.

Now she was among the Maddened crowd jostling and clawing to get at the Vortex V. The sound of its engine, raucous in the silence of the city, had drawn them from all quarters. More and more were arriving by the minute. And the more that came, the less chance Michael had of getting to the helicopter himself. In point of fact, it was hopeless. The Vortex V was an island amid a lake of heaving, shoving, thrusting bodies. Reaching it on foot was out of the question, and even if he'd still had wings, he'd have had to fly in under the rotors and try to wrestle the cockpit door open against the crush of Maddened pressing against it. The likelihood of pulling off that stunt unscathed? Zero.

All he could do was look as the stationary chopper roared, wasting fuel while its blades spun uselessly. How long till the tank ran dry? An hour, no more than that. At which point the Maddened would lose interest, but of course then the helicopter would be of no use.

Meanwhile, downstairs, Aurora was in the throes of labour. He couldn't get her out of here to a hospital; nor could he fly to fetch help.

Michael ground his teeth and beat his fist against the wall.

'Michael?' His father appeared beside him. 'Are you all right?'

'Oh just great. Super. Never better.' He sighed. 'Sorry. Didn't mean to be sarcastic. I'm all right. How's Aurora doing?'

'Fine. The contractions have stopped.'

'Stopped? Isn't that a bad sign?'

'According to your mother, no. It sometimes happens. There are lulls and then it all starts again. At least it means Aurora can have a rest. She's asleep right now, with your mother watching over her. You should probably try and get some rest too.'

'Not a chance. Couldn't if I tried.'

'I know. I feel the same.' Gabriel Enochson glanced out of the window, wincing at what he saw. 'Look at them. You say Naoutha Nisrocsdaughter's behind this? Why? I mean, how could someone want to turn innocent people into . . . *that*?'

'I don't know. She's crazy.'

'A crazy person making more crazy people like herself. There's a sort of logic to that.'

'How come you didn't get out of town, Dad? Patrollers were evacuating people.'

'They didn't get this far. In any case, your mother wouldn't leave. The first glimpse she had of those things out there roaming the street, she told me to close the shutters and board up the door. I tried to convince her that we could fly out but at our age neither of us is a great flyer any more. We have to stop for rests if we're going any distance, and that would leave us vulnerable to . . . them. Anyway, Ramona wouldn't even consider it. She insisted we'd be safer if we stay put. She said the Patrollers would soon sort it out. So what was I to do? I couldn't leave her. And now, alas, we're trapped here, and so are you.'

Michael looked forlornly at the Vortex V. 'Yeah, looks that way. I mean, I could probably . . .'

His father knew what he was going to say. 'No, you couldn't. They'd get you. I've seen it happen. Miss Rampelsdaughter out there, I watched her come out of her house earlier to yell at a couple of the creatures. She had no idea what they were and what they could do. She just thought they were rowdies come to disturb the peace and quiet of her street. I shouted from the window, trying to warn her, but she didn't hear. They fell on her, bit her, and now . . . Well, there she is. Part of the pack. As bad as any of them. In fact, look at her. What's she up to?'

Outside, Miss Rampelsdaughter had managed to clamber up on the shoulders of the other Maddened. Her features, normally etched with disapproval, were now a howling mask of rage. It was as if all her feelings about helicopters had boiled to the surface in uncontrollable loathing. Perhaps, in some vague way, she even knew the Vortex V was Michael's, giving her twice the reason to despise it. She scrambled across the top of the throng of Maddened on her hands and knees, desperate to get at the noise-making machine. Just beneath the rotors, she rose up in order to launch herself head-first at it, lifting her wings for balance.

Michael and his father realised what was coming, but neither of them could avert his gaze in time.

Miss Rampelsdaughter's wings got snarled in the whirling blades. She was snatched up and spun around in a blinding blur. Once, twice, three times she circled, flailing helplessly, and then her foot became caught in the hub of the rotors, and there was a crunch that could be heard even above the sound of the Vortex V's engine, and a scream, and blood sprayed across the crowd. The blades still spun, and Miss Rampelsdaughter's leg was ground to mincemeat as she was dragged in towards their whirring centre. Suddenly her whole body wrapped around the rotor mast and was reduced to mangled shreds. Then came a sickening shriek of metal. The mast tilted at a sharp angle, and the blade tips struck the pavement and the blades themselves crumpled and snapped. Shards of metal hurled in all directions. Several struck the fuselage. There swiftly followed an explosion. The Vortex V rocked on her undercarriage. Flames bloomed outward, scorching through the Maddened, incinerating many of them where they stood. The rest reeled away in primal dread. There was a second, larger explosion. The window in front of Michael and his father shuddered in its frame. The helicopter jumped up; came down on its side, a mass of burning glass and metal. Fire billowed from the wreckage, sending black smoke churning into the sky. Around it, charred bodies lay sprawled in contorted poses. Some of the Maddened, seared all over but still living, writhed on the ground. Some, with their wings flaring like torches, staggered to the pavement's edge and plunged over. The rest milled in panic.

Michael and his father exchanged grim, disbelieving looks.

'Well,' he said, 'there you have it, Dad. No more chopper. Our goose is well and truly cooked.'

His father slowly nodded, then started shaking his head.

'Not necessarily,' he said.

'What do you mean?'

Gabriel Enochson gave a thin, unsteady smile. 'I think your inventor of a dad may just have had a brainwave.'

CHAPTER 78

Troublesome Telegram

Inspector Gavin Treadwell lit his pipe, as he was wont to do countless times a day but especially in moments of tension or when deep thought was required.

The telegram before him on the desk qualified on both fronts. It was from Den Grubdollar and it read:

```
AIRBORN IN REFUGEE CAMPS SUFFERING + STOP + DEATHS
POSSIBLE + STOP + PLEASE ASSIST HOWEVER YOU CAN +
STOP +
```

Beneath that were the time and date of transmission, earlier that afternoon, and the name of the telegraph bureau of origin, Rivermouth Quay.

Treadwell looked over at the boy who had brought the slip of paper up from the police station lobby, where it had been delivered by a runner from the Craterhome central telegraph bureau. Toby Nimblenick was standing expectantly on the other side of the desk, waiting to be consulted.

'Well?' said Treadwell.

'Well what, Mr Treadwell?'

'I be assuming you took a peek at the message on your way up here.'

'I handed it to you folded, guv.'

'That means nothing.'

Toby gave a guilty wince. 'I may have happened to glance at a couple of the words. But I be'n't much of a reader.'

'Keep going to school and you will be. What's you reckon?'

'About school? Not much, but you said if I doesn't stick it out you'll arrest I once a day every day for the rest of my life, so . . .' He shrugged. 'School be lovely.'

'I meant about Den's message.'

'Oh! Well, I'll tell you what my first thought were.'

'Yes?' said Treadwell.

'It be'n't from he. It'm a con job. That posh bloke, Jasper Longnoble-Thingummy, him sent it, pretending to be Den.'

'Why's you say that?'

'For starters, it doesn't read like Den speaks.'

'But that'm the case with all telegrams,' Treadwell pointed out. 'Usually the telegrapher helps you compose the message, keeping the words to a minimum. It'm a very impersonal form of communication. And then, more importantly, there'm the question of motive. What's Longnoble-Drumblood stand to gain from sending it?'

'Him's hoping you'd do something like send back a reply asking what Den be doing in Rivermouth Quay when you thought him was in, you know, wherever. Some other place. Then Longnoble-Thingummy would know where the Grubdollars really be and him could go get they.'

'Cunning, Toby, very cunning.' Treadwell blew out a plume of smoke as a sign of approval. 'You has a devious mind.'

'Thank you, guv, I know.'

'That'm the kind of reasoning I employs you for.'

'My "insight into the logic of a wrongdoer", be'n't that what you called it?'

'In this instance, though,' Treadwell said, 'I think you'm wrong. Longnoble-Drumblood might well have thought of sending I a bogus telegram, for the reasons you's given, but him'd never have come up with contents like this. Him'd have said something along the lines of 'Be it safe to come out of hiding yet?' I doubt him has the imagination to have brought the refugee situation into it. Him doesn't strike me as the imaginative sort. No, this seems genuine to I. Den *would* care about the plight of the Airborn.'

'Care enough to break cover and ask you for help? Even though it could put he and his family at risk?'

'I think so. You know that him has Airborn friends.'

'Friends? Az'm practically a Grubdollar.'

'Exactly. So now, having established this message be really from Den, what us must ask ourselves be . . .'

'. . . what can us do?' Toby finished. He scratched his head. 'It'm a puzzler. I mean, me personally, I can't do a thing. I be no one. And you? You's a well respected Craterhome copper but you be'n't really, what'm the word? Influential. No offence meant.'

'None taken. You'm right. Such authority as I has be to do with investigating serious crimes in this city. I be'n't in government. I be'n't "connected" in any way. The refugee crisis be a countrywide matter. It'm massive. I appreciates the faith Den has in I but I could no sooner fix a problem that big than I could scrub the clouds from the sky.'

'Besides, you'm very busy already. You's got work piling up to your ar—' Toby checked himself.

'Toby.'

'Armpits,' Toby finished, as if that was what he'd been going to say all along.

Treadwell eyed the half-metre-high stack of documents in the in-tray on his desk and the second, even taller stack on the floor: files, case folders, witness reports, forms to be completed. Most of it related to the Dominic Slamshaft affair, which was a paperwork highway he thought he was never going to get to the end of.

'Too true,' he said, his lips curling sourly around the pipe stem. 'On the other hand, I hold Den in very high regard. Him's a man of integrity. Him and his family helped stop a war, dammit. And them's paid a heavy price for that. I reckon I owes he one.'

'I does too,' said Toby. 'Without he I'd never have met you, and without you I'd still be a street pickpocket, sleeping rough. Whereas now I be going to school every morning, living in a hostel, earning a pittance as a police inspector's errand boy . . .'

'But making a valuable contribution to society.'

'Those was going to be my very next words, Mr Treadwell,' Toby said with a sly grin. 'But even though you be willing to help, and so be I for that matter, it comes back down to the same question as before. What can the likes of we actually do?'

'It'm been troubling I ever since I first heard about the refugees,' Treadwell said. 'I can honestly say I's lain awake at night wondering how it can be sorted out. *Something* ought to be done, but what?'

He sat back and puffed on his pipe for several minutes, filling his office with aromatic fumes. Toby, while he pondered the matter too, practised rolling a coin to and fro across his knuckles then making it magically vanish into thin air. Treadwell had suggested he learn a few conjuring tricks like this in order to keep his hands busy. Agile, dextrous, pilfering fingers such as Toby's needed something to occupy them, lest they give in to temptation.

'Hmm,' said Treadwell.

'What?' said Toby, flipping the coin and holding his shirt pocket open so that the one plopped neatly into the other.

'My old mentor, Sergeant Archerfine – you know what him used to say?'

'Don't smoke so much, it'll turn your fingertips yellow?'

'No-o-o. And him didn't say I should take any cheek from minors either. What him *did* say was, if you's collared a suspect and you knows him's guilty but can't prove it, make as though you has some damning piece of evidence. Don't let on what it be. Leave the suspect stew for a while, thinking you's got he bang to rights. Nine times out of ten, him'll break eventually and confess.'

'I doesn't see how that applies here. The refugee camps be'n't a crime, for one thing.'

'Be'n't them?' said Treadwell, raising an eyebrow.

'Not as I understands it. Them's terrible, straight up. The Airborn be'n't getting treated fairly and squarely. The opposite. But a crime as in a felony . . . ?'

'There'm such a thing as criminal negligence.'

'Eh?'

'Put it this way, our government surely has a duty of care to these people who's fetched up here with we on the ground through no fault of their own. Somebody comes cap in hand to you, in desperate need – you does all you can for him, doesn't you?'

'I suppose so.'

'You does, Toby,' Treadwell said firmly. 'And I doesn't believe the Westward Territories government *be* doing all it can.'

'Some of the politicians'd rather us did nothing at all, just leave the Airborn to rot.'

'Precisely. So what'm needed be someone to suggest to they that them ought to be aiding the Airborn because them's breaking the law otherwise.'

'That someone being you, yes?'

Treadwell nodded.

'But there be'n't any such law.'

Treadwell nodded again. 'But by calling the authorities' bluff, I goad they into action.'

'Or else you gets stomped on. Folk who sticks their necks out often gets their heads lopped off.'

'I be aware of the risks. What I's contemplating is the kind of thing that could end a man's career, just like that.' He snapped his fingers. 'But it'm got to be done anyway. And I need your help.'

'What can I do, guv?'

Treadwell outlined what he had in mind. Toby liked the idea of it very much indeed. The inspector's plan needed to be set in motion straight away, so Toby raced off out of the police station, chortling with glee.

Treadwell took out his tobacco pouch and lit a fresh pipe. He was glad he had made the effort to locate Toby after the Slamshaft affair and take the boy under his wing. In much the same way that Sergeant Archerfine had saved the young Gavin Treadwell from a downward spiral into criminality and put him on the road to reform, he himself was trying to save Toby and, he felt, succeeding. He was passing the favour on to another generation. He had hopes that under his tutelage Toby would, in time, become a productive citizen. A cop even. Or was that raising the bar a little too high?

His fellow officers insisted he was on a hiding to nothing, and complained to him whenever some small item went missing around the station, laying the blame on the most obvious culprit. Treadwell, however, was convinced that Toby was innocent; the items had been mislaid, not stolen. And more often than not they turned up again and he was proved right. Toby was no thief any more. He was trying very hard to do good.

If Treadwell's scheme worked and all went well, Toby would do a great deal of good.

And if it didn't, at least no harm would befall the lad.

Treadwell wished he could say the same about himself.

CHAPTER 79

The Fledging Of Jasper Longnoble-Drumblood

Longnoble-Drumblood lay panting on the floor, slick with sweat and blood.

He had never known such pain. The worst was over now. All that remained was a dull, creaky ache between his shoulderblades. But the past few hours had been gruelling. He didn't want to go through anything like that ever again. None of the techniques he'd been taught in the army for withstanding torture had been any use. The agony was beyond anything he could have imagined, deep-seated and remorseless, and neither chanting repetitive phrases nor imagining himself in another place had made a scrap of difference.

He'd not even been able to use screaming as a vent for his distress. Just as the pain had begun to become intolerable, the Gabrielson boy had heard his cries and come to snoop around. Longnoble-Drumblood had been within a whisker of getting caught, at a moment when he'd been completely vulnerable. Only the presence of that cat in the corridor outside had saved him.

Thereafter, to keep noise to a minimum, he'd rolled up a strip torn off his shirt and bitten down on it. The rope-like piece of shirt was now chewed to ribbons but it had done the trick.

He felt exhausted. Beyond exhausted. All but empty.

But it had worked. The genomorph serum had worked. Professor Emeritus had successfully re-created Professor Metier's original compound, and Longnoble-Drumblood had injected himself with a sample of it taken from the freezer cabinet. The results were plain to see. Clambering to his knees, Longnoble-Drumblood looked over his right shoulder, then his left.

The wings were magnificent. They arched behind him, broad and white. Every feather was there, perfectly in place, nestling neatly against its neighbour. He stroked them. They felt petal-smooth.

These things had come out of *him*. It seemed almost inconceivable. They were his, a part of him. He was new now. Forever different. The thought would have made Longnoble-Drumblood's head spin, were it not spinning already from tiredness and the ordeal of the transformation.

He tottered upright. The wings arched a little, as if to assist him. He didn't consciously move them. They did it of their own accord.

Holding a workbench for support, he leaned sideways experimentally. One wing stretched out to compensate for the imbalance. He could feel unfamiliar muscles in his back working stiffly. These were the same muscles he would have to learn to operate by effort of will if he was to learn to fly. There had been little in Metier's journal about this particular aspect of the process. He would just have to figure it out for himself.

He tried. At first all he did was manage to lift his shoulders a lot and wave his arms up and down. He couldn't get to grips with where the wing muscles were and how they meshed with his body's pre-existing muscles.

He let out a grunt of frustration. Then he caught sight of his reflection in the polished steel door of a storage cupboard. Another Jasper Long-noble-Drumblood stared back, a strange, almost unrecognisable version of himself. The wings altered everything. They added height, breadth, status. Power.

He studied his bare torso. His chest seemed larger, his sternum slightly more prominent. He turned round to look at the wings themselves. The flesh around their roots was raw and swollen. Beneath the skin, the new muscles bulged.

He stepped back and, concentrating hard and using his reflection as a guide, urged one wing to flap. In the cabinet door, the reflection's wing twitched.

He tried again. The twitch became a definite up-then-down action.

Gradually the new muscles started to make sense. It was like learning a new language. No, simpler than that. A new alphabet. He began to understand how they fitted in with the others. For a downstroke of the wings, one set came into play. For an upstroke, another.

The transition between using the two sets grew smoother and smoother. The wings – his wings – flapped with increasing confidence, increasing strength. They made a pleasing *whoosh* and *whoomph* as they beat the air.

Soon he could move them without having to think too hard about it. It began to feel natural, as natural as walking or gesturing.

It wasn't until he happened to check his reflection, and couldn't find it any more, that Longnoble-Drumblood realised he was aloft. He had risen off the floor. His eyeline was no longer level with the storage cupboard.

He was hovering with at least a metre of clearance beneath his feet, his head close to the ceiling.

He started laughing.

Deliriously.

Triumphantly.

Horribly.

CHAPTER 80

The Human Key

Toby Nimblenick, despite all his efforts to turn over a new leaf, had not yet severed all connections with his past.

It had been only a couple of months, after all, since Inspector Tread-well had persuaded him to give up picking pockets and go straight. That was after years of street-thievery, a whole of lifetime of it indeed. He couldn't be expected to make the change that quickly, could he? Nor could he be expected to abandon the friends and associates he'd known from before, not altogether. That wouldn't be right or natural.

Treadwell was aware that Toby still hung out from time to time with members of 'the criminal fraternity'. That was what he called them, 'the criminal fraternity'. It made them sound quite grand, like they all belonged to some kind of club, or even a family. The truth was drabber than that. There was no wide-ranging underworld brotherhood that lived by a shared code and protected its own. Something like that would require trust, honesty, faith in your fellow man – and crooks did not have those qualities. That was why they were crooks.

There were places, however, where crooks were apt to gather. Pubs mainly – the grubbiest, seediest, scabbiest, scuzziest dives in all of Craterhome, tucked away in alleys where no sane citizen travelled after dark or even during the day. Crooks drank in these dim and dingy watering-holes and talked shop, swapping stories and exchanging tips. They discussed the jobs they had pulled or were about to pull, the wallets they had lifted, the homes burgled, the safes cracked, the cons perpe-trated, the stolen goods fenced, the dodgy wares peddled. They did this safe from fear of being overheard by someone who might be appalled by these tales and go running to the police.

Treadwell knew Toby was a familiar face in such drinking dens. He had instructed him to visit as many of them as he could, looking for a certain man.

The man's name was Terry 'The Human Key' Sharptouch, a safecracker of extraordinary skill and dexterity, someone to whom any form of security device was a puzzle he could unscramble within seconds. Doors opened like magic to Terry Sharptouch. The tumblers of the most complicated combination lock danced under his fingers. Bank vaults swung wide for him. Padlocks fell apart in his hand.

He was wanted in connection with a dozen robberies on the pending-case file and suspected of involvement in least twenty more. He had made himself rich enough, however, to bribe his way out of trouble, in common with a lot of crooks in Craterhome. The talent that enabled The Human Key to undo locks and steal whatever they were supposed to be protecting gave him the financial wherewithal to open up policemen's wallets and place money inside.

Toby scoured the Third Borough for him, making forays into the Second and Sixth as well. He visited all the pubs he knew, The Coshman's Arms, The Blowtorch And Jemmy, The Fawney-Drop, The Bolthole, and so on. In some he was less welcome than in others. 'Go back to the cop shop!' he was often told, and he was called a ratfink and a turncoat and a lot of even less complimentary names. Just as often, though, some old-timer would offer to buy him a drink – a half-measure, of course, watered down – and congratulate him on trying to straighten out. 'A life of crime be'n't all it'm cracked up to be, young Toby,' these generous, sentimental souls might say. 'I'd've got out myself, if I'd had the opportunity you's had.'

Eventually Toby tracked down Sharptouch at the bar of The Blagger's Rest. He tapped him on the shoulder and requested a quiet word. In a darkened nook of the pub, he slipped Sharptouch a ten-note which Treadwell had given him out of petty cash. In his back pocket another four tens waited, snugly folded.

'What'm this about, lad?' Sharptouch demanded, making the tenner disappear with a flick of his fingers. The Human Key had thin, straggly hair, some of which he combed sideway across the top of his head to make it look as though he had more of it than he did.

'A favour,' said Toby.

'Ah, for your friend the policeman, no doubt. And how be dear Inspector Treadwell? Can't be much a life, being just about the only straight copper in Craterhome. Must get lonely for he.'

'Him's in fine fettle,' Toby replied, 'and yes, the favour'm for Treadwell. It'm very simple. Him'd like you to claim you's stolen something you hasn't.'

Sharptouch cackled. 'What? Own up to something I's never done?

While there'm a hundred things I *has* done that I'd never dream of owning up to? That'm absurd. Why? What would I get out of it?'

'For one thing, a bit more money from I. For another, an amnesty.' Inspector Treadwell had had to coach Toby over that difficult word. Even so, he still had trouble pronouncing it. 'An amnesty on all your crimes that'm still under investigation.'

Surprise, bafflement, scepticism, rippled across Sharptouch's face in waves.

'Treadwell be offering to wipe the slate clean for you,' Toby went on. 'All those outstanding warrants for your arrest, all those unsolved cases that you be in the frame for, all those potential jail sentences that'm hanging over your head – them can all be made to vanish, just like that. The files'll disappear like they were never there. You gets to walk away scot-free.'

'But I be'n't bothered about any of that,' said The Human Key with a dismissive sniff. 'I pays my dues like everyone else. As long as I keep the right palms greased, I's never going to see the inside of a prison cell in my life.'

'But imagine what it'd be like not to have to keep coughing up to the rozzers. Imagine how much more cash you'd have in your pocket every week. Think about that.'

Sharptouch stroked his chin with his long, slender, almost delicate fingers, the same fingers that could coax a strongbox into giving up its contents with just a few caresses of the lock dial.

'I can't deny,' he said, 'that I'd be a lot better off. Paying my regular bribes be a huge drain on my resources. Sometimes I has to pull off a job simply so as I can keep up with the kickbacks. Ordinary working citizens has taxes to cope with. Us crooks has the police.'

'There you be, then,' said Toby. 'Treadwell be giving you a tax break.'

'When you puts it like that . . .' said Sharptouch, nodding. 'All right. So what'm involved?'

'All you has to do be put it about that, during one of your recent jobs, you's uncovered a document.'

'What sort of document?'

'The minutes of a closed-session meeting at City Hall.'

'City Hall!' Sharptouch exclaimed. 'I'd never break into there. Them hasn't a thing worth taking, and them barely even locks their doors besides. It'd be like raiding a nursery for sweets. A cracksman of my stature . . . !'

'But try to pretend you did,' said Toby, 'and let everyone know that the minutes of this meeting contained a specific claim about the Airborn refugee camps.'

'About the . . . ? What's *them* have to do with anything?'

'Just go along with this, Mr Sharptouch, please.'

'All right, all right,' Sharptouch grumbled. 'The refugee camps. What about they?'

Toby outlined the wording of this nonexistent document. He got Sharptouch to repeat what he'd said back to him several times, till he had it exactly right. Then he handed over the remaining four ten-notes in his pocket, which The Human Key again made disappear with a flick of his fingers.

'You need to promise to I that you'll do this,' Toby said.

'On my honour, I will,' said Sharptouch.

Toby knew that a thief's honour was not worth much. 'Swear by the tools of your trade.'

Sharptouch looked at him askance. 'You doesn't want much, eh, lad? Only the most serious oath a fellow in our line of work can make.'

'Go on,' said Toby. 'Swear.'

The Human Key spat on his palm, wiggled his fingers, rubbed both hands together, and said, 'I, Terry Sharptouch, do solemnly swear on the tools of my trade that I shall do as young master Toby Nimblenick requests.'

'And I swear back,' said Toby, copying the spitting, wiggling and rubbing action, 'that Inspector Treadwell will dispose of all casework relating to your past felonies.'

'It don't mean as much, you being out of the trade now,' said Sharptouch. 'But still, I accept. Your policeman pal, though, him's not going to make himself very popular with this, be him? Several of his colleagues be going to sorely miss the extra income them gets from I.'

'Inspector Treadwell be'n't in it for the popularity,' said Toby, with some pride. 'Him's in it to do what'm right.'

CHAPTER 81

Chief Superintendent Coldriser

The next morning, Inspector Treadwell rapped on the door to Chief Superintendent Coldriser's office.

'Come!'

He entered, bracing himself for the reek of Chief Superintendent Coldriser's cologne. It filled the room with a floral miasma, eye-wateringly pungent. Anywhere else in the station, you could smell the chief superintendent coming a good twenty seconds before he arrived. The scent preceded him like a breeze before a thunderstorm.

'Ah, Gavin,' Coldriser said, looking up from a sheaf of telegrams. All of them were printed on pale blue paper, signifying that they were messages that had come via the constabulary's internal wire service, the system by which each branch of the Territories police force was kept up to date with what the other branches were doing. Apart from the telegrams, a blotter, and an ornamental fountain pen and inkwell, the chief superintendent's desktop was otherwise remarkably clear.

'Take a seat,' Coldriser said, with a nod of the head. His slicked-down, centre-parted hair shone like pure jet. 'This is a coincidence. I've just been reading some extraordinary reports from various of the provincial forces, and they seem to involve your friends the Grubdollars.'

'What, Den and Robert? Funny you should mention that, sir, because—'

Coldriser waved a hand. 'No, no, not them. Another two, the girl and the other brother.'

'Cassie and Fletcher. Really.'

'Yes. It all starts in Easterntip, where they were missing at sea for a while and then turned up in some sort of oceangoing vehicle. Never heard the like of it before. Huge thing, and it doesn't sail like a ship, it goes along on wheels. They did some damage with it, although as I understand it that's par for the course for the Grubdollars, doing damage. The locals are upset about that but what they're truly incensed about is an unpaid bar tab, of all things. Apparently the brother, this Fletcher fellow, went off in the vehicle without coughing up for a sizeable round of drinks at a pub.'

'Fletcher did a runner?'

'Yes, and the landlord is mad keen to prosecute. That was three days ago but, being far-flung Easterntip, it's taken a while for the report to come through. And now, as of just this very morning . . .' Coldriser shuffled through the messages. 'Yes, here we go. The same vehicle has made an appearance off the coast at Blackcrab Lee. The police there have had several eyewitness reports of it arising from the waves. Some of the more, ahem, credulous locals mistook it for a sea monster, but reliable sources say it's a vast wheeled vehicle. It's still sitting there just offshore, as far as I can gather. I thought you told me that the Grubdollars were lying low.'

'Them was,' said Treadwell. 'But not any more, obviously. And in fact, it'm in connection with they that I's come to talk to you.'

'You knew of this vehicle?'

'No, this'm the first I's heard of it. The other two Grubdollars, though, has recently got in touch with I. Them's drawn my attention to the situation in the Airborn refugee camps. Them's very concerned about it.'

'Ah yes, a bad business,' said Coldriser, with not much depth of feeling. 'Terrible. Somebody should do something.'

'I agree, sir.' Treadwell steeled himself for what he had to say next. Ideally he'd have had his pipe to hand, to help steady his nerves, but the chief superintendent did not permit smoking in his office. It was bad for the lungs he said, although Treadwell thought it couldn't be any worse than breathing in that much cologne every day.

'As it happens,' he said, 'somebody *be* doing something. Or be about to, at any rate.'

Coldriser cocked an eyebrow. 'Really?'

'Yes, sir. Me.'

'You personally are going to take some supplies to these people, is that it? Good for you. I'm all for a bit of charity and initiative. I'll authorise a short leave of absence for you, if you like. And if it's a little financial support you're after . . .' The chief superintendent delved a hand into his pocket.

'No, sir, thank you. It be'n't anything like that. What I's going to do, actually, is launch an investigation into the activities of the Craterhome civic council.'

'You . . . what?' Coldriser's jaw dropped. 'Did I hear you right? An investigation?'

'That'm right, sir, a criminal investigation. I has reason to believe that the civic council, and the mayor himself, be aware that them's bound by law to give the refugees all possible aid and assistance, even though them's not doing so. All the camps that'm within the jurisdiction of Craterhome and environs ought to be receiving every last scrap of food, water and medicine that the city can muster. It'm on the statute books.'

'It is?'

'One of the oldest, longest-standing by-laws us has, sir, states that "In times of dire need special dispensation shall be made for the indigent and displaced, such that they shall want for naught and be deprived of none of the necessities for healthy living." I looked it up in the station library. It'm an obligation that the city's ruling class has to follow, and right now them appears to be shirking it. At any rate, them's paying lip service to it and doing the bare minimum for the Airborn.'

'But – but it's an ancient, obscure by-law. The civic council could hardly be expected to know of it. Besides, it doesn't strictly speaking apply here.'

'Why so?'

'Because it doesn't mention the Airborn.'

'But it doesn't *not* mention them either, sir. And if these refugees doesn't fit the description of "displaced" and "in dire need", I doesn't know who does.'

'So City Hall isn't abiding fully by the law of the land,' said Coldriser tersely. 'That's an oversight on their part, perhaps, but hardly worthy of our attention. We've plenty of other fish to fry.'

'With all due respect, sir, I have evidence that the council *be* aware of the law and have chosen to ignore it.'

Coldriser's eyebrows shot up. 'Is that so?'

'Several informants of mine has told I that a notorious safecracker, name of Terry Sharptouch, uncovered minutes of a closed-session council meeting in which several officials, including the mayor, explicitly rejected the by-law. Them said the city don't have the funds or the manpower to do what'm expected of it.'

'You have proof of this?' asked the chief superintendent.

Treadwell looked him straight in the eye. 'I has the word of informants who's never provided unreliable or false information before. If you like I could get they on record, saying that that'm what they heard Sharptouch say.'

Coldriser thought for a moment. 'These are serious allegations, Inspector.'

'The refugee situation be a serious business, sir. A terrible one, too, to use your own word.'

'But you can't prosecute a case against the Craterhome council, this city's ruling elite, on the strength of – of hearsay.'

'No, sir, but I be willing to try.'

'But the shame of it.' Coldriser's face was turning an unhealthy shade of pink. 'It would reflect very badly on everyone. Including me. You may not realise it but I have friends on the council. The mayor is a member of the same gentlemen's club as me. I've had dinner at his house. Several times.'

Treadwell in fact knew all this. He knew it very well indeed.

Coldriser stared at him. 'And for an inspector on my own force to start bandying about this sort of accusation . . .'

'It would make you look very bad, Chief Superintendent. I understand that. It would put you in an unenviable position.'

'Not just me, not just me. Relations between City Hall and the police department have been very cordial for years, thanks in large part to my own efforts. I've worked hard to maintain a decent level of council funding for us. The mayor himself is aware that the force doesn't have the cleanest of reputations, nor the most impressive of clear-up rates. Time and again he and the council have threatened to withhold money if we don't sort out our act, and time and again I've managed to convince them not to. They want to incentivise us into being more honest by slashing our budget.'

'But budget slashing would have the reverse effect,' said Treadwell. 'Cut police salaries, and most officers will just make up the shortfall by taking more and bigger bribes.'

'Precisely the argument I've made, over and over. For years it's been my skilful, nuanced diplomacy that's kept the council on our side . . . and now you'd like to charge in there like a rampaging bull and ruin everything.'

'I be sorry, sir,' said Treadwell, doing his best to look contrite. 'It be'n't my plan to ruin all the good work you's done. But I can't help it. When a law'm being broken, justice needs to be served.'

Coldriser nodded unhappily. 'You're right, Gavin. I don't suppose, though . . .'

'What, sir?'

Coldriser steepled his fingers in front of his nose. 'Just a suggestion. You don't have to go along with this, but . . . what if I were to go to City Hall and ask the council, in the politest terms, to comply with the law?'

'Rather than have I haul them in on charges, you mean?'

'That's just what I mean. I won't mention what was said at that closed-session meeting, according to the minutes. I'll leave that out of it altogether.'

Treadwell masked a smile of relief. 'And then?'

'I'll simply point out that more could be done for the refugees.'

'A lot more, sir.'

'A lot more. I'll say to the council, the mayor as well, that it would save them a lot of trouble if they dug deep into the city coffers and used the money to send truckloads of provisions to all the refugee camps within a fifty-kilometre radius of Craterhome.'

'A hundred-kilometre radius, I'd say.'

'A hundred-kilometre radius, then. I'm sure they'd agree to it. I could leave the threat of prosecution unsaid but implied. I'm sure that would galvanise them into action.'

'I's sure it would, sir. I imagine it would persuade councils in other parts of the Territories to do the same, too. There'm nothing like setting an example.'

'Yes, no one would want to be outdone by Craterhome in displays of generosity. What do you think, Gavin? Would what I'm proposing satisfy you? Justice would still get done but it wouldn't have to involve arrests or trials or any of that sort of thing. The public would never have to know.'

Treadwell did an impression of someone giving the matter a great deal of thought, someone wrestling with his conscience. Finally he nodded slowly and said, 'I could see how that might work for I, Chief Superintendent.'

'Great!' said Coldriser, slapping his desk. 'Good to hear. Thank you for bringing this matter to my attention, Gavin. I'll get onto it right away.'

Treadwell hurried out, fumbling for his tobacco pouch even as he closed the door behind him. He lit his pipe tremblingly. As the smoke hit the back of his throat, his body unstiffened and he sighed.

'Toby!' he hissed, as he strode off towards his office.

Toby appeared from a nearby alcove where he had been lurking, eavesdropping on the conversation between Treadwell and Coldriser.

'You did it, guv.'

'*Us* did it, Toby,' Treadwell said, ruffling the boy's hair. 'And now I need you to take a message to the central telegraph bureau. It'm for Den.'

In his office he scribbled on a piece of paper:

> Moves afoot to alleviate Airborn situation. If looking for
> Cassie and Fletcher, try Blackcrab Lee.

He handed this to Toby, along with some money, and the boy was off in a flash. Then Treadwell collapsed into his desk chair and reflected on the past few minutes, in which he had laid his career on the line and it had paid off.

'I will never,' he said out loud to himself, 'ever do anything as flat-out reckless bonkers as that again.'

The tobacco crackled warmly in the bowl of his pipe. The smoke had rarely tasted sweeter.

CHAPTER 82

Antipterine

Af Bri was talking to his wife.

His dead wife.

She was standing in the corner of the room where he lay. Coré and Tariel were beside her. Liwet was listening as Af Bri told her how he had killed Naoutha and received a crossbow bolt in his gut for his pains.

'I knew she'd shoot,' he said. 'I also didn't care. I thought, *My life for hers? Seems a fair exchange.* We'd relied on each other for so long, she on me for my medical expertise, me on her for, well, the direction she brought to my life. False direction, of course. Misdirection. But still, our relationship was a weird sort of co-dependency affair, so it felt right that my life would end at the same time as hers. There's a symmetry about it.'

Liwet nodded, understanding. She'd always been a good listener. She'd always understood.

'After she shot me,' Af Bri went on, 'it didn't take me long to realise two things. One, I wasn't dead. Two, I would be soon. The bolt went clean through me. A couple of the Regulars helped staunch the wound. They stopped the bleeding from both the entry point and the exit point. Only trouble is, a stomach wound is a killer. A slow killer. I can tell you the pathology. A perforated bowel means peritonitis. Peritonitis means septicaemia – blood-poisoning. Septicaemia means death. It takes time but it's inescapable. You suffer fever, chills, nausea, vomiting, hallucinations possibly. Not much fun.'

He gave a fragile laugh.

'But some good is going to come of all this. I'll tell you what's happening. We're working on an antidote now. A cure for the ultrapterine. Yes! We're trying to undo the damage we've done. Righting the wrongs we've committed. We've freed all the Gyrians, and they're chipping in. They've fired up their Ultimate Reckoner and it's whirring away, working on calculations, running through formulae that'll help us gauge the quantities of antidote we'll need and the best methods of distributing it across the realm. We're hard at it, with Sarafinah Yakelsdaughter leading the way. She's a chemist, you know. She's largely responsible for developing the ultrapterine in the first place, so if anyone can figure out a way of reversing its effects, it's her.'

Liwet gave him an encouraging smile.

'Yes,' he said, 'and I've done my bit as well. Given advice. Offered the benefit of my knowledge of the workings of the human body. Otherwise, I've just been lying here in my sickbed, waiting for the inevitable. I'm comfortable. There are drugs circulating round my system, drugs from my own bag, strong ones, keeping me nice and numb. I'm fine. I'd rather not be dying, of course. But if it hadn't been for my sacrifice, maybe the Regulars wouldn't be striving to make amends. I think I inspired them by my example. Sounds arrogant to say so, but I think it's true. Naoutha had got away with so much. Shooting me was a step too far. The final straw. The Regulars vowed she wasn't going to get away with any more. They were going to turn things around. Everything that lying, manipulative bitch had set in motion, they would reverse.'

Tariel sniggered. Liwet frowned disapproval.

'Sorry,' said her husband. 'Bad language in front of the children. Naughty Daddy. It is great to see you all, by the way. You look beautiful. Happy. Perfect. Whole. And I know we'll all be together again soon. Properly together. Not me in this bed, you over there. As one. As a family. Won't be long till—'

'Dr Mumiahson?'

Af Bri turned his head. The Count of Gyre had appeared next to the bed. He was leaning down, looking puzzled. Behind him were two of his junior actuaries.

'Ah, Count. Hello.'

'Who were you talking to?' the Count enquired.

Af Bri glanced back at the corner of the room where his family had been. They were gone. Had they even been there at all?

Af Bri thought yes. They had. If he had been a patient of his, he would have diagnosed them as a hallucination. He would have told his patient-self that he had imagined them. They'd been a symptom of the septicaemia. He'd been talking to thin air.

But they'd definitely been there.

'No one,' he said to the Count. 'Just jabbering to myself.'

'Well,' said the Count, 'if you're feeling up to it, would you like to take a trip downstairs? Miss Yakelsdaughter says she has something to show you.'

'The antidote? It's ready?'

'Yes. They're about to test it. But don't come if you don't feel strong enough.'

'I can manage.'

In fact, Af Bri was too weak either to walk or fly. But the junior actuaries were able to carry him between them, and so, like that, they set off down through Gyre. Af Bri recalled Naoutha being transported through the city in this way. Just as he'd said to his wife: symmetry.

Halfway there, the Count said, 'Just so you know, there are no hard feelings here. In my way, I've behaved as shamefully as any of you lot. Everything that's happened to my citizens, I take full responsibility for. Like you, I forged an unwise alliance with an untrustworthy person. I should have been bolder, less weak. I should have had the courage to stand up to her, rather than taken the safer, easier route.'

'Shouldn't we all?' said Af Bri.

'And now we all must atone,' said the Count. 'Pulling the realm back from the brink of disaster is a good start, but I wonder if more might not need to be done later.'

'That'll be your concern,' said Af Bri, with a twist of his lips. 'For me, there's not going to be a later.'

'Yes. Of course. How insensitive of me.'

'Don't feel bad. I'm dying. It's a fact of life.'

'You're not scared?'

Af Bri thought of his family. 'Not at all.'

Down at the base of the city, the five original test subjects and Jazar, the Regular who'd got bitten, were still locked in the pantry. The floor was littered with biscuit crumbs and gnawed apple cores. The six looked even more listless and miserable than Af Bri remembered, and they were smeared with dirt and their own filth. The stink coming off them was dreadful.

'Sarafinah,' said Af Bri, as the two actuaries sat him down in a chair. 'You look shattered.'

She yawned, rubbing her eyes. 'I've been working for thirty-six hours non-stop. Haven't had a wink of sleep. And you . . . ?'

'Never better,' said Af Bri gamely, even though he was starting to feel shaky and clammy all over. He should have stuck to his bed. But then he didn't want to miss this. 'So what's that?'

Sarafinah had rigged up a sort of pump-action device, using a beer barrel, a sink plunger, a spigot and some rubber tubing.

'A pressure sprayer for aerosol dispersal,' she said. 'It's the only safe method for administering the antidote. This way, we don't have to get too close to the infected.'

'And the antidote itself?'

'As you suggested, there was only one place to look for it.'

'I was right, then.'

'You were.'

'Her.'

'Her.'

'Her?' said the Count. 'You mean . . . ?'

Sarafinah nodded. 'The human body, you see, when confronted with an organic poison, mounts its own defences. It develops a system for coping – antibodies in the bloodstream that fight the poison's effects. Ultrapterine being a derivative of pterine, we thought if we used blood from someone who had built up a significant tolerance to the original drug, someone whose body had adjusted to years of sustained pterine use . . .'

'Naoutha,' said the Count.

'It was Dr Mumiahson's idea. We drew a specimen of blood from the corpse, then set about trying to synthesise an inorganic equivalent of Naoutha's antibodies. Then we had to make it water-soluble, although that was relatively easy. And here it is.' She patted her homemade pressure sprayer. 'We're calling it antipterine.'

'Naoutha's own blood will reverse the effects of the plague,' said the Count. 'Ironic, yet somehow apt.'

'I know,' said Sarafinah. 'There's only one way to find out if we've done it right, though.'

She pumped the handle on the sprayer, then held up the tubing, undid the spigot at the end and aimed a jet of fine mist through the bars of the pantry door at the six within. They roused themselves and snarled as cool wetness fell over them. They lunged for the door, but Sarafinah kept her distance and continued to spray them.

'Breathe,' she said softly. 'Breathe in. That's it.'

Slowly, exquisitely slowly, the snarls of the six began to subside. The redness in their eyes faded to pink, the pink to white. Their movements became erratic, twitchy, confused, like those of people waking out of a profound sleep. All at once the Calculator Savant gave a cry of distress and sank to the floor. The arrow wound had gone septic but the ultrapterine had prevented him from noticing or caring.

'Success,' said Af Bri. 'He feels pain again.'

'Let him out, then,' said the Count. 'Immediately. He should have his leg seen to.'

'Not yet,' said Sarafinah. 'We have to leave it a little longer. Just to be sure.'

One by one the other five blinked and shook their heads. Their faces seemed to lighten, like the sky after an eclipse.

Jazar was the first to speak.

'Wha– what's happened? What am I doing in here? I feel terrible. Like absolute guano. What's going on?'

The Gyrians joined in.

'Have I been asleep?'

'I drank that stuff and then . . .'

'Everything aches.'

'My leg!'

'. . . a nightmare. The world full of horrible faces. Everybody hating me. Me hating everybody.'

'Cloudy. Blurred.'

'My leg really, really hurts.'

'What *is* that smell?'

'How long have I been like this? An hour? Two?'

They barely seemed to remember what they had done under the influence of the ultrapterine, what they had been like. It seemed like a dream to them. Af Bri was glad of that.

He watched Sarafinah unlock the pantry door. He watched Jazar and the Gyrians come out, one of them helping the Calculator Savant to hobble along. No one was paying Af Bri any attention at this point. He felt cold and his breath was coming in gasps. No one noticed him begin to shudder.

He glimpsed movement out of the corner of his eye. He looked round and there was his wife.

Liwet beckoned to him. Framed by each of her wings, Coré and Tariel did the same.

They were just within reach. A step away. All he needed to do was get up and go to them.

With a grateful sigh, Af Bri did.

He slumped in the chair. Sarafinah saw this and ran to his side. She felt for a pulse, listened to his chest.

But Af Bri wasn't there. He was elsewhere, with his family, in a world where everything was a pure and pristine blue. He was uninjured, whole again. His family was whole again. There was a moment of foreverness, an unending instant of now.

Then darkness and calm silence.

CHAPTER 83

Wings

Aurora let out yet another terrible howl of pain. Ramona Enochson said something soothing and mopped her brow with a cold, damp flannel. Aurora swore at her mother-in-law, then bent double and screamed again. Mrs Enochson did not look shocked. Aurora had been swearing at her consistently for the past hour, and Mrs Enochson knew that the girl barely realised what she was saying. At any rate, she hoped so.

'The baby's nearly here,' she told Aurora. 'Stay calm. Just concentrate on your breathing.'

'Pluck off, you vile old witch! Stay calm while I've got a baby tearing my insides out?'

'That's it, dear. You're doing a great job. Keep it up. Won't be long now.'

'Why don't you just eat guano and die?'

And so on.

Michael looked on from the living-room doorway, feeling all kinds of useless. This was a women-only domain. A man could bring nothing to the situation and would probably just get in the way. His mother had given birth to two children and knew what was involved. She would get Aurora through this as best she could, till help came.

Speaking of which . . .

He went to the trapdoor in the middle of the hallway floor and rapped on it. Shortly, it opened up and his father's head poked out.

'Done yet?' Michael asked.

'As a matter of fact, yes.' The old man looked weary but pleased with himself. He'd been toiling through the night down in his basement workshop. 'It's ready. Would you give me a hand getting it up out of here?'

He went back down and returned bearing a large, folded structure of fabric and wood, which he and Michael grappled up through the trap-door. Then between them they carried the thing upstairs. Every time one of Aurora's screams rang through the house, the two men shared a pitying, helpless look.

'Why childbirth has to hurt so much, I'll never understand,' said Gabriel Enochson. 'Conceiving a baby is fun but having one isn't. Where's the sense in that?'

'Mother Nature can't have been a mother herself,' Michael replied.

His father shot him a quick, mirthless smile.

They gained access to the roof via a skylight. There, in the fresh morning air, they paused while Gabriel Enochson caught his breath. Michael peered over the edge of the roof into the street. The Maddened were still milling about down there. The blackened husk of the Vortex V smouldered away. In places the wreckage was still alight, and the move-ment of the smoke and the crackle and flicker of the flames entranced the Maddened. They were torn between that and the noises coming from the house. Whenever Aurora screamed, they turned and drifted in the direction of the sound. Then they forgot about it and wandered back towards the burning helicopter. They were like some sort of strange crowd-tide, washing this way and that. Occasionally they moaned, almost inquisitively, and now and then a fierce squabble would break out if one of them happened to bump into another or tread on another's toes.

Michael cast his gaze further afield, to a line of private aircraft parked down the street. He had already selected which one he would com-mandeer. It was an Aerodyne Cygnet, one of his company's range of mid-price commuter planes. Neither fast nor flashy, the Cygnet was utterly dependable, the sort of small aircraft that never failed to start first time and would always get you where you wanted to go. He knew for a fact that the owner, Mr Maionson, was in the habit of leaving the key in the ignition. This was a safe neighbourhood, and besides, the type of person who was out to steal a plane wouldn't look twice at a Cygnet. It had no resale value and was too slow for joyriding.

Speed wasn't a concern for Michael. He just wanted to get to the perimeter of High Haven safely and securely, and the Cygnet was the plane for the job.

First, however, he had to get to the Cygnet.

Which was where his father's invention came in.

Gabriel Enochson started unfurling the fabric-and-wood contraption. Lengths of dowel slotted together to form an armature. The fabric, con-sisting of sections cut from several bedsheets, was stretched rigidly over this framework.

Once assembled, what he'd constructed overnight was a cross between a kite and a swept-back aeroplane wing. It spanned nearly six metres and it had a central bar slung beneath it, somewhat like a trapeze, from which a person might hang.

'Your transport awaits,' he said to Michael, patting this one-man gliding device.

'Looks safe,' said Michael dubiously.

'It's as sturdy as I could make it while keeping it lightweight. It only has to get you a few hundred metres.'

A gust of wind caught the glider and made it rear off the rooftop. Michael's father held it down firmly in place, preventing it from being blown away.

'Your bodyweight will give it stability,' he added. 'You steer by leaning to either side.'

'OK.' Michael felt a surge of that weird feeling, that vertigo. His stomach gave a lurch.

'Michael, listen, you don't have to—'

'No, Dad,' Michael said, swallowing. 'I do. I really do have to. Mum's coping fantastically well but Aurora needs proper medical care. She needs to be in hospital, with a midwife and other people who know what they're doing.'

'But surely it would make more sense if *I* fly to the Cygnet under my own steam.'

'My wife, Dad. My baby. My responsibility.'

Gabriel Enochson looked at his son and knew there was no arguing with him. 'Very well, let's get you launched then.'

He lifted the glider up so that Michael could duck beneath it and grasp the bar. The glider bucked and juddered in the wind. It seemed keen to be off.

'This is the second time I've given a wingless son flight,' Gabriel Enochson mused.

'Yeah, well,' said Michael, 'let's hope this time it doesn't work out as badly as those copper wings of yours did for Az.'

His father laughed grimly. 'Good point. Do you want me to say goodbye to Aurora for you?'

'No. It's better if she doesn't know I've gone. She's got enough on her plate without having me to worry about as well. But I love her, Dad, and I love you and Mum, and I'm sorry I've been such a miserable bustard these past few weeks, and I'm coming back for all of you. I'm coming back with Alar Patrollers and an air ambulance, and nothing's going to stop me.'

'I hear you, son. Ready?'

Michael ran his tongue across suddenly dry lips. 'Ready.'

He crouched down, bracing himself against the rooftop. His father counted, 'One, two, three!' and gave the glider a mighty shove. Michael kicked off at the same time.

The glider, this fragile thing of wooden poles and woven cotton, hurtled off the rim of the house, carrying Michael with it.

CHAPTER 84

Close But No Cygnet

Michael flew.

For about three metres.

Then he began to plummet towards the street.

A downwards gust of wind caught the glider, sending it on a collision course with the pavement.

Michael, hanging onto the bar for dear life, swung his whole body backwards in a desperate effort to counteract the nosedive.

It worked. The glider angled back and started to climb. Michael's toecaps scraped the pavement. Then he was rising, the glider catching the wind, pulling him up with it.

From behind he heard his father hoot with joy and relief. Michael's teeth were too tightly clamped together for him to respond in kind.

The glider sailed straight, till another wayward gust caught it and it lurched laterally, taking Michael towards the side of a house. He leaned the opposite way, and the glider responded, veering back onto its original course.

What do you know? he thought. *The old man got the aerodynamics spot on!*

He focused his attention on the Cygnet. He was passing above the heads of the Maddened, who blinked up at him in surprise and consternation. A few of them leapt at him as he went, trying to grab him, but he was just too high. The Cygnet got nearer and nearer. Michael realised, with a kind of wild jubilation, that he was going to make it. A few seconds from now and he'd be clambering into the plane's cockpit and firing up the props. The Maddened would be eating his backwash.

Then . . .

Crack!

The sound of wood snapping.

Crumple-flump.

The sound of a taut piece of bedsheet flailing loose.

'Aargh!'

The sound of Michael yelling as the glider pivoted onto its side and dropped to the pavement like a rock.

He barely felt the impact. All he knew was that one moment he was aloft, the next he was lying amid a tangle of sheet and splintered wood. The glider had disintegrated around him. Under strain, a single length of dowel had fractured, and the whole thing had instantly fallen apart.

Michael fought his way out of the debris. He'd take issue with his father over his engineering skills later. He struggled to his feet, knowing that at least the glider had got him to within striking distance of the Cygnet, knowing also that the Maddened would soon be coming for him.

He was right. They were lumbering towards him already, arms outstretched, teeth bared.

He spun round. The Cygnet was a few paces away. He set off. He stumbled. He fell over. Pain was shooting up from his ankle. Instead of a bone joint it felt as though there were shards of glass in there, crunching and crackling. Michael hissed in agony.

Broken. His plucking ankle, broken in the crash!

Never mind, he told himself. *Forget about it. The plane. Get to the plane.*

He pushed himself off the pavement. He hop-hobbled along. Every time his injured foot touched down, however lightly, he groaned. The Cygnet was so near and yet seemed such a long way off. He could do this. He must keep going.

A careless misstep. His ankle doubled up under him. His leg gave way and he fell again. He hit the pavement chin first, and the pain from his ankle was so bad he wanted to throw up. Tears of frustration burned his eyes.

He'd still make it. He began to crawl. It was brutally slow and clumsy. The Maddened were closing in. He could hear their awful moans, getting louder. He could hear, too, his father shouting, saying that he was coming for him. He wanted to tell the old man to stay away. Not to risk it. But all his energies were tied up in keeping himself going forwards. Crawling, slithering, and his broken ankle grinding, his foot trailing . . .

The Cygnet.

He laid a hand on the tail section.

He hauled himself upright.

Using the plane for support, he limped along towards the cockpit.

A Maddened lurched into his line of vision. A clutching hand reached for him. Michael slapped it away. The Maddened came at him again, grabbing his shirt. A red-eyed face loomed just centimetres from his own. A gush of bad breath. Teeth gleaming.

Michael brought his fist up, smashing it into the Maddened's cheek.

The Maddened barely felt the blow. A flinch, and then the teeth were exposed again, clacking loudly together, chomping on air in readiness for chomping on Michael.

Michael would not become one of them. He refused to.

Leaning back against the Cygnet, he grasped the Maddened's head with both hands and sank his thumbs into those blood-crazed eyes. Neighbour, good citizen, decent, upstanding, honest, a parent, kindly – Michael didn't care who the Maddened used to be. He cared only about not getting bitten and catching the infection. He dug his thumbs further in, hard as he could, and the Maddened growled and then shrieked as something within the eye sockets popped. There was a squelch and a spurt of liquid. Blood and a thick, jelly-like substance leaked out over Michael's hands. The Maddened reeled away, still shrieking, with ragged holes where there had once been eyes. Staggering, blind, the Maddened toppled over the edge of the pavement and fell out of sight.

Michael turned and clawed his way along the side of the Cygnet, trying to ignore the hot wetness on his hands and the smears of stuff he was leaving on the plane's fuselage.

More Maddened caught up with him. One seized him from behind. Another latched onto his arm. Michael writhed in their grasp, fighting to break free. Maddened swarmed about him on all sides. He knew then that there was no hope. He was surrounded. He had got to the Cygnet, but that was as far as it went. It was not enough. He had failed.

'Aurora . . .' he whispered.

And then he heard wings.

The beating of wings.

His father?

No, lots of wings.

And a warbling whistle. A shout.

He looked up. His eyes went wide.

The sky above was filled with women.

Women.

And eagles.

CHAPTER 85

Aquila Flight To The Rescue

Beaks agape, talons splayed, the eagles hurtled down onto the throng of Maddened. They were fast, dazzlingly fast. Each swooped, slashed, soared, all in the space of a couple of seconds, before wheeling round and returning for another attack. They came in waves, in interlacing arcs. The onslaught was continuous, relentless. The Maddened didn't know which way to turn or how to retaliate.

Zwitchh! One eagle neatly removed a Maddened's ear.

Splitttch! Another took out an eye.

Shrrrikk! Talons raked a face, tearing through the flesh clean to the bone.

Above, the women of the Aquila Flight whistled and called, guiding their birds with the deftness of puppet-masters. Their voices were the strings with which they made the eagles dive and turn and strike. Each move was practised and precise. The eagles never had to swerve to avoid one another and never missed their targets. They went for the Maddened only. Michael didn't get so much as a scratch on him, for all that he was in the thick of the crowd. The only physical contact he had with any of the birds was a wingtip inadvertently brushing the crown of his head.

Steadily the eagles drove the Maddened away from him. With repeated, harrying assaults they herded them against the side of a house. The Maddened lashed out as they retreated, flailing with their hands, but they couldn't beat the eagles away. They couldn't even touch them. Wounded, bleeding, they howled in anger and frustration.

Then, as one, the birds withdrew. Each flew back to its mistress and alighted on her leather-clad arm.

At the same time, more Cumulans appeared. There were about thirty of them, flying in orderly formation. They were armed and armoured.

At a command from their leader, they fanned out around the huddled Maddened. Arrows were nocked. Bowstrings were drawn.

'Fire!'

A volley of steel-tipped shafts was unleashed.

And the Maddened fell.

'Fire!'

A second hail of arrows descended on the Maddened. Heads, chests, limbs were pierced. Any who had been missed the first time round weren't this time.

'Fire!'

The third volley finished off the Maddened who'd survived the previous two. Bodies lay on the pavement, quilled with arrows. A few of them twitched for a while, then lay still.

Michael, slumped against the side of the Cygnet, could think of nothing to say or do. The Cumulans had saved him. But they had saved him by ruthlessly eliminating every Maddened within sight. He didn't know whether to be relieved or appalled.

It was over. That much he did know. For him, at any rate.

But not for Aurora.

'Hey!' he called out. 'Hey!'

The leader of the Cumulan troops alighted in front of him. She was the biggest, burliest woman Michael had ever set eyes on.

'Are you hurt?' she demanded, levelling her sword at him. 'Did any of them bite you?'

'Yes,' said Michael. 'I mean, no. I've got a busted ankle, but nobody bit me. I'm OK.'

'Good.' The sword was sheathed.

'But there's a woman in that house back there, the one with the man standing on the roof – she's in the middle of having a baby. My baby. We need help.'

The woman summoned several of her subordinates to her side and sent them off to the house. Michael's father saw them approaching and waved them to him. He showed them the skylight, and they descended inside.

Meanwhile, overhead, the Aquila Flight dispersed to take up lookout positions all along the street.

The large woman inspected Michael's ankle, which was by now horribly inflamed and purple.

'Definitely broken,' she said. Without asking, she tore a strip of material off Michael's trouser leg and began wrapping it around the joint and foot in a figure-of-eight pattern, none too gently. 'What's a Groundling like you doing here anyway? Didn't you know there's an emergency on?'

'I'm not a Groundling,' Michael replied, wincing and gritting his teeth. 'What are *you* doing here? Cumulans don't leave the Collective.'

'You should be glad we did. Let's just say our Mother Major was persuaded into thinking we could be of use out in the realm, combating the Maddened. High Haven's the worst affected city, so that's why we came here. We came to this actual street because we spotted the smoke from that burning helicopter over there. Thanks to that, you're alive.'

'And lots of civilians are dead.'

'It's how we Cumulans deal with things. I wouldn't start complaining, if I were you.'

She tucked in the end of the makeshift bandage, then examined her handiwork. 'As field dressings go, not bad. You'll need a plaster cast, though, when you can get one.'

'Thanks,' said Michael. 'And I didn't mean to sound ungrateful before. You came in the nick of time. And those eagles . . . amazing.'

'I know,' said the Cumulan with an upward glance. 'It's the first time they've been used in a full-on conflict situation. They couldn't have performed better.'

One of her subordinates landed nearby and snapped off a salute. 'Protectrix Esme? The area is secure. The Aquila Flight report no more Maddened in immediate range.'

'Good,' said Protectrix Esme.

'And are you Michael?' the Cumulan asked Michael.

'Yeah? Why?'

'Message from your father. Your wife's asking for you.'

Michael tried to walk but couldn't. The ankle, in spite of the bandage, hurt too much when he put pressure on it.

'Let me give you a hand.' Protectrix Esme scooped him up in her arms and took off, carrying him aloft with ease.

At the house, Michael's father ushered them down through the skylight. 'Come on. Quickly.'

Protectrix Esme flew Michael down to the living room, Gabriel Enochson following. They found Aurora lying on the sofa, exhausted, soaked in sweat. Michael's mother was kneeling beside her, rolling up some very messy towels.

There was something in Aurora's arms: a bundle of blankets, it looked like.

'It all happened rather fast,' his mother said. 'Suddenly, after all that refusing to come out . . .' She looked tired too, but extremely happy.

Aurora smiled up at Michael, wan, brave.

'Hi, Mike. I hear you tried to play the hero again.'

Michael looked furtive. 'I was just . . . It seemed like . . .'

Aurora shot a glance at the woman in whose arms he lay. 'And who's your new friend?'

610

'Protectrix Esme of the Cumula Collective,' said Esme. 'Where do you want him?'

'Right here next to me, if you don't mind.'

Esme set Michael down on the sofa.

Just then, the bundle of blankets wriggled and let out a faint, raspy cry. Aurora opened up a gap in the blankets, and a small, purple-tinged face peeped out. It was encrusted with blood and bits of some dried, yellow stuff. A pair of eyes blinked owlishly, gazing around with pupils so wide they were almost entirely black. The eyes fixed on Michael. Michael felt a strange, shivery shock of recognition. Somehow he knew this little creature, the owner of the wizened face that was looking back at him. Somehow, in some deep, unfathomable way, he had known this person all his life.

'That's . . .' he said. 'Is it . . . ?'

'A boy,' said Aurora. 'Our boy. Our son, Michael.'

Michael stared at the child for several seconds.

Then promptly fainted.

CHAPTER 86

The Majesty And Mystery Of A Vast Vessel

In the bridge of Bathylab Four, parked just off Blackcrab Lee, consternation reigned.

'No power!' Fletcher exclaimed. 'Everything'm just gone and . . . shut down.'

He rushed from console to console, but each was a dead as the next. No lights glowed. No dials flickered.

'Nothing!' he said.

'But us was rolling along nicely not so long ago,' said Cassie. 'All us did was go to bed for a few hours, then get up . . . and now us can't move?'

'Not just can't move, girl. Can't do anything. Can't open automated doors, can't flush ballast, can't even turn on a light.'

'Straight up?'

Fletcher rounded on her. 'What part of "shut down" doesn't you understand? The whole system's gone phut. There'm no electricity running through it. Us is just sitting here. Bathylab Four now be nothing more than a – a big, waterlogged house on wheels.'

'Clip it down, Fletch. I's sure it'm just some glitch. Maybe a loose connection somewhere. Us can look for the problem and fix it. You knows that.'

'How big be this damn thing? Huge! I wouldn't even know where to start.'

'With the storage batteries, I'd suggest,' said Cassie.

'Yes,' said Fletcher, calming down somewhat. 'Yes, that'm not a bad idea. Where be them?'

'How should I know? But there'm a drive plant down on the lower levels. It'd make sense if the batteries was close to that.'

'Good thinking, Cass. Let's go.'

Exiting the bridge, they passed Az and Colin, both of whom wanted to know what the hold-up was.

'I thought we were going to head to shore,' Az said.

'Us will,' said Fletcher breezily. 'Electrics is down, but once that'm sorted, us'll be on our way.'

'Him's Mr Confident now,' Cassie confided to Az, 'but you should have seen he a minute ago. Him were fretting like an old maid.'

'I were not!'

'You'd've thought the Bathylab were about to explode or something.'

'I just doesn't like it when things just go wrong for no good reason,' said Fletcher. 'Come on, Cass. Quit dawdling. Work to be done.'

'See you,' Cassie said to Az and Colin, as Fletcher yanked her away.

Az looked at Colin. 'What do you reckon? Think they need our help?'

'I be'n't much of a mechanic. Them can sort it out between they.'

'I agree. Breakfast, then?'

'Why not? Let's see what us can rustle up. The cooker won't be working but there'm one of those little gas-cylinder camping stoves – probably there in case of power cuts like this. Us can at least make coffee.'

In the galley, Colin got the camping stove working, at the same time feeding Platypuss titbits of salted cod. Az, meanwhile, peered out of one of the portholes in the dining area. Bathylab Four's arrival had sparked some interest among the inhabitants on the coast. A small flotilla of boats had come out and were now circling warily around it. Along the shoreline he could make out clusters of minuscule figures, curiosity seekers come to gawp. He was reminded of *Cerulean* and the fascination that the airship had held for people, himself included. The majesty and mystery of a vast vessel. That men could build such immense machines and make them move!

Amid one of the clusters of figures he made out a large, hulking vehicle. It was so far away he couldn't be sure, but it looked like a murk-comber. Was it . . . ?

No. Couldn't be. What were the odds of *Cackling Bertha* being at Blackcrab Lee?

He turned his thoughts to the day ahead. Once this delay was over and the electricity restored, they would break out the motor launch and head for land. Then he would embark on his journey to Gyre. He'd be at the sky-city by noon, and there he would, with luck, be able to clear up the riddle of what had happened to Mr Mordadson. After that, he intended to fly to High Haven. Aurora ought to have given birth by now, and he wanted to be there to greet the new baby. He had a feeling that the baby was going to be just what his family needed. They'd been at odds with one another for a while – and he couldn't deny that a substantial portion of the blame lay with him. A new addition to the family might be just the thing to bring them all back together. It would give them something to think about other than themselves. It would give them a focus again.

Besides, he wanted to see how Michael coped with fatherhood. There was fun to be had, watching his brother grapple with nappies and bottle-feeding and sleepless nights.

Noises from the galley interrupted his gleeful musings. There was a rustling, a shuffle of feet, then a weird, choking sound.

'Colin?'

No answer.

Then Platypuss came backing out of the galley, ears flattened, fur bristling all over. The cat looked terrified. Abruptly, he turned tail and scurried off to hide under a chair.

Az approached the galley entrance on high alert. He slowed his breathing. His hands balled into fists. Something was very wrong here.

He peered in.

No one there. The room was empty.

He entered, scanning into every corner.

Where was Colin? And why had the cat . . . ?

Az felt a drip of wetness land on the top of his head. Another plopped onto his shoulder. He looked at his shirtsleeve.

Blood.

Blood from . . . above?

He didn't want to look up. He would rather have done anything than crane his head back and turn his gaze towards the ceiling.

But he did. He had to.

Colin was lodged overhead atop an extractor fan unit. He was unconscious, his body limp, his head hanging forwards. The blood had come from a small incision on his cheek.

There was someone behind him, mostly obscured by Colin's bulk, partly supporting him with one arm around his chest. This same someone was holding a carving knife at Colin's throat. The blood drips had been caused deliberately, to attract Az's attention.

Az glimpsed wings.

An Airborn? Here? On the Bathylab?

Lord Urironson.

That was his immediate thought. Az had helped thwart Lord Urironson's plans. Having escaped the Patrol's custody, Lord Urironson had stalked him and had finally caught up with him, bent on revenge.

But that was impossible. No way could this be his lordship. If nothing else, Lord Urironson could never have overpowered Colin. Not in a million years.

Who, then?

'Gabrielson,' said the figure lurking behind Colin.

Az recognised the voice – those posh, well-modulated tones – but couldn't match it to a name straight away. It didn't belong to any Airborn he knew, that was for sure.

Then a face appeared from over Colin's shoulder.

'Watch,' said the face.

The knife touched Colin's neck.

'Watch closely.'

Jasper Longnoble-Drumblood grinned.

'Watch as I slit your hillbilly friend's throat from ear to ear.'

CHAPTER 87

Divide And Conquer

Far below, Cassie and Fletcher had located the Bathylab's batteries. There were twenty-four of them, each a glass-sided box the size of a steamer trunk, with comb-like arrangements of nickel-cadmium plate inside, immersed in clear acid. The chamber that housed them was festooned with insulated cables.

The thickest cables of all were the input ones that fed in power from the turbines. They hung down from the ceiling in pairs and were attached to steel terminals atop the batteries.

The next thickest cables were the output ones, which were plugged in to a distributor unit.

Or rather, were supposed to be.

The output cables had been yanked from their sockets. They lay on the floor, coiled around one another like beheaded snakes, each tipped with a brush of loose copper filaments.

Cassie looked at Fletcher. Fletcher looked at Cassie.

Both said the word as one: 'Sabotage.'

'But who?' said Fletcher. 'Who'd do this?'

'None of *we*,' Cassie stated firmly. 'Someone else. There must be some-one else on board.'

'Not possible.'

'It'm the only explanation.'

Her next thought sent a chill through her.

'This'm a diversion,' she said. 'A way of splitting we up.'

'What for?' said her brother.

'Be you thick? Divide and conquer! Us is under attack!'

'Under . . . ?'

'Look, you stay here,' Cassie said. 'Reattach those cables as best you can.'

616

'What about you? What be you going to do?'

'What's you think?' Cassie replied, rushing out of the room. 'Make we less divided!'

Up ladders. Up companionways. Up through the Bathylab's levels. Back the way she had come.

Colin.

Az.

Hurry.

CHAPTER 88

Cauterisation

Az was beyond disbelief. He was in a world where nothing made sense any more. Nothing was right.

Longnoble-Drumblood – here?

And not only here but *with wings*?

It was almost too much to take in.

Amid all his confusion, however, a simple fact stood clear. Colin was in danger. Saving him was paramount.

Az focused on that. His hand groped across the worktop behind him. Colin was out of his reach. He couldn't jump up and grab the knife out of Longnoble-Drumblood's grasp. He needed a weapon. A projectile.

His fingers closed around the handle of a frying pan. It would have to do. He snatched it up and flung it. It whirled through the air like a discus. It missed Longnoble-Drumblood's hand but hit Colin square on the forehead. Colin gave a start. The movement jerked Longnoble-Drumblood's arm, preventing him from making the cut.

But only for a moment.

The knife returned to its position over Colin's throat.

Az searched frantically around for something else to throw.

The knife dug in.

But Colin was awake now. The blow to the head had roused him. As the knife blade began sawing into his skin, he let out a roar of pain and indignation. He writhed, shaking himself out of Longnoble-Drumblood's clutches. He fell, landing on the floor with a huge thump, fetching up in an ungainly heap.

Longnoble-Drumblood descended too, alighting beside Colin, knife poised. Colin tried to rise, but his legs failed him and he collapsed to his knees. Blood was pouring from his neck. He clamped a hand over the wound, but the blood spilled out through his fingers in a crimson slick.

618

Meanwhile Az hunted around desperately for another weapon. A proper weapon this time. He didn't dare tackle an armed Longnoble-Drumblood without one.

His gaze fell on a meat cleaver that was hanging from a hook on the wall. He plucked it down. He whirled, holding it at the ready.

Longnoble-Drumblood eyed the cleaver, then the person wielding it.

'Got your attention then, have I?' he said. 'Good.' And with a single beat of his wings, he exited the room backwards.

Az ran to Colin's side. The blood was now soaking all of Colin's shirtfront. His face was turning ashen.

'Az,' he gasped. 'I be sorry. I never saw he.'

'Don't try to talk.'

'From behind . . . above. No chance. Him were choking I. Blacked out.'

'I said don't talk. Save your strength.'

Az prised Colin's hand away from the wound. The cut was deep and long but, as far as he could tell, no major blood vessels had been severed.

The blood flow needed to be stopped all the same. A bandage wouldn't do. Something else was called for.

Az saw the camping stove. Its ring was jetting out a pale blue flame.

'Keep your hand pressed tight over the cut,' he told Colin. He grabbed an ordinary table knife from a drawer, then held its blade over the flame, turning it this way and that until it was as hot as it was likely to get.

He went back to Colin. Colin looked at the knife, groaned, and shut his eyes.

'Do it,' he said, taking his hand away from his neck.

Az pressed the flat of the blade hard against the wound. There was a sizzle, a bubbling, a wisp of smoke, a smell like bacon frying. Colin let out a sound through his teeth like a cross between a grunt and a roar.

The sizzling sound died away. Az lifted the knife off, revealing a long welt of seared red flesh. It was ugly, but there was no more bleeding. The hot knife had cauterised the wound, sealing it shut.

'Who taught you to do that?' Colin asked. His eyes glistened with tears of pain. 'Mordy?'

'Yes.'

'Then next time you see he, you give he a message from I. Tell he, it bloody well hurts.'

'I will.' Az grabbed his meat cleaver. 'But first, I've got a message to give to Jasper Longnoble-Drumblood.'

'Longnoble-Drum . . . That were him?'

'None other.'

'But him had wings.'

'Don't think I'm not as flabbergasted about that as you are.'

'Let I come with you.' Colin made to get up, but then teetered, dizzy with blood loss.

'No. You're in no fit state. Besides, the message I've got for him is personal.' Az hefted the cleaver in his hand. 'From me to him.'

CHAPTER 89

Wingless Airborn Versus Winged Groundling

Questions buzzed through Az's brain as he raced out of the galley. How had Longnoble-Drumblood found him? How had he got aboard the Bathylab? And, most crucially of all, those wings. How in the name of all that's high and bright did a Groundling come by a pair of fully-functioning, fully-fledged wings?

He could only assume that Longnoble-Drumblood must have followed him and Colin. Someone *had* been tailing them, all the way from Grimvale.

As for the wings . . .

He heard a voice in his head, Mr Mordadson's, butting in to say that none of this mattered right this moment. He must concentrate on the task at hand, nothing else. The hows and whys of the situation were distractions. He must clear his mind of them. His one and only consideration was Longnoble-Drumblood himself. The man was here and he was out to kill. It was Az's job to stop him. That was all he needed to know.

Where would a winged person go so that he could use the power of flight to his advantage?

Most of the Bathylab's rooms were small. The corridors were narrow. Wings weren't much of a help in confined spaces. They could even be a hindrance.

But not in the bridge, the largest open area the Bathylab had by far.

Az headed straight there.

He knew this was probably what Longnoble-Drumblood wanted. That was why he had fled the galley. Az was being lured. He was being drawn into an arena where the enemy had the upper hand.

So what? The plucker had tried to murder Colin. He'd do the same to Fletcher if he had the chance. To Cassie. Az couldn't think about the

621

danger to himself when others' lives were at stake. Especially when one of those others was the person he loved most in the world.

Cleaver at the ready, he raced up the companionway to the bridge.

Sure enough, Longnoble-Drumblood was there. He was hovering high above the platforms and consoles. Framing him was the massive viewing window and its vista of sea, boats, coastline and cloud.

'Hello again,' he said. As Longnoble-Drumblood wasn't wearing a shirt, Az could see he was in frighteningly good physical condition. The muscles in his torso rippled as he beat his wings to stay in position.

Az recalled that Longnoble-Drumblood was a soldier. He kept himself in trim. He knew about hand-to-hand combat. All of that was another score in his favour. One more reason why Az was unlikely to win this fight.

'Come down here,' Az said. 'Come down and we can talk about this.'

'Talk!' Longnoble-Drumblood snorted. 'What have we got to talk about? You killed my friend. Now I'm going to kill you. End of conversation.'

'I didn't kill him,' Az said. 'That hackerjackal did.'

'And who let the beast into the house? Your common-as-muck girlfriend, that's who. And you were right beside her when she did it.'

'Slamshaft had a sword. He was about to kill *us*. What else could we do?'

'Ah, self-defence. That's your excuse, eh? It was him or you.'

'Well, it was.'

'But what were you doing in his house in the first place? If you hadn't been there, Dom would still be alive.'

'And thousands of Airborn would be dead, to add to the hundreds his troops had already slaughtered. We were stopping a war, pluckwit! Slamshaft was a raving madman. A solid-gold loony. We did what we had to.'

Longnoble-Drumblood bristled. 'Don't you dare talk about him like that!'

'Why not? The man attacked the Airborn realm to *make money*. How else would you describe someone who'd do that? Mad. Psychopathically greedy.'

The aristocrat's face lit up with rage.

To Az, this was a good sign. An angry opponent was an opponent not thinking clearly, and therefore not likely to fight at his best.

'You little bastard. Dom was worth a million of you.'

'Financially, maybe,' Az said. 'But otherwise? He was the sort of thing I'd scrape off my shoe.'

'Oh, I'm going to fix you,' Longnoble-Drumblood snarled. 'I'm going to catch you and pin you down and gut you like a pig.'

He reared back, then came down in a breakneck dive. Az softened his knees, tensing, ready to spring out of his way.

The carving knife flashed. Az leapt sideways at the very last moment, ducking beneath its arc of swing. The knife whooshed through the air above him, missing him by a hair's breadth. Az tucked and rolled and came up, lashing out with the cleaver. He missed too.

Longnoble-Drumblood shot upward, turned, then swooped again.

This time Az stood his ground. He kept his eye on the knife, nothing but the knife. As Longnoble-Drumblood closed in, he brought the cleaver up. Knife and cleaver clashed. The impact shivered up Az's arm. The knife was knocked from Longnoble-Drumblood's hand and went clattering to the floor.

Az lunged for it, wanting to kick it out of the way before Longnoble-Drumblood could retrieve it. But his enemy was quicker. Longnoble-Drumblood spun in midair and darted back, booting Az between the shoulders as he passed. Az was sent sprawling. The cleaver slipped from his grasp. At the same time, Longnoble-Drumblood landed and scooped up the knife. Az staggered to his feet, weaponless. The cleaver lay metres away from him. His back throbbed where Longnoble-Drumblood's foot had struck.

'I do believe,' Longnoble-Drumblood said smugly, 'that now I'm holding *all* the aces.'

'You've still got a sad moustache, though.'

'Says the boy who thinks a couple of longish bristles make a beard. Face it, Gabrielson, you're outclassed, outmanoeuvred, out*manned* in every way. Accept your fate. I'm going to kill you. It's beyond doubt. You and your little trollop of a girlfriend too. Why not just give in without a struggle? It'll be easier that way.

'You don't know me very well. I never give in without a struggle.'

Longnoble-Drumblood offered a philosophical shrug. 'Fair enough. It wouldn't be fun for me anyway if you did.'

He came at Az at a run, then launched himself off the floor. The knife-point was aimed at Az's navel. *Gut you like a pig.*

Az did the last thing Longnoble-Drumblood was expecting. He didn't try and get out of the way. He moved straight towards him.

He twisted aside as Longnoble-Drumblood reached him, pushing the aristocrat's knife arm outward at the same time. Then he grabbed him by the wing roots, swung him around through 180° using his own momentum, and let go.

Longnoble-Drumblood hurtled headlong into one of the control consoles. He struck it with a crunch and an 'oof!' The carving knife flew from his hand again and went skidding over the edge of the platform they were on. It dropped with a clang onto the platform below.

Az didn't hesitate. He leapt onto Longnoble-Drumblood's back, pressing his wings down with his knees, and started pummelling.

'I was trained. By someone with wings,' he said, between blows. 'He showed me . . . how to bring your sort down . . . to my level.'

The assault ended when Longnoble-Drumblood retaliated with a devastatingly accurate backhand slap. His knuckles caught Az on the mouth with stunning force, splitting his lip wide open. Az reeled, blood spurting down his chin and also over his tongue.

'And *I* was trained,' Longnoble-Drumblood said, getting to his feet, 'by the Westward Territories army. Do you seriously think a snotnosed kid like you is going to be any kind of worthwhile adversary to *me*?'

He shook out his wings.

Az was on the floor, on his back. Longnoble-Drumblood loomed over him.

'Now,' the aristocrat said. 'Enough pussyfooting around. I don't need a knife. I don't need anything but my hands to tear you apart.'

That was when, as if on cue, Platypuss entered the fray.

CHAPTER 90

Ungentlemanly Conduct

The cat pounced from the top of one of the consoles. He was a spitting, hissing ball of fur and fury. He seemed to have overcome his fear of Longnoble-Drumblood and, like Az, resented the man for hurting his friend Colin. He went at him with claws outstretched, slashing at his face.

Longnoble-Drumblood cried out in shock. Within seconds, however, he had pulled Platypuss off him. He grasped the squirming cat's head in one hand, neck in the other. And then he twisted. Platypuss screeched. There was a ripple-pop of snapping neck bones. Platypuss went limp. Longnoble-Drumblood tossed the cat's lifeless body aside.

And Az kicked Longnoble-Drumblood between the legs, and it was Longnoble-Drumblood's turn to screech.

Az scrambled to his feet. Platypuss had provided a brief diversion, giving him enough time to recover his wits and lash out at his opponent. The cat was dead, but Az was pretty certain the little creature had saved his life.

Longnoble-Drumblood stood doubled over, hands cupping groin. Az slammed into him, shoulder-barging him. Longnoble-Drumblood toppled over the edge of the platform.

Straight away Az realised he had made a tactical blunder. Longnoble-Drumblood reappeared, flying. And he had his knife again.

'Trust you,' he said. Scratches webbed his face, and his voice was hoarse with pain. 'Trust you not to fight like a gentleman.'

'No reason to. Seeing as who I'm fighting isn't a gentleman.'

'Oh, but I am, Gabrielson. I'm your better in every way. You Airborn, you think you're so superior. But some of us Groundlings know a bit about good breeding. I come from a long line of—'

'Long-winded guano-heads,' said Az, charging at him.

625

He caught him in the midriff. They went hurtling through the air together, then tumbled down a short flight of steps onto an adjoining platform, which was the central one. They rammed into the command chair, sending it spinning round. They bounced off, fetching up on the floor. Longnoble-Drumblood was on top, Az beneath. Longnoble-Drumblood had managed to keep hold of the knife, and now he brought it up between them. Its tip quivered above Az's face. He could see smears of Colin's blood still on its blade.

Longnoble-Drumblood pushed the knife down with all his might. Az, holding his opponent's forearms, pushed up. The aristocrat's face was a maniacal leer of determination. The knife began to descend. Az continued to resist, putting every bit of effort he could into it. The point was getting closer to his face, slowly, steadily, inexorably. He let out a low, desperate growl. Longnoble-Drumblood answered with a ferocious laugh. He was bigger than Az. Stronger. Plus, he was able to use his weight to help press the knife down. Az was doing all he could, but he was losing. He knew it. Longnoble-Drumblood knew it.

Now the tip of the knife was mere centimetres from Az's face.

Now mere millimetres.

It was going to go straight into his eye.

CHAPTER 91

Throwing Down A Gauntlet

Cassie sprinted onto the bridge. She took in the situation at a glance: Az, Longnoble-Drumblood, the knife poised between them. She didn't think, didn't hesitate. She bounded up to the command chair platform and threw herself bodily at the man trying to plunge a knife into her boyfriend. She collided with Longnoble-Drumblood. Both of them collided with the master console. They became tangled up together. Then, next thing Cassie knew, a hand was gripping a hank of her hair and she was being hoisted to her feet.

'How splendid,' said Longnoble-Drumblood, placing the knife to her neck. 'Here's the other one. The other murderer. I have you both. Now I can make one of you watch while the other suffers.'

Az sprang up off the floor and ran at him with a growl.

'Oh no you don't,' said Longnoble-Drumblood. He shoved Cassie forwards, so that she and Az crashed into each other. Then, taking off, he seized Az by the shoulders, swung him around and let go. Az went skidding helplessly over the edge of the platform.

It was a drop of at least three metres, and he fell head-first and heavily. His skull thudded hard against the platform below.

For a time he couldn't think where he was or what had happened to him. All he knew was the ringing sound in his ears. He sensed that he should try and get up, but lying down was so much better, so much more comfortable. Reality felt a long way away from him, or else he from it.

Then somebody grabbed him. Somebody was shouting at him, seemingly from a great distance away.

Longnoble-Drumblood?

Az lashed out with a punch.

'Whoa!' the person said. 'Whoa, Az, it'm only I. Fletcher.'

'Fletcher?'

Az sat up woozily. Fletcher was kneeling over him, looking aggrieved.

'Yeah,' he said, rubbing the spot on his arm where Az's fist had made contact. 'You know. Fletcher, your pal, who you doesn't hit, thank you.'

'Sorry. I didn't know it was you. Where's Cassie?'

'No idea. Last I saw of she, her were coming up to find you. What'm going on? Colin in the galley said him were attacked by Longnoble-Drumblood. Be that true?'

'Yes. And now he's got Cassie and I'm going after him.'

Az stood. Swayed. Staggered. Fell down. His head felt like a pillow stuffed with feathers.

'Maybe you should . . .' Fletcher began.

'No.' Az got to his feet again. The fog in his brain began to clear a little. 'He's taken her somewhere. He's going to kill her. I need to find her. Where could he have gone?'

'Well, er . . .' Fletcher raised a hand, pointing towards the viewing window. 'I think there'm your answer.'

Az turned.

Longnoble-Drumblood had appeared outside. He was on his own. Cassie was nowhere to be seen. Az narrowed his gaze, peering anxiously at the knife that hung from Longnoble-Drumblood's right hand. Was there more blood on it than before? He thought there wasn't. Prayed there wasn't.

The aristocrat, with a gloating grin, beckoned to Az. He was inviting him. Calling him outside. Throwing down a gauntlet.

Az nodded to him, showing acceptance.

Longnoble-Drumblood flew up out of sight.

'How did he get out?' Az asked Fletcher. 'I thought we couldn't open any doors.'

'Power'm back on. I got it going again. Most likely him used the wet dock entrance.'

Az was off before Fletcher had finished speaking. He headed for the companionway, pausing only to snatch up his cleaver.

'Wait!' Fletcher called after him. 'What can I do? I has to do *something*.'

'Figure out some way of killing him,' Az replied over his shoulder. 'In case I don't manage to.'

CHAPTER 92

Outside

The wet dock doors stood wide. Az leapt into one of the motor launches, gunned the engine and drove out into the open, slewing wildly. He steered around the side of the Bathylab, scanning for Longnoble-Drumblood. People from some of the nearby boats called to him – 'Ahoy there!' – but he ignored them.

Finally, near the front of the Bathylab, he spied his quarry. Longnoble-Drumblood was perched at the summit of one of the squat, round towers that projected from the vessel. Cassie was there too, on all fours. At this distance Az couldn't tell if she was hurt but she seemed not to be.

Longnoble-Drumblood waved down to him, contemptuously. Az halted the launch right beside the Bathylab and yelled up, 'Longnoble-Drumblood! Let her go! Come and get *me*! Come on! You know you want to!'

Longnoble-Drumblood either couldn't hear or pretended he couldn't. He cupped a hand around his ear, shrugged, then grabbed Cassie by the throat and dragged her upright. Cassie immediately started hammering at him with her fists and kicking him. Longnoble-Drumblood held her at arm's length and strode to the edge of the tower, leaning out so that Cassie was suspended over the drop. Her toes just remained on the tower, scrabbling for purchase. She had to cling on to his arm with both hands to keep from being strangled.

If Longnoble-Drumblood let go, it was 200 metres straight down to the ocean's surface. From that height, falling into the water would be as fatal as dropping onto solid concrete.

The aristocrat was too far away for Az to make out his expression but everything about him, his stance, his attitude, said, *See how things stand now, Gabrielson? Now what are you going to do?*

Az examined the superstructure of the Bathylab in front of him. It consisted of dozens of different planes at angles to one another. Each was steep and, apart from the rivets that held its steel plates together, smooth. The rivets were spaced far apart and no larger than the heads of mushrooms. They'd be no use as handholds or footholds. Climbing, therefore, would be impossible without a rope of some sort.

His eye fell on the launch's anchor. It was had four curved prongs made of lightweight metal, and it was attached to twenty metres of stout hawser, the other end of which was tied to a cleat on the aft gunwale.

Az raised his cleaver and hacked through the cleat knot with a single blow. Then he took the anchor and whirled it around and around above his head, meanwhile paying out a short length of the hawser. He let the spinning anchor go, and it shot up, hit the side of the Bathylab, slithered down and fell into the sea.

He hauled it in and tried again.

On the third attempt his makeshift grappling hook snagged on a narrow ledge about ten metres up. He tugged. It seemed secure. He stepped onto the prow of the launch, holding the rope with both hands. The boat bobbed and lurched under him. Waves spilled over the bows, splashing his feet. He leaned back, then leaped. He swung across the gap between the launch and the Bathylab, planting both soles firmly on the vessel as he slammed against it.

The anchor continued to hold fast. Az started to climb, pulling himself up the rope, hand over hand.

Gaining the ledge, he unhooked the anchor and whirled it again, aiming for the next spot where two of the Bathylab's external planes met.

Like this, slowly, painstakingly, laboriously, section by section, he ascended.

CHAPTER 93

Gravity's Vast Hand

From above, Longnoble-Drumblood watched Az's progress with lofty disdain.

Cassie watched too, teetering on the tower's edge, holding onto the aristocrat's arm for dear life. She wished she could tell Az to give up. He mustn't try to save her. That was exactly what Longnoble-Drumblood wanted. She was bait, and Az was being reeled in.

But it would have been no use warning him to stay away, even if she'd been able to. He wouldn't have paid any attention. He was climbing to get her, come what may.

'That's it, Gabrielson,' Longnoble-Drumblood murmured, talking mostly to himself. 'Up you come, you little dribble of snot. You want her? Here she is. Clamber away like a monkey. It won't make any difference. Soon as you're within spitting distance, I drop her. Can't wait to see the look on your face when that happens.'

His words were a chilling confirmation of what Cassie already suspected. Whether or not Az reached her, she was going to die.

She could feel the empty air below her, the space that yawned between her and the waves far below. Her body seemed to want to go there. It was almost a physical thing, as if gravity were a vast hand, tugging at her, summoning her down.

It would be quick. Probably painless.

Might as well get it over with.

She let her feet slip free from the edge of the tower. The sudden increase in the amount of weight he was supporting took Longnoble-Drumblood by surprise. He lost his balance and his grip on her throat, and Cassie plummeted.

This'm for you, Az. Goodbye.

CHAPTER 94

Falling

She fell.

Fast.

Longnoble-Drumblood was staring down at her, aghast, dismayed at losing his hostage. She was plunging away from him. He was shrinking.

She felt strangely content. Now Az had a chance. With her out of the picture and Longnoble-Drumblood deprived of his hostage, Az might be able to win the day.

She fell. Longnoble-Drumblood was now just a dot against the sky, a tiny winged silhouette.

She heard wings.

A man shouted, 'Go limp! Cassie, go limp!'

She fell.

She was no longer falling. Arms enfolded her tightly. She was being carried towards the side of the Bathylab, then up, up.

'Got you.'

Mr Mordadson?

Mr Mordadson!

Cassie stared up into the face of Az's friend and mentor. Mr Mordadson – it was definitely him, although his battered features and the absence of his spectacles meant she had to look twice to be sure.

Wings straining with every beat, Mr Mordadson wheeled around and landed on the very apex of the Bathylab. He set Cassie down. Collapsed with her, to be honest. The effort of carrying her was almost too much for him.

'Are you all right?' he asked.

'Yeah, f-fine,' she stammered. 'What the hell happened to *you*?'

'Long story,' came the reply. 'Who's that fellow who had you by the throat?'

'Jasper Longnoble-Drumblood. Him wants to kill we.'

'Clearly. But Longnoble-Drumblood's a Groundling. A Groundling with wings? How?'

'Beats I.'

'Well, stay here. I'll deal with him.' Mr Mordadson took off.

Cassie glanced around her. The Bathylab's superstructure shelved steeply away on all sides.

'Stay here?' she muttered. 'Like I be able to *go* anywhere.'

CHAPTER 95

Setback

The Airborn dressed in black had caught the girl with mere metres to go before she hit the sea. He had saved her from certain death. Who was he? How dare he!

Longnoble-Drumblood ground his teeth.

Well, it was a setback, but a temporary one. These two teenagers were proving wretchedly hard to kill, but Longnoble-Drumblood had no doubt he was going to be able to finish the job.

He fixed his gaze on the Gabrielson boy. The boy had stopped climbing. He was hanging from the side of the Bathylab on his rope. He'd just seen his girlfriend nearly plunge to her doom. Even though she'd been rescued, he was numb, frozen in shock.

Pain pulsed from Longnoble-Drumblood's thumb where the Grubdollar bitch had bitten him. The digit dangled uselessly from his hand, half severed.

Cursing her, her boyfriend, the world, everyone, even himself, he sheathed the knife in his belt and launched himself off the top of the tower. Wings swept back, he dived towards the boy.

The boy spotted him at the last moment.

Too late.

Longnoble-Drumblood was heading straight for him and there was nothing he could do.

CHAPTER 96

No More Last-minute Reprieves

There was nothing Az could do . . . except let go of the rope.

He slip-slithered helplessly down the side of the Bathylab. He hit a ledge with shin-jarring impact. He lost his footing and slid further. He bounced over the next ledge down, but managed to catch hold of it with his fingers.

He hung there, his feet scrabbling for purchase, trying to haul himself up to the ledge. Longnoble-Drumblood descended from above with merciless slowness, wings spread. Alighting on the ledge, he hunkered over Az.

'Nice move,' he said. 'But it only bought you a few seconds. Really now, let's call it a day, shall we?' He rested a foot on Az's hand, applying just enough pressure to keep it, and Az, in place. 'No more tricks. No more last-minute reprieves. Time to finish this.'

He reached for the knife.

'Aren't you forgetting something?' Az said.

Longnoble-Drumblood frowned. 'Such as?'

'Him.'

Mr Mordadson sheared in from the side, knocking Longnoble-Drumblood off his perch.

The aristocrat swiftly recovered his equilibrium and flew up to meet Mr Mordadson.

The two of them engaged and grappled in the air, wings beating furiously. Az clawed his way up onto the ledge, confident that the tide had turned against Longnoble-Drumblood and there could now be only one outcome to the conflict. Mr Mordadson would beat him, surely. Both men were skilled combatants but Longnoble-Drumblood was new to flight, whereas Mr Mordadson had been doing it almost his entire life.

It quickly became clear, however, that all was not well with Mr

Mordadson. He was flying, and fighting, weakly. He was managing to hold his own against Longnoble-Drumblood, but only just. As they grappled in the air, he parried, he blocked, but he wasn't getting any blows in.

His face. Those injuries.

Az realised, belatedly, that Mr Mordadson was in a great deal of pain. In fact, more than that, he was struggling simply to stay aloft. As he and Longnoble-Drumblood fought, they were rising, but it was the aristocrat who was doing most of the wing-work. Mr Mordadson was more or less clinging on, letting himself be drawn higher and higher.

Then, to his horror, Az saw Longnoble-Drumblood reach for his belt. He saw the carving knife flash out.

He saw it sink into Mr Mordadon's chest.

Deep.

To the hilt.

CHAPTER 97

A Profound, Hollow Silence

Cassie saw it too. She gasped in anguish.

Mr Mordadson shuddered. Longnoble-Drumblood let out a bark of a laugh.

Then Cassie felt Bathylab Four begin to vibrate beneath her. Not far from where she was crouching, a large panel slid open.

The Focused Sonic Amplification Unit emerged.

Fletcher must have mended the power cables. Juice was flowing through Bathylab Four again, and now he was trying to do something to help his sister and Az – the only thing he, and the Bathylab, *could* do.

Despondently, Cassie thought it was too little, too late. Mr Mordadson was still alive but barely. He had latched onto Longnoble-Drumblood in a death grip. They were both still ascending. Mr Mordadson's wings were still beating. But blood was pouring from him, glistening against the blackness of his jacket. Longnoble-Drumblood kept trying to extricate himself from the other man's grasp. He was shoving Mr Mordadson's head back, tugging at his fingers. Mr Mordadson hung on implacably. He would not let go.

But how much longer could he last?

The Amplification Unit started to hum, and the hum deepened, and the air around its arrangement of dual-pronged arms quivered and rippled, and at such close range the noise was the loudest thing Cassie had ever heard or would ever want to hear. It resonated through her, so that her teeth seemed to rattle in her gums, so that the segments of her skull seemed to grind together, so that her bones felt as though they were turning to jelly inside her. She wrapped her arms around her head, covering her ears, for all the good that did. She wanted to scream, but what would have been the point? The scream would have been lost, even to herself.

Now the beam of sound erupted from the node, shooting high into the air, almost vertical. It punched into the clouds, making first a dent, then a tunnel.

Mr Mordadson saw it, this long, lancing cylinder of pure, focused sonic vibration. He and Longnoble-Drumblood were rising towards it. They were both stunned, deafened by the onslaught of noise, but still flying. Mr Mordadson took the initiative and flapped hard, as hard as he could, giving it everything he had left. He drove Longnoble-Drumblood backwards, upwards.

Cassie looked on through half-closed eyes, her vision blurred by the Amplification Unit's reverberant rumble.

Down below, on the ledge, Az looked on too.

The two winged men, propelled by Mr Mordadson, entered the beam.

And were pulverised.

It hit them like a freight train. Their bodies crumpled. Blood burst out like wine from smashed bottles. Flesh and feathers exploded in all directions.

A mangled tangle of Airborn and Groundling, emissary and aristocrat, they were rocketed high into the sky by the force of the beam, then started to fall.

It seemed to take ages for them to fall.

They fell, shedding a trail of feathers.

They fell so far from Bathylab Four that when they hit the sea, the splash seemed tiny.

And then Cassie howled. Az too.

Their voices were nothing compared with the almighty bellow of the Amplification Unit. It swallowed their cries whole.

Yet still they howled.

And when the tripod-like device eventually went quiet and withdrew back into the Bathylab, the silence that followed was as profound and hollow as eternity.

CHAPTER 98

Rainbow Snow

The planes came.

They flew over the infected sky-cities, to the centre of each. Then they turned and began to cruise outward in a widening spiral. While they did this, they released a mist. Each plane had been modified, fitted with a large pressurised container and a length of broad-gauge hose, the end of which protruded from the fuselage. They sprayed the air above the sky-cities, filling it with a hazy suspension of vapour which the chilly high-altitude temperatures turned to crystalline droplets. These fell slowly, like fine snow. They twinkled, iridescent, as they drifted down.

Antipterine.

Over Azuropolis, over Goldenfast, over High Haven and others, down the antipterine came. Down it came as rainbow snow. Down into streets, into plazas, into parks. Down through the cities' interleaving levels and layers, penetrating deep, melting as it went, ambient urban warmth converting the snow back to mist.

Soon the mist lay everywhere, stirred gently by the winds. Amid its pale coils and tendrils, the Maddened moved. Their shuffling footsteps slowed. They halted. Stood. Their heads twitched in confusion. Some sat down. Others sagged to their knees. Many remained upright, looking around themselves, perplexed.

The mist thinned. The mist faded. The mist vanished, like a bad dream.

The Maddened awoke, mad no more.

CHAPTER 99

Good News From Above

In the refugee camps, life had got better.

All across the Territories a massive aid effort was under way, inspired by the example of the Craterhome civic council. Now there was food in the camps. There was drinking water. Blankets arrived, and more tents, and clothing. The army had been properly mobilised, providing plenty of willing workers, and there were lieutenants and even captains to marshal them. Latrines had been dug. Sheds had been erected to serve as soup kitchens. The Airborn were amazed and flattered and grateful.

Doctors came and attended to the sick. Those in dire need of treatment were taken to hospital, the rest left where they were because their conditions weren't so serious. Many were recovering already, thanks to a few hot meals and the simple fact that someone, at last, was helping them.

Life in the camps improved even further when Alar Patrollers turned up to announce that the Maddened had been cured. The crisis was past. Unfortunately nobody could return to their homes just yet. The sky-cities had to be checked out thoroughly first, to make sure there were no lone Maddened lurking anywhere, ones who had somehow managed to escape the airdrop of antipterine. But once that was done, within a matter of days the refugees would be able to go back.

The Patrollers who brought this news were cheered and treated like conquering heroes. They stayed long enough to soak up the adulation, even though, strictly speaking, they had done little to earn it . They felt they deserved praise for staying to guard the cities, if nothing else. Then they ascended again to the Airborn realm and set about the painstaking task of going through the cordoned-off areas, searching for any remaining Maddened.

Whenever they found some, they dosed them with antipterine. The Regulars had come forward, handing themselves over to the Patrol in their home towns, asking to be arrested. Along with confessing to their crimes, they offered canisters of antipterine for the Patrollers' use. It was a way, they hoped, of mitigating what they had done. It might even count in their favour when the time came for them to face trial.

Soon enough, the sky-cities were cleansed of the Maddened. By the end of the week, the refugees were filing into the former Chancels and riding the elevators up.

CHAPTER 100

Naming Ceremony

Serena Second-House found Az in his room. He was sitting on the end of his bed, staring at his feet. He looked like someone on the edge of a precipice, contemplating the drop.

'They told me you'd be here,' she said. 'It's your nephew's naming ceremony. You should be downstairs with everyone else. This is a big day.'

Az turned to her, flashing a brave but patently false smile. 'I'm coming down. I just needed some time to myself.'

'I understand. I'll leave you be.' She went to the door.

'No,' said Az. 'Milady – I mean, Serena. Wait. Please.'

She halted.

Az paused, putting his thoughts in order.

'Do you miss him?' he said at last. 'You must do.'

'Mordadson?' Serena took a deep breath. 'More than words can say. He wasn't just someone who worked for me, you know. He was far more than that. He was one of the very few people I could trust. Trust implicitly. I was an only child, never had any brothers or sisters. I felt about him the way I imagine you feel about Michael. He was a brother to me. He looked after me. He looked after everyone. He wasn't an easy person to get to know, but you could always . . .' Her voice trailed off to a choked whisper. She ran a finger across both eyes, scraping away tears.

'I let him down,' Az said bleakly. 'That's all I can think about, and it's driving me nuts. He needed my help and I let him down. Naoutha had him. Her people did horrible things to him. And I just left him to it and went off and did what I thought was important instead. I will never forgive myself for that.'

'You should. You must.' Serena sat down next to him. 'He understood

642

that things were difficult for you. He told me so. I'm certain he wouldn't want you to flay yourself like this.'

'And in the end,' Az went on, as if she hadn't spoken, 'after everything I did, or didn't do, he came and saved me. He was with Den and Robert. They'd picked him up at one of the refugee camps. They wanted to take him to hospital but then they found out that Cassie and Fletcher were at Blackcrab Lee and he insisted they all go there instead. He put their needs before his own. Then they saw us from the coast, fighting with Longnoble-Drumblood, and Mr Mordadson flew out to help even though he was half crippled with pain. He barely had the strength to flap his wings but he weighed in anyway. He must have known he might get killed, and it didn't stop him. He should have stayed on the sidelines. He had every right to.'

'That's the kind of man he was. The kind of man you are too, Az.'

'No. No, I'm not. I'll never be.'

Serena placed an arm around his shoulders. It was something she would never have done – never have permitted herself to do – as Lady Aanfieldsdaughter.

'All right,' she said, with kindly sternness. 'Enough of this. Today is a happy occasion. Downstairs there's a beautiful little baby – so beautiful I want to kidnap him and take him home with me.'

'Don't you dare.'

She smiled. 'I wouldn't be allowed to keep him anyway. A boy child in the Cumula Collective? Can you imagine the outcry? But it's *his* day, Az. The day he's named and officially becomes a citizen of the realm. And there are some very proud parents down there, and some very proud grandparents. There are friends and other family members. The Grub-dollars as well. There should be a very proud uncle there too.'

'I said I was coming.'

'I know. My point is, you have to try and forget all that's happened. Even if only for today. Life goes on. That's what this baby is here to tell us. People die, people are born. Life goes on.'

'Forget?' said Az. 'How can I forget, even for a moment? It's not just Mr Mordadson. For pluck's sake, the whole realm was in terrible trouble and I didn't even know about it till afterwards! That's just absurd. I acted selfishly and Airborn were dying, and I wasn't here. My family were in danger and I *wasn't here.*' He thumped the bed in anger.

'Your family coped admirably,' Serena said. 'Other than Michael's ankle, they came through it unscathed.'

'But if the Aquila Flight hadn't arrived when they did . . .'

'But they did.'

'We have you to thank for that, don't we?'

'And the Mother Major, who is now beginning to review the

Collective's isolationist policy. Given that the Aquila Flight proved so useful and acquitted themselves so well, she's wondering whether greater interaction with the rest of the realm would be such a bad thing.'

'Which you're pleased about.'

'Naturally. It's an encouraging sign. People can change. But listen, Az. No, you weren't there to help. But if there's one thing I learned in my time as a Sanctum resident, it's that you can't help everyone. You can't *save* everyone. You have to do as much as you can and be content with that.'

'I don't accept that.'

'You're going to have to.'

There was silence for a while between them. The only sound in the room was the burble of voices coming up from below.

'Can I ask you a question?' Az said.

'Of course.'

'If you did have the power to help everyone – to do something that might change the whole world, probably for the better – would you do it?'

'I don't know. Depends what it is, I suppose. Change isn't always easy, or welcome.'

'But you just said you're glad the Cumula Collective is changing.'

'It's a relatively small thing, and it was overdue. You seem to have something much more wide-ranging in mind.'

'I do.'

'"Pivotal to the future of the Airborn race,"' said Serena, 'isn't that what the Ultimate Reckoner predicted about you?'

'And the Groundling race as well. And it's them I'm thinking about, really. Them and Michael.'

'What is this all about? I'm very intrigued.'

'It's to do with Bathylab Four. And Longnoble-Drumblood. And Metatron.'

'Metatron!'

'Yeah.'

'And? Aren't you going to tell me any more?'

'Not for now. I haven't yet decided what I'm going to do with what I've found out.'

'Well,' Serena said, rising, 'I'm sure that when you do decide, we'll all know about it. Right now, however, I feel we can't dally any longer. Downstairs is where we should be. I imagine the officiator is getting quite impatient. Before we go, though . . .'

She reached into a fold of her robe and took out an envelope.

'This is for you.'

The envelope was blank, no addressee.

'Who's it from?' Az said, frowning.

'Guess.'

'Mr Mordadson.'

'He told me to give it to you if anything happened to him.'

'And it did.'

'It did. Read it. I have no idea what it says. Read it, then join us downstairs.'

'OK.' Az slit the envelope flap open with a finger. 'Serena?'

'Yes?'

He held her gaze. Her stratospheric blue eyes were as blazingly brilliant as ever. 'Thanks. For talking.'

'Not at all.'

She left the room. Az fished out the letter inside the envelope. It was short, written in a neat, precise hand. He read it twice, quickly first, lingeringly the second time, then tucked it back in the envelope.

With a sad, rueful smile he went downstairs to the living room, where everyone was waiting: immediate family and not so immediate, a number of family friends, Cassie and the other Grubdollars, Colin Amblescrut too, along with a jowly and very self-important officiator who peered disapprovingly over his half-moon spectacles at Az.

'Harrumph,' the officiator said. 'All here now? No more delays? Then let us begin.'

The baby let out a squalling cry.

Cassie took Az's hand and kissed him.

'Ladies, gentlemen,' the officiator said. 'Honoured visitors from below. We are gathered here today to celebrate the addition of a new life to the ranks of the Airborn . . .'

And so little Mordad Michaelson was introduced to the world, formally given his name, greeted by all the guests, showered with gifts, this baby who had been born in the midst of chaos, a symbol of a realm quietly, hopefully restoring itself to order.

CHAPTER 101

Mr Mordadson's Letter

Dear Az,

If you're reading this, the worst has happened. Too bad for me. I trust all is well with you.

We've had a rocky time of it lately, you and I, haven't we? I'm taking the precaution of writing you this letter so that I might be able, in death, to tell you things which I would have found hard to say to you in life. I'm not very good at expressing my innermost self face to face. I've spent far too long disguising my thoughts and emotions, a necessity in my line of work.

In spite of things turning sour between us, I have never been anything but proud of you, Az. I admire you greatly. I cannot think of anyone I would rather have had as a protégé. You've fought for the realm. You've overcome hardships, personal and otherwise. You will become, if you aren't already, a force to be reckoned with.

If I have any advice left to give you, it's this. Never give in to despair. Never let fear or hopelessness overwhelm you. It's a dark world but there is always light in it if you know where to look. Life's lows invariably yield to highs. You may feel as if you are losing and the fight isn't worth it, but battle on and you will win.

I am glad I met you, glad we have been friends. In retrospect, I am somewhat ashamed that you've never got to call me by my first name. I've made a point of being 'Mr Mordadson' to everyone, in order to maintain distance, to cloak myself in an air of professional mystique. I regret that I have done this even with you.

I rectify that oversight now, if a little too late for it to be of any practical use.

I remain,

  Your friend,

    Lucifer Mordadson

CHAPTER 102

Destination: Anywhere

Bathylab Four plied the ocean depths, on no particular heading or course. Destination: anywhere.

It carried a crew complement of two, Az and Cassie.

They were travelling together, just them, no one else. They'd told their families they would be away for a couple of months, perhaps longer. They deliberately left it vague. They *would* be back, they promised. For a while, though, they simply wanted time to themselves. They had earned it. They deserved it.

And their families agreed and did not begrudge them their time together. Bathylab Four was theirs, to do with as they pleased. It was their own world, a private, secret place in which they could explore the seas and share each other's company and be free from interruptions and intrusions.

As Den Grubdollar put it: 'I be losing my girl beneath the waves again. But her'll be coming back, just as her did last time. And I's happy to let she go. For a while.'

Bathylab Four itself had been renamed. Fletcher claimed 'Bathylab Four' was too dull, too technical. Something snappier, zippier, was needed. A proper name, like a ship had.

He and Robert had done sterling work, blacking over the large white characters and painting a fresh set of their own.

Now the vessel was known as *Molly Wetbones*.

Several days into the voyage, Cassie was stationed in *Molly Wetbones*'s command chair, Az sitting cross-legged nearby. He had Professor Metier's journal in his lap.

'I still can't quite believe it,' Az said, leafing through the antique, frail pages.

'Believe what?' said Cassie. 'That Longnoble-Drumblood used that book and Emeritus's serum to grow wings?'

'Well, yeah, but also that Metier was Metatron.'

Cassie nodded. Emeritus had lied about evolution being the reason the Airborn gained their wings. Metier had been the one responsible after all. It gave her no satisfaction to know that she had guessed right about him the very first time Emeritus mentioned Metier's 'big project'.

'Metatron be an Airborn myth, right?' she said.

'Yes.'

'So, a lot of myths has their roots in the truth. No reason why him shouldn't have been a real person.'

'I know. It's just so . . . Not disappointing. Bland. He was a man, and he made us.'

'But what did you expect?'

'I suppose I thought if Metatron was a real person he'd be this heroic figure. Not some nerdy scientist.'

'You'm a hero and you'm quite nerdy.'

'Hey!'

'Just saying. Anyone can be a hero. It'm their actions, not who them is, that counts.'

. Az mused on this. 'I take your point. The thing is, it's all here, in this book. How to make an Airborn. How to get wings.'

'I know. What'm you going to do about it?'

'That's the question, isn't it? It's the future of two races. I'm holding it in my hands. Literally. The future in my hands. Just think what I could do. Mike could get his wings back, for starters. I'm sure it would work. And that would be good. Wouldn't it?'

'Certainly would,' said Cassie. 'Him's not obsessing too much about himself right now, what with little Mordad to care for and all that, but there'll come a time when the baby be less demanding and him'll start to miss his wings again.'

'But if he gets them back, what about other people? What about Groundlings? Won't they want wings too, if they're available? Metier's genomorph serum could be re-created in quantity, and everyone could be injected with it. Everyone could fly. *I* could.' His voice went soft. '*I* could fly.'

'And nothing'd be the same again,' said Cassie.

'Exactly. It'd be as huge a change as the Great Cataclysm itself. And . . . and it's up to me. To us. We have this knowledge here in the Bathy-lab. We're carting it around with us. And it's potentially devastating stuff.'

'You makes it sound like dynamite.'

'Worse. Infinite times worse.'

Cassie engaged autopilot and stood up.

'First Mate Az. Come over here. That'm an order.'

'Aye-aye, Cap'n.' Az laid down the journal and went over to her.

'You'm worrying too much,' she said, taking him by the arms. 'There'm a choice to be made, and at the right time, whatever it be, you'll make it. Now, roll up your sleeve.'

Az did.

'Let's take a look at that tattoo.'

Az showed her.

The downward arrow had been joined by an upward-pointing one. The new part of the tattoo was still puffy and reddened, but it was clear that when inflammation settled down the two halves, old and new, would mesh seamlessly.

Now the tattoo mimicked exactly the original symbol offered up by the Ultimate Reckoner:

All that was missing was the question mark in the middle.

'What were it Mordy said in his letter?' said Cassie. ' "It'm a dark world . . ." '

' " . . . but there is always light in it if you know where to look," ' Az finished.

'Choices,' Cassie said simply. 'That'm what him meant. That'm what the Ultimate Reckoner be getting at too, I think. The choices you make. The choices everyone makes. Them determines how us lives, or doesn't live. How us gets to be heroes, or not. You has it in you to go either way. Up or down. Into the light or into the dark. So does all of we.'

'But this particular choice we're talking about . . .'

'. . . you'll deal with when it needs to be dealt with,' she said. 'For now, you'm free, Az. It'm just the two of we, here in this world of our own. Here, with all that out there.' She waved at the viewing window. 'All that. All of the world's oceans. All twenty kajillion square kilometres of they. I made that figure up, by the way.'

'I'd never have guessed.'

'Old Mr Mordadson – Lucifer – him's given we all of this, by sacrificing himself and saving we from Longnoble-Drumblood. Him's given we a chance to take a rest from care and responsibility. To just be ourselves, by ourselves. Let's enjoy it while us can, eh?'

Az looked at the darkly magnificent scenery outside, an oceanscape alive with fish. He looked at the shifting columns of dimmed daylight, and the towering outcrops of rock, and the reefs with their fans of intricate coral.

Then he looked back at Cassie.

He lowered his shoulders.

He sighed.

'Is that an order, Cap'n Cassie?'

'It be, First Mate Az.'

'Then I choose,' Az said, with a faltering, then strengthening smile, 'I *choose* to obey.'

The End